The flames grew hotter and more insistent in Beneto's body, and he could not entirely push them away.

He struggled so hard that a long crack split along his thickest bough, and the glowing golden blood of his sap spilled out into space. The flames bit deeper, jumping into the point of weakness.

Nearby in space, two more verdani treeships lost their battle to possession by the elemental fires. They weakened, faltered, and then each spiny battleship became a corona of gleeful flames.

Even so, the infested treeships refused to let the faeros possess them. Rather than becoming full-fledged torch trees, the two lost verdani battleships intentionally allowed themselves to crumble into ash. Fragments of embers sparkled and drifted apart in space.

Although Beneto kept fighting, the flames ate at him, pushing deeper into his core, and he could not stop the burning.

BOOKS BY KEVIN J. ANDERSON

Terra Incognita

The Edge of the World
The Map of All Things
The Key to Creation

The Saga of Seven Suns

Hidden Empire
A Forest of Stars
Horizon Storms
Scattered Suns
Of Fire and Night
Metal Swarm
The Ashes of Worlds
Veiled Alliances (graphic novel)

THE ASHES OF WORLDS

THE SAGA OF SEVEN SUNS

7

KEVIN J. ANDERSON

www.orbitbooks.net

Copyright © 2008 by WordFire, Inc.
Excerpt from *The Edge of the World* copyright © 2008 by WordFire, Inc.

Orbit
Hachette Book Group
237 Park Avenue, New York, NY 10017
Visit our website at orbitbooks.net

Orbit is an imprint of Hachette Book Group. The Orbit name and logo are trademarks of Little, Brown Book Group Limited.

Printed in the United States of America

Originally published in hardcover by Hachette Book Group
First Orbit paperback edition: May 2009

10 9 8 7 6 5 4 3

ATTENTION CORPORATIONS AND ORGANIZATIONS:
Most Hachette Book Group books are available at quantity discounts with bulk purchase for educational, business, or sales promotional use. For information, please call or write:
**Special Markets Department, Hachette Book Group
237 Park Avenue, New York, NY 10017
Telephone: 1-800-222-6747 Fax: 1-800-477-5925**

To Rebecca Moesta
Not just for this novel, but for all the books in the
series and all the novels I've written. You have
helped me find my Guiding Star not
only in my writing, but in my life.

THE STORY SO FAR

The hydrogue war had ended with a devastating final battle at Earth. Adar Zan'nh sacrificed much of the Ildiran Solar Navy to destroy the deadly warglobes. Jess Tamblyn and Cesca Peroni led the wentals and the verdani to fight the hydrogues inside their gas-giant planets; the Roamer engineer Kotto Okiah developed a new weapon to shatter the diamond spheres. Finally, the defeated hydrogues were bottled up within their gas planets, where they could cause no further harm.

The Earth Defense Forces, led by General Lanyan, had already been crippled in a revolt by the black robots, and the final battle around Earth smashed many more EDF ships. Sirix and his black robots hoped to use their stolen fleet to help the hydrogues achieve victory, but the tides of battle turned against them, and Sirix and his comrades were forced to run for their lives.

The turmoil of the battle gave King Peter and Queen Estarra the opportunity to escape the increasingly irrational Chairman Wenceslas. With the aid of Estarra's sister Sarein, Deputy Chairman Cain, and Captain McCammon of the royal guard, they slipped away from the Whisper Palace. The Teacher compy OX purged his precious memories to obtain the mental capacity needed to operate a small hydrogue derelict, and he flew them safely to Theroc. There, Peter and

Estarra declared a new unified government for humanity, the Confederation. All green priests refused to serve the Hansa unless Basil Wenceslas resigned, which the Chairman would not do. Seeing few people he could trust, Basil resorted to more reactionary tactics. As Therons, Roamer clans, and orphaned Hansa colonies joined the Confederation, Chairman Wenceslas grew more and more isolated.

On Llaro, the EDF had detained many refugees including Orli Covitz, Hud Steinman, Davlin Lotze, and many Roamer prisoners of war. While the EDF guards were waiting to be rotated home after the end of the hydrogue war, Llaro's transportal walls activated and hordes of monstrous insect creatures marched through—the ancient race of the Klikiss, long thought to be extinct. They had returned from their distant Swarming and now wanted their colony worlds back.

The long-lost xeno-archaeologist Margaret Colicos and her compy, DD, accompanied the Klikiss. Relying on her wits and the odd tune played by a small music box, Margaret had found a way to survive among them for many years. Now she became an interpreter for the hapless Llaro colonists as the Klikiss fenced the people into their colony town.

Meanwhile, unaware that their hated creator race had returned, Sirix and his black robots attacked any former Klikiss world on which humans had established colonies. As replacements for DD, whom he had tried to reprogram, Sirix had wiped the memories of two other compies—PD and QT—and taught them how to kill humans without remorse. Believing that the former Klikiss planets belonged to them, the robots struck mercilessly, obliterating any settlements. Sirix had resurrected thousands of black robots over the years, and they were all ready to form a unified robot force to destroy humanity.

Then the transportals activated on the colony Sirix had conquered, and a host of ravenous Klikiss marched through, immediately attacking the robot forces. With PD and QT, Sirix barely escaped this unexpected battle and was forced to eradicate the transportal and retreat to Maratha, an Ildiran world where the robots were establishing a powerful base of operations.

On Ildira, the Mage-Imperator ordered Adar Zan'nh to launch a frantic program to rebuild the Solar Navy, erecting shipyards in orbit and diverting the resources of the Empire to the project. Zan'nh also made use of the innovative skills of the humans who had been forced to remain at Ildira, including Sullivan Gold and Tabitha Huck. With Gold's administrative abilities and Huck's engineering ideas, the manufacturing proceeded at a furious pace.

Sullivan's companion green priest Kolker felt isolated and confused. For a long time he had been cut off from his beloved telink with other green priests, and even after he was given access to a treeling, the sensation felt lacking to him. When he saw how the Ildirans — all Ildirans — were linked through *thism*, he wanted to understand how it worked. Lens kithmen rebuffed him, telling him that he could never grasp the *thism*, but Nira's five half-breed children were able to show him the key. As Kolker struggled to understand, he finally comprehended in a way he had never dreamed. Incredible mental vistas opened for him; better still, he knew how to share his discovery. He converted Tabitha Huck and many of her coworkers at the shipyards, though Sullivan refused. Soon, with this unique synchronicity available, Tabitha and her crew led the Ildirans in phenomenally increased productivity.

As the Solar Navy began to be restored, Jora'h's daughter Yazra'h formed a plan with Adar Zan'nh to begin recapturing lost Ildiran worlds, particularly Maratha, which had been taken over by the black robots. Yazra'h convinced the human historian Anton Colicos and Rememberer Vao'sh to accompany the military force. This was a terrifying prospect for them, since Anton and Vao'sh had nearly died there in the robot takeover, and Vao'sh had barely survived the isolation madness when the two of them had flown alone to Ildira. But they agreed to witness the events in order to record them in the *Saga of Seven Suns*.

Reaching Maratha, the Solar Navy bombarded the robot base, then went to the ground to wipe out the last machine survivors. While they were embroiled in battle, a large Klikiss swarmship arrived and dispatched thousands of warriors, who also meant to destroy the black robots. After the battle was won, a tense moment followed when the Klikiss insisted that they would reinhabit all of their own worlds, but Zan'nh held his ground, asserting that Maratha had never been a Klikiss planet, and the swarmship departed. Shortly afterward, Sirix and his black robot refugees arrived at what they expected to be a thriving base on Maratha, only to find utter devastation. Once again, they fled, seeing their plans fall apart.

The black robots and the Klikiss were not the only threats to concern the Ildiran Empire. The mad Designate Rusa'h, after suffering a severe head injury during a hydrogue attack on Hyrillka, had led a destructive but ultimately unsuccessful revolt to overthrow the Mage-Imperator and establish his own *thism* network. Unwilling to surrender in defeat, Rusa'h flew his ship directly into one of Hyrillka's suns. Instead of being incinerated, however, he was intercepted by the faeros, fiery entities that lived within stars.

Though the Ildiran Empire believed him dead, Rusa'h—who had become a faeros incarnate—continued his work. In their war with the hydrogues, the faeros had suffered many terrible losses, millions of their fireballs eradicated, whole suns extinguished. But Rusa'h showed them new ways of fighting, and the faeros swiftly began to inflict great damage upon the hydrogues, weakening them before their battle with the allied forces around Earth.

Gathering power, Rusa'h led the faeros first to the splinter colony of Dobro, where he confronted former Designate Udru'h, who had betrayed him. The ravenous faeros, needing to increase their numbers, burned Udru'h and stole his soulfire to create more newborn fiery entities. Jora'h's eldest noble-born son, Daro'h, who was destined to become the new Prime Designate, faced faeros incarnate Rusa'h, who delivered a warning for the Mage-Imperator. Before departing, Rusa'h declared that the whole Ildiran Empire would burn if necessary, until he removed the "false" Mage-Imperator. Daro'h raced back to Ildira to warn his father of the threat.

Meanwhile, as the hydrogue-faeros battles had raged in Hyrillka's sun, the young and inexperienced Designate Ridek'h had overseen the evacuation of Hyrillka, and all the refugees were taken to Ildira. Ridek'h had never expected to become a Designate responsible for an entire planet, but his mentor Tal O'nh, an old one-eyed veteran commander of the Solar Navy, tried to teach him to become a strong leader. Under orders from the Mage-Imperator, Ridek'h and Tal

O'nh went to all the ravaged systems in the Horizon Cluster
to reassure those who had suffered during the revolt.

Rusa'h had also traveled across the Horizon Cluster, his
faeros burning population after population. On his journey,
he encountered Designate Ridek'h and Tal O'nh. Though
they tried to escape, the faeros chased them down, surrounded their warliners, and incinerated their crews. Rusa'h
burned Tal O'nh, blinding him, but he refused to kill young
Ridek'h, claiming he would face the boy again. He left the
scorched and empty warliners drifting in space, while he and
the faeros headed off to Ildira.

Basil Wenceslas, seeing his Hansa crumbling, grasped
at straws. Because his captive green priest, Nahton, flatly
refused to send or report any messages, he felt cut off. Basil
called upon General Lanyan and Admiral Willis to recapture
the worlds that were defecting. He dispatched Lanyan with
military ships to secure the fledgling colonies recently established on abandoned Klikiss planets. Since they had small
populations and no defenses, they were thought to be easy
targets. For her part, Admiral Willis received orders to take
an EDF battle group directly to Theroc, crush King Peter's
outlaw government, and take him into custody. Though she
was reluctant to do this, Willis prepared to follow orders.

Sarein, Captain McCammon, and Deputy Cain came up
with a plan to warn King Peter about the impending invasion. They secretly freed Nahton, so that he could run to a
treeling locked in a greenhouse and send a telink message
to other green priests. While their involvement remained secret, Nahton was caught just after transmitting his message.
The damage was done. Nahton tried to surrender, but the

Hansa guards gunned him down. Basil Wenceslas seemed very smug about the results.

Warned about the impending EDF assault, however, the Confederation members scrambled to find a way to defend themselves. Tasia Tamblyn and Robb Brindle had joined the Confederation to rebuild their military (much to the dismay of Robb's father, Conrad Brindle, who insisted on remaining loyal to the Hansa). Under their guidance, and with the help of Kotto Okiah, new military-grade ships were being built, but that small fleet would not be enough to deflect an EDF battle group. Estarra and her sister Celli recalled the gigantic verdani battleships, led by their brother Beneto, who had fused himself into one of the giant trees. When Admiral Willis's ships arrived, they suddenly found themselves facing not only a surprisingly vigorous Confederation military defense, but also Jess Tamblyn and Cesca Peroni's wentals, and the huge thorny treeships. Knowing she could not win, and sure that this invasion had been a bad idea from the start, Willis retreated and returned to the Hansa.

General Lanyan's consolidation of the scattered colonies, meanwhile, went no better. He traveled to Rheindic Co, the hub of the transportal network, and marched his soldiers through to the first colony planet on his list, Pym. Arriving there, though, they found that the whole colony had been overrun by a huge subhive of Klikiss. As soon as his soldiers encountered the giant insects, they opened fire. The battle was much worse than anything General Lanyan had prepared for, and he lost a great many soldiers before he finally called his men to withdraw to Rheindic Co. The Klikiss followed them though the transportal, and the battle continued there. Lanyan barely escaped and was forced to destroy the Hansa's main transportal nexus to prevent more of the bugs from passing through. He raced back to Earth to inform Chairman Wenceslas of this shocking new threat.

With the failure of both Admiral Willis and General Lanyan, the Chairman was more frustrated than ever. The Hansa had no King (though Basil had a mysterious new candidate undergoing training), and so he put forward the religious leader, the Archfather of Unison, to build a fervor among the populace, declaring the monstrous Klikiss to be demons and cursing King Peter. Though Deputy Cain was highly skeptical, the gullible people accepted the fanaticism.

Next, the Chairman dispatched Lanyan and the Archfather to make an example of the weak but rebellious colony of Usk. The leaders of Usk had torn up the Hansa Charter and sworn allegiance to the Confederation, but they had no defenses and no real political aspirations. When Lanyan and the Archfather arrived, they unleashed a bloody pogrom, wiping out homesteads, slaughtering livestock, burning towns, and finally crucifying the leaders who had defied the Chairman.

Since the Usk pogrom had been such a success (as far as the Chairman was concerned), he dispatched Admiral Willis and her executive officer Conrad Brindle (Robb's father) to crack down on another upstart colony, the luxurious reef world of Rhejak. Willis set up her base despite the vehement objections of the locals and settled in, trying to govern the people. She used a light touch, granting them the freedom to go about their daily lives. When some of the locals committed brash sabotage, however, she was forced to crack down. After meeting with the local leaders, she reached a compromise that everyone could live with, and she thought she was giving the Hansa what it needed.

The Chairman, however, was not pleased. He dispatched General Lanyan to complete the job properly—to unleash another pogrom on Rhejak, murder the leaders, and punish the populace. By the time Lanyan's battle group arrived, Willis had become quite fond of Rhejak and its people, and she did not want to see them massacred. Finally, after so many grievances against the Chairman's handling of the numerous crises, she could no longer follow a fundamentally criminal government. She tricked General Lanyan, stunned him, and took over his ships before he could launch his attack on Rhejak. It was an outright mutiny, but most of her officers and crew had similar misgivings and they followed her. Conrad Brindle, though, refused to break his oath to the Hansa. He and a handful of others accompanied General Lanyan back to Earth in disgrace.

On the Klikiss-infested colony world of Llaro, Orli Covitz and Hud Steinman struggled to survive as the bugs built their hive city all around the stockaded town. Accepted among the Klikiss, Margaret Colicos and DD could come and go as they liked, and Margaret explained how she had survived among the Klikiss for so many years, showing a small music box that her son Anton had given her. Orli herself was quite proficient in playing her own synthesizer strips, and the Klikiss hive mind, the breedex, summoned her into its great chamber to play. Frightened for Orli, Margaret helped the girl survive the encounter. Orli played her music, and the hideous hive mind let her go.

Margaret finally informed the captive colonists what the Klikiss had in store for them. The Llaro breedex was continuing its many wars with other subhives and also finding and destroying any enclaves of black robots it could find. In order to increase its numbers and expand its army, the breedex needed to fission—and for that it needed new genetic material. The Klikiss would slaughter all the colonists and use them as catalysts to create a much larger insect force.

Hearing this, the appalled colonists began to develop defenses and desperate plans. Davlin Lotze slipped away from the stockade and established a secret hideout where others could be safe. Once his sheltered cave complex was ready, small groups of Llaro colonists began to slip away, but only a fraction had gotten to safety before the Klikiss made their move. A large force of insect warriors marched to the stockade to kill all the humans, but the captives did not go down without a fight. They used makeshift defenses, explosives, and firearms to kill many of the Klikiss.

In the midst of this, Sirix led his black robots to attack the Llaro subhive. After so much damage had been done to his robots, he wanted to destroy every breedex he could find. The ferocious attack by the black robots, as well as the desperate fighting from the colonists, caused a great deal of damage to the Klikiss. In the turmoil, Orli, DD, Hud Steinman, and many others managed to get away. When they finally reached Davlin's distant hideout, the refugees didn't know where they could go or how they could find safety.

Margaret Colicos, though, had insisted on remaining behind. Back at the blasted stockade, she watched in dismay as the victorious Klikiss devoured the human survivors in order to acquire their memories and genetic material, after which the wounded breedex underwent a massive fissioning to expand its hive and recover from its losses.

Stinging from his defeat on Llaro, Sirix pulled his remaining robots to safety and tried to come up with a new plan. During his attack on the Llaro breedex, he had lost many of his irreplaceable comrades. While the Klikiss could recover from their casualties, black robots were unique storehouses of ancient experiences. PD and QT suggested an unusual solution—that Sirix should seize an appropriate manufacturing facility and build new black robots. These replacements would not have the memories of the lost robots, but they could become a key part of Sirix's army. The black robots searched for a suitable facility they could take over.

Many of the Llaro colonists were Roamer prisoners, and they had not been forgotten. Tasia Tamblyn, Robb Brindle, and Nikko Chan Tylar (whose parents were both detainees on Llaro) flew a rescue ship to Llaro, expecting to see a handful of bored EDF guards and a lot of surly colonists and detainees. When they arrived, though, they ran into the Klikiss. Caught unprepared, Tasia's ship was shot down; it crashed in a remote ravine, where it lay damaged, needing significant repairs before it could fly again. They were found by Davlin Lotze and taken back to the hideout, where they all made plans to repair the ship and fly away to safety, far from Llaro.

Just as they completed fixing the ship, however, the Klikiss captured Tasia, Robb, Orli, Nikko, and Davlin. They were brought back to the hive city and held as raw material for the next upcoming fissioning. Margaret Colicos and DD agreed to help free them. When another powerful subhive attacked the Llaro breedex, the chaos of Klikiss fighting Klikiss gave the prisoners the opportunity they needed. They had only to get back to Tasia's repaired ship, load it up with the rest of the refugees, and go. Davlin remained behind, using Orli's synthesizer strips to play a music that paralyzed the hive mind. After making it possible for the others to escape, though, he found himself trapped.

Orli and her friends reached their ship, with the Klikiss

in hot pursuit. When Margaret tried to go with them, anxious to be away from the insect creatures, the Klikiss warriors singled her out and refused to let her get away. They also crushed her music box, removing the only weapon she had. Having retrieved the rest of the survivors, Tasia flew off, sad at being forced to leave Davlin and Margaret behind.

Davlin almost got away from the Klikiss. He reached one of the transportals and tried to pass through, but he was caught. Gravely injured, he was brought before the breedex, which was on the brink of another fissioning. The singular larva of the new breedex came forward to Davlin, interested in the independent and troublesome human. Before it could subsume him, though, Davlin threw himself on the breedex larva, trying to impose himself upon it. The hive mind swallowed him up.

After Adar Zan'nh eradicated the black robots on Maratha and delivered his startling news about the Klikiss, Nira urged the Mage-Imperator to send Solar Navy assistance to other besieged human colonists on former Klikiss worlds. Zan'nh was reluctant to do this, since he believed the humans had caused their own problems by settling planets that did not belong to them. However, when he witnessed how many innocent humans had been massacred on several devastated colonies, he was deeply moved. Arriving at another besieged world, he used an ancient translating routine to convince the breedex to release the captive colonists.

After their return from Maratha, Anton Colicos and Rememberer Vao'sh were given an unexpected task—to remove the lies and correct the errors in the supposedly infallible *Saga of Seven Suns*. This caused great distress among other rememberer kithmen, particularly the conservative

Chief Scribe Ko'sh, but no one could refuse the orders of the Mage-Imperator.

From Ildira, the green priest Kolker continued to spread his telink/*thism* philosophy like a new religion, even converting many green priests on Theroc. Sullivan Gold, refusing to be converted despite pressure from Kolker and Tabitha Huck, left Ildira and returned to his family on Earth. Meanwhile, Kolker also converted the Roamer trader Denn Peroni, Cesca's father, and he became an outspoken advocate of the marvelous new philosophy.

After leaving General Lanyan and the EDF, and "borrowing" his grandmother's space yacht, Patrick Fitzpatrick III searched among the Roamers for his lost love, Zhett Kellum. He finally found her on the gas giant Golgen, where the Roamers had reestablished skymining operations. His reunion with Zhett did not go as expected, however; she refused to speak to him. Trying to come clean, Patrick confessed what he had done earlier, destroying a Roamer trading ship to eliminate a witness; though General Lanyan was ultimately responsible for the murder, Patrick had given the order to fire. After a trial, Patrick was sentenced to "walk the plank" over the open cloudy skies. He bravely accepted his fate, but at the last minute Zhett spoke on his behalf and convinced her father to pardon him. Patrick then became a strong supporter of the Confederation and transmitted a damning message that squarely laid the blame for the Hansa's problems on General Lanyan and Chairman Wenceslas. Upon hearing this message, Basil rebuked Patrick's grandmother, former Chairman Maureen Fitzpatrick, for the actions of her grandson.

King Peter and Queen Estarra continued strengthening the Confederation. Seeing the King and Queen as potential allies against the Klikiss and the faeros, Mage-Imperator

Jora'h announced that he would travel to Theroc and publicly proclaim an alliance between the Ildiran Empire and the Confederation. Nira accompanied him, as well as Anton Colicos and Rememberer Vao'sh. Standing together under the worldtrees, the Mage-Imperator and the King swore a firm alliance. This was truly the death knell for the few remnants of the Hansa still loyal to Chairman Wenceslas.

Upon learning of Jora'h's announcement, the Chairman took drastic measures. He ordered Admiral Esteban Diente to take a powerful EDF battle group to intercept the Mage-Imperator after he departed from Theroc. Admiral Diente was appalled at the orders, but he could not refuse, because the Chairman had taken his family hostage.

After Mage-Imperator Jora'h made his promises to King Peter, he felt that he had strengthened the Ildiran Empire. However, Rusa'h and the faeros had just begun their worst ravages. They tracked down Denn Peroni and Caleb Tamblyn, who were flying a water tanker filled with wentals, and destroyed the ship near the icy planetoid Jonah 12. Denn was killed, but Caleb escaped in a lifepod and was marooned. The faeros also went to the primary wental planet of Charybdis and overwhelmed the living seas with their flames. Jess and Cesca could feel the agony of the dying wentals, but by the time they arrived the oceans had been scorched, the planet burned. The faeros had declared war on the wentals.

An armada of fireballs emerged from the dead Ildiran sun of Durris-B, reigniting the star and flooding out like a meteor shower. When Tabitha Huck took a newly built warliner on a shakedown cruise, the faeros were able to sense her presence because of her conversion to the telink/*thism* religion. They destroyed her and the new warliner, then flew toward Ildira, where they also targeted Kolker and all his converts there. Mijistra began to go up in flames.

Prime Designate Daro'h, left in charge of the Prism Palace, was forced to flee as the faeros incarnate Rusa'h came for him, demanding to know where the Mage-Imperator was. Osira'h and her siblings used their unique powers to protect the Prime Designate and Yazra'h; they all escaped through water channels beneath the Prism Palace.

Returning from his rescue of the human colonists on Klikiss worlds, Adar Zan'nh found the burned warliners of Tal O'nh's septa. As soon as O'nh and Designate Ridek'h warned him about the impending holocaust on Ildira, Zan'nh raced off with his ships. When they arrived, the Solar Navy warliners attempted to battle the fireballs, but they had no effective way to combat the living fire. The Adar did, however, rescue Daro'h, Yazra'h, Osira'h, and the other half-breed children. But they needed the leadership of the Mage-Imperator.

On his flagship warliner, Jora'h could sense the horrific events unfolding on Ildira. Through her treeling, Nira received news that the faeros were burning Mijistra, but her contact abruptly ended when the lone treeling in the Prism Palace turned to ash. Desperate to get back, Jora'h ordered his warliners to increase speed—only to run into Admiral Diente's EDF battleships. Diente fired upon the warliner, damaged its engines, and captured the Mage-Imperator. Despite Jora'h's urgent pleas about the disaster on Ildira, Diente escorted him and all the Ildiran captives to the EDF base on Earth's Moon. Chairman Wenceslas came to see the prisoners, pleased at his easy victory, and told the Mage-Imperator that he must remain a "guest" of the Hansa until he abandoned his alliance with the Confederation and denounced King Peter.

The faeros had conquered Ildira, and Rusa'h installed himself in the Prism Palace. Now that he had discovered the telink/*thism* pathways through his other victims, the faeros incarnate was able to follow them back to the worldforest. Suddenly, green priest converts on Theroc burst into flame. From there, the hungry elemental fire spread to the towering worldtrees. The forest on Theroc began to burn.

THE ASHES
OF WORLDS

1 ☀ ADMIRAL SHEILA WILLIS

Ten Mantas and one giant Juggernaut cruised across empty space, leaving Earth behind—possibly forever, as far as Admiral Willis was concerned. Though her ships still bore the markings of the Earth Defense Forces, their crews no longer served the Hansa. No, not after everything they had seen.

Chairman Wenceslas would have called them mutineers. *How could anyone not feel bitter about that?*

There'd been a time when Willis was young and naïve (or perhaps just insufficiently jaded), when she had thought all decisions were clear-cut, all answers black-and-white. She had believed that the good guys were fundamentally different from the bad guys. Well, she'd left that attitude behind on Rhejak when General Lanyan's brutality had forced her to make a previously unthinkable decision.

By seizing a whole battle group and turning her back on her beloved EDF, she had set wheels in motion—wheels that might well run her over. After dumping Lanyan, Conrad Brindle, and a handful of hard-line loyalists on the outskirts of Earth's solar system, she was taking her ships to Theroc, to join King Peter and his Confederation.

No matter how many times she tried to rationalize her decision, though, it still felt like desertion. Her brain was simply wired that way. She scanned the people on her bridge for signs of uneasiness. Willis was surprised at just how many of them had volunteered to burn their bridges and join her. Abandoning their homes, friends, families, and possessions was not a decision to make lightly. Obviously, she wasn't the only one who had smelled something rotten in the Hansa.

The last time she had brought these particular Mantas to Theroc, Willis had been under orders to arrest Peter as an outlaw ruler. . . .

"Approaching destination, Admiral," said her helmsman.

"Make sure you announce our arrival politely. We don't want them to pee their pants when all these warships show up." She took a few moments to adjust her posture, her uniform, her expression. Ready to go meet the new boss.

As soon as the eleven ships entered planetary orbit, however, Willis saw that something was wrong. A flurry of mismatched Roamer ships had been launched into erratic orbits. Cargo craft, fast scouts, lumbering barges all lifted off from the forested continent and raced away from the planet in all directions. Two of the larger Roamer ships nearly collided with each other.

Her young comm officer's skin turned prominently pink. "Admiral, it's total pandemonium down there! Frantic distress calls, screams—Theroc is being attacked, but I can't see how."

The threatening verdani treeships that circled the lush forested world like a crown of thorns were in trouble. Thrashing their enormous thorny branches, they did not even react to the oncoming EDF war vessels. They were battling some pervasive, unseen enemy.

"Ask how we can assist them," Willis barked. She looked around for any unexpected threat . . . perhaps the return of the hydrogues or one of General Lanyan's vessels. "Get close enough to respond as needed. We're supposed to be the cavalry here—I'd like to make a great first impression."

The feedback shrieks coming over the comm system were worse than fingernails scraping across a chalkboard.

Cruising directly in front of them, its boughs twisting and snapping as if in extreme internal pain, one of the thorny tree battleships literally burst into flames. Despite the cold vacuum of space, bright yellow-orange fire cracked out of its core and spread across the branches, devouring the energized wood.

On the high-res surveillance scans of the forests below, Willis saw intense blazes appear, spontaneously igniting and beginning to spread through the dense worldforest . . . exactly where she knew King Peter had established the Confederation's headquarters.

2 ✹ KING PETER

Another worldtree shuddered and then erupted into flames as the faeros possessed its heartwood. With sounds like cannon shots, the malicious fires crackled through the delicate fronds, striving toward the canopy—burning, but not entirely consuming the heartwood.

High up within the fungus-reef city, King Peter shouted for the people to evacuate. The smoke and heat in the air bit the back of his throat. From an opening in the organic walls, he and Estarra saw the flames race greedily up one trunk after another, but none of the living verdani turned to ash. Not yet.

The green priests who remained inside the white-walled tree city clamped hands like vises against their smooth emerald scalps as pain surged through the worldforest mind. The followers of Yarrod and Kolker, who were joined in their tightly bonded *thism*/telink web, had already suffered most of all.

A male green priest stuttered to a halt, then raised his arms in agony. The priest bent backward and with a wordless wail burst into flames. Other green priests stared at the smear of ash and burning coals that marked where the man had stood. Some wept; others collapsed to their knees.

Queen Estarra tugged her husband's sleeve as they ran from the shuddering throne room. "Peter, we have to get Reynald and go!" Her beaded braids clicked and bounced behind her head.

In their private rooms, Estarra snatched their baby son from the arms of the Teacher compy OX, who had already gathered him up for the evacuation. Little Reynald was crying from the loud commotion and the smoke from brush fires.

OX was not at all panicked. "Before we hurry to the lift platforms, Queen Estarra, I suggest we soak a blanket with water. I will wrap it around the baby for protection as I carry him." When Estarra was reluctant to relinquish the child, OX pointed out, "I am physically stronger than either of you, and neither the fire nor the smoke will affect me."

"He's right," Peter said, yanking a blanket from the bed and running to the water basin that Roamer engineers had installed. "It's his best chance."

Outside, the elemental fires continued to spread. After being transmitted through the few hapless green priest conduits, the faeros had formed a parasitic bond with the verdani, converting them into torch trees. From there, secondary blazes had spread to the underbrush, consuming smaller shrubs and plants.

Peter and Estarra wrapped the wet cloth around the squirming infant and secured the wailing bundle to OX's chest with a utility cord. The Teacher compy held Reynald firmly, keeping pace with the King and Queen as they rushed through winding fungus-reef passages to the outer balconies.

Breathing heavily, Peter stepped out into the choking hot air and watched the faeros flames jump from one tree to the next. Normal fires raced across the fringes of the clearing, where people ran pell-mell away from the fungus-reef tree.

Therons crowded the small lift platforms, trying to ride the cables down to the ground. But the elevators were equipped to carry only a few people at a time, not to accommodate such a massive evacuation. When sixteen people crammed onto one platform, clutching the side rails and each other, the overloaded lift groaned and gave way, spilling the passengers to their deaths. Watching in horror, Peter shouted, but he couldn't help them.

For just a moment the scope and suddenness of the disaster knocked the wind out of him. Even if everyone got to the ground, how would they cross the meadow safely through growing curtains of flames? There was no time to wonder how this had happened and no time for panic or grief either. Peter had to keep his wits about him and somehow get his people, and his family, to safety.

Estarra saw it, too, and quickly made her decision. "We'll have to climb." In answer to Peter's concerned expression, she gave a confident nod. "It doesn't matter that I've just had a baby. I spent most of my life scrambling up and down worldtrees. If OX can carry Reynald safely, we should be fine. Can you manage?"

Flashing her a determined smile, Peter shouted to the frantic people, "Every able-bodied person, climb down! Treedancers, help the others. Use the platforms only if you can't climb."

A few of the overcrowded elevators managed to reach the ground, and the people sprinted across the meadow toward the ring of fire. By now, the fungus-reef tree had caught fire from eager sparks that spread from the initial torch trees. Tongues of flame raced up the golden bark, consuming small fronds, scorching the bark plates, until part of the city began to smolder.

Some people swiftly grasped knobs and handholds in the bark scales. Peter could see they didn't have much time. "Let's go."

Because OX had lashed the blanket-wrapped baby to his torso, his polymer arms were left free. Without further comment, the compy swung himself over the edge and began to climb down. Peter had never seen OX do anything so nimble or athletic before, but the Teacher compy seemed perfectly capable of working his way down.

Estarra went next, calling out encouragement to the people still evacuating. Peter followed. Smoke and steam oozed from between the bark plates, burning his hands, but he didn't let go.

The compy reached the ground first and turned to wait for the King and Queen. He adjusted the wet wrappings around the infant, keeping Reynald secured to his solid chest. By now the wildfire had caught on the grasses and flowers; shrubs burst into fireballs. Above them, the fungus reef was fully engulfed, and orange flames spat from the upper balconies and windows.

Peter dropped the rest of the way to the ground. "To the edge of the meadow!"

Like solar flares, living arcs of fire sprang from torch tree to torch tree. With a crack like an incandescent bullwhip, another majestic worldtree succumbed to the fiery elementals. Its interlocked canopy of fronds became a ceiling of orange embers; smaller branches caught and transmitted sparks to adjacent ones.

While OX hurried ahead of them, carrying the baby, Estarra kept her head down and ran. But, before they could follow the evacuees into the dense surrounding forest, flames cut them off. The perimeter of the grove formed a burning wall, forcing OX to halt ahead of them.

With a crack and a roar, a thick branch broke loose from above, and a clump of flaming fronds crashed directly down onto the compy in a feathery spray of sparks and embers.

Estarra screamed for the baby. Peter shielded his stinging eyes and dove toward them, but he knew he was too late to save his son.

The little compy pushed his way out, knocking aside the blazing fronds. He kept his synthetic body hunched over, arms wrapped protectively around Reynald. OX's polymer skin was damaged; ash and soot were smeared like war paint on his smooth face, but his systems still functioned.

Estarra raced forward in panic to retrieve Reynald. Peeling the steaming blanket away, Peter checked to make sure the baby hadn't been burned. The little boy was wailing, but very much alive.

Green grass smoldered around them, making the smoke burn like acid in their lungs. Estarra pointed desperately across the meadow to the diamond sphere of the hydrogue derelict, which OX had flown during their escape from Earth. "There! That's our only way out!"

With nowhere else to run, they crashed through the embers of underbrush until they reached the small alien ship. Thankfully, the hatch had been left open. As flames flicked at their heels, Peter and Estarra, along with OX and the baby, clambered inside. Peter sealed the doorway behind them, and the sudden silence made his ears pop. They slapped at the ashes burning their garments, wheezing, coughing, frightened, and shaking with exertion. But safe.

Through the transparent curved wall, they watched angry flames engulf the rest of the meadow and then rush over them.

3 ☀ CHAIRMAN BASIL WENCESLAS

Outside in the Palace District's main square, the Archfather of Unison carried an elaborate shepherd's crook. He wore golden damask robes ornamented with frills and simulated brocades, and he looked like a jovial old uncle with a long, bushy white beard. The religious spokesman delivered another rousing speech, carefully scripted by Chairman Wenceslas.

People could so easily be distracted without a firm hand to guide them.

When properly motivated, the Archfather, a former actor, could really tug on the heartstrings of an audience. Unfortunately, though, during recent coaching sessions the man had begun to express doubts about the Chairman's agenda. The Archfather had spent altogether too much time reviewing images of the bloody Usk pogrom. Initially, he had been enthusiastic about delivering a stern message to the upstart colony world—razing the farming town, crucifying the defiant town elders—yet he now questioned the necessity of such actions.

In times like these, Basil expected his underlings to do what they were told for the good of the Hansa and, by extension, the human race. They were not supposed to have second thoughts. With harsh words and overt threats, he had put the man back in his place, leaving him white and shaking.

Making certain the Archfather had learned his lesson, Basil watched the show from the Whisper Palace observation gallery, accompanied by a concerned-looking Sarein and an unusually contemplative Deputy Eldred Cain.

"The Archfather is doing well today," Sarein pointed out. "You talked to him, didn't you?"

"I had to fan the flames of his enthusiasm a bit. This time he seems to have gotten the point."

From the square below, the bearded man bellowed his words. "Yes, the Klikiss are *demons*, but demons cannot help what they are. They may be evil, they may be destructive, but it is in their very nature. Far worse are those who *choose* evil—people who ally themselves with the Klikiss, with the demons, with our enemies. By this, I mean our treacherous King Peter and his rebellious Confederation."

The sermon was, naturally, being transmitted across Earth. Cargo ships and fast traders would deliver recordings of the Archfather's message to the handful of colonies and industrial worlds that still paid lip service to the Hansa.

In his seat, Deputy Cain looked decidedly uncomfortable, and Basil could tell he wanted to say something. He sighed, waiting. "What is it, Mr. Cain?"

The deputy answered promptly. "Complaints have been forwarded to me by several law-enforcement stations, sir. The police don't know what to do about them."

Basil's eyebrows drew together. "Complaints? There are always complaints."

"These seem to have some merit. It appears that a well-organized vigilante group has taken it upon itself to quell certain public discussions." Cain pulled out a report. "For example, here are two incidents in which the group smashed businesses and roughed people up. They target anyone who speaks out against the Hansa. They don't even try to hide themselves." He presented surveillance images and pointed to a young woman wearing a dark uniform. "This costume appears to be based on early EDF uniform designs. I have identified one of the ringleaders responsible for these strong-arm tactics, a woman named Shelia Andez, an EDF officer."

"Yes, I know. I reassigned her myself," Basil said. "She spearheads an elite force to help maintain order and loyalty on Earth. I call these soldiers my cleanup crew, though I suppose they deserve a more formal name."

"You're actually aware of this? Their activities go against any number of laws."

"Andez is doing the work I've assigned her. What you

call strong-arm tactics, I view as a last-ditch effort to maintain much-needed order. The Hansa is in an extremely fragile state right now."

The people in the square below suddenly cheered, and the Chairman turned to watch, brushing aside Cain's concerns. The Archfather bowed. Basil tried to recall what particular line might have evoked such a reaction; he decided to review the tapes later. That way he could also critique the man's performance.

The Archfather lowered his voice as if he were telling a secret to billions of listeners, delivering the preposterous suggestion with complete gravity—the very part of the speech to which the man had objected so strenuously before Basil had vetoed his concerns. "King Peter and his fellow traitors in the Confederation may actively be playing into the plans of the Klikiss. Roamer clans may be assisting the demon creatures in their conquests. In an insidious plot to destroy our beloved Hansa, the Confederation rebels and the Klikiss have agreed to split what's left of the Spiral Arm between themselves."

The audience gasped, predictably and on cue.

"That's ridiculous, Basil," Sarein muttered. "Please be cautious. When accusations get so extreme, you can't really expect people to believe them."

Basil gave her a hard sidelong look. "I disagree. It is a perfectly reasonable conclusion, considering what else the people have been told. We can't afford to lose popular support right now. Our attempted pogrom at Rhejak was a complete mess." He felt his face flush with anger and embarrassment. "Admiral Willis deserted us, taking a Juggernaut and ten Mantas. General Lanyan returned home like a whipped dog, in total disgrace."

"You've kept his ignominious defeat very quiet." Cain looked up at him. "Where is the General now?"

"I've had to remove him from public view until he can fix the problem that he caused."

"How is he going to accomplish that?" Sarein did not seem to look forward to the answer. "I thought you would consult with us—"

"It was straightforward enough. I gave him the opportunity to achieve a clear victory." Basil laced his fingers behind his head, careful not to mess his steel-gray hair. "King Peter's outlaw Confederation is our enemy, and we must treat them as such. They have resources that we require, primarily ekti. Therefore, we'll raid Roamer facilities and take what we need. After all, we're at war." His lips quirked in a smile, willfully ignoring the horrified expressions on his companions' faces. "General Lanyan's battle group is on its way to a known Roamer skymining center. Our intelligence suggests they have no viable defenses. It is my fervent hope that the General can finally redeem himself."

4 ☀ GENERAL KURT LANYAN

The Juggernaut *Goliath*, five Manta cruisers, a Thunderhead weapons platform, more than two thousand Remoras fully loaded with jazers and explosive projectiles — yes, that would keep even the most unruly clans in line. General Lanyan was quite certain of an EDF victory at Golgen.

He was glad to be at the helm of his Juggernaut again. The *Goliath* had been heavily damaged in the fighting at the end of the hydrogue war, but the giant vessel had finally been repaired and placed back into service. One small step toward having a fully capable EDF again.

Acquiring plenty of stardrive fuel . . . that was the next step.

When the gas giant came into view, Lanyan transmitted to the lead Manta in the attack group. "Admiral Brindle, verify that all personnel are at their stations, all Remora pilots ready to launch, and all weapons ready to fire. I don't intend to leave anything to chance here."

The older, dark-skinned commander acknowledged. Recently promoted to fill one of the officer slots vacated by the decimation of the Earth Defense Forces, Conrad Brindle left no doubts about his competence or dedication. When the rest of the Rhejak battle group had mutinied, Brindle had been one of the few who remained loyal to the EDF. The promotion and this new assignment were his reward.

Lanyan straightened in his command chair, loudly cleared his throat, and addressed his subcommanders. "Ac-

cording to our fast recon and recent intel, Golgen has more
than a dozen skymines, but they're industrial facilities, not
military bases. Once we've knocked down any resistance, our
objective is to seize their stores of stardrive fuel." Now his
voice held a cautionary tone. "But cause as little damage as
possible. We want these facilities to remain functional. The
Chairman wants to return and administer the facilities under
Hansa auspices. For now, the EDF just needs the ekti."

Sounding battle stations, the warships raced toward a
buttery-yellow globe laced with white cloud bands. Long-
distance sensors spotted towering cities that rode the cloud
tops converting atmospheric hydrogen into ekti.

As the main attack group fanned out, the Mantas each
approached a different Roamer skymine, while the Thunderhead remained in a stationary position, a citadel on higher
ground. "Remember, Roamers are cowards at heart," Lanyan
continued. "They like to run and hide. They sneak around
in unmarked ships, keeping their locations secret. It's not in
their nature to fight." The *Goliath* headed toward the largest
skymine, a complex of many floating platforms abuzz with
space traffic and support vehicles.

He shook his head in disgust. "Just look at them all!"

Once, as a boy, he had turned over a rotten log to find
it squirming with tiny black beetles. Suddenly exposed to
the light, the insects had scattered, seeking dark corners and
holes in which to hide. He had taken a stick and spent more
than an hour hunting down and crushing the small bugs.

These Roamer ships reacted as the beetles had. Instead
of mounting an orderly defense, the mismatched clan ships
flew in all directions, every man for himself. The General
found it pathetic. He gave his anxious weapons officers permission to take as many potshots as they liked.

On the crowded screen, he identified the spidery cargo escorts holding canisters of ekti. He pointed his index finger, raising his voice. "There! Those are the ships I was telling you about. Remember my orders."

His weapons officers fired at the evacuating cargo escorts, aiming carefully and missing intentionally. The barrage, however, was merely a diversion so that tiny pingers could attach to the hulls without the Roamer pilots noticing. The locator beacons would activate later so that Lanyan could track the cargo escorts to other fuel-distribution depots. If the EDF made a diligent effort, they could unravel the whole Roamer network and find all of their hidden facilities.

As the raid commenced, Lanyan ignored the outraged cries and threatening comm messages from the skymine managers. "Prepare to be boarded," he transmitted to the largest facility. "With your unconditional surrender, we can eliminate — or at least minimize — casualties."

A gruff voice yelled back at him, "This is Del Kellum, and I'm in charge of this skymine. I do not — repeat, *do not* — grant you permission to land."

Lanyan chuckled. "Exactly how are you going to stop me? With harsh language and a disapproving look?" He switched off the transmission, stood up, and stretched.

An hour later, from a troop transport filled with heavily armed EDF soldiers, Lanyan looked out at the enormous floating city with its many decks and docks, its antennae, sensor probes, and observation balconies. The *Goliath* hung nearby, huge and ominous in the sky. Admiral Brindle had already reported a swift victory at his assigned skymine, as had the other EDF Mantas. Chairman Wenceslas was going to be pleased when he heard how much stardrive fuel this operation would yield.

Before disembarking, the General checked his uniform, quickly combed his dark hair, and surveyed the guards ready to exit the transport with him. Lanyan thought of the successful commanders he had learned about in military school, their proud victory speeches on conquered ground. He wanted to make a memorable impression here when he set foot on the beaten skymine and showed everyone that he was not to be trifled with.

The hatch opened, and he stepped proudly down the ramp. "I hereby take control of this new facility in the name of the Hansa."

A group of agitated Roamers waited for him. He recognized bearded Del Kellum, with his barrel chest and his angry expression. Next, he saw a completely unexpected young man, who would have looked more familiar had he been wearing an EDF uniform.

"General Lanyan," said Patrick Fitzpatrick III, "I see my new opinion of you was absolutely correct."

5 ☀ JESS TAMBLYN

Once, Charybdis had been a primeval ocean world whose turbulent seas hosted countless thriving wentals. And then the faeros had come.

Jess and Cesca had not been here when angry fireballs

had rained down to blast the elemental seas, but now they stood together on the smoking ruin of the planet. The air was laden with heavy sulfurous steam, the cadaverous smell of dead wentals. He drew a deep breath, felt the anger burn through him.

This is war.

"The Roamers can help us," Cesca said, her voice brittle with fury at the sight of the blackened, glassy landscape that had once been a calm and fertile sea. "We should ask the clans to join our fight."

Kneeling, Jess put his fingers in a warm, scum-covered puddle. The water felt oily and dead. He shook his head, trying to find an independent reservoir on Charybdis. *Something* must have survived. "What possible weapons could Roamers devise against them?"

Cesca raised her eyebrows. "Jess Tamblyn, are you really doubting Roamer ingenuity?"

He took hope from that, and with his fingers still dripping, he began to walk across the wasteland. Understanding the wentals all too well, he did know what the largest problem was. "Wentals and verdani are forces of life and stability. Hydrogues and faeros are the embodiments of destruction. When they clash, the chaos and aggression inevitably overwhelm the quiet and peace. The wentals don't know how to fight effectively against an enemy like this."

Cesca followed him. "Unless we change the rules of engagement."

A small crack opened up in the ground, and steam sighed out like the last gasp of another wental that had surrendered to its fate.

Ten thousand years ago the wentals and verdani had nearly been annihilated in the great war. Sorely beaten, the hydrogues were driven into their gas-giant planets, and the faeros took up residence in their stars. When hostilities had flared up again, the unresolved conflict triggered into full fury. But now the landscape of the Spiral Arm was quite different.

From his contact with the wentals, Jess knew that the faeros had nearly been defeated by the hydrogues until the fiery beings had changed their old chaotic tactics. The former Hyrillka Designate Rusa'h had caused that difference. He had fled into the fires of a nearby sun where the faeros consumed and joined with him, much as the wentals had with Jess and Cesca. As a living embodiment of the fiery creatures, Rusa'h had showed them new ways to fight, and they had overwhelmed the hydrogues at one battleground after another — and won. His guidance had made all the difference.

Jess stopped as these thoughts roiled through his head. When the wentals had been weak and few, they had saved him by permeating the tissues of his body, rescuing him from his exploding ship. Out of gratitude, Jess had led water bearers to disperse wental seedpools from planet to planet.

Now he and Cesca had an even greater challenge. Like Rusa'h, they had to take charge and guide the wentals in an effective fight. They had to *show* the watery elementals how to take aggressive action.

He turned to Cesca, and his eyes seemed to fill with steam as he looked at the blasted landscape. "It's time for the wentals to be angry, time for them to become warriors — to fight in a way that is more than just defensive."

Power surged through his bloodstream, and he felt an overwhelming urge to strike something. Jess wasn't normally an angry man, but now with his hard fists, he struck the glassy eggshell surface and felt the baked barrier crack. He pounded again. Yes, he sensed something deeper here! The oceans of Charybdis had been blasted away, but there was always water, always life.

He struck a third time and broke through the crust. Water filled the hole he had made, liquid percolating from deep aquifers. The water was hot, near boiling. Steam drifted about—not putrid brimstone steam, but vaporized water. *Wental water.* More and more of it welled up, as if trying to break free.

Cesca thrust her hands into the thermal pool. Bubbling water spurted out of the hot spring and flowed across the baked ground. Another geyser blasted through the crust, where more wentals had awakened from the hot aquifers.

Cesca stood up and clenched both fists. "As we touch and spread these wentals, our just anger will charge them with fresh purpose. Together we will find new ways to fight back."

Beside her, Jess felt the power sing through his body, assuring him that all of the wentals would awaken and follow them. "We have a new Guiding Star."

6 ☀ TASIA TAMBLYN

After escaping from the Klikiss on Llaro, the damaged ship limped back to the Roamer shipyards. Tasia refused to leave the piloting deck, afraid that if she let her attention waver, some other crisis would hit these beleaguered people.

"Almost there, Tamblyn," Robb Brindle said from the copilot's chair, afraid to relax unless she did. "Almost there."

"You've been saying that for days."

"And each time we're closer to home, aren't we?"

The ship had originally been sent to rescue Roamer detainees held in a small EDF camp, but none of them had expected to fight a planet full of Klikiss. Damned bugs!

"Almost there," Robb said again.

"Enough already."

The Osquivel rings were a wide, sparkling disk, paper thin in relation to the bloated gas planet they encircled. Clear infrared signatures marked the largest industrial operations dispersed throughout the orbiting rubble: spacedocks and construction bays, admin asteroids, storage bunkers, independent complexes that specialized in ship construction or component fabrication, debris plumes that fanned out into space like rooster tails.

Tasia sent out their ID signal and requested an approved approach vector. In the large passenger compartment, the refugees began to get restless. Looking through the window-ports, they watched the gas giant growing larger and larger.

"Is that a Roamer base?" Orli Covitz entered the pilot deck, her interested eyes fixed on the front screens.

"Beautiful, isn't it? Bet you've never seen anything like it."

Hud Steinman, a scrawny old man who always looked disheveled, came up next to the fifteen-year-old girl. "Looks *crowded*. How many different habitation domes and industrial facilities do you have?"

"Exactly enough," Tasia said. "No, strike that. We could use a few more. We're building up the Confederation's military against the Big Goose . . . and now we've got the bugs to worry about, too."

"It's probably noisy," Steinman grumbled.

"If you prefer Llaro, we could send you back," Robb teased.

"We're docking within the hour," Tasia said. "There'll be quite a few Roamer families anxious to welcome us. Go tell everyone to get ready."

"All we have are the clothes on our backs," Orli said.

"And lucky to have *that*," Steinman added.

As their ship came into the center of the complex, numerous craft converged around the largest artificial structure. Small cargo pods and transport flitters raced in from other complexes as people gathered to welcome the refugees. Once Tasia gave them an earful about what had really happened at Llaro, she expected to rile up the whole Confederation before any more human colonies were trampled by the waves of returning Klikiss.

While she docked at the hub and went through the tedious lockdown and verification procedures, the eager passengers crowded against the hatches. Finally, after the equalization lamps blinked green, Tasia opened all four side doors at the same time and extended the ramps. In a flood, the survivors of Llaro exited into the bustling complex. Many looked shell-shocked. Many wept. Some couldn't stop laughing.

Standing together, Tasia and Robb enjoyed watching the happy reunions. Without even looking at each other, they reached out at the same moment to clasp hands. "I'm proud of what we did, Brindle, but I'm also mad as hell. We're going to have to do something about the Klikiss, and pretty damn quick."

Robb followed. "You're ready to lock and load, aren't you, Tamblyn?"

"I'm anxious to go back to Llaro and clean up the mess. I want to teach those bugs a lesson." Too many—including Davlin Lotze—had sacrificed their lives during the rescue so that others could get away.

"At least let me grab a shower before you jump headfirst into another battle."

"This is a Roamer complex with standard resource-management protocols." She looked into his amber eyes. "We'd better take that shower together—to conserve water."

Kotto Okiah, who was acting administrator of the ship-yards, scratched his curly hair and blinked his owlish eyes at all the people who had showed up unexpectedly. When he spotted Tasia and Robb, he hurried over. "Well, it looks like you've got this under control." Tasia wasn't sure he even recalled why the rescue ship had gone to Llaro in the first place.

She said, "Kotto, there's another danger that the whole Confederation needs to prepare for. We're going to need some brand-new weapons and defenses."

"Oh? That's excellent." The engineer raised his eyebrows. "Which enemy are we talking about now? I thought the hydrogues were defeated. There's the Hansa, of course, but nothing really new. Is there something I'm missing?"

"Worse than the Big Goose, maybe worse than the drogues." Taking Kotto by the elbow, Tasia said, "You've still got a green priest at the shipyards, right?"

"Yes. Liona should be on her way over here. I, uh, sent for her in case the clans wanted to hear news of their loved ones. Planning ahead—"

Tasia cut him off. "We need to send out messages to rally all the Confederation fighters. King Peter knows the Klikiss have returned, but I doubt he knows they're attacking colonies. No time to lose."

The din in the reception bay was deafening as refugees chattered eagerly with clan members. When the female green priest finally entered the admin complex through the metal-lined hall, many Roamers rushed toward her, hoping to send telink notices to friends and family.

But something was wrong with Liona; Tasia picked up on it immediately. The green priest looked aghast as she pushed her way into the clamor. She gripped her small potted tree, and the delicate fronds seemed to shudder. Liona's distraught shout brought everyone to a startled silence.

She looked around wildly. "The faeros are burning the worldforest!"

7 ☀ CELLI

A searing, sentient heat engulfed the stately trees and worked its way to their very cores. Yet the verdani heartwood refused to burn, so that the possessed trees shone like torches, unable to throw off the fiery elementals. Meanwhile, a normal fire had spread to vulnerable wood and underbrush, ravaging the forest as well.

At the edge of the meadow, Celli clenched her fists. "What can we do for the worldtrees, Solimar? How can we help them fight?"

"The faeros are torturing the trees they've captured." Her friend pressed his hands against his smooth scalp, wincing and then forcing his eyes open again. "Burning! It is hard to concentrate."

Though new to her abilities as a green priest, Celli could hear the wordless agony of trees. When the fires attacked one of them, they all felt the pain. Many green priests in the forest nearby were overwhelmed by the tragedy, unable to disconnect from their bond. Others fought back the clamor and the horror, afraid to open themselves to telink at all.

Though most of the trees in the central grove were caught up in elemental fire, Celli realized that the large trees were struggling to *hold on to* the faeros, to keep the fire from jumping to other worldtrees. She could feel the verdani fighting, but they were losing the battle.

With a shudder and then a surge of dismay, one of the weakening trees could no longer maintain its hold, and the faeros gleefully leaped to another towering trunk. Energetic flames raced up the golden bark scales to reach the vulnerable fronds, and within moments that tree had also become a living torch.

Solimar turned to her, his face drawn but determined. "Those faeros were transmitted through telink along mental pathways opened by Yarrod and his green priests. But these faeros are different somehow from the ones we've seen before."

Celli sorted the information from the bedlam in her mind. The telink/*thism* connection had inadvertently created a passage for faeros sparks to hurtle through. After consuming the green priest conduits, they had possessed the nearest trees. Yarrod himself had been the first to die, and Celli was unable to drive the horrible image of her uncle bursting into flames from her mind. He had tried to do a good thing, and it had incinerated him.

"These are newborn sparks—and they aren't as strong as the others," Celli said. "We can fight them, if the green priests will rally. We can strengthen the trees, give them hope, just like you and I did with our treedancing!"

She felt a rush of optimism. When the worldforest had nearly given up after the first hydrogue holocaust, she and Solimar had danced for the trees. That exuberance, that show of *life*, had awakened a new strength in the worldforest, had let the deep roots tap into something the verdani had not previously known how to summon. Their human spirit had shaken the worldforest out of its old malaise.

She and Solimar could do the same thing now. "We have to tell the other green priests!" Impulsively, she placed her palms against the bark of a nearby tree and opened her mind to telink.

Solimar shouted, tried to stop her. Too late, Celli realized her mistake. As soon as she made the connection, the mental uproar hit her like a cannon blast. She could not block the overpowering cacophony.

Solimar threw himself to the tree beside her, held her with one arm and touched the bark with his free hand. Instead of dragging her away and breaking the connection, he added his strength, helped her hold on. Celli squeezed her eyes shut and fought the background roar. Her narrow shoulders shuddered, but she forced herself to keep her palms in place. For the worldforest. She shouted through telink. *We are here for you. Draw on our strength.*

She suddenly realized who else might be able to help them, just as he had helped the verdani understand the power behind the treedancing. Beneto had fused with one of the giant verdani treeships circling Theroc, and he was still up in orbit. Even in cold, dark space, the great battleship trees struggled against the newborn faeros trying to reach them through the telink conduits. Two of the treeships out there had already caught fire and were surrounded by an unnatural blaze.

Celli sought out the distant mind she missed so much, and Beneto broke through to her briefly. *The burning trees must cut themselves off. Stop the spread of the fire before the faeros conquer all the worldforest.*

Like the sound of shattering crystal in her mind, a burst of pain nearly deafened her. Traveling invisible pathways, the faeros had jumped to Beneto—and now his immense battleship body became a torch high above Theroc . . . too far away for her to help him, burning and burning, but not dying.

Huddled inside the sealed hydrogue derelict, Estarra held the baby close. In the panicked flight from the fungus reef, she hadn't even noticed how her hands and arms were blistered and smudged from falling embers. Peter's face was scalded, his voice raspy from inhaling so much smoke.

Outside the insulated diamond walls, the flames roared so brightly that she had to shield her eyes. The meadow was entirely ablaze, and another huge branch crashed down.

"I can still fly this vessel," the Teacher compy offered. "Its systems are functional. I am perfectly capable of guiding it out of the fire."

Estarra felt a surge of relief. "Of course you are, OX!"

The compy placed his polymer hands on the crystal knobs and accessed the complex etched circuitry. The hydrogue engines made no sound; there was no roar of liftoff or blast of rockets, but the small sphere heaved itself up from the ground. OX guided them higher, above the conflagration, above the torch trees.

Across the sweep of the canopy Estarra spotted other islands of fire where faeros had caught on specific trees, perhaps weak points in the telink network, or places where Yarrod's green priests had inadvertently created a vulnerability. But most of the worldforest had not yet succumbed. It was bad, she knew, but it could have been worse.

Past the circle of fire that had trapped them, they saw many Therons running to scattered Roamer cargo craft.

"Better land among them, OX," Peter said, his eyes darting from side to side as he raced through possible options. "We might need those vessels to take people to safety."

"Eleven large military ships have just arrived in orbit, King Peter," the Teacher compy announced. "They belong to the Earth Defense Forces."

Estarra felt sick inside as she jumped to the obvious conclusion. "The EDF is attacking us *now*?"

Peter's left hand unconsciously tightened. "Damn the Chairman! Send a message, OX. Tell them that we intend to vigorously resist any Hansa aggression. Don't let them think we're vulnerable."

An older woman's voice replied to the transmission in a hard drawl; Estarra recognized Admiral Willis. "King Peter, I'm not here to give you a black eye—I came to offer a help-ing hand. Looks like you could use it, too. My ships and I no longer serve Chairman Wenceslas."

"That's good news, Admiral, but as you can see, we're in the middle of an emergency here. I don't have time for formalities."

"Then I'm glad we got here when we did. I'm coming down in a shuttle—if you promise not to shoot me out of the sky."

"That's a promise."

OX guided the derelict into the open area among sev-eral intact worldtrees where Therons had gathered. Peter and Estarra emerged from the hatch and tried to organize all the people. Before long, an EDF command shuttle descended to-ward their position, alarming many of those gathered there, especially Roamers, but Peter called for calm.

When Willis disembarked, she ran an appraising eye over the royal couple. She straightened, gave a salute, then a bow, as if she wasn't sure which gesture was expected. "I was hoping to be a bit more diplomatic about this, King Peter, but the circumstances are unusual. The eleven capital ships under my command have come to throw in our hats with the Confederation. Could you use a few battleships?"

Estarra couldn't believe the offer, especially considering what she'd expected. "We certainly wouldn't turn them down, Admiral — but right now we've got our hands full with other problems. Can you help us?"

Peter added, "I don't suppose you have any experience with wildfires?"

Willis answered with a shrug of bravado. "How about we consider this our first assignment on your behalf?"

9 ☀ NIRA

As the only green priest imprisoned on the Moon with the Ildiran captives, Nira felt cut off, unaware of what else might be happening in the Spiral Arm. The base commandant kept them separated in randomly chosen groups "for security reasons" — guard kithmen, Solar Navy soldiers, attenders, bureaucrats, even Rememberer Vao'sh and his companion Anton Colicos.

The rock walls of the lunar base were cold and dry, sealed with transparent polymer, but Nira tasted dust in every breath. The lights were painfully artificial, too bright, too white. She longed for something green and alive.

But she felt a much greater concern for the Mage-Imperator than for herself. She could see in his red, haunted eyes and jerky mannerisms that Jora'h was desperate and lost. Her heart went out to him, filled with love, fear, and indignation at what Chairman Wenceslas had done to him—and Nira's pain could be only a whisper of the ragged agony Jora'h must be feeling through the *thism*. His people needed him!

The Mage-Imperator knew that Rusa'h and the faeros had unleashed an inferno in the capital city of Mijistra, driving Prime Designate Daro'h out of the Prism Palace, and destroying many warliners in Adar Zan'nh's Solar Navy. When the fiery attack had begun, Nira had briefly received information through a treeling aboard the warliner. Through his *thism* connection, the Mage-Imperator had sensed the panic and death of many Ildirans. And just when the people needed their leader more than ever before, Chairman Wenceslas had seized Jora'h's warliner and brought them all here as political prisoners. *Hostages*.

"I can still feel it," Jora'h said to her. The star-sapphire glint in his eyes showed an edge of frenzy. His hands trembled, and his long braid had begun to unravel. "Ildira is wounded."

The Chairman refused to set him free. Though he knew the faeros were attacking Ildira, he remained oblivious to the urgency—or perhaps, Nira thought, he was well aware of the situation and was using it for his own purposes.

The dozen bestial-looking guard kithmen growled and flexed their clawed fingers as they prowled the perimeter of the former mess hall where the hostages were allowed to gather. Though stripped of their crystal katanas, the hope-lessly outnumbered guards were ready to tear the humans apart, given the slightest signal from their Mage-Imperator. Nira tried to calm Jora'h, and as he relaxed, so did the guard kithmen.

At the sound of approaching footsteps, Jora'h turned to whoever was coming, setting his face in a hard, command-ing expression. Even under these appalling circumstances he clung to a pride and dignity that Nira admired. She moved next to him, offering all her support.

Five EDF soldiers with rifles on their shoulders marched to the doorway and stopped. Base Commandant Tilton, a man with large, slightly bulging eyes, entered next and scanned the chamber to assess where everyone was. He had a weak chin that seemed designed for a beard, despite EDF regula-tions prohibiting facial hair. When Tilton finally spoke in a reedy voice, he addressed someone behind him in the hall. "The room is secure, Mr. Chairman."

Basil Wenceslas stepped in alone, wearing a business suit that set him apart from all the military personnel. The guard kithmen closed in around the Mage-Imperator, and Jora'h did not tell them to back down. He coldly faced the Hansa Chairman, refusing to address his supposed counter-part with any title or formalities. "My Empire is under attack. Millions, if not billions, of my people are dying because you keep me here. Release me."

"Certainly . . . provided you agree to a few simple terms. I thought I had made my expectations perfectly clear." He responded with an obviously false smile. "Break your agree-ment with Peter and the outlaw Confederation. Declare that he's a rebel and publicly support me. You can do it all in a single speech."

Jora'h's voice was ragged and distraught. "I am the Mage-Imperator. My promises are more than wind. By holding me here, you have declared war on the Ildiran Empire. My Solar Navy will hold you responsible for every Ildiran death that—"

The Chairman gave him a dismissive wave. "Your Solar Navy is in a shambles. Bluster all you like, but now that I know your battleships are busy fighting the faeros, I have even less to fear from them."

Jora'h's journey to Theroc to cement an alliance with the Confederation had been a dramatic move. He had admitted the errors of previous Mage-Imperators, and King Peter had suggested that the two great races put their pasts behind them. New leaders, new times, a new future.

But now the relationship between Ildirans and humans—at least these humans—had forever changed.

Ironically, Nira realized that Jora'h's father, like Chairman Wenceslas, would have betrayed anyone necessary to achieve his own ends and to protect the Empire. He would have had no qualms about breaking his alliance with the Confederation and making a pact with the Hansa if it served his purpose; nor would he have balked at breaking the newly made pact to be safe again. Mage-Imperator Cyroc'h had kept many secrets from the Ildiran people and even killed his own rememberers when they discovered too much.

Jora'h, however, was most emphatically not his father. He would never give in to the Hansa's coercion.

Chairman Wenceslas continued to prod him. "Where is the Confederation now? Are they here to help you? Have they responded to your alleged crisis on Ildira, or have they left you entirely alone? Why remain loyal to such fair-weather friends? Why not end this? You can be on your way in no time."

"I don't believe he has any intention of freeing you, Jora'h," Nira said. "His actions speak clearly enough."

"I agree. It makes my decision even more straightforward."

The Chairman was not impressed. "In the meantime, we've finished an analysis of your flagship. Or should I say the newest addition to *our* fleet? Since the Earth Defense Forces have been severely depleted, we need every viable ship. Enemies continue to abound . . . in all directions."

Jora'h said in a cool voice, "Then perhaps you should not have made so many enemies. I will not permit you to incorporate part of the Ildiran Solar Navy into your military."

The Chairman shrugged. "It's a perfectly functional ship. I can't let it go to waste." He turned to Commandant Tilton. "Send word to Admiral Diente to prepare for a thorough test cruise." Recognizing the name of the man who had ambushed the Mage-Imperator's warliner on its way from Theroc, Nira scowled.

The Chairman flashed Jora'h a distasteful smile. "Admiral Diente will take your ship far outside our solar system to see what it can do. And, since you still need to come to your senses, I have decided that you will accompany him—all alone, so you'll have uninterrupted time for contemplation."

"If you isolate him from all Ildiran contact, he'll go insane," Nira cried. "Even the Mage-Imperator can't bear that."

"Oh, dear. That hadn't occurred to me." The Chairman's voice was rich with sarcasm. "He can change his mind anytime he likes." He waited, but Jora'h did not respond. Annoyed, Basil Wenceslas shook his head. "I am so tired of people being obstinate and intractable instead of pulling their own weight to solve a crisis that affects us all." As if a timer had gone off, he signaled the guards in the hall. "That is all the time I can devote to the matter. I must get back to Earth. Admiral Diente has his orders. Enjoy your solitary journey, Mage-Imperator. I trust it will help you to think more clearly."

10 ☀ PRIME DESIGNATE DARO'H

Mijistra was on fire, and the faeros reveled in it.

Thanks to the sacrifices of countless guard kithmen, Prime Designate Daro'h had escaped from the Prism Palace along with his sister Yazra'h and Nira's five half-breed children. They had barely gotten away from the flaming avatar of Rusa'h as he surged through the crystalline corridors, destroying everything in his path.

On a barren hilltop far outside of Mijistra, Daro'h ached as he observed the sprawling shape of the glorious city. In the distance, the faeros continued to bombard the Ildiran capital.

To save as many of his people as possible, the Prime Designate had commanded a mass exodus, ordering all kiths to flee into the countryside while fireballs continued to hover over the skyline. Crowds of refugees streamed into the open hills, following rivers, looking for places to hide. Several Solar Navy warliners cruised low to the ground, delivering more survivors and supplies.

Next to Daro'h, Yazra'h also stared at the spectacle, her eyes like hard chips of topaz. His sister's mane of long, coppery hair drifted in the breeze. "Clustering together makes the people vulnerable. They have no defenses if the faeros decide to incinerate them. They cannot fight." Although one of her Isix cats had been burned to death during Rusa'h's conquest, the remaining two prowled around her legs.

"So far the faeros have not chosen to attack," Daro'h said. "I must postulate—I must *believe*—that annihilating the Ildiran people does not serve the faeros plans. Rusa'h seems to be in control of them. He wants something more—the Mage-Imperator, perhaps."

But their father was not on Ildira. In fact, no one knew where Jora'h was.

Yazra'h crossed her arms over her chest. "Nevertheless, I will not let *you* stay in one of the open camps or exposed villages, Prime Designate."

"You want me to hide."

She gave him a hard look. "I want you to *survive*. I swore an oath to protect you." With the Mage-Imperator missing, Ildirans had no one else to look to; Daro'h was their de facto leader.

Yazra'h had found a set of deep caves and mining tunnels in the mountains not far from Mijistra. "I have chosen the best defensive location I can. Adar Zan'nh is anxious to take you there." She glanced uneasily up at the sky. "He feels you are too vulnerable out here, and so do I."

Daro'h held his overwhelmed emotions in check, so they would not bleed into the *thism*. "Although it pains me to surrender our city to the faeros, we must choose our battles wisely." He took a last look at the troop carriers and supply streamers crisscrossing the skies. "I will do as you suggest. Summon the Adar."

Riding aboard a small, swift cutter, Daro'h sat next to one of the windows, staring out at the landscape, shocked by how much it had changed. Osira'h and her half-breed siblings had joined him as well, singed and bedraggled but very much alive.

"We are establishing as many camps as we can," Zan'nh reported, piloting the cutter himself. "The Solar Navy is delivering food, medical supplies, tools, and prefabricated shelters."

The Adar had already learned that his warliners could not fight the blazing ships directly; to extinguish a single fireball, he had sacrificed two warliners with their full crews. Now only five warliners remained of the septa he had brought to Ildira. The rest of the Solar Navy, the ragged remnants of his cohorts that had survived the climactic battle against the hydrogues, were dispersed thinly across the Ildiran Empire to watch over all the splinter colonies. Tabitha Huck and her work crews had been rapidly assembling new warliners in the orbiting industrial facilities when Rusa'h had arrived.

And so Zan'nh had explicitly instructed the captains of his few ships trapped at Ildira not to engage the faeros in direct conflict. Solar Navy ships returning from their routine patrols received transmitted orders to station themselves at the edge of the star system, waiting for an opportunity to move. They could not win, and he could not risk losing more warliners. Daro'h knew how much it galled Adar Zan'nh to issue those "cowardly" orders; nevertheless, the warliner captains obeyed and kept their large vessels ready—and safe.

"With your permission, Prime Designate, one of my captains has requested to take a warliner filled with refugees and attempt to flee this planet." Zan'nh turned from his piloting controls. "We can load ten thousand of them from the most exposed camps and fly them to safety."

Daro'h considered. "That warliner would not be able to return. Can we afford to lose it?"

"My warliners cannot fight the faeros, Prime Designate. At least this could save ten thousand lives."

"Then it is a good choice. Tell the captain he has my blessing to make the attempt."

The cutter flew toward the barren cliffs, and Daro'h saw small holes in the overhangs, caves accessed by wide gravel roads laid down centuries ago by digger kithmen. They landed on a broad rocky ledge. "Tal O'nh and Hyrillka Designate Ridek'h are already in the tunnels," Zan'nh reported. "They have begun to set up the necessary equipment for our new command center."

Daro'h emerged from the craft, looking in dismay at the round tunnel that was to be their new home for now. Yazra'h gave him a scolding look before he could say anything. "For all its magnificence, the Prism Palace is merely a structure. Remember, *you* are the Prime Designate. *You* are currently our leader. *You* matter more than Mijistra."

Daro'h tried to convince himself that it was true. He had to make sure he was worthy of that faith in him.

11 ☀ FAEROS INCARNATE RUSA'H

Rusa'h settled into his rightful place like a bright coal at the heart of a blazing bonfire. With its towers, minarets, and gemlike ceilings, the Prism Palace was meant to be his—not for his own ambitions, but for the Ildiran race . . . and for the resurrection of the faeros and the bright igniting of the universe. Rusa'h had taken action for his people, for Ildira, for all those who had lost their way to the Lightsource.

Once he was ensconced in what remained of the skysphere, his power should have begun spreading like wildfire. He had tried to weave another *thism* web, to save some Ildirans by the necessary purging and sacrifice of others. But this new victory was not what Rusa'h had expected. Though bright soul-threads bound him to the faeros and the Ildiran people under his care, he still felt alone.

Although the faeros had helped him, they wanted more . . . always more. Every combustible object in the Palace had already burned. If he gave them free rein, the fireballs would surge across the landscape consuming everything, stealing every Ildiran soulfire they could find in order to spark new young faeros. He did his best to prevent a total Armageddon.

Rusa'h had shown the flaming elementals how to defeat

the hydrogues. He was the faeros incarnate, but he was also the savior of the Ildiran Empire.

At the moment, his faeros were sweeping around the Spiral Arm to reclaim their cold, dead stars. The fiery elementals had already extinguished a major concentration of wentals on Charybdis and, thanks to the discovery Rusa'h had shown them, newborn faeros had raced along soul-threads of *thism*/telink to Theroc. The battle with the worldtrees was already raging, burning . . . burning.

But Rusa'h had to keep at least part of Ildira intact. He had to hold the faeros in check.

Inside his Prism Palace, he drank in the crackling sound of flames around him. Yet Mijistra itself seemed too quiet and empty, most of the people having fled into the hills and wastelands. He was disappointed that true Ildirans would abandon their sacred metropolis, but they continued to stream away as if the new light were too bright for them. They hid in scattered encampments, huddled together for comfort and perceived protection. In spite of their desertion, he would shield those people from the faeros whenever he could. After all, Ildira was *his*.

Huge numbers of them were evacuees from his own beloved world of Hyrillka, people who had sought sanctuary on the Empire's capital world. Rusa'h felt such compassion for them, such responsibility, but many of the reluctant refugees had never found homes here, nor had they been able to return to Hyrillka. That was Jora'h's fault.

All would have been well if the Hyrillkans had just stayed where they belonged.

Rusa'h alone could save them, or he could let the faeros incinerate them.

Now that the hydrogues were defeated, the faeros needed

to propagate. The bright, pulsing fiery entities wanted more soulfires. Insatiable, they demanded to burn more of the refugee camps, to obliterate whole splinter colonies.

Inside the dazzling skysphere his voice and thoughts boomed out to the fireballs. "You will not harm the people of Hyrillka." The faeros shuddered and thrummed against his command. He could sense them blazing brighter, but he remained firm. "*You will leave them alone.*"

A searing backlash made the faeros response clear. They were hungry. The flaming elementals demanded more, and Rusa'h was required to give it to them. He had to find something to appease them.

Up in orbit, he detected a lone warliner quietly departing from the abandoned shipyards. Rusa'h was well aware that Adar Zan'nh's few Solar Navy ships continued to deliver supplies that helped the evacuees . . . but this particular warliner held ten thousand Ildirans, all of them seeking to escape to some distant colony in the Ildiran Empire. The pilot had loaded his warliner with as many survivors as it could carry and had flown off, intending to take them far from Rusa'h.

He could not allow that to happen.

Once the moving warliner had attracted the attention of the faeros, Rusa'h knew this was an acceptable sacrifice, his best compromise. He groaned, then surrendered to the need and unleashed the fireballs. They raced off to the new target.

From the Prism Palace, he watched through blazing eyes as the fireballs swiftly closed on the crowded vessel. Through the *thism*, he could feel both hope and terror emanating from the refugees aboard the warliner. Ten thousand of them . . . all desperate to find sanctuary on some other Ildiran planet.

At least they weren't the people of Hyrillka . . . he drew some consolation from that.

The faeros ellipsoids strained, ravenous as they began the chase. When the ornate battleship detected the approaching fireballs, its flight pattern became erratic, heading back toward the complex of heavy spacedocks and industrial facilities, as if hoping to find a place to hide.

The desperate warliner tried to dodge through an obstacle course of girders and half-built ship frameworks. Flying magnificently, the Solar Navy pilot dove beneath a tethered stockpile of armored plating. As they streaked past, the weapons officer fired an energy blast that severed the clamps holding the plates in place. Vibrating from the impact, the metal sheets spread apart, twirling like an artificial storm of flat meteors.

The faeros careened into the plates, flashing into blinding brightness as they vaporized the metal, leaving only a shower of molten globules in their wake. The fireballs barely slowed.

After a brief attempt to hide, the warliner accelerated away from the abandoned shipyards at maximum thrust, trying to get far enough away for the pilot to engage his Ildiran stardrive. Three comets of fire clipped the rear engines, melting them. The warliner spun out of control, its solar sails flapping outward like loose and tattered garments. In a final gesture of defiance, the warliner's captain fired all of his weapons at the oncoming faeros ellipsoids.

Flames surrounded the Solar Navy ship, ate through its outer hull, and incinerated the vessel. Ten thousand Ildiran

refugees and many more Solar Navy crewmen flashed into a
bright blaze. Every soulfire aboard was absorbed.

And the faeros grew brighter.

In the Prism Palace, Rusa'h sighed. He hoped that would
keep them satisfied . . . for now.

12 ☀ BENETO

His body was more than human, an extended tree whose
branches spread into space, whose trailing tendrils and
mental roots connected with the overall worldforest
mind. And now his body was on fire.

Beneto and his fellow verdani battleships had been orbiting Theroc as guardians, but the faeros had found a secret
vulnerability in him, jumping through telink, seizing onto
the union of wental and verdani that created his treeship
body. Now, high above the continents, he felt the flames
from below surge through his heartwood. He could hear the
other treeships screaming.

He shouted his thoughts out to all green priests, thinking
of the worldforest rather than himself. *Give the trees your
strength. Do not despair.* Celli was right to remind him, and
he tried to help her by concentrating on the efficacy of hope,
the foolish but brave human drive to fight even when a battle
seemed lost.

By treedancing, his little sister and Solimar had once reawakened the seeds of life in the worldforest. The verdani and their wental counterparts simply did not have the dogged, foolish determination to wring a victory from almost certain defeat—but humans did. Now, even as the elemental fires caught on his gigantic body and fought their way deeper into him, Beneto called to the remnants of green priests inside the other verdani battleships, insisting that they not give up.

Beneto made a defiant stand against the newborn faeros even as flames flickered at the thorny ends of his outermost branches. A chain of sparks ricocheted up and down the bark plates of his wide trunk, but he quenched the first waves of fire. There was hope!

Around him, the verdani battleships smoldered, on the verge of crossing the flashpoint and bursting into living bonfires. Far below, Beneto could feel the main worldforest struggling as young faeros flashed from tree to tree. The fiery elementals waged a fierce battle for each victory among the towering groves, but the trees could fend them off. It could be done! He had demonstrated that himself, and he wasn't alone in his fight.

The other verdani battleships, along with green priests on the ground, were joining together. His sister Celli was one of the strongest fighters. She and Solimar used every mental skill they had to defend the forest.

Beneto's thoughts thundered through telink. *We can snuff out the faeros before their fire overwhelms us.*

The verdani battleships shuddered as they pulled strength from the worldforest mind, wrung it from their own heartwood, forcing themselves to endure the pain.

The flames grew hotter and more insistent in Beneto's body, and he could not entirely push them away. He struggled so hard that a long crack split along his thickest bough, and the glowing golden blood of his sap spilled out into space. The flames bit deeper, jumping into the point of weakness.

Nearby in space, two more verdani treeships lost their battle to possession by the elemental fires. They weakened, faltered, and then each spiny battleship became a corona of gleeful flames.

Even so, the infested treeships refused to let the faeros possess them. Rather than becoming full-fledged torch trees, the two lost verdani battleships intentionally allowed themselves to crumble into ash. Fragments of embers sparkled and drifted apart in space.

Although Beneto kept fighting, the flames ate at him, pushing deeper into his core, and he could not stop the burning.

13 ☀ ADMIRAL SHEILA WILLIS

With hundreds of small EDF craft in her battle group—Remoras, fuel tankers, cargo carriers, troop transports, and survey flyers—Willis was able to mount one hell of a bucket brigade. This wasn't exactly something she had covered in basic training, but her people called up all their available databases on wildfire-fighting techniques. They would figure it out as they went along.

Using her own landed shuttle in the middle of a clearing as a field command post, she watched her display screens, frowning or cursing as images rolled in from recon flyovers. The Admiral activated the comm system and shouted, "I'd better see water dumping on these trees within the next five minutes, or you're going to think serving under General Lanyan was a Sunday picnic."

"On our way, Admiral," came a crackling voice. "First squadron ETA in four and a half minutes, just under the wire."

The first Remoras and fuel tankers swooped low, then opened their cargo bays to dump water onto the blazing worldtrees. Smaller ships emptied their reservoirs, releasing water they had scooped from Theroc's lakes. Steam gushed into the air, rising through the dense forest canopy.

The faeros blazed paradoxically brighter as they drew energy from the worldtrees to fight off the quenching water.

Willis heard a groan, saw Celli and Solimar hunched over their treelings inside the command shuttle, both of them connected through telink. The green priests had come aboard her shuttle to act as intermediaries. Their eyes were squeezed shut, faces drawn in identical grimaces as they fought with all their hearts and minds. Celli hissed in pain and gripped her treeling. She blinked, but didn't focus on anything around her. Her words sounded hollow. "That hurt them, but not enough. The faeros are ravenous."

The small ships, now empty, circled back toward the nearest sources of open water. "Second squadron inbound, Admiral."

"The drenching will be continuous now," Willis said. "I don't care how tough these fires are. We'll stomp them again and again until there's nothing left but a puff of smoke."

A second barrage of water hindered the further spread of the fire. The torch trees shuddered and thrashed as if undergoing some kind of internal conflict, an elemental battle that Willis couldn't understand.

"Four more green priests have died," Solimar announced. "They were unable to wall themselves off from the trees they were helping through telink."

"Green priests have spread the alarm across other planets," Celli said.

"For whatever good that'll do us now," Willis said.

"The wentals are also aware," Celli said. "Jess Tamblyn and Cesca Peroni have arrived at Osquivel. Liona has told them what's happening here."

"And what can they do?"

"They can bring the wentals."

As the third group of EDF water tankers cruised in, the flaming trees tensed, and the fires intensified at the crowns. Celli suddenly screamed, and Solimar reeled backward. The torch trees shot out tendrils of fire that curled upward like solar flares and incinerated two of Willis's ships before they could dump their loads of water. Another blast of targeted fire raged from the clustered burning trees, vaporizing a large tanker.

Willis shouted into the microphone, "Scramble! Scramble! Evasive action."

Her crews responded instantly. A thick pillar of fire knocked out another Remora, but the remainder of her ships scattered. Now they were too dispersed to provide a good target for the brute-force blasts; on the other hand, they could no longer drop their water effectively.

"Circle around and stand ready," Willis growled into the comm. "We must've hurt the bastards or they wouldn't be lashing out like that. You'll have to dump your water from a greater altitude. It won't be as accurate, but those flame plumes can reach only so high."

Most of the EDF pilots responded with anger instead of fear. More and more ships streamed in, released their loads from a great height, and circled back to nearby lakes to refill, relentlessly drenching the worldforest.

Finally, through the steam and rain, Willis saw several of the smaller torch trees begin to gutter and go out. She sat back, crossing her arms. "Another couple thousand trips, and we might just have this thing under control."

14 ✦ PATRICK FITZPATRICK III

In the belly of the Golgen skymine, shouting EDF soldiers and complaining Roamer skyminers created a remarkable din. Men dropped tools onto the deck with loud clangs; ekti tanks were rolled into clusters, then lifted with levitating forklifts. Outside, the high-altitude winds whipped and roared in a continuing storm. The *Goliath* hovered nearby.

No one was able to stop the continued outrage. Patrick stood beside Del Kellum, noting the trim EDF uniforms, the determined soldiers following orders. "I used to be just like them."

"No wonder Zhett was always picking on you."

Once, he had believed everything that General Lanyan told him. The Hansa had been at war with the hydrogues, and the Earth Defense Forces needed stardrive fuel, which the Roamers had "unjustly" withheld. Therefore, when they had seized a Roamer cargo ship, the decision to destroy the witness and remove the evidence had seemed perfectly reasonable. Patrick hadn't thought twice about it: The EDF took what it needed.

Just as it was doing now. Patrick's stomach knotted. Yes, he understood what drove these soldiers, and now he was ashamed of it.

A constant flow of military ships landed in the skymine's open cargo bay, loaded up with ekti canisters, then returned to the nearby Juggernaut. General Lanyan followed a coterie of administrative aides; he wore a dress uniform rather than rugged combat fatigues, as if to show his contempt for any possible resistance from the Roamers.

A young lieutenant with soft, innocent eyes stepped up to Lanyan and reported in a clear voice, "General, we have reports from the consolidation squadrons. All Roamer skymines have been placed under EDF jurisdiction."

"*Your* jurisdiction?" Kellum bellowed. "You know the Hansa has no claim on these mines—or is your head so far up your ass that you're suffering from oxygen deprivation?"

Patrick said quietly and calmly to him, but for the General's benefit, "Pure bullshit is a standard ingredient in EDF rations, Del. Have I told you what the EDF's motto is? 'Honor and bravery in service of the Earth.'" He pointedly looked at General Lanyan. "There's a word for attacking unarmed, independent facilities to steal their property: *piracy*. Why not round things out with a bit of raping and pillaging?"

"They're pillaging quite enough right now, by damn," Kellum said.

Not rising to the bait, the General scanned the report that listed the amount of stardrive fuel the troops had seized. "My, you Roamers have been busy."

Kellum growled. "We *earn* what we have, unlike some people."

Lanyan continued to scan the inventory, not interested in what Kellum had to say. "Hmm, a supply of orange liqueur. Where did it come from?"

With pride, the bearded clan leader said, "I make it myself."

"Is it any good?"

"Too good for you."

"I'll accept your recommendation. Have it loaded into my personal shuttle." The General finally gave Patrick his full attention. "I am disappointed in you, Mr. Fitzpatrick. You had a great future in the EDF, but you pissed it all away—for *this*?" He raised his hands to indicate the cluttered complex. He leaned closer, smelling of cologne and sweat. "I'm going to take you back to Earth and treat you to a full court-martial. The Hansa has already arrested hundreds for illegally rebroadcasting that foolish condemnation and confession you recorded. That recording did no good, but we can still use it against you."

Patrick could not hide his satisfied smile. "Really—hundreds arrested? My message must have been distributed widely, then." Lanyan was flustered, and Patrick decided to call his bluff. "I'd love a public opportunity to explain how the Hansa broke treaties, killed innocent people, provoked hostilities, destroyed the capital of a sovereign people. In fact, my grandmother will make certain I get the forum I need. Take me back, I dare you. What you're doing here is illegal."

"Roamers have no legal standing in the Hansa."

"Not true. My grandmother entered into an agreement with clan Kellum, speaking officially as a former Hansa Chairman. She promised them their freedom and guaranteed that neither they nor their facilities would be harassed by the EDF in exchange for them surrendering a valuable hydrogue derelict. The Roamers held up their side of the bargain. You've reneged."

Lanyan shrugged. "Once King Peter stole the derelict back and delivered it to the Roamers, all bets were off."

Patrick was startled by this information; he hadn't been aware that the alien ship was back in the hands of the Confederation. He hadn't expected Lanyan to know about the deal at all.

Lanyan motioned for him. "Come to the operations center, Fitzpatrick, and help me go through the databases to make sure we haven't missed anything."

"I won't help."

"Then you can watch as I blunder around in your computerized systems. Who knows what damage I might cause?" Patrick grudgingly followed him to a lift, while Kellum remained behind, glowering as soldiers continued loading tank after tank of stolen stardrive fuel.

In the ops center that crowned the skymine dome, broad windows looked out upon the endless yellowish skies. Zhett was single-handedly trying to keep soldiers from the database control panels, but they ignored her. That had put her in a murderous mood. "You clods shouldn't be allowed to run an abacus!"

One of the technicians fumbled with a touchpad, frowning when the systems froze on him.

A soldier shouted, "General Lanyan on the bridge!"

"It's not a bridge," Patrick said. "It's an operations center." In the distance, he could see another skymine, Boris Goff's, also surrounded by EDF ships.

"Status report," Lanyan demanded. "Have you run a full inventory?"

"As near as we can tell, sir," said the blundering technician. "It's a very disorganized system, not to military specs at all."

Zhett stood close to Patrick and put her fists on his shoulder as if she wanted to pound on something. He slipped his arm around her waist and drew her close, restraining her.

When the General saw him holding the young woman, he seemed greatly amused. "So the well-bred Patrick Fitzpatrick III has found himself a pretty little Roamer mistress. How sweet."

"She's not my mistress. She's my wife."

Lanyan burst out laughing. "And would your grandmother still support you if she knew about that?"

Patrick remained cool. "I'm sure her wedding gift is already on its way." He didn't mention that he had neglected to send the old Battleaxe an invitation.

The technician had finally succeeded in calling up screens full of numbers. "Looks like we got it all, General. Other than the expected losses on cargo ships and a few ekti escort haulers that initially escaped our net, we have secured and transferred all the available fuel on these skymines."

"Our work here is done, then." Lanyan raked a self-satisfied gaze across the glowering Roamers in the operations center. "We'll be back when the time is right. I'm sure

Chairman Wenceslas will want to manage this in his own particular way."

The innocent-eyed lieutenant burst into the ops center, looking flushed. "There you are, General! We've picked up the tracer signal on one of the cargo escorts we tagged. We can follow it to another Roamer depot or industrial facility, if you like."

"I would like that very much. Tell the *Goliath* to prepare for immediate departure." Snapping orders for his crew to finish up, he left Fitzpatrick and Zhett standing together in the operations center.

Before long the EDF raiders departed in a ponderous group, like bumblebees overloaded with pollen.

15 ☀ MARGARET COLICOS

Trapped on Llaro and surrounded by Klikiss, Margaret wondered if all those escaped colonists had been only a dream. Orli Covitz, Hud Steinman, Tasia Tamblyn, Robb Brindle . . . She no longer even had her faithful compy DD. Yes, they had gotten away. Margaret was completely alone . . . except for the monsters.

But she *had* helped those people escape. If she were going to become delusional, she could have done so long ago. After years of living at the bare edge of survival, knowing that the incomprehensible hive mind might kill her on a whim, Margaret had used the Klikiss behavior against them. She had made it possible for the doomed colonists to slip away before the insects could slaughter them. Nearly a hundred people had fled from Llaro. Including dear DD.

But the breedex refused to let her leave. While the others escaped, a group of Klikiss warriors had singled her out and captured her again. The hive mind wanted *her*, but she had no idea why. As an ambassador? A sounding board? A pet human being?

She shouted at the milling insects. "Why did you capture me if you don't want me to do anything?"

But the new breedex chose not to answer through them. She threw a rock at a mottled brown digger, but the stone merely bounced off the chitin armor. The insects went about their bloodthirsty business, continuing the relentless assaults on other subhives, massacring countless rival Klikiss.

And ignoring her.

Her head pounded with the sound of their chittering. The smell of caustic powder, decay, and bitter insect pheromones caught in Margaret's throat and nose. The tans and browns of the desolate landscape seemed harsher now, the edges sharper, even under pastel skies. Her eyes ached, as did her heart. She was stranded here.

Again, she cursed the Klikiss for holding her prisoner. It had felt so good to be among humans again. She missed DD. She missed Orli. She missed her son, Anton, whom she hadn't seen in years. She still didn't know what had happened to Davlin Lotze, though she assumed he was dead.

And, because the Klikiss had ceased communicating with her, she could get no answers to her questions. Though she walked among the hulking insects, pushing her way into their ranks, the creatures treated her as if she were no more than a tree or a rock to avoid. "Tell me why you want me here."

In their constant chittering and humming, she heard no discernible reply.

Margaret made her way to the boundary of what had been a thriving human colony, which was now only ruins. The cultivated land had been completely subsumed by Klikiss structures. Insect warriors moved about, intent on urgent, incomprehensible missions. Builders slathered polymer resin cement on frameworks, erecting new towers to house even more Klikiss, expanding the subhive in preparation for further conquests.

The insects never ceased moving, never stopped pushing forward. Since their return from the Great Swarming, the warring subhives wanted to *annihilate* everything — all other breedexes, the hated black robots, and any human colonies that happened to get in the way. The Klikiss wouldn't stop until it was all finished, until only one breedex remained.

Shortly after the few Llaro colonists had escaped, after the breedex had fissioned again and expanded its armies, the new-generation hive mind had thrown its warlike creatures into a bloody, almost maniacal wave of offensives, ripping apart one rival after another.

Always before, the different breedexes had attacked each other, striving for dominance and assimilating their conquered rivals into larger and larger forces. It was the way of their species. But the new Llaro breedex exhibited a berserker's frenzy of violence, turning engineer sub-breeds loose to develop new weapons that *annihilated* rather than incorporated most of the defeated insect hordes. Only a few representative members of the crushed subhives were taken into the hall of the breedex to be used in the next fissioning; with their own breedex dead, the rest were sent out as expendable shock troops in an assault wave against the next subhive. Each time the Llaro subhive obliterated another breedex, it moved one step closer to being the sole hive mind of the species.

Margaret looked up, sensing a change in the air. Unified by some silent call, the Klikiss gathered around the trapezoidal wall in the middle of their city. The stone face shimmered, and figures took shape within, an entire army of the Llaro breedex's warriors marching back through the doorway. Many of them were battered, their carapaces cracked and oozing globs of clotting ichor after a terrific battle, but the Klikiss warriors carried the spiny heads of the rival subhive's domates. They had torn the other hive apart.

Another victory. The annihilation of another breedex.

Margaret felt sickened at the thought that the monstrous Llaro hive mind might actually win the struggle for species domination and control all of the Klikiss.

16 ☀ CAPTAIN BRANSON ROBERTS

On the day he got his rebuilt ship back from the Osquivel shipyards, BeBob hoped for a certain amount of fanfare. At the very least, he would have liked a small crowd to admire the new *Blind Faith*, wish him well, and offer a toast for the old ship, which the EDF had blown up.

Instead, no one came for the christening. In this damned unending war, a new crisis seemed to appear every single day. Tasia Tamblyn and her group had come back from Llaro, clamoring about the Klikiss invasion, and then the green priest had raised the alarm about the faeros attacking Theroc. Just that morning, Jess Tamblyn and Cesca Peroni had arrived at the shipyards in their wental ship, asking for help against the fiery elementals, and then *they* had rushed off.

Always an emergency. BeBob felt left out.

Like a proud parent he walked around the vessel. The paint was perfect and unscuffed, with no corrosions from cosmic radiation, no scratches or pits from micrometeoroids. And the Roamers had finished building the ship ahead of schedule!

During the reassembly he had hovered near the construction site every day. He had watched the frame put into place, the hull panels riveted on, extra armor layered over standard reinforcement alloys. The attitude-control thrusters, the in-system engines, and the stardrive had been tested on racks, then installed and tested again in situ. The modified computer systems and the full range of defensive weapons checked out. The old *Faith* had never sported projectile launchers or jazers, but in times like these, no ship could afford to be without them.

The new *Blind Faith* was seven meters longer than the original, with an expanded cargo bay and more compact engines, which yielded a twenty percent increase in carrying capacity; according to the specs, she was faster, too. BeBob couldn't wait to see what the ship could do.

He particularly would have liked Rlinda Kett to fly with him on the maiden voyage, but he wasn't going to wait around for her to come back from Earth. Long ago, she had helped him inspect the original *Blind Faith*, back when he had joined her shipping company. And then there had been their ill-advised marriage . . . but all that was so much gas down a black hole. Now the EDF had a death warrant out for him and probably one for Rlinda, too.

He still felt nervous that she had gone to the Hansa by herself. BeBob had wanted to go along, but Rlinda had laughed at him. "I'm the Confederation's Trade Minister. I can take care of myself—but I'm not letting *you* anywhere near that planet. It was enough trouble breaking you out of EDF prison in the first place." He had lost his ship, and they had lost Davlin Lotze in the process.

BeBob had every confidence in Rlinda Kett. He just wished she could be here for the launch. He had his first delivery mission already on the books, and he could set off at any time.

Toying with the external controls, he opened the main entry hatch. The boarding ramp hummed out smoothly, all tracks perfectly oiled. Bright panels lit the ship's interior. He could smell the polymers of the control deck, freshly welded compartments, polished doors, and soft upholstery.

Poking his head back out again, he saw a curly-haired Roamer man enter the chamber. "Sorry I'm late, Captain Roberts," Kotto Okiah said. "I see you've begun the inspection already."

"Everything's fine." BeBob ran his hand along the inner hull. "Hand over the keys and I'll take my ship out for a shakedown cruise."

"Keys? We don't use keys anymore. I have your access codes and authorization—"

BeBob held up a hand. "Just kidding. An archaic reference."

"I should have caught that." Kotto looked around. "Would you like us to schedule an official ceremony later on, when things settle down? There's just so much going on here."

"Oh, that's not necessary," BeBob said, though he didn't mean it. "If you're going to wait until things settle down, we'll have to send out invitations to my grandchildren."

"You know, of course, about all the Llaro refugees that just came back? Someone wanted to see you. It seems you have friends among them."

"I don't remember anyone from Llaro—" BeBob turned as more visitors entered the bay. He recognized a skinny old man with grayish-white hair and unkempt clothes and a young girl with short brown hair and large sepia eyes, accompanied by a Friendly compy. "Orli! Orli Covitz—and Hud Steinman!" He had rescued the two from Corribus, the only survivors of the black robot attack. "What were you two doing on Llaro?"

"Being chased by bugs, mostly," Orli said. "Is that a new ship? Doesn't look at all like the old one."

"Forget the battered old vessel. Now everything's shiny. The engines and power systems purr instead of clatter." Grinning, he gestured to the ramp. "Step aboard my new *Blind Faith*."

Orli trotted up to the control deck and poked around with a fascinated expression. "Maybe I can be your copilot or first officer someday."

When BeBob saw she was serious, he realized that he could do worse. "I'll think about it. Hey, I was about to take a test flight with a load of supplies for Relleker, and I wouldn't mind the company. Want to come along? Sounds like we've got plenty of stories to exchange."

"What do you think, DD?" Orli asked. The Friendly compy, obviously pleased to be with her and away from the Klikiss, seemed perfectly amenable.

"*We* would like that," said Mr. Steinman. The old man glanced around the rock-walled landing bay in which the ship rested. "We don't have anything better to do. Might as well make ourselves useful."

hough she had changed her call sign and obscured the ship's name with a strategically applied scorch mark on the hull, Rlinda never stopped calling her ship the *Voracious Curiosity*. However, she took care to avoid any unwanted EDF entanglements.

Her ship carried a profitable cargo of comfort items that people facing austerity and rationing would very much welcome: preserved foods, jungle delicacies from Theroc, difficult-to-obtain cocoon-weave fabrics, thermal-resistant equipment from Constantine III. The Hansa simply couldn't get such things anymore.

However, since Chairman Wenceslas had imposed extreme wartime tariffs, she would never enter into a formal agreement with Earth's industries and merchants. Rlinda would find her own customers through unofficial channels, thank you very much. She still had plenty of black-market connections, and she could get her goods into the hands of customers who needed and appreciated them.

As the *Curiosity* passed the Moon and headed in toward Earth orbit, she was surprised to see a large, dark Ildiran warliner being towed into position above the lunar base. "What the hell is the EDF doing with an intact warliner?" Maybe it was better if she didn't know.

Calling no attention to herself, she began weaving in among the orbital traffic. The *Curiosity* flew in stealthily. Rlinda cut her transmissions and kept a low reflective profile on any surveillance networks. She mixed in with local ships and sent a burst signal so that her contacts would know what items she had to trade and what her asking price was.

"Sneaking around like an illegal smuggler," she muttered to herself. "Ah, the glamorous life of the Confederation's Trade Minister."

That afternoon, settled in, Rlinda waited on an uncomfortable wrought-metal chair out in the sunshine. The wafting aroma of dark-roasted coffee beans gave the café a pleasant atmosphere, though she was annoyed at having paid vastly too much for a cup of coffee. Rlinda had the equipment to make herself a better one in the *Curiosity*'s galley.

Outside in the tiled square, a group of white-painted mimes—of all things!—had begun a performance, wearing garish costumes and using exaggerated motions. Their silly pratfalls garnered chuckles from the few passersby who stopped to watch. The mimes were all playing characters, and Rlinda realized with a start that they were meant to be King Peter, the Archfather of Unison, and the Hansa Chairman. She doubted many other people recognized what the mimes were doing, but their political leanings were clear from the noble nature of the King, the inept buffoonery of the religious leader, and the sheer evil of the Chairman. She watched, newly impressed, and wondered how many other quiet symptoms of rebellion were manifesting themselves on Earth.

She heard an astonished, but carefully hushed woman's voice. "What are you doing here?"

Rlinda turned. Her guest had arrived. "Hello, Sarein. I wasn't sure you'd get my invitation."

The Theron ambassador had disguised herself in plain

Earth clothes with no traditional garments or any mark of her political position. "Are you supposed to be here? Are you allowed?"

"Of course not, but I couldn't let that stop me. Sit down." Rlinda lowered her voice, maintaining a scandalized tone. "I hope you brought your Hansa budget authorization. The coffee here is very expensive."

Sarein stood motionless. She looked around, suspecting a trap. "There's probably a warrant out for your arrest. I'm sure Basil hasn't rescinded it."

"Relax, Sarein." Rlinda drummed her fingers on the edge of the table. "It's just me. We've known each other a long time. Now please *sit down*. People are going to stare if you keep standing there like that."

That was all the other woman needed to hear, and with a quick, compact movement she slid into a chair and sat across the table from Rlinda. After ordering an iced tea for herself, Sarein leaned forward and whispered, "How did you send me that message? It wasn't traceable."

"It wasn't threatening, either, so I hoped you might be intrigued enough to come."

"Even though I'm one of the few people Basil still trusts, he's always monitoring me."

"Well, why don't you just leave him?" Rlinda set her meaty elbows on the table. "If you're afraid of a man, he's not worth staying with."

"I'm not staying *with* him, but I can't leave. Not now. It wouldn't be right."

"Ah, one of those kinds of relationships."

Sarein pressed her pale lips together. "It's not much of a relationship anymore, certainly not a romantic one. I won't kid you—things are getting very bad, Rlinda. You shouldn't be here. It's dangerous. When you and Captain Roberts escaped last time, you threw the whole security net into question."

"Security *net*?" Rlinda chuckled. "That's an apt term—it's so full of holes I can slip in and out anytime I like."

"Well, I can't," Sarein said. "Basil's cut himself off from so many things, I'm one of his last remaining advisers—for what it's worth. If I leave . . ."

"Hell in a handbasket, I get it." Then she grew more serious. "Every time I come back to see you, things seem more messed up than they were on the visit before. Are you *sure* it's not time for you to leave? I could take you back to Theroc."

Sarein clutched her iced tea and peered from right to left. Rlinda wondered if she somehow imagined that Chairman Wenceslas had put her up to this as a test of her loyalty. "I . . . I couldn't."

"Really? Aren't you the Theron ambassador? Doesn't that mean your home is back there? Since the Hansa has cut off all relations with King Peter and Queen Estarra, what exactly is your role on Earth?"

"I might be one of the only stabilizing influences Basil's got left." Sarein's words tumbled out in a rush, as if she were trying to convince herself. "That's the most important role I'm able to fill. I can still talk to him. Sometimes."

"Then talk some sense into him," Rlinda said in a loud voice. Sarein quickly looked around to see if anyone had overheard.

"That's why I have to stay," she insisted. "If there's a chance I can help change his policies, soften some of his reactions, then I could save a lot of lives."

Rlinda heaved a sympathetic, put-upon sigh. "All right. If you're trying to make me feel sorry for you, then I'll pay for the coffee." She sniffed. "Still, I have to say, it doesn't look like you're making any headway with the Chairman."

Sarein took a drink of her iced tea, swallowing hard. "Maybe not, but I have to keep trying. I'm not willing to give up yet."

Rlinda shrugged. "Suit yourself. If you change your mind, and I'm still around, the offer stands . . ."

Sarein got up so quickly she jostled the table. Leaving her iced tea unfinished, she fled.

18 ☀ CELLI

As the continued water bombardment progressively weakened the faeros, the green priests, unified by Celli and Solimar, added a measure of defiance and strength to the trees' inherent quiet passivity. But the young faeros would not relinquish their hold on the worldtrees. An entire grove, including the fungus-reef tree, blazed hot with their resistance. The snap and crackle of fire and the sizzling sigh of steam filled the normally quiet forest.

While the Admiral directed her operations from inside the landed command shuttle, Celli and Solimar left to be outside among the trees again. They touched the living, embattled forest and threw their energy into the fight.

In her mind, Celli called out to Beneto's treeship high overhead, but she could hear only her brother's resonant pain from the fire growing within him.

Green priests shouted and staggered as a living ball of flame launched itself from the crown of a possessed torch tree and rocketed to an old worldtree on the other side of the barricade. The ancient tree shuddered as its upper fronds caught fire.

She and Solimar ran over to the old tree and wrapped their arms around the great trunk, pouring their strength and hope into it via telink. But it wasn't enough. The elemental fire was about to jump to other weakened trees in the grove. They could sense it.

With tears streaming down their ash-powdered cheeks, they connected with all the nearby verdani at risk. The group of endangered worldtrees knew they had to act before the blaze could leap farther. Their own line of defense.

The threatened trees voluntarily surrendered their hold on the Theron soil where they had been rooted for centuries. Celli and Solimar moaned in dismay as the sacrificial trees leaned *toward* the already blazing fires and fell with an immense simultaneous crash to create a firebreak. Geysers of sparks exploded upward, but the faeros could not spread across the charred ground.

It was only a small victory. The green priests refused to let go, continued to shore up the forest's strength. Celli was trying to reach Beneto again when she saw that the verdani had other allies as well. "Solimar! Look at the clouds."

Mountainous, unnatural thunderheads began to roll in overhead, faster than any wind could blow, gathering more and more water from the atmosphere. Celli's green skin prickled with an electrical charge in the air. The fires seemed to shudder, preparing to stand against something far more difficult than another EDF water bombardment.

Blinking her reddened eyes, she scanned the lumpy outer fringe of clouds until she spotted a silvery blue sphere that streaked in low above the blazing trees like a bullet made of water. The verdani sensed that the water elementals had come, and excited cries rippled through the green priests. Celli had seen Jess Tamblyn use wental water to create the treeships in the first place. Now he had come back.

Jess and Cesca's wental ship flitted back and forth as the rain clouds converged. The dark and roiling masses swelled, loomed larger, and closed in above the concentration of faeros-possessed trees. With a huge thunderclap that resonated across the sky, the clouds burst. Wental water spat down toward the faeros, each raindrop a deadly projectile.

The young faeros clung to their possessed trees and shot flames hopelessly into the air, but thunder boomed in response as the wentals expressed their anger. An *angry* sound—from the wentals! Celli laughed with joy to hear it. The clouds gathered over the burning last stand of new-born faeros, and released torrents of rain in an exuberant downpour.

Shaking off any remaining fear, the green priests embraced the tree trunks, adding their strength, urging the verdani to fight back. Celli and Solimar turned their faces to the sky, letting the fresh droplets drench their skin and soothe their burns.

19 ✸ BENETO

High above the planet, Beneto's treeship fought the invasive fire that coursed through his sap—his blood. The arrival of the wentals had unleashed an elemental rainstorm below, energizing the worldforest root network.

Through his own unwanted connection with the living flames, he felt the agony of the young faeros as they were extinguished, one by one. Though he could not snuff out the deadly fire within him, he could impose control over his huge spiny body. *He* would guide it where he wished; he would control the fight. Beneto felt himself gain the upper hand.

We are coming, Beneto said to Celli through telink.

Trailing smoke and fire, the group of treeships descended through the sky. Trapped within him, the fiery creatures writhed, tried to make him deflect his course, but Beneto had greater strength now. He drove his battleship body into the thick grayish clouds, soaking his massive form. The wental rain ate away at the living fire in his body like acid, and the faeros recoiled. Through telink he heard his fellow verdani pilots cry out as they plunged into the energized clouds.

Beneto's tree, sizzling with steam, dropped toward persistent faeros concentrations that had not been quenched by the wental downpour. He sent his thrumming voice to the doomed torch trees in the main grove. *We can save the trees that surround you.* Surrender your grip on the earth. *We will take you away so the faeros cannot continue to spread.*

The verdani had no individuality as humans did; each

separate tree was merely a manifestation of the overall mind, each one connected to the others. Beneto had to excise all faeros-infested trees from the worldforest—including himself and his fellow verdani battleships.

As the rain continued to pour all around, the blazing treeships began their work above the fiery grove. Beneto could hear Celli weeping through the worldforest mind. He tried to reassure her, but there was little he could say.

The clustered battleships grasped the burning trunks with thorny branches, then rose upward until they uprooted the trees. Inside the verdani wood, the newborn faeros thrashed and fought, knowing they could not win, could not escape. Beneto and the other verdani battleships rose far above the worldforest canopy, dragging the sacrificial trees into the rarefied atmosphere, passing once more through the wental-infused thunderheads.

Beneto took the tainted and doomed trees far, far from Theroc.

Originally, after the defeat of the hydrogues, all of the verdani treeships had departed from Theroc in what should have been a majestic seeding journey, never to return. Though Beneto and his comrades had been called back to assist Theroc, they remembered what they had seen along the way—and Beneto knew of a perfect place where he could dispose of these treacherous young faeros.

The burning verdani battleships flew at breakneck speed, as if they could outrun the agony from the elemental flames. They swiftly approached what had once been a binary star system; one of the stars, a blue giant, had exploded in a supernova, leaving behind an ultra-dense remnant.

A black hole.

Its companion star had also swollen, becoming a red giant now. The black hole's gravity pulled streamers of loose gas from the red giant's outer layers, siphoning it in an ever-accelerating spiral down to the infinite vanishing point.

Dragging the fiery, uprooted forest through space, they followed the river of hot gases being pulled from the red giant. The syrupy threads of gravity pulled them closer, and soon their grip would be irresistible. The living flames within their treeship bodies became frantic, blazing brighter, struggling to get away. The additional shockwave of pain inside Beneto made Celli cry out, far away on Theroc.

Although his treeship flew in a procession of inferno-infested worldtrees, he remained connected with his little sister. Though the flaming verdani battleships could barely endure their pain, they kept the young faeros leashed within their wooden forms. Ravenous living flames continued to eat away at the branches, and Beneto knew the treeships had to hurry before they succumbed. He could not let the faeros loose now.

Through telink, he saw Celli standing in a scorched meadow surrounded by the wental-drenched worldforest. She blinked once, looking skyward, and when she blinked again, she was with him surrounded by the empty gulf of space. He knew she could feel the searing damage in his heartwood, his bloodsap, his outspread branches. He could not hide it.

Many green priests could not bear to maintain a telink connection, but Celli's love for her brother gave her the strength to endure the pain. She refused to let go, and even as he raced across the gulf of space, he could feel the hot tears burning down her cheeks, hotter than the faeros fire in his heartwood.

The giant, thorny ships swirled around the black hole's vortex. He and his companions released the uprooted trees, and one by one, they vanished with silent gasps, telink echoes of both dismay and victory. One at a time, the remaining verdani battleships spiraled in, passed the event horizon, and dropped into the blackness.

As each one disappeared, he knew that Celli could feel a permanent loss. She sucked in great breaths, no longer aware of her surroundings in the meadow. "Beneto . . ." Hearing her, he drew strength from her companionship.

Beneto had done what he needed to do. He had dragged the faeros away from Theroc and saved the rest of the trees; he had brought the fiery elementals to a place from which they could not escape to cause further harm. He felt Celli shaking as she lowered herself to the singed ground. His sister would grieve, but she understood what Beneto had accomplished. She loved him, and she was loved. Love and hope had the power to heal. She and Solimar had taught the verdani the truth of that. Beneto was glad.

Celli turned to Solimar, buried her face against his muscular chest, and let the sobs come. She knew it was over.

In the last instant before he passed the point of gravitational no return, Beneto embraced the distant worldforest again with his mind and poured himself into it. His pain dissolved as his worldtree body fell into clean ash that mixed with the cosmic dust and gases . . . then swirled down forever.

20 ✹ HYRILLKA DESIGNATE RIDEK'H

The entire population of Ildira could not hide from the faeros, but they scrambled for whatever protection they could find. Young Ridek'h, the true Designate of Hyrillka, took shelter deep in the old mines along with Prime Designate Daro'h.

Digger kithmen worked to expand the tunnels and create large grottoes in the bowels of the mountain, as well as numerous new escape passages, should they be needed. Watchmen stood at posts outside the cave openings, always alert for faeros fireballs.

Ridek'h preferred to sit under the overhang, staring across the sunlit openness, trying to come up with some solution that he could offer the Prime Designate. On Hyrillka — the planet he supposedly ruled — the great, windy plains had been used for agriculture. He wasn't meant to live underground in tunnels. No Ildiran was.

Though engineers had brought blazers to light the underground chambers, it had become Ridek'h's habit to slip out and use surreptitiously gathered brushwood to build a modest fire — a *safe* fire. Sitting by the bright flames outside the mine entrance, he looked out into the never-ending daylight of multiple suns, and contemplated. Though he was no more than a young man with little experience who had become Designate completely by accident, Ridek'h was determined to help.

When the ten thousand Ildirans who had attempted to escape in a single warliner had lost their race against the faeros, he had felt the dagger of pain as all those innocents were incinerated, their soulfires stolen. Ridek'h had considered going with them, but more than a million of his displaced people were here on Ildira, and he would not leave until he found a way to save them.

While he was deep in thought, Tal O'nh joined him. Oftentimes he and the blind man sat side by side for hours without speaking, just drawing strength from each other's company. The veteran's face was still scarred and burned by the faeros; one socket was empty, and the other eye was milky and sightless, partially covered by a shriveled lid.

Upon becoming the new Hyrillka Designate, Ridek'h had gone to visit his planet and all the splinter colonies in the Horizon Cluster, accompanied by Tal O'nh and a septa of warliners. Their encounter with an enraged Rusa'h and his obedient fireballs had left all of the warliners' crews dead, two of the warliners destroyed, and the tal's eyesight blasted away.

Blindness would have driven most Ildirans insane, but O'nh was strong. Outside the mine opening, the orange glow of the small fire played across his face, though he couldn't see it. "I can endure," he told Ridek'h. "Long ago, knowing that I might lose my remaining eye, I made up my mind never to live with anxiety and fear. Humans can tolerate darkness whenever they choose, and if humans can survive this, then I certainly can."

"You are brave, Tal O'nh."

The veteran made a dismissive gesture. "I have merely

had practice. You will find your own courage, should it become necessary."

"We will need more than courage to drive out Rusa'h and his faeros."

"You have what you need. *You* are the true Hyrillka Designate, and Jora'h is the true Mage-Imperator—titles Rusa'h now attempts to claim for himself. He will not succeed."

The young man nodded before remembering that the tal could not see him. "I will hold on to hope if you tell me to."

The blind tal leaned closer to the fire and extended his hands as if to draw the light into his skin. "There is real reason for confidence, Designate. Though he has vanished, we know the Mage-Imperator is not dead. We can still sense him, however distant he may be. Jora'h lives."

Ridek'h considered that. When the previous Mage-Imperator had poisoned himself, their entire race had been crippled by mental shock and misery. Likewise, all Ildirans would have felt Jora'h's death like a discordant scream through the *thism*. Therefore, Jora'h remained alive . . . but where was he?

"Has he abandoned us?"

"I do not believe so. I must assume that something prevents him from returning."

With the Mage-Imperator missing, Mijistra lost, and the faeros in the Prism Palace, this could well be the worst time the Empire had ever known. Ridek'h knew it was time to demonstrate his confidence, to rally the old veteran. "Tal, we have every opportunity to make things better. And I swear we will."

21 ☀ MAGE-IMPERATOR JORA'H

Jora'h gazed at Nira, touched her cheek one last time, then stoically turned to follow Admiral Diente and his military escort. *Diente.* The Mage-Imperator barely acknowledged the man who had ambushed his flagship.

The Admiral's claim that he had been following the Chairman's orders did not exempt him from blame. By kidnapping him, Diente might have single-handedly doomed the Ildiran Empire, allowing all of Jora'h's people to be consumed by the faeros.

The dark-haired officer showed little expression as he walked along. "We have finished our inspection and analysis of your warliner, Mage-Imperator. All seems to be in working order, and we're ready to depart."

"So, you fixed the damage your own EDF ships inflicted upon it?" Jora'h said, staring ahead. "Are you certain you understand Solar Navy systems?"

Diente answered crisply, "Our engineers acquired a working knowledge of Ildiran warliners when we helped repair many of your vessels after the hydrogue battle here. We put that knowledge to good use." He paused, then added apologetically, "Our shots were precisely targeted when we subdued your ship. We caused no more harm than was absolutely necessary."

"You cannot begin to know how much harm you have caused, Admiral."

As he ushered Jora'h aboard the warliner, Diente gave a

slight, stiff bow, but averted his dark eyes. "I will show you to your accustomed stateroom. However, once we depart, my orders are to allow minimal interaction between yourself and my crew. You are to have privacy and solitude."

Jora'h felt a chill in his soul. Already missing Nira, he tried to reinforce the strength of his heart and mind against the coming ordeal. "And do you understand what that will do to me, leaving the other Ildirans here on the Moon?"

Judging by his mannerisms, he guessed that even Diente did not approve of what Chairman Wenceslas was doing . . . but then, the Chairman no longer sought approval from anyone. "I understand that I have no choice in the matter."

Jora'h shook his head bitterly. "I thought humans always have a choice."

"Then you don't have all the pertinent facts. Follow me." In leading him up the ramp and along the primary corridors, Diente made a point of showing him all the troops stationed aboard the warliner. "Though this is only a test cruise, we have five hundred EDF soldiers aboard. Please don't make me do anything I would regret."

"I am not a fool, Admiral Diente. I must stay alive so that I can save my people. No matter how long it takes."

"We have an understanding, then." Diente gestured him into his former elaborate cabin, the large stateroom he had shared with Nira. The entire vessel seemed cold and bleak without her, without his crew.

The Admiral sealed the door behind him. Jora'h did not check to see if it was locked. He didn't want to know the answer.

Chairman Wenceslas had not bothered to see him off, though no doubt every moment, every movement had been recorded. The Chairman was probably smiling with smug self-congratulation for coming up with this strategy.

For now, with the warliner still orbiting above the lunar base, Jora'h could feel the *thism* from the Ildiran captives nearby. Later, though, when he felt the warliner's engines powering up and the great Solar Navy ship began to cruise away, the tenuous lines became more diffuse, stretched out. His people quickly slipped farther away.

Jora'h sat by himself in his brightly lit quarters, clenching his hands, concentrating. He was the Mage-Imperator. He had to master his fear. Though the connection grew fainter with every moment, he could not allow his people to sense his anxiety through the *thism*. They needed to be strong now — stronger than ever.

When Admiral Diente engaged the stardrive and the warliner leaped into the emptiness of space, Jora'h felt those last strands snap like the strings of a delicate musical instrument played by rough and violent hands.

Gone.

He collapsed onto the comfortable bed, where he and Nira had shared their thoughts and hopes, where they'd had such quiet contentment. He felt as if he couldn't breathe, as if all the oxygen in the warliner had been sucked out into the frigid, unforgiving vacuum. He had never imagined such incredible emptiness.

Jora'h closed his eyes and clenched his teeth. He spread his arms, concentrated, and threw his mind out into the void as far as he could. He searched for anyone, but he felt only cold madness clamoring at him.

"*I* am the Mage-Imperator!" he cried through clenched teeth. His search continued for any friendly thought to help anchor him. But the universe was a vast and empty place.

To his horror, Jora'h realized that only a few seconds had passed.

22 ☀ SIRIX

In the ruins of the Roamer outpost of Forrey's Folly, Sirix and his black robots marched down the stone tunnels, penetrating deeper into the fortress asteroid. All of the weak human inhabitants were dead, and bodies lay strewn about.

Though the honeycombed asteroid was protected by erratically orbiting chunks of rock, it had been a trivial operation for Sirix's robots to plan and carry out an invasion of the outpost. In one swift operation, they had collapsed the atmospheric domes, opened bulkheads to space, and broken through blast doors and into cargo bays. Some of the Roamers had tried to flee; others had attempted to defend the installation. Either way, they had been slaughtered. Per Sirix's instructions, no one would be allowed to survive.

His two compy protégés, PD and QT, followed with brisk footsteps. At an access port to the base's central computers, QT worked to connect to the systems. "Roamers often have fail-safes rigged to their computers. We must be cautious." He paused. "Yes, an electrical and radiation pulse is poised to erase all stored information in the event of a security breach."

Sirix spun his flat head plate. "Can you deactivate it to allow a scan of the database?"

"Yes." The compies sounded anxious to please.

"Then do so."

Because both compies were familiar with Roamer systems from previous conquests, PD and QT worked together until they had deactivated the automatic purging protocols. "We now have access to the data summaries, inventories, and lists of known facilities."

While robot squads continued to explore the asteroid tunnels, rooting out the last few frantic survivors and killing them, the two compies took turns rattling off statistics about how many ships came and went to the asteroid outpost, how many metric tons of various ores were shipped away annually, how much raw metal the processing plants produced.

PD asked brightly, "Is this place acceptable, Sirix?"

"No, it is not." He was very disappointed. His crimson optical sensors glowed a deep ruby shade in contrast to the still-flashing scarlet emergency lights. "This is a bulk-processing plant designed to produce large sheets of alloys, heavy girders, construction ingots. This facility does not have the technological sophistication we require."

With each disappointing result, he grew more desperate. Circumstances beyond Sirix's control had led to defeat after defeat, and most of the original black robots had been annihilated in recent battles. Very little of his massive army and only a few dozen of the stolen EDF battleships remained intact. His options had seemed quite limited until the two naïve compies had suggested their bold and previously unthinkable scheme.

Given facilities with proper technical sophistication, they could build more black robots, *new ones,* to replace the ranks of those that had fallen. Even though the new-generation robots would not have the vital memories and experiences of the lost originals, they would still replenish his army. Sirix could use them to complete his plans.

However, manufacturing new Klikiss robots was not as simple as constructing a spacecraft or a clumsy habitation dome. The fabrication process required extreme sophistication. Forrey's Folly was inadequate. This entire operation had been a waste of Sirix's time.

Flexing his fingerlike leg clusters, Sirix stepped over two human bodies that blocked the rough floor of the deep tunnel. He turned back to the two compies. "Search all the information in their databases for any other outposts and assess their capabilities in advance. Find me a place to manufacture my robots."

"Yes, Sirix," PD and QT said in unison.

"The Roamers themselves will point us to our next target."

When the two compies came to report to him on the bridge of his ship, Sirix could tell they were pleased. "Have you found an acceptable alternative?"

PD presented a datapad, and QT spoke up. "We suggest Relleker. It is a former Hansa world with a very desirable climate. Hydrogues destroyed the settlement and killed every colonist. Roamers recently returned there to establish an extensive base, now that they are safe from the hydrogues."

"They are not safe from my robots," Sirix said. "Why do you believe this place will be satisfactory?"

"The Roamers have installed a new industrial grid with many capable workers and cutting-edge technology," PD said. "The data indicates that their fabrication plants are excellent."

"So they believe," Sirix said. "Let us see Relleker for ourselves. If it proves adequate, we will seize it and begin our work." He studied the report. According to the records the compies had downloaded, the planet did have everything necessary for the construction of new robots. The existing facilities could be converted into a proper assembly plant without difficulty. And with no significant defenses, Relleker would easily be subsumed.

"If the human colonists are technologically proficient, perhaps they will assist us in creating more robots," QT suggested. "After all, the current fabrication lines are designed for human hands."

"And we could use the help," PD said. "We should keep them alive."

Sirix grudgingly agreed. "Some of them, perhaps — *if* it serves our purposes." He contacted his ships to inform them of the mission priorities. The robot fleet altered course and flew off toward their new destination.

23 ☀ GENERAL KURT LANYAN

A s his battle group followed the pinger signal on the runaway Roamer cargo escort, Lanyan felt genuine satisfaction. At Golgen, he had put all the skyminers in their places and showed the clans that they had to line up in support of the Hansa for the good of the human race. His troops had also captured enough stardrive fuel to run the whole fleet for six months or more. Definitely a good day's work. As he sipped a cup of black coffee on the *Goliath*'s bridge, Lanyan mulled over how much the Chairman would appreciate what he'd done. For once.

Tight supplies of ekti had hampered the EDF for years. How could a space fleet perform its work properly if they had to account for every fume, every discretionary patrol run? Now that his ships were pursuing one of the "escaped" cargo escorts, Lanyan was sure he'd soon have even more to show for his efforts. Yes, he felt very good about himself and his crew.

"That was a bad business back at Golgen, General." Conrad Brindle had come aboard the flagship from his Manta for consultation and debriefing. He didn't sound enthusiastic at all.

"Bad business? It was a complete success."

"It was a civilian target, sir. We had no legal justification for seizing their assets without due process —"

"They were enemy sympathizers at the very least, if not actual combatants." Lanyan wished the other man had the decency to voice his objections in the privacy of the ready room, rather than on the bridge where the rest of the crew could overhear.

Brindle stood his ground. "At the Academy I taught students in ethics, the Hansa Charter, and the fine points of EDF regulations. During our Golgen mission, the proper procedures were not followed. What we did was tantamount to piracy."

Lanyan cut him off, annoyed that this man would rain on his parade. Years earlier, Lanyan himself had hunted down and executed the Roamer pirate Rand Sorengaard; this was completely different. "Mr. Brindle, you made the right decision when you chose not to join Willis's mutiny at Rhejak. You showed an admirable strength of character when you left your own son and his Roamer 'friend' on Theroc and remained loyal to the Earth Defense Forces. Don't fail me now when things are going so well."

His tactical officer interrupted them. "General, the pinger signal has stopped! The cargo escort's gone to ground in the system ahead."

Lanyan set his coffee aside, hoping Brindle wouldn't press the matter further. "Tell me about the system. What's there?"

"Nothing that I can see, sir. Metal-rich rocks in erratic orbits—barely worth noting on a starmap. The only name I could find in the records is Forrey's Folly. I can't tell if it refers to any particular asteroid."

Lanyan nodded slowly, smiling. "Ugly, useless, and out of the way—exactly the sort of place Roamers like." He scanned starmap archives where a tangle of ellipses showed the orbital paths of the many out-of-ecliptic planetoids around a small dim sun. The cargo escort had gone directly to one of the asteroids. "Proceed with caution. We'll probably find another clan hideout."

The sensor operator scanned the rock. "The presence of processed metals and geometrical shapes clearly indicates artificial constructions."

"Charge in with our weapons ready, but don't open fire unless I say so. We don't want to lose any ekti stockpiles they might have—or damage facilities that may continue to be productive."

"We should also avoid unnecessary casualties," Brindle added, making sure everyone on the bridge could hear him.

The sensor operator brought up a report from the long-range scans. "Detecting no energy signatures, comm traffic, or heat sources. Just the cargo escort. He's transmitting, but getting no answer."

Lanyan leaned forward, elbows on his knees. At the speed the EDF ships were moving, the outpost approached in a flash. The asteroid had once been covered with domes, tank farms, docking frameworks, and habitation tunnels, but the place was entirely destroyed. Explosions had riddled the already cratered rock of the asteroid. Blackened holes and melted cuts showed where the facility had been torn apart.

"That was done by EDF jazer blasts, sir," said the sensor operator.

"Jazers? I gave no order to attack this place. Hell, I didn't even know it was here."

Before Lanyan's ships could close in on their attack run, the cargo escort spun about. A profanity-filled transmission came across the open band. The Roamer pilot had a long, thin beard, and a braid that dangled over his shoulder; he was so angry his face was red, his eyes wide and bloodshot. "You Eddy bastards! You've killed everyone here. *Why?* Isn't piracy enough anymore? You have to engage in mass murder, too?"

Lanyan looked over at Brindle, as if his second in command might have answers. "Are you sure there's no record of any military operation taking place here?"

"None, sir."

"Open a channel to the Roamer pilot. Tell him we didn't cause this massacre."

"He's not inclined to believe us, General," said the comm officer a moment later. "His exact response is, um, quote, *Bullshit.*"

The cargo escort's engines brightened with acceleration thrust. Lanyan sighed. "Now where's he going? Does he think he can actually run from us?" But the Roamer ship turned and accelerated directly *toward* the Juggernaut. "What the hell? He's trying to ram us! That's ridiculous."

"The *Goliath*'s shields are sufficient to withstand the impact," Brindle said.

"I don't care—open fire." Then he added quickly, "Engine damage only . . . if possible."

The cargo escort headed toward them like a projectile, but at the last moment the pilot disengaged his cargo of ekti tanks, dropping the twelve metal cylinders like spreading space mines directly into the path of the battle group. The Roamer ship veered slightly aside, weaving a complicated path through the clustered EDF ships even as their jazers crisscrossed space. Two spinning ekti cylinders slammed into the bow of Lanyan's Juggernaut, and the resulting explosions shook the bridge.

"No significant damage, sir. No casualties," Brindle reported. "One of our Mantas was struck by an exploding ekti tank. Repair crews are already on their way."

Lanyan was more interested in the fleeing cargo escort. "Dammit, where did he go?"

"Still tracking him, sir—he's heading out of the system."

The Roamer pilot activated his stardrive and flashed away before Lanyan could turn his much larger battleships around and chase after him. Lanyan stood from his command chair and took a step toward the main screen. "Do we still have his homing beacon? Tell me we haven't lost the signal."

"I've got it, General."

"Then follow him. This chase isn't over until I say it is."

24 ☀ PRIME DESIGNATE DARO'H

Still feeling hunted inside the cave camp, Prime Designate Daro'h tried to understand the abrupt emptiness in the *thism* where the Mage-Imperator should have been. Until recently, they had all sensed a whisper of his distant presence, but now he was simply *gone*. Every Ildiran could feel it.

Attender kithmen desperately clung to the pretense of a normal routine by serving the Prime Designate. They prepared food and warm spiced drinks, brought cushions for Daro'h to sit on, and adjusted blazers for better light in the tunnel shadows. But no matter how servile they tried to be, they could never make this dusty, primitive camp into the Prism Palace.

While grim and silent sentries continued to watch for fireballs, Daro'h met with Adar Zan'nh, Yazra'h, and Tal O'nh. Chief Scribe Ko'sh, the head of the rememberer kith, sat near them, ready to quote from history and record new events. The knuckles on Yazra'h's right hand were torn and bloody from when, unable to quell her frustration, she had lashed out at the unyielding rock.

Zan'nh delivered a report from his most recent surveys. His hair was pulled back from his face, his uniform rumpled. He had wasted little time following meticulous military dress codes since the crisis had begun.

"The Prism Palace glows like a bonfire at all hours, and many other buildings have burned down. From what I can tell, Mijistra is empty." The effort of making such a statement was plain on the Adar's face. "The faeros have cemented their control over the skies. Ten more of my patrol cutters failed to return. Whenever a ship attempts to make a run from Ildira, the fireballs pursue and destroy it." He looked around, narrowed his eyes. "They will not let us leave the planet."

Daro'h thought of all the splinter colonies in danger, the lost settlements across the Spiral Arm. All had been distraught that the Mage-Imperator was missing during their most tumultuous crisis, and now it was much worse. Jora'h had vanished entirely from the *thism* web, and the silence in the racial mind reverberated like an unending scream.

Now it was his responsibility, as Prime Designate, but he had no way to lead them, especially not hiding deep in a tunnel.

"We are in limbo," Ko'sh interrupted. The lobes on the

rememberer's face shifted through a chameleon rainbow of colors, helping to convey the alarm in his voice. "No one can sense the Mage-Imperator!"

"That is news to no one," Yazra'h answered in a growl. "But we are not in a position to do anything about it."

"You *know* what must be done, Prime Designate," the Chief Scribe said, focused only on Daro'h. "We need a leader. There is a precedent. You must undergo the ascension ceremony and become our new Mage-Imperator."

Louder than the outcry from the others, Yazra'h shouted, "The precedent set by mad Designate Rusa'h? You are a fool to suggest it unless we know our father is dead!"

Tal O'nh said in a quiet voice, "The rememberer's logic is valid. You give the people what guidance you can, Prime Designate, but you cannot fulfill the same role unless you have all the *thism* under your control. And that requires the ceremony."

Daro'h had been present after the death of Mage-Imperator Cyroc'h when Jora'h underwent the castration ritual, the painful yet obligatory passage that transformed him from Prime Designate into Mage-Imperator. As a young man, Daro'h remembered the sudden rush of warmth and confidence as all the *thism* strands were taken in the new Mage-Imperator's mind and heart. His father had instantly brought strength and direction to the lost and frightened Ildiran race, filling them with confidence, hope, and security.

Yes, his people desperately needed that security now. If Jora'h was truly gone, then the Prime Designate was required to become Mage-Imperator.

But if his father still lived, Daro'h could not simply ascend to become a new Mage-Imperator. That would cause terrible confusion, possibly even tear the remnants of the Empire apart. Rusa'h had already proved that.

Daro'h closed his eyes. To make an appropriate decision, he needed more information. If the Mage-Imperator was dead, then his path was clear. But his father's death should have struck him like a hammer blow to his chest and mind. Instead, all Daro'h had to go on was utter mental silence . . . no *thism*, thoughts, or the faintest glimmer that Jora'h still existed.

He shook his head. "That is an irrevocable act, and it is tantamount to abandoning hope. Since I do not believe the Mage-Imperator is dead, any such action would therefore be premature. I will not do it."

"There are those who say that if you do not do this, then you are a coward, Prime Designate," Ko'sh retorted.

"There are those who say many stupid things," Yazra'h snapped.

The Prime Designate squared his shoulders, drew a deep breath, and turned to all of them. He had to be strong. "Even though he is not here, the Mage-Imperator left me in charge. I was not born to be Prime Designate, but that role has fallen to me. You are my best advisers; that is the role that has fallen to you."

He gave them a stern look. "Ildirans have trouble producing new solutions to problems. My father said that if we did not learn to change, it would be our downfall. I charge you with this task: Find me a solution. We are the Ildiran Empire! I do not care how desperate or unorthodox the plan may seem—suggest a way that we can fight back against the faeros."

25 ✸ FAEROS INCARNATE
RUSA'H

Inside the seared-clean remnants of the Prism Palace, Rusa'h continued to burn the lines of his new *thism* to guide the Ildiran people. The soul-threads were bright and hot like the filaments in a blazer. He had to go out and see what he had accomplished.

Rusa'h summoned flames from the floor and walls, pulling curtains of fire around him until they formed a fireball that enclosed him like a cocoon. He drifted through the already blasted passageways, shattering a heat-brittle door to reach the open air. His incandescent body floated above the now-slumping towers and minarets of the Palace, and from that vantage point, he surveyed his domain. He turned his flashing gaze out across the intricate metropolis of Mijistra that had been the jewel at the heart of the Ildiran Empire.

Rusa'h was torn between two driving obligations: guiding and controlling the Ildiran people, and continuing the resurrection of the faeros. The fiery elementals within him didn't care about the Empire; their battle had far vaster implications. But *he* wanted to save his people.

He had learned to his frustration that the new faeros sparks on Theroc had been extinguished. The verdani had fought back with unexpected strength, aided by wentals, green priests, and even human military ships. It had been a setback for the faeros, but not for Rusa'h. He had everything he needed here on Ildira . . . except for Mage-Imperator Jora'h, who refused to return to his people, despite their loud outcries.

Sooner or later, Rusa'h would find his brother. It was only a matter of time.

In his flaming ship, he flew over the rooftops of Mijistra, gazing down on monuments, museums, and now-dry fountains. The Hall of Rememberers was empty, its interior charred. Most of the artisans' quarters and communal dwellings for craftsmen, metal workers, technologists, and chemists had burned down. He passed over a medical center, a vehicle landing field, warehouses that held food for a populace that was no longer there.

The sheer sense of emptiness saddened him. Now that the hydrogues were bottled up in their gas giants, the faeros had the freedom to run. They could destroy whatever they wished, grow unchecked until they became the dominant force in the Spiral Arm and beyond.

Stretching his mind out to vast distances, Rusa'h joined the faeros leaping from star to star through their transgates. They frolicked in the reawakened Durris-B, where they had reignited nuclear reactions and set that star alight again. The faeros had reawakened many other old stellar battlegrounds, as well, reclaiming territory the hydrogues had taken from them.

But Ildira was *his*. The Ildiran people were *his*. Again, he hammered that fact into the faeros.

Below his flaming ship, Rusa'h spied a group of desperate refugees leaving a food warehouse from which they had retrieved supplies for one of the poorly hidden camps. True Ildirans should have stayed in Mijistra to praise him for restoring his people to the Lightsource.

But when these people saw him, they ran in abject terror, many dropping the supplies they had taken. Rusa'h could have pursued them. With little more than a thought, he could have sent a surge of flame to burn down the buildings in which they hid. He could have swept in and stolen their soulfires to stoke the flames of the faeros.

But he chose not to. Though he could feel the restless elementals within him, he held them back. He could not allow the faeros to run rampant. He had meant to use the fiery elementals to achieve his own ends, but his influence extended only so far. Their chaos was quite powerful.

His fiery chariot circled over Mijistra and returned to the Prism Palace. A dozen of the giant fireballs appeared in the air overhead, milling about, always hungry, capricious, uncontrollable. They were eager for something to destroy.

Perhaps the faeros could help him find Jora'h. . . .

26 ☀ MAGE-IMPERATOR JORA'H

Desperately alone aboard the warliner—far from Earth, far from Ildira, far from *anyone*—Jora'h struggled to remain sane. Huddled in his private quarters, he had no idea how many days had passed. He felt only the gulf of emptiness extending forever.

For most of his life, he had believed the Ildiran Empire to be all-powerful, all-encompassing. Splinter colonies spread across the Spiral Arm so that the *thism* web extended everywhere. He had been so misinformed.

Though weak to the marrow of his bones, Jora'h made himself get up from his bunk. As Mage-Imperator, he must not allow himself to look defeated. He took three stuttering steps toward the bright blazers built into the wallplates, staring all the while at the dazzling light, using it as an anchor.

At least it wasn't dark. Chairman Wenceslas hadn't inflicted that particular torture on him—not yet.

If he cried out, if he surrendered, if he swore he would do as the Hansa demanded, would the EDF Admiral deliver him back to his people? Once he returned to the lunar base, though, he knew Chairman Wenceslas would probably string him along. The Chairman would never simply let him go.

After an abrupt signal at his stateroom door, Admiral Diente entered without waiting to be invited. Jora'h forced himself not to shiver at the terrible, freezing aloneness that coursed through his veins. "What . . . do you want?"

Diente kept his voice emotionless, as if delivering a bland report. "My software experts have been studying this warliner's database. We found what seems to be some sort of a translation system designed to converse with the Klikiss. Is this true?"

Jora'h closed his eyes, trying to concentrate in spite of the swirling vortex of solitude. He searched his memory. "In ancient times we communicated with the Klikiss."

"Does it still function?"

"We have not used it in thousands of years." He paused, struggling as other memories came back. "Wait. Adar Zan'nh used it. Yes, he spoke to the Klikiss . . . at Maratha."

Diente nodded. "Then we may be able to use it for negotiations with the Klikiss."

"Negotiations . . ." Jora'h heaved a breath, intending to laugh, but he could not find the strength to do so. "You have trespassed. You have angered them. The faeros may be Ildira's greatest enemy, but the Klikiss are likely to be yours, Admiral. You are too blind to realize it."

Diente seemed very sad and weary. "We're our own worst enemy." His voice was so quiet Jora'h barely heard him. "I am acting under orders, Mage-Imperator. I do not wish to do this to you. It is . . . demeaning to the leader of a great Empire. I always admired your Solar Navy."

Now a flash of anger surfaced, allowing Jora'h to sharpen his thoughts. "Then how can you allow this? If you know your actions are wrong, why do you follow your Chairman?"

Diente stared for a long moment, the focal point of his dark eyes far away. "Because, Mage-Imperator, the Chairman has my wife, my son, and my two daughters hostage. He has threatened to murder them if I show a hint of disloyalty." He clenched his fists at his sides. *"He has my family."*

Jora'h was too distressed by his isolation to understand the full import of what the Admiral was saying.

From the pocket of his uniform, Diente pulled out a small display screen the size of the palm of his hand. Activating it, he showed a sequence of images: a beautiful woman, a teenage daughter, a handsome young man, and a smiling little girl, then another image with himself in the picture, a unified and happy family.

"Perhaps I have said too much. Thank you for the information about the Klikiss translation system." He abruptly switched off the images and pocketed the screen, embarrassed. As if dispensing a well-deserved reward, he added before he left the stateroom, "We should get back in a few days. Not so long after all."

"Not so long . . . ?" Jora'h said through clenched teeth. Time had already stretched out to a wintry infinity.

After Diente left, Jora'h's knees gave out, and he collapsed onto his bed.

A few more days. He did not know how he could bear it. Days . . .

27 ☀ MARGARET COLICOS

When the new breedex finally summoned Margaret into its hive fortress, she determined that she would have her answers. For so long she had watched the insect creatures slaughtering rival domates, wiping out rather than incorporating the defeated subhives. At last, though, the Klikiss had stopped ignoring her, and she hoped to learn why this hive mind was so different from all the others . . . so much more vicious.

Margaret considered running to the trapezoidal frame of the main transportal. Before the hive mind guessed what she intended to do, she could punch any coordinate tile and simply *leave*. But the transportal network went only to other

Klikiss planets, and any gateway would just take her to another insect-infested world. She was better off here.

No, she would stay here and take her chances with the Llaro breedex. Though this one seemed more bloodthirsty than any of the others, it had intentionally kept Margaret safe. Therefore, the breedex must want something from her, if only she could understand what it was. She had no reason to be afraid. The Klikiss had kept her alive this long.

From outside, the hall of the breedex appeared tall and lumpy with twisted candlewax towers on either side. Spiny warriors ushered Margaret into the dark opening of the central structure, and she went willingly. With their razor-edged serrated limbs, the Klikiss could have chopped her to pieces in an instant . . . but they could have done that at any time over the past several years. She knew they wouldn't harm her—not yet, at least.

Margaret was still a scientist and had spent many years with Louis studying the ancient ruins of the supposedly extinct race. She knew the Klikiss as well as any human could know an alien species. She straightened her shoulders and kept pace with the armored creatures along winding corridors like the chambers in a spiral seashell. The closeness of the numerous Klikiss intensified the smells that reminded her of sour bile, rotten eggs, decaying fish, and old sweat, a symphony of pheromones and chemical signals.

Her warrior escort guided her into a buzzing, humming central grotto filled with horrors. The heads of more than a hundred vanquished domates lay stacked like trophies. In the middle of the chamber, beside the grisly trophies, lay a stirring heap composed of millions of squirming, shifting bodies. She had seen the breedex before, but she did not look forward to this encounter.

Margaret stopped. The stench made it hard for her to breathe as the Llaro hive mind formed itself into a structure that could face her. The myriad mound began to move as hundreds of thousands of components assembled like the pixels of a broad and complex image. As the shape began to grow definite, Margaret realized that something else was different from the previous incarnations of the Klikiss hive minds.

Not only the warriors, but hundreds of large workers, diggers, and other sub-breeds stood together like worshippers in a church. The background noise became more than just the incessant rustling of limbs and wings and shell casings. She heard a clacking of mandibles, a buzzing of chitin plates being rubbed together to create musical sounds. It became recognizable as a language.

In her years among the Klikiss, Margaret had developed a rudimentary ability to communicate with the creatures. She comprehended some of their tones and chirps, and could make similar noises herself. Now, however, the background drone changed. Though it was slow and unpracticed, the sounds became recognizable. A word.

"Margaret."

The warriors and workers made a single voice in an extended, eerie choir. *"Margaret Colicos."* Never before had the Klikiss attempted to speak human words. Never, as far as she knew, had the creatures even understood the concept of names.

Startled, she took a step backward and bumped into the spiny body of a warrior, but the Klikiss creature did not move. She faced the breedex, which continued to form itself like a gigantic, interlocking puzzle.

"You're different from the last breedex," she said.

The breedex mound finally completed shaping itself until it vaguely resembled a giant human head made out of clay by a clumsy child. Its mouth moved, and noises came out like swirling breezes that picked up sharp-edged sticks. *"Margaret Colicos . . . I know you."*

Something had definitely changed. "What are you?" she demanded.

"I was . . . in part . . . a man." The human features continued to resolve themselves into finer detail. *"A man named Davlin Lotze."*

She stared. "Davlin?" She had never learned what had happened to the man; obviously, the Klikiss had assimilated his genes as well as his memory. But Davlin must have done something to the formative breedex, retaining some kernel of his own mind, which was now coming to the fore.

"After several fissionings, my subhive has gathered enough human DNA to make us more human." The pieces shifted like an image coming into focus, and now the rough approximation of a face became more clearly Davlin's. She could easily distinguish his features. *"I fought the breedex larva, and I am now part of it."*

"Your mind is the Klikiss mind?"

"Part of it. We became stronger, and I struggle for dominance." As he remembered how to communicate, the Davlin-breedex seemed to grow more proficient with his words. *"I won't let the faint human traces from the colonists be diluted further."*

She saw a heartbreaking change of the portrayed expression, a slight alteration in the tone of voice. The image blurred and then sharpened again. *"We now have . . . an uneasy peace, the Klikiss and I."*

Margaret stepped closer to the horrendous mass. "Then

why are you so bloodthirsty? Can't you stop these hive wars and impose peace? The Llaro subhive has been more vicious than any other." It made no sense to her.

"Because we must be more vicious. I . . . we must eradicate all the others."

"Why?"

"To save humanity. The subhives will attack, and dominate, and destroy. In the end, only one breedex will survive. One breedex will control all. One breedex will be the *breedex."* He paused for a long moment, and Margaret struggled to understand what Davlin was implying. *"Therefore, I must be that breedex. Humanity has no chance unless I conquer the other subhives."*

Margaret caught her breath, though many questions tumbled through her mind. Was this why she had been saved? To become a liaison? "You want the human race to deal with you, instead of another breedex."

"Yes."

"And then there will be peace between the humans and the Klikiss? We'll no longer have to fear you?"

"I am strong, but I am not the only mind here. Even if I win, there are no guarantees. I am still part Klikiss."

Staring at the monstrous form, Margaret felt a chill go through her. "How many subhives do you still need to defeat?"

"Five other subhives still fight on the Klikiss worlds, spreading outward. Two are battling at Relleker." The face shuffled itself, crystallized again. *"I remember Relleker from when I was . . . merely Davlin. My subhive will wait, and then crush whichever breedex wins there."*

"And how can I help?"

"Stay here. Do not let me forget my humanity."

When the last few crates were loaded in the *Blind Faith*'s cargo bay, Orli, DD, and Mr. Steinman climbed aboard, and the ship departed for Relleker. Captain Roberts was glad to be setting off again on a regular trading run, and very pleased to have such good company.

The *Blind Faith* sailed smoothly across space. On the tablescreen, Roberts checked his manifest. All three of them had heated up mealpax of something called "nourishing stew."

"When we get to Relleker, those people will be so thrilled they'll throw a feast in our honor," Roberts said. "It used to be a resort, you know."

"Relleker was a well-respected and wealthy Hansa colony," DD chimed in, reciting from his database, "best known for its spa cities, its comfortable climate, and its wineries. Only the wealthiest people settled there."

"And the snootiest," Roberts said. "The colony head was a real piece of work, refused to lend us a hand saving the people on Crenna, tried to charge us docking fees while our ship was gathering emergency supplies." He frowned. "Now, I'm not a man to hold a grudge, but maybe it was karma. The drogues wiped out Relleker, blasted every building to the ground, killed every last colonist." He took three quick slurping mouthfuls of the alleged stew. "But it's a whole new colony now, a fresh start."

"I can't wait to see it," Mr. Steinman said.

When the *Faith* arrived, the planet looked like a beautiful blue-and-green gem mottled with clouds, a place to tempt human settlers. Grinning, Roberts transmitted, "Hey, down there! Send out the welcome wagon. We've brought a shipful of supplies, if anybody's buying." When the comm system remained quiet, his smile faltered. Glancing at Orli, he transmitted again, more formally now. "This is Captain Branson Roberts in the *Blind Faith*. We have a load of cargo for the settlement. Please transmit landing instructions."

"I thought they'd be anxious to hear from us," Mr. Steinman said.

"A Confederation ship's been scheduled on this run for weeks. Can't imagine why they're so quiet."

Roberts waited again. Orli grew concerned. "Perhaps they are using other communication bands," DD suggested. "We could search for signal traffic."

Roberts punched the comm system, but received an error message on the complicated new controls. Orli leaned over and reentered the instructions, fixing the glitch. Suddenly a cacophony of screeches, clicks, whistles, and tortured songs poured from the speakers.

Mr. Steinman put his hands against his ears. "What a racket!"

"Some kind of feedback or distortion." Roberts slapped the control panel, as if that would fix the problem. "The Roamers must have put in a faulty comm system."

"It is not faulty," DD said. "That is the Klikiss language."

As the *Faith* came around the planet's night side, they nearly careened into two gigantic swarmships battling each other high above the atmosphere. The alien vessels were immense conglomerations of smaller craft packed into a fluid mass, like a colliding pair of globular clusters with blazing stars flung in all directions. Splashes of light, energy weapons, and power discharges crackled between the giant vessels as they tore each other apart.

"This doesn't look good," Steinman said.

Roberts activated the comm system again. "Relleker! This is the Confederation ship *Blind Faith*. Can anyone respond?" He heard only static, then more Klikiss screeching.

"I spent much time among the Klikiss with Margaret Colicos. I can translate." DD stood close to the speaker, listening. "Two rival subhives are battling for control of Relleker. They arrived at nearly the same time, and now they are attempting to destroy each other."

Clusters of smaller Klikiss ships attacked their opponents in a drunken, disorganized fashion. The gigantic swarmships seemed to be disintegrating as they continued to pick apart one component after another.

As the *Faith* raced over the night-dark hemisphere, Orli could see glowing patches of the planet's surface below—huge areas burning. She shuddered, remembering that the insect creatures had already murdered so many people she had known on the Llaro colony. She could tell there wouldn't be any survivors left down on Relleker, either. With two powerful subhives fighting over their planet, those colonists hadn't had a chance.

As the enormous clusters continued to battle each other, a segment of the nearest Klikiss swarmship separated from the main ball like a wad of sparkling clay torn off. The group of tightly packed component ships angled toward the *Blind Faith*.

"They've spotted us," Orli said.

"And we're not in any shape to fend off an attack, Roberts," Mr. Steinman yelped. "Time to get the hell out of here."

Captain Roberts agreed. "Let's see how good those new Roamer engines are." He laid in the course for their swift retreat.

The artificial gravity generators struggled to compensate for the ship's rough acceleration. A flurry of energy bolts shot past them, but the *Blind Faith* was out of range. Roberts looked behind them as they outdistanced the lumbering Klikiss component ships. "Straight back to Osquivel—we've got to tell somebody what's happened here."

29 ☀ SIRIX

When they finally reached Relleker, eager to take over the technical facilities there, Sirix and his black robots were shocked to discover that the Klikiss had already arrived. Urgently shutting down power, the robot battle group remained out of sensor range while the two swarmships tore each other apart. Even though the breedexes were locked in mortal combat, Sirix suspected the rival subhives would put aside their differences the moment they spotted the black robots.

He observed the battle while PD and QT stood beside him on the bridge. Part of him wanted to inflict great harm on the loathsome creator race, but logic prevailed. Sirix would wait until the primary battle was over, let the Klikiss damage each other, then send his battleships in to annihilate the remnants of whichever subhive survived.

"What about the colonists down on Relleker?" QT asked. "We should try to protect them."

"We may need them to help operate the industrial facilities," PD added.

Sirix had already studied the scans. "It is too late to save the factories, or the humans." He had placed a great deal of hope on Relleker, and the loss of those facilities angered him greatly, but he would not risk his remaining robots to help human colonists — if any had survived. Klikiss warriors were already swarming over the settled areas of the planet below.

The two swarmships decimated each other, neither admitting defeat. Finally, when Sirix analyzed the numbers and calculated that he could not possibly lose, he made his move. "Our firepower is now superior. It is time for us to eradicate both breedexes."

Responding to his orders, calm robots mounted the weapons stations on the stolen EDF ships. PD and QT, who had trained and practiced, were ready at the gunnery consoles. Sirix issued the command for his small fleet to power up, advance toward Relleker at full speed, and open fire.

Before the Klikiss swarmships could react to the unexpected black robot attack, EDF jazers and volleys of explosive projectiles scattered the cores of the clusters. The repeated detonations left nothing more than sparkling wreckage, like fireworks against the starry blackness. Component ships flew in all directions, without guidance.

"Sirix," QT said, "numerous Klikiss warriors remain on the ground. They have infested the established colony and are continuing the battle."

"They would have come here to conquer." Sirix ran his weapons inventory swiftly through his efficient cybernetic mind. He still possessed four nuclear warheads that could vaporize part of the continent where the Relleker colony had been. He could not risk allowing any portion of the two wounded subhives to remain. If he could not have Relleker for his own purposes, he would certainly not leave it for the Klikiss.

The warhead drop was precise, and flashes of atomic fire spread outward, disintegrating the remaining Klikiss and purging Relleker of the infestation . . . along with any hidden humans who might have survived.

When the stolen EDF ships slowly withdrew from the system, Relleker was totally dead. "It is good to have a clean victory for once," Sirix said aloud, though he remained discouraged that he had not acquired the technological facilities he had hoped for.

The two compies stared at the screen as the planet receded. "Our problem remains unsolved, Sirix," PD said.

30 ☀ KING PETER

Every breath smelled like wet ash.

Because the fungus-reef city had burned to the ground, Peter needed to establish a new temporary headquarters for his government. Admiral Willis's troops cleared the few still-smoldering trees, leveled the ground, and set up modular barracks.

She reported to Peter. "With your permission, sire, I'd like to get my corps of engineers working to ensure we have clean water and proper food supplies. Our standard ration-packs aren't gourmet fare, but they'll do in a pinch. Besides, you people eat bugs, so I don't suppose you're too picky."

Peter let the joke slide. "You and your ships couldn't have arrived at a better time, Admiral."

"Better late than never. Does this mean you accept us as part of the Confederation military?"

"Part of it? Most of it, I'd say. When you finish basic operations here, I want you to report to the Osquivel shipyards. That's where most of our fleet is being constructed. You'll have to work out the details with my current . . . commanding officers, I suppose you'd call them. Robb Brindle and Tasia Tamblyn."

Willis chuckled. "Brindle and Tamblyn? I should have known they'd find themselves in the thick of things. Brindle's father served as my exec, but he . . . elected not to change his employment at the present time."

"You left him behind when your ships mutinied?" Estarra clarified.

Willis tried not to look scandalized by the Queen's choice of words. "Some people are just a little slow to make the right choices."

Estarra adjusted the baby tucked against her side, careful not to wake him; he had finally fallen asleep with salve on his burns. "Peter, if Admiral Willis is going to the Osquivel shipyards, she should take the hydrogue derelict with her. We need to get it to Kotto Okiah."

He nodded. "Yes, it's about time for that—although I'm glad it was here when we needed it."

The silvery wental ship landed in the middle of the meadow, where droplets from the sparkling downpour continued to drip from the high trees. Jess Tamblyn and Cesca Peroni, crackling with internal wental energy, stepped through the flexible membrane of their vessel and stood glistening, coated with a permanent sheen of living water. They exchanged smiles of hard satisfaction.

"I'm glad we got your message," Cesca said. "The green priests signaled this emergency loud and clear."

Jess looked very pleased with himself. "We needed to show the wentals how they could fight. The faeros have already done them enough harm. It's time for us to go on the offensive."

A shadow crossed Cesca's face. "The faeros will strike and burn everything they can: the Confederation, the Hansa, the wentals, the verdani—*everything*. That's why we need everything to fight them."

Jess added. "As you saw here, the wentals have truly awakened, and we'll lead them." He looked at the sky, watching the colorful sunset deepen. "I've already summoned my water bearers to help spread the wentals, as before. We met with Nikko Chan Tylar and his father in the Osquivel shipyards, and they are already taking the *Aquarius* on new missions."

A deeply satisfied expression overlaid Cesca's anger. "The faeros don't know it yet, but the rules have changed. They're in for a surprise."

31 ☀ CALEB TAMBLYN

Cold. Lonely. Hopeless.

During the seemingly endless days he'd been stuck here, Caleb had thought of many words to describe his situation. Escape pods weren't designed to be luxury accommodations, but at least he was alive. Still . . .

Stranded. Isolated. At his wits' end.

When the faeros had closed in on the Tamblyn tanker, Denn Peroni and Caleb had been on the edge of the Jonah system, minding their own business, carrying a load of wentals. Who could have foreseen that Denn's bizarre new religion that allowed him to see the interconnected universe would make him vulnerable to the fiery elementals?

Denn had known that he himself couldn't get away, but he'd forced Caleb to stumble into the escape pod, and the emergency engines had blasted him free before he'd known what was really happening. The water tanker exploded behind him, and the fireballs had dragged the dispersed wentals into the sun. . . .

Caleb had tumbled for a day in empty space before crashing on the icy lump of Jonah 12. Not long ago this place had been a Roamer outpost, a hydrogen-processing plant designed by Kotto Okiah himself. But it had been devastated . . . something to do with rampaging Klikiss robots, if he remembered correctly.

Little remained on Jonah 12's cratered ice fields — no transports, no buildings, no way of transmitting an emergency signal . . . and no one within range to detect it even if he could shout out. Caleb didn't have the slightest idea how he was going to get out of this.

A sophisticated and serviceable Roamer model, the escape pod had its own life-support engine and batteries designed to keep passengers alive for a week at most. Even though he rationed his supplies and kept exertion to a minimum, Caleb wouldn't last long enough for anyone to notice he was missing.

He did, however, have a survival suit, a basic chemical generator, and a few tools. He spent the first day and a half cobbling together a simple chemical extractor, the kind of device a ten-year-old Roamer child could build. With it, he derived all the water and oxygen and hydrogen fuel he needed from the ice outside. With his Roamer know-how, Caleb would be able to extend his survival for a few more weeks — a remarkable achievement, though he doubted anyone would ever find him to admire his fortitude.

Halfway between boredom and desperation, he suited up, cycled through the small airlock, and went outside into the "daylight." The distant sun was no more than a bright star among all the others. Jonah 12 was a rock, a bleak and cold one at that. He took a toolkit and sample-collection container and trudged off across the rough, frozen surface.

Taking giant strides in the low gravity, he needed less than an hour to reach the large melted crater and the wreckage of what had been Kotto's hydrogen-extraction facility. He hoped to find some ruined huts, perhaps something he could patch up and use as a base camp. As he strode along, Caleb had dreams of discovering a generator, a cache of food supplies, maybe even a satellite dish transmitter.

Instead, he found only wreckage, a few scraps of metal,

some melted lumps of alloys . . . nothing that seemed immediately useful, but he scavenged it anyway. Most of the outpost had been vaporized in a reactor explosion, and anything
else had vanished permanently into the flash-melted ice,
which then froze into an iron-hard steel-gray lake with a few
slushy patches kept liquid by the heat of radioactive decay.

As Caleb stared, reality sank in: He would probably be
here for a long while, and his last days without food would
not be pleasant. He stood in total silence for several minutes,
but no flashes of inspiration came to him.

He turned and made his way back to his little escape
pod.

32 ☀ NIRA

Knowing that Jora'h must be battling to hold on to sanity itself, Nira was too upset to concentrate on anything
else. When Sarein and Captain McCammon arrived at the
lunar EDF base and asked to see her, she feared they brought
terrible news.

"Come with us to the Whisper Palace, Nira." Sarein
sounded almost compassionate. "The Chairman needs your
green priest skills."

Nira struggled with her anger. Sarein wore her Theron
ambassadorial garments, but she was acting as the Chair-

man's puppet. Ambassador Otema had once worn those traditional cocoon-weave garments; now, Nira thought, Sarein soiled them.

"No green priest will provide telink services to the Hansa," Nira said. "Certainly not me."

"Even if it would bring the Mage-Imperator back safely?" McCammon said. He seemed to be standing closer to Sarein than was actually necessary. He lowered his voice. "All you need to do is come with us."

Sarein seemed very earnest. "I know I can convince the Chairman to order Diente's warliner to turn around. You'll have the Mage-Imperator back, but first you've got to show some cooperation."

Nira's heart leaped. Jora'h would hate her for bowing to coercion . . . but she could literally save his life. If he died, or went mad, the consequences to the Ildiran Empire were unimaginably bleak. "I want this agreement in writing, and witnessed." Nira crossed her arms over her chest. "And within the hour."

"I'm afraid you're not in a bargaining position." Despite his words, McCammon's eyes showed a depth of feeling that surprised Nira, a compassion that he could not entirely cover. "And we are in no position to grant you anything."

"Done," Sarein said, putting a hand lightly on McCammon's arm. "I will write up the document, in my own hand." Then she threw in her last bargaining chip. "And the Chairman will have to let you use a treeling, at least for a little while. Keep that in mind."

Nira considered the advantages of even a brief contact with the worldforest. Yes, she could inform King Peter—and all green priests around the Spiral Arm—of their captivity, maybe learn something more about the faeros on Ildira.

Whatever the Chairman had in mind must be important to warrant such a risk; he wouldn't make an offer like this unless he needed her.

Through green priest memories that were accessible through the worldforest, Nira was familiar with the grandeur of the Whisper Palace, but she paid little attention to the majesty of her surroundings. Behind all the fabulous architecture and shouting crowds, Nira saw the rot deep in the Terran Hanseatic League.

Sarein led her to a colorful orange pavilion at one corner of the Palace Square; it had been decorated as a special box for the "esteemed Theron ambassador." Sarein had probably done it herself, since Nira doubted the Chairman would display any particular respect for the Confederation's new capital.

From the pavilion, they could view the central speaking podium, the rapt crowd, the numerous guards. As twilight deepened into dusk, numerous torches blazed atop the Whisper Palace towers. The whole District was extravagantly lit, as if for a celebration.

Nira wrestled with second thoughts. "What am I expected to do?"

Sarein said, "The Chairman wants to make certain King Peter hears this announcement—immediately. Report what you see. Deliver your message and let Peter decide what to do. Be a green priest!" She lowered her voice, and her words surprised Nira. "Afterward, I have to take the treeling away, so make the most of this time. Do what you need to do."

Chairman Wenceslas sauntered up, accompanied by a guard who carried a small potted treeling as if it were a time bomb. Nira realized how much she had hungered for the touch of a worldtree. For years she had been completely deprived on Dobro, and again recently in her captivity on the Moon. She could not hide her longing.

The Chairman gave her a stern look. "Once you connect to the worldforest, I know I can't control what other details you send into the verdani mind. I don't intend to try. So long as you share what you see here tonight, Peter will have his hands full."

Nira stood her ground, forcing herself not to take the potted treeling. "And the Mage-Imperator? When are you bringing him back? I demand to know—"

"Don't presume to dictate the terms of this agreement. Sarein has already convinced me to recall Admiral Diente's warliner if you cooperate today, though I still have my reservations. A little cooperation from the Mage-Imperator would have made many things so much easier. When he gets back in a few days, he may find that public sentiment has changed toward him somewhat."

The Chairman looked around the crowd. He smiled as Nira's own image was displayed on the spectator screens surrounding the huge square, a battered old photo that showed her haunted eyes, her gaunt features, her obvious suffering. The mood of the crowd grew decidedly uneasy, even ugly.

"What—what are you telling them?" She looked around wildly. Sarein averted her eyes, obviously upset.

The Chairman explained. "I decided to take down the Mage-Imperator's supposed 'nobility' by a notch. My press corps has released the full story of what the Ildirans did to you: how Ambassador Otema was murdered, how you were repeatedly raped as part of an insidious breeding program, and so on. Those abominable, inhuman Ildirans." He made a *tsk*-ing sound. "And it's quite effective, too. Ties in perfectly with the religious enthusiasm the Archfather is engendering. Best of all, it's entirely true. From now on, no human will accept empty Ildiran promises. Your story proves what treacheries the Mage-Imperator is willing to commit."

"Those things were perpetrated by the previous Mage-Imperator," Nira retorted. "Jora'h has done everything possible to make amends. And I'm not your pawn."

"Unless you wish to prolong the Mage-Imperator's suffering, you *are*. Now let's get on with it. Busy day." At the Chairman's nod, the guard handed her the treeling. Nira grabbed it, more interested in its delicate fronds and quivering potential than in the activity out on the square.

Basil turned to Sarein. "Deputy Cain and I have business to discuss inside. I wish you could go with me, but I'm trusting the green priest to you. Make certain Peter knows about our new King—especially his name."

"I will, Basil." The Chairman slipped away after briefly stroking Sarein's short hair—a mechanical gesture, as if he had reminded himself to do it; Nira detected no depth of feeling there, but she did see Sarein respond with the faintest shudder.

When they were alone in the observation pavilion, Nira touched the treeling, focused her thoughts into the world-forest network, and sank into the waiting information. In a flood, she learned everything that had happened, everything that had been kept from her since the capture of Jora'h's warliner.

She knew that the faeros had struck Ildira, but now she also knew of the newborn faeros attacking Theroc, possessing worldtrees, spreading a living fire. Although that disaster was already over, the pain still stung.

Nira sent her own waves of information, explaining how

the Mage-Imperator had been kidnapped, and how the Chair-man was trying to coerce him into betraying King Peter. Did Basil Wenceslas truly want the Confederation to have that information? It didn't matter. As soon as this event ended they were going to take the treeling away from her again. Nira decided not to tell Sarein what she had learned about Theroc; she saw no compelling reason to do so.

Engrossed in telink, she barely noticed when the ceremony started. The Archfather came forward in his robes, carrying an ornate shepherd's crook. He moved with slow strides, dragging a wake of hushed anticipation through the crowd.

Seeing her preoccupation with the treeling, Sarein chided her. "You must watch *this*. Please."

Nira retreated from the sea of secondhand events to see the Archfather at the speaking podium with an unfamiliar young man waiting behind him. He had dark hair, dark eyes, and an expression that reminded her of someone out of his depth but trying hard not to show it. He wore fine and color-ful raiment, a design similar to what Old King Frederick had worn on the throne years ago. The bearded religious leader boomed out another rant about the Klikiss demons and King Peter's supposed collusion with them, but his words seemed reluctant, without fervor.

"Before we can be saved," the Archfather intoned, "be-fore humanity can return to the path of righteousness, we need a visionary leader. We need a King who is more than a King. Someone who can undo the terrible damage Peter has wrought."

Though she did not quite understand why she was asked to do so, Nira dutifully reported these words. The green priests were even now distributing them; she could hear Celli reporting to King Peter.

"Today I announce the Hansa's new King, a young man who is destined to be our savior. All hail, *King Rory!*"

The young man stepped forward, standing straight and looking regal, as if he had practiced this entrance over and over. He seemed likeable enough, a perfect figurehead. But a savior? Nira doubted it.

And now Peter would know that the Hansa had formally replaced him as King. But surely he must have been expecting that for some time now. Why had this particular announcement been so important to the Chairman?

33 ✹ DEPUTY CHAIRMAN ELDRED CAIN

During the coronation ceremony, Basil stood next to Deputy Cain on the high, hidden balcony. The Chairman seemed in a particularly good mood. "There's definitely something special in the air tonight."

Cain wasn't sure he wanted to know what the Chairman had in mind.

Basil Wenceslas prided himself in having countless

irons in the fire, all supposedly for the benefit of the Hansa, though often they were petty gestures, such as revealing a distorted version of the green priest Nira's story.

General Lanyan had recently sent a scout back with a full and overblown report of his great success at the Roamer skymines, claiming to have secured a breathtaking amount of ekti. The General was continuing his "mission," but now Chairman Wenceslas needed to figure out how to keep the defeated skymines producing stardrive fuel for the Hansa. Cain doubted that would be an easy task. . . .

Before the Archfather's coronation of King Rory got under way, two smiling people arrived behind them on the balcony. One was a short, wide-faced man whose torso seemed longer than his legs; beside him, in comical contrast, stood a tall, dark-skinned woman. The statuesque woman had high cheekbones, lovely brown eyes, and an unusually long neck.

"Mr. Chairman, everything is prepared," said the man in a deep, gravelly voice. He carried communications equipment.

The tall woman nodded with a graceful bow of her head, like a giraffe dipping down to drink from a pool of water. "The metal dust is evenly distributed in the air overhead. With these weather patterns, it will hold the impedance paths for another fifteen to twenty minutes. The time constraints are tight, but we are ready."

With a confident smile, the Chairman introduced the newcomers. "Deputy Cain, meet my new scientific advisers, Dr. Tito Andropolis and Dr. Jane Kulu."

Kulu said in an elegant voice, "We are here to create technological miracles, thereby proving that God is indeed on our side." The woman seemed completely serious.

"Technological miracles?" Cain asked. What was the Chairman up to now?

"Smoke and mirrors," Basil murmured.

"Sometimes faith requires a nudge in the correct direction," Andropolis said with a chortle. "The truth is the truth. Why should it matter if we need to use a heavy hand to guide people along the right path?"

Below in the illuminated square, the Archfather summoned King Rory forward. Cheers, whistles, and delighted screams erupted from the crowd; the people happily swallowed everything the Archfather said.

Enjoying his high vantage point, Andropolis bobbed his square chin up and down. "After tonight's demonstration, they will worship Rory as a conquering hero."

"That is the point," Basil said.

Below, the Archfather said, "God has blessed this young man to be our chosen leader. Rory will guide us away from the demons, away from the traitors, and back to prosperity." Cleverly arranged spotlights cast an angelic glow over the newly crowned Rory.

Kulu spoke with a deep, self-assured voice into her small communicator, "Prepare discharges. On my mark."

Up in the sky, extravagant fireworks blossomed in a truly impressive show, delighting the crowd. Basil wore a mysterious smile. "This is just the warmup."

After the traditional pyrotechnic bursts had faded into smoke, Rory spoke in a quavering voice that quickly became more assured. "I am your King. I will lead you, my chosen people, and show all others the true power of the righteous."

Andropolis was nearly beside himself with excitement. Kulu clicked her communicator. "Commence discharge."

On cue outside, Rory raised his hands and shouted, "I call down the lightning!"

Suddenly, with perfect choreography, a blinding shower of spectacular electrical discharges laced the sky. One blast after another struck the tallest buildings in the Palace District like incandescent bullwhips, then anchored themselves to the highest tower of the Whisper Palace and the top of the Hansa pyramid. The searing bolts sustained themselves for four blinding seconds, weaving a blazing spiderweb of electricity across the starry dome overhead. Cain had never seen anything like it.

Viewed on the close-up screen, Rory seemed to be counting to himself, and when he lowered his hands at the appropriate moment, the discharge vanished, as if at his command, leaving the crowd in awed silence.

After the deputy blinked the afterburn from his eyes, he expected to see towers devastated, fires blazing on the roof-tops. But he quickly realized that no actual damage had been done. Not only had King Rory called down the lightning, but he had protected them all. *Perfect.*

"Well-grounded lightning rods placed beforehand," Basil explained. "They should be removed before anyone thinks to look around. See to that, please."

Cain nodded, more uneasy than awestruck.

Basil surveyed the stunned crowd, looking very satisfied. "That should keep those annoying anti-Hansa protesters quiet for a while. Have there been any further incidents?"

Cain struggled to bring his thoughts back to the present. "Always, Mr. Chairman. The resistance groups are becoming more organized."

"Then find them."

Kulu and Andropolis were on their feet, congratulating

each other. "God has certainly shown his will tonight," Andropolis said with a satisfied sigh. "Who could question it?"

34 ☀ KING PETER

When Celli delivered Nira's announcement on Theroc, Peter turned pale. "King *Rory*? It can't be."

Estarra glanced at him, sharing his confusion and uneasiness. Peter knew that the Queen understood, although no one else did—except for Basil. Damn him! This was a lower blow than he could have expected, even from the unstable Chairman.

Rory . . . How could he possibly still be alive?

First Nira said the Chairman had kidnapped the Mage-Imperator and tried to force him to renounce his alliance with the Confederation, torturing him with isolation to break him. And now he had hauled out Rory . . . long-dead, sweet Rory. It was not possible.

"Oh, Basil is an evil bastard," he said. "Describe it to me again, Celli. Every minute. And describe the young man."

Surprised by his reaction, the green priest repeated Nira's message, and Peter nodded slowly to himself, feeling sick inside. "Excuse me. I need some time alone. Estarra and I have to talk."

The Queen was already on her feet, and Peter followed

her into their temporary quarters. When they were alone, he rested his elbows on his knees and his head in his hands. "Everyone else thinks that was just a political announcement, finally putting a replacement king on the throne, but Basil knew it was vastly more personal to me. He intended to twist the knife. It's his way of threatening me."

Sitting down, Estarra cradled little Reynald in her arms and leaned back so that she could nurse the baby. "You think it's really your brother? Could it be a trick?"

Peter tried to work it out in his mind. His whole family had been killed almost ten years ago when their apartment building exploded—the result of sabotage conducted by Hansa henchmen to clear away all connections to Peter/Raymond. They wanted no one who could challenge his identity with any sort of genetic proof.

And now King Rory could not be a coincidence. Basil had made that perfectly clear by insisting that Nira send the message.

Estarra tried to sound sensible. "The very idea that your little brother could still be alive, held out of sight all these years, is absurd."

Peter drew a deep breath. "And yet if anyone could be so insidious, it'd be Basil."

"But if he really had a secret weapon to keep you in line, why would he wait until now? You could just denounce this new King Rory—explain that he must be a complete fake. That would take away whatever hold the Chairman thinks he has over you."

Peter shook his head. "If I chose that course of action, I would be forced to denounce my own rule. I'd have to admit *I'm* just a street kid given a makeover and thrust into this position. Whether Rory's my brother or not, I'm as much a fake as he is." He paced around the room. "No, it's less obvious than that. Basil will use him as a subtle hostage. As long as Rory behaves, the Chairman has exactly what he wants—a figurehead, as I was supposed to be. And if I have even a shred of hope that Rory is who I think he is, then Basil will think he has me under his thumb."

When Reynald finished nursing, Peter took the baby from Estarra to burp him. Afterward, he held his son, looking down at the small face that had such sweet features, a blend of his own and his wife's. Peter thought of his brothers, Carlos, Michael . . . Rory. Yes, Rory. He felt a swell of love in his chest, a clear sense of loss for his family and the simple yet endearing life he'd had—all destroyed by Basil's schemes. Was it possible that the Chairman had saved one small piece as a human shield?

"Basil's ploy isn't going to work, is it, Peter?"

"No," he answered quickly, then added in a softer voice, "At least I don't think so."

35 ☀ TASIA TAMBLYN

When the eleven EDF battleships arrived at the Osquivel shipyards, Tasia remarked to Robb, "They're damned lucky we've got a green priest to forewarn us. Otherwise, I might have opened fire the moment they showed themselves."

"Admit it, Tamblyn—you're happy to see them. And Admiral Willis, too."

Tasia relaxed her stern expression. "Damn right, I am. And we sure as hell could use someone who knows more about command than either of us does."

"So, you've been faking it all along?"

She clapped him on the shoulder. "Never with you, Brindle. Let's send out the welcome wagon. With all those weapons and ships, we could go on a real bug hunt!"

When the two of them formally presented themselves aboard the *Jupiter,* Tasia looked around the bridge with fond nostalgia. Willis had put on her best uniform and told all her officers and crew to make themselves presentable: polished shoes, razor-edged creases, neatly combed hair. Tasia wasn't sure why the Admiral felt the need to impress anyone, since the Confederation was in no position to turn down the offer of functional warships.

Willis returned Tasia's salute. "I swear, I never thought I'd see you two alive again."

Tasia dropped all pretense of formality and gave her a

quick hug. "Glad to see you, too, Admiral—and doubly glad to be on the same side again."

Robb, brought up in a more rigid military family, settled for a warm handshake. "I prefer combat duty to being held prisoner among the hydrogues, ma'am."

"Well, I did bring the hydrogue derelict back here to deliver to Kotto Okiah, in case you have further pie-in-the-sky ideas," Willis said.

"No thank you, ma'am. One excursion down into a gas giant was enough for me."

Leading them into her ready room, the Admiral ran her eyes up and down their grease-smudged jumpsuits. "Your uniforms could use a bit of attention. Is this the look of the Confederation military these days?"

"Roamers and colony volunteers don't need costumes to know which side they're fighting on," Tasia said, feeling defensive.

"We haven't had time to design new uniforms," Robb admitted. "In fact, I don't even know what rank we should call ourselves."

"Sounds like you need an organizational chart," Willis said. "Though I shudder to think about imposing that kind of structure on a Roamer-based society."

After Willis had called up coffee and a plate of sugar cookies from the *Jupiter*'s galley, Tasia said, "The EDF has more than its share of butt-head commanders, but you weren't one of them, Admiral. Even back when the Eddies were preying on Roamer clans, you had second thoughts."

Willis raised her eyebrows. "I may be slow, but I do get it eventually." She plucked a third sugar cookie from the plate, then told the story of how she had left the EDF after General Lanyan's crackdowns at Usk and Rhejak.

Robb was clearly sad to hear that his own father had refused to switch sides. "He'll have his head set on staying with the EDF, no matter what."

Tasia cleared her throat. "I'm not sure how best to integrate your ships and soldiers into the Confederation military, ma'am. Our setup is certainly different from what you're used to."

"No matter how it shakes out, this old dog can learn new tricks," Willis said. "All my soldiers understood what they were getting into, and they're ready for it. You're welcome to interview the crew if you like."

Tasia snorted. "Like I don't have anything better to do than chat with several thousand soldiers? If you vouch for them, Admiral, I'll take your word for it."

Willis's ships traveled to the far side of the sweeping rings where Kotto had unveiled a brand-new spacedock facility that could accommodate the entire battle group at once. "Quite an operation, Tamblyn," the Admiral mused. "Not at all like what we saw when we ran our operation here against the hydrogues. Was all this built in the last couple of years?"

Tasia flinched. "Oh, it was all here before, ma'am. We just didn't want you to see it. Back then, Roamers were content to lie low and let all the fighting pass over them, but now we've changed our philosophy. Considering the persecution we've faced, we can't just be merchants and couriers anymore—we have to be warriors, too. You can thank Chairman Wenceslas for that."

The Juggernaut pulled into a huge construction framework. Dazzling lights illuminated the geometric hull lines as docking clamps secured the giant vessel, anchoring it into place for the work to begin. Roamer engineers in environment suits swarmed over the hull, beginning a full assessment.

Tasia quickly issued orders to the spacedock crews. "Every one of these ships needs to be checked out and refurbished."

Over the next few hours, shipyard managers juggled the scheduling of the whole refit facility so that Willis's ten Mantas could settle into individual slips. Connectors, telescoping bridges, and fuel lines extended across to the hulls.

When the work was ready to begin in earnest, Tasia and Willis peered through the angled observation window of the spacedock's management center. Grinning, Tasia clicked her comm and transmitted to the busy crew, "First things first — get some abrasive blasters and take off that EDF logo! I want Confederation markings painted on every hull."

36 ☀ ORLI COVITZ

The *Blind Faith* rushed back to Osquivel with their startling news about the Klikiss at Relleker. When Captain Roberts displayed their images to the Roamers inside the main admin dome, Robb Brindle was baffled. "But what were the bugs doing there? They never had a claim to Relleker. That was a legitimate Confederation outpost."

Tasia was even more incensed. "The bugs want to conquer everything. I say we mount an offensive! As soon as Admiral Willis's ships get out of spacedock, we'll have more than enough firepower to squash those critters."

"There's no one left to save at Relleker," Orli said. "Nothing to salvage."

Roamers were grumbling, especially those who hadn't previously faced the Klikiss. "There's been too much running and too much hiding," said a leathery-faced old female pilot. "Somebody needs to teach those bugs a lesson."

"But what about the faeros?" asked Liona, the green priest. "They just attacked Theroc."

"And the Eddies just attacked Golgen," Robb pointed out.

"It sure is wonderful to have plenty of enemies to choose from," Mr. Steinman said.

Despite his muttering about wanting to relax and retire, Steinman spent most of his days in the lab chambers where Kotto Okiah dabbled with new concepts. Steinman had been a risk taker in his earlier career, exploring the uncharted Klikiss transportal network. Now he wanted a quieter life, but events kept preventing him from having the quieter life he wanted, so he decided to find a purpose.

With DD walking faithfully at her side, Orli found the two men in Kotto's lab. She didn't have any other home to go to, and she was old enough to take care of herself, to shoulder responsibilities. Among the Roamers, any girl her age already knew how to pull her weight, and Kotto seemed amenable to letting both her and Mr. Steinman help him.

The small research facility was a hollowed-out rock not unlike an empty walnut half covered by a dome of interlocking transparent plates. Reflected light from the gas giant shone down into the chamber.

Inside, Kotto and Mr. Steinman were intent on the small hydrogue derelict, which Admiral Willis had recently delivered. Even after what it had been through, the derelict's slick crystalline surface gleamed with rainbow reflections. Kotto hummed to himself as he poked his head into the open hatch. His two Research compies, KR and GU, worked at his side, taking notes, applying probes, and completing numerous tasks that Kotto started.

When she and DD entered, Mr. Steinman looked up from where he had been sorting tools. Kotto looked over his shoulder at her, distracted. "I hope you don't have an administrative problem for me to take care of."

"I'm just making sure Mr. Steinman isn't causing problems," she teased.

He looked offended. "I may be retired, girl, but I've got a good head on my shoulders."

Kotto retrieved an electronic datapad he had left on the transparent floor of the derelict. "I've got to go over the test reports those Hansa engineers compiled. A Dr. Swendsen had performed some early studies, but he's dead now. I think compies killed him. Anyway, King Peter and OX provided most of his records."

"Can I help?" Orli asked.

DD piped up. "I am an excellent assistant, too. My first owners wanted only a Friendly compy, but my masters Margaret and Louis Colicos modified my programming so I could be a research helper."

Mr. Steinman said, "If you can figure out something to do, DD, then by all means do it. Always plenty of work.

Wash the windows, if you like. Kotto and I were just trying to figure out how to get the compies up there."

Orli looked through the interconnected skylights of the research dome, at the stars and the bloated gas giant beyond. In the ring disk, small lights indicated ships constantly coming and going between the facilities.

An exceptionally fast-moving streak caught her eye, a cargo escort flying pell-mell, plunging into the rings as if a pack of slavering wolves were after it. "That ship sure is hell-bent on something. What could it be running toward?"

"Or from?" DD added.

Kotto climbed out of the derelict and craned his neck. "He must be running from all those Eddie battleships."

A Juggernaut and a group of EDF cruisers charged in after the frantically dodging cargo escort. Alarms began to sound throughout the shipyard facilities. As soon as the EDF ships arrived, they opened fire.

37 ☀ GENERAL KURT LANYAN

When he saw the thriving facilities in the rings of Osquivel, Lanyan could hardly believe his eyes. From this high above the plane, the ring disk appeared to light up with a thousand glimmers from processing stations, thermal plumes, and cargo traffic. According to reports, this place had been completely abandoned after former Chairman Fitz-patrick had kicked the Roamers out, but the gas giant certainly was infested again.

The fleeing cargo escort from the ruins of Forrey's Folly had led them directly here. Lanyan could not suppress a gleeful grin.

Within moments of the EDF's arrival, though, the Roamer ships had begun to scatter. Standing on the bridge, Conrad Brindle nodded somberly. "Looks like they're ready for us, General."

"No surprise, with all the caterwauling from that cargo escort." The fleeing pilot had blown their element of surprise, though Lanyan didn't think the man realized he'd been followed. "Weapons officer, eliminate that ship. We've already hit the jackpot here."

Brindle's eyes widened. "General, is that really necessary?"

"He's an enemy fugitive fleeing EDF pursuit. What more justification do you want?"

The weapons officer targeted the spidery craft and opened fire as soon as he had a jazer lock. The cargo escort exploded in a flash of expanding debris.

Brindle stood with his eyes narrowed and expression stony, but he chose not to comment further. Instead, he turned to the *Goliath*'s tactical officer. "Search our database and call up images of the old facilities from our previous recon missions. We'll want to know how best to shut them down without further casualties."

Lanyan was surprised by the sheer number of Roamer ships, artificial spacedocks, and habitats listed on the summary screens. This had to be one of the primary Roamer complexes.

In the disorganized jumble of evacuating spacecraft, many clan ships fled into the outer system, while others dove into the demolition derby of the inner rings. A brash handful flew directly toward the EDF ships, taking potshots before swerving away. They reminded Lanyan of tiny barking dogs, but the surprisingly powerful impacts of their shots made the Juggernaut's hull ring. Damage lights blinked. "What the hell was that? Did they actually hit us?"

Brindle studied the results. "Those weapons are more powerful than our jazers, General. They do pose a threat."

"Roamers never fought back before." He ordered his Mantas to spread out in a close-and-control pattern.

"They're the *Confederation*, sir—not just Roamers anymore."

"I've had enough of this nonsense. Use any known Roamer bands so I can address them." Lanyan cleared his throat and leaned forward, making sure that the imagers would pick up his stern glower. "This is General Lanyan of the Earth Defense Forces. You are hereby ordered to surrender. All of your facilities and raw materials are forfeit to the Hansa war effort."

"We aren't part of the Hansa, you flatulent pus-bag!" one of the captains transmitted as he streaked past, launching another barrage of jazer blasts.

"Destroy that ship!" Lanyan shouted. "In fact, destroy any Roamer vessel that takes a potshot at us. Teach them a lesson."

Brindle cautioned, "General, are you sure Chairman Wenceslas wants open warfare? Previous hostilities and casualties have been kept—"

"Of course it's open warfare!"

The Roamer ships didn't have a chance against the concentrated EDF weaponry. Horrified curses flooded the communications arrays, but Lanyan was deaf to them as he drove his battle group toward the heart of the shipyard facilities. "Now start blasting the habitation domes and fabrication plants. Scorched earth."

Even the other members of the bridge crew seemed uneasy about that. Brindle said quietly, "Those are *civilians,* General."

"In this kind of war, there are no civilians. Continue transmitting our demand for surrender. The moment they capitulate, we'll stop hurting them."

As soon as the *Goliath* and the Mantas began strafing the automated smelters and metal-storage depots, a man's voice came over the communication lines. "General Lanyan, you have been declared a war criminal. We demand that you submit yourself to the Confederation authorities to face justice."

Lanyan couldn't stop himself from chuckling. "Who the hell is this?"

The voice paused, then said, "This is, um, Commodore Robb Brindle, second—no, *third*—in command of the Confederation military."

Conrad looked shocked. Lanyan glared at him. "Admiral, I wish you'd keep better control of your son."

"I knew he'd joined the Confederation, but I never dreamed . . ." He shook his head. "*Commodore* Robb Brindle?"

Detecting a hint of pride in the man's voice, Lanyan switched off the comm unit before Brindle could respond. "We don't need to answer that ridiculous demand." He sat forward, pressed his palms together. "Spread out and continue our barrage. Pound them into debris until they surrender."

38 ☀ ADAR ZAN'NH

Deep in the protected mountain tunnels, Zan'nh studied the disposition of his Solar Navy. After the destruction of the warliner carrying ten thousand refugees, he had only nine large battleships left on Ildira. Any ships that tried to leave the planet, even smaller craft, were targeted and destroyed. Hundreds more Ildirans had also died while attempting to escape.

The five damaged warliners from Tal O'nh's processional septa had recently reported in. The teams of workers Zan'nh had left on the empty, smoke-filled vessels had finished their repairs, and now the scarred battleships had limped back to the system. The Adar swiftly ordered them to remain out of danger, to join the rest of the patrol warliners that dared not approach Ildira. Even though the numbers of his battleships were increasing out there, they were maddeningly out of reach.

Even more large warliners returned, their pilots and crews confused by the disappearance of the Mage-Imperator from the *thism*. They wanted orders and explanations, but Adar Zan'nh had little reassurance to offer. He ordered them to wait. Because he could not know what the Mage-Imperator's orders would be in such a situation, he made the best decisions he could.

His nine remaining warliners were combing the landscape for survivors, checking on refugee camps, helping Ildirans to remain marginally safe from the faeros — or so he hoped. His other warliners scattered through the Spiral Arm could do little to support the many parts of the Empire left adrift. Meanwhile, he was stuck here, forcibly separated from the bulk of his Solar Navy.

The Ildiran Empire needed him to come up with some kind of brilliant strategy that would overthrow the faeros and free the people. Zan'nh had made his career by wrenching some kind of solution out of seemingly impossible circumstances. He had proved his mettle many times. Doing the best he could, he now tried to develop a strategy.

But against the faeros, he had nothing yet. He had racked his brains for days, consulted with his best advisers, and could think of no way to stand against the fiery elementals that would not end in total disaster.

In the central grotto, Rememberer Ko'sh had gathered a group of listeners for a tale recently approved to become part of the revised *Saga of Seven Suns*. "This is how Adar Kori'nh struck a devastating blow against the hydrogues."

Zan'nh flinched, wondering if the Chief Scribe had chosen that story as a particular jab at him. Yes, Adar Kori'nh, his heroic predecessor . . . Even when the hydrogues had seemed invincible, *Kori'nh* had found a way to inflict harm.

Zan'nh's thoughts folded inward like serrated blades, cutting into his memories as the rememberer described how the old Adar had sacrificed a whole maniple of Solar Navy warliners to annihilate an equivalent number of enemy warglobes. In the process, Adar Kori'nh had shown the rest of the Ildiran Empire a way to hurt the deep-core aliens.

Zan'nh's eyes glittered in the well-lit grotto; he ground his teeth in frustration. He would gladly have followed the other Adar's example, but against the faeros the sacrifice would be pointless. Nor would he waste his remaining Solar

Navy ships in suicidal crashes against the fireballs. He had too few ships, and they *must* remain undamaged for the defense of Ildira.

During the Chief Scribe's story, young Ridek'h sat on the stone floor beside Tal O'nh. Yazra'h paced back and forth with her Isix cats, as restless and frustrated as the Adar was. Prime Designate Daro'h stood by himself, clearly disturbed.

Suddenly Zan'nh reeled backward, losing track of the rememberer's sing-song voice. A great quake passed through the *thism*, and he felt a thousand screams erupt inside his head. Ko'sh's voice faltered as he detected it, too.

On the other side of the chamber, Daro'h sank to his knees, gasping for breath. "The faeros have attacked again. Thousands of people just died."

More affected than any of them, Ridek'h placed his hands against his forehead. "Those were people from Hyrillka. One of the resettlement camps." He stared around in the underground chamber. "I could hear them shouting, pleading in my head. And then it just stopped."

Moving impulsively, Zan'nh marched toward the lift platform that led to the mine tunnel's exit. "I will take the cutter and investigate. Maybe I can help the survivors—if there are any."

Ridek'h got to his feet. His voice was strained when he spoke. "I am going with you."

"It is too dangerous."

The boy crossed his arms over his chest. "Then it is too dangerous for *you*, as well, Adar."

Tal O'nh smiled into his personal darkness. "Take the boy, Adar. The experience will make him stronger." Zan'nh

was reminded of his own relationship with Kori'nh, his
teacher. He could not say no.

The glare of smoky daylight was unrelenting as the cutter flew low over the open terrain. In the secondary pilot's
seat, Ridek'h hunched forward to look out the front win-
dowplate. Swift fires had rushed across the croplands and
prairies, blackening fields and hillsides. Off in the distance,
columns of smoke rose into the air from Mijistra's ever-
burning fires.

Zan'nh felt the *thism*-ache within him and intentionally flew toward it. The cutter arrived at one of the largest
concentrations of Hyrillka evacuees, a geometrically laid out
camp with prefabricated buildings and flash-paved streets.
The pain in his heart grew sharper from all the recent, sudden deaths.

The camp was nothing more than a smoldering wound.
Every structure had been destroyed, the refugees cremated,
their soulfires absorbed. "The faeros have been feeding
again," Zan'nh said.

Ridek'h shook his head in dismay. "We evacuated Hyrillka's entire population, told all those people it was dangerous there. We never told them it would be worse on Ildira."
His reddened eyes showed both disgust and fury. "If Designate Rusa'h once cared for the people of Hyrillka, why
would he let the faeros do this? Why?"

In the sky above, many fireballs whizzed about at high
altitude, bright and hot. Zan'nh knew they must see him.
They could plunge down and kill him and Designate Ridek'h
in a flash. But the faeros just hovered there, observing.

Taunting?

Zan'nh hated them. It seemed that the fiery elementals

were flaunting the fact that they could come for the rest of the Ildirans at any time.

39 ☀ MAGE-IMPERATOR JORA'H

Aboard his own warliner, secluded in his chamber, the Mage-Imperator shuddered and set the interior lights to maximum brightness. Despite the harsh and supposedly comforting glare, he could barely feel it, barely see it.

This was *his* private stateroom. *His* warliner. *He* was Mage-Imperator of the Ildiran Empire.

He was powerless.

And alone.

He knew Nira was waiting for him, and he vowed to hold on. But thoughts of her were not enough under circumstances like these. Even if she had been there to hold him and talk to him . . . in spite of the closeness they shared, she could not have given him strength in the *thism*.

Another second passed, and another.

His mind was filled with a hollow silence. *Nothing*. His thoughts were as empty as the void between stars where this stolen warliner now sailed. Yes, the isolation could indeed drive him mad, exactly as Chairman Wenceslas wanted. Damn the man! The Chairman was not to be trusted, and the entire Ildiran Empire, the great and glorious civilization and its great and glorious ruler, had been driven to its knees.

Less than three days—how he clung to that thought. He wondered how much time had passed. He hadn't had the presence of mind to mark the chronometer when Admiral Diente had left following his last visit. This lonely silence had already lasted years, it seemed. Had it been three days? Two? Or only an hour? A few minutes?

Jora'h could no longer tell. He had no idea whatsoever.

"Nira . . ." he whispered to himself, but no one answered.

He recalled when Anton Colicos had brought a catatonic Rememberer Vao'sh back to the Prism Palace following their long, isolated journey of escape from the black robots. As Mage-Imperator, Jora'h had felt a distinct echo of the anguish Vao'sh had endured. But he had never imagined it would feel like this.

Trapped in nightmares, he could not forget how his son Thor'h had been drugged and locked in a sealed room—by Jora'h's own order. The power generators had failed, shutting down the bright blazers in the chamber. Thor'h had died alone and in the dark, a hideous fate for an Ildiran. . . .

Jora'h pressed himself closer to the bright blazers mounted on the wall, but even the light did not help.

Feeling faint, he doggedly sent out his thoughts yet again, trying to find any echo out there. He tried for hours . . . or perhaps it was only minutes . . . until he was too exhausted to keep trying. He let his thoughts drift aimlessly in the cold, black wasteland.

Unexpectedly, familiar strands of *thism* brushed the edges of his mind. The mental touch startled him, and he reached out to grasp the threads so desperately that the tenuous connection almost scattered. Almost. The distant thoughts drifted back toward his. He struggled to recognize them, but it was so hard to think straight.

Finally, it came to him—Osira'h and her siblings! Once he understood who they were, the connection strengthened. They helped from their end, securing the link.

"Osira'h!" he said out loud, and the children seized his wandering mind like rescuers throwing a lifeline to a drowning man. Their connection through the *thism* grew bright and clear. He caught flashes of Ildiran refugees sheltering in mountain caves, absorbed secondhand memories of searing fire.

Slowly, Jora'h began to understand exactly what had happened on Ildira. He had had only the vaguest fears before, but now he learned how Rusa'h and his fireballs had driven everyone from Mijistra and taken over the Prism Palace. The Empire itself was trembling, on the verge of collapse.

Jora'h used their thoughts as an anchor and drew strength from them. But his determination was his own, as was his outrage over what Chairman Wenceslas had done to him.

Yes, now he had the strength and the will to last until this warliner returned to Earth. And then he needed to find a way to save the Ildiran people.

40 ☀ OSIRA'H

Huddled in a small rock-walled alcove in their underground shelter, all of Nira's children joined together and searched with their minds for the Mage-Imperator. Osira'h had suggested the idea even before the faint *thism* pulse from her father had gone so silent.

Though the rest of the Ildirans were stunned and disoriented by the abrupt change in the comforting mental web, she didn't believe her father was dead—only lost. And if Jora'h were lost, then Osira'h vowed to find him. She simply needed the help of Rod'h, Gale'nh, Tamo'l, and Muree'n.

Together, they could achieve what other Ildirans could not.

Earlier, in comparatively "normal" times, the five halfbreeds had generated a strong rapport through touching the lone treeling atop the Prism Palace. The children had used a synthesis of their mother's telink and their Ildiran *thism* to form a unified new force that was stronger than, and different from, anything either Ildirans or green priests had ever known. Unlike other adherents of the *thism*/telink philosophy, the five special children had been able to protect themselves by cutting off the vulnerable paths through which Rusa'h had tried to burn them.

Throughout their time here in exile—while Prime Designate Daro'h, Yazra'h, Adar Zan'nh, and Tal O'nh struggled to piece together a military solution, and refugees in hundreds of scattered camps hid or died according to the whim of the faeros—Osira'h and her siblings continued to shield themselves.

But she believed that their skills gave them a responsibility to do more than hide. So the five of them had linked their minds and cast out into the *thism* in a concerted search for the Mage-Imperator. For days, no matter how far they spun out the soul-threads, he simply wasn't there. Osira'h had refused to give up.

Finally, they found him.

When the five children came running into the central chamber, Daro'h looked up, startled. Osira'h knew that some people wanted the Prime Designate to undergo the ascension ceremony and become the new Mage-Imperator, but if Daro'h acted too soon, the results would be catastrophic.

She called out in a high, clear voice. "The Mage-Imperator is alive! We found him in the *thism*."

The Prime Designate lunged to his feet, and Zan'nh and Yazra'h could not hide their joy; O'nh remained seated with a contented smile on his ravaged face. With overlapping chatter, the half-breed children explained how they had come upon Jora'h's drifting thoughts; the Mage-Imperator had been driven nearly insane by loneliness and isolation, but he was alive. Captive, but alive.

Osira'h and her brother Rod'h had to raise their voices into the outraged clamor as they told how the Hansa Chairman had kidnapped Jora'h, seized his warliner and Ildiran crew, and tried to coerce him into recanting his support for the Confederation.

"They isolated him," Rod'h said, his voice shaking with horror at the cruelty. "They cut off the Mage-Imperator from any contact with *thism*. He has been alone, star systems away from the nearest Ildiran."

"How could anyone survive that?" Chief Scribe Ko'sh said.

"Through us." Osira'h let herself show a small smile. "He might have survived alone, but he was getting weak. Now he has our help and strength. We will not let him give up."

"Also," Rod'h said, "we know how to find him now. The human military commander is returning him to Earth's Moon."

Zan'nh and Yazra'h wanted to launch an immediate attack against the Hansa, but Daro'h reminded them that the Solar Navy did not have the strength, equipment, or manpower to engage in such battles. Though many warliners remained safely in position at the edge of the Ildiran system, they could not tackle the entire human military.

Tal O'nh said in a quiet voice, "Rusa'h wants nothing more than to find the Mage-Imperator. Even if we brought Jora'h here, the faeros would gladly destroy him. Perhaps he is safer where he is."

"Then what do we do?" Ko'sh said.

"Now that we know the Mage-Imperator is alive, I will hear no more nonsense about the ascension ceremony," Daro'h said. "If he can survive his ordeal, then we can survive ours."

Adar Zan'nh squared his shoulders. "We have learned one other thing. The Mage-Imperator cannot help us from where he is. We are on our own."

41 ✺ SAREIN

Working in Queen Estarra's devastated greenhouse was somehow therapeutic for Sarein. Her sister had loved this conservatory, where she'd planted and tended representative Theron flora to remind her of home. But Basil had ordered everything killed. Out of spite.

Only a few of the flower beds still held shriveled brown plants; the rest were bare dirt. Sarein had set flats of small flowers, seedlings, and dwarf fruit trees on the edges of the planters. She hadn't been able to get any new Theron plants, though she still kept a few in her own quarters, but these would have pleased Estarra, nonetheless. Sarein went about her work with quiet determination, getting her fingers dirty, planting what she could. She remembered too many times when she'd been unable to intercede in Basil's decisions, to prevent him from going to extremes.

When the guard escort brought Nira into the conservatory, Sarein pushed aside all her qualms. The female green priest remained in the Whisper Palace pending the return of the Mage-Imperator in another day or so. At least Basil had allowed that. By now, Nira must be frantic with worry about Jora'h, but Sarein had no way to allay her fears. She could, however, do something else.

From the doorway, Nira spoke in a sharp voice. "Replanting a few flowers and shrubs won't atone for the destruction that's been done."

Sarein drew a long, slow breath. "I'm doing what I can.

A lot of us are." She picked up a small cluster of geraniums and pushed a hole in the dirt to plant them. "It's a very delicate process, and you don't always see what happens behind the scenes."

Nira remained aloof. "Did you know Theroc was attacked by the faeros? I found out through telink on the night of the coronation."

Sarein recoiled. "Why didn't you tell me? If Theroc was in trouble, they should have called us to help!" As she spoke, Sarein knew how foolish it sounded. Even she could never have convinced Basil to do *that*.

Nira gave her a withering look. "King Peter didn't think the Hansa would offer assistance. Think of it—your own sisters couldn't call upon you for aid. To me, that speaks volumes."

Ignoring the insult, Sarein concentrated on the real concern. "Is the attack over? Did the worldforest survive? How much damage?"

"The verdani fought off the faeros with the assistance of green priests, Roamers, wentals, and even Admiral Willis's former EDF battleships. They all fought to defend the trees—everyone but the Hansa. Your brother Beneto was also there. He's dead now."

Sarein stiffened. "His treeship?"

"He burned fighting the faeros." Nira's voice held condemnation. "And where were *you* during all this? As the official Theron ambassador, shouldn't you have been involved in this crisis? Aren't you supposed to have the best interests of *Theroc* at heart? You replaced Ambassador Otema. What would she have done?"

Stung, Sarein could not stop herself from lashing out. "Otema was murdered by the Ildirans. You were her apprentice, yet not only do you willingly remain with them, but you became the lover of their leader." *Just as I became Basil's lover.* "You and I are not so different. Loyalties change as circumstances change, and we don't always have freedom to take the purely noble course of action."

"Right and wrong don't change."

They stared at each other for a long moment. When Sarein looked into the other woman's eyes, she saw strength there, along with the scars from countless rugged wounds. Even before Basil released the story to the Hansa newsnets, Sarein had heard about some of the nightmares that had fundamentally changed Nira from the bright-eyed young green priest Sarein had met in her younger days on Theroc. But if Nira could survive and retain her strength and her humanity after all she'd been through, then surely Sarein could. . . .

"Why did you bring me here?" Nira remained distant.

Sarein looked over at the guards and dismissed them. "We wish to talk in private."

The royal guards seemed uneasy, but she remembered one of the men as a close companion to Captain McCammon. She gave a slight nod, hoping he was the ally she expected. The guard gestured to the others. "Let's give Ambassador Sarein a few moments. The Chairman would want us to follow her instructions." They stepped into the hall outside the conservatory.

Sarein led a suspicious Nira around some of the planters toward a thicket of dry twigs that had once been a dense flowering bush, now brown and partially uprooted. Here they were blocked from view. When Sarein brought out a small potted treeling, Nira's eyes lit up.

Sarein said, "I've been cut off from my mother and father and sisters for so long. All I ask is that you send word.

Tell Estarra that I wish her well. Has she delivered her baby yet? And Celli — tell my littlest sister that I miss her. Is it true that she's taking the green herself? And my parents . . ."

Nira narrowed her eyes. "Why should I trust you?"

"As you said, I am the Theron ambassador. I helped Estarra and Peter escape. I arranged for Nahton to send messages about their plight, and to warn Theroc." She lowered her voice. "Can you guess what the Chairman would do to me if he knew what I'm telling you?"

The green priest softened somewhat. "I'll send your messages." She touched the treeling, and within moments she was lost in telink, her lips moving quickly and silently as she described all her news. Sarein waited anxiously, sure that the guards would come back and see what they were doing.

When Nira withdrew, Sarein pressed her. "And what is the news? Do you have anything to tell me?"

"They are rebuilding on Theroc. Many died in the faeros fire, but most were saved. Yes, Celli is now a green priest. Yes, Peter and Estarra are now the proud parents of a little boy. They named him Reynald."

Tears welled up in Sarein's eyes.

Nira's brow furrowed as Sarein hid the treeling again. "Now all the Confederation has to worry about is what foolish action Chairman Wenceslas will take next."

eafening alarms rang through Kotto's research dome. An enormous EDF Juggernaut streaked overhead, spitting fire, while clan ships darted in and out like wasps. So far, the Roamers' defense didn't seem to be having much effect.

"It's all right. We're safe here—I think." Kotto looked up at the broad skylights. "I don't see why anyone would target this particular rock."

"They seem to be shooting at everything." Mr. Steinman's eyes darted from side to side.

The three compies clustered together not far from the hydrogue derelict. "If we are safe here, shall we continue working?" GU suggested. "Or have we finished with our research for today?"

DD suggested, "I can organize and collate the previous results so we do not duplicate efforts."

KR seemed to be the only compy who understood their precarious situation. "This is quite a conundrum."

Through the dome skylight, Orli watched Roamer cargo ships and armored courier vessels harass the Mantas. One of the EDF cruisers soared directly above their nondescript laboratory station, firing jazers at any reflective metal. An energy bolt struck a nearby floating fuel tank, which erupted in a silent fireball.

Even the lab's reinforced dome could not withstand the shrapnel hurled by the shockwave. Three of the transparent triangular panels cracked, splintered, and finally shattered.

In the sudden outrush of air, four more of the geometric panels failed, blasting out into space.

Orli's ears popped. The roaring and whistling air seemed deafening, though some of the Roamer mitigation films snapped into place. But not enough. Trying to protect her, Mr. Steinman tackled her to the smooth floor. Caught directly beneath one of the gaping holes in the dome, GU was drawn into the vortex of evacuating atmosphere. He lost his footing and rose into the air, but KR shot out a polymer hand and caught his companion by the ankle. The compy yelled for help as GU continued to be sucked toward the open ceiling. When KR lost his footing, as well, and began to fall upward, DD clasped *his* foot. The Friendly compy also had the foresight to grasp the lip of the sphere's open hatch to anchor them. The waterfall of wind tugged at the chain of three compies who continued to call for help.

Kotto staggered across the floor and grabbed Steinman by the back of his shirt, propelling him and Orli along. "Get into the derelict," he shouted, but his words were barely audible in the thinning air.

Steinman got to his knees, pushing the girl ahead of him. "Come on—seal the hatch."

The air was disappearing rapidly and the chamber was growing very cold, but Orli stopped at the doorway. "I won't leave DD out there."

"He's a compy, kid. He'll survive," Steinman said.

"Not if he gets blasted by those weapons. DD, can you get inside?"

"I would have to release my grip on KR."

"I have another idea," GU announced. At the end of the chain, dangling close to the jagged hole in the dome, he bent over to clasp the second compy's arm on his ankle. Then he began pulling himself back to the floor like a man climbing an upside-down rope. When he could reach far enough, GU grasped DD's shoulder and clambered toward the open hatch. Orli helped pull the battered compy into the derelict, while KR followed GU's example. Everyone wrestled to bring them closer. Finally, all three compies collapsed inside the derelict chamber.

Kotto had already run to the central controls in the small sphere, where he stood trying to figure out how the derelict worked. "We used vibrating membranes to open the hatch in the first place, but now I can't remember how to shut it!"

"All of the control documentation should be in the database," GU said, getting to his feet. Roamer analytical equipment sat beside the incomprehensible crystalline nodules that the hydrogues had used to control the vessel. Together, KR and GU quickly found the correct systems. With a thump, the diamond hatch anchored itself into place.

Orli crumpled to the floor. Mr. Steinman's hair floated around his head like a dandelion puff. Thin streaks of blood came out of his ears, and the whites of his eyes had hemorrhaged.

A second fuel tank exploded outside, but they were unharmed inside the transparent sphere. GU pointed out, "King Peter and the Hansa engineers left us with enough information to fly this ship, if we wish."

"There's a transportal, too," DD pointed out, "though I am reluctant to go through to unidentified coordinates. In order to operate it, I would require all of my memory capacity and perhaps the capacity of KR and GU as well. Shall I tell you the story of how I—"

"Not now, DD," Orli said.

"No transportal for me," Mr. Steinman said. "I'd rather just fly out of here."

"Let's test the engines," Kotto said. "KR and GU, you may take the helm."

Riding the current of the last evacuating air, the diamond-hulled derelict floated up through the twisted framework and transparent plates that had formed the dome. The portable comm system squawked with overlapping shouts, accusations, and commands.

Once free of the ruined dome, they had an excellent view of the half-lit gas giant, the expanse of the rings, and the predatory EDF cruisers. Dozens of Confederation ships flitted about, trying to protect the primary habitation complexes and main admin facilities. They looked quite insignificant.

"The story of David and Goliath is the exception to the rule," Mr. Steinman observed. "Most times with odds like this, the little guy just gets squashed."

43 ✸ TASIA TAMBLYN

During the EDF bombardment of the ring shipyards, Roamers evacuated from numerous orbiting rocks and industrial complexes, sealing themselves inside boltholes. The clans knew how to plan for crisis situations, because they had so much practice with things not going right.

Tasia stood with Robb in the admin dome, surrounded by monitor screens and communications links set up to monitor the everyday activity of the shipyards. Practically every screen flashed red. Dozens of administrators scrambled to shut down docks, laboratories, and fabrication plants, calling all hands to emergency shelters.

Lanyan was not going to be reasonable, despite Robb's foolish optimism. "General, please respond. You are attacking civilian targets. Cease fire! These facilities are no threat to you."

As a second wave of jazer strikes rippled across a line of ore asteroids, Tasia gave a rude snort. "Shizz, Brindle, did you really think he'd just turn around and run away from your biting criticism?"

Robb switched off the communications link, frowning in disappointment. "No, but it made me feel better to vent a little steam."

"I'd rather vent some exhaust ports. The manifest says we've got two cargo vessels in the main bay, newly upgraded to warship status. How about I take one and you take the other?"

"Good enough."

"And who gave you the rank of Commodore, anyway?"

He brushed his shoulder, as if imagining the immaculate braid there. "I made it up. I didn't suppose you'd complain—especially since you're above me in rank."

"Hell of a way to run a military," Tasia said as they ran out into the rock-walled corridors. Lanyan's demand for surrender continued on a repeating loop over the loudspeakers until one disgusted clan engineer disconnected the intercom wires and shut off the blowhard's words.

They reached the docking bay, where volunteer fighters rushed aboard the two battleships, ready to go as soon as somebody took command. Both upgraded vessels were blocky with add-on modules, but lack of streamlining didn't matter in space, and no one could complain about the ships' efficiency.

She gave Robb a quick kiss as they separated—"For luck," she said—then raced toward the ship on the left.

Three scruffy-looking Roamer men and a middle-aged woman had already jumped to the available consoles. Tasia settled into the captain's chair, shouted for her makeshift crew to hurry through the start-up procedures. Since this ship had a standard set of controls, most Roamers could run any station. As they completed their launch checklist, they squabbled over who would get the chance to operate the new weapons.

With Brindle's ship right at her side, Tasia accelerated out of the docking bay. She snapped at the members of her crew. "There'll be plenty of Eddies to shoot at, so get your act together before we hit the targeting zone!"

The Roamers quickly decided on positions, settled into their seats, and coordinated their functions mere seconds before Tasia began her first attack run.

The EDF raiders continued to pummel the heart of the shipyards, blasting any structure they could find. Many Roamer ships had already rallied to the defense of Osquivel. The pilots had no discipline, but plenty of newly installed armaments, and they played havoc with the regimented EDF battle group. Sadly, though, Lanyan's raiders were much more practiced at blasting things.

"This is damned disappointing. I really would have preferred to fight the *Klikiss* today," Tasia transmitted to Robb as the ships swooped after the attacking EDF vessels. Robb was obviously uneasy at the prospect of blasting his former comrades in the EDF, so she added, "We didn't ask for this, Brindle. They came gunning for *us*."

The rings of Osquivel had turned into a shooting gallery. With a sickening feeling Tasia remembered an earlier battle here, when all the EDF ships had joined in a massive assault against the hydrogues. That battle had been an utter disaster for the forces of humanity.

Tasia and Robb added their two ships to the flurry of harassing fire, trying to deflect the EDF march against the most heavily populated facilities. As she had promised her crew, they all had plenty of targets to choose from.

With a precise shot, Tasia took out a quad bank of jazer cannons mounted on the *Goliath*'s bow. Before she could pat herself on the back, though, three Mantas began to concentrate their fire on her ship. The shields barely withstood the barrage, and she had to do some fancy flying to get out of range.

When her starboard engine was damaged, Tasia knew they were in deep trouble. Robb gallantly tried to come to her rescue, drawing fire, but he, too, spun out of control, leaking gases from a ruptured tank.

Then, rising from the planet's tenuous limb came another group of giant battleships — a Juggernaut and ten Mantas, all sporting fresh Confederation insignia on their hulls, outnumbering and outgunning General Lanyan.

"Sorry we're late to the party." Admiral Willis's jazers fired a widespread pattern long before they came into range, purely to show off. "Wasn't Rhejak enough humiliation for you, General Lanyan? Ready for more so soon?"

Robb said, "What took you so long, Admiral? We've been busy for an hour!"

"Exactly how fast do you think I can disengage eleven ships from spacedock?"

"Roamers could have done it faster," Tasia said aloud to her grinning crew, but did not broadcast the comment.

Admiral Willis raised her voice over the command channel. "General Lanyan, how about we use the same surrender terms you proposed a few minutes ago? I assume you considered them to be fair and reasonable."

Her battle group raced in to join the Roamer defenders, all of whom redoubled their attacks. Her Juggernaut matched the General's, and the rest of the outnumbered EDF ships were unable to recover from their surprise.

After a moment of tense standoff, Lanyan's ships all turned about and exited from the Osquivel system in an embarrassing retreat. He didn't even bother to transmit a response.

44 ☀ SULLIVAN GOLD

After being released from the Ildiran Empire, Sullivan Gold had hoped for a quiet retirement with his family on Earth. He had run a Hansa cloud harvester, survived a massive attack by hydrogue warglobes, rescued Ildiran skyminers, and endured a lengthy and unfair detention in Mijistra before finally going home. He deserved a little bit of time to himself.

But Chairman Wenceslas had other ideas.

Sullivan had been with Lydia and the extended family for two weeks. Wanting to live in peace for a change, he had made no announcement of his homecoming, asked for no media attention. Nor had he made a point of reporting to the Chairman. That turned out to be a mistake.

A group of paramilitary troops dressed in unfamiliar uniforms pounded on the door of his city townhouse. A cinnamon-haired female officer stood with four burly, well-armed men. She would have been pretty, Sullivan thought, if the hard edges of her features had been sanded smooth. The woman compared his face to an image projected on a palmscreen. "Are you Sullivan Gold?"

"Yes . . . yes, I am. May I ask what this is about?"

"We have orders to search your home in order to determine your whereabouts and your activities."

"Well, my whereabouts are right here. And I haven't really been taking part in any activities. Just relaxing."

Lydia came up behind him, teasing, still not sure how serious this might be. "What have you done now, Sullivan?"

"Nothing I can think of." He made no move to let the security troops in.

"You did not report to the Chairman upon returning from the Ildiran Empire." The female officer's voice was hard. "You should have been debriefed. That was your priority."

Lydia huffed. "I hardly think so, ma'am. His *family* was his priority. He was certainly gone long enough. Who are you, anyway? I don't recognize your uniforms."

"We are a special cleanup crew appointed by Chairman Wenceslas. I am Colonel Shelia Andez." She glanced down at her palmscreen again. "And you must be Lydia Gold." She scrolled down, making disappointed noises, but didn't elaborate on what she found in the record. "We need to complete our search so that we can present an accurate report to the Chairman. Mr. Gold, he has requested to meet with you as soon as he can fit you into his schedule."

Lydia's voice grew hard, as it always did when somebody pushed her too far. "I don't recognize your authority. Who do you think—"

"Lydia," Sullivan cut her off. "Please, don't add to the trouble we're already in."

"And why are we in trouble, exactly?" She stood protectively beside him. "What have we done?"

Without waiting for permission, Colonel Andez pushed past Sullivan and his wife. The five members of the "cleanup crew" spread out and began going through cupboards and drawers, opening bedroom closets, looking behind the furniture. They seemed deaf to Lydia's persistent indignation, which only made her angrier.

Ever since his return, Sullivan had been carefully watching the newsnets. The Hansa was no longer the same place he remembered. In the wake of King Peter's departure, many unpleasant crackdowns had occurred. Not liking the repression she saw, Lydia wasn't shy about expressing her opinions.

Sullivan had very much tried to keep a low profile, but the Hansa had come to his doorstep anyway.

"Colonel Andez, you'd better see this!" One of the guards pulled a box from under the bed. "Alien contraband!"

Sullivan's heart sank. Inside the box were numerous etched gems and Ildiran credit chips. For his service to the Solar Navy, the Mage-Imperator had paid him in jewels and credits before his departure for Earth. Jora'h had asked Sullivan to stay in the Empire and manage their splinter colony of Dobro, but Sullivan had chosen to return to his wife and his family.

"Currency from the Ildiran Empire?" Andez asked.

Sullivan said patiently, "Payment for services rendered in the defeat of the hydrogues. It's perfectly legitimate."

"Then you admit you're working for the enemy?"

He was baffled. "Since when was the Ildiran Empire our enemy?"

"Since they formed an alliance with the Confederation. Haven't you heard?"

"Oh, this is just plain ridiculous," Lydia said, exasperated on his behalf. "Even if what you say is true, Sullivan completed that work before the Chairman even imagined any hostilities with the Ildirans."

"Can you prove this?" Andez said.

Lydia looked at the young officer as if she were a complete idiot. "He's been back home since before the announcement was made. Do your math."

"Sarcasm will not help the case against you," Andez warned.

"There's a *case* against us? On what grounds?"

"Lydia, please!" Sullivan had always loved the way she refused to let herself get pushed around, standing up for her family and her rights, but often her sharp tongue got her in trouble.

The burly man picked up the case of Ildiran gems. "This will have to be confiscated."

"We need that money to survive," Sullivan said in dismay. They had nothing else.

When he had originally agreed to run the Hansa cloud-harvesting facility on Qronha 3, the promised pay had been excellent, but it came with many strings attached—strings they hadn't seen until too late. The Hansa had purposely delayed paying his family benefits when everyone assumed he and his crew were dead. And now that they knew he was alive after all, the situation was even more dire. If Sullivan really had been killed, the family would have gotten some sort of insurance payment, but since he'd lost a very expensive facility, the Hansa would make sure he forfeited any profits.

"Take it up with the Chairman," Andez said. "Whenever he calls you."

45 ☀ KING PETER

Peter found it awkward to conduct government business with his infant son on his lap, but he didn't want to give up a moment of it. Wrapped in a soft blanket, Reynald was comfortable and happy (for the time being) in the noisy ops center that Willis's corps of engineers had erected. Estarra dangled a bright featherthread toy in front of the baby's face. His eyes followed it, his expression screwed into one of confusion, fascination, and then delight.

Celli pushed her way into the room, practically bursting with her news. "An EDF battle group just attacked the Osquivel shipyards, led by General Lanyan himself. Casualty count is unknown."

"What the hell does he think he's doing?" Peter's exclamation disturbed the baby. "First he ransacks the Golgen skymines, and now this!"

Oddly, Celli didn't look terribly distraught. "Don't worry, the EDF got their butts kicked. The Roamers defended the shipyards, and then Admiral Willis showed up. General Lanyan ran away so fast he didn't even leave an exhaust trail."

Estarra was defiant. "That's a lesson the Hansa needed to learn."

Peter turned white as he struggled to control his anger. "Basil wants to escalate this into a full-scale civil war, and we're not prepared for that. Our military isn't ready, and our planets are still reeling from the hydrogue war. Those are still my people on Earth, no matter what they've been coerced to do."

"Don't forget, by kidnapping the Mage-Imperator, he's basically declared war on the Ildirans, too," Estarra added in disgust. "Why do the people put up with the Chairman? How can we get them to overthrow him?"

Peter had been struggling with the same question. "We've sent condemnations, but Basil cracks down as fast as the news spreads. He keeps the people too frightened to look for alternatives."

Estarra said, "But can't they see how much harm the Chairman's doing every day? He's on a downward spiral, and he's taking the human race down with him."

"Not if I can help it." Peter's stomach was knotted. He paced the room, still cradling Reynald in the crook of his right arm. "If we could work through an intermediary, someone with enough power and respect to show a clear path through the transition—that might do the trick. The people would act decisively, if they were shown a viable alternative, but there's going to be turmoil and bloodshed, any way you look at it."

"We need an insider who can rally support and do an end run around the Chairman," Estarra said. "What about Deputy Cain? Or Sarein? They helped us escape."

"No, Basil watches them too closely. We need another respected voice, someone who isn't afraid to speak out." Peter suddenly looked up, his eyes sparkling with excitement. "Former Chairman Maureen Fitzpatrick."

"The Battleaxe? How will you convince her to switch sides?"

The wheels were already turning in Peter's mind. "I'll send word to Patrick Fitzpatrick on Golgen. He's her grandson. I'm hoping he can make her an offer too good to refuse."

46 ✷ MAGE-IMPERATOR JORA'H

Admiral Diente called a shaky Jora'h to the command nucleus as the warliner settled into orbit above Earth. When he first emerged from his stateroom, the Mage-Imperator moved slowly, angry that his weakness was so apparent.

The stony EDF escort soldiers gave no indication that they noticed any change.

But he had survived the madness of isolation. He had found reserves of tenacity, both inside himself and in his half-breed daughter—reserves that Chairman Wenceslas had never known existed. Yes, Jora'h had beaten the Hansa leader. And now he was back.

In a concession to the Mage-Imperator's plight, Diente had stretched the capabilities of the warliner's engines, racing back with all possible speed. Bolstered by the thread of contact with Osira'h and her half-breed siblings, Jora'h had been able to cling to his sanity. Now that he could feel the proximity of other Ildiran captives in the lunar base, the strands of their *thism* spun around him in a coalescing mist.

Safe again . . . though still a prisoner. The isolation he had just endured, and Osira'h's revelation of what was happening on Ildira, made him yearn more than ever to be where his people needed him most. Jora'h gripped the rail in the command nucleus and drew a deep breath to steady himself.

The warliner went directly to Earth, and Diente gestured for Jora'h to follow him. "Come with me to the shuttle deck. I have an immediate appointment to see Chairman Wenceslas at Hansa HQ. He is extremely interested to hear more about the Klikiss translation system we found aboard this warliner."

"What does he intend to use it for?"

Diente seemed to think the answer was obvious. "Diplomacy."

Jora'h shuddered to think what that might entail. "I hope he is more successful than his current attempts at 'diplomacy' with the Ildiran Empire."

Diente did not comment, merely nodded respectfully. "The Chairman has instructed me to send you to the Whisper Palace straightaway." With a wan smile, he added, "Your green priest is there."

Knowing that Nira would be waiting for him, Jora'h felt much stronger, even rejuvenated by the time the shuttle landed in the Palace District. When he stepped out into the sunshine of the landing zone, surrounded by uniformed EDF soldiers, he managed to stand straight and proud. Diente had already gone to see Chairman Wenceslas in the Hansa headquarters pyramid.

Nira stood behind a line of royal guards next to Captain McCammon. One glance at her was all Jora'h needed. He strode away from the shuttle, ignoring the EDF soldiers who were supposedly escorting him. The look on his face made the royal guards falter, and McCammon told them to let the Mage-Imperator pass. He released Nira, and she ran to meet him.

"Jora'h, are you all right?"

"Chairman Wenceslas will not defeat me," he said in as strong a voice as he could manage. He folded her in his arms.

McCammon gave a slight salute, a clear gesture of respect. He wore his dress uniform, complete with a ceremonial gold-hilted dagger at his hip. Taking the two of them aside, he lowered his voice in private conversation. "The Chairman instructed me to tell you that if you declare King Peter a renegade and swear to support the Hansa, we can begin the process of returning you to Ildira."

"That is all I need to do? Truly? One simple statement, and I am free to leave Earth immediately and save my people?" Jora'h scowled in disbelief. "Do you trust him, Captain McCammon?"

The man remained silent for a long and disturbing moment. "That is not for me to say. I only convey his message."

Nira was also skeptical. "What's to stop Jora'h from recanting his statement after you let him go? Nothing. So the Hansa wouldn't really release us, would they? There'd be excuses, postponements, administrative setbacks. We would never be allowed to leave."

McCammon stared straight ahead at the landed shuttle, past the stiff-backed guards, as if not speaking to her directly. "In such complex bureaucratic matters, many unforeseen delays and difficulties might occur before your actual release. It could take years."

Jora'h had suspected as much. Continued resistance was his only leverage.

He held Nira more tightly and looked at the guard captain. "Then I am afraid I must decline the Chairman's offer. The terms are not acceptable to me."

Sarein was shocked to see the changes being made to her quarters. Now what was Basil up to? Claiming to be under the Chairman's orders, a work crew methodically removed the bright cocoon-weave hangings, a tangle-web macramé, and four small potted flowers, colorful favorites from her native worldforest.

She was incensed that he would do this without consulting her. Was he merely demonstrating that he could exert control, even here? It seemed indicative of his desire for domination. Basil did things his own way, and liked all the pieces to fall neatly in place. The very knowledge that Sarein's private space still reflected her Theron heritage must have been a persistent thorn in his side.

She doubted he cared how much this would bother her. For Basil it was all part of putting the Hansa in order, keeping as many elements in check as possible. She would try to talk to him about it, but she doubted it would do any good.

"We'll repaint this in a nice, neutral color, Ambassador," said the foreman of the crew, a roly-poly man with a deep voice and thick brown hair. "I can display catalog images of standard-issue Hansa furniture. Pick out the interior decorations yourself if you'd like, but frankly I'd rather you trusted me." The man gave her a weary grin.

"Do what you have to," she said, feeling sad and cold. It hardly mattered, since everything that expressed her personal taste was being taken away. "Obviously, the Chairman does not approve of my preferences."

When she had first arrived on Earth years ago, Sarein had scorned the quaint, provincial nature of Theroc. She had felt trapped among the worldtrees and green priests, but invigorated by images of the Whisper Palace and the wonderful cities on Earth. Leaving her home planet to follow her dreams, she had achieved a level of status beyond her expectations.

Now, though, most of her influence had gone. She was an ambassador from a planet with which the Hansa had cut off all relations, yet she couldn't go home. She represented . . . nothing. Basil kept her in his inner circle, but she had to fight continually to be a sounding board for his decisions. More and more often, he made up his mind without consulting anyone. Despite what she had told Rlinda Kett during their surreptitious meeting in the coffee shop, she despaired of finding a way to get through to Basil. Not for the first time, she wished she had accepted Rlinda's offer and simply fled Earth.

The workers roughly stuck her plants into a crate marked for storage, but she intercepted them. "Save those—I want them delivered to the greenhouse wing. The Queen's conservatory is being restored."

The decorator shrugged. "If you like. They're no longer allowed in private quarters. Some Ildiran plants are known to be poisonous."

Captain McCammon walked briskly down the hall toward her chambers. His eyes always seemed to light up when he saw her, though he had been well schooled in maintaining a neutral expression. She often found herself smiling, too, when she saw him, but she didn't dare show any affection for the man. Now he stopped at her doorway, amazed by the flurry of redecorating.

She read McCammon's expression of disapproval. "It's how the Chairman reacts when he feels insecure," Sarein said quickly.

He lowered his voice, showing genuine compassion. "Then right now he must feel very insecure."

Basil's plan to break the Mage-Imperator had backfired. Sarein couldn't help but silently cheer the Ildiran leader. No matter how often she tried to caution him, the Chairman refused to acknowledge the damage he was causing. But other people were seeing the cracks appear in the government.

Just that morning she had heard reports of a new outspoken group calling themselves "Freedom's Sword," which had hijacked several newsnets and rebroadcast Patrick Fitzpatrick's damning confession that accused the Hansa of provoking war with the Roamers. The best security crackdowns had been unable to trace the saboteurs, and so they had gotten away.

Furious, Basil had assigned Colonel Andez and her cleanup crew to investigate the problem. A cold thought struck her. Did the Chairman doubt Sarein's loyalty? Had he seen something? Her little meeting with Nira and the treeling, perhaps?

Seeing her concern, McCammon touched her arm, and she felt an irrational desire to move closer to him, but she didn't dare, especially in front of these workers. Realizing what time it was, she cleared her throat and spoke in a formal voice. "Have you come to escort me to the meeting, Captain?" Basil had been excited about meeting with Admiral Diente in the Hansa HQ, and she had asked to be included.

She had also requested that McCammon take her there, since it was the only way for him to be present.

"Yes, Ambassador."

Paying no more attention to the bustling redecorators, she walked briskly down the hall with the royal guard captain. "We'd better go, then. The Chairman won't wait for us."

Chairman Wenceslas sat at his deskscreen across from Admiral Diente, tapping fingertips on the polished surface. The Admiral stood rigidly at attention, while Deputy Cain sat off to the side in a chair, taking notes like some medieval scribe. The silence had already dragged out for several seconds.

Basil looked up when Sarein and McCammon entered. He wore a puzzled look, as if interrupted in the middle of a complex thought; then he remembered that she had been scheduled to attend. "Ah yes, thank you for coming, Sarein. I wanted you to hear my announcement."

She felt a quick stab of alarm. "Announcement? I thought we were having a discussion."

"The decision has already been made."

Cain rose to his feet, discouraged but doggedly doing his job to bring her up to speed. "On his shakedown cruise of the Mage-Imperator's flagship, Admiral Diente made a remarkable discovery. During the ancient wars, the Ildirans developed a translation device for direct communication with the Klikiss. It's uncomplicated Ildiran technology, simple to operate."

Now Basil sat up, engaged in the conversation. "This translation system gives us a remarkable and unexpected opportunity to approach a very destructive enemy. In recent months the Klikiss have retaken many of their old planets, which were part of our Colonization Initiative. We depended on their transportal network, and now that's also been denied to us. But there's no reason our two races should be enemies. We should be able to find common ground."

He folded his hands. "We know too little about the Klikiss, and I want to nip this conflict in the bud. We must engage in diplomacy instead of immediate destruction. I've concluded that it is the swiftest, most efficient way to solve the crisis. So, we are sending an emissary to talk to them."

McCammon spoke up. "We sent an emissary in a containment chamber to meet with the hydrogues, too. That didn't turn out very well, if I remember correctly."

"This is completely different," Basil snapped, obviously wondering why the guard captain was still in the room. "The Klikiss were once a great civilization. They invented the transportals and the Klikiss Torch. They must be reasonable. I am sending Admiral Diente to Pym, where General Lanyan conveniently located a large subhive. He will negotiate a mutual nonaggression pact with the Klikiss. After that, we'll have one less thing to worry about." He paused for just a moment. "And we can concentrate on bringing down the Confederation."

Diente seemed decidedly uncomfortable, as stiff-backed as a toy soldier placed as an ornament in the office. He still hadn't spoken.

Sarein looked at him. "And what do you believe, Admiral Diente? Can you pull it off?"

"The Mage-Imperator assures me the translation system will work." It wasn't much of an answer.

"He has sufficient incentive," Basil answered for him.

"If he succeeds, I have promised to free his family from custody, with no encumbrances whatsoever."

The temperature in the room seemed to drop. Diente nodded brusquely. "Yes, Mr. Chairman. I am confident that I will succeed in this mission."

48 ☀ SIRIX

The satisfaction of eradicating both warring subhives at Relleker swiftly faded. Yes, Sirix had destroyed two major groups of Klikiss, but now his main concern was for the survival of his robots.

The Klikiss had annihilated the desirable facilities at Relleker and killed all of the technically proficient colonists. Sirix was no closer to being able to manufacture robots and replenish his armies, and he was growing quite impatient. He turned back to his two compies. "Find me another option."

PD and QT delved once more into the Roamer and EDF records, studying asteroid outposts, lunar bases, drifting orbital complexes. Most clan facilities specialized along specific lines of endeavor. Constantine III produced only fibers and exotic polymers; the Hhrenni asteroids were primarily greenhouses; Eldora mainly produced lumber and forest products.

Lacking a better alternative, the stolen fleet flew to what

had once been the capital of the Roamer clans. *Rendezvous.* Now only wreckage remained, rocks and metal debris in wildly disturbed orbits, since the Earth Defense Forces had destroyed it. At times Sirix thought that those chaotic, violent, and capricious people might well exterminate one another more efficiently than any of his grand schemes could.

Cruising in silent mode in case some Roamers had come back to their former home, Sirix's ships drifted through the rubble searching for any still-functional complexes. They found none. Another wasted effort. Sirix and the two compies studied the records yet again.

Finally, QT spoke up. "PD and I would like to suggest an unorthodox candidate. We believe it has the sophisticated operations and technological facilities we require."

PD agreed. "The place has demonstrated skill in manufacturing compies, and already possesses a working knowledge of Klikiss robots."

Sirix's optical sensors flashed as he realized what the two compies were suggesting. "You propose that we return to Earth, conquer the Terran Hanseatic League with our few remaining ships, and take over their factory complexes for ourselves? We could never succeed."

"No, we suggest you negotiate an agreement directly with the Chairman."

"Go to the Hansa and simply request the use of their facilities," PD added. "QT and I can assist you as ambassadors."

It was a naïve and absurd suggestion. Completely impossible.

PD continued. "Human history is filled with examples of former enemies becoming allies, given sufficient motivation as circumstances change."

Sirix considered further. Could it possibly work? He did

not comprehend humans. Their contradictory moods and decisions were unfathomable. "You both understand humans better than I do. How would you convince them to do as we demand?"

QT lifted his polymer face. "Issue a sincere apology. Show the Hansa Chairman that we share an enemy in the Klikiss."

Sirix considered the strange suggestion. With his handful of remaining ships and weapons, his robot force posed no credible military threat to Earth, but the Hansa didn't know that. He could use the fact that he had just wiped out a significant concentration of Klikiss at Relleker to demonstrate his good intentions, even though the Hansa had not factored into his attack at all.

"The Terran Hanseatic League should see the black robots as a valuable ally," Sirix said, "provided we can work out an acceptable agreement."

This would take careful maneuvering, indeed.

"Change our course. Head directly toward the Earth system."

Sirix began his calculations.

49 ☀ MARGARET COLICOS

Margaret felt unafraid when the ferocious tiger-striped domate approached her and lifted its serrated praying-mantis forelimbs. She put her hands on her hips. "What do you want?"

As part of her work with the Davlin-breedex, she was trying to force the individual Klikiss to actually *communicate* with her using Davlin's memories, Davlin's abilities. Each time she did that, she hoped to bring positive human traits to the fore and keep the natural violence of the insect race at bay.

The hard plates of the tiger-striped creature's exoskeleton slid smoothly against each other as the domate fidgeted. Its face was a mosaic of interlocked plates that shifted into an eerie, humanlike visage for just a moment, but the thick pieces fitted more comfortably into its monstrous form.

"Breedex," it said in a voice that sounded like a knife edge being dragged across a washboard. "Two . . . more . . . subhives . . . defeated."

"Where? Name the planet."

A long pause, as if the complex mind were trying to summon a name that would be comprehensible to her. "Relleker."

"Good." In their last conversation, Davlin had mentioned the Klikiss subhives battling there. "Take me to the breedex. He can tell me more himself." She knew that Davlin could not carry on extended communication through the mouths of domates or warriors. She followed the gigantic creature past bustling workers, diggers, excreters, harvesters, and other sub-breeds.

In years past, her visits to prior incarnations of the breedex had been fraught with anxiety and danger, but now Margaret walked boldly alongside the domate. While her guide remained behind at the entrance, she presented herself before the squirming mass. "What is it you want to tell me, Davlin? Two more subhives conquered? Both breedexes destroyed?"

With a buzzing, staticky sound, the numerous components piled together, each tiny unit knowing its place, assembling into the crude sculpture of a man's face. It took the simulated head a few moments to remember how to speak, then the buzzing background noise became words. *"They defeated themselves. Two rival subhives clashed."* After a pregnant pause, the Davlin-breedex continued. *"The rest were destroyed by black robots . . . nuclear explosives . . . EDF ships."*

"So the black robots are still out there." Margaret wasn't sure if the hive mind could hear the hatred in her own voice. "You want to destroy them, don't you?" This was an anger she could allow Davlin to keep. Sirix had killed Louis long ago, back on Rheindic Co. . . .

"All of them."

She had seen more domates march through the new transportal, carrying the remains of Klikiss victims. "How close are you to finishing your work with the other subhives? How many breedexes remain?"

"All pieces are coalescing. I will be the One Breedex soon. A single rival subhive remains. A powerful subhive . . . on Pym."

"And once you defeat that subhive, you will control the

whole race? And you promise to keep humanity safe?" She waited a long moment. "Davlin?" She had to continue focusing the human presence that remained. Recently, she had seen troubling instances when the man had lost ground to the insects.

"Then we will control all the Klikiss."

"And you will keep humanity safe?"

"First I must fission. I must consume many more Klikiss, make them part of me, rather than just obedient to me."

Margaret was alarmed. "No, that will dilute your human fraction. You told me." Until now, the Davlin-breedex had maintained control by refusing to let his domates devour the fallen subhives. His hold was already tenuous. And she could not suggest the obvious and unpleasant solution of allowing the breedex to consume and incorporate more human DNA.

"Must increase numbers and strength. Otherwise, I will fail."

"You will also fail if you lose your grip, Davlin. Don't loosen your control."

"It is the only way. Incorporate the strength and superior traits of all the other hives we have crushed. Our domates will gather their songs." The distinctive features sloughed away as the breedex began to refer to itself in the plural. She listened as it seemed to wrestle with itself; then Davlin's face appeared again. *"I will not let . . . myself be diluted, Margaret. I am still here."*

She wasn't certain how much she could trust this bizarre hybrid. Was it human enough, or would the Klikiss genes become dominant with another fissioning? She had to keep reminding him. "Do what you must, Davlin, but keep your control—and I'll do everything I can to help."

On the fast EDF shuttle that took them away from the Moon, Anton sat next to Rememberer Vao'sh. One escort guard remained rigidly alert on the nearby passenger bench, his sidearm prominent. Never in his life had Anton considered himself a threatening person, and now he had a vigilant guard at all times.

He had no idea what Chairman Wenceslas could possibly want with the two of them.

Anton tried to look on the bright side. At least he and Vao'sh were on their way to Earth, where the Mage-Imperator was now being held. The Ildiran prisoners in the lunar base had been frantic when Jora'h had been taken away and isolated. Given his own similar ordeal, Vao'sh understood more than any other Ildiran Jora'h's sheer nightmare of solitude, his risk of slipping into catatonic madness.

Now, as they rode the swift shuttle, the rememberer's facial lobes changed to a more grayish color, indicating his anxiety. "I am very confused by your Chairman's actions. He does not understand what he is doing."

"There's no excuse for it." Anton had no explanations to give. "No one has the right to treat people this way." He sounded far braver than he actually felt.

When the shuttle flew in over the Palace District, Vao'sh placed his hands against the windows and smiled wistfully at Anton. "I always wanted to see the Whisper Palace for myself—although I wish my first visit were under better circumstances."

Anton felt sad and apologetic. "I'm ashamed. I can't ask you, or the Mage-Imperator, or any Ildiran to forgive us."

"The Chairman did this, Rememberer Anton. Your whole race should not be condemned for the choices one man makes."

The shuttle landed on the rooftop deck of the Hansa HQ. The two of them were briskly led to the penthouse office levels, where they waited under guard. And waited.

More than an hour later, they were ushered to the Chairman's office. Surrounded by banks of windows, Basil Wenceslas sat at a broad deskscreen, which portrayed not spreadsheets or productivity graphs, but a shifting grid of surveillance images. He seemed intent on watching everything around him.

When they entered, the Chairman stood up. The expression on his handsome face was guarded, but his demeanor was one of expansive cordiality—as if they were old friends. "Anton Colicos. I am pleased to see you again! So much has happened in the years since our last communication."

"I'm surprised you even remember, Mr. Chairman. My mother was never found, and my father's body was discovered in the ruins on Rheindic Co. Not a very successful rescue effort."

"Ah, but your request to find your missing parents set in motion key events in our history, though we didn't realize it at the time. When I sent Davlin Lotze and Rlinda Kett to Rheindic Co, they discovered the transportals, which have been such a boon to us—until recently." He seemed preoccupied with the surveillance images on his deskscreen. "But

Admiral Diente is on his way to the Klikiss, so even that problem should soon be neatly solved."

"Glad it worked out for you," Anton mumbled.

The Chairman now turned to Vao'sh. "I understand that you are one of the greatest Ildiran historians. You can help me." Basil's voice had an odd edge, though he was clearly trying to sound reasonable. "I need to understand Ildirans. I have obviously misjudged the Mage-Imperator. He has not been rational. Is it a cultural thing, or a personality flaw in Jora'h alone? I would have thought his long voyage of contemplation would be sufficient to make him see what is best for both the Ildiran Empire and the Hansa. Yet he refuses to make the trivial effort necessary. Doesn't he want to return to his people, who — according to him — urgently need his leadership? What kind of ruler is that? I am at my wits' end. I don't understand why the Mage-Imperator does what he does."

"And we do not understand you, Chairman Wenceslas." Vao'sh was not inclined to be helpful. "Your side of the story, frankly, is incomprehensible to us. It will be difficult for me to portray the Hansa in a favorable light when I record these events in the *Saga of Seven Suns*."

The Chairman visibly fought down a flash of anger. "I am not interested in Ildiran propaganda or bedtime stories, but in acquiring intelligence the Hansa vitally needs." He turned to Anton, who flinched. "Mr. Colicos, you will remain on Earth with Rememberer Vao'sh. Take him to our Department of Ildiran Studies at your old university. I want our scholars to debrief him thoroughly."

51 ☀ DEPUTY CHAIRMAN
ELDRED CAIN

N ice enough . . . for a prison." Cain looked through the small one-way observation block into the family holding chambers.

While walking around the nondescript building's exterior on a brief inspection with Sarein, Cain had been intrigued by the clever camouflage, seeing nothing to distinguish it from any other moderate-income living complex. But inside, the five apartments were isolated from each other, accessible only through the strictest security. And the inhabitants could not leave.

"I doubt Admiral Diente would be comforted by the homey touches," Sarein said.

"At least his family is alive. And the Chairman has promised they'll be released unharmed as soon as he returns from his mission to Pym." Cain's voice carried no inflection to hint at how much he doubted Chairman Wenceslas would keep his end of the bargain. Nevertheless, he had sent the two of them here to make certain, with their own eyes, that everything was in order. He claimed he couldn't trust anyone else; Cain supposed that was probably true.

Expander lenses from the inset spy-hole brought the view to them, so that he and Sarein could watch the family of Admiral Diente go about their daily tedium. Sarein leaned close, keeping her voice low but not conspiratorially quiet. "Basil probably thinks he's being quite generous, giving them all the comforts they could need. I'll ask him for a little more leniency, but I doubt he'll act on it."

"These people aren't actually aware that they're being held hostage." Cain's pale lips quirked in a cold smile. "They think they're being kept inside for their own protection. In a way, that's merciful."

The only thing that mattered, Cain realized, was that the Admiral knew they were there.

The family had four rooms to themselves, a living area, two small bedrooms, and a tiny toilet/shower combination. The man's wife, two daughters (ages fifteen and six), and son (twelve) must have felt quite crowded. As a man who relished privacy and solitude, Cain couldn't imagine living under such conditions.

Sarein watched the teenaged daughter slump into a hard-backed chair, while her brother tried to cajole her into playing a game. The mother sat stiffly at the tiny kitchenette table reading, but though she stared at the book, Cain noted that she hadn't turned a page in six minutes. On the wall near her hung an image of her husband and family, all together and smiling. The image appeared to be old.

"Can't we talk to them?" Sarein asked. "How are we supposed to verify that they are all in good mental and physical health?"

"No interaction whatsoever. We are just supposed to observe."

"I hope our word matters to Basil."

In the spy-hole image, the son was now pestering his little sister to play a different, much simpler game with colored cards.

"Of course it matters."

Sarein turned, and Cain could tell she was genuinely curious. "Why? He's been cutting us out more and more often."

"Even so, he realizes he can't do everything alone. He's got to rely on someone, and he is convinced—correctly—that I have no interest in robbing him of his power. Even as deputy, I have risen in prominence much higher than I desire. And you—he knows that you both love him and are afraid of him. That makes you perfectly safe, in his view."

Sarein blinked her large, dark eyes. "You're a very odd man, Mr. Cain. How can you be so perceptive?"

Before he and Sarein made their way back to the Hansa HQ, Cain received the expected call. He had intentionally timed it that way. He wanted her with him when they went to "investigate."

Like Chairman Wenceslas, Cain couldn't do everything himself. Captain McCammon should also be on his way.

Colonel Andez and several members of the cleanup crew had already responded to the fire that had gutted a small storage chamber in a block of personal warehouses. The self-contained locker was unremarkable in a beehive complex of identical units. It had been fitted out as a mail drop and wired as an office cell—barely room enough for one person with a chair and an upload terminal. It had served its purpose.

Andez picked through sodden bits of electronic equipment slimed with fire-suppressant foam. Cain noted that the primer-painted metal door had been physically bent from its hinges—exactly the sort of boneheaded enthusiasm he had expected from the cleanup crew. They had torn their way inside, sure they would find a nest of rebels in a two-meter-square cubicle.

When she saw Deputy Cain and Sarein arrive, Andez straightened. Falling short of an actual salute, she brushed a smear of soot from her cheek, making the mark worse. "They keep springing up, sir. When will they learn? This group calls itself Freedom's Sword. Nobody had ever heard of them until a few days ago."

Cain pursed his lips. "You are in error, Colonel. Freedom's Sword is an active and widespread organization that has been operating quietly, but effectively, for many months. My own people have been tracking them. You'd best keep a close watch. Did you find any leads here?"

Her expression hardened even further. "We arrived too late, unfortunately. The fire destroyed the equipment, and our electronic autopsy specialists claim it was thoroughly wiped even before that. But we do know that this site was a transmission point for seditious messages. The perpetrators rebroadcast Patrick Fitzpatrick's condemnation statement" — her face twisted briefly, and Cain remembered that Andez and Fitzpatrick had been POWs together among the Roamers — "as well as King Peter's message calling for the resignation of Chairman Wenceslas."

"The resignation *or overthrow* of the Chairman," Cain amended.

"That only makes it worse," Andez said.

Sarein clearly wondered why Cain had wanted her to accompany him here. "Nothing new in all that," she said. "Those messages have been seen plenty of times before. Why would anyone bother with such a setup?"

Cain nodded solemnly. "Yes, with a group as sophisticated as Freedom's Sword, there must be a far more insidious purpose. Colonel Andez, I suggest you find the exact messages they broadcast and devote significant manpower to analyzing them. It's possible there's another, more sinister message coded into the carrier signal. Pay particular attention to irregularities in background static."

Cain enjoyed watching her enthusiasm. Those orders would keep Andez's people busy for days.

Finally Captain McCammon arrived with four of his hand-picked royal guards. McCammon smiled at Sarein. "Glad to see you, Ambassador." Then he got down to business, looking completely professional. "Colonel Andez, my men will take over the on-site investigation from here."

She bristled. "This job clearly falls under our purview."

Cain interceded. "Colonel Andez, the unrest fostered by Freedom's Sword is a direct threat to the authority and rule of King Rory. Therefore it is fitting that the royal guard should be in charge. Your people are dismissed."

"Don't you have transmissions to analyze?" Sarein added.

"These rebels endanger the Chairman and the very stability of the Hansa."

Cain continued in a reasonable voice. "You know Chairman Wenceslas doesn't like to be in the spotlight. If we present this as a threat to our beloved savior and King, there's a better chance the people will turn against Freedom's Sword."

After a few more moments of confusion, the cleanup crew packed away their shards of evidence and sample scrapings and departed, leaving Captain McCammon in charge of the site.

When they were gone, Sarein turned to Cain wearing a no-nonsense expression. "Now, what was all that about? Why did you bring me here?"

McCammon watched his men comb over the wreckage

in the cramped office cell. He looked very skeptical. "And what do you really expect me to find in there that the cleanup crew missed?"

"There's nothing to find." Cain smiled, then said in a low voice, "But it certainly got Colonel Andez worked up, didn't it? The diversion will keep them chasing shadows so that they have less time to harass innocent people."

Sarein drew a quick breath as she jumped to the obvious conclusion. "You knew about this. You're a member of Freedom's Sword."

Cain shook his head. "Not exactly. Freedom's Sword is entirely my creation, a will-o'-the-wisp. I needed a conduit to disseminate certain information—such as when I leaked the news about Queen Estarra's pregnancy before the Chairman could force her to have an abortion. It can be very useful to imply the existence of a much larger organization calling for the Hansa to join the Confederation. Many others are now taking independent action, as well, and the movement seems to be growing on its own. Any random dissident activity is chalked up to the work of a larger organization."

McCammon stared, then laughed. "So you plant little seeds like this to divert attention from yourself."

"To divert attention from all three of us, Captain." Cain looked at Sarein and the guard. "None of us has clean hands when it comes to the escape of King Peter and Queen Estarra . . . and plenty of other minor actions, any one of which would be considered treason if the Chairman decided to define them that way. Freedom's Sword is a facade, but a useful one."

McCammon's guards had removed the inner layer of scorched metal plating from the office cell and with great excitement uncovered a lump of fused polymers and wires, the incendiary trigger.

"Keep looking," McCammon gruffly told them.

"You've given a focus and a voice to all the dissatisfied and frightened people that we know are out there," Sarein said. "That's something to be proud of. But Basil will never resign, you know—especially if he ever finds out the organization of dissenters is only a sham."

"Not a sham. They're out there. I'm merely providing the catalyst. As people hear more and more about a large and organized group, I believe Freedom's Sword will become a self-fulfilling prophecy."

52 ☀ ADMIRAL ESTEBAN DIENTE

The closer his Manta got to the known Klikiss hive at Pym, the less convinced Admiral Diente was of his chances of success. The Chairman had given him only one cruiser for the ambassadorial mission, blithely putting all his faith in the old Ildiran translation system (though he hadn't sent an Ildiran engineer along to monitor it) and in Diente's negotiating skills.

Basil Wenceslas was confident that the Admiral had sufficient *incentive* to work miracles—and Diente hated him for it.

He had been the commander of the Grid 9 forces. He had always been quiet, almost taciturn, except when at home with his family. His house had been filled with love; he had giggled and wrestled with his children. He hadn't seen any of them in more than a month, been denied even a letter from his wife.

The Chairman assured him they were well and being held in "protective custody." They had been taken hostage shortly before Diente received his orders to seize the Mage-Imperator's warliner. That had been the first instance of blackmail; this was another.

He was Admiral Esteban Diente . . . "the Tooth" in Spanish. As he had worked his way up the ladder of command during his military career, his comrades had joked that he had "fangs," that he could clamp onto a problem and not let go until it was solved. Now, though, he felt toothless.

And he had to make some sort of pact with the Klikiss. It was a naïve and human-centric view to assume the hive mind would comprehend, much less agree to, standard negotiating tactics. Did anyone really know how the Klikiss thought or reacted? To prepare himself, he had studied all available background information. General Lanyan had delivered a full report after his disastrous clash with the Klikiss on Pym, but his sparse information was unobjective and, frankly, questionable. In his reports Lanyan had been unable to hide how shaken he'd been by the encounter.

The General had begun shooting at the Klikiss as soon as he saw them. Not a good foundation for peaceful negotiations. Diente hoped to do better, but he was hampered by not knowing anything about the psychology of the insect creatures. What made them tick? How would they react? Diente had no idea where to begin. Such musings did not inspire him with great confidence, yet he had to take the old Ildiran translating device and do his best.

"I'll be in my ready room." He stood from the command chair. "I need time to think. Let me know when we arrive at Pym."

"It'll be less than two hours, Admiral."

"Then that's two hours I need to myself." He left the bridge and closed the door to the quiet chamber. Although he knew that he needed to be alert, he had slept poorly for several days. He ordered a double-strength coffee from the dispenser and gulped it quickly.

Even though the alien insects would not understand EDF uniforms or rank insignia, Diente pulled his dress uniform from the wardrobe unit and made his appearance as authoritative as possible. He even imaged pictures of himself to be stored in the ship's emergency log for his family, just in case something happened.

Following the set mission profile, his Manta came in over Pym making no threatening moves, its weapons systems on standby. Diente would personally take an armored diplomatic shuttle down to meet with the hive mind on the surface, while the Manta hovered overhead, supposedly to show its muscle.

His legs moved mechanically as he climbed aboard the small craft, accompanied by twenty-eight guards, just enough to form an impressive entourage, though he doubted the Klikiss would understand such gestures. His stomach felt leaden. He did what he was expected to do.

The ambassadorial ship dropped out of the lead cruiser. Diente drew careful, even breaths, centering his thoughts. He could feel the tension in the men around him. Two of

the soldiers nervously tried to joke with each other, but their
comments fell flat, so they dropped into silence again.

Below them, the convoluted hive complex came into
view on the blindingly white alkaline desert, where murky
bad-water swamps bubbled up from evaporated lakes. The
organic-looking city was a spreading infestation with giant
towers, knobby battlements, and spearlike fortifications. It
sprawled for kilometers and kilometers.

Diente's heart sank. In General Lanyan's previous attack
here and his rescue of the few surviving colonists, his soldiers
had inflicted a great deal of damage. Diente had reviewed
the images recorded by combat suitcams. Now, though, he
saw no signs of damage whatsoever. Not a mark. Everything
had not only been repaired but greatly expanded.

Assailed by an overwhelming sense of dread, for just
a moment he was tempted to abort the mission, to return to
Earth and ask the Chairman to reconsider his approach. But
Chairman Wenceslas was not a man to reconsider; he saw it
as a sign of weakness to change his mind once he had made
a decision.

The shuttle descended toward the heart of the hive complex. Everything he did and said was being automatically
recorded and uploaded to the Manta above. Unfortunately,
since the EDF no longer had access to instantaneous telink
communication via green priests, Diente had no way to
maintain a direct line to the Hansa. He had insisted that log
drones be launched back to Earth hourly once the mission
began. That way at least someone would have a record.

On its landing approach, the diplomatic craft came in
unchallenged, though Diente expected swarms of insect
ships to rise up and intercept him. He thought the Klikiss
would sound an alarm and rush out to destroy his ship, or at

least demand to know his intentions. The translation system was ready.

But as far as he could tell, the Klikiss merely ignored the intrusion. He did not understand these creatures at all.

The shuttle set down in a powdery white clearing near the center of the enormous hive city. The Admiral closed his eyes for two seconds, pictured his wife and children, and remembered why he was here.

Swallowing his instinctive revulsion, Diente stood at the hatch, straightened his uniform, and opened the hatch to taste the bitter air of Pym. Each breath felt choked with a caustic dust. His eyes began to burn, but he marched down the ramp and onto the cracked alkaline ground. Per his instructions, the honor guard followed several steps behind him.

The Klikiss were a riot of different shapes and forms, all of them covered with hard body armor; some were ponderous workers and diggers while others looked designed for combat and mayhem. He couldn't tell if they were curious, or hungry.

Diente tried to identify one creature that might be a spokesman. He activated the Ildiran translator from a transmitter box at his hip. "I am a human. You have encountered us before. We mean you no harm." He allowed a moment for the translation device to process the words. "The Terran Hanseatic League has no quarrel with the Klikiss."

With hissing, clacking sounds, four of the ominous-looking warriors stepped closer. Behind them towered two larger creatures, gigantic forms whose shells were striped with black and silver. They clicked and whistled, but Diente received no translation from the device, although it appeared to be functioning properly.

"Can you understand me?" He gathered his courage and

continued. "There is no need for conflict between our races."
He waited; again no answer, but more bugs crowded toward
the shuttle. The guards behind him muttered nervously. "If
there has been any trespass, it was inadvertent. In the interest
of cooperation between our races, we offer to withdraw from
any former Klikiss worlds."

The warrior insects raised their sharp limbs. The EDF
soldiers unslung their weapons and held them defensively.
Diente did not feel he was getting through to the Klikiss.
"Please, this is an overture of peace."

Without warning, large ground-based artillery tubes
belched fire from the tops of hollow turrets in the hive city.
Enormous energy projectiles rolled upward like solidified comets and slammed into the Manta that cruised low
overhead.

"Stop!" Diente shouted.

"Holy shit!" Screaming in terror and fury, the twenty-
eight guards opened fire on the nearby Klikiss, mowing
them down.

Above them, the Manta was ripped open, its engines
destroyed. Huge chunks of flaming debris fell out of the
sky like meteors, before the hulk itself hurtled downward.
It crashed into the outskirts of the hive city and erupted in
a huge fireball that flattened half a kilometer of the insect
structures. The Klikiss didn't seem to care.

"There is no need for this!" Diente shouted into the
translator. He glanced at the Klikiss translation device and
came to the sick conclusion that the hive mind didn't understand the very concept of peacemaking or negotiation. The
Klikiss had no interest in coexisting with another species.

With continuous fire from their weapons, his guards

massacred hundreds of bugs. But they were in a nest of millions.

Tears streamed down the Admiral's face as Klikiss warriors marched forward. Diente doubted that Chairman Wenceslas would ever realize the extent of his folly here. At least, though, there would be no further reason to hold his family hostage.

He felt an odd sense of release, maybe even a feeling of relief, as the tension of these past months reached a culmination. He drew his sidearm and faced the oncoming insects. Yes, at least his family would be free.

53 ☀ ORLI COVITZ

At Osquivel, many storage domes, laboratory complexes, and admin centers were scarred and blasted from the recent EDF depredations. Busy Roamer workers flew about in construction pods rebuilding domes, sealing habitats, and linking damaged structures together.

On her way through the shipyard complexes to the new lab chamber Kotto Okiah had set up, Orli stumbled upon the Governess compy UR, whom she remembered from Llaro. UR had been courageous in defending the Llaro children from Klikiss attacks, losing her left arm to a vicious insect scout. Once the Llaro refugees had returned to Osquivel,

Roamer engineers had not taken long to find a donor arm from a previously decommissioned compy. The colors of the polymer skin did not match — the new arm was blue and orange, in contrast to the more sedate indigo and gray of the Governess compy's body — but UR seemed quite pleased with it.

The compy was surrounded by students ranging in age from five to nine. On the coated stone floor, she had spread a colorful mat divided into squares overprinted with a lush yet confusing pattern of writhing snakes — vipers, cobras, pythons — meshed with a spray of arrows that flew in various directions. The snakes and arrows connected squares on the game board. While UR gave calm advice on strategy, the children threw dice and moved their pieces.

"What are you doing?" Orli asked.

"I am teaching the children," UR said.

"Looks like you're playing a game."

"I am teaching the children to play the game. It is an ancient Hindu game called Leela, or Snakes and Arrows, thousands of years old. The grid has seventy-two squares, each named for a state of being. When the player rolls, the die is guided by his or her karma. If the die takes you to a square with an arrow, you ascend to a higher plane. If you fall on a square with a serpent, you slide down."

One boy shouted as he landed on a particularly good square.

"So . . . it has nothing to do with the Klikiss? Or the EDF?"

"Snakes and Arrows deals with all aspects of life in a metaphorical sense," UR said. "Would you like to play, Orli Covitz?"

"Not right now." The idea of the battered compy speaking of karma, states of being, and planes of existence was too unsettling for her. "I'm helping Kotto Okiah and Mr. Steinman. We're working on ways to defend the Confederation against . . . well, against everything."

In his new laboratory, Kotto activated one documentation screen after another. Mr. Steinman lifted a flat metal case of tools and slid it onto a chest-high shelf that was bracketed to the wall. "Sure, but who's the real enemy? The EDF attacked Golgen and Osquivel. The faeros attacked Theroc. The Klikiss attacked Llaro. The Klikiss robots are still out there. Which one do we concentrate on?"

Kotto stared at a data projection, then blanked it. "Do I have to pick one in particular?"

Following him, Steinman activated the same screen and jotted down a file name. KR and GU circulated, cleaning, organizing, arranging the new lab; Orli had noticed that the clutter created by the two men kept the compies quite busy. DD was also there, eager to make himself useful.

Orli spoke up. "I pick the Klikiss. After Llaro—and Relleker—we need to stop the subhives from expanding."

Kotto scratched his curly hair. "It would be easier to do that if I had a specimen to study. I don't know enough about them."

Orli pulled up a chair and folded her legs beneath her in a comfortable position. "Well, Mr. Steinman and I have some firsthand experience."

"As do I," DD said. "We have considerable data to share."

Kotto brightened. "Then maybe I won't be working in the dark, after all. Give me a starting point."

Orli thought for a minute. "The Klikiss have songs and

music. They communicate with intricate melodies as well as pheromones. When I played my synthesizer strips and bombarded the bugs with my songs, it seemed to shut down the thoughts of the hive mind." She didn't think the specific tune mattered, only that the music had to be different from anything they had heard before.

Kotto was already deep in thought. "I could develop a kind of random melody generator. Maybe if we played it at sufficient volume in the right place, we could paralyze the creatures."

"There, we have a new project to sink our teeth into." Steinman rubbed his hands together. "And the Klikiss annoy me even more than General Lanyan does."

54 ☀ DEPUTY CHAIRMAN ELDRED CAIN

An unannounced ship arrived at Earth, causing a flurry of alarms and consternation. A Roamer ship.

Deputy Cain studied the traces projected on the Chairman's deskscreen. "No ID beacon, no explanation, just a small flyer with a passenger capacity of five. It's not a cargo ship or a military vessel."

"The ship can't possibly be a threat, but I want to know what the hell he thinks he's doing here."

Finally a transmission came from the Roamer craft. In an uninflected voice, the pilot said, "We are on a peaceful mission that concerns a matter of mutual survival."

The Chairman looked at Cain as if he should instantly have an answer. "They could be Roamer deserters," Cain suggested. "If so, they could provide valuable information about the Confederation. Valuable enough for us to talk to them at least."

"Nevertheless, we should prepare to shoot it down, just in case." The Chairman took charge of the communication console himself. "Roamer ship, I am sending you coordinates for landing. We will have Remoras prepared to destroy you if you take any threatening action."

"We are not a threat," said the calm, androgynous voice.

"I'll be the judge of that."

Chairman Wenceslas ordered the entire Whisper Palace landing square cleared and then surrounded. Captain Mc-Cammon hurriedly marched out with a large group of royal guards.

The small ship came down without deviating a centimeter from the imposed path. The vessel's design had a weird grace and functionality, unlike anything Cain had ever seen; the Chairman merely commented how ugly it was.

At a signal from McCammon, the guards stood ready. The ship locked down its landing pads; the rectangular hatch disengaged and slid open.

Instead of a man in a gaudy Roamer jumpsuit, as Cain

expected, a chrome-and-green compy stepped out. "We mean no harm."

A second compy appeared behind the first, similar in size and design but with a bronze and copper body. "I am PD, and this is QT. We are compy representatives."

Everyone kept their distance. The compies stood at the bottom of the ramp and waited to be acknowledged. Finally Cain called, "Who else is aboard your ship? Who's the pilot?"

"We both have pilot programming," said QT. "There are no humans aboard our ship."

Standing back with a scowl on his face, Chairman Wenceslas gestured for the guards to advance. "Conduct a full search. Check for weapons, listening devices, tracking beacons. They've got to have something up their sleeves."

"We have no sleeves," said PD. The Chairman ignored him.

"Where did you get a Roamer ship?" Cain asked, taking a step closer.

"From a fuel depot called Barrymore's Rock," QT said.

PD added, "Once the depot was destroyed, the former Roamer inhabitants no longer needed their ships. We thought they might be useful." Neither compy explained further.

A squad of technicians crowded into the small Roamer vessel with scanners, but they found nothing. "It's just a stripped-down ship, sir. The life support doesn't even seem to be functioning."

"We do not require life support," said QT. Guards surrounded the pair of compies, who looked ludicrously harmless.

Studying the two small robots, the ship, the whole tableau, Cain was convinced that they were worried about the wrong thing. "I don't believe the danger is aboard that ship. It's in what these compies have to say."

The Chairman slowly nodded. "I believe you're right, Mr. Cain."

Cain turned to the compies. "Why are you here?"

"We have a message and a proposal for Chairman Basil Wenceslas of the Terran Hanseatic League," said QT.

The Chairman looked down at them. "Who sent you?"

"We were once the personal compies of Admiral Wu-Lin of the Grid 3 battle group," said PD. "Now we serve the Klikiss robots."

Though Cain remained silent, many other listeners responded with cries of outrage. Even the Chairman's face reddened. He worked his jaw. "And why would the treacherous robots ask you to come here to speak to me?"

The two compies answered in perfectly synchronized unison. "Our master Sirix wishes to discuss forming an alliance against our mutual enemy, the Klikiss."

"Why the hell should we believe you?" McCammon growled. "Those black robots turned our Soldier compies against us, massacred the EDF, destroyed the bulk of our space fleet."

QT said, "The return of the Klikiss race forced Sirix to take actions that he now regrets. We acted out of desperation, only to protect ourselves."

Cain frowned. The explanation seemed too convenient. Sirix couldn't have known about the return of the original Klikiss until well after the black robots had seized the EDF ships. "Remember, we're still waiting for word from Admiral Diente about his negotiation mission. By now, we may already have an alliance with the Klikiss."

To his surprise and dismay, Cain saw a look of deep concentration on Basil's face. "That doesn't mean we can't open a dialog with the black robots, does it? We should keep our options open."

Captain McCammon looked at him as if he had gone insane, but the Chairman cut off any comments with a hand raised like a hatchet blade poised to strike. He turned to the compies. "This is a most unusual and unexpected offer, and you must accept my healthy skepticism." Wheels were obviously turning in his mind. "But alliances have changed many times in Earth's past, and I won't turn down an opportunity until I learn more about it." He crossed his arms over his chest. "Explain yourselves further."

55 ☀ PATRICK FITZPATRICK III

As the *Gypsy* flew off bearing a message from King Peter, Patrick could hardly believe he was actually going back to visit his grandmother. Voluntarily. He remarked on the impossible turns his life had taken.

"Some people just start out going in the wrong direction," Zhett teased. "You were so spun around you didn't even know you *had* a Guiding Star, much less where to look for it."

"That's not how my grandmother will see it." His lackluster parents were living in obscurity away from Earth, but since the Battleaxe had believed in him and wooed them to let her take him under her wing, Patrick had been raised in the upper crust of Earth society. Frankly, he had grown up to be a spoiled and ungrateful little snot. If the Battleaxe had ever suspected he would one day run off to join the Roamers, she might have drowned him at birth.

And now he had to convince her to leave the Hansa and endorse the Confederation government. Patrick prayed she would at least give him two minutes to explain himself. After all, the King had chosen Patrick to be one of the most important ambassadors in the Spiral Arm.

"My grandmother is a smart and sensible woman," he had told King Peter when he responded to the original request. "She can't be blind to what Chairman Wenceslas is doing, but she won't take drastic action for purely altruistic reasons. However, she may jump at the chance to be important again. She hates being retired."

"Use your discretion, Mr. Fitzpatrick. Promise her anything you think is reasonable in order to secure her cooperation. She can pave the way for Earth to join the Confederation."

"I'll flatter her, call on her patriotism . . . but she'll make up her own mind," Patrick said.

Once they had packed, refueled, and said their farewells to Del Kellum and the skyminers on Golgen, Zhett piloted the *Gypsy*. Although the space yacht's systems were state-of-the-art, she still complained about the inefficient and non-intuitive setup. "We should have taken a Roamer ship."

"But this yacht was owned by the former Hansa Chairman. It's got access codes and pass routines that'll let us slip through Earth security without raising any alarms. Nothing trumps that." He frowned to himself. "Besides, I *did* promise to bring this ship back after I . . . borrowed it."

He sounded more confident than he felt, and he knew that Zhett could see through him. "I bet your grandmother's not as big a monster as you make her out to be, Fitzie."

He gave her a wry smile. "You two should get along just fine. You have a lot in common."

She punched him lightly on the arm. "Don't pretend for a minute you meant that as a compliment."

Upon reaching Earth, he transmitted the stored authorization identifiers from Maureen's private log. As they approached what he had once called home, Patrick took over the controls and flew the *Gypsy* over the Rocky Mountains, zeroing in on the former Chairman's private mansion. He landed on an empty pad outside the house, hoping his grandmother wasn't in the middle of some diplomatic reception or cocktail party with wealthy industrialists.

Jonas, Maureen's longtime personal assistant, acknowledged their arrival on the comm, his voice a barely restrained squawk. As Patrick and Zhett emerged from the ship, smiling hopefully, the old woman marched out onto the deck alone. Patrick studied her expression and let the silence hang for just a moment, surprised that she hadn't taken charge of the conversation already.

Before either he or the old Battleaxe could say anything, Zhett broke the ice by extending her hand. "You must be Maureen Fitzpatrick. Very pleased to meet you. Patrick has told me so much about his grandmother."

Maureen turned to her with the gaze of a hunting falcon. "Charmed, I'm sure — but who the hell are you?" She swung back to him. "I don't like surprises like this, Patrick."

"Yes, you do. This is my wife, Zhett Kellum. She's

the daughter of one of the wealthiest and most influential Roamer families."

"Did you say *Roamer*?" She blinked.

"I said 'one of the wealthiest and most influential.' I assumed that would be good enough for you."

Maureen was having trouble catching up with the conversation. "Did you say *wife*?"

Zhett broke in wickedly. "I understand how you feel. My father wasn't exactly pleased that I married the grandson of a former Hansa Chairman, but we all have to make concessions in these difficult times."

Maureen was stunned into silence by the audacious comment. Transferring her annoyance until she could process the information, she frowned at the new name painted on the space yacht's hull. "You've got a lot of nerve stealing my ship, deserting the Earth Defense Forces, then flying back here as if nothing's happened. Where the hell have you been?" She gestured briskly to the door. "You'd both better come inside before any EDF spies spot you. I wouldn't be surprised if they shot you on sight. With your damn fool messages and accusations, you've caused a world of trouble here. Freedom's Sword is having a field day."

"What's Freedom's Sword?" Patrick and Zhett both said at the same time.

"Some new dissident group—taking a page out of your book. They've been distributing your confession about Raven Kamarov and doing a lot more rabble-rousing of their own. It's embarrassing." She flashed a small smile. "The Archfather is ranting against the protesters, but I get the impression he's secretly pleased. That puffed-up boy, King Rory, stood in front of a cheering crowd and said 'Any insult to the

Hansa Chairman is an insult to my Royal Person!' Bunch of bull crap."

"Somebody's finally listening." Patrick found himself smiling. "Are there actual protests in the streets?"

"And are they accomplishing anything?" Zhett added.

"Nothing substantive—yet. You've become quite a little folk hero around here, Patrick. My grandson, a world-class thorn in the side."

"He can be a pain in the butt, too," Zhett said, "but he's brave, and I love him. He faced a Roamer court and admitted his own part in starting the conflict between the clans and the Hansa." Her voice noticeably cooled. "Did you know the EDF is raiding Roamer skymines, attacking industrial facilities, murdering civilians? Your government has a lot to answer for, Madame Chairman."

The old woman pointed a large-knuckled finger at Zhett, and her tenor changed. "You be careful which words you use, young lady. Don't go calling that *my* government. When I was Chairman, I never allowed any of this nonsense."

"Ah, yes. The golden, peaceful times," Zhett drawled, her words rich with sarcasm. "Roamers still sing songs about those glory days of Hansa open-mindedness and understanding—"

Patrick interrupted them. "See? I knew you two would get along."

Maureen finally allowed herself a laugh. "Well, Patrick, I'm glad you found a woman who can stand up for herself. You learned that much from me, at least."

56 ☀ CHAIRMAN BASIL WENCESLAS

Now that he was familiar with Sirix's treachery, Basil was sure he could outscheme the black robots. Deputy Cain urged him to wait until he heard back from Diente's embassy to the Klikiss on Pym, but he saw no need to delay. In the worst-case situation, the EDF could turn the black robots over to the Klikiss, or perhaps destroy them all to demonstrate humanity's good intentions. But first he wanted to hear what Sirix had to say. No harm in *private* exploratory talks.

"The two compies have already transmitted my instructions. Sirix will land in the Palace District at night in an unmarked EDF shuttle — one of the shuttles he stole. As far as anyone else is concerned, it'll be logged as a routine military transport."

"Might I suggest instead that we meet at the lunar EDF base, or some other neutral territory?" Cain said.

"No. It will be on my home ground. I want full control of every detail."

Out of courtesy, and because for some indefinable reason he wanted her there, Basil invited Sarein to join them. She told him quite plainly she thought he was making a deal with the devil. That amused him. Her constant criticism and second-guessing, though, were growing tiresome.

In preparation, he gave explicit instructions to Captain McCammon. He wanted ten guards standing in full view, and fifty more hidden as sharpshooters, each carrying a high-powered jazer rifle. Altogether, it would be enough firepower to turn Sirix into a pile of obsidian slag if he made the slightest wrong move.

"This doesn't feel right, Mr. Chairman," Cain said as they all stepped out under a star-strewn night sky.

Basil gazed upward, expecting to see the tiny dot of the landing shuttle any minute now. Even after full dark, the Palace District was dazzling. The blinking lights of air traffic crisscrossed the sky. "Don't be pessimistic."

"I prefer the term pragmatic, since my concerns are backed by hard data."

"Everything will turn out for the best, you will see," PD said brightly. "Sirix will follow your instructions exactly."

Basil had allowed the two compies to attend. He supposed he could use them as hostages, threaten to destroy them if Sirix got out of hand, though he doubted the black robots had any compassion for such things.

Next to him, QT added, "We will assist your negotiations."

The Earth Defense Forces were on high alert in close orbit, warily watching the robot-commandeered battleships that had approached under a flag of truce. Since General Lanyan was not due to return from his raiding mission for several more days, Basil had assigned Admirals Pike and San Luis, his only two remaining grid admirals, to set up a defensive line.

When the ragtag group had arrived in orbit, Basil was shocked to receive Admiral Pike's report on how few EDF vessels the robots still possessed. Sirix and his comrades had stolen the bulk of the Earth's fleet, and they had squandered most of the ships. Basil was anxious to learn what dire mistakes had forced the robots to come crawling here for help.

Each of the compies extended a polymer hand to the sky, pointing. "That one is Sirix's ship." A bright light like a shooting star descended directly to the small private spaceport that Basil had designated for this meeting.

McCammon and his guards shifted their weapons warily. Cain and Sarein moved closer to the Chairman. Basil began to have second thoughts about having so many additional witnesses. What sort of preposterous proposal was Sirix going to make? And what sort of leverage did he have?

"Captain McCammon, tell your men to be alert, but do not open fire except at my express command. Anyone who takes a preemptive shot will face summary execution."

After an uncomfortable pause, McCammon nodded. "Understood, Mr. Chairman."

Basil's face remained stony as the EDF shuttle landed, though he felt deep outrage to see an Earth ship piloted by the black metal abomination. PD and QT stepped forward, but Basil sternly waved them back.

The hulking robot clambered out, barely able to push himself through a hatch designed for human beings. In a buzzing voice, Sirix said, "Chairman Wenceslas of the Terran Hanseatic League, thank you for agreeing to see me. I am alone and unarmed. As you requested."

"And what business brings you here?"

"I seek your help and offer our assistance in return. I wish to make a bargain with you."

Basil remained detached and implacable. "We made a bargain with you once before. It did not work out to our advantage."

"Circumstances have changed significantly," Sirix said.

"The original Klikiss have returned, and they are far more vicious than any other enemy you have faced. We black robots have stood up against them before, but now our numbers are depleted."

"Don't expect my sympathy for your difficulties," Basil said.

"Those difficulties are yours as well. The Klikiss mean to destroy us all. Together we can fight them. Helping us conquer the remnants of our creator race is to your advantage."

Basil considered. "I'm willing to entertain the possibility that we can find a mutually acceptable arrangement regarding our common enemy, but only under the strictest precautions."

"I would rather be allies than enemies," Sirix said. "You can help replenish our numbers. Your manufacturing facilities can create more black robots, which will be dedicated to the war against the Klikiss."

Basil ignored the gasps and grumbles behind him. "Your robots caused immeasurable harm to the Hansa. Why in the world would I want to create more of them? We have already learned not to trust you."

Sirix paused as if to consider, but Basil didn't doubt that he had already calculated every word of his response. "We will release the EDF vessels that we have taken. I am certain your Earth military could use them. All we ask in return is that you help us replace the black robots that we have lost in recent massacres. If we continue fighting the Klikiss, you would benefit as well."

Basil let out a dry laugh. "You have the audacity to offer us a handful of ships—*our* ships in the first place. They're probably damaged, their weapons depleted. That is hardly sufficent payment. And if we help to create more of your kind, what is to stop you from turning them against us?"

"We have no standing grudge against humans," Sirix insisted. "We knew the Klikiss would hunt us down and exterminate us, and therefore we needed ships to defend ourselves. We were merely fighting for our survival. We had no alternative but to take them from your EDF."

"You could have asked," Cain suggested. "Made an alliance with us in the first place."

Sirix swiveled his flat head. "Would you have simply surrendered the bulk of your space fleet? That is not likely. We were pushed to extremes. We face total annihilation if we do not defeat the Klikiss."

"I wouldn't lose sleep about that," Sarein muttered.

"And once the Klikiss annihilate us, they will annihilate you."

Cain's brow furrowed. "If you return our ships, what will the robots use for transport? You'll need vessels of your own."

"We are resourceful. We can cobble together stripped-down vessels to take us to safe star systems. We will be no bother to you."

Basil folded his hands together, annoyed that the others were talking so much. "Before I can even consider the possibility, I'll need more than the surrender of our own ships. They're too few to make a difference. I must have a significant fleet back, strong and ready to defend Earth."

Sarein and Cain gawked at him, unable to believe that he would genuinely negotiate with Sirix, but Basil ignored them.

"Many more EDF ships were damaged in battle here. Right now, hundreds of wrecks remain in orbit. Since your robots function perfectly well in space, I want you to rebuild those damaged ships. Give me my fleet back, and—provided you perform satisfactory work—I will direct some of our compy facilities to build your robots, but only under the most stringent supervision. We'll exchange a certain number of robots for a certain number of recommissioned ships." He shrugged, an imitation of benevolence. "You can even use some of the useless components in orbit to build your own vessels . . . if only to let your robots leave here as swiftly as possible."

Cain could restrain himself no longer. "Mr. Chairman, you know what Freedom's Sword will say when they hear of this. There'll be rioting in the streets!"

Basil scowled; the very existence of the dissident group was like a personal affront to him. "There are always whiners and naysayers. I need to do what is best for the Hansa. And this may be an opportunity we can't afford to pass up."

Though the black robot showed no emotions, Basil felt that even Sirix was surprised by the easy agreement. Basil offered him his most trustworthy smile.

It had been a long trip, with too many stops. Though she enjoyed sneaking through the Hansa's supposed "security" measures and dealing with black-market merchants, both on Earth and their few holdout colony worlds, Rlinda was glad to get back to the Confederation, to the Osquivel shipyards . . . and to BeBob.

When she landed the *Curiosity*, BeBob was there with a huge grin on his face. He greeted Rlinda with enough enthusiasm to satisfy even her. "I've been waiting for you! I got my ship back, good as new, and I've already put her through her paces. We can fly out together again, the *Blind Faith* and the *Voracious Curiosity*, just like old times."

"Not exactly like old times, BeBob." She kept her arms locked around him, refusing to release him from the hug. She had already gleaned reports of General Lanyan's clumsy attack on the shipyards here, as well as BeBob's encounter with the Klikiss at Relleker. "Not until the Chairman gets his head out of his ass and lets us get back to business as usual."

He looked deeply serious. "So is it bad on Earth?"

"Not so much bad as annoying. I met with Sarein, and even she's fed up, but I'm pretty sure she's too scared to do anything about it. She thinks she has a chance to keep the Chairman on the straight and narrow. I actually feel sorry for the poor girl."

BeBob snorted. "She chose the Chairman as her play-mate. Now she has to live with him."

"Excuse me, Mr. Holier-Than-Thou Roberts? I chose a few bad partners in my life, too. Didn't mean I couldn't get over it."

BeBob was unable to cover his smile. "And sometimes you find yourself back with somebody who was a good idea in the first place. You can be taught."

"I'm still reserving judgment, so make sure you keep behaving yourself. Now, then, would you prefer a squabble, or are you going to offer me a shower and a bed, preferably large enough to fit the two of us?"

"You mean the shower or the bed?"

"Both."

Later, they went together to the mess hall. Rlinda sniffed the air. "I want to make sure these shipyard chefs still remember how to cook."

"It always tasted good enough to me," BeBob said.

"Cardboard tastes good enough to you. That's why you need me around."

While BeBob accepted his plate of noodles and protein cubes mixed with the sauce of the day, Rlinda leaned her elbows on the serving counter and consulted the chefs about the spices they used, how they stretched their ingredients, what they could produce directly from hydroponics labs and what had to be imported.

"Well, it just so happens that while I investigated trade opportunities on Earth, I stocked my cargo hold with certain items, such as fresh chili peppers, ginger root, long curls of cinnamon bark, and saffron—I have a *kilo* of saffron that cost almost as much as a tankful of ekti. Ever had saffron?" The server shook her head, overwhelmed by Rlinda's enthusiasm. "I'd be willing to part with some of my stash, so long as I'm here to make sure everything is prepared properly. Your cafeteria food will never taste the same."

Rlinda followed BeBob to a table and took a seat across from Tasia Tamblyn and Robb Brindle. Instead of EDF uniforms, the pair now wore Roamer jumpsuits on which they had embroidered the new logo of the Confederation. While she wasn't close with Brindle or Tamblyn, Rlinda had met them back on Theroc while consulting with King Peter on setting up the new government.

Rlinda inhaled deeply of her plate of food, took several bites, and pronounced the meal "adequate." Tamblyn, as usual (according to BeBob), needed little incentive to get on her soapbox about the threat of the Klikiss. She and Brindle seemed to have personal axes to grind. "So, then, I take it you've both had some personal experience with the bugs?" Rlinda asked.

"Shizz, you could say that," Tamblyn said. "Too damned much experience."

"As hosts, they're about as pleasant as the hydrogues were," Brindle added. They described their struggles on Llaro and how only a few of them had gotten away. "Davlin Lotze and Margaret Colicos bought us time to escape."

Rlinda looked quickly at BeBob. "Did you say Davlin?" The last they had seen of the "specialist in obscure details," he'd been aboard BeBob's original *Blind Faith* when the EDF destroyed it. "I knew it was a trick! He got away. He's still alive."

"He was alive when we left him on Llaro," Tamblyn said, her expression glum. "But he didn't have a chance against the bugs. He went into the main hive to slow them down so the rest of us could get away."

"He's dead," Robb added, swallowing hard.

BeBob shook his head sadly. "Poor Davlin."

Rlinda found herself growing both angry and stubborn. "Right. I've heard that one before. We saw the *Blind Faith* destroyed before our very eyes, and he managed to survive." Rlinda leaned across the table, scowling at Tamblyn and Brindle. "I can't believe you just left him there! What were you thinking?"

Tamblyn didn't flinch. "Davlin did it to buy our freedom, and I sure as hell wasn't going to let him waste the sacrifice."

"Thanks to him, we saved almost a hundred other people," Brindle added.

Rlinda sat back, crossed her heavy arms over her breasts, and clung to her optimism. "Some people have a knack for getting out of desperate situations. After all I've been through with that man, I know not to underestimate Davlin Lotze."

58 ☀ CALEB TAMBLYN

Caleb had never much liked people, but this maddening solitude was getting on his nerves. Lost on a barren planetoid, he felt like Robinson Crusoe. From what he remembered of that old tale, Crusoe had been ingenious at using scant materials to make a functional home for himself.

Caleb figured he could achieve a lot more than that. After all, he was a Roamer.

Having scavenged the few marginally useful items at the melted ruins of the hydrogen-extraction facility, he used them to reinforce his modest habitat. After that, he resigned himself to utilizing the slim pickings in his escape pod. The only other technological items on Jonah 12 were orbiting ekti reactors, automated cargo-transfer satellites, and communications boosters, but they circled high above the frozen planetoid.

Eventually, with all the time in the world to think, Caleb convinced himself that those items might not be out of reach after all.

Though the pod's transmitter wouldn't reach beyond the Jonah system, he could use it to send coded commands to the mothballed equipment in orbit. It might take a while to decipher the protocols and Roamer programming, but it wasn't as if Caleb had anything else to do. Tinkering with the emergency transmitter, he scanned through hundreds of possible frequencies and tried different electronic handshake routines as he attempted to wake up at least one of the satellites. Though he was wasting battery power, he considered the gamble worthwhile, given the potential payoff.

Finally, his constant pleading ping was answered when a production satellite recognized the signal. Caleb lurched over to the slanted control panel and keyed in the secondary protocol, which locked the two signals together. "Gotcha!"

The production satellite dutifully transmitted its schematics so that Caleb could see what he had latched onto. It was little more than a box with attitude-control thrusters, a storage unit holding supplies for passing cargo ships so they would not need to drop into Jonah 12's shallow gravity well.

Now, if he could remember his basic celestial mechanics.

Since Jonah 12 had no atmosphere to speak of, he couldn't use drag to slow down the satellite; that meant he would have to bring it down under its own power. At least he had a good estimate of the planetoid's gravity, and that was the main thing he needed.

Under his command, the satellite's rockets fired, decreasing its orbital velocity and forcing it to spiral down. It was easy to make the satellite crash; the tricky part was making it crash *nearby*. Even bounding along in the low gravity, he wouldn't be able to cover much distance in an environment suit.

Four more orbits, and the satellite had spiraled down until it raced only a thousand feet above the surface. Caleb suited up, carefully checking his seals, locking his helmet down, closing the faceplate, and pressurizing his suit. One more orbit, he guessed, and the satellite was going to come down.

He stood outside, watching for the tiny glimmer to pass

overhead as he stared up at the stars. They all looked like lonely, cold eyes.

The satellite came over the foreshortened horizon and roared past him, so close and so fast that he jumped—accidentally propelling himself ten meters off the ground. At the apex of his leap, he watched the production satellite keep going on its final plunge until it scraped along a line of frozen hills no more than a kilometer away. A starburst pattern of fresh ice and steam marked the bull's-eye where the satellite had come in for a hard landing.

Caleb bounded across the ice, each leap seemingly carrying him halfway to the small planetoid's horizon. When he reached the crash point, he saw that the satellite's metal walls had buckled, but at least the contents weren't strewn across the cratered terrain. With clumsy gloved hands he pried apart the broken pieces of metal, eager to see what equipment and supplies were inside. Again, he felt like Robinson Crusoe finding a cargo crate washed up on his shores.

The Roamer engineers had thought of everything: spare energy packs, generalized components that could be assembled into any number of useful gadgets, a standard emergency kit with basic medicines, even concentrated rations (though Caleb couldn't imagine why anyone would really need such a thing out in orbit).

As he looked at the remnants of the large satellite, Caleb thought he might be able to cannibalize some of the structure itself, put a nice addition on his cramped escape pod. If he was going to be stranded here for the rest of his life—however long that might be—he could at least be comfortable.

Knowing he would have to make several trips, Caleb gathered the most vital objects, made one of the flat solar-panel wings into a sled, then happily began his jaunt back to the pod. He climbed up over the low, frozen hills, raced down into the valleys, and skipped around wide, black fissures.

As he approached his small camp, Caleb was startled to see a glow permeating the ice, shimmering as if from an inner fire. The eerie luminescence spread out to the width of a broad lake near his landed escape pod.

He stopped in his tracks, feeling a chill go down his spine. Still moving under its own momentum, the loaded solar-panel sled bumped into his heels, startling him. Something very strange was going on here. . . .

But he couldn't stay outside to wait and watch; his suit's battery pack and air tank were already down to twenty-five percent. Gathering his courage, Caleb headed toward the strange glow that surrounded his pod.

59 ☀ ANTON COLICOS

While the Mage-Imperator remained a "special guest" in the Whisper Palace until Chairman Wenceslas figured out what to do with him, Anton was under orders to take Rememberer Vao'sh to the university. He had no idea what sort of interrogation or debriefing the other professors would inflict upon him, but he supposed Vao'sh could hold his own.

Anton had spent most of his scholarly career here, and

this should have been a happy return for him . . . but it didn't feel that way. "I've wanted to show you this place for a long time, Vao'sh. I'm afraid the Hansa's actions have dampened my enthusiasm for all the things I used to be proud of."

The old rememberer, though, was surprisingly accepting of the circumstances. "Even in troubled times, a rememberer should always observe and absorb. I intend to learn as much about your human culture as your experts intend to learn from me."

Anton looked closely at his friend, trying to read his moods from the colors of his expressive lobes. "How are you holding up so far away from the rest of your people?"

"I can bear it, for now. The Mage-Imperator is close, and I know where the rest of my people are. I do not feel entirely alone." With forced good cheer, the rememberer took Anton's arm as they walked together onto the campus grounds. "After my previous ordeal with the isolation madness, perhaps I have a greater tolerance than other Ildirans."

The expansive parklike campus was crowded with earnest young students who were not yet scarred by the cynicism of real life. As a researcher here, Anton had been oblivious to the treacheries and convolutions of faculty politics, which were a far cry from mythic story arcs and great epic cycles. His goals had seemed lofty to him at the time: striving for tenure, submitting a unique interpretation or a new translation, engaging rival professors in vehement but irrelevant academic debates. Since then, he had experienced so much more—from the Ildiran Empire, to treacherous black robots, the hydrogues, the worldforest . . . and now, betrayal by his own government. Yes, university politics seemed laughably insignificant by comparison.

As the two walked across the campus, Anton tried to

ignore the veritable army of security guards that accompanied them at a not-terribly-discreet distance. He stopped by a mirrored fountain whose design had been copied from a counterpart in Mijistra. "This section of the campus is the Department of Ildiran Studies. This is where we'll be spending most of our time."

Before Anton's departure years ago, the dean had promised that as long as he was on his remarkable mission to Ildira, Anton would be considered a great asset to the department, a feather in the university's cap. Now, when he led Vao'sh into the old college administration building, he didn't realize what a stir he would cause. Hansa guards rushed ahead to sweep the building, to inform the administrators and their staff. Anton was embarrassed by all the attention.

The dean bustled out to greet them, speaking with a German accent. "I am so pleased you have finally returned to us, Dr. Colicos." He held out a big hand. "And Rememberer Vao'sh, we have heard much about you." The dean, an older man whose thick red hair was obviously dyed, had somewhat heavyset cheeks and lips too large for his face. He was said to have an acid wit, especially at cocktail parties after a glass or two of wine, though Anton had never been invited to such a prestigious department function.

Looking askance at the Hansa guards who stood by the doorway, the dean shook Anton's hand, then did the same to Vao'sh. "We were absolutely delighted to receive your first translations of the *Saga*, Dr. Colicos. They were delivered here—smuggled, actually. We're greatly indebted to the trader captain, whoever she was."

"I could tell you her name, but I'm afraid the Hansa might punish her."

"Pffft! They are perfectly happy with our Ildiran studies. In fact, I've assigned four full professors to study your translations. You have given us fodder for years of work."

"That epic took my people millennia to compose," Vao'sh pointed out.

"Of course. Of course," the dean said, grinning. "These translations are worth more than a hundred dissertations. Come, we've restored your office exactly as you remember it."

Restored it? So the dean had reassigned his office in the meantime, but must have scrambled to put everything back in order as soon as the Chairman's instructions had come down.

"We found your notes for the biography of your parents. Fascinating people." The dean stumped down the hall on short legs. "I glanced at a few of your drafts. I hope you don't mind." Actually, Anton did mind, but he decided not to make an issue of it. "For the time being, however, your Ildiran work must take priority."

Hansa guards waited at the far end of the hallway, still cautious, still watching. The dean looked uncomfortable. "And I understand Rememberer Vao'sh will be helping us with a research project for the Chairman?"

Let our scholars debrief him thoroughly, Basil Wenceslas had said. Anton wasn't surprised at how the dean had interpreted it.

"I am willing to tell parts of the *Saga*," Vao'sh said. "That is my purpose as a rememberer."

"So, you will deliver guest lectures? We can host an entire series of talks, as many as the rememberer chooses to give. Would they be private affairs, or open to the entire student body?"

Anton tried to hide his surprise. "Oh, we'd like to make them as public as possible."

60 ☀ HYRILLKA DESIGNATE RIDEK'H

He found Tal O'nh sitting outside the caves again, staring with impunity into the multiple suns. After returning from the obliterated camp of Hyrillka refugees—the people *he* was supposed to protect—the young man no longer felt like a mere substitute for his father, whom Rusa'h had killed. Now he finally, wholeheartedly thought of himself as the true Hyrillka Designate.

Ridek'h joined his mentor. "I should not be hiding here in these caves."

"No, you should not. None of us should . . . but do we flee? Do we provoke the faeros? Do we engage in a direct battle—and all die? We will get no guidance from the Mage-Imperator, as long as he remains imprisoned by the humans, and we have no way of rescuing him. And what can we do ourselves?"

"Indeed," Ridek'h said. "What can we do ourselves?"

He voiced it as a challenge rather than an admission of failure.

After the Mage-Imperator had been returned to the *thism* web, his presence had shone like a reignited blazer. Across the Empire all of the panicked and dismayed Ildirans would have felt at least a glimmer of reassurance. In response, Tal Ala'nh, who commanded one of the remaining cohorts of free Solar Navy ships, had gathered his dispersed warliners and charged back to Ildira. Seven complete maniples, 343 battleships, all ready to throw themselves at the fireballs.

Adar Zan'nh had stopped them, refusing to let so many warliners be destroyed in a pointless sacrifice. And so a frustrated Tal Ala'nh waited at a distance, in nominal command of the gathering off-planet military force, with orders to remain intact, ready, and unobtrusive.

After what he had seen in the burned refugee camp, Ridek'h's attention was focused on the remaining Hyrillkans on Ildira. More than a million of the people evacuated from his world were still scattered across the Ildiran landscape. The faeros could exterminate them at any time they chose, whenever the mad Designate let them. Ridek'h could barely contain himself, quivering with the need to act.

"I should challenge him. *I* am the rightful Hyrillka Designate. I have faced Rusa'h before, and he didn't kill me."

"Some would call that a miracle," O'nh said, his scarred face troubled by memories of that awful encounter. "What would it accomplish to tempt fate again?"

"I will sacrifice myself if I must."

"I would prefer you did not, young man. I can see no way it would be helpful."

Ridek'h tried to make his decision sound less impulsive than it was. "In the command nucleus of your warliner,

Rusa'h said we would face each other again. I want to do it now, on my own terms. I will make the long journey back to Mijistra alone, enter the Prism Palace, and confront him. If Rusa'h was going to kill me, he would have done it already."

"And what can you say to him?"

"I will make him realize what he is doing to his own people! If he is still Rusa'h, at least in part, then he must see the horror of what he has let loose. Who is truly in control—him, or the faeros? Maybe an Ildiran heart still beats within him."

O'nh let out a sigh, though he clearly longed to do something himself. "You are being foolish. I forbid it."

The young man raised his voice. "I am the Designate. You follow my commands, not the other way around. Need I remind you of your own teachings? Followers follow, but leaders must lead. I have the blood of the Mage-Imperator in me. You told me that if I could think of something that might save us, then I am morally obligated to *do it*."

The veteran allowed a small smile to cross his face. "So, you were listening to me after all."

"Yes, to every word. There I will stand, Hyrillka Designate to Hyrillka Designate. This is a time for desperate acts. The Mage-Imperator is no longer with us, and so we must make these decisions for ourselves." He found himself breathing heavily.

Tal O'nh remained seated, still staring at the suns. "Desperate acts. Perhaps we should all consider them. I see no other way to save the Empire."

61 ☀ MAGE-IMPERATOR JORA'H

Now that the Chairman had become busy with his new co-operative scheme with the black robots, his interest in the Mage-Imperator waned. Young King Rory and the Arch-father of Unison had announced the retooling of existing groundside compy factories while the black robots diligently repaired and reassembled EDF vessels in orbit.

Though Jora'h was no expert in the nuances of human emotions, even he could see that the Archfather looked nauseated by the words he was forced to speak. The bearded Unison spokesman seemed offended by the very idea of suggesting, on religious grounds, that the black robots were tantamount to saviors.

If only the Archfather had been so obviously offended by the idea of kidnapping the leader of the Ildiran Empire. . . .

Frustrated, and dismissive, now that the Mage-Imperator had failed to yield, the Hansa Chairman abruptly removed Jora'h and Nira from their quarters in the Whisper Palace and sent them back to the Moon, accompanied by Captain McCammon and a group of royal guards. Holding their heads high, Jora'h and the green priest boarded the shuttle and prepared to depart. No newsnet imagers were allowed to attend the event.

Though he would be closer to his fellow hostages, being returned to the lunar base brought Jora'h neither joy nor satisfaction. He needed to be back on *Ildira*. He needed to be fighting the faeros.

As the EDF transport ship made the passage to the Moon, Jora'h sat quietly with Nira on the cold metal seats. She clutched his hand, and he loved her nearness; yet he needed more than that.

Captain McCammon watched them, saying nothing. The guard captain was hard to read, possibly sympathetic, definitely reticent.

After the shuttle docked inside one of the enclosed lunar craters, Jora'h took Nira by the arm and emerged from the shuttle into the dusty landing zone, looking cool and imperial. McCammon and his royal guards followed closely.

The Ildiran guard kithmen, stripped of their weapons, stood against the back wall to watch the Mage-Imperator's arrival. The bestial-looking guard kithmen swelled their armored chests, simmering with the desire to do something. Many prisoners from the captured warliner had been allowed into the chamber to witness the reception. Jora'h guessed that his people had been unruly and agitated in his absence. He did not try to hide his grim smile.

An EDF squad led by Commandant Tilton stepped forward to receive them formally. "I didn't expect to say this, but I am glad to have you back here, Mage-Imperator. I hope that now I can expect a return to order on my base." He had never wanted to host these hostages in the first place.

Jora'h faced the embarrassed-looking lunar commandant. "The Chairman has sent us to rot here while my planet burns and my people die by the thousands each day."

Though they were heavily outnumbered, the growling Ildiran guards flexed their enlarged muscles and claws. If Yazra'h had been here, she would have thrown herself upon the enemy without a second thought.

Commandant Tilton paled, and his men seemed uneasy,

holding their weapons ready. Another squad of EDF soldiers marched into the landing bay, guarding the doors, as if to remind the Mage-Imperator that it would be foolish to try anything.

Through the *thism*, Jora'h could feel the barely contained fury of the guards. They were ready to explode, desperate to do something, with no concern for their own well-being. He knew that every Ildiran here was willing to sacrifice himself so the Mage-Imperator could get away.

The wave of emotion pushed against him like a strong wind. Jora'h knew that further talk wouldn't help, and that bowing to the Chairman's foolish demands wouldn't work. There would be no opportunity to carefully plan an escape. The guard kithmen waited for any hint of instructions from him, seething for their chance.

He knew that each of his soldiers could easily take down several humans. They were not as outnumbered as they appeared to be. And his own warliner was right here at the lunar base.

Jora'h made his decision. Desperation demanded desperate moves. With the tiniest of motions, connected to all of his guards through the *thism*, the Mage-Imperator gave his implicit permission for them to act. *Go*.

The response was blindingly swift. Moving in a wild, coordinated flash, the unarmed guard kithmen threw themselves upon the EDF soldiers crowded in the docking bay. With whipcord muscles and long fangs, they killed several men in the first few seconds, breaking necks, tearing out throats. They ripped handguns and jazer rifles from dead hands. Within another five seconds they had armed themselves and begun to open fire, cutting down the EDF soldiers that came yelling into the chamber.

Commandant Tilton screamed orders, unable to believe what was happening. The Ildiran guard kithmen attacked like whirlwinds and made their way toward the Mage-Imperator. The EDF soldiers fought back, cutting down three, then five Ildiran guards. A dozen more soldiers ran into the chamber and opened fire. Jora'h could barely count the casualties as they happened.

"Mage-Imperator!" a voice roared. "Order your guards to stand down—*or she dies*."

Jora'h whirled and saw that Captain McCammon had seized Nira. Though she struggled and fought, the captain's arm was locked around her waist and his ceremonial dagger was against her smooth green throat. His voice was hard and determined. "If you do not tell your guards to surrender right now, I will kill her."

Jora'h saw the fear on Nira's face change to a flicker of defiance. But he would not allow her to die in what was already a futile attempt. He would not let Nira be harmed.

McCammon did not move. His sharp blade pressed hard against her neck, and his cold blue eyes did not waver.

He couldn't bear to lose her.

"Lay down your weapons," Jora'h shouted. "Stop!"

His surviving guard kithmen shuddered. Then, in unison, they ceased. Absolutely obedient to their Mage-Imperator, they could not refuse his order, no matter how filled with bloodlust they might be. The surviving Ildiran fighters cast their stolen weapons to the ground, as if in disgust.

Jora'h desperately searched for some other way out, but he knew he could not fight his way through an entire base of human soldiers. The plan had been hopeless from the beginning. "We surrender."

McCammon's shoulders slumped. He seemed entirely

relieved as he withdrew his dagger from Nira's throat and let her go.

Commandant Tilton looked like a scarecrow, wrung out and shaken. His voice was shrill. "Seize them! Put them in separate cells." He heaved deep breaths as if about to retch.

More than half of Jora'h's loyal guard kithmen had been slaughtered, though they had dealt far more damage to their human captors. He folded his arms around Nira, and she began to sob.

McCammon looked at the Mage-Imperator. "It was the swiftest and most efficient means to end the crisis," he said, as if in apology.

62 ☀ GENERAL KURT LANYAN

After being trounced at the Osquivel shipyards, Lanyan wasn't in a hurry to get back to Earth. In spite of his good news about locating one of the Confederation's major industrial operations and seizing enough Roamer ekti to supply the EDF for months, he knew the Chairman could read between the lines.

He would consider Lanyan a failure. Again.

He ordered his battle group to stop at two other potential targets on the way, stalling by more than a week, but both turned out to be abandoned. Finally, and without much fanfare, his raiding group returned to Earth.

He went directly to the Hansa HQ to make his report. The Chairman remained silent at his desk for a long moment while Lanyan's uneasiness grew. He stood at attention, feeling like a cadet about to receive a dressing-down, and his practiced smile of pride began to falter. When he swallowed, his throat had become unexpectedly dry. He thought at least the Golgen report would have satisfied the man.

Finally the Chairman sighed. "Now I'm going to have to see about sending someone to administer the Roamer skymines or we'll lose all that potential, too. At least you got the ekti."

Lanyan was glad he had not mentioned finding Patrick Fitzpatrick; no doubt the Chairman would complain that the young man should have been brought back to Earth in chains. Probably so, Lanyan thought, but given a few moments of media spotlight, Fitzpatrick could have caused a lot of damage.

"Yes, sir. Those facilities are vital." He didn't know what else to say. "During the raid, I was careful to keep the manufacturing capabilities intact—"

The Chairman's voice dripped with scorn. "While you and your ships have been on a boisterous raiding expedition, and getting chased off by a few ragtag Roamers and deserters from the EDF, I've made difficult decisions about the very future of the Hansa." He didn't even bother to look at Lanyan as he spoke, but when he finally glanced up, his gray eyes were as cold as liquid nitrogen. "Come with me, General. I have to inspect the new robot facilities. It's time you see what has been happening in your absence."

Flustered, Lanyan followed him out of the Hansa HQ.

He had left Conrad Brindle in command of his ships in orbit, where the battered robot-controlled vessels were being surrendered to human control again. The sight of all those stolen EDF craft had made him furious. No wonder protests and complaints were popping up all over the newsnets. How could anyone forget what the black robots had done? What the hell was Chairman Wenceslas thinking to agree to an alliance?

The two men barely spoke a word during their trip to one of the retooled factories. Lanyan shuddered as he remembered the murderously programmed Soldier compies — and now the Hansa was placing its head into the same noose again? He was certain Basil Wenceslas must have some plan, but he hadn't been able to determine what it was. No one had.

The whole manufacturing facility, with its cavernous warehouse bay, thermal stacks, and thrumming assembly lines, produced a deafening background roar. Dozens of monstrous black robots paraded about the assembly floor, inspecting ebony components, circuit plates, programming modules intricately etched in supercooled baths. For every black robot, thankfully, Lanyan observed at least ten human soldiers and inspectors.

Basil dismissed his obvious anxiety. "Nothing to worry about. Our inspectors maintain round-the-clock surveillance on every aspect of the production line."

"Even so, I don't trust these *things*."

The Chairman gave him a paternal smile. "We also have this whole factory rigged with explosives, and I can destroy it with the snap of a finger. It is to the robots' benefit to cooperate with us. I understand how Sirix thinks. His hatred for the Klikiss supersedes any disagreements he had with us in the past."

"Sir, our last 'disagreement' cost us two-thirds of the EDF fleet and close to a million human soldiers!"

Deputy Cain walked out of a floor-level office, followed by the Hansa's new lead scientists, Jane Kulu and Tito Andropolis. Lanyan had met the two before, and thought their enthusiasm extended beyond their technical abilities. Cain, on the other hand, kept his true feelings hidden. "The robots finished retooling this facility, and Sirix pronounced the production line to be satisfactory."

Kulu interjected. "The robots have helped us modify and improve the efficiency of our own process lines."

"Didn't we say that last time?" Lanyan said, looking around in alarm. "When we copied the robot programming modules?"

"This is completely different," Andropolis insisted. "This facility should be fully operational within days."

"And the robots will begin reassembling our own warships," the Chairman said. "I have promised them one hundred new robots for every EDF ship that is placed back into service. Over just the past few days, Sirix has finished reconditioning fifteen Mantas and one Juggernaut—much faster than we could do it ourselves. So you see, if we cooperate, then everyone is happy."

Lanyan had no real alternative but to agree. "If the robots deliver on their promises and they restore our fleet, then I will withdraw my objections."

"I'm sick of people voicing objections." Basil walked smartly away from the process line.

Lanyan followed him, first swallowing his angry retorts, then searching for a politic way to raise the questions still plaguing him. Finally he stepped in front of the Chairman and blocked his way. The cold inside him went as deep as his bones, but he swallowed his pride and said, "Sir, I know that some parts of my recent performance have not met your expectations. Please tell me how I can earn back your trust and confidence. Give me a mission to prove myself."

Basil considered, then said, "Two hours ago we received a series of log drones launched from Admiral Diente's *Manta*. I dispatched him to Pym in hopes of opening a dialog with the Klikiss there, but they destroyed the ship and killed everyone. Another failed mission." He seemed more disappointed than shocked or outraged.

Lanyan struggled for words. "You sent Admiral Diente to *Pym*? To *talk* with the bugs?"

"I had hoped our two races could find common ground, but the Klikiss have no interest in negotiation. Therefore, the Hansa will no longer attempt to negotiate." He continued to pace. "On your first mission to Pym, you fled in terror and shame. Now you can make up for that."

Lanyan went pale. His prior experience with the Klikiss had been the most frightening event in his life, and he maintained a knee-jerk hatred of the bugs. He already knew what the Chairman was going to suggest.

"We must not let the Klikiss believe they can treat official Hansa ambassadors in such a barbaric way. You, General, will lead our appropriate response. Firm, clear, and incontrovertible."

With the rattle and hum all around them, Lanyan managed to cover his gasp. He didn't dare show outright fear in front of the Chairman. "And what exactly is our appropriate response, sir?"

"Why, a military one, of course. Teach them a lesson.

Take a battle group to Pym and eradicate the Klikiss. Sirix promises that the new Juggernaut will be ready within days." The Chairman smiled. "After you have achieved that victory, we can discuss your possible return to a position of trust. Then we'll see about squashing the Confederation resistance. You'd like a chance to get revenge on Admiral Willis, wouldn't you?"

Lanyan nodded automatically, though he was still dealing with the idea of facing a planetful of Klikiss warriors. The Chairman strolled out of the factory toward the waiting transport that would take him to the Hansa HQ. "My plan, General, is to have the black robots fight the Klikiss for us. Ideally the two will wipe each other out, though we may have to make some sacrifices of our own."

Lanyan was uncomfortably aware that the Chairman might consider *him* one of those potential "sacrifices."

63 ☀ SULLIVAN GOLD

Chairman Wenceslas was not in a forgiving mood when he summoned Sullivan to the Hansa HQ. "I was astonished to learn you were back on Earth, Mr. Gold. Didn't you think I might be interested to hear from you firsthand? And as soon as possible?"

It wasn't difficult for Sullivan to act confused about the

uproar. "I had quite an ordeal, sir, and I haven't even begun to get my life back together."

"You have had more than long enough." The Chairman sat down behind his desk. "I know exactly when you returned."

Sullivan glanced out the penthouse windows at the gorgeous skyline of the Palace District, impressed by the view from the top of the towering Hansa pyramid. Noticing his distraction, Chairman Wenceslas swept his fingers across a control to opaque the windows. Now they appeared to be in a shielded bunker, and for some reason the Chairman seemed more content.

Sullivan sighed, then told his story. "Sir, a few of us escaped when the hydrogues destroyed our cloud harvester at Qronha 3. We rescued many Ildiran workers and returned them to Ildira, where we were pressed into service, helping outfit the Solar Navy to defend Earth—successfully, I might add."

He saw no softening of the other man's expression, but he pressed on. "Sir, lately my family's suffered a great deal of financial hardship, and the Hansa reneged on the contractual terms of my employment. I believe I deserve some compensation."

The Chairman remained sitting stiffly at his desk. "That's what you believe, is it? I disagree, Mr. Gold. You were in charge of that extraordinarily expensive facility, which is now completely destroyed, along with its entire stockpile of ekti. I would say the Hansa's financial losses far outweigh your own."

Sullivan had been an administrator and a negotiator long enough to know not to let his irritation escalate an already tense situation. "At the very least please return the reward the Mage-Imperator gave me. I earned that."

"Currency from an enemy empire will do you no good, Mr. Gold. In fact, even possessing it casts suspicion on you. It's a good thing that we took it into safekeeping. We wouldn't want there to be any misunderstandings. Colonel Andez and her cleanup crew sometimes get overly zealous."

Sullivan had been watching the newsnets, and more than once he heard glowing reports of how the cleanup crew was cracking down on anyone whose words "shattered the morale of our brave fighters." They were most incensed about Freedom's Sword. According to the reports, the "enemy" took great comfort from the Hansa's internal strife, though Sullivan doubted the Klikiss were listening to human newsnets.

After the cleanup crew's outrageous illegal search and seizure of their townhome, Lydia had gotten herself into a high dudgeon, and made sure to tell her family, friends, and neighbors. "How can we let them get away with that?" Lydia would say. "And if I don't complain about it, then the next person won't complain about it, or the next. And those storm-troopers will just walk all over our rights. I don't intend to just sit back and let that happen. Not on my watch." Sullivan often had to drag her back inside the house just to keep her quiet. Her heart was in the right place, even if she was dead set on getting into trouble. . . .

Now the Chairman lectured Sullivan. "With the hydrogue war over, the Hansa must become more self-sufficient. We need secure and independent supplies of stardrive fuel."

Sullivan dreaded what the man was about to suggest. "And you want me to manage another Hansa cloud harvester? Surely you have a better candidate."

Chairman Wenceslas frowned at the interruption. "No,

not another Hansa cloud harvester. You may have heard of General Lanyan's recent successful resource-gathering mission in Roamer-held territory? He took possession of a group of skymines at Golgen and relieved them of an extensive supply of ekti. Now that their defenses are broken, I intend for you to administer those facilities under the auspices of the Hansa."

Sullivan had to sit down without being invited to do so. "I'm not trained to manage a hostile workforce. That's a military job, and I'm just a simple administrator." He was so upset that he no longer felt cowed. "The Roamers would sabotage the process line every chance they got. I'm not inclined to do it, Mr. Chairman."

Basil Wenceslas looked at him in disbelief, as if no one had ever turned him down before. "I urge you to reconsider." His voice held a clear threat.

But Sullivan had had enough of coercive tactics, the cleanup crew's intimidation, the freezing of his financial assets. He had faced a hydrogue armada that had destroyed his cloud-harvesting facility right out from under him. He could survive the disapproval of Chairman Wenceslas. He stood and went to the door of the office. "Sorry, Mr. Chairman. You'll have to find someone else. I've retired, and my decision is final."

Maureen Fitzpatrick actually proved to be a gracious hostess. Over the course of several days, Patrick told his grandmother what he'd been doing since flying off with her space yacht to find Zhett. Someone more romantic might have found it a heartwarming tale, but the old Battleaxe said that she simply considered him foolish and sappy.

But Patrick didn't allow himself to think of this as a merely social visit. King Peter had sent him here to plant a few provocative ideas in the former Chairman's mind and find out what she really thought about the Confederation and about Basil Wenceslas.

One afternoon the three of them sat together on a large open porch, looking out at the snowcapped peaks and breathing cool mountain air that was fresher than anything he had tasted in a Roamer facility. Maureen had newscreens playing in the background, as she always did. Though it had been decades since she had served as Hansa Chairman, she nevertheless surrounded herself with current events, as if she were still a vital cog in the wheel.

Feeling distinctly uncomfortable, Patrick finally blurted out something he had been meaning to say since he arrived. "Grandmother, I know you used to think of me as headstrong and selfish and immature—"

"Used to?" she broke in.

"I'm trying to apologize here!" He flushed red, and Maureen fell awkwardly silent. Neither he nor his grandmother was good at this. "I was a lazy, spoiled pain in the ass, but I've learned that I need to work for what I want, whether it's respect or belongings."

"Not much room for lazy people in a Roamer outpost," Zhett said. "We straightened him out, eventually."

The former Chairman narrowed her eyes. "You showed some of that when you got in the middle of the EDF and the Roamers, when you made me broker a cease-fire at Osquivel. I could see you weren't the same old Patrick." She grew serious. "I always knew you had a lot more potential than your parents did. That's why I was so hard on you. You just needed to get your head on straight."

Patrick felt a lump in his throat. He squeezed Zhett's hand. "When I came home, I sulked around, didn't do much of anything, but I knew what was really going on out there. I had to take a stand. I couldn't go back to serve the EDF when I knew that *they* had started the war with the Roamers. So I ran. I'm sorry I abused your trust by stealing your space yacht. I didn't think of anyone but myself. I was rationalizing, taking what I needed."

He thought of how Chairman Wenceslas and General Lanyan justified raids on Roamers, Ildirans, human colonies—even committing murder—simply because they "needed" something. But Patrick refused to think like they did.

Maureen made an awkward gesture of dismissal. "I've got plenty of personal ships. You didn't cause me a moment's hardship—I was more annoyed that you'd run off just because you were heartsick for some girl." Before Zhett could interject, Maureen continued. "I can't say I'm pleased that you deserted the EDF, but I didn't listen to you either. I thought you needed therapy to get over your delusions, but dammit, you were right—at least for the most part. I watched the rah-rah images of the pogrom on Usk; I listen to the crazy Archfather; I see what the Chairman's special cleanup crew is doing every day." She shook her head in disgust.

General Lanyan came on one of the newscreens, suddenly drawing all of their attention. With great fanfare he announced the launch of a new military initiative against the Klikiss in order to "avenge the senseless murder of Admiral Diente and his peaceful diplomatic mission to Pym." In a bold, gruff voice, he vowed to "teach the vicious insect race to fear the Earth Defense Forces." Patrick noted that the newsnets mentioned neither Lanyan's piracy at the Golgen skymines, nor how he had been resoundingly beaten at Osquivel.

"Asshole." Maureen rolled her eyes at the General's bravado. "Lanyan's come crawling home with his tail between his legs so often he's getting calluses on his backside."

Patrick scowled. "I can't believe I used to admire him."

"You used to be remarkably ill informed, Fitzie," Zhett teased, "not to mention thickheaded."

"Thanks."

Maureen couldn't tear her eyes from the newsnet screen. "Lanyan's latest boondoggle isn't half as stupid as Basil's boneheaded new plan to cooperate with the black robots. Why the hell is a Hansa *Chairman* agreeing to manufacture more of those damned alien machines?"

Patrick said, "Is it any wonder the opposition groups are growing louder, even though he tries to stomp them down? He pumps up the fear to keep the people believing his iron fist is better than the alternative—but they don't think about any alternatives."

"They don't bother to think at all," Maureen said with a sniff. "Bunch of sheep. At least Freedom's Sword is pointing in the right direction."

Using his grandmother's sophisticated media-watch network, Patrick and Zhett had been admiring the ingenious ways dissidents had managed to insert condemnations and seditious messages into a variety of communications venues; his old shipmate Shelia Andez and her cleanup crew were driving themselves crazy chasing down rumors and supposed propaganda strongholds, only to come up empty-handed time and again.

"It sure isn't the way I would run the circus tent," Maureen grumbled. "In fact, when I was Chairman —"

Patrick seized the perfect segue. "That's actually why we're here, Grandmother. King Peter himself asked us to speak with you."

"King Peter? So you're rubbing elbows with the high and mighty. The Hansa calls him an outlaw — I've read the official press releases." She seemed to find it amusing.

Zhett didn't. "Outlaw? King Peter leads the majority of the human race. Basil Wenceslas is the real criminal. For months now, King Peter has been calling for him to resign."

"Like that'll ever happen," Maureen said.

"Then maybe he should be deposed," Patrick suggested quietly. He was sure his grandmother had thought of it herself, many times.

Pretending to ignore what he had just said, Maureen switched off the newscreen in disgust. "You don't have to tell me all the things the Chairman has done wrong. But I'm not at the helm anymore."

"Funny you should mention that. We have an official

offer from the Confederation that you'll want to hear. It's right up your alley."

Patrick made his pitch, explaining how the King wanted her to provide a counterpoint to the propaganda of Chairman Wenceslas, while acting as an official liaison between the orphaned colonies, the government of Theroc, and the failing Hansa. "It's extremely prestigious and important. Think about it, Grandmother—what are you accomplishing around here?"

"Why, I thought you always resented my political work." Her lips quirked in a smile, playing him.

"Like I said, I've changed." Patrick could see she was not entirely averse to the idea he had proposed. "After spending time among the Roamers, I realized that I never understood how hard you worked for what you have. You've got skills, contacts, influence, and behind-the-scenes knowledge that no one on Earth or in the Confederation can hope to match."

Zhett spoke up. "Ma'am, do you want to stay on a sinking ship, or would you rather deploy the life rafts?"

"Don't call me 'ma'am.' It makes me feel old." Maureen leaned back in the chair and stared out at the landscape. "There's a name for people who leave a sinking ship, you know. They're called rats."

"Or survivors," Zhett countered.

"Touché. Patrick, I think I like this girl after all."

"Don't call me a girl. I'm not that young." This elicited a burst of laughter from the old Battleaxe.

"Grandmother, Chairman Wenceslas got us into this mess, and you can help get us out of it. I can tell you're ready to be at the helm again. How much more incentive do you need?" Patrick said with a quick smile; then he grew serious again. "By sending General Lanyan to attack the Golgen skymines and the Osquivel shipyards, the Hansa declared war on the Confederation. The Chairman kidnapped the Mage-Imperator, making enemies out of the entire Ildiran Empire. He agreed to manufacture more black robots even after they massacred the majority of the EDF. And now he's sending part of Earth's limited fleet on an offensive against the Klikiss race, which will probably start an all-out conflict with the bugs. Tell me again—why exactly would you stay here and support this government?"

"Why indeed?" Maureen played coy. "On the other hand, do you expect me just to jump aboard your ship and fly off, leaving everything I hold dear? And what about my assistant, Jonas? My God, he's been in my household since the first mammals appeared on land."

Patrick said, "With your help, this can all be over soon. Once the Chairman has gone, and the Hansa unites with the Confederation, think of how many people will be clamoring to get into your good graces. You'll still have your house, your possessions, your political connections—*and* more clout than you ever had."

"I've still got plenty of clout."

"You'll have more."

"I'll get us some tea." The old woman stood up and walked briskly away. "What kind would you like?"

"Strong," Zhett answered for both of them.

Patrick called after her, "I know you want to say yes."

"You should also know that you won't get an immediate answer from me. It would look far too eager—not very astute. Haven't I taught you anything?" Maureen returned with the tea from an instant dispenser. Patrick was surprised she did it herself, rather than calling for Jonas.

She got down to brass tacks. "I'll want an official title, naturally—something impressive and with real authority. You two go on ahead, and make sure King Peter has all the right documents prepared. Besides, you're a fugitive, Patrick. I shouldn't be seen with you during delicate negotiations. I'll come to Theroc in my own ship with my own retinue."

"The King needs someone soon, and he'll be interviewing other candidates."

"No, he won't. If he thinks I'm on the hook, he'll give me all the time I need."

"Two weeks," Zhett said. "If you don't come to Theroc by then, my own father just might apply for the job."

"Two weeks," Maureen said with a smile.

Patrick had a difficult time keeping the grin off his face. "I know I just brought your space yacht back to you, but would it be all right if we borrowed it for a little longer—to get back to Theroc? We'll return it to you there."

The old woman heaved an exaggerated sigh. "Oh, keep the ship. Consider it my wedding gift to you."

J ess and Cesca had rallied their former group of water
bearers, launching them all on a mission to spread the
new warrior wentals and also to recover ancient seedpools
from long-forgotten reservoirs throughout the Spiral Arm.

Although the water bearers were all enthusiastic, Jess
and Cesca feared that their efforts were still too limited and
conventional. The powers of the wentals had not been sufficient in the previous war, and even with the water entities'
more aggressive stance, the coming battles against the faeros
would require much more ingenuity. The energized water itself, though ready to go on the offensive, needed to become
more effective somehow. The wentals couldn't do it alone.

For as long as Jess could remember, Kotto Okiah had
been the brightest star of Roamer innovation. As their ship
floated into the Osquivel shipyards, Jess was anxious to see
how Kotto could combine Roamer technology with wental
powers.

A space traffic controller directed them to a primary lab
complex in one of the larger ring asteroids. Their liquid ship
floated into the designated hangar bay, and the heavy doors
sealed behind them. As atmosphere was restored, the ship's
surface tension dissolved, leaving a deep puddle around their
bare feet.

The living water pooled itself and divided into two thick,
cylindrical blobs, rolling like transparent clay. When Jess and

Cesca walked forward, the eerie ovoid shapes oozed ahead of them, rising and rolling down the rock-floored corridor.

Roamer workers in the facility peered through doorways, amazed at the procession. One woman backed away in fear of getting too close to a wental blob, but Cesca raised her hand reassuringly. "The water is safe — the wentals won't disperse their energy."

Jess added, "Just don't get too close to the two of *us*."

Kotto Okiah kept the diamond-walled hydrogue derelict inside the largest lab chamber. At the moment, however, he was hard at work on some sort of new acoustic transmitter, a large dish formed of components spread across his tables. Three compies worked with him, as did Orli Covitz and Hud Steinman. Kotto was so startled to see the two visitors, along with the pair of self-contained wentals, that he dropped a curved spanner. The tool clanged on the floor.

"We brought something unusual for you to study," Jess said. The two ovoid wental shapes rose up, one each behind Jess and Cesca, like tubes of cohesive gel.

"You call that 'unusual'?" Steinman said. "I'd try a few more emphatically descriptive terms myself."

Cesca stepped forward, smiling at Kotto. She had always been able to wring the best work out of him. "A long time ago, when your mother designated me as Speaker, I asked Roamers to find new ways to survive after the hydrogues prevented us from skymining. You truly answered that call, Kotto, and helped the clans survive those terribly austere years."

He was embarrassed, shuffling his feet. "I just did what I do best."

"That's exactly what we need from you now," Jess said. "And it's more important than ever before."

Intrigued, Orli moved closer to the shifting, flexible water shapes. "Can I touch them?" Once Jess assured her the strange water was safe, the girl touched her fingertip to the shimmering quicksilver skin, then plunged her hand in all the way up to the elbow.

"Don't you have a speck of caution, girl?" Steinman cried.

"When it's appropriate." Orli withdrew her hand. Her skin glistened for a moment, but then it dried as the droplets pulled themselves back into the self-contained wentals. The two shapes twisted, jiggled, then braided themselves together to form one large, bouncing shape.

Kotto observed, amazed and delighted.

Cesca spread her hands. "The wentals need your help to stand against the faeros."

"The faeros . . . I've been trying to figure that out, but I'm stumped. Thermal armor? Some kind of cold beam? Heat-resistant technologies?" Kotto grinned, trying to impress her. "In the meantime, we've been working on a gadget to use against the Klikiss. A melodic siren that could shut down the hive mind—"

"The *faeros*," Jess said, forcing the engineer to return his focus. "Maybe you just need the right raw materials." He stepped aside so the wental shape could lurch forward. "These wentals are here for you, as specimens. I promise they'll cooperate in any way possible."

Kotto blinked. "To do what? You mean . . . experiment with them?"

"Help them become effective weapons. We need you to be brilliant, Kotto." Cesca's eyes glowed warm with pride. "Do things that have never been done before—that's your specialty, isn't it?"

Kotto bent over to pick up the curved spanner he had dropped on the floor. He walked around the pulsing, shapeless mass of water, both perplexed and fascinated. "When have I ever let you down, Speaker?"

66 ☀ CALEB TAMBLYN

Even with the extra equipment he had brought down from low orbit, Caleb didn't stand much of a chance for long-term survival. But he felt less edgy, less desperate.

After he returned to the crashed escape pod with his last sled full of recovered material from the satellite, Caleb recharged his suitpack, used the air regenerator to refill his tanks with fresh oxygen cooked out of the ice, and finally went out to investigate the strange lights that glimmered across the landscape.

For hours now, the ice around the great meltdown crater had shimmered as if auroral curtains had somehow been locked into the frozen matrix. Caleb had never seen anything like it. In his years living in the water mines under the thick Plumas ice sheet, he had experienced some bizarre things, and these sparkling lights reminded him of the wentals he had seen.

He wasn't particularly keen to face another tainted elemental force like the one that had reanimated Karla Tamblyn. On the other hand, Jess and Cesca had used the power of wentals to restore the ruined water mines . . . so the exotic water entities couldn't be all bad. Besides, he wasn't in a position to be choosy.

As he trudged around the rim of the frozen crater, he saw more lights sparkling deep beneath the iron-gray lake. The whole disaster site seemed to be awakening. Far below, he saw liquid water, quicksilver streams that spread out in a network like a circulatory system. Runnels flowed of their own accord, changed direction, gathered strength.

Yes, these were wentals. He could tell. Standing on an uphill slope at the edge of the blasted rim, Caleb watched trickles of water flowing *upward* against gravity—directly toward him. The ground beneath him became uncertain as ice turned to slush. Clumsy in his protective boots, he tried to move away, but the frozen surface melted further, and he started to sink into a sort of icy quicksand.

After a moment of hesitation he decided not to flee. Jess had said that the wentals meant no harm. Caleb stopped in his tracks and braced himself. He stopped sinking.

The ankle-deep slushy water around his boots ran up his suit, covered his legs, then his waist. He felt tingling energy pass directly through the fabric, but there was no fundamental physical change in his cells. The wentals sensed him here. Were they trying to understand him?

Slowly, Caleb began to walk away from the crater back toward his cramped escape pod. The wentals followed him. His boots left clear footprints in the slushy ice. As he took more plodding steps, he saw identical footprints spontaneously forming *ahead of him*, a trail of ghostly steps marking a path all the way to his pod.

So, the wentals knew who he was and where he had come from.

Picking up the pace in the low gravity, Caleb returned to his small simple home. Silvery lines of liquefied water shot through the ice, and the glowing lights became brighter.

"Are you trying to communicate? What do you want?" he shouted into his suit radio. "By the Guiding Star, can you at least give me a hint?"

Either the wentals couldn't speak in a language he understood, or they couldn't pick up radio transmissions . . . or they simply chose not to respond. He waited outside the escape pod for a long time, watching the light show, but little changed.

When he cycled back through the airlock into his shelter, he was astonished to discover that all of his power sources, including his system batteries, were now fully charged. His gas exchangers operated at full capacity; he had plenty of air, water, and power. And with what he had retrieved from the satellite, he even had a little extra food.

The wentals were consciously trying to keep him alive. Caleb decided that, for once, he wasn't going to complain.

Talking with Rlinda Kett had gotten her worked up again, and Tasia was ready to launch every ship available with every weapon installed. She had wanted to charge after the Klikiss as soon as she got back with the Llaro refugees, but the faeros crisis on Theroc—and more recently, General Lanyan's stupid attack on the shipyards—had sidetracked everyone.

Nevertheless, she and Brindle had time to plan and prepare.

Admiral Willis joined them in the admin complex, where wallscreens reported the large number of vessels in spacedock and temporary repair facilities. After the surprise EDF strike here, Willis had declined to send her ships back into the Osquivel docks for a complete refit and reconditioning. "We can't afford to have them out of service right now, considering what might drop in our laps at any moment."

On the screen, Tasia spotted a fast space yacht entering the Osquivel system. Since it broadcast an appropriate Confederation ID signal, the ship triggered no alarms, but Tasia perked up when she saw the pilots listed as Patrick Fitzpatrick III and Zhett Kellum.

"I heard Fitzpatrick had gone over to your side," Admiral Willis mused. "*Our* side, I mean. Caused quite a scandal, considering who his grandmother is. Deserted the EDF and went off to points unknown. It could be useful to hear what he's got to say for himself."

The three went to meet the *Gypsy* as it docked. Since Fitzpatrick had been her nemesis during their training days on the lunar EDF base, Tasia couldn't wait to see the expression on his face. When the space yacht's hatch opened and he and Zhett stepped out arm in arm, his eyes went wide. "Tamblyn—and Robb Brindle? You've got to be kidding me."

Though years had passed, it was hard for her to forget all the mistreatment Fitzpatrick had heaped on her, how he had bullied her and sneered at her Roamer heritage. "Don't expect a big hug and a kiss on the cheek."

He looked away sheepishly. "Yeah, I was an ass back then—although you stood up for yourself perfectly well, Tamblyn."

"I keep him in line," Zhett teased. "Even the most insufferable jerks can be redeemed with a little hard work and patience—well, maybe not General Lanyan."

Tasia gave Zhett a disbelieving look. "I'll believe that when I see it." She was shocked to see how close the two stood, adoring each other. She and Robb had never been so sappy . . . at least, she hoped not.

Fitzpatrick turned to Willis with an automatic salute. "Admiral! Good to see you again. I heard you'd come to join the Confederation forces."

"You figured it out well before I did. It's not my place to throw stones and muddy up the water that's already under the bridge, to mix a handy metaphor." The older woman turned sternly to Tasia and Robb. "And it's not for either of these two to do, either."

Fitzpatrick explained how he had spoken to his grandmother on orders from King Peter, and that she would be coming to Theroc to work against Chairman Wenceslas. The

Admiral nodded. "It'll be all over for the Hansa soon. Now, if we can only find a fat lady to do the singing. And if General Lanyan stops poking his battleships where they don't belong."

Fitzpatrick smiled. "The General's taking a large group of battleships to fight the Klikiss on Pym. It's his next big mission."

"Now that's good news for a change!" Tasia's eyes brightened. "At least he's after the right enemy for once."

Robb saw her expression shift. "Don't even think about it, Tamblyn."

"Too late." She spun to face Willis. "Admiral, I've been ready to launch a similar offensive of our own. Seems to me that two fleets would be better than one." She shrugged. "Besides, we can't let the General do a half-assed job."

Willis blew air through her lips, considering. "It's certainly one way to wrap this mess up with ribbons and bows. But we'll need to depart immediately if we're going to fight alongside the EDF ships. It'd be damned embarrassing if we arrive *after* the General's already done the hard work."

"Shizz, I've been writing mission proposals for weeks now," Tasia said. "Let's get going."

Robb cautioned, "Even if we help him, don't expect the General to become a real convert to our cause."

Tasia couldn't stop grinning. "Either way, this is going to be fun."

68 ✺ SIRIX

Aboard the former flagship of Admiral Wu-Lin, Sirix inspected the work his robots had completed as part of the agreement with Chairman Wenceslas. Sirix had nearly finished the restoration of the stolen EDF vessels, including this Juggernaut, which had now been rechristened the *Thunder Child*. Surrendering these hard-won ships was a high price to pay, but in return he would receive thousands more black robots to replace all those that had recently been lost.

General Lanyan was taking this Juggernaut off to fight the Klikiss on Pym, and Sirix wanted the *Thunder Child* to function perfectly, so long as the humans fought against the sub-hive, rather than turning their weapons against the black robots.

"This alliance is advantageous to both sides," PD said brightly. The two compies had been returned to him as a goodwill gesture. He was proud of them; their behavior was exactly what he had hoped to achieve from DD.

"We're glad we suggested it," QT added.

But Sirix knew how quickly things could change. Humans had very short memories and limited attention spans. They could not hold a grudge long enough to achieve any significant historic impact. Throughout their existence, they had forgotten feuds at the drop of a hat, switched from enemies to allies and back again and again; it was dizzying. Conversely, Sirix and his robots had hated the Klikiss without wavering for more than ten thousand years.

"For now, the terms are indeed mutually beneficial. Come with me."

PD and QT dutifully followed him as he stalked down the Juggernaut's corridors. The black robots and the remaining Soldier compies were hard at work scrubbing decks, removing old bloodstains, repairing obvious damage from weapons blasts, like torn doors and smashed wall plates, which had occurred during the trapped human soldiers' final desperate hours.

"All EDF ships will be polished and ready to present to the Terran Hanseatic League by tomorrow," QT said. "In time for General Lanyan's departure."

"Good as new," PD added. "The humans will be very happy."

Such cosmetic repairs did not require a great deal of effort. The stolen ships already functioned correctly because the robots had maintained them properly. The work primarily involved cleaning, the reinstallation of unnecessary life-support systems, and the removal of any modifications that increased the power in the EDF engines. Sirix had no intention of giving the humans such advantages.

The next step — the reassembly of damaged ships and the construction of new robot vessels from the piles of un-cataloged space wreckage — was far more ambitious. Sirix had already dispatched the majority of his black robots to comb the orbital battlefield and round up any salvageable components of damaged battleships. From there, his robot workers speedily began assembling new ships. Though humans in spacesuits could perform this labor, the black robots were far more efficient at it.

Despite the supposed goodwill of the Hansa, however, any restored EDF ships could conceivably be turned against the robots. Sirix had taken measures to ensure that would not happen.

He and the two compies entered the *Thunder Child*'s engine room, where large stardrives filled the giant chambers. Stripped-down compies with specially modified maintenance programming had crawled deep inside the reaction chambers, then inserted tiny automated drones that would pass into the smaller and smaller constrictions of the drive train. They would sit like Trojan horses, waiting to be activated.

From the engineering console Sirix uploaded detailed readouts to learn where the surreptitious modifications had been made. EDF construction engineers and Hansa inspectors watched every part of the work, but they were easily fooled. Modifications could be so subtle, and the complex military vessels had so many weak points. . . .

While PD and QT observed attentively, Sirix confirmed that any one of the restored vessels could be detonated, whenever he chose.

Sirix was pleased. General Lanyan could prove the worth of these ships against the Klikiss at Pym. But if Chairman Wenceslas reneged on his agreement or ever attempted to trick and destroy the black robots . . . or if Sirix believed it would be to his advantage, he could scuttle the EDF fleet at any time.

69 ☀ SAREIN

When she met Deputy Cain and Captain McCammon in the rarely used canal levels beneath the Whisper Palace, Sarein was fully aware of what they were doing. She realized with a heavy heart that this would be no game with hooligan "dissidents" dropping subtle messages into newsnet broadcasts. The time had come to do something more concrete.

There was no polite word for plotting the overthrow of the Chairman, but it had to be done if they were to salvage anything of the Hansa. She wished she could have made Basil see the truth for himself.

Few people maintained the dank grottoes now that King Peter's private yacht had been decommissioned. Peter and Estarra's last colorful procession had been a spectacular event years ago, though it held dark memories for Sarein. That had been the day hydrogues attacked both Theroc and Corvus Landing, killing both of her brothers. Later, Sarein learned that Basil had also intended to blow up the King and Queen's boat, then blame the assassination on the Roamers.

For too long, she had called Estarra's suspicions nonsense. For too long she had refused to see the obvious. Not anymore.

She, Cain, and McCammon had concocted a cover story, suggesting that the royal yacht should be renovated so that King Rory could make a similar procession. After all (they would argue to Basil, if he should question them), why not invest Rory with at least as much majesty and grandeur in the people's minds as the former King and Queen had enjoyed? The Chairman wouldn't disagree with that.

The three conspirators followed the mossy stone walkway next to the calm, algae-filled canal. Both Cain and McCammon had checked the Whisper Palace's security surveillance systems to confirm that no one monitored these tunnels. Before long, Basil was sure to make up for the oversight, but right now he was understaffed and had too many other things to worry about.

"We have to remove him," Deputy Cain said in a low voice, barely more than a mumble. "Even the Archfather has been raising warning flags, as you might have noticed, changing some parts of his speeches, arguing about content. It's making the Chairman quite upset."

"The Archfather is a fool if he thinks the Chairman cares about his opinions," Sarein said. *Basil barely listens to me nowadays.*

"The Chairman is impervious to public opinion," Cain said. "He marches ahead no matter what, refusing to believe he might have to change course. Or admit he made a mistake."

"Like the way he's treated the Mage-Imperator?" Sarein said.

A grim McCammon fingered the dagger at his side. "Seventeen dead in total, humans and Ildirans, in that botched escape attempt on the Moon." He shook his head, deeply affected by what he had witnessed there. "And who can blame them? The Chairman has placed the Mage-Imperator in an untenable situation."

"We're all in an untenable situation—a dangerous one," Sarein said.

McCammon turned to her with great sincerity in his eyes. "I can't guarantee I'll be able to protect you, Sarein."

"I don't need protection."

"Yes, you do. The Chairman might once have loved you, but that won't save you anymore. Don't be oblivious."

Sarein perceived carefully hidden emotion in the guard captain's voice, and it made her anxious. "Please don't put yourself in danger on my account, Captain."

"I'll do what I have to." He sounded resentful.

"We all will," Cain insisted. "It's clear that one way or another this whole situation is going to implode soon. But protests in the streets can only accomplish so much. The cleanup crew ransacks businesses and arrests anyone who speaks out against the Chairman. It's all highly symptomatic of a repressive regime *in its last days*. History has plenty of examples for anyone who cares to look. I, for one, would rather be driving the vehicle of change than be crushed under its wheels."

McCammon said, "Chairman Wenceslas poses a clear and present danger to the survival of human civilization."

Since every moment they talked put them at significant risk, Sarein decided to get down to practicalities. "How do we go about it? Do we oust him? Force him to resign? We could detain him until we complete a governmental changeover."

Deputy Cain's answer was blunt, but inarguable. "Half measures won't succeed. The Chairman is sure to have taken precautions." He looked from Sarein to McCammon. "We have to kill him."

70 ☀ CHAIRMAN BASIL WENCESLAS

Closed off in his office, Basil reviewed surveillance tapes.

Again and again he studied records from the Whisper Palace, especially those taken on the night of the hydrogue attack on Earth. Too many questions remained about how Peter and Estarra had escaped, despite the tight security, despite putting Captain McCammon in charge of the King and Queen. Still, the upstart Peter had gotten away.

He had pinpointed that as the turning point in his problems, when the situation had grown substantially worse. This required much closer scrutiny, and alas, like so many things, Basil could count on no one to do it but himself. Everyone else was either criminally unreliable or actively plotting against him.

He'd kept his eyes on Sarein for some time now, at first as a precaution and then with keener interest. She and Deputy Cain "bumped into each other" altogether too often and in conveniently private places. Sarein also met with McCammon much more than was strictly necessary. That morning the three of them had even gone down into the old disused docks beneath the Whisper Palace, and Basil immediately requested the installation of hidden observation measures there, but it was too late for him to learn what they had been doing.

Captain McCammon? Deputy Cain? The answer was

obvious, even amusing in a way. Sarein used to be Basil's lover, but it had been a long time since he'd had sex with her. Now that the whole Spiral Arm had gone to hell, Basil no longer had time for such distractions. So naturally Sarein had turned to the next person on the list, the Deputy Chairman. She and Cain were having an affair. Or maybe it was with McCammon. Or both. She had been quite an ambitious woman.

While he didn't like the idea that he was being cuckolded, Basil was not surprised that they had succumbed to such a typical human weakness. In a way, he supposed, it kept Sarein from being so needy and demanding, and he could concentrate on important things. On the other hand, maybe it would be a good idea to devote a little more time to Sarein to keep her happy and loyal, more than just redecorating her quarters. He doubted that sending flowers would suffice. . . .

The Archfather was due to arrive momentarily for a review meeting, and Basil wanted to have words with him. Stern words. Tabling the Whisper Palace records for the time being, he compared the Archfather's firebrand delivery at the beginning of the Klikiss crusade with his decidedly lackluster recent performances.

As a result, the crowds were responding differently. Their reaction to Basil's agreement with the black robots had not been overwhelmingly enthusiastic. They hadn't been primed properly, and he could lay that directly at the Archfather's feet.

Originally, the man's fervor in demonizing the Klikiss had been truly inspired, but lately his passion had waned, as if he didn't believe his own sermons anymore—and that just wouldn't do. Basil needed to light a fire under the man's feet.

Alternatively, perhaps a preferable alternative, it was time to find someone else who could do his job. He saw no reason why King Rory couldn't fulfill both roles, as puppet secular leader and puppet religious leader. Two for the price of one. *Amen.* Basil smiled at the thought.

The Archfather arrived in his robes, clutching a printed copy of the new speech in his hands. His ringed knuckles were white, and he was clearly flustered, swelled with his own perceived importance. Basil covered a sigh, already expecting problems. Why was it so impossible for his underlings just to do what they were told?

The Archfather held up the printed document as if it were an accusation. "I cannot read this, Mr. Chairman."

Basil intentionally misunderstood. "Oh? Do you need a translator?"

"It will cause a revolt. It could create unnecessary bloodshed, and it's . . . it's *appalling*. This isn't what I believe. This isn't Unison."

"What is Unison? We define it however we like. That's the point of a state-sponsored religion. Don't believe your own script, Archfather."

The bearded man gave a sad, paternal shake of his head and looked down at the Chairman seated at his desk. "I have studied Unison for many years. Even as a child I followed and believed it. The Usk pogrom was a turning point for me. I review those awful images every night before I go to sleep, and every day when I wake up. That was *wrong*, Mr. Chairman. We committed those heinous acts in the name of religion, but it was not religion. Unison is being hijacked for political purposes — your purposes."

Basil could barely stop himself from laughing. "Unison was never a religion to *believe* in. It's a set of rituals to comfort people who are incapable of developing their own philosophy of life, death, and morality. Would you like to see the original classified Hansa memo defining it?"

"Unison is much more than that, if you would open your mind and your heart. Many people have."

"Don't get delusions. You're just a paid actor." Yes, indeed, he would have to do something about this man.

The Archfather flushed. "I am not just playing a role—I *am* the role." He set the papers down on the desk with finality. "I've done unsavory things in the past, but I cannot give this particular speech. I have more important things to say."

Basil kept control of his expression, though he was tempted to call in the guards and sit back while he ordered them to strangle the bearded fool. But he thought of a better option that dovetailed neatly with other goals he wanted to accomplish. Yes, this could be very effective indeed, even earthshaking.

"And what would you really like to say, Archfather?" He gave the man an encouraging smile. "Would you like to write your own speech?"

"You . . . you would allow me to do that?"

"Passion has been sorely lacking in your recent presentations. If you feel so strongly about this, then put your passion into your speech. I'll give you this one chance to make a difference." He could not imagine the sort of naïve nonsense the Archfather would end up blathering about. Holding hands and singing songs, probably.

The Archfather's eyes grew fiery. "I can put these people on the straight-and-narrow path—I can really do it."

"I'm sure you can. I'll postpone your next scheduled address for a week to give you all the time you need. Make it perfect. Break a leg. I don't want to be disappointed."

Basil was happy to let the man jump off a cliff. It was time to play more heavily on King Rory's messianic aspects anyway. The leader of Unison would have to step aside and let Rory play his role.

71 ✸ PRIME DESIGNATE DARO'H

When they discovered that Hyrillka Designate Ridek'h had vanished from the sheltered caves, the Ildirans were in an uproar. Daro'h and Yazra'h marched to the mine opening to stare out across the bright landscape, desperately searching for him.

In the sky, faeros fireballs cruised back and forth, always watching. The open plains below the foothills spread out in great blackened swaths. Smoke curled into the sky from numerous smoldering flames. The Prime Designate stared, but he saw no figure moving out there.

Adar Zan'nh emerged from the tunnels, accompanied by four equally worried guards. "There is no sign of him in any of the chambers."

Blind Tal O'nh sat cross-legged on the rocks outside, as he often did. Daro'h went to him to deliver the grim news. "Designate Ridek'h is missing, and I fear for his safety."

"I know where he is," O'nh said, unperturbed. "Ridek'h went to face the faeros incarnate in Mijistra."

Yazra'h was ready to go after the young man with her two Isix cats. "Then he will die. Why did you not stop him?"

Adar Zan'nh responded immediately. "My scout ships could comb the landscape and intercept the Designate before he reaches Rusa'h."

"And what would that accomplish?" The old tal's expression was implacable as he faced the harsh light of the suns. "Though Ridek'h is just a boy, he understands what the rest of us are afraid to admit: We grow weaker every day. We must take *action*. The Mage-Imperator is being held prisoner by the humans and cannot help us. Hundreds of warliners remain in a holding pattern outside the system, impotent. Nine more are trapped here. We have several days to lay our plans and prepare to act while Ridek'h makes his way to Mijistra. If we do not, the Designate's challenge and sacrifice will be wasted."

Daro'h clenched his fists in frustration. "Give me a course of action that is not futile, and I will take it immediately!"

"Call Tal Ala'nh to bring back our warliners," Yazra'h suggested, prowling back and forth like one of her cats. "If we launch a tremendous assault on Mijistra and seize back our city, it would deal a profound blow to the faeros."

The Adar's face was troubled. He had already watched most of his warliners obliterate themselves in an effort to weaken the hydrogues, and many had also been lost against the faeros. "They would destroy our Solar Navy—to no purpose. As Adar Kori'nh showed us, sacrifice must not be pointless." He turned away. "Yet now it seems Designate Ridek'h is intent on throwing his life away."

"Even failure in battle is preferable to this endless hiding!" Yazra'h cried. "Look what the faeros have done to our people, our world—our Empire. We must fight them. We must do something truly significant."

Adar Zan'nh spoke slowly, an idea clearly forming in his mind. "We cannot win a direct combat—against *them*. The faeros are too powerful. But they are not our only adversary."

Daro'h came to a conclusion he should have thought of much sooner. "The Solar Navy cannot fight the faeros, but they can go to Earth and free the Mage-Imperator."

"Would that not mean going up against the entire human military fleet?" Yazra'h asked.

Zan'nh was shaking his head. "I understand the Earth Defense Forces. I am familiar with their ships, their command structure, their placement at Earth. If I joined my nine warliners with Tal Ala'nh's cohort, my force could strike swiftly, rescue the Mage-Imperator, and depart without ever fully engaging their military."

"We could have the Mage-Imperator back . . ." Yazra'h breathed.

The Prime Designate began to feel the surge of possibilities. "But how do we get the warliners away from Ildira? The fireballs *will* intercept and destroy them as soon as they try to move."

Tal O'nh got slowly to his feet. "Let the boy make his attempt. We do not know what he might accomplish. He may die, but he will preoccupy Rusa'h long enough for us to take extreme action." He turned toward the Adar as if he could watch the expressions play across his face.

Zan'nh stared stonily. "An extreme action . . . something that Adar Kori'nh might have taken, provided there is a chance it could work." He faced Daro'h, nodding slowly. "Prime Designate, we cannot waste our warliners, but we do possess another playing piece. When the tal first discussed it, the prospect seemed too terrible to consider."

"We must consider everything," Daro'h said.

"What is more terrible than granting the faeros free rein over Ildira?" Yazra'h asked.

Zan'nh looked up into the sky. "Our shipyards and spacedocks are hanging in Ildiran orbit—massive, unoccupied industrial facilities."

The Prime Designate remained puzzled. "They are not armed. They cannot maneuver. How can the shipyards help us?"

"We know Rusa'h is ensconced in the Prism Palace," Zan'nh pointed out. "We have a chance of destroying him, or at least hurting him, if we strike a powerful enough blow. But first we must accept an unspeakable reality: We will never get Mijistra back."

72 ☀ RLINDA KETT

This was really stupid, Rlinda knew. Unconscionably, ridiculously stupid. If BeBob tried to do something like this, she would have sealed him in an airlock chamber until he came to his senses.

But Rlinda did it anyway. The *Voracious Curiosity* was fully fueled and supplied, and she had checked out the new weapons systems. BeBob was due to leave on his next standard trading run, this time to a place called Eldora, so she waited until he left. She flew off when he couldn't do anything to stop her, leaving only a brief message for him to find when he got back. It was the only way.

She already knew she would regret not asking for his help if—when—the situation got hairy, but BeBob's new *Blind Faith* was too perfect, too clean, and he was just too damned proud of it. She was taking a huge risk and didn't want to worry about anything but herself and her ship.

She would find Davlin Lotze, if he was still alive.

Though she had filed no flight plan, BeBob would figure out where she was going. It was fairly obvious. Nevertheless, she hoped to be back before he could do anything equally stupid. . . .

Though Llaro had been a Hansa colony, it wasn't one of her usual destinations. Not a terribly scenic place, but Rlinda didn't plan to do any sightseeing. From space, the world looked as if it had been used roughly, scraped clean, and left exhausted.

Her planetary database identified the site of the former colony. There, she found an extensive complex spreading for many kilometers, a maze of towers and tunnels and incomprehensible structures. "If you're down there, Davlin, I'm going to have a hell of a time finding you," she muttered.

She reminded herself again that this was a really stupid idea, but she owed the man too much to give up now. Davlin had saved her too many times, even though she had done her best to return the favor.

Opening a channel on the *Curiosity*'s comm system, she broadcast on a private EDF frequency—one that Davlin would know and monitor, if he could. "Hello, Davlin? Davlin Lotze. If you're there, please respond. This is Captain Rlinda Kett, cavalry of one. Remember me?"

From the size of the infestation down there, she wasn't sure how Davlin would get to a transceiver, but if it was humanly possible, she was willing to bet he'd do it. In fact, Davlin might even have found a way to escape on his own. Via transportal wall, maybe? In that case, he wouldn't be here anymore . . . and then she didn't know what she'd do.

Alert, she circled overhead, unrealistically hoping that the Klikiss wouldn't notice her. She kept herself ready at all times, prepared to throw the *Curiosity* into an immediate retreat. Then, unexpectedly, she received a signal on the EDF band. She did not recognize the voice. The strange tone sounded synthesized and mechanical, not human.

"Captain Kett."

A chill went up her spine. "Who is this? I'm trying to contact Davlin Lotze."

Suddenly, a swarm of small Klikiss ships came toward her, hundreds of identical component vessels. They launched from the colony structures below while others swooped down from orbit, rapidly converging on her poor little *Curiosity*. "Oh, crap!"

It was time to check out the new weapons the Roamer shipyards had installed. She shot jazer blasts at all the bug vessels that swirled around her, and in less than a minute she had obliterated a dozen of them; high-velocity projectiles smashed another seven. But the Klikiss ships kept coming. There were far too many of them.

She accelerated, trying to ram her way out. "Getting a little crowded around here." Two of the component craft caromed off her hull as they attempted to evade her charge. Red alarm lights flashed on the *Curiosity*'s status indicator array, and sparks spat out of the copilot's control panel. Good thing BeBob wasn't there. He'd be panicked right now.

"Captain Kett, please land."

She realized then that the Klikiss component ships could have wiped her out, but the precise shots had merely crippled her engines. As she descended, alien component ships surrounded her, herding her. She had about as much maneuverability as a square asteroid. She used up all of her favorite curses on the way down and made up a few more before the *Curiosity* skidded across the dirt and rocks, clipping one of the termite-mound towers.

Crash webbing exploded around her, pinning her to her seat while cushioning foam spurted against her body. She spluttered and cursed again as the *Curiosity* came to a grudging halt. The bottom hull was ripped, the engines wrecked. "Oh, dammit a hundred times over!"

Outside, thousands of Klikiss emerged from their tunnels and towers, scuttling toward her.

This wasn't exactly how Rlinda had pictured the mission ending. She considered launching an emergency buoy into space with a brief last message for BeBob, but that would just be treacly sentiment, and she couldn't bring herself to do it.

While peeling off the crash webbing and smearing away the soft, slimy foam that had saved her life, she heard scraping and scratching on the outside of the ship. Even though the lower hull was already compromised, she couldn't bear to see the bugs rip open her beloved ship as if it were nothing more than a food package. That would just be too much.

Opening the hatch, she stared out upon a sea of polished chitin, segmented limbs, and faceted eyes. Offensive odors filled the air—like a mixture of ammonia, sulfur dust, rotting meat, and vomit. Then she saw an old woman standing among the creatures. A human woman. Leaving the insects behind, the stranger approached the *Curiosity*'s hatch. "Captain Kett, I'm Margaret Colicos. I've been sent to meet you."

Rlinda blinked in disbelief. It took her a long moment to form a response, and she couldn't decide which part she found most astonishing. She had spent a lot of time in the ruins of Rheindic Co with Davlin, helping him search for any sign of the Colicos team. "I tried to find you years ago!" She glanced nervously at the insects. "I'm looking for Davlin Lotze now. I think he was abandoned here on Llaro. Any idea where he might be?"

Margaret hesitated, then said, "Davlin is here . . . but he's not the Davlin you're expecting."

73 ☀ CHAIRMAN BASIL WENCESLAS

The looming black robot seemed to fill much of the Chairman's office with his armored body. Captain McCammon and three heavily armed royal guards stood at the doorway, visibly concerned, their weapons drawn and ready to fire if the robot should make any threatening moves.

Basil leaned back in his chair, entirely unafraid. He had plenty of things to worry about, but Sirix wanted something from him, and the Chairman wanted something in return. "The EDF ships you returned all passed inspection, and General Lanyan has departed this morning on schedule."

"Your human inspectors were very thorough. All systems will perform properly," Sirix said in his buzzing voice. "Many of my black robots would like to have gone along on the mission, to assist in destroying the Pym subhive."

"I understand, but the General was quite adamant."

Basil wasn't sure whether Lanyan had been more worried about the robots or the Klikiss themselves. He doubted Sirix would be so stupid as to betray them, since the Hansa manufacturing facilities had not yet delivered the replacement robots Sirix so desperately needed. Nevertheless, Basil had acceded to the General's demand; only human soldiers accompanied the battle group off to Pym.

"Your robots' work so far has been acceptable." He leaned forward and put his elbows on the deskscreen. "I see no reason why we cannot proceed with our arrangement, provided I receive daily updates on your progress on the ships."

Sirix remained motionless. "We are on schedule. We will deliver five rebuilt EDF ships to you within seven days, in exchange for five hundred new comrades."

"Our modified facilities are ready to begin the assembly process, but we will carefully control the release of all completed robots."

Sirix backed away. "We recognize your need for caution and will abide by your rules, Chairman Wenceslas."

Basil tapped his fingers on the polished desktop, remembering the public's lukewarm response to his announced alliance with Sirix. That needed to change. "We should have an event to commemorate the release of the first black robots. Mr. Cain, see to it."

His deputy remained seated in his usual chair off to the side. "An excellent suggestion. Perhaps you should give the speech personally? Your presence would make the people understand the real business reasons for this operation."

He frowned at Cain, not sure why he seemed so interested. Basil didn't often like to step into the spotlight, but maybe this wasn't something he wanted to place on the shoulders of King Rory. "All right. Make sure there's appropriate fanfare, positive media coverage — schedule it for a few days after the Archfather's next rally." (And what an interesting event *that* was going to be!) He maintained his calm expression. "We need the right sort of spin on this new relationship to overshadow the complaints of Freedom's Sword." He narrowed his eyes. "Any further progress on capturing their ringleaders, Mr. Cain?"

"None, sir. They are extremely clever."

Colonel Andez appeared in the doorway of his office and gave a smart salute. When McCammon tried to block her entrance, she gave him an indignant glare. "I have important news for the Chairman." Not surprisingly, McCammon did not like Andez or her cleanup crew, who had begun to usurp many long-standing duties of the royal guard. As Basil had given her more and more responsibility, Andez had definitely risen to the task.

Basil stood up. "Deputy Cain, Captain McCammon, please escort Sirix to the factory. In our new spirit of openness and cooperation, let him perform whatever inspections he desires." He motioned for Andez to enter his office. "In the meantime, I need to speak with the colonel in private."

When they were alone in the office, Basil drew out the silence. She did not blurt questions or show any sign of impatience; she simply waited, looking at the Chairman with her steely gaze. Finally, he allowed himself a smile. She had passed his little test. "Very well, Colonel," he said. "What do you have to report?"

"It's Former Chairman Maureen Fitzpatrick, sir. She plans to betray you to our enemies, perhaps even resume her old position."

Basil hadn't expected this at all, not even an inkling. "Explain."

"When you first aired your suspicions of the former Chairman, we established covert surveillance on her mansion. You will be interested to know that she recently had a visitor: her grandson, Patrick Fitzpatrick."

Now Basil was incensed. The young man was a deserter who had publicly denounced the Hansa and blamed the Roamer ekti embargo on EDF atrocities. Not only had King Peter used Fitzpatrick's confession to spread sedition throughout the Hansa, Freedom's Sword had used him as their poster child. "What was he doing here?"

"Recruiting her for the Confederation. The former Chairman intends to defect to Theroc and join King Peter."

"Is everyone in the Spiral Arm hell-bent on stabbing me in the back?" Once retired, a Hansa Chairman was supposed to be respectful toward the person currently in charge, not meddle in politics or voice objections to the current government. His immediate predecessor, Ronald Palomar, had led the Hansa for seventeen lackluster years, and when Basil took over, Palomar quietly and gratefully disappeared from public view. In fact, Basil didn't even know if the man was still alive. But Maureen Fitzpatrick had led the Hansa for only nine years before she chose to retire; she had been out of office for nearly a quarter of a century, and now she wanted to come back? The power-hungry bitch.

"Contact Admiral Pike. I need his ships to intercept the former Chairman before she can do something stupid that irreparably damages the Hansa."

"Yes, Mr. Chairman." She turned briskly to leave.

Pike might have objections, but he would do exactly as he was ordered. After all, Basil held the man's family hostage, as well.

In addition to their primary duties of reassembling EDF ships, the Chairman had secretly asked the black robots to perform a strange yet vital task in Earth orbit. Sirix did not question his reasons, since the human leader had offered him an additional one hundred new robots in exchange for this minimal service. Humans often did not make sense.

After inspecting the frenetic ship-repair operations, Sirix flew a small vehicle to where five black robots tinkered with a long-mothballed weapons satellite, a directed-energy projector abandoned in orbit more than a century ago. Basil Wenceslas had given them access to detailed schematics and new components.

Sirix was perplexed at the extent of the man's trust in him. Was this some inexplicable test of the robots' reliability? He could find no logical explanation for what they had been instructed to do.

The Hansa Chairman had asked Sirix to put his "most reliable" robots on the assignment; obviously, the man did not understand that all black robots were equally trustworthy, since they shared the same programming, the same goals. They would never betray each other, as humans so often did.

Now, floating in black vacuum with the immense cloud-swathed sphere of Earth beneath them, the five robots extended articulated limbs and attached the requested tools to the large orbiting device. They expanded and tested new circuitry, reconfigured and polished the focusing mirrors, replaced the long-depleted power sources. Out of common caution, they added their now-standard safeguards to disable the equipment if anyone should attempt to turn the weapons satellite against the black robots themselves. But Sirix didn't think that was what the Chairman had in mind.

With meticulous care, the robot workers removed all traces of corrosion, fixed a circuit board marred by micrometeoroid impacts, then ran all necessary diagnostic routines. The systems were quite primitive, but they would work.

When the control programming was set to active standby, ready to be used at a moment's notice, the robots withdrew from the forgotten satellite. Their mission was complete.

The high-energy beam was aimed down at the Palace District. Sirix had already calculated how much damage such a strike could cause — its maximum output was enough to obliterate the whole of the Whisper Palace and the Hansa Headquarters. He was curious to learn what the Chairman intended to do with it.

He had long suspected that Basil Wenceslas was not a completely rational man.

75 ☀ FORMER CHAIRMAN MAUREEN FITZPATRICK

Maureen knew how to work the system, how to doctor paperwork, and how to slip under the radar of pencil pushers and lackluster bureaucrats. Old Jonas was a master at inputting vague and uninteresting answers on the clearance forms. Nobody would guess the real reason she was leaving Earth.

Though she had retired voluntarily ages ago, the former Chairman maintained a thriving career as a consultant and adviser. She sat on the boards of numerous companies, think tanks, and foundations; every week she appeared at charity functions, commencement ceremonies, and steering-committee gatherings. She had more consulting work than she could possibly finish. But life was all about choices, and Maureen Fitzpatrick had to put her considerable skills to their most advantageous use. She had made her decision.

In the months following Patrick's stint as a prisoner of war, she had worried about her poor grandson, sure that he'd been brainwashed by the Roamers. But now, much to her chagrin, Maureen realized that the young man had been right after all. Chairman Wenceslas was the threat, not the Roamers or the Confederation.

Before her departure, she spent days making preparations, leaving a few little surprises for Patrick in case the deal went south. She had learned never to underestimate the likelihood of a worst-case scenario, or the amazing number of ways that things could get screwed up.

Maureen wandered through her mansion, staring at all the things she knew and loved. She'd never had much patience for insipid nostalgia, yet here she was acting in a way that would have sparked her scorn if she'd observed it in anyone else. At first she wanted to crate art objects and mementos to take with her, but Maureen quickly realized that unless she commissioned a whole cargo hauler, she could never take everything she wanted. In the end, frustrated, she made a command decision and left everything behind. As part of her compensation package for services rendered, she might even bill King Peter for all she had sacrificed.

Besides, if she straightened out the mess, she'd be back soon anyway.

With no particular fanfare, her small ship flew away from Earth's security zone and past the EDF patrol ships around the Moon. Her ship had a registration number, but no name. It amused her that her grandson had christened the stolen vessel the *Gypsy;* despite his upbringing, the boy had a soft heart and a soft head. Maureen had always considered the practice of naming a ship—as if it were some kind of a pet—frivolous.

Nevertheless, Patrick had surprised her. He had certainly begun to shine.

Ostensibly, the private yacht's flight plan said that she was going to meet with an industrial contractor; the asteroid belt industries needed a firm management hand. Her entourage consisted of twenty people. Jonas had served at her side since her days as a deputy division head overseeing nothing larger than a continent; Maureen had kept him around forever because it was so difficult to find competent and reliable employees. Her pilot was also loyal, as were the other assistants in this hand-picked group. If she had to take on a role equivalent to Hansa Chairman, Maureen needed her best people with her.

Everyone aboard knew where they were really going and what they were giving up. She had been surprised at how easily they all agreed to leave—a clear barometer of just how bad things were on Earth. Since she led a privileged life, Maureen had little exposure to most of the Chairman's ruthless crackdowns; her companions, though, had seen the writing on the wall.

Her ship followed their documented course until they reached the asteroid belt complex. The pilot spoke over the intercom to the passenger compartment. "Ready to deviate from the flight plan, Madame Chairman. Should I power up the Ildiran stardrive?"

"Yes, let's head off to Theroc before anyone notices." Patrick was waiting there for her, and she was ready to *go*.

But nothing ever went as smoothly as expected.

The pilot transmitted back with clear anxiety in his voice. "Two EDF Mantas are coming to intercept. Admiral Pike insists that we stand down and surrender."

"What is his problem?" Maureen pushed her way to the cockpit. "You may have to pull some fancy evasive maneuvers to get us out of here."

Little beads of sweat sparkled on the pilot's forehead. "I can't fly like a smuggler or a blockade runner, ma'am."

"We haven't done anything wrong, Captain. Your service record is completely clean—I checked. This must just be a routine stop. Apparently, the EDF doesn't have anything better to do."

He pointed to the bright traces on his navigation screens.

"They were waiting for us, Madame Chairman. There's plenty of other traffic, but they're heading straight toward us. This is no routine stop."

Maureen felt cold. Somehow the Chairman had learned of her plans. Paranoid bastard! "I'm going to have to ask you to bend a few rules. How soon can you align our vector and engage the stardrive?"

"Right away. I was about to—"

"Then do it."

He swallowed hard. "There'll be hell to pay when we get back."

She frowned at him. "You know we're not coming back."

"Right you are."

The two Mantas raced closer at full speed. She said rather urgently, "It would be a good idea if we got out of here before they're in weapons range."

The pilot engaged the stardrive, and her space yacht leaped across the light-years. With a mocking gesture at the screens, Maureen waved goodbye. So much for the worst-case scenario.

Her staff was amazed that the EDF had tried to prevent them from leaving Earth, that they had run for their lives and gotten away from the bad guys. They all felt as if they were in an action vidloop. A lifetime of government service had given them few opportunities for excitement. Now they had no doubt that Chairman Wenceslas was afraid of what Maureen might do! She could tell that they were all quite pleased with themselves, especially Jonas.

After two days of travel, the pilot disengaged their stardrive and arrived without incident at the edge of the

Theron system, punctual as always. She sent out a long-range message as they made their way into the inner system. She was sure Patrick and his Roamer wife had arranged to roll out the red carpet. "This is former Chairman Maureen Fitzpatrick. Can somebody manage an escort and a reception committee? We're on our way in."

Maureen wished she had at least brought some of the best bottles from her wine cellar so they could toast their new lives. She had never tasted a Theron vintage before, but she doubted it could measure up to her private collection. Nevertheless, the green-and-blue planet looked very welcoming as it grew larger with their approach.

Two EDF Mantas roared in from either side, so close they nearly collided with the yacht. Maureen lost her balance and fell to the deck, grabbing for a handhold. The pilot squawked in panic and began to fly erratically.

Admiral Pike's face appeared on the comm screen. "Chairman Fitzpatrick, we warned you not to flee. I have orders from Chairman Wenceslas to prevent you from committing a treasonous act. I cannot allow you to reach Theroc."

Maureen was livid. They must have known her destination from the start. She opened the communications channel, leaned close to the screen, and brought to bear all of the fury that had gained her fame as the old Battleaxe. "Admiral, you are no longer in Hansa-controlled space, and you have no jurisdiction here. My ship has arrived at the behest of King Peter and the Confederation."

Pike's squarish face was stony, but she could see a troubled glimmer of uncertainty there. "Maybe so, but I cannot allow you to proceed."

A cluster of ships had already launched from Theroc: Roamer vessels and even a single Manta, apparently one of

Admiral Willis's battle group. As she expected, Patrick was out there flying the *Gypsy*. Now that the Confederation reception committee had seen the threatening EDF ships, they increased acceleration.

Maureen responded to Pike with a cold smile. "Admiral, if you try to take me prisoner, I will create such a shitstorm of scandal your great-grandchildren will still be cringing from it. Cut your losses and go home. You don't belong here."

"Neither do you, ma'am. Unfortunately, the Chairman's orders are clear."

The two Mantas circled around before the Confederation ships could close the distance. The pilot looked to her frantically for instructions. Maureen assumed the EDF ships were going to use a tractor beam to seize her yacht, but instead the two Mantas pointed their bow weapons clusters at her. She saw their jazer banks powering up.

"He has my family hostage," Pike said apologetically. "He has all of our families."

Maureen opened her mouth in disbelief, and all words suddenly left her.

The Mantas opened fire.

The explosion flared on the *Gypsy*'s cockpit screens as he accelerated toward his grandmother's ship. Though Patrick demanded all possible speed from his engines, he knew he would be too late.

For days now, he had been filled with optimism. King Peter had pressed him for details on his grandmother's reaction to the invitation. "Is there any chance you misinterpreted her answer?"

"She'll come. She knows the Chairman has to be stopped. She'll be a strong advocate for the Confederation, and she'll convince what's left of the Hansa." He looked forward to being on the same side with her; the Chairman wouldn't stand a chance against their combined skills and determination.

But now his hopes vanished in a sparkling cloud of shrapnel, incandescent gases, and vented atmosphere. Somewhere among that wreckage, curling and drifting out in empty space, was all that remained of his grandmother, her crew, her companions.

"Damn you!" Patrick shouted into the comm system. "Murderers!" Before he knew what he was doing, he had accelerated violently toward Admiral Pike's Mantas. He needed no more reason to hate the Hansa, hate the Chairman, and hate the dark and twisted abomination the EDF had become.

The pair of cruisers hung in space, their weapons ports

still hot as the *Gypsy* rushed toward them. He simply could not let the EDF continue its atrocities with impunity.

In the copilot's seat, Zhett was white with shock, yet sharp enough to realize the danger. "Fitzie, they'll blow us out of the sky — just like they did to her."

"They won't," Patrick growled, sounding more confident than he felt. But this was a fool's response, and he knew it.

To his surprise, the rest of the Confederation reception committee followed him, also spoiling for a fight. Maybe all together they did have enough combined firepower.

Oddly, though, Admiral Pike's heavily armored ships did not engage. The older man appeared on the comm screen, and he clearly recognized Patrick — probably because his face had been displayed so prominently on the Most Wanted boards.

"I'm sorry." Pike sounded sincere. "Believe me, Mr. Fitzpatrick, I had no choice."

Patrick took several potshots with the *Gypsy*'s minimal weapons, which were far too insignificant to cause harm to either Manta. Ignoring the provocation, the two EDF ships turned and accelerated away before any of the Confederation ships could catch up with them.

As soon as the Mantas were gone, Patrick felt the echoing emptiness of shock. He dug inside himself, found his hot anger again, and clung to it. She had come here because *he* had asked her to. She had been doing the right *thing*!

In dismay, he turned the space yacht around and headed back toward where his grandmother's ship had been obliterated. With tears in her dark eyes, Zhett leaned close to touch him, but she found no words. Patrick sat back stiffly, clutching the piloting controls and staring straight ahead, not sure what he was searching for. A few sparkles of cooling wreckage were the only trace that remained of the woman who had raised him.

77 ☀ HYRILLKA DESIGNATE RIDEK'H

The young man walked across open country in the unrelenting daylight. Normally he would have taken comfort from the seven suns, but now their light revealed only how bleak and empty Ildira was. He felt no weariness or despair, only a determination to do what he had been born to do, to follow the destiny that had been handed to him. Though he was an untried Designate, Ridek'h meant to hold the faeros incarnate accountable.

Perhaps he would even earn himself a place in the *Saga of Seven Suns* . . . if any rememberers survived to write it.

He rested when he needed to, always heading toward the majestic capital city that his people had been forced to abandon. Blackened hillsides and charred fields bore mute testament to the brutality of the fiery elementals. Up in the sky, the ever-present fireballs drifted like ominous predatory fish. Ridek'h was sure they saw him, but he did not hide.

The hot glare made his eyes sting with tears, but he pressed onward—for days.

He found several crowded refugee camps, and none of the people he talked to believed they were safe. Even though most Ildirans did not know who Ridek'h was by sight, they understood that he belonged to the noble kith. They all begged to know when Mage-Imperator Jora'h would return to save Ildira.

Ridek'h straightened. These people deserved an answer, the best one he could give. "The Prime Designate and Adar Zan'nh will find a way to bring him back." He paused, giving them an intent look. "And the Ildiran people must do everything possible to help."

They murmured their agreement. Designate Ridek'h remained with them for a short while longer before moving on. Even if he failed on this audacious—or foolhardy—mission, he hoped to inspire Prime Designate Daro'h and all Ildirans by his example. He refused to believe that his actions would be fruitless. This was the stuff of legends.

He understood that he wasn't likely to survive—he and Tal O'nh had discussed that at great length—but the faeros incarnate would certainly remember the encounter. The young Designate would get through to him, even if it cost him his life. Rusa'h could not keep inflicting such horror on people—*his* people!—without being challenged.

Finally, he reached the outskirts of glorious Mijistra. Fires had run rampant through the streets, charring and melting the crystal, stone, and metal structures. Warehouses and habitation complexes were gutted, covered with soot. The seven symmetrical streams that had flowed up the elliptical hill overlooking the city were bone dry.

Ahead, the magnificent Prism Palace, with its bulbous

domes and tall spires, minarets, and transparent shafts, glowed with a dazzling, hateful light, like a gem in a furnace. That was his goal. Faeros incarnate Rusa'h waited there for him. The young man was afraid—he was not a fool—but the mad Designate had not killed him in their previous encounter.

Head held high, Ridek'h entered the city without any pretense of hiding while a dozen more fireballs swirled overhead, their flames brightening. He walked through the dazzling streets, remembering the glory of the Ildiran Empire under Mage-Imperator Jora'h. Heat shimmered in the air, reflecting off the numerous flat, mirrored surfaces.

He followed the long, winding pilgrims' path toward the Prism Palace. Supplicants had once taken this road on their way to behold the Mage-Imperator. His own purpose was not to submit to the mad Designate, but to indicate his resolve by facing the hardship and doing what was necessary, despite the pain.

The faeros incarnate came out to stop him before he could enter the Palace. Clothed in flames, his skin incandescent from the living thermal energy that permeated his body, Rusa'h stood blazing in front of the arched entrance and faced the young Designate. His eyes were brighter than novas.

"You know who I am." The boy spoke first. "I am the Hyrillka Designate."

"*I* am the Hyrillka Designate," Rusa'h roared, flames flickering from his mouth.

Ridek'h flinched but did not back away. Though he expected to be incinerated at any moment, he would at least speak the message he had come here to deliver. "If you were a true Hyrillka Designate, I would not need to come here in order to beg for the lives of the Hyrillkan people." He spread his arms and added an accusatory tone. "Look around you at the empty city. All Ildirans have fled Mijistra. Is this how you lead, how you represent our race? The people of Hyrillka — supposedly *your* people — are being decimated by the faeros. Have you visited the burned refugee camps to which they fled for safety? Have you touched the blackened bones of your own former subjects?"

Rusa'h seemed to waver. "The faeros do what they must."

In that answer, the boy Designate received his first ink-ling that the faeros might not be entirely under Rusa'h's con-trol. This startled him. He had believed, perhaps falsely, that the fireballs were in the madman's thrall. But what if the fallen Designate did not have as much power over the fiery creatures as Ildirans had all assumed?

"Why are you *allowing* so many of your people to be killed? Would a true Mage-Imperator allow it?" He took a step closer, defying the heat. "Neither is this how a Desig-nate cares for his subjects. Why do you not protect them?" He stood there before the flaming man. "Both as Designate and as Mage-Imperator, you have failed them absolutely."

Ridek'h had intended to challenge the faeros incarnate, to anger him and make him *think*. He realized he had suc-ceeded in at least one of these goals when the fires around Rusa'h intensified with rage.

The hovering fireballs plunged down toward the Prism Palace.

With her special sensitivity to changes in the *thism*, Osira'h felt the disruption from Mijistra like a roar in her mind: vibrations, stresses . . . danger. She knew that Designate Ridek'h had arrived at the Prism Palace and confronted the faeros incarnate.

She raced down a mine shaft to gather her brothers and sisters, but they had sensed the threat too and were already running toward her. No one but the half-breed children of the green priest Nira could turn the *thism* against the flames that Ridek'h was facing.

Everyone else had already given up on the young Designate, assuming him to be dead. Adar Zan'nh and Prime Designate Daro'h had set events in motion that could not be halted. Tal O'nh was on his way up to the orbiting shipyards with a very small crew; together they would create an incredible diversion that should buy Adar Zan'nh all the time he needed to get his ships away unharmed.

"Concentrate!" Rod'h urged.

"We need to protect Ridek'h long enough for him to get away," Osira'h agreed.

With his impetuous mission to Mijistra, the young Hyrillka Designate had unwittingly done his part in the bold and risky plan to rescue the Mage-Imperator, and now the half-breed children would not let go of him.

Sitting in a circle on the stone floor, the children joined hands and cast the *thism* net in their minds far and wide to create a sort of shield for the young man. Riding the *thism* forward, they found Mijistra, the Prism Palace . . . and brave Ridek'h, as he faced the flaming fury of the mad Designate, whose heat made the air blister and shimmer.

While he had the boy trapped, Rusa'h attempted to rip away his soulfire and add the fresh life force to the growing faeros — but Osira'h and her siblings cut him off. Combined, they protected the young Designate's *thism* and all the threads that surrounded him with a sort of mental insulation, making him impervious to the first wave of attack.

Rusa'h blasted his victim, but he was unable to crash through the unexpected barrier. When the mad Designate could not seize the soulfire he wanted, he was momentarily stunned. But if the faeros incarnate should choose to lash out with physical, incinerating fire . . .

Run! Osira'h shouted to the young Designate through her mind. *Come back to us!*

Ridek'h heard them, but echoes of the mental shout also resonated through the barrier, and the faeros incarnate realized that someone was helping his victim. Burning Rusa'h stood nonplussed at the blackened dry mouth where the seven streams converged, curious about what could be powerful enough to prevent him from taking what he wanted.

Run, Ridek'h!

Osira'h caught a ripple of the young man's thoughts, feeling his resolve as he faced death, his satisfaction that he had accomplished what he had wanted to. She shouted out again, penetrating his awareness with a glimmer of the plan that was under way to destroy the mad Designate and divert the faeros. *Your work is done, Ridek'h. Go — we will help you escape.*

Reeling, the boy scrambled from the blazing Prism Palace while the faeros incarnate was momentarily paralyzed with surprise. Ridek'h ran headlong down the well-trodden path that led away from the hill.

Nira's five children found the strength to maintain their shield, but now the mad Designate came after them along the mental pathways. Tracing their *thism* connections, Rusa'h used all his strength to lash out at Osira'h and her siblings. But they thwarted him, diverting his concentration using the protective powers of *thism* and the verdani telink, as well as their own synergy.

Rusa'h bellowed in their minds, demanding to take all of their soulfires for the salvation of the Ildiran people. Osira'h could feel him battering at her mind, trying to rip information from her. The faeros incarnate sensed something was about to happen.

And young Ridek'h kept running.

In her mind, Osira'h felt the mad Designate become suspicious. He had caught a glimpse of the trap about to be sprung.

She clenched her brother's hand tightly. They had to keep Rusa'h busy for at least a short while longer. The boy Designate had far to go before he could hope to escape the impending holocaust. The timing would be close.

Adar Zan'nh was ready to launch his ships. Prime Designate Daro'h remained in the cave shelter, prepared to seize back the Empire. Up in the shipyards Tal O'nh had implemented the initial stages of his plan.

The end was coming.

Somehow, in their efforts to protect Ridek'h, fear and anticipation trickled through the barriers the children had set up around themselves. A few revelatory thoughts slipped free—and the faeros incarnate caught a hint of what the Prime Designate planned to do. He knew his danger.

Osira'h could hear his flaming roar throughout the web of *thism*.

By the time he unleashed his fury from the Prism Palace, Rusa'h was no longer concerned about one defiant boy, but his own survival.

79 ☀ GENERAL KURT LANYAN

General Lanyan had already faced the subhive on Pym with a small group of soldiers, and he had no interest in repeating the escapade, but Chairman Wenceslas hadn't given him a choice. So, he kept reminding himself that this was an opportunity to show what he was made of. At least this time he had a strong enough military force to really do some damage to the bugs.

Though he was glad to be at the helm of a Juggernaut again, feeling secure in the giant ship's mass and armor, he still had plenty of concerns. In a single Manta, Admiral Diente had been too easily overwhelmed. With the *Thunder Child* and seven accompanying Mantas, though, Lanyan had a great deal of firepower, including atmospheric-dispersal bombardment capabilities that would turn half a continent into a lake of molten glass. From what he had seen of Pym before, that could only improve the scenery.

This time, he vowed the Klikiss wouldn't take him by surprise. Unlike Diente, Lanyan did not plan to negotiate.

As his ships approached, Lanyan transmitted over a coded channel (not that he expected the bugs were eavesdropping on EDF transmissions), "Admiral Brindle, I want this to be a swift and devastating operation. As soon as we acquire a target, drop the scorchers and level any structures down there. Wave after wave, constant bombardment. That should do the trick."

"Yes, General," Brindle said from the helm of his own cruiser.

He sat stoically in the command chair. He had to achieve a victory here that exceeded the Chairman's expectations. He had ships full of armaments, and he would bomb the living daylights out of everything even remotely resembling a bug structure.

He would rather have been aboard his own Juggernaut, but on the other hand, it was gratifying to fly these once-stolen EDF ships, which the black robots had been forced to return. The Mantas and the *Thunder Child* had passed a complete detailed inspection; absolutely everything had checked out. Even so, Lanyan would never trust the robots again. He had lost too many good men to those tearing mechanical claws.

He had also lost plenty of men to the Klikiss—these particular Klikiss on Pym, in fact. He couldn't wait to see how well these battleships performed.

On tactical screens, his weapons officers brought up projections of Pym, the location of the original Colonization Initiative settlement, and the site of the known transportal wall. The hive had spread out in concentric waves from the salty inland sea where the human settlers had built their colony.

Tactical officers on the eight ships divided up the approach, and as soon as the planet came into view, they began their attack runs. They had enough powerful flash-melters, thermal-wave warheads, and even a dozen old standby nukes that could peel the top layer of crust like an orange.

With the *Thunder Child* in the lead, the EDF vessels cruised in high above the chalky white landscape, the alkaline flats, and the rivers of tainted water. They dropped loads of atmosphere-dispersed armaments. Before the bugs even realized they were under attack, the initial bombardment sent deep shockwaves and additive blasts to wipe out a significant section of the hive complex for kilometers around. The nukes made the biggest flashes, but the new-design weapons caused deeper damage.

Destruction continued to rain down in the second run, flash-melters literally *erasing* parts of the expansive bug city, penetrating deep to hit even the lowest tunnel complexes. As he scanned the smoke and vitrified desert below, Lanyan felt real satisfaction. Nothing—no bug *or* human—would ever live here again.

While a human settlement would have responded with panicked confusion to the surprise attack, the Klikiss hive mind launched a smooth, efficient counterstrike. Lanyan was amazed that so much of their infrastructure remained intact even after such a hellish bombardment. He ordered another attack run.

Thousands upon thousands of Klikiss component ships shot like fireworks from protected underground bunkers. A roiling, coordinated cloud of them came directly toward

Lanyan's seven Mantas. Each alien component craft had only two energy-weapon cannons, but thousands of stinging blasts caused cumulative damage. Lanyan diverted his bombardment of the hive city below to turn his Juggernaut's jazers against the numerous small ships.

"General!" Brindle reported, "we've got company coming in from above."

"Where did they come from?"

"Four large cluster vessels were on the far side of the planet. We charged in too fast to detect them on our initial run, but now they're on the way here."

"Great, a cockroach cavalry." On his tactical screens Lanyan watched four giant spherical masses composed of countless linked component ships. "Continue our bombardment of the ground colony while we can! Don't let up." Supposedly, once they managed to crush the central mind, the bugs wouldn't know how to attack anymore. On the other hand, the hive mind might be aboard one of those swarmships instead.

He directed three of his Mantas to peel off from the main group and engage the giant clusters in orbit. When the Mantas opened fire, the jazer blasts carved away sections of the conglomerate vessels, but the swarmships simply recoalesced, shed their debris, and continued to bear down on them.

Lanyan swallowed hard. This was not good.

One of the swarmships shifted its internal structure to form a deep pit in its middle, like a giant cannon mouth. Lanyan was trying to figure out what kind of threat it posed when a gout of whitish-yellow light vomited out of the swarmship weapon. The lavalike beam played across the bow of the nearest Manta, peeling it down into slag.

Two more swarmships shaped themselves into similar weapons, but before they could fire, the EDF ships whipped about in evasive maneuvers. Their captains didn't need specific orders to scramble. The huge energy blasts struck out repeatedly, at last destroying a second cruiser. The third Manta managed to evade, but Lanyan knew it was only a matter of time.

Below, an endless stream of component ships continued to launch from the burning hive cluster. With all the damage the Juggernaut and Mantas had already inflicted, he couldn't understand how he suddenly found himself facing a hopeless *defensive* battle, when he'd been in the midst of a headlong punitive attack only moments before. He was supposed to arrive in great force, lay waste to the hive, then depart.

Considering how many alien vessels were all around them, along with the four swarmships closing in, Lanyan couldn't even see a clear path to retreat. His ships were trapped here. Emergency alarms made a deafening clamor on the bridge. The *Thunder Child* no longer seemed so powerful.

Those waves of component ships fundamentally altered the tactical scenario. He had to change his approach, and fast. "Launch all Remoras for one-on-one dogfights. It's the only way to deal with so many targets."

With commendable speed, thousands of Remora attack ships streaked out from the five remaining Mantas and began to engage the Klikiss component vessels in individual battles. His pilots were good, their weapons training extensive, and they did a lot of damage . . . but Lanyan was sickened to count the tremendous number of casualties they suffered.

Suddenly, one of the huge swarmships received a furious blast from the rear, struck by a barrage of unexpected

firepower. It broke apart into a disconnected cloud of component ships. High-energy shots continued to pepper the dis-
associated wreckage, slicing the cluster into pieces.

"What the hell was that?"

Dozens more ships roared in from outside — a Juggernaut, several Mantas, and some odd vessels that he didn't
recognize.

"This is *Fleet* Admiral Willis calling," a voice drawled.
"General, it looks like you could use some help. What's it
gonna be, allies or enemies?"

Lanyan couldn't believe what he was seeing. The new
set of battleships opened fire on the Klikiss ships from above.
Confederation battleships. The Juggernaut — Willis's *Jupiter*, he saw — raked a swath of destruction through a second
swarmship.

Speaking without authorization, Conrad Brindle responded on the open channel. "We're sure glad to see you,
Admiral! We appreciate your assistance."

On a direct, coded channel, Lanyan scolded him not to
open communications with the other ships.

A young man's voice joined the conversation. "I kinda
prefer fighting at your side, Dad. We should do it more
often."

A cheer went up on the bridge of the *Thunder Child*.
Lanyan's beleaguered Mantas responded with a surge of
hope, lashing out at the Klikiss attackers with unexpected
fury. The balance was still precarious, but maybe — just
maybe — they could turn the tide against the Klikiss.

"About time you shot at the correct enemy instead of a
made-up punching bag, General," Willis said. "Any fool can
see that we need to worry about these bugs, not a bunch of
innocent traders and shipbuilders."

Lanyan swallowed his pride and answered. "Any Klikiss you kill, Admiral, is one we don't have to." Not overwhelming enthusiasm, he supposed, but it was the best he could manage. He had vowed never to trust Willis again after the way she had completely humiliated him . . . more than once.

As a remarkable idea began to take shape in his mind, he transmitted to Conrad Brindle on the private, coded channel, "String the traitors along and let them take the brunt of enemy fire. Maybe we can kill two birds with one projectile."

80 ☀ DEPUTY CHAIRMAN ELDRED CAIN

The Chairman looked much too smug when he invited the three of them to observe the Archfather's speech. He even brought out refreshments for Cain, Sarein, and Captain McCammon. The Chairman did not seem concerned, even though the discontented Archfather had written his own script. Lately, Cain found Basil's calm and content moods more disturbing than his tantrums.

The Chairman took a sip of his ice water with lemon as he gazed at the familiar scene below. "When people grow complacent, they become sloppy, and right now we need everyone to serve the Hansa with full devotion and concentration. It is time to shake them up."

"What are you planning, Basil?" Sarein said guardedly. It was clear the Chairman hadn't consulted her about this any more than he had consulted Cain. "What is the Archfather going to say?"

"I have no idea." He seemed actually jovial. "He disagreed with the speech I asked him to give, so he wrote this one himself. Still, I expect the audience will be quite amazed."

"You don't leave anything to chance," Cain said. "You're giving him just enough rope to hang himself."

Basil chuckled. "Oh, hanging is much too primitive." He changed the subject abruptly. "Next agenda item. Is my presentation ceremony on track for the new robots rolling off our assembly lines? Three days from now? I expect everything to be in order."

Cain had made the arrangements, taking care of every subtle detail. "We're ready for you, Mr. Chairman."

"Good. After today, I expect the Hansa to run more smoothly."

Before Cain could ask questions, the Archfather plodded to the podium dressed in his usual robes. His snowy white beard glistened in the sunshine under a perfectly clear blue sky. The crowds cheered on cue, and newsnet cameras recorded every movement, every word. King Rory was nowhere in sight.

The Chairman hushed them. "Observe."

The Archfather activated the voice amplifier and spoke abruptly, without preamble, as if afraid the Chairman would shut him down at any moment. "Unison has been hijacked.

Our religion. The condemnations I have issued from this po-dium were not my own. I, your Archfather, was coerced into making them. You have been tricked and misled. This is not what Unison is about."

The people muttered and gasped. Many reacted with anger, but Cain couldn't tell if the anger was directed toward the supposed betrayal or toward the Archfather's unorthodox words. Sarein was obviously astonished; Cain expected the cleanup crew to come rushing in at any moment.

Now that he had built up some momentum, the Archfa-ther's voice grew louder, more passionate. "I call for you to look into your hearts, into the core of your beliefs, and do what is right. The *Hansa* is not your religion. The *Hansa* does not speak for God. Unison does!"

Basil flexed his hand into a fist, then straightened his fingers again. "My, he does go on and on." He depressed the button on a small hand communicator. "I have heard enough."

Jane Kulu's deep voice answered calmly. "Yes, Mr. Chairman."

The accented voice of Tito Andropolis crackled over the speaker. "After this, no one will doubt God's intentions."

Basil sat back, his gray eyes glittering.

With an astounding whistle, as if the air itself were rip-ping apart, a bolt of energy streaked through the crystal-clear sky. The lightning shot straight down to strike the Archfather in the middle of the podium. The searing flash vaporized the bearded man, leaving no clothes or bones, only a flash of smoke, a crack of superheated air, and the smell of a crema-torium. A glassy crater marked his place. The most faithful in the crowd, who had stood closest to the podium, were bowled backward by the shockwave.

Sarein put her hand to her mouth in horror. The crowd screamed, and a ripple of evacuating people spread outward from the podium.

"What have you done?" Cain said in a barely audible voice. "My God, *what have you done?*"

"Wait," Basil said with a cool smile. "It's not over yet."

While the crowd remained stunned by the lightning flash, King Rory appeared like a vision amidst the dissipating smoke at the edge of the crater. His young voice boomed out with such strength and confidence that he must have rehearsed many times. "No law and no court could be more plain. God will smite those who try to weaken us. The Archfather was a heretic. I am your chosen King, and it is God's will that I also become the leader of Unison. I, King Rory, will save the Hansa and the human race."

Sarein was appalled, her face pale. "Basil, how could you? That was murder!"

The Chairman took a long sip of his water. "Quite the contrary. That was the will of God. You heard King Rory."

Blasting bug vessels with total abandon—now, that was the kind of battle she could really sink her teeth into. But though Admiral Willis had brought Confederation battleships loaded with every weapon they could scrounge, the Pym infestation was a lot more extensive than she had expected.

General Lanyan's ships had gotten themselves into a pickle, and it made her feel warm and fuzzy to be the knight in shining armor.

The Confederation ships caused an uproar among the bugs. Two swarmships had been destroyed, or at least disassembled. But for every thousand component ships they vaporized, another thousand rose from the hive structures below or detached and attacked from the remaining swarmships. Willis had never seen anything like it.

Over the basic EDF comm channels, Lanyan was telling his ships to continue to fire. The *Thunder Child* blasted a small intact section of the hive city and attempted to retreat back to the imaginary safety of orbit. So far he hadn't bothered to express much gratitude to his Confederation rescuers.

Willis wasn't sure where the General had come up with a new Juggernaut—she didn't recognize the name—but he wasn't using it to full advantage. His battle group's combined surface bombardment had been the right idea, but as usual, Lanyan had overestimated his own competence. He just hadn't bombed the planet heavily enough.

"General, keep hitting the bug city. If we can squash the hive mind, we'll be done here."

"Look for yourself, Willis. We *have* been bloody well blasting the city!"

"If you want something done right . . ." she said with a sigh. Willis transmitted to Tasia in one of the Mantas flying close beside the *Jupiter*, "Commodore Tamblyn, if you would do the honors?" She had not only approved of Robb keeping his flag officer rank, but she had insisted that Tasia accept at least the equivalent rank.

"My pleasure, Admiral."

Her *Jupiter* cleared a swath through the bugs that were harrying Lanyan's vessels. The General's flagship climbed higher in the atmosphere, trying to reach orbit while the surviving EDF ships continued to fire, covering his tail.

Tamblyn grumbled over the comm, "He better not run away before we're all finished with this job."

Robb shouted to his father across the comm, "Dad, we've got enough firepower to put an end to this. Concentrate your jazers on the center of the hive city below. Do you have any more nukes for surface bombardment?"

The surface of Pym already looked like a moonscape after the flash-melters, nukes, and several rounds of carpet bombing, and now the Confederation ships increased the destruction tenfold. Ignoring individual battles with the broken-apart swarmships, Willis led another Armageddon run over the insect city. "Use all of our penetrators and the full load of strata crumblers. They've probably hidden their breedex deep, or we'd have hit it by now."

They left a holocaust behind them. Every remaining

structure was smashed to powder. Shockwaves hammered the entire Pym hive city. The surface itself was halfway molten.

"Damn, that's got to be enough," Robb said.

"We'll know when it's enough," Tasia said, "because once we kill the breedex, all those other bugs won't know which direction to fly."

Lanyan's ships kept shooting haphazardly at Klikiss vessels. Though Robb continued to call his father, he received no response. Willis was annoyed that Conrad Brindle wouldn't reply to his son's repeated transmissions.

"Let's give it our biggest, balls-out bombing run." Willis intentionally used an open transmission line so the EDF ships would hear as well. "General Lanyan, what have you got left? Flash-melters? Thermal-wave warheads? Atomics? Throw down everything but the kitchen sink—that ought to do it."

"Yes, Admiral." He sounded strained. "One last round to finish the job. I'll have the *Thunder Child* follow you in."

Willis was confident this last bombardment would eradicate one more deadly breedex from the Spiral Arm. Best of all, Lanyan might actually learn a lesson in brotherly cooperation.

The EDF ships followed her on the bombing run, as she'd hoped. The smoking, cratered landscape directly below showed that the insect city had been reduced to complete ruin.

The *Jupiter* dumped its full load of surface armaments. No sense in being stingy now, she thought. The destruction was absolutely glorious, giving her a childlike thrill. Hot, intense waves scoured the surface, obliterating every last speck of the hive structures below. Behind her, the loaded Confederation ships dropped their weapons, slamming deeper, shattering the crust.

"Nobody's going to want to settle down there for a long, long time," Willis said. "Better take Pym off the Colonization Initiative list."

Three of the EDF Mantas also made a final bombardment, even though it seemed redundant. There was absolutely nothing left on the surface.

"I think that's a job well done, Admiral Willis," Lanyan said.

Suddenly, from behind her, the *Thunder Child* and two EDF Mantas began to open fire *on her*, targeting the Juggernaut's engines.

"What the hell?" She slammed her fist down on the comm panel. "General, you're either a bad shot or more boneheaded than I can describe."

"I am acting on behalf of the Earth Defense Forces. You are deemed as great a threat to human civilization as the Klikiss are. Now that the Pym subhive has been eradicated, I plan on taking care of the second threat." He called upon the *Thunder Child* to open fire again.

Willis ordered her ships to take evasive action. Disgusted, she did not keep her opinions to herself. "That man has three testicles, and one of them is in place of his brain." The EDF ships kept firing on her Juggernaut. "Get us out of here. Pym has lost its charm."

As Lanyan's ship closed in to fire upon the Confederation vessels, one of the Mantas flew directly between the *Thunder Child* and the *Jupiter*. For a moment Willis thought it was one of her own ships, but then she clearly saw the EDF chain-of-stars logo.

Conrad Brindle spoke over the channel as his Manta

took heavy damage by intercepting shots fired by Lanyan's weapons officers. "Robb, Admiral, you'd best get out of here. You've helped us pound the Klikiss, but if you stay any longer this isn't going to end well."

Willis glowered down at the smoldering remains of the hive city, then sounded a call for retreat across her battle group. "You heard the man. Pack it up and save your bacon while you can. We've done our part here. General Lanyan just never learned how to play well with others."

82 ☀ TAL O'NH

Even without his eyesight, Tal O'nh could sense the mass and geometry of the structures around him—the sounds, the vibrations, the *solidity* of the big shipyard complex.

The Solar Navy construction yards had been abandoned since the return of the faeros. When the fireballs had burst out of the dead sun of Durris-B and swarmed to Ildira, construction teams had evacuated the facility. The spacedocks, fabrication lines, administrative hubs, and skeletal frameworks of four incomplete warliners hung together above the planet's atmosphere. It was a ghost town, a massive junkyard in space.

O'nh knew what to do with it.

Though corrupted by the fiery elementals, Rusa'h still

thought like an Ildiran. He still believed, in some distorted way, that he was a guardian of his people. He would not be able to conceive that any Prime Designate could order something so drastic, so unspeakable. No Ildiran could—until now.

Though he had no eyes, the old commander knew the controls by touch. Aided by his few obdurate assistants, he had already activated the main panel, fired the attitude-adjustment rockets, and initiated the descent of the gigantic shipyards. None of them found any need for words; they all knew full well what they were doing.

The complex circled Ildira, losing altitude, touching the outer atmosphere, first with a whisper, then with a roar. The structural girders began to heat up with friction from the sky itself. He imagined it must be generating a bright light.

"Our course is true, Tal." The voice belonged to one of the few men who remained with him. "The intercept point is locked in."

When they had finally decided to do this, Prime Designate Daro'h had offered to send a full crew to assist O'nh. Knowing what was at stake, hundreds had volunteered their services, but the old veteran had argued that a small ship had a better chance of reaching the orbital facility without being stopped by faeros. Also, he wanted no unnecessary casualties; the cost was already unbearably high. "Every Ildiran life is precious, Prime Designate. Give me five volunteers, and we will change history."

He had heard the awe and appreciation in Daro'h's voice. "You will burn your name in the *Saga of Seven Suns*. I will see to it that Chief Scribe Ko'sh records all you have done."

"By our actions today, I hope to make certain there is still more of the *Saga* to write," O'nh had said.

The thought of what young Designate Ridek'h had been willing to do gave him strength. On their flight up to the shipyards, his heart had felt heavy with the knowledge that the boy must be dead, but he was also proud of his protégé. And now O'nh hoped to put an end to the mad Designate who had caused so much harm and pain.

The five volunteers had operated the cold controls, re-awakening the mothballed systems. As a blind man, he could make none of the actual modifications, but he gave them instructions and did not let them falter.

At the edge of the system, Tal Ala'nh and his warliners waited, unaware of what was happening here. Adar Zan'nh had not wanted to risk a transmission to inform them, fearing that Rusa'h might somehow intercept it. But O'nh knew Tal Ala'nh well enough; he and his cohort would be ready. The Adar should be watching intently, ready to race away with his nine warliners to join the rest of the Solar Navy.

After a few more moments passed, O'nh could feel the great structure shudder around him, buffeted by the thickening atmosphere. "What are our fuel reserves?" Unable to look at the people inside the control chamber, he stared into his own darkness.

"Enough to adjust our course if necessary, Tal." The thin voice belonged to an engineer kithman. "But we used most of our supplies to send us on as rapid a descent as possible. We will strike the target."

O'nh nodded. "Good. There is no going back."

"No, Tal. No going back."

"Our place in the *Saga* is assured." He sat back and waited, imagining that all of the framework must now be glowing a cherry red, thermal waves flying off as ablation peeled away the outer layers of metal. He wished he could see true light one last time, but soon this frail body would be gone and his soul would be on the plane of the Lightsource.

Rusa'h could not know what was coming directly toward him.

Though these four warliners would never be completed, the huge skeletal ships would perform a great service for the Solar Navy. What mattered now was not weaponry or maneuverability, but sheer *mass*. The orbital descent was set.

The control chamber shuddered violently, and he gripped the sturdy arms of his chair to hold himself steady. He heard hissing sounds, the screaming whine of air as it whipped through the girders. "Today we strike a blow the faeros can never forget, one that Ildirans will forever remember."

The spacedocks, unassembled hull plates, gigantic engine components, girders and assembly bays, all of the useless heavy junk, tore down through the atmosphere. O'nh could feel the heat as the falling city turned into a meteor.

Though most of their sensors had burned out, one of his assistants cried, "Faeros fireballs! Ten of them, heading straight toward us."

"Rusa'h has finally guessed what we are about to do." A smile formed on his scarred face. "But he cannot stop us."

The flaming ellipsoids launched gouts of fire at the descending complex, but though they melted some of the framework, the shipyards were a falling projectile that could not be deflected.

Just then, he received a static-filled transmission from Prime Designate Daro'h. "I have good news for you, Tal O'nh. Ridek'h is alive! Osira'h and the others protected him. He is safe."

O'nh drew a large breath, though it burned his lungs. He felt a deep, satisfying contentment. "Thank you, Prime Designate."

The faeros fireballs continued to pummel the shipyards with increasing desperation. Flames licked through the framework, but even when two of the spacedock components and one warliner frame sheared away from the central mass, the separate projectiles continued to descend on the same trajectory.

Sitting in the middle of it all, protected for only a few moments more, the old veteran wished he could see. The nearest engineer kithman shouted, "There are flames all around us, Tal, but the clouds have just parted. We shot through them like a projectile."

"What do you see?"

"Mijistra—it is beautiful! The city spreads out, but it is empty. And there's the Prism Palace. I am glad I got to see it one last time. The whole Palace glows. It is lit up with the fire from within."

O'nh nodded. "Good, then Rusa'h is likely still inside. He cannot get away."

In the last moment, Tal O'nh felt as if he were bringing the very Lightsource itself to Ildira.

With Yazra'h at his side, her hair blowing wildly in the warm breeze, Daro'h stood on a hill far from the outskirts of Mijistra. With tears in his eyes he stared at his beloved majestic city and the shining gem of the Prism Palace. Having said his farewells to Tal O'nh, he set aside the communication device.

Words failed him as the flaming hand of vengeance descended toward Mijistra.

He heard a deafening shriek as the shipyards ripped a hole through the sky. They trailed a plume of vaporized metal like a comet's tail of clotting blood. Fireballs harried the plummeting mass, but they could not stop its descent.

Yazra'h stared, unable to blink. Daro'h clutched his sister's arm. Chief Scribe Ko'sh silently joined them.

The shipyards came down in a colossal explosion, as if an asteroid-sized hammer had slammed into the heart of Mijistra. Into the Prism Palace.

Daro'h covered his eyes from the blinding flash. Ripples of destruction flattened the buildings, erasing the greatest achievements of the Ildiran Empire. The capital city vanished in a rumble of unleashed kinetic energy.

The shockwave took only a few seconds to arrive, but it was strong enough to knock them to the ground. The explosion seemed to go on and on.

After a long, stunned moment Daro'h got to his hands and knees, then slowly, unsteadily, climbed to his feet. "My heart has been ripped from my chest." His voice sounded strangely muffled in his ears.

Yazra'h had a feral look in her eyes, anger at what Rusa'h had forced them to do. "It is a devastating blow."

"But a necessary one." The Prime Designate was shuddering. The path of the descending shipyards left a scar like a black gash in the air.

The Chief Scribe brushed off his robes as he climbed to his feet. He was speechless as he watched tumbling waves of smoke and fire pour into the sky. The wondrous capital city had vanished, leaving only a vast, boiling crater. Finally, he said, "The Hall of Rememberers is lost! Our history, our *Saga*."

"Our city, our Prism Palace," Daro'h added. "But our race survives. Maybe this was an unforgivable act, but it is a second chance."

"But the *Saga*—" Ko'sh moaned.

"You are a rememberer! We will remember in our hearts and minds. Do not lose sight of what this has bought us. Now Adar Zan'nh can rejoin the Solar Navy. Without the faeros pursuing him, he will free the Mage-Imperator." Daro'h prayed that his father would someday find a way to pardon him for what he had done.

As his head throbbed from the shockwave and his eyes burned from the flash, he made out a figure coming closer, a silhouette stumbling away from the holocaust. Daro'h tried to catch his breath, but his lungs burned. He shaded his eyes, then pointed.

Yazra'h saw the young man staggering along, exhausted, stunned. She shouted, "It is Designate Ridek'h! He survived!" She began waving her arms.

The brave boy looked burned, shell-shocked, but determined. He saw Yazra'h's movement, though he seemed unable to hear her calling for him. Daro'h led the way, and they met him on the hillside. The Prime Designate caught Ridek'h just before his legs gave out. "You are safe now. You have escaped."

The boy blinked several times, disoriented. Finally he shuddered, then used the support of Daro'h and Yazra'h to get back to his feet. He turned and stared at the still-smoking impact site and the raging fires on the perimeter of what had been Mijistra.

"I ran and ran," he said, his voice ragged. "I did not look back. Not until now." He began to cough, his chest spasming; the sounds turned into sobs.

"Do you think Rusa'h is dead?" Yazra'h said.

Daro'h stared at the holocaust. He could not imagine how the faeros incarnate could have survived that, but he was unwilling to assume anything.

84 ☀ ADAR ZAN'NH

At the moment of obliteration, Adar Zan'nh seized his chance. The massive spacedocks and construction yards crashing down from orbit provided more than enough diversion for his nine warliners to escape from the faeros on Ildira. He felt a deep ache in his heart as his ships put distance between themselves and his beloved home planet.

The beautiful, ancient city from which Mage-Imperators had ruled since the beginning of the Empire was no more. He knew what had been lost, knew that Ildira would never be the same. The impact was like a bright splash of blood and fire on the landscape. Mijistra . . . the Prism Palace. So much history, so much culture . . . all gone.

And, he hoped, faeros incarnate Rusa'h as well.

Yet the desperate tactic was their only hope of surviving as an Empire, perhaps even as a race. At last, the Adar had a mission he could expect to accomplish. If he could indeed rescue the Mage-Imperator from captivity, the Empire would be far stronger with its rightful ruler.

"Even when we free our father, the war will not be over," said Osira'h, who had asked to accompany him while her four siblings remained with the Prime Designate on Ildira. "Even if Rusa'h is dead, the faeros are still a threat."

Zan'nh looked down at the strange little girl. "All the more reason why we must free him."

"Yes, we must."

As the warliners raced away from the planet, they broadcast instant commands to Tal Ala'nh and his hundreds of waiting warliners outside the system. The Adar no longer needed to keep his plans secret. He could tell the cohort commander their objectives and reveal where the Mage-Imperator was being held. With all the fiery elementals stunned and distracted, the bulk of his Solar Navy prepared to depart en masse.

Behind them, the faeros ricocheted like sparks in a frenetic storm. Zan'nh had hoped the conflagration of Mijistra would occupy them for some time . . . but as his nine warliners sped away, several of the fireballs streaked after them. They seemed attracted by the movement, seeking anything to destroy.

"Increase acceleration. Prepare to activate stardrives." He had not gained as much distance as he had hoped. With or without Rusa'h, the faeros could act.

In the command nucleus, his well-trained soldiers worked like machines despite the dread that gripped them. They knew full well what was at stake.

"The faeros are closing in on us, Adar."

His warliners strained to get out of the system, gaining speed, changing course, ready to activate their stardrives. An increasing number of fireballs followed them like flaming projectiles. "Tell Tal Ala'nh to set course for Earth and to depart immediately. We will follow as we can."

Osira'h said in a small voice, "Whether or not the impact destroyed him, Rusa'h learned what we intended to do, and so the faeros knew. They will still try to come after you. They know we are going to Earth."

"But they will not catch me." Zan'nh flashed a hard smile at his half-sister. "We will have the Mage-Imperator back before they get there."

"Stardrives are ready, Adar," said the helmsman.

"Activate them." On the screen he watched the ravenous flaming ellipsoids closing the gap. Tal O'nh had made an immeasurable sacrifice, not just of his life but of the heart of Ildira. Zan'nh refused to let it be in vain.

The warliners leaped ahead, leaving the fireballs behind with a terribly scarred planet.

H e wasn't surprised that Admiral Willis and her rebel ships would simply run, but Lanyan was shocked that his own gunners couldn't shoot down the *Jupiter* in the first volley of weapons fire. A target as big as a Juggernaut, flying right in front of them! The *Thunder Child* should have made swift work of it.

He wondered if the systems were sluggish—some flaw in the robot repairs, perhaps? Or maybe the rebels had upgraded Admiral Willis's ships more than just scouring off the EDF logo and painting a new sign on the hull plates. On the other hand, he could blame the botched job on new recruits, insufficient training, and even a dash of blind bad luck. And on Conrad Brindle.

Of all the people he knew in the EDF, Brindle was one of the most dedicated and unshakeable. But at the crucial moment, he had intentionally placed his Manta in the line of fire, blocking shots that should have decapitated the rebel Confederation force. And it could not have been an accident.

"Brindle, damn you—keep shooting! That's an order. Admiral Willis is a mutineer. This is our chance to destroy them along with the Klikiss."

The other man's answer was calm and cool. "I will not fire on them, sir. Our enemy is the Klikiss. In this battle, Admiral Willis is our ally."

Lanyan pounded his fist on the *Thunder Child*'s command console as Willis and her Confederation battle group beat a hasty and indignant retreat. The General attempted to pursue, but most of the jazer blasts went wild. His weapons officers must be either unskilled or insufficiently motivated.

"General, this is insanity!" Once again, Brindle's Manta crossed in front of the lead cruiser, blocking Lanyan's clear line of fire and buying the rebel ships just enough time to get away. A jazer burst scorched the Manta's lower hull. On the comm, Brindle's face was filled with disgust. "General, cease fire immediately, or I will relieve you of command on the grounds that you are unfit to lead."

The soldiers on the *Thunder Child*'s bridge deck were clearly uneasy.

Before Lanyan could respond, the supposedly neutralized Klikiss vessels began to open fire again, and this time his ships were the only targets in the vicinity. "What the hell?"

Even after the total devastation down below, which should have killed the Klikiss hive mind ten times over, the giant swarmships had begun to move again. Apparently, they'd been stunned, but now the component craft buzzed around, seeking new targets. He had underestimated how swiftly the remaining components could coalesce into new alien conglomerate ships.

Below, on the bubbling, seared landscape, craters opened up to reveal access holes to incredibly deep tunnels. Another wave of component craft emerged from undamaged hive complexes far underground.

His gunners independently retargeted their weapons and began to shoot at the Klikiss that closed in on them. An explosion rocked the *Thunder Child*, sending it reeling off course. The scattered alien vessels had now managed to reconstitute two complete swarmships, each of which molded its geometry into a gigantic cannon-barrel weapon. A crackling bolt spewed out of the nearest cluster and vaporized another of Lanyan's Mantas. More than a thousand crewmen dead in an instant, one more EDF capital ship obliterated.

This wasn't good. Not at all.

An announcement came across the command channel, a priority signal that preempted all other transmissions. "Attention EDF ships! This is Admiral Conrad Brindle. I have assumed command of this battle group. General Lanyan is hereby relieved of duty. We are leaving Pym. Return to Earth."

"You will not retreat!" Lanyan roared.

Another explosion struck his Juggernaut, a bad one, ripping out two of his engines. His navigation officer struggled against a shower of sparks on her console to keep the gigantic ship from spiraling down to the planet.

Hundreds of Klikiss component vessels continued pecking away at the *Thunder Child*. On the screen, Lanyan saw Brindle's cruiser and two others pulling away. Only one other Manta survived, and he was relieved to see that it remained at his side. But the cruiser looked hopelessly crippled, with smoke pouring from prominent breaches in its hull.

Sensing easy prey, the Klikiss closed in.

He had expected Chairman Wenceslas to applaud his foresight for not only striking the bugs, but also wiping out the human traitors. Now, instead of a double victory, he had botched the whole mission. He could already imagine the scorn the Chairman would heap upon him as soon as they got back to Earth. *Not one of the high points in my illustrious career*. If there was any chance of salvaging the situation, he needed to arrive back at Earth before Brindle made his report. He needed to tell his side of the story first.

"Get us out of here," he snapped. "Maximum speed."

The navigator turned to him with an astonished, sickened look on her long face. "General, I can barely keep us in a stable orbit! Two engines damaged, all control linkages fried — we're not going anywhere."

"Then activate our stardrives. I don't care where we are. Get us away from this planet."

She frowned at him as if he were a mentally deficient child. "Too late for that, sir."

His Juggernaut was rapidly falling apart, and space was thick with Klikiss component ships still slashing and slicing. He hesitated only a second before opening up the comm channel again. He had to act before the retreating EDF ships could get out of range.

"Admiral Brindle, we are declaring an emergency. I order you to return and assist us." He swallowed hard. "We're abandoning ship."

The *Thunder Child*'s bridge crew didn't need to be told twice. They scrambled to escape pods. Loud Klaxons echoed up and down the metal-walled corridors. Entire decks were on fire, and hundreds of his crew were already dead from the numerous hull breaches.

Lanyan continued to shout into the comm system, "Admiral Brindle, it is your obligation to retrieve our escape pods." At any other time, the man would have obeyed without a second thought. He would have done his duty. But on the static-filled screen, Brindle and the surviving Mantas continued their retreat.

The Klikiss kept pummeling the *Thunder Child*. When the deck started to split beneath him, Lanyan had no choice but to dash to the small escape pod built into his ready room. Everyone else had shot themselves away in the larger life-boats, though with so many Klikiss ships in the vicinity, he doubted anyone would get away for long.

On a viewscreen behind his desk he saw Admiral Brin-dle turning his Manta around to retrieve whatever pods he could, even though he put himself and his ships at great risk to do so. At least the man had a tiny bit of honor left.

Lanyan jumped feetfirst into the round hatch and pulled the lid shut. He hammered the activation buttons that locked down the airtight seal, blasted free the retention bolts, and disengaged the pod. As the small chamber spun, Lanyan grew dizzy watching through the single observation port.

In orbit above, the *Thunder Child* was little more than a skeletal structure held together by a few hull plates and con-nective girders. He saw other escape pods flying into space like the spores of a swollen mushroom, heading out to safety, but he was falling in the other direction, toward the planet's surface, nowhere close to Brindle's retrieval operations.

As the pod decelerated through Pym's atmosphere, the white expanse of desert and brackish lakes looked uninvit-ing. The automated systems could manage an intact landing, but he didn't know how he was going to arrange a pickup and rescue from down there. At least he was on the other side of the continent from where the repeated bombardment had annihilated the hive city.

Slowed by its landing thrusters, the pod struck the ground and tumbled, scraping up a rooster tail of glitter-ing gypsum powder and alkaline dust. His small window was completely covered, and Lanyan bounced around like a man going over a waterfall in a barrel. Stupid, not to have strapped himself in.

As the pod finally came to rest and his adrenaline slowly ebbed, shock still rang in his ears. He realized that the sharp pain indicated he must have broken his elbow. More stupidity.

First things first. With one hand he found a first-aid kit and cracked open a dual stimulant/painkiller shot. That should be enough to keep him going. He couldn't think very far ahead, though. Lanyan couldn't believe that Brindle would not follow his duty and come to retrieve him, but for now he would be on his own. He'd have to live off the land and survive somehow.

Next step, he activated the locator beacon on the off chance that someone would come back to scoop him up. He gathered a survival pack, a handgun—the only weapon stored aboard the pod—and braced himself as he popped open the hatch.

Outside on the flat, white landscape he saw no towering insect structures, no alien buildings. Nevertheless, Klikiss were swarming out of deep tunnels, their spiny carapaces glittering in the sun, their scythelike limbs flailing in the air. Though his pod had landed many hundreds of kilometers from the heart of the Klikiss city, their tunnels apparently extended across and under the entire continent. He hadn't killed all the bugs on Pym—not even close. And the breedex must still be alive and controlling them.

Now Klikiss warriors were emerging to investigate the crashed escape pod. Millions of them. And they had spotted him.

As the creatures scuttled forward, he held his weapon in his good hand, took careful aim, and fired. He kept firing. He counted thirty-eight splattered bugs before his charge pack was almost depleted. Swallowing hard, he decided he should keep the last shot for himself; the gun's power levels read nearly zero. The stimulant burst he had given himself wasn't working. His elbow ached like a son of a bitch.

As chittering and clacking Klikiss surrounded his escape pod, Lanyan dropped back inside and sealed the hatch. Hunkering down, he could hear them pounding and scratching against the hull. The pod was not designed to serve as a bunker in an all-out attack.

There was a long, ominous pause, then Lanyan heard cutting tools and sharp claws. In four different places, the wall of the vessel broke open. The enormous bugs clawed their way inside. Lanyan backed against the wall, holding his weapon.

Everything was happening too fast, but he could accept reality. These things were monsters from his worst nightmare, and they came at him now, all claws, pincers, and mandibles. With a final defiant howl, he squeezed his eyes shut, pressed the weapon against his temple, and activated the firing stud.

The charge pack had only enough energy left to burn his skin. Lanyan stared at the empty weapon in helpless dismay. The curved hull fell apart behind him.

From all directions, the Klikiss swarmed over him. Their chittering, triumphant music drowned out his screams.

Cain felt no emotion about this at all, which he found odd, since (unlike Chairman Wenceslas) he had never committed outright murder. But this was necessary. The assassination of the Archfather, the cold-blooded murder of former Chairman Maureen Fitzpatrick, the appalling bargain with the black robots—Cain could not let the downward spiral go any further.

Basil Wenceslas had to be removed, permanently.

McCammon had helped Cain set up the trap, while Sarein had tried to convince the Chairman to consider less extreme alternatives to some of his actions, to no effect. Cain had chosen not to tell Sarein too much about the specific plot. She wasn't so much weak as she was *breakable*. Nevertheless, she was part of what was about to happen, and she had performed admirably.

After the "bolt of heavenly fire" had annihilated the outspoken Archfather, the people flocked to their supposed savior, King Rory. Never before had Cain seen such an explosion of religious fervor. The most gullible people were also the most vociferous, and the Chairman encouraged the newsnets to carry only coverage that proclaimed the Archfather's death to be a dark miracle, an unmistakable sign from God, a blow from Heaven.

Though many were plainly skeptical, curious investigators could find no sign of what the true cause of the lightning had been. Cain suspected that Chairman Wenceslas had deleted all records of whatever he had used. Freedom's Sword had proposed a handful of explanations, which the newsnets consistently mocked as "ridiculous conspiracy theories."

The murder of the Archfather was just one more terrible thing. There could be no saving Chairman Basil Wenceslas.

Now on a bright morning, Basil rode with Sarein and Deputy Cain in his protected ground vehicle. The driver pulled up at the small parade field in front of the retooled compy factory, where a small receiving stand had been set up outside the wide warehouse doors.

Modular warehouse annexes and squarish industrial structures were part of the manufacturing facility. This particular factory had been put online as a secondary complex to pick up the slack in assembling Soldier compies, but after the compy revolt it had become the primary site.

McCammon had already gone ahead to arrange for security during the Chairman's speech, although King Rory wouldn't be there. Sarein sat close to the Chairman in the vehicle, obviously uncomfortable, while Cain remained apart, saying little, keeping a poker face.

A small crowd of Basil's most conservative supporters had gathered at the edges of the parade ground; several had brought their own banners. Industrialists took their places on the flat seats of the VIP bleachers, watching the royal guards line up to one side of the compact group of stands.

Captain McCammon's guards surrounded the speaking area. Colonel Andez and her dark-uniformed cleanup crew stood closer to the podium, as if symbolically protecting Chairman Wenceslas even against the royal guard. Not a good sign, Cain thought.

When the people noticed the Chairman's vehicle, a dull cheer went up. Cain did not detect the enthusiasm he had expected. Perhaps even these people were uneasy about Basil's Faustian deal with the black robots.

"You two wait here," Basil said. "I'll make the announcement, and we can get back to work." He slipped away from the ground vehicle and headed toward the podium without a backward glance at them.

Cain allowed no sign of his relief to show; he'd been afraid Basil would ask them to accompany him. As he and Sarein emerged from the vehicle, she pointedly did not glance at him. Knowing what was to come, she seemed to be counting the seconds. He certainly was.

They watched with distaste as three brand-new black robots marched out of the factory doorway to be presented as a symbol of Hansa industrial acumen. The Chairman stepped up to the podium and faced the spectators. With abrupt and businesslike movements, he placed himself at the center of the podium exactly on his mark, exactly where Cain knew he would be.

"It is the measure of a great leader to put misunderstandings behind him. It is human to admit a mistake." Basil's words were flat and clipped, without the passion he would have demanded of either the Archfather or King Rory. "Despite our past differences, we and the black robots can be far stronger together. It may be the only way we can survive against the dangers abroad in the Spiral Arm." He smiled. "The robots will restore our Earth Defense Forces, and in return we will replenish their numbers so that they can fight against their destructive Klikiss creators. Together, we become powerful, a force for our enemies to reckon with."

Basil surprised Cain by summoning Sirix and his companions forward. The deputy blinked. He hadn't expected the black robots to be so close to the Chairman. Sarein flashed him a quick, nervous glance, then looked away. She appeared nauseated. He didn't acknowledge her.

Moving on clusters of fingerlike legs, Sirix led the two identical machines up beside Basil Wenceslas. Cain felt sweat glistening on his pale forehead, but he did not dare reach up to wipe it away.

"These are the first new robots we've released from our factories," the Chairman announced. "They and others will be exchanged for more newly reassembled EDF battleships."

Sirix stepped forward, his crimson optical sensors bright. Basil discreetly moved back half a step to give him room. Cain closed his eyes.

The first shots rang out.

A patter of projectiles whizzed through the air and stitched an embroidery of sparks against Sirix's black body core. McCammon's guards and Andez's men shouted, trying frantically to locate the sniper. Andez pointed to one of the rooftops where an automated self-guiding gun had risen up from where it had lain hidden among the pipes and heat radiators.

Basil threw himself to the ground as projectiles ricocheted off the black bodies of the other two robots. Andez pointed to the warehouse rooftop and barked orders. McCammon's men were already opening fire, though they could not see any sniper. Within seconds, they had blasted the automated weapon to pieces.

McCammon raced to the podium, panting, while Colonel Andez sprinted ahead of him, apparently wanting to be the first to reach the Chairman's side. Afraid it would appear that he had waited too long to respond, Cain grabbed

Sarein's arm and they ran forward as soon as the gunfire stopped.

Stumbling, Sarein gasped at Cain, "What do we do now?"

"Why, we try to save the Chairman," he said, struggling to play the expected role. "We need to say that Freedom's Sword must be behind this. They are the ones who wish to assassinate the Chairman."

Sarein looked stunned; then she nodded briskly. "Yes, I'm sure that's it."

Sirix and the two other black robots extended their multiple sharp-tipped arms, ready for close-in combat, if necessary. "Who dares attack us?" he demanded.

"Those shots weren't meant for you," Basil snapped. "Somebody was trying to kill me." His face was red with anger. He drew deep breaths and said coldly to Andez, "Find out who did this."

"We will," McCammon answered.

87 ☀ FAEROS INCARNATE RUSA'H

Following the impact of the shipyards, Mijistra was an inferno. But this was not a cleansing, reviving fire such as the faeros might cause. The magnificent Prism Palace, the legendary Hall of Rememberers, the museums, sculptures, and fountains—all of them erased, vaporized in a fiery flash of impact.

At the heart of the blaze, embers and shards of superheated crystal stirred. Dozens of brilliant faeros fireballs swirled around the impact point like angry hornets. They added their energy, nurturing the flames, pulling upon the lava.

Rusa'h emerged, his form intact and wreathed in flames like the corona of a sun. His skin glowed, and his soulfire quivered with fury for what had been done to him and to this glorious city. The part of him that still remembered being an Ildiran recoiled from the appalling act. The Prism Palace! Mijistra! And an *Ildiran* had done such a thing.

Now, because of the thoughts he had glimpsed in the *thism,* he knew it was all because of Mage-Imperator Jora'h.

In a shower of sparks Rusa'h cast the wreckage away. He stood powerful, throbbing, his fists clenched. His transitory flame garments billowed in a windstorm of his own making. The wild fireballs circled overhead, barely under his control, hot with their need for destruction. The faeros wanted to sweep across the landscape now and incinerate every remaining Ildiran in every camp, every sheltered tunnel, every town and settlement.

Rusa'h was barely strong enough to hold them back. He would not let them exterminate his people. "No, we have a far more important goal."

The crucial target.

From the *thism* of the half-breed children, he had learned to his shock and disbelief what Tal O'nh was doing, but too late to stop the disaster. The orbital shipyards had already been on their way down, and neither Rusa'h nor his faeros could prevent the impact.

Even as Mijistra exploded all around him, he had reeled with shock at the revelation gleaned from the children who were shielding young Ridek'h: Jora'h was being held prisoner among the humans! Now he knew why the Mage-Imperator had not come to face him when the faeros took control of Ildira, why he had left the Adar and the Prime Designate to fight in his stead.

The Terran Hanseatic League had captured the mighty Mage-Imperator! Another sign of Jora'h's weakness and corrupt rule.

Now, though, he also understood what Adar Zan'nh meant to do. The destruction of Mijistra had been meant both to kill him and to let the warliners escape the faeros. He would not let that go unchallenged. The nine Solar Navy ships had already left Ildira. He could pursue them, even though they thought they had gotten away.

And at last, he could confront Mage-Imperator Jora'h.

Rusa'h raised his glowing hands and summoned the flaming ellipsoids overhead. He called one down, its outer skin rippling with sharp tongues of fire. The fireball enfolded him like a hot embrace.

Thanks to the soulfires they had absorbed over the past several months, the faeros had vastly increased their numbers. Rusa'h would take the fireballs with him as reinforcements—all of them—and by doing so he would also ensure that they did not capriciously exterminate more Ildirans here.

Rusa'h was the one who would save the Ildiran people.

Mage-Imperator Jora'h was the one who must suffer.

Like a meteor shower, Rusa'h and his tremendous armada streamed away from Ildira toward the Earth system.

88 ☀ RLINDA KETT

D ealing with bugs was never much of a problem aboard a spaceship, you understand," Rlinda said to Margaret Colicos.

The older woman walked ahead, unfazed by the squealing, whistling, and clattering of the armored insects. "I don't like them either, Captain Kett, but I have survived among them for many years."

Rlinda was amazed the bugs hadn't hurt her as they led her away from her damaged ship, a sad and lonely hulk crashed on the ground. "I hope they plan on fixing the *Curiosity*. It's their fault the ship is wrecked."

Margaret paused. "They believe you shouldn't have come here at all." Then she allowed a faint, mysterious smile. "But if Davlin agrees, I suppose the Klikiss could be convinced to make repairs."

"Well, what's happened to Davlin?"

"We are going to the hall of the breedex. You'll have your answers there."

Rlinda frowned back at the sprawling hive city. By now she was hopelessly lost. "I suppose I should tell you that I came here to save him."

"I'm afraid you're too late." The older woman sounded deeply saddened. "Davlin is beyond saving . . . or perhaps he'll save us all. I can't be sure."

Rlinda let out a long, frustrated sigh. "I still don't know what you're talking about. Is Davlin alive, or is he dead?"

"Yes," Margaret said. "It's something you have to see for yourself."

The insects continued to lead the two women toward an enormous, domelike structure. When Margaret voluntarily entered a noisome black tunnel, Rlinda wasn't overly enthusiastic about sharing the dark and crowded passages with so many armored monsters. But the old xeno-archaeologist pressed onward, looking for all the world like a woman simply going about her business.

Rlinda kept up with her rapid pace, taking sudden turns, following a path that only Margaret could see. Being out of breath kept her from asking too many questions. She'd never been particularly claustrophobic, but Rlinda felt as if she were suffocating inside the slick tunnels.

The large central chamber was even worse.

Margaret stopped and began talking to what appeared to be a churning mass of small grubs, black bits of smashed insects, broken debris, like a garbage heap that was somehow alive and crawling with maggots. "You remember Rlinda Kett—I brought her with me." She glanced back. "The breedex wishes to speak to you."

Rlinda's stomach lurched as the squirming mass shifted, changed. She wanted nothing more than to run . . . until she realized that the components were pulling together into a sculpture of a face. A human face.

The face of Davlin Lotze.

"You have got to be kidding me."

The head was like a colossal statue filling much of the central vault. Davlin's simulated lips moved. *"Rlinda Kett."* The voice was not Davlin's; it wasn't even close to human. *"I issued orders to guarantee your safety."*

"Very hospitable of you, Davlin." She fell back on humor as a means of self-protection.

"I am not . . . entirely Davlin. My mind encompasses all of the Klikiss in my hive. I have destroyed most other subhives . . . refused to incorporate their DNA . . . refused to fission."

Margaret spoke to Rlinda. "I'll explain Klikiss reproduction to you later. It's quite bizarre."

"I can't wait." Pushing back her fear, Rlinda forced herself to inch closer to the eerie sculptured head.

"I have one more subhive to destroy. That will be soon. Then I will be the One Breedex."

Rlinda looked at Margaret, then back at the hive mind. "Congratulations. What happens next?"

"Then I will do a great thing," the Davlin-breedex said. *"I will be much more powerful than ever before."*

"Davlin conquers the universe? Doesn't really sound like you."

"I am not Davlin."

In a low voice Margaret said, "He changes with every subhive he crushes, even if he doesn't assimilate it. But I think he means the Klikiss will exterminate the black robots next."

"Getting rid of the black robots doesn't sound like a bad idea to me. And what happens to all the other Klikiss subhives he's defeated? Do they join his army, does he kill them? What?"

"In this case, I'm not sure."

"The Pym subhive is nearly destroyed," the breedex said.

Margaret explained what she had learned over her years of research among them. "Left to themselves, the Klikiss would sweep like locusts across any planet they find—including human-inhabited worlds. But Davlin thinks he's strong enough to stop them. We have to pray that *he*—not the breedex of some other subhive—becomes the One Breedex."

Rlinda waited, but heard only the rustling, buzzing, and skittering of millions of small creatures. She wanted Davlin to tell her that he was not evil, but the simulated face said nothing. "Remember that old cliché about picking the lesser of two evils?" Feeling immense sadness, she murmured, "Sorry I'm late. I meant to rescue you."

"And I meant to escape intact. Instead . . . I have had to adapt."

The mosaic form of the man's head shivered and vibrated as if the pieces had lost their resolve to remain together in a particular pattern. Rlinda could hear a great flurry of Klikiss moving outside in the hive city. Something big must be happening.

The breedex was not forthcoming with explanations. Davlin's mind—or whatever part of it remained—was preoccupied with some great turmoil.

After a few tense moments, a procession of Klikiss warriors marked with crimson and maroon splotches marched into the presence of the breedex. They carried the heads of four enormous bugs, silver with jagged black stripes like lightning bolts across their horned head-crests. Ganglia and dripping cords hung from the severed necks; the faceted eyes were dull.

The warriors presented the four dead creatures as an offering, and the trophies were placed amongst the other piled clutter and debris. More warriors streamed in, crowding the vaulted chamber and chittering in celebration.

Margaret explained to Rlinda, "Those are domates from a rival subhive."

"Does that mean something important just happened?"

The writhing, shifting mass remained indistinguishable, the human personality drowned within the chaos, but finally the crude face formed itself from the squirming components once more.

"*EDF battleships severely damaged the Pym subhive. They killed several domates, but departed without destroying the breedex.*" The Davlin face paused. "*We arrived immediately afterward. My warriors achieved an easy victory. I have eradicated the Pym breedex.*"

"Then it's done." Margaret's voice was filled with awe.

"What does that mean?" Rlinda whispered to her.

"*I am now the Klikiss race. I am the hive mind that controls them all.*" The simulated head shifted, but the face it formed was not even remotely human, with no hint of Davlin Lotze. It looked like a giant spiny insect. *"Now I will change. Surviving members of every subhive will travel here, and my domates will devour them at last. Then I will embark on a great fissioning."*

Margaret looked alarmed. "But, Davlin, that will drown you out—your personality will be lost in the noise!"

The sculptured insect head crumbled into a mound of individual chaotically moving pieces. As far as Rlinda could tell, Davlin Lotze was already little more than a whisper in the cacophony of the gigantic hive mind.

89 ✹ DEPUTY CHAIRMAN ELDRED CAIN

He did not want to be at the execution ceremony, but Chairman Wenceslas had given him no choice. Deputy Cain and Sarein must be visibly present, Basil insisted, so that the public could see their unwavering support. Cain thought he might be sick, but he took refuge in his role as the unflappable deputy.

Sarein's voice carried a faint, forlorn tremble. "I remember when I used to love to watch the pageants, parades, and spectacles, Basil. Why don't we do something positive for a change, show the people the true core of the Hansa?"

The Chairman looked at her with an unreadable expression. Did he suspect something? "Oh, this will be a spectacle—just as Freedom's Sword expected my assassination to be a grand show."

Playing his part as never before, a somberly uniformed King Rory sat on a temporary throne high above the square, where he would mete out the Hansa's retribution. Rory's dark hair was perfectly cut, and the folds of heavy cloth disguised his thin body.

"Where is Captain McCammon?" Sarein asked, unsuccessfully trying to keep the alarm out of her voice. "Shouldn't he be here?"

"This work goes beyond the duties of the royal guard," Basil said. "I have come to question McCammon's enthusiasm, if not his loyalty. He failed to find a single confirmed member of the dissident group, but my cleanup crew discovered plenty as soon as they looked hard enough."

"Rounding up the usual suspects?" Cain asked.

"The evidence Colonel Andez provided was suitably convincing," the Chairman said.

As Rory sat on his throne, looking gravely important, a staccato burst of gunfire echoed across the plaza, but it was just part of the military parade. Dark-uniformed soldiers with red piping and red armbands marched into the plaza.

The Chairman's elite cleanup crew came forward carrying long jazer rifles on their shoulders, hustling along a group of eighteen bound and gagged prisoners. Their faces were gaunt, their eyes hollow; some were frantic, but all were secured in tight restraints. They stumbled as they attempted to keep pace with the military march. At the front of the group, Colonel Andez was actually grinning. Everyone could smell execution in the air.

Finally, King Rory recited his words. The boy knew not to deviate from the script. He could not entirely hide the quaver in his voice, though otherwise he valiantly acted his role. "Our enemies are not only those who attack us on distant planets or out in space. Our enemies are not limited to the Klikiss, the hydrogues, or the faeros, or even Peter and his rebellious Confederation. Sadly, we also have enemies right here among us — in our neighbors, our supposed friends! It is a rot working its way through our society.

"A group known as Freedom's Sword is a poison to humanity. There can be no doubt of this after their recent failed attempt to assassinate Chairman Wenceslas. Fortunately, the plotters of this foul murder have been apprehended, thanks to the diligence of my people." He raised his hands in benediction.

After the young King had finished, a lesser functionary came forward and in a ponderous voice read the names and crimes of the eighteen bound prisoners. One of them was a man still wearing mime's makeup.

Cain listened to charges of "unspeakable" crimes, alleged proof of involvement in the assassination plot. He doubted any of them were genuinely members of Freedom's Sword, but they made convenient scapegoats. No doubt they had been caught speaking against the administration. That was good enough to condemn them.

As soon as the assassination plot had failed, Cain knew the reactionary response would set in. He had been so careful to cover his tracks, to hide every hint that he or Sarein or McCammon might have been involved. He had left no evidence, no proof.

Chairman Wenceslas, however, didn't need any evidence or proof. He simply made up his own mind.

"We can all rest easy, now that the perpetrators have been brought to justice," Basil said.

The cleanup crew backed away to leave the group of prisoners standing in full view. As Colonel Andez unshouldered her jazer rifle and the other dark-uniformed soldiers did the same, the "conspirators" were herded together.

The knots grew tighter in Cain's stomach. Sarein seemed about to faint, and he reached over to steady her. Basil's eyes were fixed on the eighteen prisoners. One of them lurched against the group and tried to push toward the crowd despite his restraints. His movement was the trigger Andez had been waiting for. The cleanup crew fired their jazer rifles in a buzzing lightning storm of ozone and blinding light, flashing webs of disintegrating energy.

All eighteen prisoners were chopped into smoking hunks of meat. The carnage was over in seconds, but the reeking smoke curled upward long after. People in the crowd screamed. Basil smiled. He seemed to hear it as cheers.

With well-practiced moves, Andez snapped orders to her fellow guards. They shouldered their rifles and stepped back in perfect ranks. King Rory swayed uncertainly on his throne, as the silence hung for a long moment.

"Why doesn't he speak?" Basil muttered. "He knows what he's supposed to do."

Finally the boy remembered himself and got to his feet, starting out with a stammer but growing stronger. "Please don't make us do this again. Be loyal to your government. Help us achieve our victory. That is all I want, as your King."

Basil seemed impressed with his delivery. "Not bad."

"He's right," Sarein said in a raspy voice. "Let's hope we never have to do this again."

90 ☀ SULLIVAN GOLD

Two days after the horrific public executions, Sullivan opened the door to find a crisply uniformed Colonel Andez and six of her thugs ready to pounce. Lydia, standing in the kitchen, said sourly, "Tell them to leave."

"Please don't get in our way, Mr. Gold." Andez's voice was cold.

Wiping her hands on a towel, Lydia stormed forward, her face pinched. "Demand to see their search warrant, Sullivan. We don't have to let them in here. There are laws—"

Her ill-advised words seemed to incite the cleanup crew, and they pushed past Sullivan. "Wait a minute," he said. "This is private property. I'll call the police."

"We are the police."

Lydia got in their way. "No, you're not. You're a gang of hoodlums."

Sullivan grabbed his wife and physically restrained her. He had already seen how coolly they had gunned down the supposed accomplices in the assassination attempt on the Chairman. "Lydia, stop this."

"Tell *them* to stop it. Why are you letting them walk all

over you?" She looked hurt. "We have to stand up for ourselves. We can't just let this happen. It's not *right*!"

The uniformed men and women overturned the furniture, upended an entire bookshelf, opened the cupboards in the kitchen, and began to fling dishes, pots, and pans everywhere.

"Please, just tell me what you're looking for!" Sullivan cried.

"Evidence," said Andez.

"Evidence of what?"

"Whatever we can find. We've had reports about you, especially your wife." Andez smiled as they stood the dining room table on end as if they expected to find a secret transmitting device underneath the spindly wooden legs.

The previous day, his son Jerome's restaurant had been looted, the windows smashed. Other family members had had their homes and places of employment terrorized. The cleanup crew had gone to his daughter Patrice's private accounting office and placed an electronic lock on the door, posting that the business was "closed until further notice." Two other daughters and a son had been "detained," and his teenaged grandson Philip had a prestigious scholarship inexplicably revoked.

Now, as the uniformed men and women ransacked the home, going out of their way to overturn as many objects as possible, Lydia reached the boiling point. Sullivan saw it coming, but could not react quickly enough to stop her. She threw herself upon Andez, using bony fists to pound the woman's shoulders and back. In a flash, the others pounced on his wife. Sullivan shouted for them to stop, genuinely terrified that they would shoot Lydia. Instead, they put her in restraint cuffs.

"You can release her," he said, trying to get in the middle. "She won't cause any more trouble."

"She's caused far more than enough trouble. The Chairman gave us orders." Andez narrowed her eyes and looked at him. "He is still not pleased with your refusal to take over the Golgen skymines, Mr. Gold."

As they whisked Lydia away, she struggled like a tigress trying to protect her home. They didn't even bother continuing their search, and Sullivan felt that the whole event had been staged. He realized it must have been designed to provoke Lydia so they had an excuse to arrest her.

They had done it on purpose, just as they must have been selectively targeting his other family members. This was all about the Chairman showing him what the Hansa could do to him unless he agreed to cooperate.

He waited at home for almost a day, sure that Chairman Wenceslas would contact him with an ultimatum, and this time Sullivan would have no choice but to change his mind. But he heard nothing, and so he took the initiative and went to the Hansa HQ.

The door guards wouldn't let him inside, citing "security reasons."

Worse, he heard rumors that another round of executions would soon be scheduled. Though he never saw any list of proposed names, he felt a heavy dread in his chest. All of his family was in custody. He needed to see the Chairman. This was more than his own life and career on the line.

The first two times he begged for an appointment, his request was politely filed and then ignored, sent into a bin of low-priority items that some functionary far down in the chain of command would eventually review.

After days of being denied a meeting, Sullivan grew increasingly frantic. Finally, he tried a different administrative chain and managed to talk his way into one of the lower halls of the Hansa HQ. Fortunately, he bumped into Deputy Chairman Cain, who came through on his way to a meeting. "Please, Deputy, I need your help."

The pale-skinned man recognized Sullivan, and in a rush Sullivan explained what had happened. Cain looked grave. "Obviously you need to speak with the Chairman."

"I know. I've tried for days."

"Come with me."

Sullivan stumbled along, barely able to believe his luck. Cain walked right past the moat dragons, administrators, appointment keepers, and guards. "Mr. Chairman," he said loudly as they entered the penthouse office, "you need to hear what this man has to say."

In the spacious room, Chairman Wenceslas looked up with a scowl, recognizing Sullivan. "In due course. I have not yet replied to his requests."

"I'm happy to expedite matters for you, sir. This should take only a few moments to straighten out." He gestured Sullivan inside, as if he knew the Chairman was playing some unacceptable game, then turned smartly around and left.

Not sure what to do, but determined, Sullivan stood stiffly in front of the Chairman. "My family has been taken. I don't know why, and I don't know where they are. I . . . I was hoping you could help me, sir." He inhaled deeply. "Please."

"I'm sure there must have been some reason for their trouble."

Sullivan decided to cut to the chase. "All right, dammit. If you insist that I take over the management of the Roamer skymining complex on Golgen, then I will do my best. If you give me military support, I can probably handle a hostile workforce. Send me there immediately, if you like. Just please, leave my family alone. Keep them safe."

"These are dangerous and uncertain times, Mr. Gold. Who can guarantee anyone's safety?"

Sullivan leaned close to the other man. "*You* can, Chairman Wenceslas."

The other man smiled at the comment. "So I always believed, but recently I've had to take measures that I don't particularly like. I comfort myself with the knowledge that in the long run, history will see the wisdom in what I've done."

"I would see more of your wisdom if you released my family," Sullivan countered. "They have caused no harm and certainly meant none."

Basil tapped his fingers, aligning the fingerprints with other smudges on the polished projection surface of his desk. "The EDF base on the Moon would be a safe place to keep your family. Don't you agree? We can provide them secure housing on the base. Commandant Tilton will be a proper host. So long as your cooperation and performance at Golgen are acceptable, your loved ones will remain entirely unharmed."

Sullivan felt cold drops of sweat on his back. He couldn't believe Wenceslas was so blatant about holding hostages. The carefully honed edge of the man's political skill had been dulled by wielding his power with a heavy hand. "I suppose that's the best I can hope for, Mr. Chairman."

"Good. The Roamer skyminers on Golgen should be ripe for the picking. I'll assign an EDF squadron to help you assert your new authority."

Sullivan had little bargaining power, but he pushed as hard as he could. "Then please arrange for my family's transfer as soon as possible. Get them out of prison, or wherever you've kept them, and I will see them safely settled on the Moon — just to say goodbye and to comfort them. You understand."

Chairman Wenceslas apparently didn't understand, but he did not argue.

Sullivan pressed the matter as far as he dared. "Once I see them in place and I know exactly where they'll be, then I'll do as you say."

The Chairman called up papers on his screen. Apparently, he had already drafted the order. "Of course you will."

91 ☀ PATRICK FITZPATRICK III

Leaving Theroc after his grandmother's murder, Patrick and Zhett returned to the main skymine at Golgen, but his anger and shock did not diminish.

Maureen Fitzpatrick had never been a particularly warm person, but she had raised him to be strong. Patrick respected her, and now he began to realize how much he owed her . . . and how much he hated Chairman Wenceslas.

He and Zhett sat together in their bright and airy quarters aboard the skymine. The ever-resilient Roamers had gotten their ekti-processing operations back on track. With work shifts continuing around the clock, stardrive-fuel production was beginning to make up for what the EDF had stolen. Patrick doubted the General would be stupid enough to come back again so soon; on the other hand, he couldn't fathom anything the Earth military did anymore. Del Kellum vowed that he would rather jettison full canisters into the clouds than let the Eddy bastards have them.

King Peter had promised to send at least one of Admiral Willis's cruisers to Golgen for protection once they returned from Pym. However, Roamer skymines were now in place on dozens of gas giants, and the Confederation's fledgling military simply didn't have enough ships to patrol them all.

Patrick drew a deep breath. His voice hitched. "That should have been the most important act in her lifelong career. My grandmother could have changed things for the better—and she died for it."

Zhett's eyes blazed. "We've got to do something about that, Fitzie."

"Damn right we do." He slipped his arm around her. He had felt tangled in skeins of emotions—outrage, disbelief, a need for revenge, and horror at what the Hansa had been willing to do. He finally clarified his scrambled thoughts by trying to imagine what the old Battleaxe would have done. Then he knew.

He went to the broad window and stared out at the endless gas clouds. "Remember how my grandmother said I've become sort of a folk hero among the protesters? Well, my little confession was nothing compared to what we've got now. Vid images of EDF Mantas blasting the former Chairman's ship. And raiding the skymines here, stealing all that ekti. And the strike on the Osquivel shipyards, all those civilians killed."

"You can bet none of *that* was broadcast on any official Hansa channels," Zhett said.

"We have plenty of demonstrable proof of illegal activities. It's about time we share some of that proof with people on Earth—maybe link up with Freedom's Sword and help them overthrow the Chairman." Patrick set his jaw, imagining how his grandmother might have said the words. "I'm going to Earth, and I'm not going to come back until I've brought down Chairman Wenceslas."

Del Kellum could deny nothing to his daughter or his son-in-law. Son-in-law! Patrick still hadn't entirely wrapped his mind around *that* concept.

They gathered on the lower landing deck where cargo escorts, supply ships, and small inspection pods came and went. The breezes that filtered through the atmosphere-containment fields had an especially sour tang today, a chemical smell that indicated a new plume of gases bubbling up from below.

"All the resources of clan Kellum are at your disposal. It's time to teach the Big Goose a lesson or two, by damn. By now the Chairman's managed to piss off ninety percent of the population in the Spiral Arm."

Patrick said, "It's a critical mass. There's got to be an explosion soon."

"Just be careful. I'm way too busy to plan another couple of funerals." Kellum turned away, but not before Patrick saw the man's anxious expression. At the beginning of the war, the hydrogues had killed his fiancée and partner, Shareen Pasternak, and many years before that, Zhett's mother had also been killed in an accident. "Do what your Guiding Star says, my sweet."

"Don't worry," Zhett said, kissing her father's bearded cheek. "If I can handle Fitzie, the rest of Earth should be no problem."

92 ☼ DEPUTY CHAIRMAN ELDRED CAIN

When the battered remnants of General Lanyan's assault force returned from Pym, the acting commander explained how the Klikiss had defeated them. Conrad Brindle finished his report in Basil's Hansa office, while Deputy Cain diligently took notes.

Brindle pulled no punches. His clipped tone clearly expressed his disapproval as he laid the blame squarely on Lanyan for instigating the debacle. "There was no need for this to have happened—none whatsoever. The Confederation ships willingly offered their assistance. If we had joined forces, we could have annihilated the breedex."

"Instead, the General failed to complete either task," Basil growled. "He turned one sure victory into two total failures."

Brindle remained ramrod straight. "Yes, Mr. Chairman. Because of him, the EDF lost three Mantas, the *Thunder Child*, and a great many soldiers, including General Lanyan himself."

"And the Confederation military remains unscathed. That idiot probably thought he was going to impress me."

Cain finished with his notes, and kept his silence. He did not ask whether the assault had been a good idea in the first place, any more than the naïve plan to send Admiral Diente with an ancient translating device had been. While the Chairman searched doggedly for conspirators, Deputy Cain had attempted to be quieter and more unobtrusive than ever.

The Chairman had called up an intricate expanded grid of the command structure of the Earth Defense Forces. Many boxes in the upper tier remained empty, whole ranks decimated after the black robots' original turnabout. Now the top rank of General was also vacant.

Basil stared at the display. "Pike and San Luis are our only remaining grid admirals, and I'm not overly impressed with either of them." He barely paused before making an impulsive decision. "Brindle, you've demonstrated your capabilities and your loyalty—several times, in fact. I'm making you the new commander of the Earth Defense Forces."

The older man was startled, as was Cain. "Sir?"

The Chairman made an amendment to the command grid, used his authorization, and posted it. "Your rank is hereby raised to General, the highest military officer in the Earth Defense Forces." His face remained blank, his expression distant for a long moment before he seemed to remember to give a congratulatory smile. "Deputy Cain, arrange for an immediate ceremony. I want King Rory himself to pin on General Brindle's stars."

The next day, resplendent in spectacular robes and a crown that gleamed with gems, the young King confirmed Conrad Brindle as the new commander of the EDF.

Brindle knelt in front of the King in his crisp new uniform. The older man had served in the military all his life and now seemed amazed at his good fortune. Rory made additional pronouncements, praised Brindle's brave and loyal actions, and applied new rank insignia to his shoulders. Natalie Brindle, his wife, sat in an honored position near the portable throne, also wearing her EDF uniform.

The crowds cheered, and the newsnets recorded every second of the strange event. Cain watched without comment. The scene looked for all the world like an ancient king dubbing one of his new knights. . . .

The next evening Cain returned to his apartment suite in the heart of the Hansa pyramid, where he had no windows and no distractions. He spent more than an hour just sitting in solitary silence, contemplating his prized Velázquez paintings. He needed to center himself.

Even in his private sanctuary, though, Cain detected subtle indications that his possessions, furniture, and storage areas had been carefully searched. He felt a chill, suspecting that microscopic surveillance imagers must even now be trained on him. If he ransacked the place looking for them, the Chairman might interpret his actions as being indicative of a guilty conscience. No, it would take some time for him to put a subtle signal jammer in place, find the devices, and hook up a mirror feed of him performing innocuous activities.

Then again, he *was* just performing innocuous activities. He had nothing to worry about.

Cain knew that Chairman Wenceslas was still looking

for the traitor or traitors in his midst, determined to find the real assassins. But he also knew that Basil had never believed that the eighteen scapegoats were truly members of Freedom's Sword. He was too smart for that. The executions had been for show, not for justice or vengeance.

Cain had been careful at all times. He hoped he hadn't left any loose ends.

Unsettled but hiding his anxiety from any secret observers, he left his quarters. He was required to attend an "urgent" and mysterious meeting in the Whisper Palace . . . supposedly a late-night conference with King Rory himself, though Cain was sure the Chairman must be behind it. He always was.

Out in the dark streets, making his way through the crowds without drawing undue attention to himself, Cain noticed more than the usual number of uniformed members of Basil's cleanup crew on the streets, ever vigilant.

Cain was not a paranoid person, but he had no doubt that they were watching him.

93 ✷ SAREIN

When King Rory summoned her to the throne room of the Whisper Palace, Sarein was automatically frightened. He had never done that before, and she knew the boy wouldn't have thought of it on his own. It was late at night.

Ever since the failed assassination attempt, she'd felt as though her life had been built on a foundation of exceedingly fragile eggshells.

King Rory looked particularly young sitting on his elaborate throne. The crown on his head seemed overlarge, and his robes gave him a decadent rather than a regal appearance. So different from the somber uniform he had worn during the horrific executions of the supposed assassins.

Innocents, she knew.

Sarein had never spent time alone with Rory, had not seen him speak in an unrehearsed conversation. He was simply a mouthpiece for Chairman Wenceslas, as the Archfather was supposed to have been. And everyone in the Hansa had seen what happened when such a mouthpiece decided to speak for himself. She glanced up at the throne room ceiling, as if she might spot a newly installed set of lightning-bolt projectors.

On either side of the young King's throne stood royal guards, but Sarein did not recognize them as among the particular friends of Captain McCammon. Colonel Andez was also there with twelve members of the cleanup crew; they stood in a line with their backs to the stone wall.

Sarein was especially disturbed to see no other audience, no members of the media, no newsnet imagers. Too many guards, too many guns, and too few witnesses. Her throat went dry.

Deputy Cain and Captain McCammon arrived separately, looking similarly perplexed.

Rory rose from his elaborate seat and gestured for the three of them to step forward along a crimson carpet that flowed like a river to the raised throne. As she stopped before the dais, Sarein glanced out of the corner of her eye at her companions. Cain was as calm and unreadable as always, though right now he seemed to be working very hard to maintain his composure. McCammon was a half step closer to the throne, as if to shield her.

King Rory's brown eyes seemed to look *through* them, as if he were still practicing these words in front of a mirror. "We have long known there is a traitor in our midst. Chairman Wenceslas has brought to my attention certain evidence that proves who is really responsible—not only for the recent failed assassination attempt, but also for letting the outlaw Peter and his wife, Estarra, escape from Earth. We also know that Freedom's Sword did not plan their assassination attempt without cooperation from someone close to the Chairman."

The pronouncement reverberated like a thunderclap. All of the guards remained silent. Sarein felt her knees tremble. How could he know? What loose ends had they not wrapped up? Before anyone else could speak, she pressed forward, trying to sound perfectly reasonable. "That is excellent news, King Rory. Exactly what sort of evidence do you have? And how can we help?"

McCammon nodded, picking up on her cue. "I'll send my men to apprehend him. It is my duty to protect you, Your Highness."

Deputy Cain did not seem at all ruffled. "I thought you announced that all those involved in the assassination plot were found and executed?" He sounded as if he were explaining mathematics to a child. "And after all this time it seems frivolous to worry about the nature of the King and Queen's self-imposed exile. Considering what just happened to General Lanyan on Pym, shouldn't the Hansa be more worried about a Klikiss retaliation? Surely we have higher priorities."

Basil emerged from a side alcove and stood not far from the King's throne. His mere presence suddenly increased the level of threat that Sarein felt. "Enough games, all of you. We have significant new information. I know one of you three is behind it."

Before McCammon and Sarein could protest, Cain lifted his chin. "Games, Mr. Chairman? I recognize the tactic, and we all resent it. How many others have you brought here and accused like this, hoping to get a nervous confession? If you do it enough times, you're bound to find someone sufficiently frightened to cave in."

Sarein jumped on Cain's train. With eyes flashing, she directed her words at Basil. "You're trying to intimidate us, and frankly I don't appreciate it. We've been your trusted advisers for years."

Basil came around the throne, his face flushed. "You don't appreciate it? *I* don't appreciate someone—someone so close to me—trying to kill me!"

Sarein struggled to hide her anxiety. The three of them had done enough questionable things that the simplest mistake, the slightest missing detail, could have been enough to draw attention to them. She knew her own part in the conspiracy, and she felt color rising in her cheeks.

"Was it you?" He focused his accusatory stare on her like a high-powered jazer beam, as if he knew she was the easiest one to break. *"Sarein?"*

If she said nothing, he would assume she was guilty. If she vehemently denied her involvement, she would look guilty. "Basil, stop this. How can you believe that any of us is involved? You know you can trust me."

"Do I?" He looked like a total stranger to her. "We will take care of this today. Now."

Cain protested, drawing Basil's jazer stare away from Sarein. "Mr. Chairman, you have produced no evidence for these unlikely assertions."

Basil actually seemed relieved. "I have all the proof I need, Deputy Cain."

Sarein could see, as clearly as she had ever understood anything, that Basil meant to blame one of the three of them. He would not let anyone leave the room until he was satisfied.

She knew that she would buckle if Basil subjected her to direct interrogation—but she held on to the very slim hope that he would give her the benefit of the doubt because of his past feelings. She remembered how he had once been. He *must* still have at least a glimmer of affection for her.

On the other hand, Cain and McCammon might well face execution. He hadn't required much of an excuse to murder the eighteen alleged conspirators in the public square.

Maybe if *she* confessed, though, Basil would just exile her back to Theroc—which was what she really wanted anyway. It seemed to her that it was the only way out of this mess, a single chance to save the other two.

Sarein drew a breath and opened her mouth, ready to blurt that she was the one—the *only one*—responsible, when McCammon, after a brief glance at her, snapped, "It was me. I let the King and Queen escape."

"He's lying!" Sarein cried.

"Captain McCammon, do not speak another word," Cain said. "Do not give in to unnecessary inappropriate pressure."

"I am not lying, and I will not stop." McCammon clearly

realized that he needed to pull all of the blame upon himself if there was to be any hope of helping Sarein and Cain get away. "*I* set up the assassination attempt at the manufacturing center. *I* let the King stun me so that he could escape from the Whisper Palace." He shouted out anything he could think of. "*I* allowed the green priest Nahton to slip away from his detention quarters so he could warn Theroc about the imminent EDF attack." He crossed his arms over his chest. "*I* am the head of Freedom's Sword."

Standing in front of them, Basil's expression oscillated between smug satisfaction and fury. He slowly turned and went back to stand beside Rory's throne. "That is enough, Captain. Thank you for making this easier."

Colonel Andez gave a short, sharp whistle, and the members of her cleanup crew lowered their firearms and touched the power switches. A barely audible hum of active rifles resonated in the large chamber.

"What have you done?" Sarein said to McCammon in a hoarse whisper. Cain had turned into a statue, clearly seeing that he could do nothing to change the Chairman's decision, but Sarein wouldn't give up. Appalled, she shouted, "Basil, stop this!" No one looked at her.

Coldly furious, the Chairman said to McCammon, "I would dearly love to make a true public spectacle of you, Captain—even have you drawn and quartered." He heaved a deep breath. "But that in itself poses a problem. The alleged conspirators have already been executed, and the public is happy enough with that. There's no need to flaunt the fact that someone close to me was a traitor. Alas, your execution will have to be swift and private. It's better that way."

Sarein was prepared to insist that McCammon hadn't acted alone, but Cain grabbed her forearm and squeezed so tightly that he nearly broke her wrist. Cain cleared his throat. "Sir, Captain McCammon deserves a full trial. I must insist that you follow proper legal—"

Basil gave a signal, and without a moment's hesitation, before anyone could speak another word, the cleanup crew let loose a burst of weapons fire.

McCammon shuddered and jittered as dozens of high-speed hot projectiles peppered his body, splattering his fellow conspirators with gore. Sarein screamed. McCammon dropped to the floor, his body broken and shredded. Blood spread out in a thick pool, seeping into the crimson rug.

Cain could only stare. Sarein bit her lip, struggling against her own sobs. Even King Rory, his eyes as wide as saucers, could not control himself. He leaned over the side of the throne away from Basil and vomited with loud retching sounds. The Chairman frowned at this sign of weakness.

After a long silence, Basil snapped to the guards, "Please clean up the mess." He glanced at the vomit on the floor. "All of it."

94 ☀ SIRIX

The black robots worked together in space. Earth's blue-and-white sphere was a target tantalizingly out of reach, though probably not for long.

Watchdog EDF engineers flitted along in inspection shuttles and scanning pods, while crew "supervisors" observed the industrious black machines gathering more debris to repair the damaged EDF ships. They tried not to interfere, but their very presence hindered Sirix's efforts.

The human inspectors paid particularly close attention to the angular new robot vessels being assembled from scrap and structural components that were too damaged to be placed back into service for the EDF. Methodical robots worked in small teams to cobble together enormous vessels of radically different configurations. The inspectors could look all they liked. They had no hope of understanding the vessels or the hidden offensive weaponry.

Without remorse Sirix could have given a command for his robots to turn on the meddling humans, crack open the inspection pods, and pull their bloated bodies out into the cold vacuum. But he didn't want to do that yet. He still had much to gain from them, so the deception must continue.

Sirix boarded one of the nearly complete Juggernauts, where overworked Hansa quality-control teams and EDF engineers were combing over the systems, anxious to give their stamp of approval. When the inspectors ran their diagnostics, they would see exactly the readings they expected. The microscopic booby traps were far too subtle to be found.

On the clean, sterile bridge of the giant ship, Sirix scuttled forward on fingerlike legs to stand before the pleased-looking team. "I am ready to present this vessel to your Earth Defense Forces, if it meets with your approval."

"Oh, indeed! It's as good as new." The man clutched his electronic clipboard as if it were some kind of holy book. "Things are looking up."

"You and your robots have our gratitude for the work

you're doing," said the second inspector. "Faster and more efficient than our own crews could ever manage."

They wanted so badly to believe that the robots really intended to help them. Sirix found it ironic, even amusing. "Then I look forward to the release of another one hundred robots from your manufactories."

"We'll put in the request. Everything seems to be in order here."

The new robots would join existing work crews to keep the production moving at a rapid clip, which greatly pleased Chairman Wenceslas. As each new batch of robots was shipped up from the surface, four of Sirix's comrades saw to their indoctrination, uploading true programming so that the new replacements were as close to real Klikiss robots as possible. They even installed shared memories in the new robots' woefully empty storage modules. The new machines were like infants, but they were being educated rapidly.

Every one of them understood the overall mission.

For the first time since the end of the hydrogue war, Sirix actually began to feel strong again. Ah, yes, he and the humans, perfectly cooperative allies . . .

Even though they had provoked the Ildiran Empire, the Hansa would never be prepared for such an overwhelming attack by the Solar Navy—especially not now. With his own warliners and the nearly complete cohort led by Tal Ala'nh, Adar Zan'nh surely had enough firepower to resist the human military.

Even so, he also incorporated the five damaged warliners from Designate Ridek'h's processional septa that had been burned by the faeros. After leaving Ildira, he had found two other maniples of warliners patrolling the outskirts of the Empire, guarding splinter colonies there. Now, his fleet swelled as they rushed toward Earth.

Every pilot, septar, qul, and tal received all the information Adar Zan'nh had on the strategic makeup of Earth, its Moon, the likely placement of EDF perimeter picket ships, and the positioning of defenses closer to the planet. While helping the humans stand against the hydrogues, the Adar had spent significant time near Earth, and he used that knowledge now.

As they approached their destination, Zan'nh reviewed the plans he had made before departing from Ildira. His warliners would perform a lightning strike: plunge toward the lunar base, take advantage of the element of surprise, overcome any Earth Defense Forces they found there, and rescue the Mage-Imperator. Instead of prolonging the engagement with the human military, he would make a clean escape and then ask his father for further orders.

After days of interstellar passage, the Solar Navy charged into Earth's solar system and set course directly toward the Moon. They did not pause to survey or assess. As the warliners raced forward, he could feel the determination and enthusiasm resounding through the faint strands of *thism* that bound them all together.

The Mage-Imperator was here, and he would sense their arrival. He would know the Solar Navy had come for him. Jora'h would be ready. As the ships grew closer, Zan'nh could feel the gratifying strength of his father's *thism*. This was the reason these soldiers had accepted the destruction of Mijistra, why they had gambled everything to escape from the faeros.

The crew did not cheer in a wild and uncontained way, as humans might have. Their manner of celebrating was to complete a difficult task. Today, finally, they would free their beloved leader. The Mage-Imperator would return to his people.

Hundreds of ornate Ildiran battleships encircled the Moon in a breathtaking show of force, barely slowing enough to achieve orbital velocity. Two maniples stood off at a greater distance to forestall any EDF reinforcements that might arrive from farther out in the solar system.

Zan'nh was convinced that he could subdue any resistance from the relatively small number of soldiers at the lunar training base and free the Mage-Imperator. The rest would depend on timing. He hoped to be quick about this — in and out before a significant response could be mounted.

With the perfect coordination of a skyparade, innumerable warliners entered various orbits above the cratered surface and pointed their weapons toward the domed settlement and paved landing zones. As he had expected, the lunar base's complement of heavy battleships, small cargo haulers, troop transports, and swift courier ships was minimal. Most of the fleet was closer to Earth.

To his great indignation, the Adar saw the captured flagship warliner—the Mage-Imperator's own ship—drifting in low lunar orbit, darkened and mostly unmanned. Though it was tempting to dispatch a separate crew to board and recapture the stolen warliner, that was not his priority. He would not put the mission at risk.

"Transmit on all known EDF bands." He stood at the command nucleus rail. "This is Adar Zan'nh of the Ildiran Solar Navy. Surrender Mage-Imperator Jora'h and all Ildiran prisoners. If you resist, you will suffer great harm—and we will still take our leader back."

Alarms sounded down below. Cries of disbelief echoed across various communication bands. Within moments, troop transports rose, though it was clear they could not challenge the Solar Navy by hurling infantry at them. One Manta detached from an orbiting fuel depot and circled around as if to launch a solo attack against the entire Solar Navy, but fortunately the captain changed his mind. In a frenzy, several EDF courier craft raced away.

"Adar, numerous ships are slipping through our net. Several emergency transmissions have been directed toward Earth. They will know we are here."

"It cannot be helped. We must act swiftly."

The EDF base was locking down in what must have been standard emergency procedures. Access domes were sealed shut, and airlocks were deactivated so that Ildiran troops could not access them.

Zan'nh had not expected an immediate surrender. He issued his next command to his ships. "Dispatch all cutters to the lunar surface. *All* of them." He knew precisely the impression that would make: Anyone in charge would be awestruck. The Earth Defense Forces could not stand against such show of strength, and it was far more than just show.

While flocks of Ildiran cutters dropped down to the Moon, hundreds of warliners remained in lunar orbit with their weapons ready, surrounded by a wider-ranging defensive line. In wave after wave of heavily crowded landers, hundreds of thousands of Solar Navy soldiers landed on the lunar surface, each suited, armed, and trained . . . each with a single goal for this mission.

Zan'nh transmitted his ultimatum to the local base commander. "I am prepared to pummel every dome, every outpost, and every ship until you surrender our Mage-Imperator."

96 ☀ MAGE-IMPERATOR JORA'H

Alarms sounded deep inside the lunar base tunnels. As he watched the EDF soldiers running about with panic on their faces, Jora'h could tell that this was no drill.

"We are under attack," Nira said to him, looking through the window in the locked door of their barracks quarters.

"But by whom? The hydrogues again? The faeros? Klikiss robots?"

Jora'h felt a surge of turmoil in the *thism,* and he smiled. He pressed a flattened palm against his chest, examining the faint feelings. "No, it is something else. Ildirans are near, many of them . . . the Solar Navy. And Adar Zan'nh is here."

Nira caught her breath. She sensed it, too. "Yes, and Osira'h! She's the one who gave them our exact location."

Out in the corridor, harsh loudspeaker voices ordered detachments and squadrons to take up specific positions. Breathless soldiers rushed to the armories, pilots ran to their ships in the landing bays. Security doors slammed into place. Moments later an announcement declared that all airlock domes had been locked down to prevent any entry into the base.

"They're scared," Nira said. "Genuinely scared."

"They should be. The Solar Navy means to free me, whatever the cost." The Mage-Imperator stood as tall as he could, his hands locked behind his back. He felt invigorated by the presence of thousands more Ildirans. All of the captives would feel it, too.

He stared at the sealed doorway of their stone-walled quarters and waited. He knew someone would come for him soon.

More than fifty uniformed humans crowded the halls outside the holding chambers for the Ildiran prisoners. Apparently, some of the EDF soldiers intended to make a last stand here.

The gaunt commandant elbowed his way through the anxious troops. Tilton's bulging eyes were wild, his expression nearly frantic. He reached the entrance of Jora'h's holding room and paused to take a breath, as if gathering courage.

The Mage-Imperator faced him at the threshold, hardening his own resolve. He did not intend to compromise with this man who had willingly followed the heinous orders issued by Chairman Wenceslas.

The commandant disengaged the security on the chamber door, opened the transparent panel, and stepped inside without being invited. More than a dozen soldiers stood at the entrance behind him, ostensibly to guard it. "Your Solar Navy has come with hundreds of ships. Hundreds! They have this base under siege. I cannot fathom how they knew your exact location."

Jora'h smiled. "All Ildirans can feel their Mage-Imperator. We are connected in ways that humans are not."

Tilton sounded fearful but resigned. "I can be realistic. There is no way our reinforcements can arrive in time, but I don't think your Adar is inclined to settle in for a long engagement. He's in a hurry, and he demands your immediate release. Thousands of small cutters are dropping down to the lunar surface, and our defenses won't hold up against them." He shook his head. "Personally, I think you're more trouble than you're worth."

Jora'h shrugged casually. "Then release me."

Tilton withdrew his sidearm and held it loosely in his hand. "They would be very upset to find you dead when they arrive. You're the only bargaining chip I have."

Nira stepped directly in front of Jora'h, boldly placing herself between him and the gun. "You will not kill him."

Tilton looked more flustered than angry. "You think I won't just shoot you both if it comes to that? If I have to?"

"If you harm me, or either of us," Jora'h said in a voice

as hard and cold as frozen steel, "then you guarantee that my Solar Navy will kill every single person on this base. They will feel the moment of my death. You saw how furiously my handful of guards fought when they tried to free me. Imagine what would happen if they knew you had killed me." Even though Jora'h despised the Hansa Chairman for what he had done, he did not wish to inflict a bloodbath on the human soldiers. His true battle had always been clear—to fight the *faeros*.

Tilton was holding his sidearm halfheartedly. "Then I suggest we reach some sort of satisfactory conclusion here."

"The only satisfactory conclusion is for you to release me so I can go back and save my Empire. You and your Chairman have already done enough damage."

Sporadic gunfire echoed through the tunnels, coming closer. Tilton seemed very alarmed.

"The Solar Navy soldiers are approaching, Commandant," Nira said, stepping even closer to the man's sidearm. "If you order your troops to dig in and fight back, you know it'll be a massacre, and you'll never hold them back. In the end the Ildirans will still free us."

"The outcome is a foregone conclusion," Jora'h said. "But the path to it is not yet decided. Tell your soldiers to withdraw. Let us go free. You will be saving hundreds, perhaps thousands, of lives."

"Most of them human lives," Nira pointed out. "Do the honorable thing."

Tilton's expression was in knots, as if he were ready either to explode or collapse. He shifted the sidearm. "Chairman Wenceslas isn't going to like this one bit," he finally said under his breath. He shouted over his shoulder to his soldiers crowded in the corridor. "Pass the word on the intercom. Do not engage the Solar Navy troops!" He clenched his jaw, working his muscles. "Inform the Ildirans that their Mage-Imperator is unharmed—and will remain unharmed only if they stop killing my men."

Slowly, the sounds of sporadic resistance died away, though the chaotic shouts continued. With thunderous footsteps, bestial-looking Solar Navy soldiers charged down the tunnels, their crystal katanas ready to slash apart any uniformed EDF personnel who stood in their way. Adar Zan'nh strode at the head of the group, looking as if he had just conquered an entire planet.

As soon as the Adar approached the holding cell, Tilton again pointed his sidearm threateningly at Jora'h. "What guarantee do I have that your troops won't murder us all once you've taken the Mage-Imperator? I need assurances for me and my personnel."

Zan'nh narrowed his eyes, fixated on the hand weapon. "This is an insult. Have you not done enough harm already?"

Tilton was extremely jittery to see the sheer number of Solar Navy soldiers pressing close. Nira stepped forward and simply plucked the weapon from the man's sweaty hands. "You aren't going to shoot him, Commandant." Tilton looked ready to collapse.

Jora'h stepped forward. "Good work, Adar."

A broad smile of relief crossed Zan'nh's face. Unable to restrain himself, he embraced his father, then stepped back to salute his Mage-Imperator in a more formal fashion. "I have what I came for." He glowered at the defeated commandant. "It is time for the Solar Navy to withdraw."

When the Chairman sent his family to the lunar base "for their own protection," Sullivan had not expected the place to be pleasant. Nor had he expected to be caught in the middle of a war.

Before he agreed to go to the Roamer gas giant of Golgen with a full EDF peacekeeping escort, Sullivan followed Lydia and his family to the Moon, insisting on seeing them settled in. He tried to promise them (and, secretly, himself) that everything would be all right. This was a painful solution, but the only one he could think of.

And then the base was attacked.

"Do the soldiers have to have drills every hour of every day? Don't they ever sleep?" Lydia groaned. She turned to her husband. "I'm glad you're here, at least."

Sullivan poked his head outside their quarters, one in a row of identical rooms along the same rock-lined corridor. When intercom messages called all soldiers to battle stations to defend the base, he listened to the palpable urgency in the voices. "I don't think this is a drill."

Because they were not technically prisoners, his family could move wherever they liked, provided they remained within certain nonrestricted areas. Jerome, Victor, and Patrice had all sat around sullenly for most of the first day, unable to guess how they could ever put their lives back together. The younger children had quickly become bored.

Sullivan grabbed Lydia's wrist. "Quick, let's get the

family together. I don't know what's happening, but we don't want to lose anyone."

No one would explain what all the excitement was about, even after the turmoil had raged for more than half an hour. The frantic soldiers had other priorities, and that gave Sullivan no great confidence. Lydia was already upset at being here. "I don't know whether to be afraid, or hope that these soldiers get some sense knocked into them."

Commandant Tilton's order echoed through the loudspeakers over the commotion and the sporadic gunfire in the corridors. "Give the Solar Navy soldiers unrestricted passage to the Mage-Imperator. Do not engage. They will guarantee our safety if we do not shoot at them. The Mage-Imperator is to be released unharmed."

Sullivan blinked. "So the Solar Navy's here to rescue their people. That's good news."

"And how does that benefit us?" Lydia said, sounding hopeful.

He thought about that, weighed their options, and made up his mind. "Come with me, all of you." He rushed out into the corridor, and the whole group of them, fourteen in all, followed him along the tunnels. The younger children were crying; Philip's expression held more excitement than fear.

"Where are we going, Sullivan?" Lydia said. "If this is the best thing, I'm right behind you — but what good will the Solar Navy do us?"

"Plenty. Would you rather count on the hospitality of the EDF? Given the alternative, I prefer the way the Mage-Imperator treated me." He looked deep into his wife's eyes. "Please. I need you to trust me."

She responded with a wry smile. "I always trust you. Haven't we given each other enough headaches over the years? We came through it all. We'll go, if that's what you say we need to do."

Sullivan had a general idea of the section of the base where the Ildiran captives were being held, and he made a beeline for it, family in tow. The passageways were filled with so many confused soldiers that no one bothered to stop them.

Just before they reached the Ildiran barracks, Sullivan turned a corner and came upon a large group of armored Solar Navy soldiers standing in ranks. Waving his hands at the stony Ildirans, he tried to get the attention of anybody in charge. "My name is Sullivan Gold. Please take me to Mage-Imperator Jora'h or Adar Zan'nh — either one will do."

The ferocious-looking fighters glared at him.

Since all the Ildiran soldiers were marching toward the same point, Sullivan decided to follow them with Lydia and their large brood. "Excuse me!" He worked his way around heavily muscled guard kithmen, avoiding their sharp weapons and hard armor. Ildiran soldiers were streaming swiftly out of the tunnels in an orderly retreat, heading back toward the surface and the large paved landing zones where a veritable blizzard of cutters and troop transports had landed. "I hope we're not too late."

Ahead of them, he saw more Ildirans in different clothing, bureaucrat kithmen, attenders, then a female green priest. He knew Jora'h must be nearby. "Mage-Imperator! Wait! I need to speak with you!"

An imposingly dressed soldier at the head of the crowd turned toward him, and Sullivan recognized Adar Zan'nh. The military commander caught his father's attention, pointing back at Sullivan, who pulled Lydia along with him, whispering, "Follow me. Better not make them wait."

When he finally worked his way through the muscular guard kithmen, Sullivan faced the Adar and the Mage-Imperator. He could barely catch his breath. "My family and I request sanctuary in the Ildiran Empire. Please take us with you."

"This is quite a turnabout, Sullivan Gold." Jora'h looked at him in surprise. "Have you changed your mind about staying in the Hansa?"

"Yes, sir, we have," Lydia piped up for him. "Our whole family has."

Surprisingly, the Adar spoke in his favor. "This man has already demonstrated how much he has to offer our people, Liege. We know he would be a continued asset to the Empire."

"And my family can be just as useful. This is my wife, Lydia." He pointed to the rest of the group. "I'll introduce the others later. The Chairman had them all held hostage. Please take us back to Ildira. We'd much rather be there."

Mage-Imperator Jora'h turned a sad but understanding face toward him. "The faeros have invaded Ildira. Hundreds of thousands have already died. Mijistra itself is obliterated, as is the Prism Palace. I am no longer sure how much of my Empire remains."

Sullivan was shocked to hear the news, but he did not change his mind. "Nevertheless, we'd still rather take our chances with the Ildirans. We'll help you however we can. This hasn't been a picnic here."

The Mage-Imperator nodded, then gestured for them to follow. By the time they climbed aboard a large troop transport, Sullivan had calmed the family somewhat. "It'll be all right—I *mean* it this time."

Clusters of ships rose away from the landing fields on

the Moon to join the crowded warliners in low orbit. Sullivan was amazed at the speed of the frantic mass exodus. The whole operation was astoundingly efficient.

While the Solar Navy retrieved its personnel from the Moon, the outer ring of warliners remained ready to intercept the first reinforcement battleships that were en route from Earth. From start to finish, Adar Zan'nh's lightning strike and his near-bloodless rescue of the Mage-Imperator lasted no more than two hours.

Once all personnel were aboard, the first septas of warliners streaked away toward a prearranged rendezvous point. Sullivan and his family followed the Mage-Imperator and Nira into the command nucleus of Adar Zan'nh's warliner. Jora'h and Nira's young daughter Osira'h greeted her parents with hugs. Sullivan wasn't sure if he belonged there, but none of the Ildirans complained.

Warliners continued to streak away, one by one, as soon as their crews returned. While waiting for the rest of the evacuation, the remaining Solar Navy maniples clustered in a defensive formation, prepared to depart once they had finished guarding the retreat. Though his primary mission had been to rescue the Mage-Imperator, Adar Zan'nh insisted on remaining there until all ships had gotten safely away.

When the last cutters and troop transports landed aboard the flagship, he looked at the Mage-Imperator's warliner, which had been seized by the EDF, still in a parking orbit over the Moon. He seemed to be weighing options, deciding whether or not he had time to retrieve it.

A new set of alarms shrieked throughout the command nucleus. "Adar, incoming vessels! They are on their way to the Moon from outside the system. A . . . *vast* number."

"It's probably the EDF chasing you," Sullivan said, trying to stay out of the way. "But I didn't think they had that many ships left outside of the solar system."

Zan'nh stood with his father, staring at the main projection screen. "These are not Earth vessels. In fact, these are not truly vessels at all . . ."

Moving so swiftly that the sensors had difficulty tracking them, bright lights drove forward like flashes of fire from deep space. It looked like a frenzied cluster of stars shot into the solar system, flaming ellipsoids too numerous to count.

"If the faeros knew to come here, then apparently Rusa'h was not killed in the destruction of Mijistra, as we hoped," Zan'nh said.

In the command nucleus, Osira'h touched her father's hand. "Rusa'h thinks you are still on the Moon."

Adar Zan'nh snapped quick orders. "Move our remaining ships to the far side of the Moon. We will take advantage of the blocking shadow to finish loading our last cutters and transports."

"If the faeros are coming for us," Jora'h said, "they will find us."

The last few warliners dove below the cratered horizon, swiftly finishing their lockdown procedures. "No, Liege. I promise you, we will escape."

Behind them, like an inconceivably powerful meteor shower, the faeros armada headed straight toward the Earth's Moon.

When he discovered the damn fool thing Rlinda had done by chasing off to "save" Davlin Lotze, BeBob packed up the *Blind Faith* and went after her.

He'd come back to the shipyards, pleased with how well the *Blind Faith* had operated. The trip to the forestry colony of Eldora had been a successful run, not traumatic like the debacle at Relleker. When he disembarked, he had expected a particularly large hug (and other physical celebrations) from Rlinda. But she was gone. She hadn't done BeBob any favors by leaving him that explanatory message. He couldn't decide if he was more upset that she would pull such a crazy stunt, or that she would have gone without telling him.

And now he had to go rescue her.

BeBob took less than an hour to pack his supplies, top off the ekti tanks, and head out again, muttering to himself all the while. On his approach to Llaro, he flew casually, calling no attention to himself. He'd read the reports submitted by Tasia Tamblyn and Robb Brindle about this place, had talked at great length with Orli Covitz and Hud Steinman during their escape flight from Relleker. He had some idea what to expect. He wished Rlinda had. Once he saw the immensity of the hive city, he couldn't believe she would have willingly stepped foot into that. What a mess!

He felt sick with revulsion and anxiety. "Why did you

go without me, Rlinda?" His instruments were blurry, and he swiped away tears.

The insect colony was a nightmare of towers, tunnels, and incomprehensible organic shapes. BeBob couldn't begin to estimate the number of bugs that inhabited the place. Every scrap of ground was covered by Klikiss, from the free-form rock towers, to the canyons, to the desolate flatlands that had once been agricultural fields planted by hopeful colonists. Crowds of bugs—millions to be sure—marched around in a maddening blur of colors, sharp-jointed legs, and armored crests. They all seemed extremely agitated. The comparison to a stirred-up anthill was too easy.

Orli had told him, in vivid detail, about the horrific slaughter of the trapped Llaro colonists when the breedex decided it was time to fission. He wondered if that could be happening now . . . and who the next group of victims would be.

In the heart of the city, a large trapezoidal stone slab towered many meters high, ringed by coordinate tiles. The transportal was continuously active, and rank after rank of Klikiss poured forth from the gateway, thousands more every minute, flooding to Llaro.

"Oh, Rlinda, what have you gotten yourself into?"

And how was he supposed to get her out of it?

Then his continuous sweeps picked up the *Curiosity*'s ID beacon. No voice, no transmission—just the locator. Nevertheless, his heart started pounding. At least the ship wasn't utterly destroyed. Definitely a good sign. He descended recklessly toward where Rlinda had landed.

It didn't matter if Rlinda had landed her ship safely—the bugs would have gotten her. He realized that if he had any common sense, he would just turn around and race away before the Klikiss came after him. But he couldn't bring himself to alter the *Blind Faith*'s course. Not until he knew.

Some rescue this had turned out to be.

Finally, he spotted the *Curiosity*, a dark speck landed amidst the gray-brown structures, right in the middle of the maddening flow of insects. He increased magnification, ran a set of scans (silently thanking Orli for having shown him how to work all the new computer systems), and soon saw how much damage the *Curiosity* had suffered. The engines were blasted; several holes had been torn through the hull; dark smoke stained the metal plates.

Definitely a crash, then. And it didn't look like an accident.

He hit the transmitter, his voice breaking as he squawked, "Rlinda, it's me! Are you there?" He waited a second—it seemed like a year—then repeated his message. "I found your ship, but where are you?"

Unexpectedly, a warm voice came over the comm speaker. "BeBob, it's me. Don't worry." Before he could respond, Rlinda added, "Well, you can worry a little bit, but I think we'll be okay . . . if you don't wait too damn long. The bugs aren't interested in us. Not at the moment, anyway."

He was so shocked and thrilled that he nearly sent the ship into a spin as he fumbled with the comm controls. "I'm coming! Doesn't look too good down there. Where in the world am I supposed to land? How do I find you?"

"Are you saying you won't be able to tell me apart from a million giant cockroaches? Thanks a lot." She spoke to someone else with her, then answered, "We're inside the *Curiosity* . . . but as you can probably see, my ship's not going anywhere. Land nearby."

He wondered if this could be some kind of trick, if

the Klikiss had managed to imitate Rlinda's voice, but he doubted such creatures could have mimicked her personality so well. He altered course, descended to the wrecked vessel. "Who's 'we?' You got company?" Maybe she had found Davlin after all!

"Margaret Colicos. She's coming with us."

Orli and Steinman had told him that the long-lost xeno-archaeologist was still trapped among the Klikiss. "I'll try to land without squashing too many bugs."

"Don't worry, the breedex has plenty more where they came from, and right now the bugs are preoccupied with their superfissioning, or whatever they call it. But I'd sure appreciate getting the hell out of here."

As soon as the *Faith*'s shadow fell over them, the gathered insects shuffled aside, clearing enough room for him to set the ship down with a hard thump, kicking up dust and powdery stones. Not his best landing, but he doubted Rlinda would scold him for being sloppy.

The *Curiosity*'s hatch glided open, and Rlinda emerged with another woman. They both looked dusty and sweaty, but apparently unharmed. They pushed their way through the monstrous ranks of secreters, diggers, warriors, and scouts, dodging toward the *Faith*. They were running. Maybe Rlinda wasn't as confident as she'd sounded.

He opened the hatch and was almost overwhelmed by the smell of all the insects, but he shouted and waved. "Rlinda! Over here!" As if she didn't know damned well where his ship was.

She pelted up to him and nearly bowled him over with a hug, driving him back into the ship. BeBob had known her for so long that he could see how deeply frightened she was.

"Rlinda, what's really going on? Did you find Davlin? How did you get Margaret free from those things?"

"The breedex is letting us go. No strings attached." While he tried to process that, she continued in a rush. "The breedex is *Davlin*—at least in part. Davlin is controlling this hive . . . the whole damn race, in fact. Or he was."

Looking agitated as well, Margaret Colicos boarded the *Blind Faith* just behind Rlinda. "The race is about to complete a massive new fissioning, pooling the genetic songs of all the diverse subhives. There will be One Breedex." She looked devastated, as if only she understood what she was saying. "Until now, Davlin's humanity kept a tenuous control over the Llaro subhive, but the domates are even now devouring representatives of all the defeated breedexes. It will be a massive, final fissioning, and after the other Klikiss attributes flood into the hive mind, Davlin is sure to be entirely subsumed." She sealed the hatch. "We have to depart—now—before that happens."

BeBob's mind was already overloaded. "Is any of that supposed to make sense to me? You've both got a lot of explaining to do."

"We'll fill you in after we're all flying away at top speed," Rlinda said. She wasted no time in getting to the cockpit and firing up the engines. The *Blind Faith* raced away, unnoticed by the swarming insect creatures.

A s frantic emergency calls came from the lunar EDF base, the battleships patrolling Earth orbit rallied, while others launched from the Palace District spaceport.

From the bridge of his new flagship, the *Goliath*, General Conrad Brindle watched the ships move into position and prepare for a rapid response. "The Moon is under attack by the Ildiran Solar Navy," he shouted into the comm, as if nothing else needed to be said. "I want our response fleet to launch pronto! Battle stations, emergency checklists—finish all the details en route. *The Moon is under attack!*"

It defied belief! He was glad to be in the middle of an EDF operation he could support, for a change. He was an EDF soldier to the very core, and alien invaders could not be allowed to strike human territory with impunity. He also recalled six Mantas from the fringes of the solar system, but it would take hours just for the signal to reach them.

After only ten minutes, all of his ships signaled that they were ready to depart, and he immediately gave the order to launch. Now that the black robots had placed so many EDF ships back into service, Conrad had a significant force. Even though every one of those vessels had passed the most thorough inspections, he was glad to be aboard a Juggernaut that had been repaired by humans.

Conrad still hadn't quite grasped the fact that he was in command of the Earth Defense Forces. He and Natalie had retired, then during the hydrogue war they were both recalled to active duty as training officers, and now he found himself in the big chair. He followed orders, he did his duty . . . and his duty was to defend Earth—in spite of itself, if necessary.

"Power up weapons. All gunners to your stations. Make no mistake, we are going into battle." His stomach felt leaden as he formulated his attack plan. He was still running the numbers of how many enemy ships he was due to face. From the initial reports, the Solar Navy had brought more than a thousand warliners. Even his partially restored EDF couldn't possibly fight against that. Yet he would if he had to. He did not intend to let the Ildirans get away. For the honor of the Earth Defense Forces, he had to stop them.

By the time his ships had powered up, moved out in formation, and traversed the quarter million miles to the Moon, however, the Solar Navy had accomplished its mission. Adar Zan'nh had struck the lunar EDF base, seized all Ildiran captives, and scrambled away. Most of the Solar Navy raiders had already escaped.

As the *Goliath* and his clustered battleships closed the distance, Conrad watched the ornate warliners race off into space. Too late. He had never seen such a major operation move so quickly!

"Solar Navy, you are ordered to surrender!" Conrad's words sounded hollow as he spoke them. Adar Zan'nh had no reason to listen to him. He turned to his gunners. "Fire at will. My intent is to disable, not destroy."

"Looks like the Ildirans have no stomach for fighting, sir," said his navigator.

Conrad nodded without replying. The Adar already had what he'd come for. Considering the enormity of the Ildiran force, a part of him was glad the whole Solar Navy did not intend to engage in a full-fledged battle. It would have been a bloodbath.

The Ildirans had not taken the time to retrieve the Mage-Imperator's hijacked warliner, which was still in orbit over the Moon. Conrad saw that its systems were coming on, and an EDF pilot—a mere lieutenant left on duty with the engineering and inspection crew—announced that he intended to use it in the fight. He powered up its engines and accelerated to begin the pursuit.

Over the emergency comm system, Commandant Tilton bellowed for help from the EDF. He sounded like a bleating sheep.

The Adar's last few warliners had arced around the dark side of the Moon in a tight orbit and now emerged from below the southern hemisphere. Accelerating from the slingshot, the Ildiran ships followed a trajectory that actually threw them toward the *Goliath* and the pursuing EDF ships. "General Brindle, warliners on a collision course!"

"Are they trying to ram us?" Conrad gripped the armrests, pushing himself halfway out of the unfamiliar command chair. The cratered landscape of the nearby Moon filled the entire screen.

"No, sir. I think they're . . . running from something."

Three more ships in the Adar's group fanned out, activated their stardrives, and sped away. Meanwhile, the last Ildiran ship skimmed close to the surface in extremely low orbit, using the lunar mass as a shield until it left the Moon and headed off at full speed. Although its vector would carry it directly out of the solar system, it would also bring the gaudy alien ship unnecessarily within weapons range of the EDF battle group.

And the Ildirans didn't even seem to care.

Conrad couldn't understand the Adar's actions. "What is he thinking?" No response came from repeated hails. The EDF ships unleashed a flurry of jazer blasts, but the warliner was moving too swiftly; some of the bolts struck the ornate solar sails, but did little damage. The fleeing ship streaked away.

Conrad looked quickly to his bridge crew for any answers or suggestions. "Can anybody tell me what he's trying to do?" None of this made any sense.

A cloud of hot spheres streaked toward the Moon like incandescent buckshot. Within seconds, the shower of sparks on the *Goliath*'s main screen changed to an inferno. Impossible numbers of fireballs extended beyond the net of the EDF's sensors.

"Faeros," he said aloud. "My God!"

The flaming ellipsoids arrowed straight toward the lunar base and all the EDF ships that had launched in a confused response as soon as the Solar Navy had departed. The Mage-Imperator's confiscated warliner, still attempting its pursuit of Adar Zan'nh, had risen up over the Moon and was increasing speed. The faeros saw it. The EDF lieutenant in command of the skeleton crew called to General Brindle for instructions.

Without pause, without warning, without any communication whatsoever, the foremost faeros slammed into the warliner, engulfing it in flames. The ship's extended solar sails shriveled, and its meager shields could not possibly withstand the impact. The whole gigantic vessel was vaporized within seconds.

The stream of fireballs kept coming, and thousands of faeros began to attack the Moon. *The whole Moon.*

Elemental flames lanced down in a unified barrage,

blistering the already barren landscape, gouging new molten craters in the surface. This was orders of magnitude more destructive, more overwhelming, than any attack, any weapon, any disaster Conrad had witnessed in his entire life.

Even as a second wave of EDF ships rushed in from other stations in the solar system, he knew there was nothing his entire fleet could do against these things.

Clustering around the Moon, the fireballs threw down a holocaust. The faeros bombarded the surface with total abandon, erasing craters and turning the rocks and dust into glassy streams of lava.

They obliterated the fortified EDF base within the first few minutes. All transmissions from Commandant Tilton and anyone in the vicinity of the EDF base had fallen silent. Conrad didn't know how many people had been stationed there, but it must have been in the thousands. Those men and women were already dead, the facilities destroyed, all the nearby ships vaporized. Every ship that had managed to launch was wiped out.

But even that did not satisfy the rage of the fiery entities. The faeros bombardment continued until they succeeded in breaking through the lunar surface. Their weaponry hammered through the regolith until the Moon itself became cracked and red.

"General Brindle, do we attack?"

"No, do not engage the faeros! Maintain our distance." He shuddered, staring at the screen. "No weapon in the entire Hansa arsenal can fight against *that*." Any Earth Defense Forces that tried would be incinerated in the first wave.

Conrad didn't know what had provoked their fury. It reminded him of angry wasps stinging a blundering child who had accidentally disturbed their nest. Then he remembered the root cause of the hydrogue war: The Hansa's first test of the Klikiss Torch at Oncier had unwittingly destroyed an enclave of hydrogues; in retaliation, hydrogue warglobes had completely annihilated the four moons of the gas giant, turning them into rubble.

Now the faeros, elemental companions to the hydrogues, were doing the same to the Earth's Moon. "What the hell did we do to piss them off?"

Or were the humans just in the way?

The vengeful faeros continued to pour energy through the crust, pounding hot spikes all the way into the Moon's core, until it reached a final unstable point.

Conrad couldn't believe what he was seeing. Unable to stand, he collapsed back into the command chair.

Because of the lunar mass and size, the explosion seemed to occur with infinite slowness, a gradual crumbling and separation. The Moon cracked, fissured . . . and then literally broke apart like a ball of dried clay.

100 ☀ MAGE-IMPERATOR JORA'H

The fireballs swarmed in as the Mage-Imperator's ship angled high out of the orbital plane. The rest of the Solar Navy had successfully gotten away to the rendezvous point, and now the flagship warliner could no longer hide behind the bulk of the Moon.

Though the EDF reinforcements had finally arrived from their stations around Earth, they were by far the least of Adar Zan'nh's worries. He did not engage them, but flew past with all possible speed. Instead of pursuing them, however, the faeros concentrated their fury upon the Moon itself.

Even the Adar was astonished by the sheer number of fireballs that Rusa'h had summoned. "We must take you to safety, Liege. We cannot stay here." He turned to the helmsman. "Set course for Ildira."

Jora'h could not tear his eyes from the thermal pummeling of the Moon. "And lead all the faeros directly back there? Rusa'h wants *me*, does he not?"

"Then we have go somewhere safe for a while," Nira said.

"King Peter would offer me sanctuary on Theroc," Jora'h considered, "but the faeros already know that place. The worldforest has been devastated too many times. We need a world that has no connection with our prior dealings."

"We must make our decision now, Liege," Zan'nh said

with an edge in his voice, staring at the fireballs on his screens.

Standing pale and shaken at the edge of the command nucleus, Sullivan Gold cleared his throat. "I've got an idea. I have the coordinates, I know the facilities, and I was about to go there myself." He glanced at his wife. "There's a gas giant called Golgen with plenty of Roamer skymines. They have no love for the EDF or the Hansa, I can promise you that—and I bet they'd welcome the presence of the Solar Navy, as protection in case the Chairman decides to raid them again."

After what was happening on the Moon, Jora'h doubted the Hansa Chairman would be particularly interested in consolidating Roamer skymines. Nevertheless, he needed to vacate the solar system before the faeros spotted their single remaining warliner. "Very well. We will go to Golgen."

101 ☀ ANTON COLICOS

For weeks Anton had tried to keep Rememberer Vao'sh occupied at the university, first out of courtesy and friendship, then out of desperation. Once the Mage-Imperator had been taken back to his prison in the lunar EDF base, the comforting *thism* that had protected the old historian had stretched thinner and thinner.

But Chairman Wenceslas insisted that Vao'sh stay so that he could continue disseminating information about Ildira to other scholars. The dean of the Department of Ildiran Studies sent repeated glowing reports back to Hansa HQ, but Anton doubted the Chairman agreed with the academic priorities. For that, he was glad.

On the faculty, Anton had garnered a great deal of clout and prestige by arranging for the Ildiran historian to give lectures. Vao'sh entertained audiences of students for hours with dramatic presentations from the *Saga of Seven Suns*. Though the students and professors had studied the alien race and culture, they had never seen an actual rememberer perform before.

At first, the old historian had seemed pleased to have such enthusiastic audiences, but no matter how well the academic elite treated him, Vao'sh never forgot why and how he was here. And neither did Anton. Anger and resentment always remained in the background of his thoughts. There were no justifications for the Chairman's behavior, but no one would listen to the outrage of a mere scholar or an alien storyteller.

Over the past several days, the old rememberer had begun to weaken visibly. Seeing his friend's anxiety and nervousness, Anton did his best to support him, just as when the two of them were drifting alone in space following their escape from the Klikiss robots on Maratha. Even with his newfound strength and certitude, having survived the isolation madness once already, Vao'sh found it difficult to grasp the tenuous strands of *thism* when his people were so far away. The Moon was not so close after all. . . .

Maintaining appearances as best they could, they departed from a lecture hall that had been filled to capacity with fascinated listeners. Anton and the rememberer had stayed for an appropriate amount of time to greet friends and colleagues. Vao'sh was such a consummate performer that few others would have noticed his uneasiness, but Anton was attuned to how much his friend was hurting. He was amazed by Vao'sh's strength and adored his determination. He was sure no normal Ildiran could have survived.

Outside the lecture hall they found the students and teachers abuzz, shocked by something that was occurring in the news. Emergency announcements blared from a current-events transmission screen mounted on the wall of a student lounge. Anton had seen plenty of emergencies lately, but this one must be different from the usual Hansa propaganda, judging by the reaction of the university audience.

Vao'sh stared at a sequence of long-distance images that showed a group of Ildiran warliners fleeing from the lunar base. He quickly understood what was going on. "The Solar Navy is rescuing the Mage-Imperator, and I am here." He turned meaningfully toward Anton. *"And I am here."*

Anton caught his breath. "They'll come back for you. They have to. You're an important rememberer."

"I am expendable. They have come only for the Mage-Imperator."

"The Ildirans are attacking our Moon!" cried a blustery professor. "Do they think they can get away with that? How dare they!"

Anton snapped at him, "We kidnapped their leader and held him hostage. How did you expect the Solar Navy to respond?"

One young female student shook her head sadly. "They shouldn't have resorted to war. We never need to resort to war. Diplomacy could have solved the problem."

Next, the situation became worse, much worse, as the faeros attacked, then destroyed the Moon itself.

The crowd fell speechless, quickly forgetting their indignation toward the Solar Navy. Several of them dropped into chairs, unable to stand. Vao'sh stared at the screen, all color draining from his facial lobes. Images from Conrad Brindle's battle group showed the fragmented, glowing-hot rubble of the Moon driven in all directions by the liberated energy. The EDF ships had to retreat swiftly with shields on full power as they were pummeled by flying debris.

The old rememberer looked at the black emptiness of stars into which the Solar Navy warliners had disappeared. Anton turned to his friend with tears in his eyes. The others certainly misinterpreted the reason for his weeping.

In a devastatingly flat tone, Vao'sh said, "I am the only Ildiran in the entire solar system."

102 ☀ NIKKO CHAN TYLAR

Nikko Chan Tylar was pleased to be flying the *Aquarius* again on a mission as one of Jess Tamblyn's water bearers, and this time his father accompanied him. Crim was glad to be safely away from Llaro, both from the Eddies and from the bugs. He didn't seem too sure, however, about taking instructions from his son. "At least let me help with the navigation, Nikko. Admit it; that was never your strong point."

Nikko blushed. "Okay, I admit it."

"And we can't afford any lost time. In fact, I'll even pilot the ship if you want. Go take a nap or do some homework."

"I completed my schooling five years ago."

"Nobody ever completes schooling. You can always keep learning."

"You never wanted to pilot a ship before. Come to think of it, when you worked in our greenhouse domes, I don't think you liked it there either."

Crim let out a long sigh. "At least in the greenhouses I was with your mother." Both of them fell silent for a moment, remembering how Marla Chan Tylar had been killed by the Klikiss. "I guess I have a pretty dim Guiding Star. For the time being I'm satisfied to be working with you."

"I'm glad we got that resolved, then."

And they were off to Jonah 12, where Jess and Cesca had planted a seedpool of wentals some months earlier. "Did I ever tell you what happened the time I came to supply the Roamer base, but found all the Klikiss robots already there? I rescued Speaker Peroni—"

"You've told everyone that story more than once," Crim said, but not in a surly voice. "It seems to grow more dramatic each time."

"I couldn't make this stuff up."

"Well, you handled yourself well; that's all I've got to say."

Nikko was happy to accept the compliment.

The ship finally arrived at the frozen planetoid, its cargo bay ready to be filled with a swell of fresh wentals. A few old Roamer control satellites and orbital-processing stations remained high overhead; the radio bands were silent except for the background hiss of static. Nikko felt a lump in his throat, remembering the terrors he had endured in this place. As he flew the ship down toward the planetoid, his father stared out the windowports, awestruck at the size of the ice crater left by the reactor explosion.

"Look!" Crim said. "I see lights down there."

"Must be reflections from stars. Nobody's left on Jonah 12."

His father scowled at him. "I know what a reflection looks like. That's intrinsic phosphorescence. Something luminous is locked in the ice."

Nikko studied his readings, saw energy blips. "Then it's probably the wentals waiting for us." During the descent, he spotted more than just the refrozen ice of the crater or the shimmer of energy. He saw some makeshift structures—a little hut connected to an escape pod.

Frowning, he fiddled with the communications system, turned up the pickup strength, and searched standard Roamer emergency bands. Finally, he picked up a faint oscillating pulse. "Someone's crashed down there, Dad!"

Crim had already reached the same conclusion. "So land the ship already."

Once on the surface, Nikko made out a very cleverly constructed shelter that appeared to be made from the remnants of a large satellite appended to a Roamer escape pod. He detected energy sources and strong thermal readings emanating from inside the shelter. "Chances are, whoever crashed is still alive."

Crim was already suiting up, and as soon as locking bolts secured the *Aquarius* to the ice, Nikko scrambled out to join his father. "An escape pod contains supplies only for a week or so, right?"

"Depends on how many people are inside," Crim transmitted over the helmet radio as the two emerged from the airlock. "I'd be very disappointed if our survivor died yesterday because we didn't show up soon enough."

They hurried across the ice. Nikko saw splashes of glowing light beneath his feet as if each footstep ignited some kind of luminescence. He stopped in front of the pod and studied the satellite fuselage attached to its side. "Do we knock?"

The dwelling was cobbled together without neat corners and angles; flat pieces were stuck everywhere, even if they didn't fit—no aesthetic accomplishment, but it seemed functional. Nikko couldn't believe that such a hodgepodge could be airtight and structurally sound, but a cocoon of flowing ice had covered the joints and sealed them. Obviously, the *wentals* had armored and insulated this place. Maybe they had even supplied additional energy to keep the person or people alive.

Crim transmitted, "Hello, escape pod. Anybody in need of a rescue in there?" He pounded on the hatch with his gloved fist.

The pod's access door was so small that only one of them could cycle through at a time. With a knot in his stomach, hoping he wouldn't find one or more bodies inside, Nikko went first.

Inside stood a shaggy old man with beard stubble, unkempt hair, and rumpled clothes. He had a huge grin on his face. "Well, it's about damn time. I could use some company besides those flashing lights."

Nikko recognized him. "Caleb Tamblyn?" As soon as

he popped open his faceplate and took a breath, the stench made him wrinkle his nose: body odor, stale air, improperly recycled wastes. He doubted old Caleb could even notice the smell anymore (not that the man had ever smelled as fresh as a rose). The escape pod's life-support systems must have been on their last gasp. He stepped away from the hatch so that his father could cycle through. When Crim Tylar entered behind his son, the escape pod became extremely crowded.

"How long have you been here?" Nikko asked.

"About three weeks, as far as I can tell. Maybe four."

"Impossible," Crim said. "Your supplies couldn't last that long."

Caleb snorted. "Any Roamer worth his salt can figure out solutions . . . and, well, I had a little help from the wentals. They provided enough energy to get by on less food. I'm awfully damn hungry, though. You have mealpax aboard your ship?"

"Plenty of them," Nikko said.

Once aboard the *Aquarius*, Caleb wolfed down self-heating rations. He explained how the faeros had destroyed his water tanker and Denn Peroni had been obliterated. "I didn't think anyone would be looking for us, but I wasn't about to give up." Caleb shrugged his bony shoulders. "Those faeros really piss me off. We didn't do anything to deserve this. Poor Denn . . ."

He looked around for a bunk so he could take a nap, but Crim told him in no uncertain terms that it would be a wise idea for him to use the ship's sanitary facilities to clean himself up first.

"We can take you directly to Plumas," Nikko suggested. "I assume you want to go back to the water mines?"

"Wynn and Torin are probably overloaded with work

and mad at me for leaving them, but I've had a long time to sit there and think about my Guiding Star." Caleb leaned back in a hard passenger chair. "This war seems a lot more important than the family water business. If you're gearing up to fight those faeros, I'd like to see this through to the end."

103 ☀ DEL KELLUM

On the Golgen skymine, Del Kellum was happy to receive Kotto Okiah and his entourage. Whatever the engineer came up with would certainly be interesting. Kotto came to the Osquivel shipyards in a midsized Roamer transport that seemed a little too large, given his limited piloting abilities. When Kellum learned that Tasia Tamblyn was in the cockpit, however, he granted permission for the craft to land on a small mid-level landing deck. He took a lift down from the ops center, pulled on a jacket against the cool breezes, and went out to meet them.

As expected, the inventor had brought a shipful of gadgetry with him. "You never know what might come in handy," he said, as he walked down the exit ramp while Tamblyn finished shutting down the systems in the cockpit. He looked over his shoulder, back toward the ship. "I've brought some friends along. I find them very helpful in my work . . . at least nondistracting. They've never been aboard a skymine before."

Three compies descended the ramp after him; each had a different body coloration, two of them Technical models, the last a Friendly. Kotto flushed. "Well, those aren't friends, they're compies . . . although at times I think of them as friends." Finally, a teenaged girl and an older man came down the ramp. "I was talking about these two—Orli Covitz and Hud Steinman."

Steinman seemed a bit seasick; Orli, though, stared around her at the huge open skies of Golgen, the high clouds, and the bright sunlight, and she smiled in delight. Tasia Tamblyn emerged from the piloting deck, wiping her forehead and shading her eyes from the sun.

"I'll find quarters for you all. Plenty of extra room." Kellum gestured toward the other three. "Have a look at whatever you like—just don't break anything. Tamblyn, you know your way around a skymine. Give them a tour."

Tasia took her two companions off across the deck. "Look at what Kotto's brought," she called back at Kellum. "It's a military necessity. Jess put him up to it."

Kellum turned to the inventor. "Now what have you concocted? I'm sure it's intriguing."

"Oh, definitely." He jumped right into his excited spiel as they tromped up the ramp. "New defenses—a genuinely novel concept. We're dispersing them throughout the Confederation . . . although I don't have a clue why the faeros would attack you out here. They've never shown any interest in gas giant planets. Jess Tamblyn and Speaker Peroni told me to make sure the Confederation is ready, though."

Kellum paused in his step, startled. "Faeros? Here? By damn, what are you talking about?"

"They challenged me to develop new weapons to use against the fireballs, and they gave me some wental water to work with. Incredible stuff. Lots of potential."

When the two men entered the large cargo bay, Kotto increased the illumination. Bright light shone down on the gleaming hydrogue derelict that sat next to what looked like some kind of satellite transmitter dish.

"Why did you bring that damned drogue sphere?" Kellum demanded. Intellectually, he knew the hydrogues were defeated, and he hoped never to see them again, but the reminder was quite unsettling.

Kotto glanced at it. "Oh . . . never mind, that has nothing to do with the wental weapons. And this other device is a prototype to be used against the Klikiss. I was expecting to test it soon—which is the main reason why Tasia Tamblyn came along, as a matter of fact." He seemed to realize he had gone off on a tangent and brought himself back to the point. "First, though, I've got to deliver and install the new wental weapons."

Kellum shook his head. "So you brought everything along with you, just in case?"

"One never knows when some component or other might be useful. The Klikiss Siren needs a bit of tuning up when I get the time, and I might find another way to test the derelict. My investigations are never finished."

"So what's this amazing new weapon?"

Like an excited boy, Kotto went to a large cubical bin, punched in an access code, and slid open the top. The container's interior was frosty, shimmering with a bluish chemical light that emitted no heat whatsoever. Faint wisps of steam wafted upward like the breath of an ice ogre. Kellum peered inside to see dozens of cylindrical objects with pointed ends, like artillery shells as long as his forearm and a hand-span wide.

"That's frozen wental water," Kotto said. "Projectiles. I fashioned them with the help of the wentals, of course—I couldn't do anything without their cooperation. They're the right caliber to fit into the standard projectile cannons that the shipyards installed as defenses in most Confederation vessels."

"You've got to be kidding me!"

Kotto grinned. "Frozen wentals, explosive bullets to shoot at the faeros. I don't really know what'll happen, but I assume that if a fireball gets shot with that kind of shell, the effects would be . . . extreme. Frankly, I'm not anxious for a chance to test it out, since that would mean finding some faeros. But better to be prepared for anything, don't you think?"

Kellum couldn't disagree.

"Fashioning them was quite interesting—I simply made some calculations and communicated to the wentals what I wanted them to do. Then they shaped themselves, cooled down into solid ice, and—voilà!—perfect artillery shells. I wish everything was that easy."

As the two men emerged from the ship's hold, Kellum looked up into the yellowish skies. He was startled when proximity alarms howled throughout the skymine complex. "*Now* what?"

Over the intercom, voices bellowed for all skyminers to man their stations, telling any armed craft to launch immediately. "More than eight hundred large ships inbound! No, make that a thousand!"

Tasia Tamblyn came sprinting back, her face flushed. "Kellum, do you have a green priest on the skymine? I can send a message to Osquivel—call for Confederation reinforcements."

Frantic Roamer ships were launching from the lower decks, and the sky was filled with a chaos of unfiled flight plans. More craft streaked away from nearby skymines. Kellum sprinted to an intercom and demanded a report, though his people had little more information to give him. "Even I didn't think the Eddies would come back with cojones that big. We are in deep poop."

"We're in deep something," Tasia said. "I'm surprised the Eddies have any ships left after the debacle on Pym."

Kotto Okiah, standing perplexed next to them, furrowed his brow and stared at the numerous distant shapes that had begun to appear at high altitude. "Let's not jump to conclusions. That's way too many ships, and they're not behaving like Eddy raiders."

Descending through the sky in a great parade with colorful solar sails deployed, hundreds of Ildiran warliners approached the skymining levels. The ornate alien ships reminded Kellum of the frilly angelfish he had once kept in his aquariums. Behind the first wave came another, and another.

"It looks like the whole Solar Navy." He let out a long breath. "By damn, what are we supposed to do against this?" He sprinted toward the lift with the others following. He had to get to the ops center and at least pretend to be in charge. He *was* in charge, and people would want him to make decisions.

The warliners had broadcast no message. As soon as he reached the control room, Kellum sent a loud message to the incoming ships, as well as his own. "Don't shoot! There's no need for any weapons fire. We have no beef with the Ildiran Empire." On the outer tactical screens, he saw hundreds more warliners locked in orbit, forming a full cordon around the gas giant. "This is Del Kellum, chief of this skymine complex. And I'd very much like some explanations."

On the screen an image formed, showing a proud and ornately dressed Ildiran male with a long braid that hung over one shoulder. Mage-Imperator Jora'h. "Do not be concerned, Del Kellum. We also have no quarrel with the Roamer clans or the Confederation." The alien leader's smile seemed compassionate and genuine. "We request temporary sanctuary here on Golgen."

104 ☀ RLINDA KETT

After leaving the Klikiss before the One Breedex could complete its fissioning, Rlinda wanted to pilot the ship, feeling sharply the loss of the *Curiosity*. Although BeBob adored her, he also adored his new *Blind Faith,* so they compromised by taking turns.

Margaret Colicos had asked to be taken back to Earth, where her son, Anton, lived. While they were on their way, she continued to ponder what might be happening on Llaro. "Now that all the Klikiss subhives have consolidated themselves, I don't know how much information the One Breedex acquired and retained from all the humans the domates incorporated. Or from Davlin himself." She looked at them, obviously trying to get Rlinda and BeBob to hear the significance of her words. "The hive mind definitely understands something about humanity. What if the One Breedex decides it wants to control the human race, too? What if the Klikiss sweep across all of *our* colony worlds?"

"This lady is just full of fun ideas," BeBob said with a loud groan.

"We'll be at Earth soon," Rlinda said, though she did not actually feel much optimism at the prospect. "Everything will be fine—you'll see."

But when they arrived, they found that Earth had suffered the greatest devastation in human history. Rlinda was stunned by what their screens showed. "I stay away from here for a month, and the whole solar system falls apart?"

Fragments large and small, many still glowing with residual thermal heat, spread out from where the Moon should have been. A small planet's worth of rubble had dispersed into a hot cloud, most of it spreading out along its former orbital path, though numerous ejected chunks had gone into erratic orbits, slipping toward Earth's deep gravity well.

"Moons and planets don't just spontaneously explode," BeBob said. "Do they?"

Margaret shook her head. "Not even the Klikiss have that kind of firepower."

Rlinda scowled, trying to think of an answer. They stared in numb silence for a long moment, until BeBob finally said, "In the grand scheme of things, I suppose my arrest warrant isn't going to be their highest priority. We should be safe taking the ship in."

They approached, listening to the agitated chatter across the various communication bands. High-velocity lunar fragments tumbled toward Earth, and EDF ships were out in force to stop them, but the Hansa's space military was like a handful of gnats against a tornado. Rescue and salvage ships of all different types dodged the debris, trying to create a defensive map of the oncoming clusters of rubble.

Seven sharp impacts banged against the *Faith*'s hull. A much larger rock, twice the size of their ship, tumbled slowly past on a nearly parallel course and shouldered them out of the way, caroming off in a slightly altered direction. BeBob yelped as he swerved violently. "There goes the new paint job. I don't like this at all."

"Let me take the controls," Rlinda said; he did not argue with her.

The highest velocity ejecta from the exploding Moon had already reached the Earth's atmosphere. When the fragments began to burn up, bright orange and white streaks made fingernail scratches through the air, then left thicker plumes as huge chunks hurtled toward the ground. The first fragments vaporized in flashes.

Margaret watched. "Earth hasn't been pummeled with impacts like this since the Cretaceous Period. Any one of these could become an extinction event."

"You sure we want to land in the middle of that?" BeBob said in disbelief.

"I believe Anton is down there," Margaret said.

On their high-resolution imagers, they watched a succession of impacts smack the surface of the planet in bright orange explosions, flashes of liberated light. They listened to frantic calls of alarm, pleas for help, but no force could evacuate a population of billions in so short a time. And where would they go?

One massive fragment obliterated Dallas.

A few hours later, another wiped out all of Shanghai.

Margaret announced, "These are just the precursors. The largest fragments will move more slowly, but they are on their way. The most devastating impacts are still to come."

105 ✸ PATRICK FITZPATRICK III

When the *Gypsy* flew in toward Earth, Patrick was puffed up and ready to shout his accusations across all of the communication bands. He wanted to expose Chairman Wenceslas for the cold-blooded assassination of his grandmother, for authorizing blatant piracy at the Golgen skymines and the Osquivel shipyards, for causing scores of civilian deaths. He had graphic and appalling footage.

But no one paid any attention to them. They were just another ship among tens of thousands, all flying in the debris-strewn orbital lanes with no monitoring by space traffic control. After the destruction of the Moon, it was every pilot for himself. *The Moon!*

The problem was so obvious, yet inconceivable, that Patrick couldn't even place what was wrong for several minutes. It took quite a while for him to get over his shock, and finally to get some answers. After that, he needed only a second or two to make up his mind that Chairman Wenceslas must have caused the disaster somehow.

Zhett said, "Nobody is going to be interested in politics after this. Our complaints about the Chairman are going to be lost in the noise."

His eyes narrowed. "On the contrary, I can't think of a better scenario for a revolution. The population has got to be ready to overthrow him, if we can only get Freedom's Sword behind us. *If* we can make enough noise."

Once the small yacht hit the atmosphere, they headed directly for Maureen Fitzpatrick's mountain mansion. He felt a knot in his stomach and an odd reluctance as they approached. The Battleaxe had abandoned all her clout and possessions in order to take on the new position Patrick had talked her into.

And Basil had killed her.

Now Patrick was angry as hell.

When the *Gypsy* set down on the paved outdoor landing pad, the mansion appeared to be abandoned. Maureen's staff, servants, and persistent guests had all gone. With the succession of disasters in the intervening weeks, he doubted the Chairman had had time to send his goons to pick through her home and property.

Looking at the large house, he suddenly paused as he felt a lump in his throat. "I suppose this is my inheritance now."

Using his memorized passcodes to deactivate the security systems, he and Zhett entered the silent home. They carried their belongings from the space yacht into a guest bedroom, which they claimed as their own.

They went to the former Chairman's media room, a large chamber with comfortable chairs, a minibar, and a coffee-dispensing station. The walls were covered with dark news-net screens.

"Do you think we can find a way to contact the other protesters?" she asked. "How will we get in touch with them?"

"We can do some broadcasts from here, form our own little self-contained cell. Wait for Freedom's Sword to track us down."

"Unless the Hansa finds us first."

"We'll scramble our signal, make it look like we're somewhere out in space—you saw the chaos out there. They'll never be able to figure it out."

"Then how will Freedom's Sword find us?" Zhett activated the monitors and sat back to watch the numerous reports. Many screens reported on the asteroid-roundup efforts or displayed tragic stories of cities obliterated by meteor impacts. On several discussion channels guest speakers railed against the Confederation with various degrees of fanaticism. Conspiracy theorists speculated that King Peter had somehow provoked the faeros attack. Patrick rolled his eyes.

A few sporadic channels voiced genuine criticism of Chairman Wenceslas, how his bad decisions and ineptitude had dug humanity's grave; those discussions, though, were few. Many once-popular channels, Patrick noted, were no longer broadcasting.

One story was focused on the Klikiss, briefly reporting that General Lanyan had been killed on Pym. After the Moon's destruction, though, that was old news. Patrick heard the story of Lanyan's fate with mixed emotions. He had once admired the man, seen him as his mentor and the key to career advancement. How naïve and foolish he had been! Considering how many times Lanyan had thrust his hand into a hornet's nest, it had been inevitable that he would get stung. . . .

They listened to reports of massive arrests of demonstrators who demanded the Chairman's resignation. During the state of emergency, King Rory could do little to calm the people. Patrick was sure he would find a way to tap into the Freedom's Sword network; even if he never found them, he could use their name to gain additional attention. With his revelations, the dissenters would have a lot more things to yell about.

When he used his own ID and thumbprint to access the main household communication center, instead of a blank Ready screen, an image formed. His grandmother stood there looking at him. He was startled to see Maureen Fitzpatrick give him a hard smile.

"Well, then, Patrick, since you've accessed this message from my home, and since I'm not there to delete it before you can listen, I must be dead. That pisses me off. Unless I happened to fall off a tree balcony on Theroc — and I'm not that clumsy — I'll bet Chairman Wenceslas had something to do with it. Bastard," she muttered under her breath.

"I can imagine what you must be thinking. You're fired up to take on the Hansa, bring the man to justice, save the human race. You've turned into a crusader, Patrick, so listen: There are smart crusaders and stupid ones. That Roamer girl of yours has brought out an altruistic streak in you . . . which I suppose is just fine. I wouldn't mind, though, if you also wanted to get even with the Chairman for what he did to your dear, sweet grandmother." She laughed.

Patrick felt a chill to see her talking so blithely about her fate. In order for her to make the recording at all, she must have suspected that Chairman Wenceslas was capable of such a vicious action. He had never guessed how much risk he was asking the old Battleaxe to take, but Maureen had prepared for the worst-case scenario.

"Now, then, if you're going to accomplish anything, you'll need contacts and you'll need resources. I'm appending to this message a full list and access instructions to several large funds. It's not everything, of course, but it should be enough. I don't want you blowing the whole family fortune on your campaign, even if you are doing it for my sake . . . and humanity's.

"I'm also giving you a list of trusted contacts in the media and in business, people who did me quite a few good turns while I was Chairman, and I can guarantee you they're not fans of the current administration."

When she narrowed her eyes and looked right at him, he couldn't believe she wasn't really there on the other side of the screen. "I know how smart you are, and I know how well I raised you. I'm . . . proud of you. Now, go get 'em."

She looked over her shoulder, called out to Jonas, and ended the recording. Patrick stared at the screen, his eyes burning.

Zhett beamed, already pulling up the lists Maureen had left.

They had everything they needed to get started.

Using Maureen's sophisticated communications equipment, disguising the origin of the transmission through numerous layers of encryption, Patrick easily hacked into the open newsnets. Because so many popular stations had been taken off the air, leaving only dead static, he could easily broadcast on those channels. He contacted the media experts his grandmother had suggested, and they helped spread the message; several of them claimed to be members of Freedom's Sword already. Using his extensive funds, he could open doors and cover tracks. Zhett, in particular, proved to be quite good at getting new recruits.

Patrick also found a way to insert messages into a popular news discussion show, interrupting a debate about future weather shifts due to the loss of the Moon. He got his largest audience, however, when he piggybacked onto a successful music and entertainment channel; in spite of the world practically coming to an end around them — or perhaps because of it — people still watched their favorite shows.

In an anger-intensified voice, Patrick made his damning statements and laid out the facts. Letting the appalling images speak for themselves, he uploaded the images of Admiral Pike's Mantas assassinating the former Chairman because she had accepted an appointment as liaison to the Confederation. He showed the attack on the Osquivel shipyards and the ransacking of the Golgen skymines, before reminding his audience of his earlier widely broadcast confession, that General Lanyan had himself been responsible for causing the ekti embargo.

For good measure, he claimed to represent Freedom's Sword and called everyone to take to the streets. While showing an image of Chairman Basil Wenceslas, he made a sound of disgust and asked, "Why do you tolerate this man?"

He signed off and took Zhett by the hand. He would do similar broadcasts day after day until he achieved critical momentum.

Leaving Adar Zan'nh and the majority of his Solar Navy soldiers aboard their warliners so as not to make an unnerving or overwhelming show of force, Jora'h descended to the primary skymine on Golgen.

Overhead, hundreds of warliners crisscrossed the sky in tight, impressive formations. Upon witnessing the arrival of such a great military force, all the skymine chiefs were alarmed, despite the Mage-Imperator's reassurances. Kellum summoned his fellow managers so that Jora'h could address them and explain the true situation.

Nira and Osira'h accompanied the Mage-Imperator, and after due consideration, he decided to bring Sullivan Gold as well, since the Hansa manager's story would astonish the Roamers. Sullivan looked shell-shocked as he described how Chairman Wenceslas wanted him to take over the Golgen skymines and run them as a Hansa subsidiary.

Kellum gaped. "By damn, the gall of the man!"

Another skymine chief, Bing Palmer, snorted. "I almost wish the Eddies would try another pirate raid while the Solar Navy's here, just so I could watch them turn around and run home with their tails between their exhaust pipes!"

One facility chief named Boris Goff brought his own green priest to the conclave, who delivered a spare treeling to Nira, much to her delight. With a pleased smile on her face and trembling fingers, Nira touched the delicate fronds and reconnected through telink. In a burst of words and thoughts, she described all the recent horrific events, including the destruction of the Moon by the faeros. Although she was telling the story, Nira seemed to have a hard time believing what she herself had witnessed. Her fellow green priests relayed the disturbing information to King Peter.

Kellum rested his elbows on the table, leaning forward as he considered the Ildiran leader. "And what, exactly, do you need here, Mage-Imperator? I'll take you at your word that the Solar Navy isn't a threat to us. How can we help the Ildiran Empire?"

"Like you, I am angered and offended by what Chairman Wenceslas has done," Jora'h said. "But our most powerful enemies are the *faeros*. The Solar Navy is eager to face them, but Adar Zan'nh needs to make repairs, restore our weapons, and pull together our ships in preparation for a victorious return to Mijistra. We must also attempt to find effective ways to fight the faeros and make a battle plan."

Kellum smiled. "It just so happens we've got a Roamer scientist here who may be able to help you with some new weapons."

As the gas giant's sunset painted the clouds a rainbow of colors, Jora'h found Osira'h standing alone on an open deck outside a large landing bay. Precariously close to the edge, she gazed down into the restless, hypnotically layered atmospheric ocean.

Nearby sat the small diamond-walled hydrogue derelict, empty and ominous. Kotto Okiah had moved it here from his laboratory chamber, perhaps intending to run tests, but

Osira'h didn't look at it; instead, she concentrated on the deep soup of misty gases.

He stood behind his daughter, just watching her, thinking about all Osira'h had accomplished . . . yet this was still a child, one who had been forced to grow up and become something *more* than any normal girl during her encounter with the hydrogues. He didn't want to disturb her, but he could not hide from Osira'h.

Without turning around, she spoke. "The clouds seem so peaceful, but I know what they hide."

Father and daughter gazed into the swirling, cottony emptiness. Jora'h couldn't fully understand what the girl had endured when she had plunged down in a containment chamber, much like the small transparent derelict here, to parley with the hydrogues. Though they were incredibly powerful entities—arrogant, destructive, and cold—she had made them bow to her will.

Osira'h seemed wistful and disturbed. "They're down there, you know. The hydrogues may be quiet for now, but they are still here."

107 ✺ KING PETER

The moment King Peter learned of the Moon's destruction, he made up his mind to offer all the aid the Confederation could put together — and immediately. Not long after Nira sent the news via telink, traders arrived on Theroc, bringing eyewitness accounts of the catastrophic event.

When he and Estarra watched the images of slow-moving celestial fragments heading inexorably toward Earth, Peter knew that the real disaster was only just beginning. If a big enough chunk burned through the atmosphere, the shockwave would kill every living thing on the planet.

In addition, there were numerous other dire consequences. Peter had looked at the initial reports: Earth's climate was going to suffer significant upheavals. The disruption of the tidal cycle would cause immense shifts in weather patterns and even the seasons, depending on how evenly the lunar mass distributed itself across the orbital path. Marine migrations, coastal flooding, storm fronts . . . and those were only the first-order effects.

"Good thing the human race doesn't have all its eggs in one basket anymore," Estarra said, thinking like a true Theron. "The Confederation will survive."

But Peter had been born and raised on Earth. "I might despise Basil Wenceslas, but I will not abandon the rest of Earth's population when they need us so much."

Not everyone was happy with the idea of offering help, particularly people from orphaned Hansa colonies or

Roamer traders wronged by EDF bandits. But Peter was adamant, and Queen Estarra supported him. Green priests in attendance sent the King's message to their counterparts across the Spiral Arm.

"It doesn't matter that the Hansa turned its back on Theroc and all of its colonies. It doesn't matter that the misguided EDF struck Roamer facilities. I will not stoop to such pettiness in the face of such tragedy." He indicated the tangle of computed orbits on the screens. "Look at the projections!"

"No matter what path others take, we in the Confederation must do what is right," Estarra added.

Once convinced, the Roamers tackled the problem with all the enthusiasm and ingenuity Peter expected. He put out a call for anyone experienced in space construction, asteroid-field analysis, and complex multibody orbital projections.

Peter had already summoned Admiral Willis's *Jupiter* and all ten of her Mantas. He intended to lead the procession himself. Understandably cautious after General Lanyan had turned against her during the battle on Pym, Willis warned, "I would approach this mission of mercy with extreme caution, sire."

"We'll be cautious, but we will also show the people of Earth who we really are. Basil has painted us as monsters and villains for too long. When we take the high road, our actions will speak louder than his words."

Even so, Peter had no intention of being anywhere near Basil Wenceslas without a lot of firepower at his side. He had already sent the first wave of Roamer engineers to Earth to offer their services, and he knew that no reasonable person would turn down the help.

No reasonable person.

Knowing it was only a matter of time before Vao'sh succumbed to his utter isolation, Anton frantically tried to save him, praying that with his warmth and comfort he could help Vao'sh to hold on for just a little while longer. The old rememberer needed him, and Anton did not want to leave his side, wishing he could spend all day just clutching his hand, *willing* Vao'sh to be strong.

But he had to do something to help. He had to try everything. Everything! Anton personally called in favors, made calls, grabbed lapels and begged for assistance. He made lists of possibilities, then doggedly pursued every alternative, crossing off each failure, jotting down any new idea.

He barged into the office of the Dean of the Department of Ildiran Studies, but the man immediately washed his hands of the matter, ducking from a groundswell of anti-Ildiran sentiment since the Solar Navy had led the faeros to the Moon (never mind that the Mage-Imperator and a whole Ildiran crew were being held hostage there). Next, Anton went to the chancellor of the university, but the man was practically catatonic after the annihilation of several major cities, sure that the Palace District could be next. The campus itself had degenerated into near anarchy, and all classes were canceled.

Anton dispatched fourteen increasingly urgent messages to Chairman Wenceslas, implying that he had vital new information, but his calls were all ignored. Apparently, the leader had no further interest in the Ildiran rememberer. Rumor had it that the Chairman had taken refuge somewhere deep underground; he hadn't been seen for days, though King Rory remained in public view, raising his hands and promising—not convincingly—that everything would be all right.

Anton knew for certain that Vao'sh wasn't going to be all right, unless he could get some help. He would die without his fellow Ildirans, without the *thism*. That was the one thing Anton could not give him, no matter how much he wanted to.

The best thing would be a fast ship to rush Vao'sh back to the Ildiran Empire, where he could be with his people, safe in the *thism*. Any splinter colony would do, so long as Vao'sh was near his own people. Considering the current situation on Earth, Anton would have been perfectly happy to go away with him, too. *Anything,* just to help his friend.

But there were no ships to be had, and certainly none that were willing to fly off to the distant Ildiran Empire.

No matter how hard he tried, Anton could get no one to take his problem seriously. The Moon had been destroyed, and meteors had wiped out several cities. Flaming elementals had attacked the solar system. The plight of a lonely alien was an absolutely trivial concern for everyone on Earth.

Only Anton considered it important. He was desperate.

Already isolated from the *thism*, Vao'sh huddled inside the small apartment they shared. Anton urged him to go out among crowds, to be surrounded by people (although he quietly feared a lynch mob might form and attack him). The old rememberer refused, though. "I cannot get what I need from humans, no matter how large the crowd. It is the difference between seeing an image of food and eating a feast. There is no nourishment for me here."

Anton felt torn apart, but refused to despair. He would think of something. He couldn't lose Vao'sh. He did not give up.

Anton begged for coverage on the newsnets so that he could make others feel the pain of Vao'sh's problem, but every broadcast was fixated with the destruction of the Moon, analyses of the faeros, condemnations of the Solar Navy invaders. Other stories covered the devastating impacts, the destroyed cities, and dire warnings about larger fragments even now hurtling toward Earth.

Finally Anton used up his last possibility. He could think of nothing else to do, no more favors to call in. With a leaden heart, he returned to the apartment, closed the door behind him, and stood frozen for a moment, afraid to admit his utter failure. He knew what it would do to Vao'sh. He closed his eyes, drew a deep breath, and used every scrap of optimism he could summon to call out with false cheer, "Nothing yet, but I will think of something. I'm not giving up."

The old rememberer had switched on all the lights, opened the blinds and curtains. Anton found him lying on the temporary bed, shivering and clammy. His facial lobes swirled with sickly colors. Anton knelt down to clasp his friend's hand. "Be strong. I'm here! You have all my support, my strength."

It took him several moments to realize that Vao'sh was suffering from far more than isolation. The rememberer spasmed, and his lips drew back to expose his teeth. His eyes were squeezed shut, forcing painful tears between the lids. "I am glad you have come," he managed to say. "I wanted you here."

"I won't give up!" Anton insisted.

"Nothing . . . to do. Accept it."

"No!"

Anton noticed a sharp smell. He looked around and saw empty bottles of chemicals—caustic cleaning fluids from his bathroom and kitchenette, several old prescription bottles, all empty. "Vao'sh, what have you done?"

Though the old rememberer continued to shudder, he forced his eyes open. He spoke as if he were telling a tale. "Mage-Imperator Cyroc'h, seeing what was necessary for the Ildiran Empire, consumed poison so that the story could move on to its next chapter." He coughed and then retched.

Anton held the old man's bony shoulders, raising him from the bed. He felt as if the world had fallen out from beneath him. "Why did you give up on me? I was still trying! I am still here."

The rememberer clasped Anton's hand weakly, heaved a breath, and wheezed, "All stories cannot have a happy ending."

"Don't you dare do this to me!" Anton pulled away and stood up. His heart was racing, and he couldn't find the air to draw a breath. He could barely hear anything but the clamor of his own thoughts. "I'll call a hospital. They can do something."

But no Earth physician understood the slightest bit about Ildiran physiology or toxicology. Without a thorough analysis, there was no telling which of the chemicals Vao'sh had consumed were poisonous to his biochemistry, and there was no way to develop a reliable antidote in time.

Anton slammed a door on those thoughts and refused to consider them.

Vao'sh reached for his hand, forced him to come closer.

"Ah, my friend, the loneliness I endured after fleeing Maratha gave me a taste of what I experience now — and it will only get horribly worse. I know that, and so do you. This way, it is my choice. This way, *I* have control, and I die much more peacefully than if I allowed the madness to overcome me." He sounded absolutely calm.

"No!" Anton felt the sobs and anger building inside him. He refused to accept that he couldn't *do* anything, that he had let Vao'sh down.

"Promise me . . . promise that you will tell my story. Write my ending for the *Saga of Seven Suns*." Though his eyes were glazed and unfocused, Vao'sh added, "I found a poem that I like very much. It was written by a human named Thomas Babington Macaulay, from a work called 'Lays of Ancient Rome.'"

Anton pushed aside his other thoughts, seized on something normal, something he could do, and he found that he recalled the piece. "I know it."

Vao'sh gathered strength and recited in a voice that still held the power of a great rememberer:

"And how can man die better
Than facing fearful odds,
For the ashes of his fathers,
And the temples of his Gods?"

He slumped back with a faint smile. "That would make a fine epitaph, I think."

"No . . ." Anton couldn't stop weeping as he fell to his knees beside his friend. Vao'sh reached over and took his hand again. Almost an hour later, the old rememberer passed away as peacefully as he had promised he would.

109 ☀ CHAIRMAN BASIL WENCESLAS

The penthouse office no longer felt safe to him. Always before, the glassed-in apex of the Hansa HQ had placed him high enough that he could see the mosaic pattern of humanity without being bothered by the details of individual tiles. Lately, however, he did not like to be so visible. So vulnerable. The glass windows in his penthouse were proof against both jazers and projectiles, but not against mountains falling from the sky.

Even deep underground and protected by half a kilometer of rock, Basil could not be sure he would be completely sheltered. A large enough asteroid impact would kill him here just as surely as if he were standing in his penthouse. And, no doubt, a clever assassin could still find a way to get to him.

At first he had considered establishing a mobile headquarters on General Brindle's *Goliath* in orbit, which sounded like a good enough idea until he realized just how vulnerable a Juggernaut could be to external attack. What if the black robots betrayed them and opened fire? What if some of the EDF ships mutinied? What if the faeros came back? Or the Ildiran Solar Navy? Or the Klikiss? So many enemies—and even former allies had turned against him.

Yes, Basil had to be very, very careful. As the Chairman, he needed to be protected. He had to stay secure. Who else would lead the Hansa in these most terrible times?

It had been a snap decision to move his personal offices down into the tunnels far beneath the Hansa HQ pyramid. The tunnels were old, Spartan, and meant for only the most severe, and temporary, emergencies. But the rocks felt solid and, most important, he could control those who had access to him. It was the best he could do.

The sounds of construction seemed oppressive as workers completed the underground modifications he had requested. Heavy trucks and small earth movers cleared more chambers and passages, expanding the protected subterranean command post. The dust in the air mixed with the smell of engine exhaust, an acrid tang that could not be entirely filtered out despite the high-capacity air exchangers. Light panels cast sharp-edged shadows everywhere. This place reminded him of an austere hidden bunker where a deposed leader might hide from angry mobs. He didn't like the implications of that.

A network of portable communication screens had been mounted on the rock walls. While technicians sat in uncomfortable temporary chairs with hard backs and metal seats, Basil had obtained a more impressive chair that he could tolerate for the hours he would be staring at the screens, watching everything.

As his first line of defense above the atmosphere, a variety of scout ships, EDF vessels, and salvage craft were combing the vicinity for incoming shards of rock. But the empty volume of space was so vast and his ships so few that he couldn't possibly intercept, or even detect, the majority of lunar debris.

Just yesterday an asteroid estimated to be six hundred meters in diameter had wiped out half of Buenos Aires. Two more had struck the Arctic. One had slammed into the middle of the Australian outback.

And the main mass of the shattered Moon hadn't even arrived yet.

Basil listened to each report with growing dread and anger, as if physics itself had somehow turned against him, bombarding his Earth in an expression of malice toward him.

As a result, the world remained in a constant state of panic. Worse, everyone seemed to be blaming Basil. Patrick Fitzpatrick III, after reappearing from whatever rock he'd crawled under, had exposed the Hansa's elimination of the former Chairman. He made it sound like a bad thing to pre-empt treason! And Fitzpatrick entirely mischaracterized General Lanyan's resource-acquisition missions to the Roamer outposts.

Nevertheless, Fitzpatrick had sparked quite an uproar. Freedom's Sword had been increasingly vociferous in calling for Basil's resignation and the return of King Peter. They were complete, gullible fools. If Peter hadn't defied *him,* if everyone in the Hansa had simply done as they were told, if human beings had simply been *reliable,* then none of these problems would have happened. The human race would be on the right track.

It was their own damned fault. How could they cast the blame on him?

Deputy Cain stood behind Basil's black upholstered chair, having delivered his daily report from the surface, painting a grimmer and grimmer picture. After McCammon's confession and execution, Basil had been forced to keep Cain and Sarein close. He hadn't had time to do further interrogations because the Solar Navy had arrived, bringing hellfire with them. Despite his continued reservations, he *had* to rely on them.

Before Basil could issue further instructions to Cain to counter the increasing unrest, the technicians in the underground control center called to him, "Ships coming in, Mr. Chairman! A large number of them. Looks like . . . EDF ships. Ten Mantas, one Juggernaut, and a lot of smaller, unidentifiable craft."

"Are any EDF ships unaccounted for? Did Sirix hold out on us?" Basil turned to Cain. The deputy briskly shook his head.

Then, like a slap in the face, an image appeared on the screen—King Peter dressed in full regalia with Queen Estarra beside him. "People of Earth, the Confederation has come to assist you in your time of need. We have brought many Roamer ships to help chart and reroute the worst of the lunar fragments, and large military vessels to do the big work. Please accept our assistance in keeping Earth safe."

A hot flush crept up Basil's cheeks, and his nostrils flared as he inhaled and exhaled swiftly. "This is insane. Divert General Brindle's ships to apprehend him. King Peter must face trial for the crimes he has committed. Drive away the Roamer ships. They constitute an enemy military in our solar system."

Deputy Cain did not move. His voice was cool and logical. "Mr. Chairman, we can't afford to turn down the assistance. You've seen the projected scale of the impacts. We do not have the means to do this alone."

He skewered Cain with a glare. "You can see what Peter's doing, can't you? He comes here just to taunt me, to flaunt that he is unharmed while I hide underground, and to subvert the loyalties of the people—*my* people. Altruistic reasons? This is a personal thing, a way for Peter to twist the knife."

"You misjudge him, sir. Though you two may disagree on politics, Peter does have Earth's best interests at heart. I am certain of that. I got to know him quite well when he was here."

"Don't let him fool you. He's just thumbing his nose at me—and trying to take over."

"Sir, we are in desperate need of help. We cannot turn their offer down. You know this."

Basil shook his head, his thoughts in a flurry. "I've got Sirix and the Klikiss robots also studying the countless fragments. They can set up grids and response drones to help us divert the asteroids." He stood abruptly from his chair, letting it spin counterclockwise as he faced his deputy. "Don't you see? If I let *Peter* save us, that will prove the Hansa has finally fallen. He'll show that he's better than I am. He wants us to let our guard down, and as soon as our defenses are spread too thin, his Confederation outlaws will invade. Peter will seize power again. That's what he's always wanted."

Basil realized that everyone in the underground command chamber was staring at him. After a long moment of silence, one of the technicians interrupted. "Mr. Chairman, we just detected three more impacts in the southern Atlantic Ocean. They've generated tidal waves. Within the hour they will hit the Brazilian coastline. An evacuation call has been sounded, but most of the people probably won't have enough time."

Basil clenched and unclenched his fists, imagining that Peter himself had hurled those asteroids down to where they could cause the most damage. Cain said again, more insistent now, "Mr. Chairman, we *cannot* turn down the help."

"Very well, let him pretend—but I'm not fooled." Basil turned away, feeling defeated. Then his thoughts shifted, and he let a slow smile cross his face. Yes, he did possess one last secret weapon he could turn against Peter. He hadn't expected to be so direct, but now the opportunity had fallen into his lap.

He had seen the numerous surveillance files of the Aguerra family taken long before "King Peter" had been introduced to the public. Basil knew how much Raymond/Peter had loved his mother and little brothers. Peter would cling to any hope that poor little Rory had survived. That boy would be a perfect lever to force Peter back in line. Fortunately, Basil had no such sentimentality.

110 ☀ JESS TAMBLYN

For weeks the water bearers continued their travels across the Spiral Arm, conveying the new warrior wentals, locating fresh seedpools, bringing powerful reservoirs back to Theroc. Now Jess and Cesca needed to see what Kotto Okiah had managed to develop in cooperation with his sample wentals.

Traveling toward Golgen, Jess could never forget what had happened here to Ross, but he and Cesca had to keep their Guiding Star in sight—defeating the faeros and ending this elemental war once and for all.

But when their water-bubble ship approached the yellowish gas giant, they were astonished to see hundreds, possibly more than a thousand, Solar Navy warliners in orbit and cruising through the atmosphere above the skymines.

Though Jess could not understand why so many ships

were here, Cesca gave him a knowing smile. "I think the Ildirans are in the same fight that we are."

Though Del Kellum had offered his largest conference room for the war council, the chamber still felt crowded with eager audience members. Before the meeting began, Kellum paced back and forth, arranging for refreshments and trying to look busy. Eighteen people took seats at a long milky-white table, while others crowded against the walls. Jess and Cesca remained by themselves at the far corner, isolated and haloed by elemental power.

Tasia glanced at her brother and smiled, looking as sure of herself as she'd ever been. Kotto was there, full of news to share about his new weapons developments. Mage-Imperator Jora'h and Adar Zan'nh, garbed in ornate, uncomfortable-looking clothes, took seats side by side. Wearing only a brief shift, the green priest Nira held on to her new treeling, and the girl Osira'h remained attentive at her mother's side.

Cesca had been right in her initial assessment: They were all in the same fight, against the same terrible enemies. And, together, they might be strong enough to win.

Wisps of pinkish clouds drifted like gauze over the room's wide rectangular skylights, sending faint shadows across the boardroom table. Jess's eyes were bright as he listened to the Mage-Imperator talk about the faeros incarnate and how the predatory fireballs had destroyed Earth's Moon.

Listening carefully, Jess assessed the audience. He knew the determination of the Mage-Imperator and the Solar Navy, knew that the Roamers and green priests were ready, and knew that King Peter and the Confederation would offer any resources they could. The verdani had already fought the faeros in their worldforest, but as the water bearers returned to Theroc, the trees and the warrior wentals had suggested a new concept to combine their strengths, now that the giant tree battleships had proved too vulnerable to the faeros fires.

Yes, the allies now possessed many ways to fight that they had not previously used against the flaming elementals.

"Rusa'h is still searching for me," the Mage-Imperator said. "No doubt he will go back to Ildira. That is where he expects me to go."

"Then Ildira is where we will confront the faeros," Cesca said. "We can bring all of our allies together and fight with everything we have."

Adar Zan'nh seemed hungry. "I have more than a thousand warliners ready to engage in the battle."

Kotto, who had been scribbling on a touchpad throughout the discussion, spoke up from where he sat at the far end of the table. "Sure, but you can't just keep crashing your ships into things—that's not the way to win." He shook his head. "I've designed some exciting new wental weapons, though I haven't had the opportunity to test them yet."

"Thank the Guiding Star for that," muttered Boris Goff.

"I would like to consider these weapons," the Adar said. "Can they be adapted to our warliners?"

Kotto shrugged. "The wentals were perfectly happy to shape their water however we like. If you provide me with specs for your warliners' projectile launchers, I'll see what I can do." He glanced down at his touchpad, made a note, then looked up at Jess. "But the wental water you gave me was only enough for about a hundred frozen artillery shells, which I already delivered to the Roamer ships in the vicinity. If we're going to attack the faeros on a large scale, we'll need thousands more. Tens of thousands!"

"We've got to be smart about this," Tasia interrupted. "No half-assed measures. If we go to Ildira, it'll likely be our last, best chance against the faeros. We need to make it count."

"The clouds of Golgen are laden with moisture, all of which is infused with wental energy," Cesca said. "We can draw on some of that water to make new frozen shells, and we can bring water from other wental planets to build up a large stockpile. Yes, we'll be ready for the faeros at Ildira."

"The wental water here is holding the hydrogues in check," Jess pointed out. "We don't dare deplete too much of it."

The young girl Osira'h had remained quiet beside Nira, but now she spoke with a strange, obsessive look in her large eyes. "And what about the hydrogues? They hate the faeros more than anything."

Del Kellum gave a loud, angry retort. "Even more than they hate humans? After all the destruction they caused, all those skymines wrecked, thousands and thousands of Roamers dead?"

"Including my brother," Jess said.

Mage-Imperator Jora'h looked at his daughter. "The hydrogues cannot be trusted. They destroy. They betray. I made that mistake once, and we are not that desperate."

"But if the faeros are so powerful, we need equally powerful allies to defeat them," Osira'h insisted.

"We have the wentals," Cesca pointed out, and that ended the discussion.

Even though he had been stranded and miserable for weeks, Caleb Tamblyn didn't seem to be in any hurry to leave Jonah 12. He fussed and dithered inside his makeshift shelter, gathering his few possessions, although Nikko couldn't see anything worth keeping among the bits of wreckage.

Even the wentals seemed enthusiastic and impatient to depart, thawing themselves from the chunks of ice and flowing voluntarily into the cargo hold of the *Aquarius*. The whole icy planet was by now infused with them, and they were strong and eager to fight the faeros.

Finally, Crim put his foot down and told Caleb, "Enough of this, man. Get aboard the *Aquarius*—we've got places to go, wentals to deliver, wars to win!"

After boarding the ship, Caleb took one last look at the rough, frozen landscape, and sealed the airlock hatch behind him. Nikko raised the *Aquarius* from the ice, keying in the next set of coordinates. Following their timetable, all the water bearers were supposed to rendezvous back at Theroc. Thanks to Jess and Cesca, the water elementals now held a spark of courage and determination as they rallied to stand against the faeros in ways they had never fought before.

Caleb hunched behind the two seats in the cockpit, relieved and excited now that they were finally on their way. Nikko accelerated away from the small frozen planetoid and headed out of the system.

"You sure you set the right course?" his father asked.

"I double-checked the nav calculations while we were waiting for Caleb to gather all his things."

"Oh. So you had plenty of time then."

Caleb made a sour face at him.

They hadn't gone far, though, before the wentals on the *Aquarius* began to churn. Thrumming through the deck and bulkheads, straining inside the hold, the living water sent out a wordless signal of alarm. Nikko knew what it meant. He quickly sent out a sensor sweep.

Nine swollen fireballs shot toward them from the outskirts of the Jonah system. Having sensed the water elementals inside the ship, they meant to destroy the *Aquarius* and its precious cargo.

Caleb's voice turned into a squawk of anger and fear. "I bet those are the same bastards that got my water tanker."

Nikko frantically reversed course and looped around, squeezing everything he could from the *Aquarius*'s engines. The sudden acceleration smashed him and his father back against their seats, while Caleb stumbled and fell to the deck.

The ship raced away — and the fiery ellipsoids rushed after them. Nikko tried to guess the limits to which he could push the hybrid vessel. "I can't engage the stardrives yet."

"Then just dodge the fireballs, boy!" his father said.

"Sure, I'll get right on that." Nikko made another radical course change and dropped back down into the Jonah system. He could sense the wentals boiling and angry, and suddenly he knew what he had to do. The watery entities made him realize it. "I'm heading back to the planetoid."

Caleb yelped, "Where are you planning to hide down there?"

"We're not going to hide. The wentals want me to go there. They're extremely agitated right now."

"No kidding." Crim's teeth were clenched tightly together. "I thought you said you couldn't communicate with them."

"Not entirely, and not clearly, but . . . I can *feel* that it's what they want." He felt the anger of the wentals onboard, a pounding sense that was entirely different from their previous passivity.

The nine faeros poured after them, trailing fire. Nikko dodged like a maniac, but he didn't see how the pool of wental water aboard his ship could fight off the fireballs pursuing them.

Nikko hurtled toward Jonah 12, which looked like no more than a speck of cosmic lint in the vast black emptiness. The planetoid glinted, its icy surface reflecting the distant sunlight. At the wentals' insistence, Nikko calculated an orbital vector, swinging low. He would practically scrape his underbelly on the crater rims and the frozen mounds of low mountains. It was going to take some fancy flying.

He couldn't imagine what the wentals had in mind, but he trusted them implicitly.

With the faeros careening in its wake, the *Aquarius* whisked like a swift-moving shadow across the rugged landscape. His father and Caleb were so frightened they didn't even criticize his flying, and Nikko's terror helped keep his concentration as focused as a laser. He didn't know how much longer he could fly like this.

The relentless fireballs pressed ever closer, and curtains of heat rippled out, melting the surface wherever they touched.

Then, as the *Aquarius* cruised over the wide melted crater from the reactor explosion, the trap was sprung. Emerging from where they had been locked in the ice, wentals erupted as great, gushing geysers.

The faeros could not back away or change their course swiftly enough from the cannon blasts of charged water. Like watery volcanoes, the surge of liquid struck the nine ellipsoids. More living water streamed from the thick ice and engulfed the faeros, who could not fight back. The warrior wentals snuffed out the elemental fires.

A surge of exhilaration rushed through his bloodstream as Nikko raced away in the *Aquarius*.

"Neat trick," Caleb said, "and a very auspicious start to this big battle you keep talking about."

The three laughed out loud with relief. Nikko's father clapped both of the others on the shoulders. "Now let's head to Theroc and get on with it."

112 ❋ ROBB BRINDLE

Days after their arrival, Robb stood with Fleet Admiral Willis aboard the *Jupiter*, gazing out at the Earth with feelings as jumbled as the scattered chunks of lunar debris. This place had been Robb's home, where his parents had been stationed throughout his youth, where he had first filled out the forms to join the EDF, eager to go out and fight the hydrogues.

Robb felt a great hollowness in his chest each time he saw the rubble field of the Moon. Nothing left but shattered rocks flying in all directions. He had undergone his initial training at the EDF base there, the same base where he'd met the cocky Roamer recruit Tasia Tamblyn. . . . He wished Tasia could have accompanied them on this mission, but she had flown off with Kotto Okiah to Golgen and points unknown, hoping to help him test his Klikiss Siren.

No, coming back to Earth to face this extraordinary disaster—that was his own job.

He hadn't seen his mother in years, and he and his father had parted under difficult circumstances when Robb chose to remain loyal to King Peter rather than to the Hansa. It shouldn't have been a choice that either one had to make. At Pym, though, Robb had seen some hint that his father might be softening his position, maybe understanding the rot in the command structure.

Today there could be no avoiding General Conrad Brindle. The new commander of the Earth Defense Forces was coming aboard the *Jupiter* to discuss the situation with Admiral Willis. Robb had no doubt that would be an interesting meeting.

When the huge group of Confederation ships had arrived at Earth, the EDF met—or confronted—them, led by the ominous *Goliath* and a far greater number of repaired ships than they had ever expected to see. After a few tense moments, the Confederation ships had grudgingly been allowed to get to work.

Despite their diligence, the EDF ships had been managing to catch only about one percent of the Earth-intersecting objects. It was impossible to detect and deflect all of them, but with so many additional experienced helpers, Robb hoped to increase that success rate to at least ninety percent.

Still, it took only one extinction event . . .

Admiral Willis had dispersed her ships and the Roamer privateers, and they plunged into the task with dogged determination. Showing off, the clan volunteers worked like hyperactive ants repairing a damaged colony. The Admiral was initially flustered by the independence of the Roamer pilots, who did not fall neatly into her guidelines, adhere to the chain of command, or use standardized procedures. However, when they spread out in their mishmash of unique craft, they worked just fine without oversight.

Thousands of clan ships—mostly cargo vessels and scout flyers—accompanied the orderly squads of Confederation-marked Remoras. They flew wide and thorough search patterns with their sensors attuned for any faint readings. Each time they found a questionable object, they planted a small pinger to broadcast the rock's location so larger battleships could intercept it in time. Roamer craft reported back to the *Jupiter,* dumping their navigation logs to provide the Confederation with an ever-growing database of celestial hazards. Computers projected a bird's nest of orbital lines, and Robb's mind reeled at the huge number of significant objects—with many more waiting to be found.

"Never thought I'd say it," Willis commented, lounging back in her command chair, "but this looks like a job too big even for the Roamer clans—and those people are insane!"

"Insane? Or desperate?"

"One often leads to the other."

Emergency crews had to prioritize which fragments posed the largest potential danger. Using concentrated jazer fire, powerful explosives, and some of Willis's stockpiled nukes, the Confederation ships broke the largest objects into chunks small enough to theoretically burn up in the atmosphere. Some giant fragments were far enough away that carefully planted explosions deflected them into safer orbits, easing the problem at least temporarily.

Experienced Roamer scouts quickly showed the stodgier EDF pilots how it was done. Squadrons of ships combed the nearby volume of space all day long, searching the emptiness and back-calculating the projected paths of lunar rubble.

Several more repaired EDF ships had been released from the robot construction complexes to join the scout fleet. Every new vessel helped. Even so, Robb didn't view the black robots too kindly. After being held prisoner inside a gas giant by hydrogues and black robots, knowing how the robots had betrayed Tasia, and how they had hijacked much of the EDF fleet, Robb remained suspicious.

On the main screen on the *Jupiter*'s bridge, he saw the large open-architecture vessels that Sirix and his comrades were building for themselves, right in view of Earth. The alien configurations had been adapted from old Klikiss plans. Why would Chairman Wenceslas allow them to do that? It defied belief.

Willis's executive officer reported to the bridge. "The EDF command shuttle has just docked, ma'am. General Brindle will be here momentarily."

She looked at Robb, knowing full well what she was asking. "Would you please escort him up to the bridge?"

Robb's stomach was in knots, but he forced a smile that fooled no one. "Sure, Admiral. I'd be happy to."

His father came alone, leaving his protocol officers aboard his shuttle. Robb knew the man liked to do things himself. *General Brindle*. He still couldn't get used to his father's title. Of course, he himself was now "Commodore."

Conrad Brindle stood in the corridor in front of the lift, wearing a snappy new EDF uniform complete with fresh stars on his shoulders. Instead of his usual unreadable expression, a succession of emotions played visibly across the older man's face.

Robb stared at him for a moment and finally said, "I . . . I don't know whether or not I'm supposed to salute you."

His father frowned. "I wouldn't worry about a thing like that now. We've got more important matters to deal with."

"I'll take you to Fleet Admiral Willis, then." Robb gestured for him to enter the lift. Then he added, "We've always been trying to help, you know." He realized that this might be their only brief chance to talk alone. The lift doors whisked shut, and they began to ascend to the bridge. "Thank you for what you did at Pym." They both knew that Conrad's actions had probably saved Robb's life there.

"General Lanyan made it necessary." His father looked at him coolly, then finally burst out, "Robb, I was furious with you for abandoning me on Theroc. Your training, your oaths of loyalty, your impeccable service . . . all thrown away for a bunch of rebels who tore up the Hansa Charter? You turned your back on the Hansa, on the EDF."

"But not on *Earth,* and never you. I always did what I thought was best for Earth, and I stand by the course I chose." Robb stiffened, facing the closed doors, knowing they would open on the bridge at any moment.

Instead of making a bitter retort, Conrad surprised Robb by nodding slowly. "For my own part, I thought I was being loyal to Earth by remaining true to the *Earth* Defense Forces, but serving under General Lanyan made me ashamed. I participated in despicable acts, robbing the Golgen skymine complex as if we were a bunch of pirates. We went to a Roamer asteroid-processing facility, too, but it was already destroyed. Then, at the Osquivel shipyards—all those civilian . . ." Conrad looked stricken. "Casualties."

When the lift doors whisked open, the two took a moment to recover their professional composure before stepping out onto the *Jupiter*'s main deck.

Admiral Willis got to her feet. "Congratulations on your promotion, General. You were always an excellent soldier and, in my opinion, not as much of a horse's ass as Lanyan was."

Conrad was taken aback by her candor. "The consequences of my predecessor's decisions . . . speak for themselves. I hope to employ a somewhat different command approach."

Robb extended his hand. "Now's our chance to set things straight, sir." He glanced at the immensely complex tangle of projected orbits of all the lunar fragments that had been mapped thus far. "There's plenty of work to do."

His father nodded. "I've already authorized the release of our largest warhead stockpile. The Chairman objected to putting such weapons anywhere close to Confederation loyalists, but I overruled him when eight fragments left a chain of craters across the Sahara." He drew a deep breath, gazing toward the deceptively calm image of Earth on the viewscreen. He could not see the deadly storm of rubble all around them in space, but he knew it was there.

"Chairman Wenceslas didn't want us to use every means possible to prevent further impacts?" Robb said in disbelief. "What in the world did he expect us to do with the atomics—launch a warhead strike on Earth?"

Admiral Willis shook her head, looking disgusted. "These fragments are bad enough, General Brindle, but in my studied opinion, the Chairman himself is an even greater danger to Earth."

113 ☀ SAREIN

When Basil came to her quarters that night, Sarein was not ready for him.

After the murder of Captain McCammon, the sudden disaster with the Solar Navy, and then the faeros at the Moon, the Chairman had withdrawn to deal with other emergencies. Sarein had avoided him entirely and had actually been relieved when he retreated to his underground bunker far beneath the Hansa HQ.

Every shred of hope, every small confidence that she could change him and halt his plunge into irrationality, had died with McCammon.

Now, in the middle of the night, Basil stood at her door looking as if he could go anywhere he wished, and she knew she had no choice but to let him in. If she had considered it even remotely likely that he would visit her, Sarein would have found a different place to sleep . . . to hide.

Now it was too late. She didn't dare raise his suspicions, since she knew what he was capable of doing. He had given the order to kill McCammon with no more emotion than he would have shown in asking for a sandwich. Had that truly been the end of his witch hunt, or was he still suspicious?

Now he was here.

And he wanted to *touch* her.

Basil smiled at her. "That's not a very warm welcome, Sarein." She thought there was a smell of blood about him, a metallic tang that made her heart stutter. "You seem surprised to see me. You must feel neglected. Have you forgotten all the times you asked me to come to your quarters? Those were good days . . . stable days." He raised his eyebrows. "I was afraid you might think I was avoiding you, that I was too preoccupied with the concerns of the Hansa."

"I understood completely, Basil." What had he been imagining?

He walked through her remodeled chambers without bothering to look around. She had no doubt that he regularly observed her quarters with his own surveillance systems. Did he watch her undress, like a voyeur? Did he look at her longingly and remember the times they had actually been happy, or at least content together? Did Basil Wenceslas even have lustful thoughts, or was that part of him dead? As he stepped closer, she knew for certain it had died in *her*.

She could not show her anxiety, but he had to know she was still shaken by the execution. McCammon had been her friend. One moment he had been alive, protecting her, caring for her, and the next, his blood had spattered her cheek, her clothes. She drew a deep breath and tried to think of some way to stall him. "Would you like me to put on some music, Basil? Shall I call for a meal?"

He placed his hands on her upper arms, drawing her close. "We're well past the point where we need to waste time on a long, slow seduction—aren't we?" He kissed her. Sarein tried her best to respond, but she felt sick.

Captain McCammon . . . his body spasming from multiple gunshot wounds, sprawling on the floor . . . the scarlet pool leaking out.

She couldn't get enough air to breathe. She shuddered when he stroked her short hair, traced his fingers down her back, then reached around to her breasts.

"I can tell you're excited," he said.

Sarein wanted to scream.

She pulled away from him as much as she dared. "Why the sudden change in attitude, Basil?" She had to pray that he was convinced McCammon was the only conspirator, that he had dealt Freedom's Sword a mortal wound, even though Patrick Fitzpatrick had become a prominent new thorn in his side.

"Does it displease you?" he asked.

"No . . . I just don't understand the reason for this."

He explained with maddening logic. "As more and more people turn against me, Sarein, I know I can't go it alone. Who else can I rely on? Deputy Cain? Perhaps. Colonel Andez? Of course, but only to follow orders. Remember what you and I had. Who could possibly be a better companion to shoulder the important responsibilities? You were my apprentice. I taught you about politics. You and I were perfect partners."

"Yes, we were." *A long time ago . . . before you became a madman.*

He seemed certain that his comment would act as an aphrodisiac, because he found the idea so very seductive himself. But Sarein knew that Chairman Wenceslas would never surrender any real power, never allow her to make changes or decisions. When she'd first met him, she had been young and naïve. She had listened to his philosophy and studied him — for a time.

He had killed McCammon.

He had killed the Archfather.

He had killed former Chairman Fitzpatrick.

He had tried to kill Peter and Estarra, more than once.

He stroked her cheek, smiling at her. Although his hands were covered with invisible blood, Sarein had to be more convincing than ever in her life, or he just might find the excuse he needed to kill her too. Sarein felt detached and bleak as he led her into the bedroom, but she didn't show it. He never noticed the difference.

Basil did not take long to finish. For him, the visit didn't seem to be so much about sex as it was about making sure that he had Sarein under his control. Afterward, she felt soiled, and as soon as she could make a proper excuse, she hurried into the bathroom to wash up. She wanted to take a long shower to cleanse herself, but Basil was still there, and she had to go back to him, not hide. For a moment, nausea threatened to overwhelm her.

She splashed cold water on her face, drew a deep breath, and toweled off. Through force of will she regained her composure — Basil was a master at that. For years, as his protégée, she had listened to him describe the necessities of politics, how to stomp down emotions and take the required action. She had learned from the best.

She emerged from the bathroom only to hear him at the door of her quarters, surreptitiously leaving. Sarein froze, holding her breath, hoping he would not turn back. She didn't call out to him. When Basil sealed the door behind him, she shuddered with relief.

Sarein slumped back onto the rumpled bed. After a moment of paralysis, she began to tear at the sheets, uprooting them from the mattress. She couldn't stand to feel the fine fabric against her skin, reminding her that she had already felt it beneath her, with Basil on top, thrusting. She had squirmed, not in passion, but loathing. Sarein hated herself for fearing him.

She pulled up one of the pillows to rip off the case and found a package hidden beneath. Basil must have put it there — which explained why he had left so soon. Clearly, he had wanted to be gone when she found his "surprise."

Sarein stared at the package, as if it were a hidden featherviper coiled and waiting to attack: an imagepak, with a screen and a player. She dreaded finding out what it held, but she also knew — from Basil's training, of course — that the sooner one learned of a threat, the more time one had to counteract it.

She played the series of images. Basil had not recorded an introductory message, as she had expected. Instead, she saw grainy surveillance images: Sarein and Captain McCammon smuggling the green priest Nahton in to see King Peter and Queen Estarra when they had been under house arrest; Estarra's conversation with her in the greenhouse wing, during which she laid out evidence of Basil's crimes and indiscretions; whispered conversations with Deputy Cain. Sarein was in all of the surreptitious recordings. Any one of them would have been damning enough.

They had thought they were so careful . . . yet Basil had watched them all.

Cold sweat trickled down her spine. Now she understood what Basil was telling her. He knew full well that Freedom's Sword had not, in fact, been behind the assassination attempt. He knew that McCammon hadn't acted alone in his schemes. He knew that Sarein had taken part in the conspiracy. He had all the evidence he needed.

Yet he had allowed her to live—for now—with the knowledge that he could change his mind at any time he chose.

Sarein rushed back to the bathroom, and this time she did vomit, long and loudly.

114 ☀ ANTON COLICOS

Fighting the malaise of grief in his empty, pointless-seeming university office, Anton took his files out of storage and stacked them on the desk. Books and documents, handwritten notes, papers, printed correspondence from his parents, newsnet articles stored in a special scrapbook folder . . . everything he needed. The extensive biography project had been interrupted, cut short—just as his parents' lives had been.

But his heart was so heavy he could not find the initiative to get back to the work. Where once he had been enthusiastic about writing a celebratory chronicle of the renowned xeno-archaeologists Margaret and Louis Colicos, now the silence and emptiness of the office weighed upon him.

Somehow along the way, he had forgotten how to do anything without Vao'sh.

Feeling desolate, he remembered that he had also promised to write the poignant and dramatic story of the green priest Nira, her tribulations in the breeding camps on Dobro and her love for Mage-Imperator Jora'h. Now she was gone, too, escaped with the Solar Navy when all Ildirans had fled the Moon . . . leaving Vao'sh behind.

And, most important of all, he had to make sure that Vao'sh was remembered in the *Saga of Seven Suns,* seen as a real hero, part of the brave tale and not just a detached storyteller.

He didn't know how he could ever find the heart to finish any of those projects.

For so long he and the old rememberer had worked side by side, talking with each other, pointing out nuances or factual contradictions in the *Saga* or long-censored apocrypha. Anton had translated from the original Ildiran and delivered portions of the epic to appreciative Earth scholars. He and Vao'sh had been true companions of heart and mind. Even during their imprisonment on Earth, at least they had been together. He had never imagined how empty he would feel now.

All through their time at the Department of Ildiran Studies, ostensibly under "close debriefing" as ordered by Chairman Wenceslas, the two of them had gone to numerous gala events and spectacular conferences, and had given countless talks in crowded lecture halls. Now that the old rememberer was gone, Anton simply sat at his desk and stared.

The dean had recently given him the most spacious office in the building. Its large windows looked out on the parklike courtyard and the Ildiran-inspired sculptures. Four unwashed coffee mugs sat on his desk. A plant — a gift from someone? — was brown and dead because he'd neglected to water it.

At any moment, a big burning rock could hurtle through the atmosphere and obliterate the entire campus. He wasn't sure he cared.

Across the planet, the whole population lived with that fatalism. Some people had become dramatically religious; others responded with wild end-of-the-world hedonism. Many didn't know what to do. To Anton, no disaster seemed as significant as the death of Vao'sh. He heaved a sigh. Hearing somebody at his door, he looked up from his desk.

For the first time in years, Anton saw his mother.

He stared, and Margaret stared back at him. "Hello, Anton."

The silence stretched out for an impossibly long moment, and he finally blurted, "Where have you been?"

He couldn't remember doing so, but suddenly he was up from his desk and running to the office door. His mother seemed bony and rigid as he threw his arms around her. It was an automatic reaction; he couldn't recall the last time Margaret had given him a hug. His parents had always been so wrapped up in their archaeological pursuits that they didn't know how to deal with children, not even grown-up ones.

He continued, barely pausing for a breath. "I looked for you! I begged Chairman Wenceslas to send search teams, and he did. I made inquiries, but then I went off to Ildira—" He shook his head, as if to rattle his thoughts back into place. "It was so hard to get news there."

"No one knew where I was," she said. "I was too far away. Much too far. You always did enjoy epic stories, and I've got one that's a saga and a half."

"What's it about? Will you tell it to me?" Anton realized maybe he would be able to complete writing that long-planned biography after all.

Margaret seemed lost in thought. "Where do I start? The black robots? How your father died on Rheindic Co? How I lived isolated among the Klikiss for years? How I finally came back home?" She flashed him a strange smile. "Remember that music box you gave me—the one that played 'Greensleeves'?"

"It was a present for your . . . anniversary? Birthday?" He always had trouble figuring out what to get his mother, and he had bought it at the last minute. Although the little metal box hadn't cost much, it had appealed to him, and she had seemed pleased by the gift. "You actually *kept* that?"

"It saved my life. Its music was why the Klikiss didn't kill me, as they did the other human captives." She held his shoulders, studying him. "You look sad."

Once again, he was at a loss for words. "We've both got some complicated stories to tell." He shook his head. "There was a time when I thought being invited as the guest speaker to a conference was the most exciting thing I could aspire to. I liked to read about great heroes, not try to be one." Without realizing he was doing it, he suddenly found himself crying on her shoulder.

Margaret held him for a long while, and then took him by the arm. "Is there a coffee shop on campus where we can talk?"

He wiped his eyes. "We'll need more than a cup of coffee. How about we plan on having dinner together?"

Margaret smiled as they walked down the hall. "Tonight, and maybe for the next few nights. This won't be quick or easy."

115 ☀ MAGE-IMPERATOR JORA'H

Drawing a deep breath of bitter air on the open landing bay with Del Kellum, Jora'h stared out into the clouds, watching the stately Solar Navy ships. Osira'h and Nira were also with him to observe the preparations to take the battle back to Ildira. Nearby, the hydrogue derelict sat waiting for whatever tests Kotto intended to perform, but his work on it—as well as the Klikiss Siren—had been preempted by their preparations to fight the faeros. The intense gear-up had been under way since the previous day.

After the war council meeting, Adar Zan'nh had returned to his flagship to oversee yet another round of practice runs. Warliners cruised back and forth in regimented formations, practicing maneuvers, performing intricate loops and close encounters, in training for their offensive against the faeros.

"They never tire of flying in all those complicated patterns, do they?" Kellum asked.

"The Adar tells me these maneuvers help Ildiran pilots to hone their skills." As they watched, three warliners drove directly toward each other, nearly colliding, but then dodged with pinpoint accuracy.

"Impressive enough, but when those ships go into actual battle, the rules of engagement won't have anything to do with fancy dance moves."

Jora'h looked at the bearded man. At one time he would have disagreed out of sheer pride, but now he nodded slowly. "Adar Zan'nh has been learning to adapt. But who has a training program to fight the faeros? This is a new kind of war for us."

"For all of us, by damn."

They peered into the bottomless pit of calm clouds. Out there, Jess Tamblyn and Cesca Peroni flitted about the cloud tops in their silvery vessel, coalescing water droplets and then flying back to the skymine.

The wental vessel returned to the open launching bay to deposit a large spill of energized water they had retrieved from the atmosphere. "This should be enough to make a few dozen more ice projectiles," Jess said, emerging from his shimmering ship with Cesca.

The liquid flowed out onto the scuffed metal floor, and the wentals seemed to know what to do. The spreading puddle separated itself into smaller globules that formed pointed cylinders and then, in a flash of curling white steam, they spontaneously froze into icy artillery shells.

Kellum called a work team that used insulated gloves and tongs to distribute the frozen shells among the ships near the skymine, and Jess and Cesca flew off again to draw more traces of wentals from the clouds. By the time the ships were ready to go find the faeros, they would all be fully armed.

While the activities carried on all around them, Nira sent telink messages through her treeling to inform the Confederation of the plans the allies were making to fight the faeros on Ildira.

Jora'h felt satisfied. "We have waited a long time for this. And I am glad, very glad, that I maintained my faith in the Confederation and the Roamers, rather than trusting Chairman Wenceslas."

A cargo vessel loaded with hundreds of the new projectiles lumbered off across the sky to deliver them to the other skymines. Adar Zan'nh had already sent specifications to Kotto Okiah, so the Roamer engineer could create frozen wental shells for use in Ildiran projectile launchers. Soon, the Solar Navy would be armed with them as well.

Osira'h moved closer to the edge of the open platform and pointed upward. "Look."

High above the skymine, a single bright shape streaked alone across the sky, like a meteor that did not burn up. Behind it came another crackling ball . . . and dozens more, like a shower of incandescent sparks.

Jora'h instantly realized what he was seeing. His braid whipped and thrashed of its own volition. "So, Rusa'h has found me after all."

Nira's eyes widened. "Did he track one of the warliners? Or did he locate you somehow through the *thism*?"

Two more flaming ellipsoids streaked past, followed by another dozen. Flashes raced above the upper fringes of Golgen's sky in a rain of fire.

"Doesn't matter how — they're *here*," Kellum said.

The Solar Navy ships abandoned their complex exercises and quickly arranged themselves into genuine battle formations. Alarms began to sound. The skymine's intercom

flooded with an overlapping cacophony of shouts. Kellum ran
to the wall and slapped the transmit button. "I'm on my way.
Tell Kotto he's getting a chance to test those wental popsi-
cles." He turned to Jora'h, his face flushed. "The faeros blew
up the whole Moon trying to get to you, Mage-Imperator.
doubt they'll show any more restraint here."

Jora'h knew he was right. "No, they will try to destroy
everything."

116 ☀ TASIA TAMBLYN

The vanguard of fireballs left a roiling wake of hot gases
and thermal ripples across Golgen's sky. Having seen the
faeros arrive, some of the skyminers were already evacuating. The flaming ellipsoids streaked after anything that
moved.

Inside Kellum's skymine, Tasia slid down ladders
dodged stored cargo crates and industrial equipment, and
raced across the deck to the lower hangar bay where she had
left her cargo hauler. She was already kicking herself for not
bringing a military-grade vessel with her, just to cover the
bases, but she would make do. At least the ship was equipped
with the standard new armaments and improved hull plating
supplied by the Confederation.

Surrounded by the clamor of alarms, Kotto huffed down

to the hangar deck to board the ship. He arrived red-faced and winded, but he was actually smiling! "At last, a chance to test the new wental weapons."

With a sweep of her arm, Tasia encouraged him to get inside as soon as she extended the ramp. "And they'd better work. We launch in two minutes. No time to waste."

Orli Covitz and Hud Steinman had followed Kotto from the workroom, where the three of them had been fiddling with the Klikiss Siren. Tasia was anxious to test that device, as well—but it sure as shizz wasn't going to be today.

"Are we evacuating?" Steinman asked.

Tasia turned. "Not a chance. We're going to fight those bastards with everything Kotto's got."

"You should stay here, Orli," the old man said, sounding a bit too paternal. "It'll be safer."

The teenager rolled her eyes. "What, exactly, is safe about being on a skymine that's under attack?"

"Good point."

Kotto looked back into the hangar bay. "Are the compies coming?"

"They're not very good at running," Orli said. "I'm sure they'll be here in a few minutes."

"We can't wait," Tasia shouted over the roar of her engines, which she was already warming up. "Get in, or stay behind. This ship is leaving now." They all decided to scramble aboard.

When the hatch was sealed, the Confederation cargo hauler streaked away from the skymine, and they instantly found themselves in a fury of faeros, like ricocheting sparks. Steinman and Orli let out astonished gasps as Tasia pulled the ship in a tight corkscrew to evade a gout of fire; Kotto was so busy checking his system status with the ice-projectile launchers that he didn't seem to notice.

"The wental shells are ready," he announced. "I rigged a refrigerated magazine and loaded the shells onto this ship and eighteen others. We each have ten projectiles. Let's see how effective they are."

"*Ten* projectiles each?" Tasia indicated all the blazing ellipsoids. "Don't you think you underestimated a little?"

He flushed. "Well, it was originally meant for defense, and the faeros usually attack with only a few fireballs at a time. When Speaker Peroni asked me, it seemed a reasonable assumption."

Hundreds of Solar Navy warliners descended from orbit in a mind-boggling defensive array, led by Tal Ala'nh. Though it was an extremely impressive show of force, Tasia wasn't certain the warliners were prepared to face the faeros. She switched on the comm. "Stay clear, Solar Navy — we're going to try out the new projectiles."

Tal Ala'nh's gruff voice came over the channel. "We may not have your specialized armaments, but we will fight, not cower behind you."

"For whatever good that'll do," Tasia muttered. As three warliners charged forward in a foolish and suicidal offensive, she sent another communication burst. "Shizz, don't waste your ships! They're going to be destroyed."

The fireballs flared brighter, racing to intercept the ornate vessels. When she contacted Adar Zan'nh in the main force of warliners, however, he did not order the tal to have his ships retreat. The Ildiran commander's face looked tired and haggard on the small screen in Tasia's cockpit. "It is what they feel they need to do to protect the Mage-Imperator."

Exactly as Tasia had predicted, the trio of warliners

crashed into the flaming ellipsoids, ineffectually firing their weapons until the moment of their destruction. The exploding Ildiran ships released a shockwave that hammered back into the faeros, disrupting the integrity of those particular fireballs, though they soon reformed into a roiling mass. As far as Tasia could tell, the Ildiran sacrifice accomplished little.

"Our turn," Orli said.

Tasia aligned the targeting cross on her screen and drove the cargo hauler toward the nearest fireball. Flickering, ragged flames wreathed the oncoming faeros as they grew closer, hotter. "Here goes nothing." She launched the frozen projectile, subconsciously holding her breath.

The pointed cylinder streaked out and vanished into the heart of the vastly larger fireball. The flames twisted, knotted, and swallowed all trace of the frozen artillery shell.

Kotto seemed embarrassed. "I, uh, expected something a little more . . . dramatic."

With an eruption of white steam, a detonation tore apart the fireball's nucleus, expanding outward in a cold, moist cloud that engulfed and smothered the flames. When the flash dissipated, nothing remained—no faeros, no wental, just an empty clot of superheated air in the sky.

"Nine ice bullets left . . . and about a million fireballs out there," Steinman said.

"Dive toward another one!" Orli said. "We're wasting time."

Exuberant, Kotto took the communication controls and urged the eighteen other Roamer ships to launch their frozen projectiles. "It works—I encourage you all to try it!"

Tasia headed toward a faeros and shot their second icy artillery shell. One more fireball annihilated. Altogether, the clan ships on Golgen had nearly two hundred of the special shells. Maybe it would be enough to make a dent and turn back the faeros. As far as she could tell, they had no other weapons that were even remotely effective.

Her third icy projectile created yet another spectacular cold flash that extinguished a faeros. "I can start enjoying this. Your artillery is a success, Kotto—I just wish I had a full battery of them."

Now, more Roamer ships flew into the chaos of fire-balls, launching their own frozen projectiles. Numerous flaming ellipsoids were extinguished, leaving behind flashes of dying light.

Down below, skimming over the cloud tops, Tasia could see the watery vessel flown by her brother and Cesca, rallying the wentals in the atmosphere, pulling curls of mist higher into the sky. She expended her fourth projectile, and Orli and Steinman let out a cheer.

When the enraged fireballs hurtled toward them, though, she knew for certain they didn't have enough ammunition.

From where they stood inside the large bay, looking out at the landing deck and the open sky, Osira'h and the others watched several warliners being destroyed in their attempts to fight back. The daring Roamer ships flew about, and their icy projectiles were having some effect, but their numbers could not possibly be sufficient. The fireballs kept coming.

Adar Zan'nh's voice called out on the open channel of the Mage-Imperator's small communication device, "Liege, will you remain on the skymine, or do you wish to be brought up to the flagship? I do not know which gives you a better guarantee of safety."

"There is no guarantee of safety." Jora'h glanced at Kellum, then responded briskly. "However, the Roamers will have a better chance if I do not remain among them. Rusa'h wants *me*. Send a cutter to retrieve us." He gestured to Nira and their daughter to come with him.

Osira'h, though, turned toward the small diamond derelict. "No, there is one other chance." She knew it in her heart, even though none of the others were willing to consider the idea. "And by now we must be desperate enough to take it."

The hydrogues had caused much damage to so many planets, including the Ildiran Empire, but Osira'h had been linked with them. She had confronted them, formed a bridge, used her mind as well as her connection to the telink and the *thism* to force them to listen to her. She had touched their thoughts, and she knew how much they hated the faeros.

Nira's eyes widened. "It's too dangerous."

But Osira'h broke away from them and sprinted over to the small diamond sphere. The ship would fall into the depths by itself, but she needed to get it away from the sky-mine . . . just the slightest nudge would send it over the edge of the launching deck.

Jora'h's ornate robes fluttered in the thin air of the open deck. He shouted, "No, Osira'h! I cannot ask you to do this again."

Osira'h scrambled through the hatch and paused just for a second to answer him. "You did not ask—I chose."

As her parents ran after her, Del Kellum called out, "What the hell does that girl think she's doing?"

Osira'h sealed the transparent hatch just as her mother reached the hull. She couldn't look at Nira, but instead hurried to the lumpy crystalline controls. She had no idea how to fly the craft, remembered only a few glimpses of thoughts from the hydrogues. But all she needed to do was activate the engines, give the sphere a nudge. She would never be able to guide it . . . gravity would have to do the rest.

An explosion rumbled across the sky. Jora'h and Nira stood pleading outside the transparent hull, but she couldn't hear them. Instead, her small hands danced over the controls, trying to interpret them, searching for anything that made sense. One of the panels lit up, and though Osira'h heard nothing, she sensed a faint vibration. She tried similar controls, and finally felt a burst of power, a brief pulse from the alien engines.

The transparent sphere moved forward, began to roll as if someone had given it a shove across the smooth deck toward the precipitous drop-off. Her mother and father could not stop it. Faeros and Roamer ships streaked by overhead.

Osira'h steeled herself as she glanced out at the firestorm in the skies. It had not been so long since she'd established a link with the hydrogues and used the power of the verdani to coerce them. She had been raised and trained to do this, and she could do it again. Through the *thism*, the Mage-Imperator would know she remained alive.

And then she was over the edge. The derelict dropped like a stone away from the giant city in the sky. As she fell, Osira'h peered through the transparent ceiling and saw Nira and Jora'h still shouting, still reaching out for her.

She watched the gigantic skymine and the frenzied battle dwindle in the distance far above her. Then gauzy clouds engulfed her, and she felt claustrophobic and alone.

118 ☀ PATRICK FITZPATRICK III

Patrick managed to send out four more subversive broadcasts before Hansa troops stormed the mansion. He knew the resources Basil Wenceslas could bring to bear against them—especially now that the Chairman was infuriated. He had used relays to cover their origin. He thought he was clever. He thought he was safe.

He was wrong.

Though Wenceslas certainly had far more pressing problems, he ruthlessly prosecuted anyone who criticized him, never mind the facts. And, of course, he bore a particular grudge against anybody claiming to represent Freedom's Sword. Patrick was definitely in the crosshairs.

The worldwide panic and continuing threat of meteor strikes had plunged the population into near anarchy, and they took up the cry against the Chairman with great fervor. Although King Rory made plenty of impassioned speeches, he fooled no one; in fact, since the destruction of the Moon and the horrendous meteor impacts that followed, not many people listened to him anymore.

With the arrival of King Peter and his cavalry of Confederation rescuers, there could be no better time for a change of government. Patrick felt he was making real progress, but protests could accomplish only so much. Still, that didn't stop him and Zhett. Thanks to his grandmother's connections and finances, he had a powerful platform, if only for a little while. He rather enjoyed being a folk hero, but he knew he had to be living on borrowed time.

With external sensors and automatic alarms, he made his preparations to slip away at the first sign of danger, and in that he made his most serious mistake.

Since only he and Zhett were in the mansion, he was astonished by the size of the force arrayed against them: four hundred uniformed troops, fourteen low-altitude gunships, six land assault vehicles. He had expected at least a few minutes of warning, but the cleanup crew came in like a blitzkrieg. In the first minute, a projectile blew up the *Gypsy* where it sat on the small private landing pad; repeated explosions wiped out the adjacent hangar and all of Maureen's vehicle bays. The space yacht had been primed and ready to go, but now it was only a smoldering lump of wreckage. He and Zhett had counted on eluding pursuit with their Roamer-augmented engines. Now, his Plans B, C, and D had also been cut off. The Chairman's goons were very thorough.

"Sorry I got you into this," he said to Zhett as the troops swarmed around the mansion, smashing windows and breaking in through every possible entrance. They shot projectiles at the walls with loud rifles, apparently to intimidate them.

She pretended to be unfazed. "Listen, if you had left me behind, you'd be in a lot more trouble than you are with these people."

The troops found them together in the media room behind a barricaded door. The moment he accepted the impossibility of escape, Patrick had decided to transmit the whole assault live, so that people could witness the antics of the cleanup crew. More fodder for the protests. He hoped, but was not convinced, that the Hansa soldiers might exercise more restraint if they knew their actions were being broadcast. But Chairman Wenceslas was past caring about public outrage. People might well scream, but he did as he pleased.

When the dark-uniformed soldiers broke down the door and stormed the media room, Patrick was surprised to see that the assault group was led by a zealous Shelia Andez, now sporting a colonel's rank insignia. She seemed barely able to keep herself from spitting in his face. "You're a disgrace to your oath of service, your government, and your people."

"Funny, I was about to say the same." Patrick faced his former comrade in arms. "If you paid attention to what the Hansa is really doing, you wouldn't cooperate. Open your eyes."

Zhett let out a bitter laugh at the suggestion. "She knows

damned well what's going on, Fitzie. This is the bitch who's doing most of it!"

At some point during the operation, the soldiers smashed the imagers recording the incident. The abrupt termination of the broadcast would probably cause even more consternation among the real members of Freedom's Sword. Patrick doubted these guards knew what they were provoking.

Her face flushed with self-importance, Shelia said, "If you don't cooperate, we'll stun you and drag you by your feet to one of the troop transports."

"Oh, we wouldn't dream of being uncooperative," Patrick said.

They were placed in electronic restraints. He walked alongside Zhett, his head held high. The fear in his chest was no more than a dull, persistent ache. After all, he reminded himself, he'd been sentenced to death before.

119 ☀ KING PETER

Estarra's large brown eyes were full of suspicion when she heard Basil's surprise invitation. "You don't actually believe the Chairman's making a peace gesture, do you?"

"Of course not, but I don't think he'll try anything stupid. He needs us."

Any reasonable person might have responded with gratitude for all the aid the Confederation brought to Earth, but not Basil Wenceslas. Though he kept pretending the Hansa was thriving and under his complete control, even Basil could not ignore the disaster.

Young King Rory had invited Peter and Estarra (their royal titles intentionally omitted) to attend a banquet in the Whisper Palace "in recognition of assistance given," with no specific acknowledgment of the Confederation or anyone by name. It was the sort of thing that should have incensed Peter, but he let it flow past him. Childish word games were not his concern. He did, however, want to know what the Chairman had up his sleeve.

And then there was Rory . . .

He was even more interested in meeting the familiar-looking King, with his dark eyes, dark hair, and olive complexion. It had been almost ten years since the Chairman's henchmen had killed Peter's mother and his brothers, Michael, Carlos . . . and Rory. *Rory.*

He couldn't believe Basil would have thought so far ahead as to fake the boy's death and then keep him hidden on the off chance that Peter would cause problems someday. And why would the Chairman have bothered with Prince Daniel if he already had Rory in reserve? It implied a mind-boggling depth of long-range planning, a tortuous chain of paranoia . . . and profound patience.

It was exactly the way Basil Wenceslas worked.

Peter had to see for himself.

"We'll take a full guard escort. We'll also be monitored by our own imagers, not just the Hansa's propaganda patsies." He tried to sound confident. "And we'll take OX with us to record, analyze, and advise."

Basil could not afford any more bad press. As a bellwether of the public's dissatisfaction, the Chairman was condemned daily in postings, demonstrations, and random acts of arson or vandalism. The cleanup crew tried to snuff all the negative news stories, but they leaked out with greater and greater vehemence.

Peter had been observing the newsnets with interest. Just that morning, Patrick Fitzpatrick and Zhett Kellum — supposed ringleaders of Freedom's Sword — had shaken up the population with the vivid broadcast of their brutal arrest. That had only inflamed the protesters more.

Basil was not going to be in a good mood when Peter and Estarra arrived.

He and Estarra dressed in their finest clothes with distinct touches of Theron and Roamer fashion, a carefully balanced mixture of pomp and practicality. He gathered a guard escort of former EDF crewmen, Roamers, Hansa colonists, and the Teacher compy, as well as a complete "documentation" team to record and broadcast the event in real time, uncensored. All of them had instructions to watch for any signs of treachery from the Chairman.

With the concentrated efforts of nearly a thousand new ships Peter had brought, the threat of a major asteroid strike had diminished dramatically. Peter was far more worried about Basil.

Fleet Admiral Willis scowled, fidgeted, and finally spoke up. "This just doesn't feel right. We know about the executions he ordered. We're sure he was responsible for blasting the Archfather of Unison. You saw with your own eyes what he did to former Chairman Fitzpatrick. He's thrown subtlety right out the window with the baby and the bathwater. If the Chairman sees a chance, he'll take it. What are your orders if things do go south?"

Peter pondered. "If necessary, carry out a surgical strike on the Hansa HQ or the Whisper Palace, one that minimizes casualties but is sure to deliver justice. The people of Earth aren't responsible for the Chairman's reckless actions. Don't make them suffer any more than they already have."

"You don't have to tell me that, King Peter."

Estarra took his hand, and along with their well-armed ceremonial escort, they boarded a specially outfitted diplomatic shuttle. Peter had mixed feelings about going back to the Palace District. On the chaotic and dangerous night of their escape, they had flown off while tremendous battles raged around them. Back then, the two of them had done what they thought best for humanity.

Now perhaps he could come back and fix things.

120 ☀ DEL KELLUM

A Solar Navy cutter flew down through the turbulent air battles to pick up the Mage-Imperator. Jora'h raised his hands to signal the Ildiran ship, which touched down on the skymine's open deck, its engines still roaring for an immediate departure.

Before the cutter opened its hatch, the green priest peered down into the clouds where the derelict had vanished some time before, but she saw no sign of her daughter. Both of them were distraught by what the half-breed girl had done, though Jora'h said he could tell through the *thism* that Osira'h remained alive.

Kellum didn't know what the girl hoped to accomplish, and he wasn't holding his breath for a miracle to happen. Jora'h took Nira's arm and pulled her toward the small Solar Navy ship. "She is gone now—she will succeed, or she will fail. It is up to her." Once he got the green priest aboard the cutter, Jora'h shouted into the noise, "Join us, Del Kellum! Adar Zan'nh will do everything in his power to keep us safe."

Kellum shook his head. "It may sound corny, but the captain's supposed to go down with his ship. Live in the sky, die in the sky . . . that's an old Roamer saying."

As more explosions rumbled overhead, and a fireball streaked so close to the top of the skymine that it melted some of the high towers, the Solar Navy pilot insisted that they had to depart. Kellum stood his ground, refusing to leave, and finally with a brisk wave of farewell, the Mage-Imperator and Nira flew off.

He thought longingly of his dear Shareen Pasternak, killed on a skymine that had been destroyed by hydrogues. And now a little girl had gone down in hopes that the hydrogues would *rescue* them. How ridiculous was that? He shook his head. As a counterpoint to these dismal thoughts, he clung to the satisfying knowledge that at least Zhett and Patrick had gotten away. They must be safer on Earth. . . .

Now that his beloved skymine was nothing more than a gigantic, lumbering target, Kellum had to make the call. Swallowing hard, he slapped the main intercom button so hard he hurt his palm. "This is Del Kellum—listen up! I'm sounding a full evacuation of this skymine. All personnel, get to a ship. Any ship you can find. I can't guarantee you'll be safer out in the open, but we're sitting ducks here."

Most of his workers had anticipated the announcement. Dozens of ships, including tiny maintenance vehicles with a range of no more than a few kilometers, sprang away from the lower decks, putting as much distance as possible between themselves and the skymine. They wanted to be far from the huge facility when the faeros circled in.

Countless ellipsoids swooped and looped like aimless sparks searching for victims, hunting down any escaping vessels. Most of the Roamer defenders had depleted their icy projectiles and were now running.

Flaming creatures closed in on all the skymines. Nearby, six fireballs threw their fury against a helpless cloud harvester owned by clan Hobart. Exhaust towers crumpled and melted; gas storage tanks burst, spewing a jet of flames to knock the levitating facility off its axis. The flames peeled away the armored structural plates, dismantling the whole facility. Finally, the lower ekti tanks ruptured, and the Hobart skymine's emergency signals and calls for assistance abruptly ceased. The gigantic wreck became a roiling mass of smoke and explosions. Its altitude engines failed, and the once-graceful city tumbled down into the deep clouds.

Kellum watched it mournfully, wondering if this disaster was similar to what Ross Tamblyn had experienced as his Blue Sky Mine fell apart in the air.

Below he saw an unnatural storm cell bubbling up from the stirring layers of mist, and his heart froze as an ominous, yet terribly familiar, spiked diamond vessel breached the clouds like some spherical sea leviathan. "Oh, hell . . ."

Another one rose, then another.

As the faeros continued to throw themselves at the Solar

Navy warliners, and the Roamer ships expended their last few ice projectiles, an armada of hydrogue warglobes rose up to meet them, shrouded in glittering wental mist.

121 ✺ JESS TAMBLYN

With their water sphere skimming atop the cloud banks, Jess and Cesca called upon the watery entities within the depths of Golgen, drawing sparkling smoke into a windy vortex. Diaphanous wisps of sentient fog curled toward the fireballs, ready to strike.

Jess could feel the warrior wentals around and within him thrumming with unaccustomed fury. *Faeros!* He nursed that anger into a determination that he fed back to the wentals as he led the charge upward. The sky was so full of vessels in chaotic motion that even the vast gas giant seemed crowded.

Though the rising mist looked deceptively ethereal, whenever it touched a fireball, the result was like a boiler explosion. The watery entities seethed with animosity. This was vengeance for the devastation of Charybdis. Yes, the wentals had learned. . . .

Jess could sense the faeros incarnate in one of the largest fireballs, another corporeal presence guiding the elementals—an avatar like himself, and yet entirely different. Jess could feel Rusa'h like a burn on the skin, a fire in the mind. This man had single-handedly changed the war with the faeros and taught them how to defeat the hydrogues.

Jess knew that *Rusa'h* must be the wentals' main target.

Cesca understood as well. "If we can defeat him here, then there will be no need to go to Ildira. He chose this battlefield. Now let's turn it against him."

Sparking a deep and implacable determination among the wentals, the two directed their water ship up toward the central ellipsoid. Rusa'h led his charge to find and destroy the Mage-Imperator among the numerous Solar Navy warliners, but so far he had been unsuccessful.

A sudden intense turmoil occurred from below, though—different from the battle above. He could feel what was about to emerge. Cesca looked at him, startled. "Hydrogues."

Hydrogues, the wentals said inside his mind. *They will fight here.*

Jess could not curb his surge of anger and disbelief. "The drogues will turn on us! It's like letting loose a wolf to fight a mad dog."

The wentals, though, responded with a firm confidence Jess did not feel. *We will keep them chained.*

When the clouds parted, a large armada of spiked spheres shot into the open, bright skies—dozens, and then dozens more. And tumbling along with them, drawn up by the warglobes, came the small derelict. From inside the diamond globe, Osira'h used her communication systems. "The hydrogues are outraged that the faeros have come to their world. I convinced them to help turn the battle."

"I don't believe this," Cesca said.

We are warrior wentals. We learned to fight from you, said the voice inside him. *We learned to consider alternatives. The hydrogues do not battle for us, or for humanity, but for themselves. They fight only to destroy faeros, nothing more.*

"I compelled them, as I did before," Osira'h said. "They have accepted limited terms."

The wentals will contain them.

Jess was not entirely reassured, but he accepted the wentals' confidence. Osira'h had acted independently, and the water elementals believed there was some advantage to unleashing the deep-core aliens, at least for the moment.

Bottled up in the high-pressure depths, the hydrogues had stewed in their own anger for far too long. Now, with elemental chains loosened, numerous warglobes flew upward. Their abiding and ancient loathing of the fiery elementals far exceeded their relatively new resentment for humans. They chose their targets, and they did not waver.

Diamond spheres rocketed into the flaming ellipsoids, unleashing skittery patterns of blue electrical bolts. The fireballs pulsed and struggled, and some of the weaker ones diminished like candle flames extinguished by the wind.

But even as the warglobes raced into the clash, tendrils of wental vapor clung to them in a strange symbiosis. When the hydrogue spheres approached a group of fireballs, the sentient mists expanded and lifted up in filmy nets to snarl the faeros.

The hydrogues spewed their shattering cold weapons in icy white ripples that weakened and then extinguished the fireballs. Previously, the warglobes had used those terrible frigid blasts to lay waste to the worldforest, and Jess felt his stomach roiling as he observed them now. He doubted the deep-core aliens had any interest in earning forgiveness or redemption.

But they were certainly wreaking a lot of unexpected destruction here.

As the faeros fought back, however, one of the warglobes exploded, its shattered diamond hull raining back down into the clouds. Several other hydrogue ships were wiped out as well, but more of them emerged from the depths.

"Jess, we have to reach the faeros incarnate," Cesca said.

He shook free of his anger. "You're right—let's keep our eyes on the target."

Intent again, Jess drove their water sphere up into the path of Rusa'h's blazing ellipsoid. He could sense that although the other avatar was shaken by the sudden turnabout, he would not back away. He continued to dart among the Solar Navy ships, intent on finding the Mage-Imperator and destroying any warliner that got in his way.

Jess and Cesca pulled the atmospheric wentals along with them in a stream of water vapor that circled with a sharp wind into an ever-tightening spiral and coalesced into a misty tornado. Jess did not intend to let the faeros incarnate harm Mage-Imperator Jora'h.

The cyclone of fog wrapped like a straitjacket around Rusa'h's fireball. Jess felt buffeted by the faeros incarnate's surprise; the other avatar could sense them, too, but Rusa'h had not previously encountered anyone else like himself. Jess and Cesca took advantage of his disorientation and threw the energized water against the flaming shield.

Rusa'h's charge against the Solar Navy faltered as he struggled to fight off the watery hurricane. Jess guided his wental ship in circles, harrying the faeros incarnate and spiraling in. The flames diminished even though Rusa'h fought back. Sending a coordinated mental shout, Jess and Cesca called upon the wentals—and the hydrogues—to concentrate their attack here.

The battle swiftly turned. Many spiked warglobes fought beside the Roamer ships, which had expended all their frozen projectiles. Wentals splashed up to seize and smother numerous fireballs. Sparks flew everywhere, and ashes dropped down into the endless atmosphere.

Just as more wentals and hydrogues surged forward to the faeros incarnate, Rusa'h surrounded himself with dozens of fireballs to form an intense barricade. Finally, the burning man broke free of the misty cyclone. Obviously weakened as he limped higher into the sky, he called a retreat from Golgen. When another wave of warglobes shot out of the clouds, the faeros pulled together and sped away. With a surge of strength, Jess and Cesca raced after them, but the surviving fireballs vanished in a dazzling group.

Though they had failed to stop the faeros incarnate, Jess felt his heart swell to see the flaming enemies retreat. The local communications equipment crackled with a thousand overlapping cheers, while others hurled curses at the faeros, which had dwindled to mere sparks in the sky.

Though many warglobes had been smashed in the air battle, the remaining hydrogues hovered, like vicious attack dogs straining at a leash. They wanted to pursue the fireballs into space, to escape from Golgen and run free again—but Jess refused to allow that. He still felt a knotted anger toward the hydrogues, a bitterness that he could not let go, no matter how many faeros they had extinguished.

Jess prepared for another fight to restrain them. He expected the deep-core aliens to turn on the wentals. But the wentals surrounded the warglobes with strands of fog, and the surreal chains held them in place.

From her derelict Osira'h transmitted, "They will not fight to help us. They will not join in the battle for Ildira. They will stay here."

We would not allow them to leave, the combined wental voice said.

"Good," Jess said. "The risk would be too great."

Slowly, the warglobes were drawn back down into the clouds of Golgen, their prison, their home. Although the hydrogues were still contained, still defeated, Jess wondered if they felt some gratification at having beaten their enemies. He was glad for what they had done, but that was all.

When he spotted Osira'h's small diamond sphere among the hydrogue warglobes, though, he realized that it had begun to fall back down with them. Cesca saw it too, and urged their wental ship down into the thick gas layers, darting toward the derelict. They snagged the ship, and as they pulled it back up toward the damaged skymines and the regrouping Solar Navy warliners, the half-breed girl sent another message.

"Did you hear Rusa'h's thoughts?" She did not wait for them to answer. "He is taking all of the faeros to Ildira."

He thought he was prepared for this moment, but Peter still came to a faltering stop when the gold-inlaid doors swung inward. At the end of the long banquet table sat Rory, looking directly at him.

Estarra's grip tightened on Peter's arm, but he didn't take his eyes from the young man's face. He searched for a flicker of recognition, but Rory (or whoever he was) let nothing noticeable slip. Peter searched his old memories, trying to clarify the images of his little brother, then fast-forwarding to the present.

Yes, it was possible. It could be him. . . .

After an awkward moment, Rory stood. "Greetings, Peter and Estarra. I am glad you could join me in my Whisper Palace." *Was that a deliberate taunt?*

Estarra responded curtly, "Our titles are *King* Peter and *Queen* Estarra."

Before the boy could concede anything, Basil Wenceslas entered through a side door, dapper in one of his usual business suits. His expression was cold, though he managed to summon a small smile for the imagers. "Let us not begin this meeting with petty semantics. It wouldn't set the right tone."

Actually, Peter did not think the formal recognition of their titles was petty, and neither did the Chairman, but he decided not to press the issue. Peter said, "We would not want to diminish anyone's enjoyment of this gathering.

Thank you for inviting us to dinner, Rory." He intentionally left out the word "king."

Beside him, the Teacher compy gave a slight nod. OX himself had taught Peter that etiquette should be guided by local practices — and King Rory himself had established that titles were unnecessary tonight. By the narrowing of Basil's eyes, Peter could tell he had struck a nerve.

The Confederation entourage filled the banquet hall, and they mingled with their Hansa counterparts. Sarein was sitting at the far end of the table, surrounded by (shielded by?) several ministers and minor functionaries. Estarra greeted her sister with great pleasure, but Sarein remained stiff and guarded, as if she had been allowed a strict quota of words during the event. "Welcome to the Whisper Palace, Estarra."

Peter guessed that Basil had placed her in a straitjacket of rules and consequences as a condition of her attendance here. Estarra looked at her sister, clearly wanting to spend time talking with her, but that was not going to happen. Deputy Cain sat at the other side of the table, but he did not speak a word.

Leading Estarra, Peter walked directly to the head of the broad table, where Rory was seated. "Come, there is no need to be so isolated, Rory. If we move two of these chairs, there is plenty of room for the three of us to sit together, as equals." He flashed Basil an icy smile. "In the spirit of cooperation and mutual respect."

Peter's protocol ministers quickly moved to rearrange the seats, while Sarein looked away, as if to hide an embarrassed smile. Estarra and Peter sat on either side of Rory, who had to be operating under a very strict set of guidelines, just like Sarein.

As the elaborate meal was served, one appetizer after another, colorful salads, cold and refreshing palate cleansers, a variety of meats, OX remained close to Peter. The Teacher compy carefully analyzed each course, screening it for poisons, hallucinogens, or any other dangerous chemical additives. As a matter of protocol, the servants dished the food from large communal plates, so that if one item were tainted, King Rory would receive a dose as well. Nevertheless, Peter wouldn't have put it past the Chairman to give his patsy an antidote before the banquet or have him build up a tolerance to something deadly. On the other hand, though, Basil wouldn't expect Peter to be fooled easily.

Peter still wondered why the Chairman had summoned them here. Was it just so that he'd have a chance to see Rory up close? The young man certainly did look like his brother. Every chance he got, Peter glanced at the other King, studied his mannerisms, his appearance. He couldn't be certain. . . .

During the meal, Rory kept up a patter of shallow conversation, sidestepping any issues of substance and offering no hints about his past. He did not say a thing to try to convince Peter . . . which, in its own way, was all the more convincing. If this were a trick, Basil would have primed the imposter with a wealth of compelling little details. Peter dropped a few carefully veiled hints relating to his old family life, hoping that Rory—if he was the real Rory—would pick up on them. But the young King did not respond either way.

Sarein did speak up to ask about baby Reynald, and Estarra was pleased to tell her sister about the little boy.

"I hope I can see him someday," Sarein said, then stopped talking, as if sure she had said too much.

Peter turned coolly to the Chairman. "So, Basil, is it true

that you have relocated your main office from the Hansa HQ to an underground bunker somewhere? Are you really hiding under a rock during Earth's greatest crisis?"

Basil's expression tightened. "You are reading too much into the matter. I found it prudent to activate a more secure secondary command center. In the meantime, King Rory stays here in the Whisper Palace and is available for public appearances anytime he is needed."

"So you consider the Whisper Palace to be perfectly safe, then?" Peter started to make a gesture with one hand to indicate the palace around them, but his sleeve brushed over a piece of the ornate silverware and knocked it off the table. Peter tried to catch it, but it fell to the floor, and the blunder diminished the seriousness of his question. OX bent to retrieve the offending implement.

Basil smiled at the clatter. "Are you nervous, Peter?"

"Just clumsy." He made sure the imagers captured his self-deprecating smile; then he surprised the Chairman with a serious question. "I'd like to take this opportunity to officially request the release of Patrick Fitzpatrick and his wife. They are Confederation citizens."

Basil looked as if he had swallowed something sticky and unpleasant. "They are accused of sedition, a very serious crime, especially during such an extreme emergency. The Hansa is not inclined to be lenient."

"Yes, we saw how you dealt with former Chairman Maureen Fitzpatrick," Estarra said.

Basil called for the music to begin.

When the main meal was over and coffees and sweet liqueurs were served, Peter sipped his coffee—ironically flavored with cardamom, Basil's signature drink. The Chairman himself had accepted only ice water with a slice of lemon to drink.

At the opposite end of the table, Deputy Cain read a statement of gratitude for all the volunteer ships that had come to the aid of Earth. Cain so rarely spoke in public that Peter couldn't understand why he, and not King Rory, had been chosen for such a duty. Then he saw that Basil wanted the audience to be distracted so that he could speak quietly with Peter. "And what exactly is your game? Bringing all your Confederation ships here—what are you really after, Peter? I'm keeping all EDF vessels on high alert in case you try something."

Estarra made a disbelieving sound. "We came here to *help*, whether you choose to believe it or not."

"Earth has suffered incalculable disaster, Basil," Peter said. "Or hadn't you noticed?"

"What I've noticed is a full-fledged military fleet on my doorstep and a former King who has made it plain that he wants to remove me. It's time for this nonsense to stop, for the good of the human race."

"Nonsense?" Estarra asked in a low voice. "We have only offered assistance, while you have raided Roamer sky-mines, shipyards, and fuel depots. Are you trying to provoke us to war?"

He glared at the Queen like a teacher warning a difficult child. He glanced over to make sure that none of the imagers were close enough to pick up his words, then looked coldly at Peter. "Enough of your delusions of grandeur. Surrender your crown and dissolve your silly Confederation. The Hansa has guided humanity for three centuries. Now that we face the Klikiss and the faeros, and who knows what else, we must not be divided. I am the one most fit to guide us through this."

"By what measure?" Peter was surprised the man could even say such a thing.

The Chairman's expression darkened, predictably, when the conversation did not go his way. "Let me be perfectly clear. I have been a respected leader since well before you were born. It will be best for all concerned if you simply do as I say. If you force me to use my leverage, I will not hesitate—"

Peter let out a bitter chuckle. "Leverage? Like your inept ploy with this young man? It's a gesture of total desperation, and you know it." He shook his head sadly and looked at the boy King. "I know who the Chairman wants me to think you are, Rory—or whatever your name is. You do bear a close resemblance to my little brother, but tonight you've said nothing to convince me that you're really him."

"I've made no claims of that whatsoever." Rory lowered his gaze and looked away. "I'm not allowed to."

The comment told Peter a great deal. Again, he studied the young man's profile, his eyes, the shape of his nose, wondering if the features had been changed or enhanced . . . or if they were natural.

Basil's eyes looked like twin thunderstorms, and Peter could see he was ready to explode. Down the table, Sarein was watching the exchange, and though she couldn't hear their words, she looked extremely alarmed.

Abruptly, Peter stood and turned to Estarra, taking the protocol attendees by surprise. He was finished playing Basil's game. He raised his voice. "Mr. Chairman, thank you for coming up into the light of day to allow us this fine meal. Rory, please allow me to reciprocate and invite you to my

Confederation flagship so that I can demonstrate our good-will and hospitality—shall we say in two days? Of course, you are most welcome to bring the Chairman with you." He lowered his voice and quietly growled to Basil, "I'll have an answer for you then about reuniting the human race."

At a slight nod from the agitated Chairman, King Rory brightly accepted the invitation as all the imagers captured the moment.

Basil seemed to be trying to figure out how to have the last word even as Peter and the rest of his retinue took leave of the Whisper Palace and followed their escorts back toward the spaceport. Estarra cast one last glance back at Sarein, who seemed unsuccessfully to be trying to communicate something.

Peter transmitted to Admiral Willis that they had been released unharmed and would be returning to the *Jupiter* shortly. He wasn't certain exactly what the Chairman had meant to accomplish with this meeting, but Peter had achieved his own aims. "We're done here, Admiral. It was quite a successful evening."

Willis acknowledged. Estarra was disturbed and preoccupied as they boarded the diplomatic shuttle that would take them back up to the Confederation ships patrolling beyond the lunar orbit.

In his former life, as the streetwise kid named Raymond, Peter had learned how to pick pockets. Though he was now King, he had never forgotten important skills. Now, as the shuttle lifted off and flew away from the Palace District, Peter carefully held on to the piece of silverware he had discreetly slipped up his sleeve. While OX had made a show of picking up a dropped spoon, Peter had palmed the fork from Rory's plate. A fork with his DNA.

123 ✹ SAREIN

Sarein withdrew to her quarters after being released from her rigidly defined duties at the banquet—"Keep talking to a minimum," Basil had said. "You're there to remind Estarra that you are *with me*. That's all."

He had returned to his private shelter deep underground, leaving her up here. Basil hadn't spoken a word to her after the banquet, though she supposed he was still watching her every move.

As she lay back on a settee in her quarters, trying to remember every word her sister had spoken during dinner, an evacuation alarm shattered her concentration. The obnoxious racket demanded her full attention. Because of the imminent threat of meteor bombardment, everyone knew how to find the closest evacuation shelters. The thick-walled rooms would supposedly provide protection in the event of a complete building collapse, although if a large enough fragment of the Moon smashed into the Palace District, everything would be vaporized for kilometers around.

In response to the alarm, Sarein ran from her rooms, taking nothing with her. All of her favorite possessions had been removed anyway when Basil had ordered the remodeling of her quarters. She hurried down the hall, dropped down a level, and raced into the nearest VIP shelter. With the evacuation alert still sounding, she ducked into the small room—and saw that someone had arrived ahead of her: Deputy Eldred Cain.

He sealed the door and turned to her with a cold smile. "This will give us a few moments to talk in private. I wish I didn't need to cause such disruption, but I couldn't think of any other way. We don't have much time."

The bomb shelter wasted no space on comforts or decoration. The steel-reinforced walls were made of thick beige-painted blocks. A metal cabinet held food supplies and water; in the corner a polymer curtain surrounded a small chemical toilet, adjacent to which was a water recycler and sanitizer sink. The phosphorescent tiles in the ceiling would illuminate the chamber indefinitely.

Although Cain had secured the chamber, Sarein could still hear the throbbing alarm out in the corridors. The deputy kept his voice low. "It is more urgent than ever that we remove the Chairman. You know this, Sarein."

"Of course I know it! But the first assassination attempt failed, and look what happened to McCammon—and eighteen innocent scapegoats."

Deputy Cain withdrew a ceremonial dagger from his inner jacket pocket. Its ornate sheath was inscribed with the initials *RRM:* the ceremonial knife that McCammon had always worn as part of his royal guard uniform. "I recovered this from the Captain's body before his possessions were disposed of. I cleaned off the bloodstains." When he looked at her, the expression on Cain's face and the way he held the knife in his hand frightened her. "I intended to give it to his family. I thought they'd want it as a token of his years of honorable service. But I found no one. Apparently, our Captain McCammon was alone in the world. He had no family to miss him."

"We'll miss him," Sarein said, her voice catching in her throat. "We know what really happened."

Cain tapped the pointed end of the sheathed dagger against his palm. "Ironically, the Captain's death, coupled with the faeros attack on the Moon, may have bought us a little time. The Chairman no doubt believes that we have been frightened back into our places. He's moved on to the next problem, and I'm sure he thinks we'll behave ourselves."

"He showed me surveillance images! He's got proof against me."

Cain shrugged. "And he quite probably has proof against me, as well. The question is, will we act before he does?"

Remembering Basil's cold touch, Sarein shuddered and wondered if he would come to see her again. She could not let that happen. "We have to."

He smiled. "Agreed. And we have no choice but to act precipitously. You may have noticed that an opportunity arose at the banquet. Peter extended an invitation that the Chairman cannot afford to decline. I doubt he'll take King Rory with him, since that would put him at a tactical disadvantage, but he will go to the Confederation flagship. Behind closed doors, he will hammer Peter with his ultimatum and back it up with significant threats."

She lowered her voice, not convinced—even during a disaster alarm—that Basil wasn't eavesdropping. "What kind of threats?"

"Now that King Peter has seen Rory in person, the Chairman is ready for the coup de grâce. He'll threaten to kill Rory . . . and I'm quite certain he means it. Under the circumstances, the Chairman is absolutely convinced Peter will back down, rather than let any harm come to his brother."

"*Is* Rory his brother?"

"I have no idea. And neither does Peter."

"Basil thought the Mage-Imperator would bow to his demands, too," Sarein pointed out.

"We won't give Peter the opportunity, either way. There's too much at stake. While the Chairman is gone, Freedom's Sword is perfectly positioned and ready to move." Cain slowly drew the knife out of its sheath and looked down at the sharp silver blade. His meaning was clear.

"While the cat's away?" she said.

"It has to be quick, and a surprise. As soon as he leaves, we make our move. I need your help."

The very thought sent a chill down her spine, but not as cold as the thought of how much harm Basil could do — to her, and to the human race. "You still intend to kill him?"

Outside the room, the alarms fell abruptly silent.

"Better than that. We'll deprive him of his power." The blade made a whispery metallic sound as he pushed it back into the sheath. He returned it to his jacket pocket, then spoke in an implacable voice. "While he is gone, you'll slip away from Earth. Fly to orbit, lie in wait, and as soon as the Chairman leaves the flagship, request asylum among the Confederation ships. Queen Estarra will welcome you. Tell King Peter that there's a revolution just waiting to happen on Earth, and it's time for him to take the Hansa back. But he needs to move quickly before the Chairman can recover from the surprise I'm preparing. We're at the Rubicon, and we're going to cross it."

"Peter and Estarra won't abandon us." The plan made her heart leap. At last, a real chance to leave here. "And how will I get up to the Confederation ships?"

"Ask Captain Kett." He smiled at her shocked expression. "Yes, she and Captain Roberts returned here several days after the destruction of the Moon. They seem to think the Chairman has forgotten about the arrest order for both of them. Fortunately, I deleted all records before their ship could be noticed by any scouts. I'm sure she would be happy to hear from you."

Sarein could not conceal her surprise. She felt giddy at the thought of slipping away from Earth, possibly even returning to Theroc. "I know how to contact her."

Cain nodded. "Make sure King Peter knows that the whole population has turned against the Chairman, but they need an alternative in place. If he returns to the Whisper Palace, the people will be on his side."

She got up from the hard bench, listening to the movement of people out in the corridors again. "And while I'm on my way up to take sanctuary among the Confederation, what will you be doing? Can't you come with me?"

His expression was unreadable. "No, my place is here, giving Freedom's Sword the last key weapons they need. By the time he gets back to Earth, the Chairman won't have a government left."

Now that the faeros were in retreat, the Solar Navy ships were anxious to rush off to Ildira and finish the job. Adar Zan'nh issued orders for all remaining warliners to draw together and prepare for departure.

The intact Roamer vessels were also ready to join the campaign, despite having run out of frozen wental munitions. In one of the open, bustling hangar bays on the skymine, Tasia joined the others, studying the enthusiasm on their faces. Kotto Okiah flinched at every loud noise of loading spacecraft, departing ships, and hissing exhaust vents.

"We must pursue them," Mage-Imperator Jora'h insisted. "Ildira is unguarded. Once they arrive, Rusa'h and his faeros will sterilize the whole planet just because he failed here. He will stop at nothing to hurt me."

"Perhaps he is not as much in control of the faeros as we believe," Osira'h said.

Jess said, "My water bearers have returned to Theroc and are ready to throw themselves into the battle. I will call them to follow us to Ildira."

Tasia was glad to see just how pissed off everyone was toward the faeros. It reminded her of how she felt about the Klikiss since the ordeal on Llaro. The Klikiss . . . still unresolved. While she was pleased at the ten faeros she had helped to snuff with her icy artillery shells, Tasia thought the plan ill considered. "Now, don't go off half-cocked. Shizz, I can't believe *I* have to be the voice of restraint. Poor planning is poor tactics. Are you really as prepared as you can be? Sure, you can *go* to Ildira, but you won't win the fight. Take a breath, and do this right."

Kotto was also agitated. "Before we can even think about facing the faeros again, we need to reload the ships with thousands of frozen projectiles." He frowned at Adar Zan'nh. "Your warliners can't hold up against the heat of the faeros, and we know that Ildirans have a habit of crashing their ships into things. So you need better armor."

"Our armor is the best ever developed," Zan'nh said flatly. "There is nothing better."

"Then we'll have to come up with something better—maybe something a bit unorthodox."

The Solar Navy commander's expression relaxed slightly. "Yes, you human engineers are good at that."

"Ideas, Kotto?" Cesca said.

He scratched his head. "You did ask me to think of ways to use the wentals. What if we had them form a misty shield, like a cocoon, around the hulls of our ships?"

"Both the shield and the frozen projectiles would require a lot more wental water than we have available here," Cesca said.

Tasia was optimistic about Kotto's suggestion. It was a step in the right direction. "Then let's get that wental water *before* charging off to Ildira. If you want to defeat the faeros, we'll have to put up our best fight."

"We can get all the wental water we need." Jess nodded to his sister. "Tasia, you can lead the Roamer charge into battle. And, Kotto—"

The engineer surprised them by shaking his head. "I'm not going along. I already demonstrated that my weapons work, and that's good enough for me. Mission accomplished. Now I have another project to finish—something just as important, and one that we've all been ignoring. You think we've got only one enemy at a time?"

Cesca stiffened. "But we have to defeat the faeros."

"True, but you don't need me with you to do that. My Klikiss Siren has been ready to test for days, but there were so many distractions . . . If the Siren turns out to be effective, we could get rid of the *whole* Klikiss threat."

That was all Tasia had to hear. "In that case, you need my help, Kotto. I've got more than my share of experience with those damned bugs, and a score to settle with them for killing the colonists on Llaro! If you've got a weapon, I'll find you some Klikiss to try it out on."

Cesca and Jess looked at her with real consternation, but Tasia faced them. "I *should* be going with you to fight the faeros. Shizz, maybe I should even be back with Robb and Admiral Willis helping to round up lunar fragments. But my Guiding Star tells me this is what I *need* to do. Trust me, Jess."

He regarded his sister and let out a long sigh. "You've always made up your own mind, Tasia. You ran off to join the Eddies without asking any of us. I can't stop you now."

125 ☀ CELLI

With great joy Celli looked up between the parted branches of the worldtrees to watch the water bearers return. Their reservoirs were full of restored wental seedpools they had retrieved in their widespread searches, and all of the watery entities had been infused with the anger and fighting spirit promulgated by Jess Tamblyn and Cesca Peroni.

She and Solimar touched the same tree, listening to the verdani sing out their welcome. The canopy rustled as fronds moved aside, granting the Roamer ships room to approach.

Bursting with energy and anxious to be freed, the wentals convinced the newly arrived pilots to open their cargo bay doors while they were still in the sky, letting the energized water spill out. As streams of silvery liquid poured into the open air, the suspended water gathered itself into reflective globules like engorged raindrops that drifted among the towering trees.

Previously, Celli had seen the wentals fuse with damaged worldtrees, a symbiosis that converted them into enormous verdani battleships. But what the wentals were doing now was new to her. Since the gigantic thorny treeships had proved too vulnerable to the faeros, this time, the wentals and verdani would try a different tactic, a way to engulf and contain the fiery elementals, and then trap them back inside their suns.

Celli and Solimar joined other green priests, all of them intuitively understanding what they were supposed to do.

Climbing the towering trees, they harvested small treelings that grew in crevices in the gold-scaled bark. They detached the shoots and carried them gently down.

In normal times, emissary priests had planted new groves on distant planets, spreading the sentient trees across the Spiral Arm. These treelings, though, had a far different purpose.

Through telink, the green priests also knew the news from Nira about the recent faeros battle at Golgen. Jess and Cesca, Adar Zan'nh, the wentals, and the Roamers were all preparing to take the fight to Ildira. And the worldforest would join them. All of the allies had to act now, before the faeros began their vengeful destruction.

With her gaze turned to the sky again, Celli watched the numerous wental spheres drift down like a rainstorm of huge drops. She and Solimar stepped forward, carrying their newly harvested treelings. Because the verdani were interconnected, each delicate plant was as significant a part of the worldforest as any larger tree. All of them were one.

A wental sphere as broad as her outstretched arms hovered in front of Celli. When she pressed one of her spindly treelings against the curved soap-bubble edge, the water folded itself inward. She positioned the treeling at the center of the globe of water, where it floated free. An aurora of light shimmered from the core, and the water rippled with liquid power, as the verdani tree and the wental combined into a stronger force. An invincible force, Celli hoped.

Completed, the water sphere lifted into the air to hover above the treetops. Solimar also inserted a treeling into a waiting wental ball, and the second englobed tree rose to join the first. More green priests came forward to do the same, each one creating a new combined elemental weapon.

After dumping his liquid cargo in the air, Nikko Chan Tylar landed his *Aquarius* alongside the ships of ten other water bearers. He emerged, followed by his father, Crim, and another old man, whom some of the clan representatives recognized. "Caleb Tamblyn!"

"Yes, I'm joining this damned fight after what those fiery monsters did to me, and they murdered Denn."

Mother Alexa and Father Idriss came out to meet them, carrying baby Reynald, whom they were tending while Peter and Estarra were at Earth. "We can always use more fighters."

"Then I'm ready to join the fight." Caleb crossed his bony arms over his chest. "I'll make a difference, just you wait and see."

Celli's father reached out to shake Caleb's hand. "Happy to have you with us. And what is it you can do, exactly?"

The old man looked flustered.

The green priests continued to create weapons with treelings and water spheres. Fronds floated inside their wental bubbles, both drawing and providing energy. Many silvery balls lifted above the canopy, reflecting the sunlight like a cluster of polished pearls. Nikko stared upward, his almond eyes sparkling. "That's really beautiful."

"Let's hope the faeros don't think they're so pretty," his father growled.

When they were ready, the wental-verdani spheres shot off toward Ildira.

"Is that all there is to it?" Caleb Tamblyn asked, looking around uncertainly. "I expected something to *happen*."

"Oh, there's more to come," Celli said.

"Much more," Solimar added. "But it's going to take place at Ildira."

Caleb clapped Crim on the shoulder. "Then what are we waiting for?"

Nikko was already sprinting toward his ship, and the other water bearers did the same.

126 ✺ SAREIN

She and Cain formulated their plans, timing everything carefully. They waited for a blustering Basil to fly off to his closed-door meeting on the Confederation flagship; once he had left Earth for the full diplomatic process, they would have less than two days to hamstring the Hansa government.

Before he departed, though, Basil came to her quarters again, looking tense and harried. Fortunately, he did not have sex on his mind; he needed something else. "Soon we'll celebrate, Sarein. Everything will be back in order. Once I manage to make Peter recognize his untenable position, the Hansa will run smoothly again." The Chairman made no secret of the ultimatum he had issued; he was quite smug about Peter's long-lost brother Rory as his trump card. He expected Peter to quickly bow to his wishes.

Basil stood so close that it felt awkwardly intimate. The warmth of his breath sent a chill down her spine. "I wanted to reassure you." He touched her shoulder. "When I come back from this trip, I'm going to need your help much more often." He traced his fingertip along her chin, up to her high cheekbone. "I've been cold to you, I know. Distracted. But I need you by me."

Sarein's mind was a whirlwind of clashing thoughts. Did he really remember some hint of emotion toward her? Or was this just another kind of manipulation? She couldn't forget the damning set of surveillance images he had hidden under her pillow, a clear warning that he knew she had done things for which he could easily execute her. She blinked as a strange thought crossed her mind. What if Basil had meant the gesture not as a threat, but as a *favor*, to prove that he knew of her indiscretions and yet was willing to forgive her?

Basil smiled as if an idea had just occurred to him, but Sarein was sure he had planned it carefully. "While I am gone, I want you to move your possessions into my private quarters underground. Stay there with me, safe in the bunker. We'll be together every day."

Though alarmed by the idea, she found herself nodding with feigned enthusiasm . . . nothing to provoke him, nothing to raise his suspicions. She wanted nothing more than to leave immediately. "I can't wait" was all she said.

"Good. I'll look forward to seeing you when I return." He seemed convinced by her performance.

"Goodbye, Basil."

He went to the door, hesitated briefly. For one horrified instant, Sarein thought he was going to come back to kiss her . . . but then he hurried off, leaving her frozen in place.

Yes, it was time to move. No regrets.

127 ☀ DEPUTY CHAIRMAN ELDRED CAIN

As soon as the Chairman's ship left the Palace District spaceport, Deputy Cain got to work. He had a great deal to accomplish in a short time.

Cain would have preferred to have Sarein at his side, along with Captain McCammon and a mob of shouting protesters all claiming to belong to Freedom's Sword. But in a sense, solo action was more liberating, now that the Chairman was gone. Cain was free to act without coordinating with others and without the fear of risking anyone else's life. The responsibility was his and his alone. He found it more efficient.

Admiral Diente was already dead, having tried his best to meet the Chairman's unreasonable expectations. Cain saw no reason why the Admiral's family should remain under house arrest—except for the fact that the Hansa wouldn't want them out in public where they could talk. Still held in their special detention apartments, they hadn't even been informed of his death; Basil claimed that it kept the family more tractable. Once Diente's wife and children discovered the truth, though, Cain was certain they would have plenty to say.

At the apartment complex, he easily bluffed his way past the guards. "Their detention order is rescinded." He showed them an official-looking Hansa document. In all the turmoil on Earth, no one had bothered with the hostage family in some time. The guards shrugged.

Inside, when Cain opened the doorway of the secure apartment and looked at the shocked and haunted faces of the wife, the daughters, the son, he realized he wasn't the best person to pass along the heartbreaking news; he had never been particularly good at warmth and compassion. He saw the four of them staring at him.

"Are you here to let us out?" the wife asked. He chided himself for not having bothered to familiarize himself with her name. "Do you have news?"

He stated what he needed to say. "I regret to inform you that Admiral Esteban Diente has been killed on a mission to the Klikiss. It . . . happened some weeks ago, but the Chairman has kept the information from you."

The wife began sobbing, as if she had been expecting the announcement as soon as Cain arrived. The teenaged girl and the twelve-year-old boy gasped and shouted in disbelief; the younger daughter didn't understand what was going on.

Cain faltered, then continued. "All along, you were being held here under false pretenses. Chairman Wenceslas kept you hostage so that Admiral Diente could not refuse his orders. He used you to guarantee your husband's loyalty to the Hansa."

"No, no, no," the wife cried.

"The Chairman does not know I am doing this," he said. "I am here to release you."

"Release us?" the boy blurted. "Where are we supposed to go?"

The older daughter simply blinked. She seemed to be the only one truly paying attention. "We were *hostages*?"

He tried to usher them toward the door he had just unlocked. "I've made arrangements, but you must leave before Chairman Wenceslas returns. Things will go badly once he discovers you are no longer in custody. I'm sending you to a group called Freedom's Sword. They're gaining followers everywhere. You can stay with them, at least until it's safe. They're expecting you. Tell them your story, and they will let everyone on Earth know exactly what the Chairman did to you, and to your husband."

"No, no, no," the wife said. Cain doubted she knew what she was saying.

Now he wished he had brought Sarein with him; surely she would have been better at this. "Come with me."

By now, the Chairman had been gone less than an hour.

In the same building, he found the families of Admirals Pike and San Luis, also taken hostage as threats to hang over the two military commanders. Releasing the families, he gave them instructions on how to get in touch with the two officers.

"The Admirals are in the EDF crews helping to protect Earth from lunar fragments. Tell them you are free and safe. Only when they know you are no longer in jeopardy can each man follow his conscience, instead of obeying illegal orders in order to protect you." Cain decided it was best not to tell Pike's wife that her husband had been ordered to assassinate the former Chairman.

Disbelief showed on their faces, but the adult son of Admiral San Luis nodded grimly. "You know it's true, Mother. They lied to us all along."

With a growing sense of urgency, Cain led them all to the streets. "Chairman Wenceslas used each of you as an expendable bargaining chip. Tell the world that he is not fit to lead us. Now go. You—all of you—are weapons that Freedom's Sword can use to unravel the Chairman's web."

Cain's pulse raced with the awareness of what he had just done. However, to truly achieve critical mass, he needed a catalyst, a focal point. Fortunately, he knew exactly where to get that. It was in another holding cell.

During the past several days, Chairman Wenceslas had been too busy to plan an extravagant execution for Patrick Fitzpatrick and Zhett Kellum. The timing couldn't be better.

Cain slipped through the streets, hearing the loud shouts and buzzing sounds of twitchers as the increasingly overwhelmed cleanup crew tried to suppress the demonstrations. Good. Once Freedom's Sword began spreading the news from the released hostage families, there could be no stopping the tide.

If King Peter was willing to work with them. If Sarein could convince him.

Some protesters were camped out near the nondescript government building where Patrick and Zhett were being held. Though the Hansa guards refused to reveal the location of any particular prisoner, despite demands from the ever more vociferous dissidents, demonstrators staked out every possible holding center, hoping to catch a glimpse of their two heroes. Given enough dissenters, someone had been bound to get it right.

Sure that someone in the crowd would recognize him as the Deputy Chairman, Cain entered a building across the street, descended two floors underground, and took a dimly lit access tunnel across to the holding structure.

The tiled floor was white, the smooth walls painted cream, the ceilings an unbroken flow of phosphorescence.

No shadows were allowed. The cleanup crew had filled all the available maximum-security detention centers weeks ago, and these holding cells had been designed for the temporary detention of disorderly people, drunks, or rowdies, not evil masterminds.

When Cain approached the two uniformed men at a reception desk, they came immediately to attention. "I am here with orders to escort the two new prisoners, Patrick Fitzpatrick and Zhett Kellum, to an undisclosed location. The Chairman wants me to attend to this matter personally and without delay."

Trying to look official, the guards consulted their display screens. One of the men deferred to his larger companion, who nodded. "Right this way, sir."

Patrick and Zhett were in adjacent cells. As Cain arrived, both of them jumped to their feet. Gazing dispassionately at them through the transparent barriers, he snapped to the accompanying guard, "What are you waiting for? Open it."

"Shouldn't I bring in an armed escort, sir? These are dangerous criminals."

"These two are my problem. I have already arranged for everything I need. Release them into my custody."

Fitzpatrick looked defiantly at the deputy. "I was wondering if you'd come. Can't the Chairman do his own dirty work? Are you going to execute us out in the main square? Or are you going to take us to a dark room, put a bullet in our brains, then quietly dispose of the bodies?"

"Neither. Now, if you will come with me?"

When the two emerged from their separate cells, they hugged each other and stood close together. "Where are we going?" Zhett asked.

For the guard's benefit, Cain said, "An agreement has

been reached behind closed doors. Some people in the government still feel they owe something to your grandmother." That seemed to pacify Patrick. "I will explain it all as we go. Now, follow me, please."

Patrick and Zhett glanced at each other, back at the empty cells, then hurried along. The disconcerted guard remained behind to seal the doors.

As soon as they were out of earshot, Cain whispered, "I'm releasing you. The Chairman is away, and we don't have much time." He explained what was happening; he asked the two of them to focus the demonstrations, build the uproar, and pave the way for King Peter's return. He led them to a side door that exited to an alley. "Duck into the crowds and make yourselves invisible." When the two hesitated, he planted his hand between Patrick's shoulderblades and gave him a shove. "Go!"

They ran.

Once they were gone, Cain felt a heavy weight lifted from him, which was quickly replaced by a gnawing worry in his stomach. Now it was out of his hands. The rest was up to them, and to Sarein.

With forced casualness, he sauntered toward the reception desk on his way out the main door, only to find a livid Colonel Andez arguing with the cowed-looking guards. Cain hesitated for just a moment, then walked forward. He hadn't expected to be discovered quite so soon.

The uniformed men were greatly relieved to see him. When Andez turned, her face showed angry displeasure. "What do you think you're doing, Deputy Cain?"

He regarded the woman with an unsettling glare. "And who are you to make demands of the Hansa's deputy chairman?"

She squirmed for just a moment, then lashed out. "These men told me that you've removed Fitzpatrick and his Roamer whore from their cells. I want to see your authorization. Show me your orders from the Chairman."

"My orders are not for you to approve."

"But those two committed treason. Everyone heard it. Their guilt is without question."

"No one can fault you for your zeal, Ms. Andez—"

"*Colonel* Andez!"

"However, you forget your place. I am hereby putting you on notice."

"Putting *me* on notice?" She stiffened, then faltered. "I am only protecting the Hansa."

"You would do well to remember that other people bear that responsibility as well." Cain left, while Andez continued to glower at him. He had no doubt that she would report the matter to Chairman Wenceslas as soon as he returned.

By then, though, it would be too late.

s usual, Basil acted as if he owned the Spiral Arm. Peter watched the Chairman's shuttle approach the *Jupiter* without a military escort, without bluster or threats. Ever since leaving the tense banquet in the Whisper Palace, he had been waiting for the other shoe to drop. *Here it comes.*

En route to the flagship, Basil had altered the plans, not surprisingly, to demonstrate that he was in control of the details. Instead of a showy banquet with media imagers, protocol escorts, and a large audience, he wanted a private audience with Peter. And he had declined to bring Rory with him.

No matter. Basil wasn't going to like what Peter showed him, no matter how it was served up.

Admiral Willis shook her head. "Arriving in a little shuttle like that? He must be damned sure you won't shoot at him, sire."

"And we won't. He knows that."

Estarra had joined the King to watch the diplomatic craft make its way from General Brindle's Juggernaut over to theirs. The Chairman intended to dock aboard the *Jupiter* in half an hour—significantly earlier than their agreed-upon time—and expected to be received without delay.

"Basil can rattle his saber all he wants, but it's just empty noise. He doesn't know that his bargaining chip has no value." Peter took Estarra's arm in his. "Admiral, we won't be needing our scheduled banquet after all. Can you provide a secure conference room? Nothing fancy—in fact, make it pointedly *not* fancy."

"We've got plenty of empty rooms. There's even the brig if you like." Two of the bridge officers let out snickers, which they quickly covered.

"I'd prefer something closer to the shuttle deck. Let's not keep the Chairman here any longer than is absolutely necessary, regardless of what he's got to say."

Willis selected a small mess hall just down the corridor from the bay where the shuttle would be landing. Accompanied by OX, Peter and Estarra went to the room, where crewmen were rapidly cleaning and straightening up as best they could.

"Please escort the Chairman here as soon as he disembarks," Peter said. "I have no idea what sort of staff he'll bring along, but I want at least one guard for each of his. At a minimum, two Confederation soldiers to be stationed outside this door."

A few minutes later, an impatient-looking Basil Wenceslas was shown into the mess hall. He hadn't bothered to bring a single guard or adviser.

Arrogant indeed, Peter thought.

Or he wanted the discussions to be completely private.

Though Basil maintained a businesslike demeanor, Peter knew the man well enough to detect subtle changes in his mannerisms. The Chairman seemed a bit ragged around the edges, even stressed. He frowned with disapproval at their surroundings. "A lunchroom? That's how you receive me?"

"Forget the pomp and ceremony, Basil. Let's get down to business." Peter calmly sat in a hard resin chair, facing his old mentor, his current nemesis. "Are you releasing Patrick Fitzpatrick and his wife, as I requested?"

"That would be a good opening gesture," Estarra added. "We would rather have asked King Rory in person, but you seem to have left him back on Earth."

Ignoring Estarra, Basil gave Peter a withering look. "Did you really think I would bring the King here, where your Confederation mercenaries could just seize him? Don't be naïve."

"It's pointless for us to butt heads this way. Speak your piece, Basil."

The Chairman placed an elbow on the mess hall table, after glancing down to make sure the surface was clean. With his other hand he removed a sheaf of printouts from his inner jacket pocket. "I have genetic comparisons here, since I assumed you would demand them. It's proof that Rory is your brother, but I suspect you already know that." He narrowed his gray eyes. "What happens now is up to you. I can arrange an accident for him, even an assassination, and blame it on Freedom's Sword." He seemed to like the idea. "I've got no qualms against killing him if you don't behave."

"Behave? What does that even mean?" Peter couldn't believe the Chairman was still treating him like a frightened child. Basil Wenceslas had regressed a great deal.

"It means you will abdicate. You will stop this ridiculous insurrection that weakens the true government of humanity. You will dissolve the Confederation so that the scattered colonies and Roamer clans come back into the fold of the Hansa, where they belong. And you will agree to it now, before we end this meeting."

Peter let out a sigh. "Is that all?" He tapped the printouts. "You aren't even going to give me a chance to run independent DNA tests with my own specialists?"

The flippant response seemed to anger Basil. "I will not

waste any more of humanity's time. You forced me into this, Peter. King Rory's blood will be on your hands. Your own brother." He folded his arms, as if he had just announced a checkmate.

Peter surprised him by responding with a chuckle. "Oh, Basil — you yourself instructed me in leadership. One boy's life isn't worth everything that's at stake."

"You're no good at bluffing. I know you won't just abandon your brother. Mark my words, Peter — fall into line, or Rory dies."

"My brother Rory died many years ago when *you* killed him." Peter tried to match the steel in his tone with what he heard in Basil's. "I'll admit you did a good job, and I did have my doubts for a while, but now I have proof positive. I tested his DNA from a small sample on a piece of flatware. Your propped-up King is not my brother, no matter how much I may want to believe he is. The genetics don't match. He's an imposter — and a pawn, like I was."

"Don't try to con me. You can't possibly take the risk."

Peter glanced back at the stoic Teacher compy. "I can have OX display the results of our DNA comparisons, if you like. *Real* comparisons." He frowned down at the false printouts Basil had offered. "That boy is no more a relative of mine than you are. You can't use him against me."

The Chairman stood abruptly. There was no one in the room who even pretended to support him. "You are treading on dangerous ground, Peter. You have pushed me for the last time."

"If I had a tank of ekti for every time you've said that," Estarra quipped.

He turned to her with a strange flush on his face. "I wouldn't be so cavalier, if I were you." He showed his teeth in a vicious, lupine smile. "Don't forget, I have your sister Sarein as well."

Basil strode to the mess hall door and pushed his way past the two Confederation guards outside.

129 ☀ SAREIN

Now that Basil was away, Sarein had her best chance to escape and turn the tables on the Hansa.

By freeing Patrick Fitzpatrick and releasing the hostage families, Deputy Cain would fundamentally undermine the Chairman's authority, but that wasn't enough to ensure lasting change. Sarein had to convince the King to return without delay.

Basil would kill her if he guessed what she was doing.

He had said he wanted her close by his side, wanted her to move into the protection of his underground bunker. If she turned on him now, just after he had made what he considered a generous gesture, Basil would see it as the ultimate betrayal.

She had to leave.

Sarein sealed the door to her quarters, not that she expected anyone to be eavesdropping. Nevertheless, she kept her voice low as she sent a signal, using the personal code Rlinda Kett had supplied after their meeting at the coffee shop. She prayed that Cain's information was accurate, that the captain was still on Earth.

The beefy woman answered almost immediately. "Ah, wonderful to hear from you, Sarein. Sorry we haven't had time for a social visit. Things are more messed up than ever around here." Then she smiled as a thought occurred to her. "So, you finally decided to take me up on my offer, right?"

Captain Roberts was beside her on the screen. "I don't like just waiting here to be smashed by a rock falling from the sky. It's a lot better now with the Roamers helping, but still . . . We were planning to head out again this afternoon. Somebody's bound to notice us here sooner or later."

Sarein drew a breath, forced certitude into her voice. "I need you to take me to King Peter's flagship—to discuss business. After all, you're the Confederation's Trade Minister, and I'm the ambassador from Theroc."

Rlinda chuckled. "There's a bit of backbone—good to see it!"

Sarein leaned closer to the screen, her face drawn. "And we have to do this *soon*. No time to lose. Where shall I meet you?"

"When will you be ready to leave?"

"Now."

"That's soon enough, all right." Rlinda provided the grid number where the *Blind Faith* had landed in the Palace District spaceport.

Although she had made her decision, Sarein hesitated before leaving her quarters forever. Yes, she and Cain had plotted to overthrow the Chairman, but considering the alternatives, this was perhaps the only way to save his life. She had spent so many years with Basil. He had carried her with him through the rough waters of interplanetary politics. Now, though, she wanted to go home.

Feeling a tug at her heart—more for the Basil she remembered than for the one she was leaving—she went back to the comm screen and set it to record a message. Her last message. Even though she was afraid of him, her conscience demanded this of her.

Sarein spoke from the heart. "Basil, you won't find me here when you come back to Earth. For years I've turned a blind eye to your bad decisions, but I can't support your policies any longer. Your Hansa is corrupt. It tramples the rights of the citizens it was meant to serve, and I won't be part of it anymore."

She gave a bittersweet smile. "I appreciate what you did for me at one time. Though I'm sure you'll never accept it, I did love you. Maybe I still do in a way, but I can't tolerate what you've become." Tears welled in her eyes. "Whatever happens from now on is the result of your own actions. Goodbye, Basil."

She switched off the recording and set the message transmission on a proximity timer. As soon as Basil returned to the Palace District, the automated system would upload the recording to his personal communication device.

By then, Sarein would be long gone, safely away.

On the *Jupiter*'s command viewscreen, all eyes were on the Chairman's diplomatic shuttle as it departed for the cluster of EDF ships. Admiral Willis paced the bridge with her hands linked behind her. She sniffed with undisguised distaste at the receding craft. "I can't say I minded seeing him leave in a huff. But not so much as a goodbye? I thought he might leave me a gold watch for all my years of faithful service." She turned to the King. "So, what did the blowhard really want?"

Peter pressed his lips together. So far he had told no one else the truth about Rory. Exposing those details would have forced him to reveal his own humble roots, that he too was fundamentally an imposter. "He was just throwing his weight around—unsuccessfully."

As soon as Basil left the mess hall, Peter had felt the rush of adrenaline drain from his system. He had taken a few moments to compose himself before going to the bridge. Beside him, Estarra had expressed her concerns. "You can't let the Chairman execute that poor boy out of spite, even if he isn't your real brother."

Peter wore a grim smile. "Oh, Basil won't kill him now. It wouldn't gain him anything. As an ace up his sleeve, Rory is worthless. The most he can do is continue to serve as a figurehead."

"Are you really willing to take that risk, knowing the Chairman? He could murder him out of spite."

Peter felt a lump in his throat, knowing she might be right. "Rory—or whatever his real name is—may be no more than a patsy, but he's just like I was, probably nabbed from the streets and forced to play a role. Basil turns the thumbscrews, and it's all a matter of how well the kid can act. I understand what he's going through—don't worry, I won't let him get killed for my sake."

"Actually, I'm more worried about Sarein," she said.

"Me too."

Now that they had arrived on the Juggernaut's bridge, he watched Admiral Willis fume quietly at the retreating diplomatic shuttle. After a long moment of tense silence, she mused, "You know, a single jazer blast would solve a lot of our problems."

"I can't say that the thought hasn't occurred to me, Admiral." Peter knew that Basil himself would take the shot—and *had* done it, both with Maureen Fitzpatrick and with the outspoken Archfather. "But if I regain my rule through assassination, then how am I different from Basil? I can't simply kill someone because I don't like them, or because they're bad, or because they're in my way."

But, oh, it would be an easy, temporary solution.

The price he'd pay later for taking that road, though, could bring about his downfall as surely as it had corrupted Basil Wenceslas, transforming him from effective leader into monster. He let out a slow sigh. "As King, I've got to lead by example. I can't just barge in and tell the people of Earth what's good for them. They need to get rid of him themselves."

Estarra said, "You know there's a groundswell of protests. Patrick Fitzpatrick has stirred up a hornet's nest of rebellion down there. What's wrong with taking advantage of that?"

Peter had watched the demonstrations grow more intense in the newsnet coverage, even in the short time since he had come to the Earth system. He realized the people might be ready after all. "You may be right."

Basil's diplomatic shuttle continued to fly away. Admiral Willis made no comment about the King's decision, except to say, "He's out of range anyway."

131 ☀ PATRICK FITZPATRICK III

Once Deputy Cain released them from Hansa detention, the rational, logical, and safe thing would have been for Patrick and Zhett to steal a small spacecraft and fly to the Confederation battle group.

But Patrick was not in a rational, logical, or safe frame of mind.

Cain had told them how they could help bring down the Chairman once and for all, and that possibility was just too worthwhile to pass up. He still had the contacts his grandmother had left for him and a large portion of the funds. Now was the time to throw everything into the effort.

"I still can't convince myself this isn't a trick." Zhett

looked furtively at the streets behind them. "What does the deputy have to gain by doing this?"

"He's a smart man. He can see that the Chairman is herding everyone over a cliff—and he doesn't plan to be one of the lemmings."

In the crowded streets and plazas, Freedom's Sword was holding demonstrations. Observing that the protests had gotten wilder in the days since their arrest, Patrick could not help but view the groundswell with a certain level of satisfaction. "A lot of crap is hitting a lot of fans."

When they walked in among the demonstrators and added their shouts to the rising tide of anger, he was surprised to hear someone call out, "Look—it's Patrick Fitzpatrick! He's free!"

"I heard they were executed."

"They must have escaped."

"He showed us the evidence against the Chairman!"

"The bastard Chairman murdered his grandmother."

Patrick flinched, not sure he was ready to draw so much attention, but too many people had noticed him, so he decided to embrace it. He raised both hands as word rippled through the crowd. Some of the noise died down, though people at the outer fringes had no idea what was happening. "Yes, we're out of prison, and we need to continue our work. All of you are part of the solution."

"How can we help you?" someone yelled.

"We need a safe place," Zhett said. With a devilish grin, she added, "And transmission equipment. It's time to overthrow the Hansa and bring back King Peter. The Chairman's away for the moment—so there's no better time."

Patrick felt giddy with the righteous knowledge of what he could help accomplish and what the old Battleaxe would have done if she had been around. And, yes, he felt a hint of satisfaction at being able to get even for her sake. "I've got a plan."

The crowd swept them along. Even if Hansa guards had come after Patrick and Zhett, these demonstrators would have shielded them. That thought gave him a strange sense of empowerment.

In no time, the group whisked the two of them away to a sheltered place, gave them computers, network access, and imagers. While stewing in his cell, Patrick had mulled over the things he still needed to say. He had mentally rehearsed his speech over and over, polishing his anger and focusing his words.

Now that he finally had another chance, he let loose with a new broadcast, calling them all to arms.

132 ☀ JESS TAMBLYN

After leaving Golgen, Jess and Cesca guided the Solar Navy and the Confederation ships to Charybdis to make their final preparations. Surrounded by a shimmering haze of energy, the pair stood in the command nucleus of the Mage-Imperator's flagship.

What had once been a primordial ocean alive with the water elementals now appeared to be a scarred wreck. But

Jess and Cesca had broken through to underground aquifers that gurgled up into hot, eager pools. Several of his faithful water bearers had returned seedpools of living water here as part of their work, as well. Those seedpools had flowed and multiplied. Right now, thousands of the tree-bubbles were streaming across open space from Theroc, accompanied by the water bearers in their own ships.

The battle on Golgen had left many of the Solar Navy ships battered and scarred, their anodized hull plates scorched, the solar sails in tatters. Nevertheless, the warliners still formed a mighty fleet with all the Confederation ships that had joined the group.

Adar Zan'nh was impatient to face the faeros as the numerous ships descended over the newly awakened oceans, but Jess assured him the process would not take long. "The wentals know what to do."

Zan'nh clenched and unclenched his hands and spoke as if reminding himself. "A rush into battle is often a plan for defeat."

"Give Kotto's new idea a chance," Sullivan Gold said. "It sounds like something Tabitha Huck might have come up with." The Adar looked at him and responded with a faint smile before he nodded.

As the warliners swooped over the cracked landscape covered with large pools of resurrected water, the wentals simmered and rejoiced. The mass of ships cruised low over the glistening pools, and the rejuvenated oceans and lakes bubbled beneath them.

Columns of wental water leaped into the air like cyclones, and fountains of elemental liquid dispersed themselves into a thin spray. The living fog surrounded each warliner and Roamer ship in a cocoon of mist that sparkled in the hazy sunlight. As the combined fleet raced onward without pausing in their flight, each ship gathered a gauzy wreath of protective vapor.

Through their wentals, Jess and Cesca instructed the liquid entities to follow the patterns Kotto had earlier devised, forming themselves into frozen artillery shells. The ships in the combined war fleet drew more of the wental water into their holding chambers, and aboard each vessel, crewmen loaded the icy projectiles into gunports.

Also joining their fighting force, hundreds of pearlescent tree-bubbles arrived from Theroc, like foam droplets on a cosmic tide, each encapsulating a small but vital treeling. Nikko Chan Tylar and the rest of Jess's volunteer water bearers followed along in their ships.

Jess could feel the powerful wentals surging within his body, ready to challenge their opponents. "The faeros incarnate can be destroyed, and the rest of the faeros can be *controlled*. Just like the hydrogues. But it will not be easy."

Cesca took Jess's hand, and he felt the crackle of energy flow between them. She addressed the Mage-Imperator. "We will lead the charge. The faeros incarnate is as much our enemy as he is yours."

They went to the warliner's launching bay, emerged from the airlock, and shot themselves away from the ornate hull, tumbling out into the misty swath that surrounded the warliner. Gathering the droplets around themselves, Jess and Cesca formed a new wental ship for themselves.

Behind them, as the combined fleet left Charybdis and entered open space, all the ships were now veiled in misty shields. Flying their bright sphere in front of the gathered battleships, the new wental bubble shone like a Guiding Star.

In a great sparkling mass, the Solar Navy and the Confederation fleet streaked toward Ildira.

133 ☀ TASIA TAMBLYN

I hate bugs," Tasia said, sealing the hatch of the Roamer cargo hauler in preparation for leaving the main Golgen skymine. "I *really* hate bugs. And you will too, Kotto—as soon as you get to know them."

Kotto Okiah sat eagerly in the copilot's chair. "I hope that doesn't mean you're having second thoughts and would rather be off fighting the faeros. We have to test the Klikiss Siren."

"No second thoughts at all. My loathing for those bugs gives me all the more incentive to squash them. It is up to us, you know."

Jess and Cesca, the Ildiran Solar Navy, and flocks of Roamer volunteers had all rushed off to Ildira. Tasia hoped that Robb, Admiral Willis, and the volunteer Confederation ships were accomplishing what they needed to do at Earth, without the Big Goose getting in their way.

That left the group of them—and Kotto's gadget—to take care of the entire Klikiss race. Fair enough. She was up for it.

But Kotto had insisted that his research compies come

with them in case he needed to modify the device on the fly. With those two going on the expedition, DD had asked to join them. And with DD came Orli Covitz and Hud Steinman. Tasia didn't mind; they had all helped to develop the Siren.

As the hours passed, Kotto spent a great deal of time in the back with the three compies, tinkering with his Siren and running diagnostics. The device was an acoustic transmitter, about a meter across, assembled from dozens of mismatched components, circuit boards cannibalized from other equipment, and dangling power leads. Tasia had no doubt it would work. Kotto's gadgets usually did.

Kotto tapped the curved dish as he explained. "A complex burst from this siren should incapacitate a Klikiss subhive, at least temporarily. If a group of insects is controlled by the thoughts of a single breedex, and we succeed in stunning that breedex by overloading its input, then they should all freeze."

"I like the way you think," Tasia said.

"I don't know exactly how interconnected the various subhives are. We may have to do this quite a few times."

"Trial and error, Kotto. We'll figure it out."

Despite his genius, Kotto hadn't given much thought as to how they should conduct the actual test run. He had assumed they would simply fly down to the Klikiss-infested planet, land in the middle of a bustling hive, and switch on his Siren.

"Too much of a risk, if we don't even know the Siren will work," Tasia said. "Let me think about this—it isn't your job to make military plans anyway."

During the day-long journey, Tasia linked the gadget to the ship's transmitting systems so that they could send out a blast as they flew overhead—using both electromagnetic transmissions and actual acoustic waves from external loud-speakers. They wouldn't have to land and could keep their maneuverability. The bugs were going to hear the blast, one way or another.

The test would provide a real, tangible answer soon enough . . . or Tasia would find herself fighting her way out and running like hell.

At last, the ship arrived at Llaro, a planet that held only bad memories for Tasia. She flew closer, all her senses alert, ready to dodge the Klikiss swarmships she was sure would be there. She couldn't shake her recollection of her last experience at Pym.

To her surprise, though, they found not a single alien vessel in planetary orbit—no sign of them at all.

Orli and Steinman came into the cockpit, both of them obviously uneasy. "Nobody's home?" the old man asked.

"Could it be a trick?" Orli said. "Are they hiding?"

"Why would they go out of their way to hide from us?" Tasia said. "Something else is going on here."

With high-res sensors she could see the extent of the enormous hive below, at least ten times the size of the original human settlement, far more spectacular than the one she had seen on Pym. "Looks like the breedex has been busy."

Despite the size, though, she detected no transmissions, thermal emissions, or any other signs of activity whatsoever.

"It's a ghost town down there," Kotto said. "Did the Klikiss all leave?"

"Where would they go?" Tasia continued to study the empty city. "I don't like this at all."

DD also entered the crowded cockpit. "Have you found any sign of Margaret Colicos? I am sure she would welcome us."

"No sign of anyone or anything, DD." Tasia continued on course, alert for danger. "Oh, what the hell—it's time for a test run. We'll find out if anything's down there. Everybody strap in, just in case I have to do some fancy flying." She flew so swiftly through Llaro's pastel skies that she left a bright ionized trail behind her. "This should flush them out if they've got their bug eyes open. Hello, anybody home?"

The cargo hauler roared over the immense hive city, skimming barely above the twisted towers, the lumpy monoliths, the pockmarked black openings.

Nothing responded. Nothing came out to see them.

She circled around and made a second run. Kotto's fingers were ready on the Siren's transmit button, but no Klikiss showed themselves. None.

Finally, gathering her courage, Tasia landed in a swirl of powdery dust where the human colony had been, where she had fought the bugs and rescued the few remaining settlers. Once the cargo hauler was on the ground, she waited a few more tense moments, alert for any movement. Still nothing.

Finally, she opened the hatch and let the dry air and yellowish sunlight flood in. Llaro was completely silent. Completely empty.

"Shizz, where the hell have they all gone?"

134 ☀ SAREIN

When Sarein was safely aboard the *Blind Faith*, Captain Roberts took off from the Palace District without bothering to request clearance. He flew swiftly away, ignoring outraged protests from the ground control system. With the threat of rubble bombardment and the chaos of so many scout ships trying to protect Earth, nobody had time to track a single unmarked craft anyway.

Sitting in a comfortable passenger seat, Sarein breathed in the aroma of the new ship: the upholstery, the polish on the decks and bulkheads, the air from the freshly tuned atmosphere recyclers. For her, it was the smell of freedom. "We have to time this carefully," she said. "We want to be sure Basil has left the flagship before we announce ourselves and ask for sanctuary."

"We'll keep an eye on it," Captain Roberts said.

Sarein swallowed hard. Now that she was on her way, she feared more for Deputy Cain than for herself. *He* was staying behind. *He* would have to face Basil. "No, Captain Kett, our worries are far from over." She closed her eyes in the comfortable passenger seat, felt the ship vibrate as Roberts accelerated away from Earth. "Just get me to my sister and King Peter. They're the ones I need to talk to."

Pelted by the tiny rocks that continued to drift toward the planet, the *Blind Faith* headed out into orbit. They waited at a safe distance from General Brindle's EDF Juggernaut, watching until Basil's diplomatic shuttle left the *Jupiter* and returned to the other Juggernaut.

When they were safely clear, Captain Roberts flew toward the Confederation ships combing space, tightening the net so that no significant fragments passed through. When they approached, Rlinda tapped a transponder, waited for an acknowledgment. "This is Trade Minister Rlinda Kett. I've got news, and a guest, for King Peter and Queen Estarra."

The flagship Juggernaut's large hull doors swung apart to admit them, and Roberts masterfully guided the ship into an open hangar bay.

Sarein stepped out of the *Blind Faith* feeling stronger than she could remember feeling for a very long time. That was when she realized that she hadn't left home, she was *coming* home.

When she walked onto the bridge, Sarein's eyes were immediately drawn to King Peter . . . and Queen Estarra. *Estarra.*

She and her sister were so different. Sarein had been ambitious, excited by the prospect of power and its trappings. Estarra had always been more motivated by love for her family — both before and after her marriage to Peter — than a desire for influence, authority, or wealth.

It had taken years for Estarra to convince her that Basil was not the man Sarein thought he was; she had tried to get Sarein to escape with them during the hydrogue attack on Earth. *What would have happened,* Sarein wondered, *if I had changed my mind that night and gone back to Theroc? Would Basil have lost his desperate hold on power before he could do more damage?*

How ironic it was that Estarra, who had never craved

power, was no longer a mere puppet queen, but a real queen, because she wanted to help. *Queen of the Confederation!* And if Sarein had anything to say about it, her little sister and Peter would soon bring Earth into the fold. *If* she could convince them to act. *If* they would trust her.

Sarein's lips formed a tentative smile. "Hello, little sister . . ."

Estarra ran toward her, talking in a rush. "Have you finally left the Chairman? I knew you wanted to tell me something during the banquet! Are you here to stay? He threatened to do something to you if we didn't cooperate—I'm so glad you're safe."

Peter was more cautious. "Basil was just here, and I didn't fall for his tricks. Did he send you to make us change our minds?"

"No, he has no idea I'm here—and that's the point," Sarein said, squaring her shoulders. "I'm here to help you get your throne back. If you care about Earth, you need to act *now*. Are you interested?"

135 ☀ CHAIRMAN BASIL WENCESLAS

Basil hadn't stopped grinding his teeth since his extremely unsatisfying encounter with Peter. After briefly stopping at the *Goliath,* Basil was anxious to get back to Earth. He had wasted enough time on this fool's errand, and he needed to plan his next move. As the diplomatic shuttle flew away from the EDF Juggernaut, heading back toward Earth, his heart hammered, his head throbbed. He didn't trust himself to speak to anyone, not his pilot, not General Brindle. No one. He was going to have to take extreme actions to put everything back on track.

Peter had thwarted his ruse with King Rory. Basil had expected to wrap the young man around his finger and coerce him into submission, but that leverage was gone. A stolen piece of flatware—how stupid! But he knew that Peter no longer had any doubt in his mind. The DNA tests would have given conclusive results. Red and black spots danced in front of the Chairman's eyes.

Now he would be forced to use Sarein as his bargaining chip. Estarra's sister was the last advantage he had. A part of him didn't like it, and he hoped he wouldn't be forced to kill Sarein after all, but he had begun to believe that no good end would come of this.

The situation got worse, though, when he returned to Earth.

As the diplomatic shuttle approached the Palace District, his personal communicator chimed, transmitting a proximity-triggered message on his private channel. It was from Sarein.

Listening to it in private, he could barely breathe. "Your Hansa is corrupt," she said. "I won't be a part of it anymore." Another traitor, another coward had abandoned him! "Whatever happens from now on is the result of your own actions." The clamor of emotions in his head drowned all rational thought. "Goodbye, Basil."

Caught up in a whirlwind of silence, he stepped out of the shuttle feeling disoriented, barely able to stand or breathe. He had done everything for Sarein—brought her back into his good graces, showed her how valuable she was to him. He had even overlooked her proven treason and asked her to join him in his safe underground bunker. She hadn't had any inkling that he might need to use her as a hostage. Why would she turn against him, when he had given her so many chances? Under the right circumstances, she could have had the Hansa!

"Goodbye, Basil."

Colonel Andez rushed up to meet him as soon as he disembarked. "Chairman Wenceslas, you've returned! There's been a crisis while you were gone."

More than one, he thought. His body locked up, as if all his muscles had tightened to their breaking points. He felt a need to lash out at someone, and he turned as quickly as a viper. Andez gave him a smart salute, and he froze again, glad to see someone behaving as expected. "What crisis now?"

She was visibly upset. "Did you give the order, Mr. Chairman? Did you authorize Deputy Cain to release Patrick

Fitzpatrick and his wife from their holding cells? There's no telling where those two are or what further sedition they might be spreading."

That surprised him. He had been so focused on Peter's intractability, and then Sarein's betrayal . . . but *Cain, too*? And Fitzpatrick on the loose? "What are you talking about?"

"Deputy Cain freed them. He claimed he had the authority. He also released the hostage families of Admirals Diente, Pike, and San Luis—and now they're denouncing you on all the newsnets! The deputy is nowhere to be found."

Basil could feel a flush creeping up his cheeks, but he clamped down on his temper. "Apparently, Deputy Cain and I have something to discuss. *Find him*. Bring him to my bunker."

Andez looked smugly satisfied. "Shall I send out search parties for Fitzpatrick as well? If we move quickly, we could possibly round up—"

"That is not for you to do anything about, Colonel Andez. Not my immediate priority." He did not dare admit to yet another crack in his armor, a flaw in his own trusted inner circle. "I will take care of it. For now, escort me to my headquarters." He needed to be away from the madness, somewhere he could think, where he could control every detail of his environment.

"Yes, sir." She led him briskly toward the projectile-proof vehicle in which she would transport him from the landing area. Even though she chose a route that avoided the worst of the demonstrations, Basil was shocked to see the sheer number of frightened fools demanding his resignation and the return of King Peter. People with too much time and too little mental acuity would follow any charismatic charlatan who promised to change their lives for the better.

He turned away from the vehicle's window, from the angry faces and shouting mouths, from the *mob*. He wished he had tens of thousands more troops under Andez's control so he could round up every one of these demonstrators. But it was futile to continue cracking down. The stunnings, beatings, and arrests had only inflamed them further.

Why did they blame him, when the problems were caused by people who *didn't* listen to him? Did they think the Chairman could have *negotiated* with the flaming elementals, or the fanatical Ildiran Adar?

Sarein and Cain should have known better, and yet they had deserted him, too. Apparently in killing McCammon he had executed the wrong traitor . . . or maybe he just hadn't executed enough of them. Why were all those closest to him prone to weakness and betrayal? And Sarein . . . He saw a fringe of deep red around his vision.

Goodbye, Basil.

Yes, he very much wanted to go underground.

Andez and four guards accompanied him through multilayered security checks into the headquarters building and to a lift that would plunge him down to his internal, windowless office deep beneath the Hansa pyramid.

As soon as the elevator started its descent, though, security alarms began to ring. Andez touched the communications stud in her ear, listened. She visibly paled. Basil hated when other people knew more about what was going on than he did. "What's happening?"

"An invasion fleet just entered our solar system. Sensors have picked up eleven enormous vessels."

Basil leaned against the vibrating wall of the descending elevator, so that his knees wouldn't buckle. "What sort of invasion fleet? From whom?" And, he wondered, exactly how big was "enormous"?

The elevator came to a stop, and its doors hissed open. In the heavily reinforced command center, technicians rushed from station to station. The alarms were deafening. Screens displayed images from space.

Andez touched the communication stud again and finally said in a husky voice, "It's *the Klikiss,* sir. The Klikiss have come to Earth."

Basil pushed aside a technician and took his place at the primary display console. What the hell were the Klikiss doing here? Was this a belated response to General Lanyan's botched attack on Pym? He tried to focus, dragging his mind from one thought to the next, as if each problem were a heavy stone he had to lift and discard.

The eleven alien swarmships came closer, completely silent, absolutely terrifying.

Basil's diplomatic and administrative skills would presumably be useless against such creatures. Admiral Diente had proved that negotiation did not work, that the Klikiss did not understand human thoughts or expectations. They did not play by the same rules. They simply wished to eradicate anything in their way.

And now they had come to Earth.

He opened a channel, knowing that Peter was probably laughing at this turn of events. "General Brindle, prepare to stand in defense of Earth."

The older commander appeared as grim as a statue. "Fleet Admiral Willis has offered her assistance, and I intend to take her up on it." Basil noted this wasn't phrased as a request. Without waiting for his acknowledgment, the *Goliath* and the EDF ships formed a defensive line in space, their jazer banks powered up, their explosive projectiles loaded.

A transmission came across all the common EDF bands, all private frequencies used by Hansa diplomats, all commercial channels—a buzzing voice filled with eerie, scraping tones.

And it spoke in *Trade Standard*, needing no translation.

"The breedex demands to see the Chairman of the Terran Hanseatic League. Basil Wenceslas must come aboard our swarmship. In person. Immediately."

136 ☀ SIRIX

In the network of reconstruction frames orbiting above the Earth, Sirix was satisfied with the progress of the robot-specific ships, forty-two vessels of unorthodox design that had been assembled from the leftover components and raw materials the robots had scrounged. While Sirix's ships looked like no more than unpressurized frameworks, they were essentially complete and could depart, or attack, at any time.

In addition, his workers had nearly finished rebuilding fourteen more EDF ships. Once these vessels passed the ponderous human inspections, the Hansa would release thousands more new black robots . . . another major step forward for his plan. Chairman Wenceslas was so arrogant that he believed the robots could not deceive him again.

Now, on the bridge of a newly repaired EDF Manta, Sirix waited for a human engineer to complete his tedious sign-off process. The inspector was a somewhat chubby man with a good-natured disposition, and he did his work at a maddeningly slow pace. He kept muttering to himself. "Gotta be careful. No sense in rushing. Can't make mistakes."

And yet he did make mistakes, missing the extremely subtle modifications the robots had made in every one of the vessels.

While he waited for the man to finish, Sirix fixed his crimson optical sensors on the shocking readings that were suddenly projected across the Manta's long-range watchdog screens. Ships. Large ships.

Klikiss swarmships.

The clumsy human inspector took several moments to notice them. "What are those?" He jabbed a stubby finger toward the blips on the screen, as if Sirix wouldn't know what he was talking about.

The robot leader scanned through possibilities, assessing and rejecting options. He settled on the only possible alternative. "Those are swarmships," Sirix said. "The Klikiss have come for us."

During his time aboard, the man had tried to be friendly to Sirix, chatting with him as if they were old comrades. "For you? What does that mean?"

"It means my robots will require these battleships after all." Sirix extended one of the long, articulated arms from his body core. This one had a serrated edge.

"What—"

With a single sweep, Sirix severed the man's head. It

landed on the deck plates with a wet plop, rolled, then came
to a stop.

One other human worker stood close to the lift doors on
the Manta's bridge. He stared with wide eyes and turned to
run. Two other black robots intercepted him and made quick
work of tearing the man apart. At any other time Sirix would
have relished the feeling of his hard pincers cutting through
soft flesh. Now, his only concern was with the oncoming
swarmships. Eleven of them, a larger Klikiss force than anything Sirix had ever encountered.

The breedex sent a blaring signal across all channels,
asking for Chairman Wenceslas *by name,* and suddenly,
Sirix realized that *he* was the one who had been betrayed.
While pretending to form a naïve partnership with the black
robots, the Chairman had somehow been in contact with the
insect race. He must have summoned the breedex here to
exterminate them.

Sirix transmitted an immediate command on a coded
frequency to all of his black robots. "Power up our ships.
Prepare to seize every EDF vessel that is functional. Kill all
humans aboard, quickly and quietly if possible, so as not to
trigger any immediate retaliation. Our highest priority is to
depart before the Klikiss find us here."

Margaret knew she was the only one with any hope of understanding the Klikiss. "I need to contact Chairman Wenceslas. He has no idea what he's up against."

Anton let out a sarcastic snort. "He rarely does." She had moved into Anton's small apartment, and they had spent a fine few days together, catching up, recovering.

But now the enormous insect vessels had arrived with enough firepower to eliminate what remained of the Earth Defense Forces and all the Confederation ships. And after the gigantic fissioning that had been about to occur on Llaro, Margaret doubted anything remained of Davlin Lotze inside that great, teeming hive mind. And yet the oncoming swarm-ships had known to ask specifically for Chairman Wenceslas. That gave her a flicker of hope. The One Breedex retained some memories . . . but memories could be turned against the human race, as well.

She also recalled that Davlin Lotze had abandoned the Hansa and gone to live in obscurity on Llaro. Davlin had severed ties with the Chairman, strongly disagreeing with some of the man's policies and activities. If some hint of his subsumed memories had percolated to the surface of the great hive mind, including a possible animosity against Chairman Wenceslas, then humanity might be in even graver trouble.

No, the Chairman had no idea what he was up against.

Using Anton's private comm, Margaret got to work

penetrating the Hansa bureaucracy with a dogged insistence. Years earlier, when she and Louis demonstrated the Klikiss Torch, Margaret had been granted direct access to the Chairman, and she still had some of those contact codes.

Everyone was in crisis mode, but no one seemed to want to do anything. She spoke sharply with one person after another, drilling her way deeper into the system. Most people didn't recognize her name, and those who did were dubious, since they had assumed her dead for years.

Always helpful, Anton brought her a cup of tea. She took a sip. Earl Grey. She couldn't remember the last time she'd had a good cup of Earl Grey. Anton had made no secret of the Chairman's ham-handed actions against the Mage-Imperator, and how the Chairman had forced Anton to watch over Rememberer Vao'sh on the university campus so that scholars could ply him for information, and how Vao'sh had died from neglect. He was not at all impressed with the man.

Abruptly, Chairman Wenceslas's face appeared on the screen, startling her. "Margaret Colicos—a ghost from the past." He paused for just a moment, then got down to business without any preliminaries. "You claim you have some specialized knowledge that can assist me with the Klikiss? I have not yet decided how to respond."

She met him with an implacable expression. "How to respond? Mr. Chairman, you are going to do exactly as the breedex demands. Get on a shuttle and go to the central swarmship, as the Klikiss requested—and take me with you. Perhaps I can help."

He seemed to resent the very idea. "I am still considering options."

"They can wipe out every living thing on Earth.

Speak with the breedex. It's the only way to prevent your extermination."

His voice was brittle. "How do you know so much about them?"

She gave the man the bare bones of what had happened to her among the Klikiss. "You need me with you . . . as well as my son, Anton. The two of us will help guide you in these delicate conversations." Out of range of the comm screen, Anton stared at his mother in surprise, since he was barely able to stifle his antipathy toward the Chairman.

Basil Wenceslas stared coldly at her from the screen and finally nodded. "It's a relief to see someone actually willing to meet their obligations. I will have a team retrieve you promptly." Without a farewell, the Chairman severed the link.

Within minutes—an astonishingly short time, considering the distance from the Palace District to Anton's private apartment—an abrupt and insistent pounding came at the door. Colonel Andez and four men stood there in cleanup-crew uniforms.

"How did you get here so fast?" Anton said. When Vao'sh had been dying of isolation, Margaret knew he had tried for days to get any help whatsoever.

Andez answered with a supercilious scowl. "Your persistent demands to speak with the Chairman raised a red flag, and we had already been dispatched to observe and investigate the possible threat. While we were inbound, the Chairman changed our objective."

Wasting no time, Margaret strode out into the hall to head toward their vehicle. "Of course he did."

Chairman Wenceslas was already aboard his refueled diplomatic shuttle, impatient to go. As she and Anton rushed through the hatch, he looked at her sourly. Without giving them any chance to settle, he said, "So tell me what the Klikiss want, Dr. Colicos. Why did the hive mind ask to speak to me by name?"

"I don't know." Her answer startled him.

"You are not instilling me with confidence."

"It is not my intention to. I want you prepared. Realistically." Margaret chose a seat across from him, as if she did this every day.

Buckling in beside her, Anton grumbled, "The Hansa knew the Klikiss were a danger, that they had wiped out numerous colony worlds. You received reports, Mr. Chairman, but you didn't take the threat seriously."

The Chairman twitched as if he'd been stung by invisible bees. "I take all threats seriously, but there are so many." Margaret could tell he was nervous about the upcoming encounter. This situation was entirely out of his control, and Chairman Wenceslas obviously knew it. "General Lanyan and Admiral Diente were both killed by the Klikiss. From the presence of those swarmships, I'd say their aggressive intentions are pretty clear."

Margaret felt the rumble of vibrations through the deck as the shuttle's engines powered up. "Then you must reach some sort of rapprochement. I suggest you comport yourself well with the breedex."

"I can't wait to see what happens when they find out about your partnership with the black robots," Anton muttered.

"That worries me more than anything," Margaret said, and she meant it. The Chairman had no grasp of the sheer animosity the Klikiss held toward their robots. She would guide him as best she could, getting him up to speed as they traveled to the swarmships.

"I can handle it," he said, as if it were no more than a difficult board meeting. He leaned back as the shuttle launched.

138 ※ CHAIRMAN BASIL WENCESLAS

B asil would have flown the diplomatic shuttle himself if he could, just so he didn't need to worry about the pilot balking or overreacting. The man had been competent enough flying out to the Confederation flagship, but these jaw-dropping alien vessels were something else entirely.

The fate of the planet hung in the balance — again. Alas, he could not do everything himself. He had left King Rory behind and brought along Margaret and Anton Colicos, in the hope that their insights would be useful. He listened as Margaret told him as much as she knew about the insect race, about the breedex, the subhive wars, how she had been stranded among them for years, and how they had massacred and incorporated most of the colonists from Llaro. Basil wasn't sure how much all this information would help. He didn't need any help.

At the end of the day, he was the only person he could truly count on. Once Basil finally faced the breedex, leader to leader, he trusted his own political skills to make the Klikiss be reasonable. Diente must have done something wrong in his earlier attempt.

As the shuttle flew onward, Basil pushed aside his hatred for King Peter, and now Deputy Cain and Sarein. He did not worry about them. Not now. The Klikiss consumed his attention. Those other problems could wait. He clenched and unclenched his fists, drew a long, slow breath.

The breedex had not included King Peter in the invitation. That was something, at least. Obviously, the Klikiss understood who was truly important here. Always thinking ahead, he wondered in a giddy moment if he might be able to strike some sort of bargain, provided he could communicate his needs to the breedex. Maybe he could convince this insect swarmship to destroy Peter and his Confederation ships. Now that would be a neat solution!

He contacted the pilot. "Increase speed. Let's get this over with." The man must be sweating, but he didn't argue with the Chairman's orders.

Basil called for an EDF escort as the diplomatic shuttle flew out to where the eleven swarmships waited beyond the orbit of the shattered Moon. While General Brindle remained ready in the *Goliath*, Admirals Pike and San Luis flew their Mantas on either side of the shuttle. Still not a terribly impressive procession.

The shuttle pilot called Basil to the cockpit. "Mr. Chairman, I have a message from Admiral Pike. He wishes to speak with you personally."

Frowning at the interruption, Basil made his way forward. Without being invited, Margaret and Anton Colicos followed. Ahead of them, out of the shuttle's front window-ports, Basil could see the looming alien craft growing larger as they closed the distance.

The pilot gestured to the communication panel. "He's on screen, Mr. Chairman."

Admiral Pike's glowering image appeared, looking impatient. Basil leaned forward into the focal zone. "Yes, what is it?" Basil asked.

"If the fate of the world wasn't at stake, we would blast your shuttle to ions right now, just as you commanded me to destroy Chairman Fitzpatrick's space yacht. The bugs can have you, as far as we're concerned."

Basil blinked, momentarily speechless. Now what? He felt a sense of unreality, as if he had fallen into some kind of distorted mirror world. "What are you talking about, Admiral?"

Admiral San Luis broke into the transmission. "Our families have been freed. You no longer have any hold over us."

Pike lifted his chin, and his eyes were pitiless. "They're safe, Mr. Chairman. Their story is being broadcast by Freedom's Sword. Admiral Diente's family is doing the same. Everyone knows what you've done, sir. No matter what happens, you can't blackmail us any longer. When you do come back to Earth, you will not find a warm reception from us, nor from anyone in the EDF."

Basil felt blindsided. And then he realized that Pike and San Luis had broadcast on a completely open channel.

The two Admirals ended the transmission, and the escort Mantas on either side of the diplomatic shuttle altered course and peeled away, leaving the small craft all alone in space as it approached the alien swarmships.

A chain-saw ache pressed into the back of his skull. His carefully laid foundations were turning to quicksand.

Margaret Colicos looked at him. "The timing could have been better."

Basil drew deep breaths to drive back the red fringes in his vision, staring at the foremost of the huge Klikiss ships until his eyes burned. No one dared to speak a word in the cockpit.

The diplomatic shuttle drew close to the enormous sphere. Millions of component craft moved about like grains of sand trying to keep a proper configuration, shifting, blurring, shifting again.

Finally, the pilot said in a small voice, "I can't find any port or access to the interior of the swarmship, Mr. Chairman. What should I do?"

"Just keep heading forward," Margaret answered for him. "You'll see what you need."

Basil's throat was dry. His skin prickled with goose bumps. He clenched his fists so hard that his well-manicured nails cut crescent-shaped grooves into his palms. *One problem at a time. Prioritize.* He would take care of the others later . . . if he survived.

"Are we supposed to read minds?" he said testily. "Why doesn't the breedex issue some instructions?"

"The breedex doesn't have to."

As they neared the external shell, the component craft suddenly re-arranged themselves, and the outer layer of vessels broke off like gases blown from a sun's surface. The hive vessel seemed to be evaporating, spreading out.

Basil flinched as geometrical alien ships flurried around

them like a cloud of gnats, and then simply re-formed the swarmship's shell on the other side of the shuttle, swallowing them up. Though the gigantic conglomerate vessel hadn't moved, the Hansa shuttle was suddenly enclosed within the alien sphere.

139 ✸ KING PETER

The Confederation ships hung beside the EDF vessels in space, facing the enigmatically silent Klikiss swarmships. Nothing moved.

King Peter stood on the *Jupiter*'s bridge with Estarra and OX, studying the huge alien clusters as the foremost one abruptly engulfed the Hansa's diplomatic shuttle, along with Basil Wenceslas. The mass of interlocking alien components had simply absorbed it.

Good riddance.

"If there's a way to make this situation worse, the Chairman's bound to find it." Admiral Willis leaned forward in her command chair. "I'm keeping our weapons ready."

He couldn't imagine what the breedex wanted with Basil. The Klikiss arrival had certainly thrown a wrinkle into his plans for returning to the Whisper Palace. Now they had to stand together against a seemingly invincible enemy.

Peter stared at the screen until his eyes burned. Could he

really take advantage of the distraction to seize control of the government? The very existence of Earth was threatened by the massive alien ships.

On the other hand, how could he not, knowing that the situation would only grow worse in the hands of Chairman Wenceslas?

Sarein was greatly agitated. "The Klikiss have changed the circumstances, but not the main goal. It's more important now than ever. Deputy Cain is ready for you down there, and so are the people of Earth. Basil won't be able to do a thing about it."

Estarra couldn't tear her eyes from the enormous alien vessels that had swept into the system. "But isn't this the worst possible time to throw Earth into more instability? We've got a common enemy now."

"These Klikiss ships might well be the worst threat to humanity since the hydrogue war," OX observed.

Peter agreed with the assessment logically, but he made a bitter noise. "The Chairman will never set aside our differences and work together. How can I leave the fate of humanity in the hands of *Basil Wenceslas*? Given his track record, it would be irresponsible."

Sarein's dark eyes flashed. "Peter, we'll never have a better chance! The Whisper Palace is wide open."

Admiral Willis rested her chin on her knuckles. "I'm as worried about the Klikiss as anybody, but we know for damn sure that the Chairman is a threat. There's nothing you can do for Earth up here, sire."

Peter felt a steely resolve. "I can make a difference if I take my throne back. Humanity needs a strong visionary leader, now more than ever." With all their blatant signs of unrest, he knew the people were ready. One way or another, the angry people would soon overthrow the Chairman and depose his sham King Rory, and they were likely to turn the kid into a scapegoat. A fate the poor patsy didn't deserve. He turned to Admiral Willis. "Do you see any way to avoid a shooting war? We can't have our ships blasting at the EDF."

Excitement flushed Willis's face. "Right now, who's watching? Everybody's hypnotized by the Klikiss. I could easily slip one Manta away from the back ranks and take a roundabout path toward Earth. Go in quick and clean, establish a foothold, plant our flag in the Palace District, and have you sitting back on your throne by the end of the day. We'll be all settled in if, or when, the Chairman comes back. A bloodless coup."

"It is not technically a coup," OX pointed out. "King Peter never abdicated his throne. I can cite numerous precedents in Hansa law, as well as historical comparisons."

"It's true, Peter," Estarra said. "The people need you."

It felt good to be making clear decisions again, moving forward on a plan. Peter kissed her. "I'll take OX with me, but you should stay here with Sarein. If anything happens to me, the Confederation will need its Queen." He could see that she was torn by this, but understood the political necessity.

"I'm leading this operation personally," Willis said, leaving no room for argument. "Commodore Brindle can hold down the fort."

Peter followed her to the lift, glancing one last time at the looming swarmships on the main screen. "For everyone's sake, I hope this isn't the shortest comeback in human history."

The eleven swarmships had halted outside the rubble zone of the broken Moon. Sirix could not understand why the Klikiss simply didn't open fire upon the pathetic-looking group of EDF and Confederation vessels; it was not like a breedex to show any sort of restraint.

The hive mind was meeting with the treacherous Hansa Chairman—almost certainly planning the annihilation of the black robots. Sirix needed to take advantage of every second of delay to launch his retreat.

After receiving his command burst, the black robots swiftly accomplished the massacre on all fourteen flight-worthy EDF ships. Every Hansa engineer, quality-control inspector, tactical expert, and ship designer had been hunted down and killed. Only one man managed to reach a trans-mitting station in time. In a squawking voice he called out to warn the rest of the EDF. "The robots are turning on us again! They're killing—" And then nothing more. The ro-bots had crushed his larynx before he could continue. In the fear and confusion caused by the Klikiss arrival, Sirix hoped the human military would not respond swiftly to the alarm.

Nevertheless, he and his black robots had to move.

Meanwhile, commandeering the construction pods that had been used by the human inspectors, robots raced to their open-framed battleships. More than ten thousand ro-bots—mostly new arrivals from the compy factories—went to their posts and fired up the starship engines. All together, the black robots prepared for a mass exodus.

Sirix swiveled his angular head to PD and QT, who waited with him on the Manta's bridge. The two compies had wet red smears on their polymer skins from helping to haul away the mangled bodies of the two dead human inspectors. "Both of you, stand ready at our weapons stations."

"Yes, Sirix," they said in unison.

While the eleven swarmships made no overt moves either toward Earth or toward the robot ships, Sirix's sensors did detect a flurry of smaller component ships spreading out. Klikiss scout vessels had separated from the primary masses to scan the activity in space, studying the numerous vessels that still combed the Earth-Moon neighborhood in search of deadly lunar fragments.

Three of the Klikiss scouts streaked toward the highly distinctive open-framework vessels in the orbital repair docks. They would easily recognize the fundamental design and conclude that the black robots were here. They would know. He shouted orders to PD and QT. "Destroy those ships."

The two compies, well practiced in using EDF weapons, opened fire using jazer blasts, but now he feared it was already too late. The scouts would have immediately noted the black robot infestation—and what they knew, the breedex knew.

Sirix sent his command for an immediate and complete withdrawal, and the entire group of ships under his control—forty-two robot ships and fourteen stolen EDF vessels—accelerated away. He would leave the humans to face the Klikiss alone.

However, the breedex must have seen through the eyes

of the scoutship pilots. The enormous swarmships began to move.

141 ☀ CHAIRMAN BASIL WENCESLAS

Once swallowed up by the incredible swarmship, the diplomatic shuttle jolted, then began to accelerate toward the core — a large, organic-looking lump of convolutions composed both of metals and glistening polymer secretions. The central mass reminded Basil of an electrified, resin-coated brain.

The pilot lifted his hands from the controls, helpless. "A tractor beam is pulling us along. There's nothing I can do."

"Obviously, that is where we're supposed to go." Basil stared forward, trying to glean any sort of information. "Your advice would be most helpful right now, Dr. Colicos."

"At the moment, my best advice is to wait. The breedex will make the first move, and I've given you as much preparation as I can."

The tractor beam drew them into a cavernous opening within the core mass of the swarmship. The shuttle dropped heavily onto the floor inside a vaulted, slick-walled landing bay, and more than a hundred Klikiss warriors marched out to meet them.

Once the ship came to a rest, Margaret went to the shuttle's hatch, unsealed it, and casually stepped out among the Klikiss. She called over her shoulder, "Mr. Chairman, you have to see the breedex. Come."

She looked annoyingly calm before the monstrous insects, and Basil did not like someone else taking the initiative. He instructed the pilot to remain inside to protect the craft (if such a thing were possible) and followed Margaret through the hatch, with Anton close behind him. The chamber's stale but breathable air was filled with a bitter alkaline stench.

The spiny chitinous bodies looked like armored tanks. The ones Margaret identified as domates had silvery armor slashed with black stripes; their faces were mosaics of small bony plates that shifted into skeletal, almost-human visages.

He faced the nearest domate—one with a horned head-crest—as if he were addressing a formal ambassador. "I am the Chairman of the Terran Hanseatic League. I have an appointment to meet with your breedex."

Margaret said in a quiet voice, "They have no individuality. When you speak to any of them, you *are* speaking to the breedex. The hive mind is listening to all of our conversations."

"Then why didn't they just send an emissary to us?" Basil grumbled.

Margaret cocked her head at him. "Because the impact isn't the same. Follow me."

The towering domates and spiny warriors guided them with a swift and clicking gait along strangely intestinal corridors. Basil saw so many Klikiss crowding the passages that he felt certain the hive mind had no intention of letting them out of this hellish place.

When they finally reached a central chamber, Basil stared at a festering, shifting horror of mucus, broken pieces of slaughtered Klikiss, bits of debris, shiny pieces of metal, shattered glass, and grubs . . . many, many grubs. He reeled, and his ears rang with a constant deafening buzz that penetrated to subsonic levels, making his bones vibrate. All of his schemes, negotiating skills, and confidence wilted in an instant.

He had never felt so out of his depth.

Margaret stepped close to the edge of the horrific mass. "This is the One Breedex." She seemed less certain now. "It's . . . different from anything I've seen before."

Basil's legs had locked up, but he forced himself to move closer. His voice was husky. He had never felt so overwhelmed. "I am Chairman Basil Wenceslas. I believe we have diplomatic matters to discuss?"

Margaret remained close, and she called down into the buzzing, shifting mass with a hint of hope in her voice. "Are you still there, Davlin? Any part of you? Speak to us."

On the shuttle flight, Margaret had tried to convince him that Davlin's personality and memories had come to live inside the hive mind. Basil found the whole idea preposterous.

The squirming, separated pieces of the hive mind shifted like clay being squeezed by a sculptor's hands until it formed a towering face that resembled the Klikiss. Then the features flickered, softened, became familiar. He stared at it in awe as the rough face loomed up out of the mass of the shifting hive mind. "It . . . does look like Davlin."

"So, some part of him is still there, even after the last massive fissioning." She sounded relieved.

"I know you, Chairman Wenceslas." The lips of the giant sculpture moved, but the voice came from everywhere. *"Know your enemy."*

So many things had already fallen apart, but this bizarre turn of events was no stranger than the rest. Basil clung to the knowledge that the breedex had called for him by name. Even though he saw little of the man who had served him for years as a "specialist in obscure details," he knew that Davlin must remember him.

"And I know you, Davlin. You were my greatest expert, and I'm sure you remember your loyalties. The Hansa wants to make peace with the Klikiss." He thought it best not to mention Admiral Diente's previous attempt, or bring up General Lanyan's attack, or speak of the robots.

The expression on the simulated face didn't change. *"I remember you, Chairman Wenceslas. You cannot keep secrets."* A frisson of fear gave Basil gooseflesh. The real Davlin Lotze did know much about his personality, and maybe that wasn't entirely a good thing.

Then the vaguely human visage lost its features again, sharpened, enlarged, and became a kaleidoscope of the most horrific Klikiss warriors, monstrous domates, spiny insectoid beasts. *"You dispatched humans to our worlds. Your Colonization Initiative. You sent battleships to destroy our subhive at Pym."*

When Basil spoke, his voice scraped through a dry throat. "It was a misunderstanding. At the time I felt I had no alternative. The Hansa means the Klikiss no harm. We can be allies. There is no need for hostility."

"You cannot hide what you have done." Suddenly, all

semblance of the breedex's integrity—whether Davlin's face or a Klikiss head—collapsed into churning turmoil again. Even Margaret backed away in alarm. The hive mind's voice, however, continued to thunder from countless throats, echoing, accusing. *"You made an alliance with the robots. You have cooperated with our enemies."*

The domates and warriors moved farther into the central chamber, raised their serrated arms.

Basil's heart turned to ice. All around them the swarm-ship began to vibrate, humming and moving. The Klikiss shifted in agitation.

"It was part of a carefully orchestrated plan," Basil insisted. "Sirix intended to betray us. I always knew that. I set up a trap to wipe out the black robots once and for all. Nothing would please me more than to see them gone."

Startlingly, the breedex formed the face of Davlin Lotze again. *"I know you, Chairman Wenceslas. You believe in . . . situational truth."*

"I tell you it was never a real bargain, always a trap."

But any hint of Davlin Lotze, any humanity at all, was gone from the thrumming voice. *"Two of my swarmships will pursue and destroy the black robots. The rest will sterilize Earth for cooperating with our enemies."*

Basil shouted in desperation. "Davlin, listen to me. I promise it will all become clear." He tried to summon his composure again as the Chairman. "When you encounter the black robots, you'll recognize what I did, both for humanity and for the Klikiss. If you know me as you say, then you know it is what I would do."

He prayed that the subtle plan he had implemented against Sirix would function as he had designed it to. Otherwise, there was no conceivable way he could stop the Klikiss onslaught.

142 ✸ KING PETER

A ship as large as a Manta rarely landed in the Palace District. The local spaceport's tethering and support facilities could not easily accommodate the cruiser's subsidiary mooring systems and stabilizing struts.

"I'll use the hovering engines to keep us in place," Admiral Willis decided. "No need for a full-fledged landing and hours of docking procedures. Too much hassle, and we're in a hurry. We'll take our troops out on small skimmers."

In the vicinity of the commercial spaceport, Peter watched small private flyers dash out of the way. At any other time, their arrival would have been challenged by a major military response, but all of the EDF ships were deployed in a cordon facing the eleven swarmships.

The local Hansa security troops were swamped with increasingly vehement demonstrations across the Palace District—across the planet, in fact. As Sarein had promised, Patrick Fitzpatrick and Zhett Kellum continuously rallied them with new broadcasts enumerating Basil's transgressions. And Chairman Wenceslas wasn't around to issue any orders. King Rory was noticeably silent.

"One neat, clean victory coming right up, sire." Willis brought the Manta down, ignoring the objections of the spaceport authority. "I am escorting the rightful King back to the Whisper Palace, after all. I don't need to say please and thank-you. Still, I'll try not to flatten too many of your rejoicing subjects." The cruiser moved slowly enough so that other ships could get out of her way.

With OX at his side, alert for any opportunity to assist, Peter and his team prepared to disembark. Two hundred battle-ready soldiers had volunteered for this mission. When he reached the launching bay, he raised his voice to address the troops. "There will be some resistance. A few of those who stand against us will be genuinely loyal to Chairman Wenceslas, but most others have been misled. Use stun gas and twitchers—I want no casualties unless we have absolutely no other choice." He squared his shoulders. "But be cautious. I doubt the Chairman has given similar orders of restraint."

The soldiers in the swift assault group climbed into seventeen troop skimmers, and Peter joined Admiral Willis in the first transport. When the Manta's bay doors opened, all of the craft dropped out at the same time, descended beneath the hovering cruiser, then struck out on a direct flight path for the Whisper Palace. He had left here in the middle of the night; now he was coming back in broad daylight—as it should be.

Throngs of demonstrators crowded plazas, filled alleys. There were fires and banners. In many areas the overwhelmed Hansa guards did not even try to keep them in check. Peter hoped he could reassure the mobs and impose order before they set fire to the Hansa HQ.

The troop skimmers landed in a cluster just in front of

the Whisper Palace, arriving faster than the Hansa guards could respond to intercept them. The skimmer hatches hummed open simultaneously, and Confederation soldiers spilled out.

Willis and OX stopped protectively beside Peter as he paused to look up at the many-towered structure of the Palace. For the first time, he saw how ostentatious the enormous structure seemed, too cold and elaborate. Not like Theroc. And neither his family nor the Confederation could be truly safe until Peter closed the book on the dark days of the Hansa.

"Let's go finish this."

At his command, the assault troops raced up the broad stone staircase. Before his soldiers could reach the towering arches of the grand entrance, though, the glass-inset doors swung open. Colonel Andez and twenty of her fellow storm troopers stood with their weapons drawn—deadly projectile weapons, not stunners. "We have a warrant for your arrest."

Willis pushed forward. "We don't recognize the validity of any Hansa order."

From the middle of the stairs, Peter shouted up at them. "I am the rightful King, and the Whisper Palace is mine. The people are calling for change. The Chairman's time is finished, and so is yours. You can't stop this uprising by standing in my way."

Forthright and angry, Andez thrust up her chin and sneered. "You come slinking back while the Chairman is bravely facing the Klikiss. You are an opportunist, a coward, and an outlaw."

Peter's overwhelming number of troops held out their stunners and moved up the stairs. Though not cowed into submission, Andez visibly panicked. "Take them out! Shoot the King."

The astonishing order caused her troops to hesitate, but Peter's soldiers did not. With a buzzing crackle, twitcher beams engulfed Andez and her guards. The cleanup crew folded to the ground, a crowd of jittering arms and legs strewn across the grand foyer.

"I can see why the Chairman likes her," Willis said. "She's as boneheaded as he is."

Peter nodded to the Confederation soldiers. "Good work."

Willis issued orders for Andez and her companions to be disarmed, put in restraints, and locked into one of the meeting rooms just off the grand foyer. "That should hold them for now. We can deal with them once we've secured control."

As the fallen guards were taken away, Peter gestured for the others to follow him. "Now we go inside—to the throne room."

"Shall I take the lead, King Peter?" OX asked. "If we encounter additional resistance, I can draw fire, and I am expendable."

He turned to the Teacher compy, thinking of everything OX had done for him, the sacrifices he had made. The compy had voluntarily deleted all of his memory and history—his very essence—just to save Peter and Estarra. "You are *not* expendable." He looked at his troops. "I don't intend to lose anybody." He passed deeper into the familiar passageways with his team pressing around him. Willis dispatched separate squads to adjacent halls and wings to secure the Whisper Palace, but Peter headed directly for the throne room.

When they marched into the spectacular chamber,

Peter found King Rory sitting on the throne, dwarfed by the massive chair. He was alone in the big room. The boy stood indignantly when he saw them swarming toward him. "Guards! Help!"

Peter walked up the stairs to the throne and stood directly before the boy king. "You have nothing to fear from us, Rory."

The boy looked uncertain. "Colonel Andez ordered me to come here after the Chairman went to the swarmship. She said I had to sit in my place as the Hansa's King . . . but there's no one else around. The deputy's gone. I know Captain McCammon is dead, but where are the rest of the royal guards? I've heard explosions outside. The demonstrators are bound to come into the Whisper Palace!"

Admiral Willis gestured, and the guards fanned out to protect the other entrances to the throne room. "This chamber is secure, King Peter."

"You don't need to worry about the protesters," Peter said to Rory. "In fact, I might be the only one who can save your life." He spoke with genuine compassion. "I'll keep you safe from the Chairman, too. I know what he did to you, because he did the same thing to me."

The gigantic alien vessels shimmered and pulsed, like several huge beating hearts formed of countless individual specks. Sarein and Estarra waited with Robb on the bridge, all of them trying to hide their anxiety. Captains Kett and Roberts sat unobtrusively at two empty stations. Nobody spoke.

By now, Admiral Willis and King Peter should have made it to the Whisper Palace, but there had been no word from the King . . . or from Chairman Wenceslas since he'd disappeared into the gigantic Klikiss vessel.

"Anybody bring a deck of cards?" Rlinda finally said, breaking the silence.

Suddenly, perhaps responding to some kind of silent, simultaneous transmission, the eleven conglomerate ships began to move. Though Robb saw no engines, or any means of acceleration, the insect vessels lumbered through space like small asteroids, picking up speed and heading straight toward them.

Robb shouted orders. "Evasive action! Don't let those things roll over us."

His helmsman was already scrambling at his controls, but the swarmships plowed past on a course directly for Earth, barely missing the Confederation vessels. The bugs took no notice of them.

"Something's sure got the breedex riled up," Robb commented.

"Probably something the Chairman said," Estarra added.

Sarein's face was hard. "Basil can be irritating."

Robb's father spoke across the priority comm channel from the *Goliath*. "I am going to withdraw to Earth to set up a defensive line in case those swarmships attack."

Leaving the channel open, Robb called out, "You all heard General Brindle. Let's not have him fight this battle alone."

The Confederation vessels drew back into formation and sped after the *Goliath* and the EDF fleet, who were already on the move. The Klikiss seemed to ignore them altogether as the swarmships plunged forward, hell-bent on reaching Earth.

Two of the swarmships split from the others and shot off to pursue a specific target. Robb called for long-range scans and saw the exotic angular vessels constructed by the black robots. Their engines blazed as the robots headed away from Earth, rising up out of the plane of the solar system, and a group of newly repaired EDF ships flew with them.

"They're sure in a hurry to get out of here," Captain Roberts said. "With good reason, I suppose."

When the two swarmships veered off toward the robot ships, Robb realized that the breedex must have discovered the Chairman's bargain with Sirix. "That'll make the bugs really unhappy." Countless component vessels were already shooting energy weapons at the fleeing robots, but Robb couldn't say he was sorry.

More important, the other nine swarmships were still headed toward Earth. Smaller craft began to split off and bombard the ship-repair docks around the planet. "Should we open fire?" Queen Estarra asked. "Do we have enough combined weapons to damage those alien clusters?"

Robb knew how difficult the swarmships had been to fight at Pym, and this insect force was hundreds of times larger. "It would be like pricking an elephant with a needle."

"But we have a lot of needles, don't we?" Captain Kett said. "We'll fly the *Blind Faith* out there to take potshots, if it will do any good."

"I'll thank you not to go volunteering my ship," Roberts said. "You already crashed your own."

The EDF battle group, though, did not show restraint. Robb's father ordered a barrage to delay the giant clustered vessels before they could take up their positions above the Earth. Each blast destroyed at least one component ship, but there were millions. Robb directed his ships to help his father. The concentrated shots peeled off the clusters' external components, but all signs of damage were simply absorbed and erased.

Swifter, smaller human vessels passed the swarmships and turned about to form a crowded defensive line, the *Jupiter* next to the *Goliath*. It seemed an impossible stance, but they did it nevertheless.

Robb swallowed hard and sat straighter in his command chair. "It's showtime."

The nine swarmships closed around Earth—and then stopped in front of the blockade of EDF and Confederation vessels. They just hung there.

Though no one had asked him to, King Rory stepped away from the massive throne and now sat on the stone steps of the dais, looking pale. In a way, he seemed almost relieved.

Admiral Willis's troops had secured the throne room, and Peter was clearly in charge. Within the first twenty minutes, she set up holo-imagers and newsnet recorders, then transmitted a live feed of King Peter on his throne. He hoped it would quell some of the riots.

"People of the Hansa, I am ready to resume my responsibilities as your King. Chairman Wenceslas has been relieved of his duties, and Rory has surrendered the throne. The Confederation and I will do everything in our power to repair the recent damage to Earth, unify humanity, ensure the rights of every citizen, and strengthen the human race."

Outside in the streets, the demonstrations had grown in size and fervor, swelling with a giddy, celebratory mood despite the looming Klikiss threat.

Shortly after they had solidified their hold on the Whisper Palace, Deputy Cain reappeared. Even with the Hansa, and perhaps the human race itself, on the verge of total destruction, he looked as if this were any other day and he was simply attending a conference. Willis told her guards to let the man pass, and Cain approached the throne with a polite bow. "King Peter, I'm pleased to see I could count on you. Sarein obviously delivered our message. She is safe?"

Peter nodded. "She's with Queen Estarra up on the flagship. I'm grateful for what you did. You took quite a risk."

"It was necessary. The worst I'd anticipated for today was being murdered by the Chairman becausee Sarein and I undermined his authority. Unfortunately, the arrival of the Klikiss demonstrates that there are even worse things. Our priorities have obviously changed. We'll have to adapt our approach to finishing this."

Patrick and Zhett, having seen the Confederation Manta hovering in the Palace District, also arrived to offer their assistance. Peter welcomed them. "I'm relieved to see you safe, and free, Mr. Fitzpatrick. You cleared the way for my return, just as I had hoped your grandmother would."

Patrick smiled. "As you can see on the newsnets, you have a lot of support on Earth, sire. It's good to have you back."

Willis was obviously pleased to see him. "You always did excel in causing trouble, Mr. Fitzpatrick. Glad to see you using your talents in a productive way."

Patrick straightened. "News has already spread of King Peter's return, but I'd like to broadcast my own message from here. Freedom's Sword is waiting for confirmation—they'll believe this isn't one of the Chairman's tricks if it comes from me."

Deputy Cain nodded politely. "The central communications nexus is located on a sublevel of the Whisper Palace. If you transmit from there, using the governmental overrides, everyone on the planet will hear your broadcast."

"I can assist you in accessing it," OX said.

Willis dispatched five soldiers to escort the Teacher compy, Patrick, and Zhett to the comm center. Their exuberant message went out on every public channel, where it was seen by the people glued to their update screens for news about the Klikiss invasion. The Chairman didn't have a ghost of a chance of wrangling his way back into power.

Just then, Robb Brindle called on the emergency channel, "Admiral! Is the King's position secure? The Klikiss are on their way! We can't stop them." Images played across the small communications unit showing the monstrous swarm-ships charging toward Earth. "We sure could use some help up here—every Manta counts."

Peter wasted no time. "Return to your ship, Admiral. Go defend Earth."

"I can't leave you here unprotected, sire! What if the Chairman tries to pull something?"

The King frowned. "Admiral, if the Klikiss get through, there will be no one left to protect. Leave a dozen soldiers behind with me, but take your Manta and go! I'm counting on you to protect Queen Estarra."

Willis raced out of the throne room, yelling into the comm unit, "Prepare for immediate liftoff! Our day's not over yet—not by a long shot."

Shielded by gauzy cocoons of wental water, the Solar Navy warliners raced toward Ildira. Adar Zan'nh was ready to take back his world. At last, he had the weapons he needed to battle the faeros.

All of his surviving warliners flew in perfect formation, and the Confederation ships traveling with them were loaded with cylinders of frozen wental water. Those ice projectiles had destroyed the fireballs far more effectively than his sacrifice of whole warliners had, and now the Solar Navy also had hundreds of the artillery shells. Numerous water-encapsulated treelings from Theroc flitted like small pearls around the wental sphere flown by Jess and Cesca.

Yes, this would be a battle to be remembered in the *Saga of Seven Suns*.

Sullivan Gold stood at the edge of the command nucleus. Quiet until now, the old man let out a gasp as the long-range images sharpened on the screen. "My God! Is that *all* of the faeros?"

Space around Ildira was clogged with a blizzard of fireballs, an incandescent storm of new faeros that Rusa'h had created by consuming the soul-fires of helpless Ildirans.

"We will defeat them." Zan'nh allowed no doubt whatsoever to dilute his words.

His helmsman suddenly let out a surprised cry. "We are accelerating, Adar. I am no longer in control of this warliner." He lifted his hands helplessly. "We are being pulled along."

Zan'nh understood. "Yes—by our allies. The wentals are leading the charge now." He did not try to hide his anticipation. "Prepare for the first clash."

The water elementals propelled the Solar Navy ships forward like huge spearpoints, hundreds of battleship-sized projectiles. The faeros gathered, as if curious but unconcerned about this charge. Some swept toward the wental-swathed ships, while others ricocheted away like sparks on a wind.

Two anxious Confederation pilots shot several wental-ice shells in a preemptive flurry. Even though their panicked targeting was poor, the projectiles swerved of their own volition and plunged into a group of faeros, snuffing them out in a combined misty explosion.

The Solar Navy warliners accelerated as the warrior wentals raced to find targets. Zan'nh gripped the rail, forced to do nothing more than watch the battle because he could not control the movement of his own ship. As Adar, he was used to making the strategy and giving the orders.

One blazing fireball careened directly into their path, wreathed in huge arcs of fire. The flagship plunged directly toward it.

"Adar!" the helmsman yelped.

The mist-cocooned warliner hurtled into the inferno—and passed entirely through. When the scrabbling flames tried to catch at their scrolled hull ornamentation, deadly water vapor snarled around the faeros, tearing it apart. As if poisoned, the flaming creature writhed and flickered. The flagship soared away from the scraps of flame, its anodized hull plates smoking but undamaged.

Zan'nh felt an electric crackle of enthusiasm through

the *thism*. Again directed by the wentals, the big warliner shifted course and headed after another faeros.

The Adar took his own initiative. "Port and starboard gun batteries, shoot your wental artillery shells. Make every projectile count." The Solar Navy soldiers were eager to comply. He watched on his screens, pleased to see the white streaks fly out like sunlit arrows to strike fireballs. Meanwhile, commandeered by the wentals, his warliner charged from one faeros to another like the maddened mount of an Ildiran jouster.

The bulk of the Solar Navy followed, commencing similar attacks of their own. Behind them flew a wave of disorganized Confederation vessels, seeking out and extinguishing ellipsoids, firing their frozen projectiles into any incandescent target.

Zan'nh's chest swelled with pride and triumph—feelings that had been too long absent in him. So far, hundreds of fireballs had been snuffed out. After regrouping, the allied ships dove in again, seeking other targets, and now the faeros swiftly retreated to avoid the new threat.

"Never thought I'd see that—they're actually running away!" Sullivan said.

Osira'h stared, unblinking. "They are starting to realize what we have brought against them. Rusa'h should begin to fear."

The command nucleus received several transmissions from outlying Solar Navy scoutships that fought on the perimeter of the solar system. "Liege! Something is happening in the suns. The faeros have opened more transgates."

On the relayed image, the seven stars of Ildira had become gateways from hell. Thousands of fireballs emerged from the stellar furnaces. Traveling through solar transgates

from the numerous suns they inhabited across the Spiral
Arm, the faeros all came rushing toward Ildira.

146 ☀ PRIME DESIGNATE DARO'H

Even without the Prism Palace, even without Mijistra, the
Ildiran Empire remained alive. The Empire *was still alive*!
Prime Designate Daro'h encouraged everyone to remember that.

When the crashing spacedocks had obliterated the wondrous capital city, the blow might have crushed the Ildiran spirit, but Daro'h held on to certitude for his entire race. As Prime Designate, that was his responsibility.

After Designate Ridek'h had returned to tell his story, exhausted but alive, the boy seemed stronger now, and his eyes wore a different look. He had faced the faeros incarnate, expecting to be incinerated. He had not known Nira's half-breed children could shield him. Now, back in their shelters deep in the mines, the Prime Designate, as well as Osira'h's siblings, accepted his survival as another sign of Ildiran fortitude.

But with the faeros gone for a short while at least,

Daro'h's people could recover their strength. With all his heart, the Prime Designate believed that Adar Zan'nh would free the Mage-Imperator. And as he believed it, so did the rest of the Ildirans, drawing confidence from their direct *thism* connection to him.

To demonstrate his resolve, Daro'h emerged from his shelter deep in the mountains, calling his people to follow him out of their caves and mines. Beside him, Yazra'h gave a feral smile of pride in her half brother. "We cannot hide forever," she said.

Stepping out of the tunnels, the frightened people blinked in the sunlight, glad to see the comforting suns again. Through the *thism*, Daro'h could feel the rejuvenation of the collective racial psyche, the surge of confidence. That confidence waned somewhat, as the long-isolated Ildirans saw firsthand the extent of the damage to the landscape.

Through the soul-threads that connected them all, Daro'h pressed his conviction on them. With his mind, with his determination, he rallied the people. "We will go back to Mijistra!" Along the way, he decided they would bring together refugees from their camps, find the many displaced kiths that had scattered across the landscape.

Despite his recent confrontation with the faeros incarnate and the news that his mentor Tal O'nh had died aboard the flaming shipyards, Ridek'h was one of the first to volunteer to go. Nira's four half-breed children also insisted on walking in the lead, beside Daro'h.

After several long and wearisome days, the company reached the blackened ruin of Mijistra. When the Prime Designate looked out at the expanse of shattered buildings and flattened rubble, the collective wave of despair from his people nearly caused him to waver. Those who had come with him could not see beyond the charred remnants of what had once been the glory of their ancient empire.

And Daro'h knew that he himself had caused this destruction to happen. *I am responsible.* He could not stop staring. *It was the only way.*

Though he had witnessed the original impact, Chief Scribe Ko'sh was devastated to gaze upon the aftermath. His facial lobes shimmered in a storm of violent hues, and at first he could not summon words, despite his lifetime of telling tales. "It is all gone. Every scrap of our history—of our soul!"

Daro'h said in a grave voice, "No. *We* are not gone. If you are a rememberer, then *remember*. You have a greater responsibility than ever before. So long as we live, we can re-create our past glory. We must show the faeros that we are not defeated."

"But we *are* defeated!" Ko'sh cried.

Yazra'h struck the Chief Scribe across the face with a blow that knocked him to the ground. Ko'sh got to his knees, blinking, as her two Isix cats prowled around him, sensing prey.

Daro'h glowered at him. "I will not have the *Saga* say that we behaved as cowards, even in the face of great loss."

From across the blasted landscape, more refugees arrived from villages and camps. They had sensed the Prime Designate's call and followed him here, looking for answers. Daro'h intended to give them what they needed. Until his father returned, they were all *his* people. . . .

But when the storm of fireballs reappeared in the sky like an exploding globular cluster, he wondered if his followers were doomed after all. A rain of ellipsoidal fires streaked in smoldering paths overhead, thousands of fiery entities returning to Ildira along with faeros incarnate Rusa'h.

"Now they will annihilate us," Ko'sh moaned. "We are out in the open, unprotected."

Daro'h drew a deep breath, and the air felt hot in his lungs. He did not know how he could refute the Chief Scribe's prediction.

But it quickly became apparent that these faeros had not come to exterminate the population, but to make a stand. The fireballs appeared to be in retreat—from Solar Navy warliners! And Roamer ships that streaked after them, firing small white projectiles. Whenever an artillery shell struck the faeros, an explosion of cold, white steam engulfed and smothered it.

Ridek'h let out a shout; Yazra'h looked as if she wanted to spring into the air to join the fight. The Ildirans who had followed him to the wreckage of Mijistra cried out with joy and relief.

Daro'h made his voice loud and clear. "Adar Zan'nh has returned!" The strands of *thism* strengthened as he felt his father's nearness rejuvenating his spirit. "And the Mage-Imperator is with them."

Rod'h and his siblings gazed upward. "And Osira'h. And our mother."

Yazra'h shouted triumphantly at Chief Scribe Ko'sh, making him flinch. "We are *not* defeated!"

With a voice that held a wisdom far beyond his years, young Rod'h turned to Daro'h. "As Prime Designate, there is an important part of the battle you must wage here on the ground. Only you can do it—with us. Follow me."

147 ☀ SIRIX

To get out of the solar system, the black robot ships pushed their engines well beyond their design specifications. Even so, Sirix calculated that they weren't moving fast enough to outrun the two swarmships in close pursuit.

These new Klikiss had significantly advanced their technology from their race's previous incarnation. Their swarmships flew faster and could accelerate more dramatically; no doubt their armaments were improved as well.

But his black robots had made advances, too. The new framework battleships were far superior to the old Klikiss vessels, and he also had his stolen EDF ships. Sirix believed that his robots had a statistically significant chance of surviving against two swarmships, but only if he used sufficiently aggressive tactics.

The swarmships managed to close in on his fleeing group before they made it out of the solar system. Desperate to delay them, Sirix ran an assessment of the vessels accompanying him. Obviously, some would be destroyed, and he needed to choose. The slowest of the fifty-six craft was a battered Thunderhead weapons platform that had not been completely repaired. The platform lagged behind, and the swarmships were almost upon it.

Sirix decided to sacrifice it.

None of the original black robots were aboard the Thunderhead, only thirty-seven of the new robots released from the Hansa compy factories. Considering the circumstances,

Sirix decided the loss was acceptable, if it bought enough time for his comrades to escape.

Without remorse, he transmitted instructions to the Thunderhead, and the new black robots dutifully accepted their orders. The weapons platform slowed and turned about to target its jazers and projectile weapons toward the swarmships. "Destroy as many of the component ships as possible."

But the Thunderhead's jazer ports and projectile launchers remained dark and closed. The weapons platform hung motionless, completely vulnerable. Something was clearly wrong.

Alarm surged through Sirix's cybernetic mind. "Open fire." The new robots aboard did not respond.

Because of their frantic exodus, this particular Thunderhead was still under repair. Had its weapons been disabled? In a frantic staccato he repeated his order to fire, but before the robots aboard could obey, the swarmships were upon the faltering platform.

Bristling with a thousand bright needles, the two Klikiss vessels opened fire, and within moments the lagging Thunderhead exploded, spraying molten debris in all directions.

A complete failure. And now the black robots had lost time and any advantage they might have gained by the sacrifice. As the explosion's flare dissipated, Sirix commanded his remaining ships to fly faster.

The two swarmships suddenly disassembled themselves, and each spewed a heavy stream of component ships forward at impossible accelerations, like thick jets of particles. The flare of component vessels arced around to recoalesce as a third, smaller swarmship directly in front of Sirix's fleeing fleet. From behind, the two original swarmships began to open fire on the rearmost black robot ships, while the newly formed cluster shot at the lead vessels.

Two of the repaired EDF Mantas were destroyed; one of the new robot-design ships was disabled and reeling out of control.

Sirix would have to make his last stand here, at the fringes of the Earth's solar system. He continued to run calculations and reevaluate his plans. Very few options remained.

PD and QT stood at their weapons stations, ready to strike out against the enemy that Sirix had programmed them to hate. He was gratified that these two compies had not proved to be disappointments, as DD had.

"With our enhanced new weaponry, these ships are not demonstrably inferior to the Klikiss," PD pointed out. "Our odds of success are non-zero."

QT agreed. "If we attack them now, we have a small probability of victory. But we must attack."

Sirix had come to the same conclusion. Linked by instantaneous communication and programming, all his robots could command their ships to reverse course in an instant, a perfectly coordinated maneuver. A surprise turnabout—as surprising as his new weapons would be. And the sooner he did this, the less the Klikiss would expect it. He could at least cripple the pursuing swarmships. That was all he needed. He could still get away.

At his command, Sirix's group of ships fanned out, dispersing widely to render themselves more difficult targets. Next, in a coordinated effort, they all wheeled around to turn their weaponry upon the swarmships from every angle. If his robots all opened fire at once, with perfect targeting accuracy, the Klikiss would suffer heavy damage.

Before the surprised swarmships could react, Sirix instructed all his gunners to open fire. From their consoles beside him, PD and QT sent rapid bursts of enhanced jazers into the nearest swarmship.

But none of the other robots shot their weapons.

Sirix sent the command again. "Destroy the Klikiss. Open fire." Precious seconds were ticking away.

Aboard his ship, every one of the newly manufactured black robots froze in position. None of them lifted an articulated claw to activate the weapons controls directly in front of them.

The robot vessels remained silent. No shots were fired.

A few of his original comrades sent frantic signals, reporting the same fault on their ships.

Sirix swiftly noted the commonality: All of the Hansa-manufactured robots had failed, and all at the same time. Some programming snag had shut them down.

Without hesitation, the swarmships began to shoot at them from all sides.

As multiple explosions struck the hull of his Manta, he sent an urgent signal burst. "This is a priority override. Delete any programming that has hindered your obedience. Find and remove any corrupted command strings."

He received no response. All of the most sophisticated instructions he summoned from his central programming went ignored. This crippling shutdown went deep into the core of the new robots' operating systems.

"There seems to be a malfunction," QT said.

"Perhaps the Hansa installed defective programming before they released the new robots to us," PD suggested.

It was not possible. Sirix had thoroughly checked every single newly manufactured robot emerging from the fabrication lines. His comrades had performed detailed quality-control checks. He could not comprehend how the humans could possibly have understood Klikiss programming well enough to accomplish something of this magnitude.

And yet the robots themselves had given them all the tools they needed. They had offered the Hansa scientists modules to duplicate for their Soldier compies. The humans could not be sufficiently sophisticated to understand the subtleties and introduce hidden programming bombs. *They could not be!*

Yet all of his new robots had shut down as soon as he ordered them to open fire.

At his weapons console, QT did not pause in his constant firing. "The timing of this failure is very inconvenient."

Scattered, pathetic bursts of jazer fire came from his other ships, where a few of the original black robots had seized the weapons controls. But the smattering of blasts was utterly inadequate.

The three globular swarmships broke apart into a large, dispersed cloud of cumulatively deadly component vessels. They turned on the robot ships.

Sirix frantically tried to find some way to escape, but he could discern no viable alternatives.

On his Manta's bridge, one of the new black robots lifted its geometric head. Its red optical sensors dimmed, and re-corded words emerged from its speaker in the voice of Chair-man Basil Wenceslas. His tone sounded amused.

"Sirix, I was never the fool you took me for. These new robots were manufactured with an Achilles' heel. I had my cybernetics engineers install a shutdown switch in the core programming that would activate the moment you ordered them to take aggressive action. You cannot delete or override it. Your new robots are now completely useless to you." Sirix could hear the deep satisfaction in the Chairman's voice. "My only regret is that I could not be there myself to see the effects of my revenge."

When the recording ended, Sirix understood what it was to be betrayed, exactly as he himself had betrayed the humans and the original Klikiss race.

The dispersed swarmships began to open fire, and his own vessels could not withstand the barrage from thousands of components.

In the face of imminent destruction, Sirix took scant satisfaction from knowing that his own final plan would cripple the Hansa. Chairman Wenceslas was not the only one who had schemed to take his enemy/ally unawares.

The booby-trapped explosives his robots had planted in the repaired EDF battleships were tied to a "dead man" switch inside himself. In the event of Sirix's destruction, those bombs would all be triggered. It was cold comfort, though. Either way, he and his robotic comrades would be destroyed.

Though PD, QT, and a few of the original robots remained at their weapons consoles, the Klikiss continued to blast the robot vessels. They did not cease firing until nothing remained but shrapnel and stardust.

Frozen in place over Earth, nothing moved—not the EDF vessels, not the Confederation ships, not the nine remaining Klikiss swarmships. The other two swarmships had hunted down the escaping black robot fleet, and flashes of distant weapons discharges indicated an intense space battle occurring somewhere far above the ecliptic.

Though announcements about Peter reclaiming the Whisper Palace had been widely broadcast, no one had heard a word from Chairman Wenceslas inside the main swarmship; no one could guess what the breedex had done to him. In addition, Robb's father, in command of the EDF ships, had refused to acknowledge the King's return to power.

Right now, even though they all faced the swarmships, the *Goliath* and more than a hundred EDF military vessels could just as easily point their weapons toward the Confederation fleet. Robb couldn't be sure his father wouldn't do that if the Chairman gave him a direct order. But the Chairman was no longer around.

Rising from the Palace District, Admiral Willis's warliner raced up toward the human ships that hovered in two distinct defensive lines against the Klikiss. Her weapons were ready to fire, pointed at the swarmships charging in like the cavalry.

One of the EDF ships suddenly exploded. The eruption took everyone by surprise. Flames and shrapnel hurtled outward in an expanding, roiling ball where the Manta had been.

Robb yelped. "Who opened fire?"

Like a chain reaction, a second Manta erupted in flames, its fuel tanks bursting. A Thunderhead went next, then one of the two newly repaired Juggernauts, the pride of the re-constituted fleet.

Taking his own initiative, the *Jupiter*'s weapons officer shouted, "Targeting main swarmship! They're firing on us—"

"Don't shoot!" Robb hadn't seen the Klikiss clusters initiate any action at all.

"We have to help them!" Estarra cried.

Sarein looked dismayed. "But I don't see any weapons fire."

Another Manta exploded. The comm channels were filled with frantic, angry chatter. In a tumultuous reaction, the EDF battle group scrambled, powering their engines up, pulling their vessels into a defensive formation, ready to open fire.

Robb jumped to his feet, letting the command chair spin behind him. "Sound General Quarters—all alarms! Everybody prepare for attack from *any* direction. Dammit, what's causing those explosions?"

Another Manta cruiser broke apart in a gush of flames. The succession of explosions continued all along the EDF line. Admiral Willis veered her own ship away from the debris.

General Conrad Brindle's face appeared on the communication screen, yelling at Robb. "What the *hell* have you done?"

Robb frantically searched for the comm button on the

Jupiter's command chair. Even before he opened a response channel, he was already yelling, "It's not us! We didn't do it!"

"You have attacked the Earth Defense Forces. With our backs turned! We trusted you, but Chairman Wenceslas warned me—"

He cut his father off. "I never gave the order. Check your readouts—we're *not* firing."

Admiral Willis bellowed from the bridge of her Manta. "Mr. Brindle, you'd better have a damned good explanation for this." Robb couldn't tell if she was referring to him, or to his father.

Two disabled EDF battleships careened into each other. Explosions burst the hulls and spewed atmosphere. Flames spat through the breaches and ignited fuel vapor in empty space. Four more EDF ships mysteriously exploded. The rest of the ships had no place to run.

After a few seconds he realized that only EDF ships were suffering, not a single Confederation vessel.

It didn't make any sense. Robb shouted, "I need confirmation! Make absolutely sure none of our ships have opened fire. Were any Confederation jazers or projectiles launched?" He was positive none of his ships would have initiated a strike on the EDF vessels—especially with the Klikiss looming over Earth.

Everyone on the *Jupiter*'s bridge ran from station to station, calling up data, yelling at one another. Estarra was staring in disbelief at the burning wrecks that drifted away from the defensive line.

The EDF was in ruins. Ships continued to spontaneously explode. Twenty of them, then thirty, then more.

"Every single target was an EDF ship," the weapons officer said. "Fifty-three destroyed so far."

Sarein cocked her head to the side. "Could this be sabotage? Could someone have planted explosives aboard?"

"Confirmed," said the tactical specialist. "The detonations are not the result of weapons fire."

More ships exploded in a chain reaction. Seventy ships. Eighty-seven. Ninety-two. Escape pods shot like dust motes out into space, but very few soldiers had managed to escape.

"All those people," Estarra said. "How can we stop it?"

Though the *Goliath* was unharmed, it could still explode at any moment. The EDF Juggernaut spun and charged toward the *Jupiter,* its jazer banks powering up.

"The *Goliath* is coming for us!" the navigator warned.

"Get me a communication link back to my father. I need to talk with him—now!"

Estarra took a place at his side in a show of strength. "I can speak on behalf of the Confederation."

"*If* he'll listen! The Hansa's been telling him to distrust us for months, and now he must think all that paranoia was warranted."

"Channel confirmed, sir."

"Dad, those detonations were *internal* to your ships! Your fleet must have been rigged." When no more explosions occurred for several minutes, Robb watched the remaining EDF ships warily. They all seemed to be ticking time bombs.

Finally, from a corner of the main screen, Conrad Brindle glowered at him. "Rigged, how? Almost a hundred ships, Robb—two-thirds of my fleet—with full crew complements! This is exactly the sort of thing the Chairman told us to watch out for." The older man's face conveyed the extent of the disaster more clearly than any sensor readout could. Distracted, he shouted into a different speaker, "All intact ships, prepare to retrieve escape pods."

Admiral Willis flew her Manta in beside the Juggernaut, jumping into the conversation. "Check your records, General. I'll bet my last paycheck that every one of those ships was repaired by the black robots."

"I give you my word, Dad—it wasn't us!"

Estarra spoke up. "Please, General, let us help you pick up the survivors."

Robb could see that his father held his hands on the firing controls of his weapons. Finally, after a long, tense moment, Conrad's shoulders drooped and he nodded. "We could use the help." He called out to his tactical officer, "Review the records on those ships. Get to the bottom of this!" The connection cut off.

"You heard the Queen," Robb said to his helmsman. "Let's go pick up some escape pods."

On the main viewscreen, throughout all the fuss, the swarmships hung motionless. They displayed no reaction whatsoever.

Llaro was a tomb.

With the hard dry ground crunching under her feet, Tasia trudged through the ruins, looking for any signs of life. All the insect hive structures, tunnels, and expanded towers were empty and silent.

Tasia sniffed the air. "Right now, I'm more interested in answers than in the Klikiss themselves. Maybe they vanished again, just like they did thousands of years ago. I just want to make sure they're *gone*."

KR and GU followed close on Kotto's heels, recording data with their optical sensors. DD marched along with clear enthusiasm. "If we find Margaret Colicos, she will explain what happened here."

"DD, you were with the Klikiss for a long while. Can you make a guess?" Orli said.

The Friendly compy paused to reassess the overrun former colony. "It is possible that the breedex dispatched its warriors through the transportals to attack or consolidate other subhives. Maybe they are no longer here because they are . . . elsewhere."

Tasia sighed. "Then we'll have to go elsewhere to look for them. We've got to test that Siren." She glanced at Kotto. "What does your Guiding Star say?"

"I generally follow my own calculations instead of my Guiding Star. My mother never could understand that."

"Not really an answer to my question, Kotto."

Looking concerned, Mr. Steinman said, "Before we go looking for those bugs, I need to know one thing. If your gadget works, it'll *work,* right? Immediately? We find the bugs, we zap them, and we'll know within seconds?"

Kotto pondered for a moment. "In theory, the transmission of harmonic melodies should impose almost instant paralysis on the Klikiss—maybe even initiating hibernation."

"And if it doesn't work, we'll figure that quick enough, too," Steinman said. "But first we've got to find some bugs to use as guinea pigs."

"All right, then, here's my idea," Tasia said. "If the Klikiss went to some other planet, we have to track them down. We can use the transportal. First, we disconnect the Siren from our ship and use antigrav handles to carry it." She glanced at the tall transportal structure the Klikiss had erected in the middle of the Llaro hive. "Then we pick coordinate tiles and start shopping for planets. As soon as we find a bunch of Klikiss, we give them an earful of your Siren."

DD brightened. "I know of many viable Klikiss centers. I can suggest alternative worlds where the breedex might have gone."

Tasia nodded. "All of you compies, help us move the equipment; then we'll start our bug hunt."

After DD had compiled a list of target planets, he was obviously disappointed when the first two coordinate tiles opened only to silent, dusty planets similarly abandoned by the Klikiss. He seemed discouraged.

The third time, however, as soon as the transportal wall cleared and they stepped through, Tasia found herself facing hundreds of Klikiss diggers, excreters, and constructors expanding a vast insect metropolis. The creatures turned toward them, raising claws, chittering interrogatories.

"Bingo!" Tasia cried. "Serenade them, Kotto."

The eager engineer activated the Siren, and Tasia instinctively covered her ears, though Kotto had given them each a set of noise-canceling plugs. Originally, he had been puzzled by this request, since the Siren's blast should have no effect on humans, until Tasia pointed out that it would still be *loud*.

A warbling sonic thunderstorm belched out of the device. The signal didn't sound like a melody by any definition Tasia knew, and fully half of the frequencies were beyond the range of human hearing. Even with earplugs, the sonic bombardment was bone-shaking.

Steinman winced, backing away, while Orli pressed her hands flat against her ears. The three compies just stood under the noisy barrage, listening and analyzing. Kotto didn't seem bothered by the noise at all.

The Klikiss, though, were mesmerized. They paused, seemingly fascinated. All of the sub-breeds turned their armored heads toward the transportal in a perfectly synchronized motion, directing their faceted eyes at the droning sound. Then, with a simultaneous dissonant squeak, the bugs froze, like short-circuited robots.

Kotto stared. "I believe it worked."

Steinman, who seemed to have read Kotto's lips, yelled, "Then shut that damn thing off! It's pounding right through my eardrums."

Kotto shut down the device, and the subsequent silence was like a void in the air. The Klikiss did not move.

"Are they dead?" Tasia asked.

"I believe the signal has forced them into their hibernation mode," DD said.

"Good enough for me," Orli said.

Steinman looked at the immobilized insect bodies. "That's damned impressive."

"Judging by their bodily configurations, these subbreeds appear to have been members of a subhive different from the Llaro Klikiss," DD said. "They might be part of a larger consolidated hive mind, or perhaps a tenuously connected group of . . . leftovers."

Tasia grabbed the antigrav handles and hauled the bulky Siren back through the transportal wall to empty Llaro. "Definitely a successful test. Now we can get down to business." As soon as they had all returned, the trapezoidal frame shimmered back to solid rock. She turned to DD. "Give us some more possible coordinate tiles. I plan to keep hitting the bugs until we knock out whatever's left of all the subhives."

150 ☀ CHAIRMAN BASIL WENCESLAS

In the center of the alien swarmship, the breedex spoke in a shuddery voice that did not sound at all like the cool and collected Davlin Lotze. *"You were not lying, Basil Wenceslas."* The voice carried an odd and annoying note of surprise. *"The black robots are destroyed."*

"Then you saw the trap I planted for Sirix," Basil exclaimed, unable to conceal his joy and relief. "A fatal defect. I caused it. All the new robots shut down as soon as they tried to open fire."

"The black robots are destroyed," the breedex said again, finally sounding satisfied. *"Every one of them. At last."*

Margaret Colicos looked strangely at him. "Sirix killed my Louis. I am glad he's gone." Beside her, Anton put his hand over hers.

Basil ignored them, focused only on the seething hive mind. "I helped you. *I* made the black robots vulnerable so the Klikiss could wipe them out. I set the wheels in motion long before you arrived." With both Sarein and Cain stabbing him in the back, Admirals Pike and San Luis deserting him, and Peter's rebellion, Basil found himself grasping at straws. But the Klikiss were the biggest prize of all. Given the proper incentive, maybe the One Breedex could overwhelm all of the Hansa's other enemies. "You owe the Hansa due consideration. We're partners. You have no reason to harm us. You need me."

But the hive mind no longer showed any vestige of Davlin Lotze. In fact, it seemed more Klikiss than ever, as if thrown into bloodlust by crushing the last robots. He had thought that might be the end of Klikiss aggression, but now the creatures were ready to move on Earth.

Margaret and Anton looked very uneasy. The domates and warrior insects standing guard outside the central chamber shifted their serrated limbs and edged closer, poised to kill the hostages.

Suddenly, though, the warriors jittered and froze, as if they had all been stunned at once. The shapeless breedex mass quivered and cringed, and the simulated face reappeared. *"What is happening? Klikiss . . . paralyzed . . . shutting down . . ."* The artificial face slumped into millions of writhing components, but the voice continued. *"Subhive remnants . . . one after another. Too many losses from my mind . . ."*

The breedex mound writhed through a series of configurations — faces of other human colonists, random Klikiss heads, and then nothing more than a soupy, staticky mass. *"Losing segments of my mind. Treachery! Destroy— "*

Basil didn't know what was happening; apparently, neither did Margaret Colicos. She spoke in a crisp voice. "What trick is this, Mr. Chairman? A new EDF weapon?"

"I'd love to take the credit, Dr. Colicos, but I have no idea what's happening."

A shockwave rippled through all of the Klikiss warriors in the breedex chambers, and every insect nearby froze in place. One domate collapsed, falling in front of an arched doorway.

At the center of the chamber, the breedex became a quivering disconnected mass. Even the buried persona of Davlin did not respond.

Throughout the swarmship, and presumably all the other swarmships, the Klikiss had gone catatonic. If someone else—the Confederation?—had developed a weapon, Basil did not want to remain aboard the swarmship. With the monstrous creatures locked in place, he didn't dare waste this opportunity.

"We've got to get out of here while the Klikiss are incapacitated. This meeting is at an end." He felt hamstrung, not knowing how long the paralysis would last, and he could not guess how the erratic breedex would react if, or when, it regained consciousness. He did not want to be here when it did. "Run."

Neither Margaret nor Anton argued. They had seen the Davlin personality subsumed. Together, they hurried along the twisting organic corridors, trying to remember the way back to the shuttle. When they finally reached the landing chamber, they found Klikiss warriors standing around the diplomatic ship like nightmarish sculptures. Their armored forelimbs were raised, spiny head-crests tilted back as if ready for attack. They didn't move.

"Open!" he shouted to the pilot. "Open, dammit!" The hatch slid aside, and he bounded up the ramp.

"Mr. Chairman, you're alive!" the pilot cried.

"Obviously. Get the engines started." This strange species paralysis could end at any moment—or, if the Confederation was behind this, Peter could try to blow up the swarmship, and he'd certainly have no scruples about doing it while the Chairman was aboard.

With a lurch that threw the passengers off balance, the

shuttle lifted from the slick resin floor, and the pilot guided them away. They accelerated out of the mouthlike cavern and emerged from the core, passing through an atmosphere-containment field and heading toward the closely packed component ships that served as an indistinct external shell. But rather than forming a rigid barrier, the component ships now drifted aimlessly, spreading apart.

Although the small alien vessels provided an overall geometrical shape to the swarmship, they were not physically connected. Gaps between the listless component craft gave the pilot just enough room to squeak between them. Within moments, they were free and flying away from the alien vessel into blessedly open space.

Then Basil spotted the wreckage of his EDF ships. He took in the disaster at a glance: the debris, the dying fires, the twisted ruins of General Brindle's command. The carnage was appalling.

The Confederation battle group, however, was unharmed.

"Damn you, Peter," Basil yelled. "Damn you!"

W e just barely got away from the Klikiss on Llaro, and we scraped past the faeros on Jonah 12," Crim Tylar muttered. "Now look what you've gotten us into, Nikko."

"Yes. That's my plan."

Following the thousands of small tree-bubbles that swept like a deadly hailstorm toward Ildira, the *Aquarius* and the other water-bearer ships plunged into a bizarre battlefield: wental-encased treelings, mist-swathed Solar Navy warliners, and Confederation vessels from Golgen. Nikko felt the exuberance of the warrior wentals singing through the hull, the new determination that Jess and Cesca had poured into them.

Then the firestorm suddenly increased as blazing reinforcements belched out of the nearby suns. Even though a misty wental sheath protected the *Aquarius* from the faeros, he didn't think there was enough moisture to stop the sheer number of fireballs. But he flew into the fray, nevertheless.

His ship's hold still held a small reservoir of the energized water taken from Charybdis, and those wentals were restless, eager to join the battle. Some of them had formed themselves into icy projectiles, which Nikko's father and Caleb loaded into the ship's gunports.

As soon as they got close enough to the wild fireballs, Caleb launched the frozen artillery shells with great pleasure. While Confederation ships concentrated their attack close to Ildira, the water bearers and the wental-encased treelings

fought their own battle, heading off to stop the blazing reinforcements emerging from the suns. Caleb shot his projectiles, annihilating one faeros after another. Unfortunately, he
soon ran out of shells.

"Scored a hit every single time, but it doesn't look like I
made a dent," he said, exasperated. "Can't we make ice projectiles from the rest of the wental water in the hold?"

"If there's time. We're in the thick of things right now."

Like transparent pearls, the wental-encased treelings
streaked ahead to encounter the new wave of fireballs
emerging from the suns. Caught up in the flow, the *Aquarius*
was swept along with the bubbles like a leaf in a windstorm.
Nikko didn't know what the innocuous-looking globes intended to do. They looked so tiny compared to the faeros.
Nevertheless, he didn't want to underestimate them.

Closing in on a flaming ellipsoid, the nearest tree-
bubble expanded by orders of magnitude, inflating like a
huge balloon. Stretching its outer membranes, the water
sphere opened and turned *inside out*. In an instant, like a fish
gulping an insect, the bubble entirely englobed the fireball
in a filmy prison. From within the bubble, the treeling added
strength drawn from the worldforest—trapping the faeros.
Though the elemental flame struggled, caught between the
water and tree forces, it could not escape.

Before the numerous faeros could alter their courses,
hundreds of the small tree-bubbles expanded and swallowed
the fireballs, removing them from the battlefield.

"Well, look at that—they're containing the bastards,"
Crim said with a whoop.

The bubbles snared the unsuspecting faeros, scooping
them out of space. Within minutes, fully a quarter of the
freshly emerged ellipsoids had been captured within the thin

liquid walls. When a tree-bubble had encased a fiery entity, it hauled the squirming and helpless faeros back toward the nearest star.

More tiny tree-bubbles flitted back and forth, searching for fireballs to snap up. The flaming elementals withdrew, apparently in a panic, and the small pearly spheres pursued them.

Borne along with the ships of Nikko's fellow water bearers, the *Aquarius* raced into the turbulent flare zone around Ildira's primary star.

"Where do you think we're going, boy?" Caleb asked.

Nikko shrugged. "We're following them."

The first tree-bubbles dragged their captive flames down into the sun's photosphere. Without hesitation, they plunged into the roiling stellar sea, pulling the trapped faeros with them. One after another, the expanded bubbles dropped like stones into the star, sinking deep until they vanished in the plasma oceans.

His father watched with keen interest. "Looks good so far, but now what are they going to do?"

Nikko had a sense of the answer. "I think they'll hold the faeros inside the suns and seal the transgates. Those traps will keep the faeros within their stars, just like they bottled the hydrogues inside their planets."

"I wish they'd just snuff out the damned things," Caleb muttered.

Crim Tylar still didn't understand. "Don't the faeros *like* living in the suns?"

Nikko had only a tenuous grasp of what the wentals really wanted. "The wentals and the verdani have enough power to imprison them there. They *could* snuff them, but they need to achieve balance, not destruction. The wen-

tals and the verdani have to neutralize them, not eliminate
them."

Hundreds more tree-bubbles submerged themselves
and their captives in the incandescent layers of the bloated
sun. Somewhere deep inside, the elementals reached a point
where they could seal the transgate in the stellar core, permanently cutting off the flow of emerging faeros.

As the raging fireballs around the star grew more desperate, the wentals inside the *Aquarius*'s hold seemed ready
to pry their way out through the hull plates. Nikko flew directly toward the firestorm.

"What are you doing?" Caleb yelped.

"Can't you feel it?" Nikko hit the cargo doors and released all the wental water he carried. With an exuberant
leap, the spray of elemental liquid spread out in a shimmering curtain. Before the faeros could dodge around the curtain, a second wave of tree-bubbles converged on them from
behind, capturing fireballs before they could join the battle
at Ildira.

"Now, that's satisfying," Nikko said through a wash of
adrenaline. Behind him, he saw many of his fellow water
bearers doing the same. The innocuous-looking tree-bubbles
continued to engulf and remove the faeros. The new synthesis of verdani and wental proved stronger than the flaming
elementals.

"I think we can call it a good day's work," Crim said.
"And let's get the hell out of here."

A dar Zan'nh, take me down to Mijistra—whatever is left of it," said Mage-Imperator Jora'h. "I need to see the city with my own eyes."

Though apprehensive, the Adar was ready to face the disaster he had left behind. He and Osira'h had rushed away from the faeros without ever witnessing the carnage of the impact. "Yes, Liege."

Osira'h closed her eyes, already able to feel her siblings down there with Prime Designate Daro'h. She sensed how she, Rod'h, and the others could help the Mage-Imperator vanquish Rusa'h, and she was ready for it. But this would be far worse than facing the hydrogues again at Golgen. She opened her eyes, stepped forward to stand between her parents, and stared at the images of destruction on the viewscreen.

As her father and Adar Zan'nh absorbed the magnitude of what had happened here, Osira'h could feel a wave of their dismay rush through the *thism*, strong enough to produce a stab of physical pain. Buildings had been flattened for kilometers: towers, museums, political buildings, warehouses, and habitation complexes—all collapsed and burned. The Prism Palace and its perfect elliptical hill had been ground zero for the immense crash; the grand structure, the hill, the seven symmetrical streams—everything was simply *gone*.

"A part of me has died," said Jora'h as he gazed in disbelief.

"A part, yes. But not all." Nira wept to see the holocaust, but she clasped his arm. "We will save the rest."

Osira'h spoke up. "We need to descend to the surface. They are all down there waiting for us." She drew a deep breath. "I can do more against the faeros incarnate if I am with my brothers and sisters. Together, we can tap into a kind of strength that even the wentals cannot use."

Though the mist-swathed ships and the frozen projectiles had decimated the faeros, the danger was not over yet. Great numbers of fireballs continued to fly in all directions; vengeful and capricious, they struck wherever they could. The battle screens in the warliner's command nucleus showed the constant clashes all around Ildira.

Nira considered the images. "If Osira'h says it is what we must do, then I agree. After all, she was right about the hydrogues on Golgen." She held up the treeling she had carried with her. "And now we have the verdani to help."

"Descend, then," said the Mage-Imperator. "Much of our battle is yet to come. We will all fight against Rusa'h."

Flanked by a dozen intact warliners, the flagship descended into the atmosphere, flying toward the site of the capital city. Leaving Zan'nh in the command nucleus, Jora'h led Nira and Osira'h to the warliner's docking bay, where they boarded a ready cutter. Piloted by one of the soldier kithmen, the small ship passed directly through the warliner's hazy cocoon and fought its way down through the thermal turbulence in the air.

On the way down, her father stared at the wrecked capital city, unable to protect the morale of his people by dampening the shock he experienced. Osira'h could also feel the lingering pain that resonated from all the Ildirans who had survived down below, though she sensed her half-breed

brothers and sisters, along with Prime Designate Daro'h, trying to bolster the people. She directed the pilot to where tiny
figures stood at the edge of the still-smoking ruins.

As soon as the cutter landed and the hatch opened,
Osira'h bounded out. The air burned her lungs; the whirl
of fiery elementals overhead seemed to singe the very atmosphere. Grasses, bushes, and any remaining combustible
wreckage had begun to smoke.

Prime Designate Daro'h and Yazra'h ran forward, barely
able to believe that the Mage-Imperator had returned. When
Osira'h's brothers and sisters came to her, she grasped their
hands and formed a mental circuit. Preparing herself, she
retreated into her mind, then extended her thoughts outward,
both to her father and to her siblings. She had to bind them
all together. Tight . . . strong.

The faeros incarnate was out there, a cauldron of fiery
hatred, a nexus for the revived elementals. Osira'h could find
him, too, and force him to come.

She squeezed the hands of Rod'h on one side and Gale'nh
on the other. Her two sisters completed the ring. "Like we
did before," she said. "Form a barrier that's stronger than
fire, stronger than *thism*." As they worked, the air acquired
an impermeability that stopped some of the worst heat. The
children concentrated on the intangible connections that tied
the whole race together. "Reach out and strengthen the soul-
threads. Find the other Ildirans—all of them. Rusa'h has
burned his own paths. Now it is time for us to undo them and
weave our shield."

Using their exotic bridging abilities, Osira'h and her
brothers and sisters isolated and *cut off* the connecting chains
through which the faeros had entangled the soulfires they
had stolen. The fiery elementals had traveled along those

scorched pathways when they had ignited the *thism* to consume Ildiran souls. Now the five children erected roadblocks along those blackened lines. They severed intersections and sealed off pathways by which the flaming elementals could retreat, starving them of the soul energy on which they fed. She squeezed her eyes tightly shut, blocking out the world around them so she could hone her concentration.

But then Osira'h became aware of shouts nearby, cries of terror. The heat in the air increased to an unbearable level, penetrating their tenuous shield until she could feel her skin sizzling. A golden-orange light flared in front of her face, making her reel backward as a huge, angry fireball descended before them. Larger than any of the other faeros, it hovered close, a swollen, roaring knot of flames.

Osira'h sensed the seething fury even before she saw the incandescent manlike figure inside. She held fast to her siblings, refusing to break contact.

Rusa'h had answered their call.

153 ☀ CHAIRMAN BASIL WENCESLAS

The shuttle pulled away from the still-frozen Klikiss swarmships, passing through the wreckage of the Earth Defense Forces and the maddeningly intact Confederation ships. Appalled, Basil worked his jaw but was unable to find words. He could guess exactly what must have happened—a treacherous ambush. At least the *Goliath* seemed intact.

Ignoring the pilot, he took charge of the comm console and opened a direct channel to the EDF flagship Juggernaut. "General Brindle, what the hell happened? Why aren't you firing on the Confederation warships?"

The reply took longer than he expected, due to the chaos and confusion that still reigned aboard the EDF ships. Brindle sounded distracted. "Our ships were sabotaged, sir, most likely by the Klikiss robots. They must have booby-trapped our ships when they repaired them. We have ascertained that it was not in any way connected to the Confederation ships."

Basil knew Sirix was capable of doing such a thing, and in a way he was disappointed that he couldn't blame Peter for the disaster. Regardless, he felt satisfied to have caused the destruction of all the black robots . . . even if the breedex did not seem grateful for the assistance. Enemies everywhere.

Basil studied the motionless alien swarmship, considering what the Klikiss hive mind would do when it broke free of its mysterious paralysis. He might never have another chance like this. "General Brindle, are your weapons still functional?"

"Yes, sir. The *Goliath* has full armaments, and nineteen other ships remain undamaged."

"Good. The hive mind is aboard the main swarmship. Destroy it, and you destroy the entire Klikiss threat. Let's take care of this right now. Open fire with everything you have."

The General hesitated. "*Initiate* hostilities against the Klikiss? Sir, two-thirds of my fleet is gone!"

Basil bridled. "Right now the breedex is crippled, and the insects can't defend themselves. They're not going to shoot back! If those unharmed Confederation ships have any balls, they'll join the fight beside us. It's what Peter always promises to do."

"Sir, in your absence King Peter has reclaimed the Whisper Palace. The people on Earth are . . . celebrating."

Basil felt as if an airlock had suddenly popped and depressurized the shuttle's cabin. And was General Brindle pleased to deliver this news? Basil felt a rage swelling within him. "General, I gave you an order. Open fire on the Klikiss swarmship. I'll deal with Peter myself."

Before the Juggernaut could launch its first volley, though, a transmission spread like a bombarding wave across all channels, as pervasive and overpowering as the first Klikiss broadcast that had demanded his presence. The volume was thunderous through the cockpit speakers, and this time it actually sounded like Davlin Lotze—his voice, his personality!

"*Chairman Wenceslas, I do not understand this*

weapon you used against us, but I am impressed. Dozens of my separate subhives have been incapacitated. Only a few remain functional." A harsh undertone filled the speakers during a long pause before the breedex continued. *"Many parts of my hive mind are now . . . offline. Klikiss parts. Therefore, I was able to reassert my influence."*

Margaret Colicos pushed her way into the cockpit. "Davlin—you've got to stop the Klikiss advance. The One Breedex wants to exterminate humanity."

"Ah, Margaret. Many subhive remnants are stunned, and now my own mind controls them all. The Klikiss parts of the breedex are . . . safely locked away now." Basil could clearly hear nuances of wry humor in the response. *"I trust you'll find my solution acceptable. Observe."*

The swarmship began to come alive again, more ominous than ever. The components shifted and flickered. The once-paralyzed insect warriors were reawakening aboard the gigantic conglomeration vessels.

The Davlin-breedex continued. *"But you are not to be trusted, Mr. Chairman. I heard you give the order to destroy us while we were paralyzed. You are a danger to us. You have proved regrettably faithful to all of my expectations and memories of you."*

Basil was alarmed. "Remember, I booby-trapped the black robots. I betrayed Sirix—destroyed them for you!"

"It is not in your nature to be altruistic. No, you would have allowed the robots to fight us. Afterward, if any robots survived, you would have used the kill switch to wipe them out anyway, neatly taking care of both sides."

Basil froze. Davlin was right, of course.

During the transmissions, the nine separate and enormous swarmships looming over Earth re-formed into a single incredible mass—shifting, fusing, and coalescing into one conglomerate sphere the size of a small moon. The other two swarmships that had pursued the black robots also returned and joined the main mass. Basil had never seen a single artificial unit so huge, with so much potential for destruction.

The pilot looked at him In shock, as if sure the swarmships would open fire on them at any second.

"You did exactly as I expected of you, Mr. Chairman." The Davlin-breedex fell silent, and as Basil stared in awe at the inconceivably powerful conglomerate ship, he could think of no way to defend himself or justify his actions. The giant swarmship sent one last transmission. *"You are more like the Klikiss than you know."*

To Basil's astonishment, the enormous vessel did not fire, did not attack the EDF battle group. Rather, the conglomerate unit hovered in place ominously for a long moment, then began to withdraw from Earth orbit, from the scattered and ruined EDF ships, and past the uneasy Confederation defensive line.

Basil was stunned into silence.

Margaret smiled. "It seems Davlin found a way to perform one last service for humanity—by saving us."

Anton breathed, "Thank you, Davlin."

The flickering, shifting vessel hauled itself out to the edge of the system. Basil watched it go, feeling simultaneously giddy with relief and defeated. Like a swollen, swirling cloud of angry wasps, the last of the Klikiss headed out to open space. Gone . . . At last something was going right.

A substantial part of him, though, wished General Brindle had just blown all the bugs into atoms. . . .

A priority message came over the shuttle's comm system, using overrides that only a handful of people knew. *Deputy Cain*. Basil gritted his teeth . . . another traitor.

Cain's pale face was bland, showing no emotion. "Mr. Chairman, I am glad to learn you're safe and alive—and very pleased to see the Klikiss swarmships withdraw. Thank you for your efforts."

"You've got a lot to answer for, Cain. Why are you calling me?"

The deputy smiled faintly. "King Peter requests your presence at the Whisper Palace to ensure an orderly transition of power. Please come as soon as possible."

154 ☀ MAGE-IMPERATOR JORA'H

P arting the flame curtains, Rusa'h emerged from his fireball to face them. His flesh was molten, his hair twisted like thick smoke, his eyes novas in his face. The faeros incarnate looked both furious and pleased to be standing before Jora'h. "At last I can save our entire race."

The Mage-Imperator merely stared at his brother. "You will do no more damage to the Ildiran people."

Rusa'h looked almost saddened, paternal. "You weakened the *thism* and nearly destroyed our Empire. I will take the strongest Ildirans to the Lightsource and save them with my faeros alliance."

Jora'h managed to take a step forward. "Save them?" Although the heat in the air was incredible, he could feel the half-breed children blocking much of it. "Whole refugee camps incinerated by the faeros? Ships full of Ildirans trying to evacuate blown out of the skies? Countless kithmen turned to ash when the faeros took over Mijistra? I see how you tried to 'save them.' Those were *your people*, Rusa'h. *You* were supposed to protect them." Jora'h jabbed an accusing finger at him. "Now they are all dead."

Though the burning man maintained his shape and size, Jora'h saw little of his soft and placid brother there, nothing of the person who had once reveled in his celebrations and pleasure mates on Hyrillka. Now transformed into an avatar of the fiery elementals, this man wanted only to *burn*. "No . . . I did this for them!"

In the sky above, fireballs came closer, ready to incinerate the Mage-Imperator and absorb his soulfire.

"The faeros have corrupted you, Rusa'h."

Osira'h reached out to take her father's hand. He felt her electric touch, armored with an invisible strength that she drew from her unique connection to Ildiran *thism*.

Nira held on to her treeling, hunched over to protect it from the searing heat that penetrated the faltering mental shield. With her other hand, Osira'h grasped her mother's arm, connected through her, through the treeling. Suddenly the worldforest network was also drawn into this surge, the verdani mind and powers.

To strengthen themselves, the children joined themselves to their mother's telink, just as the green priest Kolker had found a way to bind the worldforest network. They also found and touched the wentals, focused through the treelings that were enclosed in the living bubbles of water, further increasing their shield. Now Yazra'h and Prime Designate Daro'h united with Osira'h, her four siblings, Nira, and Jora'h in their connected circle. The Mage-Imperator felt a considerable strengthening of the protective barriers.

Designate Ridek'h also joined the group, strong and unafraid. The boy shouted against the crackling roar of fire, facing his nemesis again, "We will stand against the faeros and against you, Rusa'h. *I* am the Hyrillka Designate."

"And I am the true Mage-Imperator." Jora'h loomed larger as he faced off against the faeros incarnate. "The Ildiran people are *mine* to save—from you."

"You are wrong, brother." Responding to the faeros incarnate's command, hundreds of surviving faeros came down in a sea of suns, as if all the stars in the sky had exploded at once. Under that thermal assault, despite the mental barricades and the safety net of strengthened *thism*, even with all the exotic allies that had come to fight at Ildira, the Mage-Imperator felt himself burning.

"I will not surrender to you!" When Jora'h's eyes watered, the tears flashed into steam. The flames seemed infinite, pressing down from hundreds of fireballs overhead.

The Mage-Imperator clung to Osira'h and Nira, feeling their strength. At that instant, he understood: Like an unfathomable well in the depths of his spirit, the profound power of *thism* resided within him. *He* guided the Empire left to him by his father and a long succession of Mage-Imperators before him. And as the nexus of the Ildiran race, only *he* could draw upon the full power of *thism*.

In order to spark the creation of new faeros, the deluded

Rusa'h had allowed the fireballs to incinerate whole populations, stealing soulfires from Hyrillka, Dzelluria, other splinter colonies in the Horizon Cluster, Tal O'nh's septa of warliners, even Dobro where they had burned former Designate Udru'h. Jora'h could not allow it to continue.

Reaching out with his mind, he envisioned the lost populations, all the souls the faeros incarnate had taken—and *demanded* that their soulfires be freed. Though the bodies had long ago been turned to ash, the suffering Ildirans had been kept from reaching the Lightsource. Rusa'h had prevented them from escaping, but Jora'h would help them.

His mind reached into the soulfires held within the faeros clustering overhead and found the *thism* threads of each Ildiran they had taken. The fireballs flared and struggled, refusing to release their captives.

But Mage-Imperator Jora'h would not be denied. He tapped into the reservoir of power—the newly discovered facet of *thism* that was his alone to use, as the true Mage-Imperator—and simultaneously touched all Ildirans here and in every splinter colony, via every faint strand. Combining this control with the strength of the circle around him—Nira, her children, his own children, the verdani and wentals—he challenged the fireballs directly. And they could not hold on to the resistant, tormented voices within them.

The surviving faeros reeled even as they streaked down to protect Rusa'h in his battle. The Mage-Imperator looked up, his eyes dazzled by the waves of light and heat, and finally he succeeded in wresting the stolen souls from the blazing elementals.

Jora'h held the soul-threads in his mind, and to him it seemed as if the heart of the flames had been removed. With great caring, he guided the recovered souls higher, higher, until they reached the plane of the Lightsource. Jora'h released their soul-threads. And laughed in a burst of joy.

They were gone, free—leaving the newborn faeros weak and disconnected.

Elementally eviscerated, the new fireballs could not retain their integrity, and they sparkled off into bright, transient lights. The thunderheads of knotted fire overhead had broken up, scattering and fading.

The mad Designate let out a wordless roar, not of defeat but of defiance, and an invisible wind seemed to blast at him. Struggling against it, his face drawn into a grimace with the effort, he staggered two steps backward. The flames that comprised his body whipped and crackled. He clenched his glowing fists at his sides and raised them in the air.

And as he came toward Jora'h, the faeros incarnate obviously had nothing to lose.

155 ☀ KING PETER

The mysterious withdrawal of the Klikiss swarmships seemed nothing short of a miracle. And now the Chairman was on his way here.

Peter had never relished the power for its own sake, but the throne was his again—by right. The people of Earth trusted him, and he had worked hard to become the leader they needed. Now that he was back in the Whisper Palace, Peter felt he finally belonged there.

The people deserved better than Basil Wenceslas.

OX had returned from the communications center with Patrick and Zhett, pleased that Freedom's Sword was helping to spread the announcements about the changeover of power. The ever-swelling demonstrations had turned into celebrations, overwhelming any resistance. Most of the Hansa guards had quietly melted away from their posts, changing out of their uniforms before they could be targeted by the crowds.

No matter what he believed, Chairman Basil Wenceslas was no longer relevant to the government of humanity.

But there were still some holdouts. Peter tried to contact General Conrad Brindle, as did Admiral Willis and Robb Brindle, but the man refused to respond, refused to turn his loyalty from the EDF. The commander had always been skeptical of the Confederation, but now with most of his fleet destroyed by black robot sabotage, he had very few straws left to clutch.

The Teacher compy stood supportively beside the throne, and Deputy Cain waited with a very downcast Rory, who looked miserable despite Peter's assurances.

"We've got a lot of work to do," Peter said. "Call Admiral Willis and ask her to escort Queen Estarra to the Whisper Palace. Deputy Cain, I'd like you to work with Ambassador Sarein to effect the transfer of the Hansa government into the Confederation—you two have done well to get us this far. We've got to return to a steady course to reassure the people. I want to communicate that the worst is over."

Cain nodded. "I would be honored. It's time for a smooth transition."

"And bring Trade Minister Kett here. She'll enjoy being able to operate openly for a change. A lot of merchants will love to have open markets again."

OX baldly stated the largest problem they would face. "I suggest that you order Chairman Wenceslas immediately detained. It would be best to eliminate any potential confusion."

"The compy's right," Fitzpatrick said. "Even if he has no power, Wenceslas can be a pain in the ass."

Suddenly, the dozen soldiers Willis had left as Peter's personal guard raised their weapons at the doorway. Rory slumped down, as if trying to hide.

"I call for *your* arrest, Peter." Chairman Basil Wenceslas pushed his way past the guards and entered the throne room, accompanied by five ruffled-looking members of the cleanup crew, whom he had freed from the temporary holding room where Admiral Willis had kept them. Colonel Andez was among them, once again sporting a sidearm. "Colonel, take him into custody."

Andez, looking embarrassed at having been knocked out and disarmed, ordered her team forward. However, since she and her four companions were heavily outnumbered by the Confederation guards, Peter didn't know what she expected to accomplish. His soldiers were ready to shoot to protect him, but he motioned for them to hold their fire. There was no need.

The Chairman strode forward, blind to all the weapons raised against him, and Peter leaned forward on the throne, unperturbed. "Are these all the supporters you have left on Earth, Basil? Five people?"

Basil blithely refused to see. "My forces are preoccupied with the madness you initiated in the streets while I was saving humanity from the Klikiss. I've alerted all the security troops in the Whisper Palace. More guards are coming down the halls. We will take care of everything here and now."

Peter doubted the Chairman would find any support in the whole city, but Basil seemed convinced.

Acting on his own, Deputy Cain touched a security pad on the wall. Thick doors slammed down across the entrance arches with loud crashes of metal. Blast shields covered the small stained-glass windows, and heavy grates blocked access to the ventilation ducts. All weak areas, all vulnerable entry points were locked down. "I took the liberty of activating the security systems. The throne room is now secure."

Peter nodded. Even if the Chairman did manage to rout out any loyal followers, they were now locked outside. Andez and her few companions looked uneasily at the Chairman, perhaps wondering if he could remedy their weak position.

Basil directed his building, frustrated anger at Rory, but when the young man flinched, he turned away in disgust.

Patrick Fitzpatrick made a rude noise. "I'm sorry Admiral Willis didn't just blast your ship away. Isn't that your approved method of problem solving, after all?"

"Maureen Fitzpatrick was executed for intent to commit treason." Basil sounded dismissive, impatient.

"I can hear my grandmother's ghost laughing at you," Patrick snapped.

Finally, Basil skewered Deputy Cain with a glare, looking for someone to blame. "*You* allowed this to happen."

"More precisely, sir, I arranged it. You gave me no choice."

Peter did not budge from the ornate throne, looking

coolly at the Chairman. "Basil, you are relieved of your duties as Chairman, and now you will officially resign."

"I will do no such thing."

"*Once* you resign," Peter ignored the interruption, "the Terran Hanseatic League will be dissolved, and the Earth-based government will be included in the Confederation. Then we can begin the long process of repairing the damage you've done over the years."

Though Basil was furious, his expression remained carefully neutral. He turned to Andez. "Colonel, I instructed you to arrest Peter. Drag him down from the throne by force, if necessary. Throw all of these people into the lower prison levels, where they will await courts-martial. I'm not inclined to be merciful."

Unable to believe Basil's blatantly irrational orders, considering the position he was in, Willis's soldiers looked to Peter for guidance. "Hold!" he said. He could only hope that Andez and her guards weren't mad enough to open fire.

Andez gestured helplessly at the standoff, and the weapons pointed toward them. She blinked. "Exactly how . . . are we to do that, Mr. Chairman?"

From where he stood beside the throne, OX said, as if giving a lecture to a novice prince candidate, "Basil, the conclusion is inescapable. It is only logical to admit defeat." He added pointedly, "It would be the most efficient solution to this problem. As Chairman, you should appreciate that."

Peter rose from the throne. "There's nothing you can do. The whole population of Earth blames you, Basil, and you can't use me—or Rory—as a scapegoat anymore. You're done."

The Chairman seemed pathologically unable to grasp that he no longer controlled the situation. He ripped the small personal communicator from his waist and activated a direct line to his EDF ships. "General Brindle, this is a direct order! Access the guillotine codes for the ships Admiral Willis took from the EDF and shut down the Confederation's space navy. Hamstring them."

After only a brief hesitation, barely a second longer than could be accounted for by the transmission lag, the EDF commander grudgingly acknowledged.

Peter felt more disappointed than angry. "Basil, this is pointless. Even if the General does as you say—"

Basil stared directly at Peter as he continued speaking into the communicator. Now his smile seemed genuine. "And once those traitorous ships are helpless, General, bombard them with everything you have."

156 ☀ ROBB BRINDLE

Shizz, we're dead in space!" Robb pounded his fist on the arm of his command chair and barked to his bridge crew, "Report—give me options."

"It's our guillotine code, sir," said the helmsman, hammering at his console in frustration. "The EDF just triggered it. All Confederation ships have been nailed."

"But how?" Estarra asked.

Robb's muscles were tight with tension, and his head

was beginning to ache. "A shutdown system built into all EDF capital ships, and the commander has the codes."

"But these are Confederation ships now."

Robb groaned. "Our codes should have been changed with a complete wipe and refit when the Admiral brought her ships to the Osquivel rings, but there was no time."

"Bit of a tactical oversight, wasn't it?" Rlinda Kett asked.

"We got a little distracted by General Lanyan's attack," Robb said. "Since then, there hasn't been time to put our military ships in spacedock."

"Too late now," Sarein said. "What do we do?"

"We talk to General Brindle," Estarra said. "Convince him not to make this worse."

Robb shook his head, feeling incredibly weary. "You can argue logic all you want, but my father believes it's his duty to follow the Chairman."

Estarra pressed her lips together. "Well, I believe I *outrank* the Chairman."

"He doesn't accept the Confederation as a legitimate government," Robb said.

Estarra glanced at her sister. "Sarein, you're the Theron ambassador—that's a title he should recognize."

"And I'm his son," Robb added. "But that won't matter if the Chairman orders him to capture us."

Sarein let out a cold laugh. "Capture? Trust me, Basil has something harsher in mind for us."

Robb went to the comm station and tried to work the controls, to no avail. With the exception of life support, even the most basic systems were dead. "Doesn't matter. We can't transmit a message. We're bound and gagged."

Estarra's eyes flashed as she stared at the darkened

screen, as if willing it to display the threatening ships, the stars and planets. But it remained blank. The silence seemed more ominous than any overt threat.

Captain Kett came up beside the Queen, grinning.

"What is it?" Estarra asked. "If you have an idea—"

"That guillotine code may have shut down all of your fancy EDF systems, but it couldn't do a damned thing to the *Blind Faith*," she said. She looked at Robb. "I assume your launching bays have manual backup systems for opening the space doors? Good. BeBob and I can take you right in front of the *Goliath*, up close and personal. We'll get the message across."

Estarra smiled. "Then we'd better make it convincing."

157 ☀ JESS TAMBLYN

As Jess and Cesca raced down to the surface, the fiery elementals that gathered over the ruins of Mijistra seemed weak, desperate, disorganized. As their wental ship bulldozed through the scattering fireballs, they both could see through the flames to the flashing conflict on the ground, where the Mage-Imperator and a group of Ildirans faced a fiery man.

"Rusa'h is like us." Jess increased their speed. "We've got to stop him."

"No, *not* like us. The faeros burned away the soul of the person he once was," Cesca said. "The wentals in us may always set us apart from other humans, but we're still who we were inside."

Jess brought the water-globule ship down fast, like the first heavy drop before a drenching downpour. As the liquid bubble touched the ground near the embattled Ildirans, the surface tension dissolved, like a burst water balloon, and its wental contents flooded out. He and Cesca stepped away from the soupy mud at their feet.

The Mage-Imperator and his companions had begun to succumb to the battering heat. "You are cut off from the *thism*, Rusa'h," shouted the Mage-Imperator. "I will not allow your faeros to prey upon my people again."

In the sky, most of the fiery shapes had flown away, leaving Rusa'h alone. But he was not weak.

Jess and Cesca approached the faeros incarnate, their bodies covered with a glistening film of water, and Rusa'h sensed their power. When he turned, his body seemed to swell, and his face showed an incredible struggle taking place within him.

"This is my Empire!" Like a wildfire let loose, Rusa'h hurled gouts of flame from his hands.

Jess intercepted the inferno, deflecting it from the weary Ildirans. Cesca joined her power to his; they had to extinguish this spark that spread destructive fire, consuming ships and cities and planets and people. They had to control the flames and stop the faeros from burning all the worlds in the Spiral Arm.

Showing no restraint, Rusa'h unleashed his furious strength, making Jess and Cesca stagger backward. The hard ground around them began to melt.

Mist sprang from Jess's pores like sweat, creating a powerful living fog. Cesca raised her hands, and steam flashed against the barrage of fire. They both drew deeply from the wentals within them, struggling against the fierce onslaught, staggering a step backward. Seeing them falter, Rusa'h hurled even more fire at them.

The two pushed back, wrapping cool wental vapors like thick ropes around the faeros incarnate. Jess surrendered more and more of his inner reservoir of wental strength. The air burned around him, and he fought back until he was at the point of collapse, but he did not relent.

The Mage-Imperator and the linked Ildirans behind their shield drained away some power from the faeros incarnate, contributing to the fight.

Jora'h lashed out at his brother. "Come back to me, Rusa'h! No matter what you have done, I know an Ildiran heart still beats within you. If you truly want to save our people, save them *now*. Drive away the faeros before they consume you entirely."

"No!" When Rusa'h screamed, a gout of fire jetted from his mouth.

The sparkling fog grew so thick that Jess could barely see what he was fighting. Flashes of blinding orange and yellow battered the wentals, but he and Cesca kept pushing closer to the faeros incarnate. Their inner water elementals were exhausting themselves, depleting their energy to protect Jess and Cesca. He hoped they could last longer than the fires.

Unable to resist the added pressure, Rusa'h stumbled backward.

Jess refused to back off, even though he could feel the wentals using up all of their energy inside him. He began to feel light-headed, empty, as if every molecule of moisture were being wrung from his pores. To summon any last vestiges of strength, he made himself remember the faeros attack on Charybdis and its pristine seas full of reborn wentals. That holocaust would always be burned into his mind—the blasted oceans, the blackened reefs and undersea rocks. Nor could he forget how the faeros had attacked Golgen, had tried to destroy the Roamer skymines . . . had burned Theroc to consume the worldtrees . . . had killed Cesca's father and stranded his uncle on Jonah 12.

The wentals within his cells pulled together and threw themselves upon the burning man.

Unable to resist the extra push, Rusa'h staggered backward into the muddy pool from their wental ship—and the trap was sprung. Living water surged up from the ground and seized his legs. Rusa'h thrashed, hurling fire everywhere.

Before he could regain his balance, Jess and Cesca threw themselves upon the faeros incarnate, entwining him in smothering blankets of mist. Jess drained his inner reservoirs dry, spending the last of the wental power that had saved him from the hydrogues so long ago in one final surge. Beside him and connected to him, Cesca did the same.

The flames inside Rusa'h were finally quenched. Extinguished from within, the faeros incarnate collapsed.

Coughing and choking, barely able to breathe through the boiling clouds of steam, Jess and Cesca staggered away to drop to their knees near the Ildirans.

Nira set down her treeling and rushed to them. Before Jess could think to warn her away, the green priest touched him, held him. Jess automatically cringed as she helped him to his feet. He looked at the unharmed green priest in amazement. "I don't understand. My touch should have killed you."

Cesca stared at her hands in wonder and drew a breath. "Feel it, Jess. They're gone. The wentals are no longer inside!"

Jess realized that his own skin seemed exactly as it once had been. He had almost forgotten the sensation of being *normal*. "We must have burned them out—used them up." Jess turned around in amazement. "We're human again. And we survived!" Joy welled up within him, mingling with sadness and admiration for the water elementals that had sacrificed themselves.

"We defeated the faeros," Cesca said quietly. "That's what matters. That's what the wentals wanted." They looked up and saw the remaining fireballs flitting away aimlessly, to be scooped up and whisked away by several tree-bubbles that dragged them to the nearby suns.

Jess smiled, feeling immensely relieved.

They heard a sound nearby. Steam still rose, scattered by churning thermal currents in the air. When the hot mist finally cleared, they saw the former faeros incarnate on his knees, wholly defeated. The fiery elementals had been purged from his system, and now he huddled there naked and weak, a mere shadow of himself.

Sobbing, Rusa'h turned his face up to the Mage-Imperator.

158 ☀ DEPUTY CHAIRMAN ELDRED CAIN

By the sharklike expression on the Chairman's face, Cain could tell that all humanity had died within him. Basil Wenceslas, who had once been a smooth and talented leader, hard negotiator, and competent administrator, had tumbled headlong down a slippery slope.

OX stood beside the throne, his optical sensors flashing. "Chairman Wenceslas, I must point out that you have no legal basis whatsoever for this order. There is no precedent for your command."

Cain positioned himself at the stairs leading up to the throne dais, between the Chairman and the King. "Sir, I urge you to reconsider."

Basil ignored the compy and showed only contempt for his deputy. "You think I don't know how you and Sarein plotted against me, Cain, subverting my authority at every turn? I'm the only one with vision, the only one who can lead the human race where it needs to go. You are such a disappointment." He swept his gaze around the sealed room. "All of you — complete failures! Peter, Fitzpatrick — even you, Colonel Andez!"

General Brindle's response over the communicator interrupted his rant. "Guillotine codes are confirmed, sir. As you ordered." He sounded stiff and displeased. "The Confederation ships have been shut down, weapons and shields are inactive. Except for the Roamer vessels among them, all are dead in space." The man's voice wavered, distorted by static. "I fail to see, however, what you intend to accomplish here. I still need their help to retrieve the escape pods from my wrecked fleet."

Basil lifted the communicator again. "General Brindle, I issued an order for you to open fire on the Confederation ships. Have you destroyed the enemy fleet yet?"

Peter spoke loudly enough to cut through the Chairman's words. "General, this is your King. The Chairman has been deposed, and I command you not to listen to him. Queen Estarra is aboard the *Jupiter*."

"Actually," Brindle said dryly, "she is in a small trader ship directly off my bow and directly in my line of fire. She and Ambassador Sarein have made quite a compelling case for me to switch my allegiance to the Confederation."

Basil clutched the communicator and shouted so loudly that flecks of spittle flew out of his mouth. "Are you threatening a mutiny, General? Your entire lifetime of honorable service speaks against it. I gave you an order—"

Brindle's response overlapped the Chairman's words in the brief transmission lag. "I do not believe this attack is warranted. Circumstances have quite plainly changed."

"I didn't ask your opinion, General. Destroy the Confederation ships!"

The EDF commander's turmoil boiled up in his words. "I cannot open fire on a sovereign leader."

Basil blinked as if he had never expected the General to defy him. "Don't be ridiculous. The Confederation is not a legitimate government. They are a clear threat to the entire Hansa. Open fire!"

After a hesitation longer than the time lag required, Brindle replied, "I will not."

His eyes flared, and his voice was like acid. "Your wife currently serves on an EDF base. I have had her watched, and now I will order her to be taken into custody. I never dreamed I would have to use strong-arm tactics to get *you* to follow simple commands, General."

Conrad's voice was brittle. "And I never dreamed that a real leader would resort to taking innocent hostages or threatening loyal citizens. I have made a grave error in not realizing sooner that King Peter is my true commander-in-chief. I won't let you use Natalie as a pawn."

Basil turned as pale as curdled milk. He shouted, "If you do not do as you're told, I will order you and your bridge crew executed as mutineers!"

Only a crackle of static came from the communicator. The EDF commander had cut off the transmission.

Basil spun to Andez, whose four guards stood close together in the sealed room. They seemed deeply unsettled now that General Brindle had abandoned the Chairman. Several of them seemed ready to throw down their weapons.

Basil, somehow, didn't see it. "Colonel Andez, it is time to end this. I order Peter's execution. Shoot him down for usurping King Rory's throne."

"He can have the throne!" the boy cried.

"You shut your mouth!"

Foreseeing a threat to Peter, OX immediately placed himself in front of the throne, using his hard polymer-and-metal body as a barricade. "I cannot allow you to harm the King. My programming prevents it. You will have to shoot through me."

Andez's hand twitched, but she did not draw her firearm from its holster. Too many of Peter's guards pointed their weapons toward her; she and her handful of comrades were heavily outnumbered. "But, Mr. Chairman, even the EDF—"

Basil grabbed her small sidearm from the holster at her hip and stalked toward the throne four steps away, as if he and Peter were the only two people in the room. All of the guards swung their firearms toward him, though Peter had given them orders not to fire.

"Mr. Chairman, drop your weapon! Now!"

Basil completely ignored them, as if they were inconsequential.

Stationed at the base of the dais steps, Cain did not hesitate. As the Chairman strode dismissively past him, he drew the ceremonial dagger that Captain McCammon had so proudly worn. Swinging the knife in a smooth arc, he threw his weight into the blow.

The blade slammed into Chairman Wenceslas's back, piercing him below his left shoulder blade, slightly to one side of the spine. Cain drove the point between the ribs and directly into Basil's heart.

The Chairman stopped as if he had walked into a wall. Cain gave the knife an extra thrust.

Everyone froze in shock. Peter pushed away from his throne and sidestepped the guardian compy.

Deputy Cain held the dagger's hilt, keeping the Chairman upright for a paralyzed instant. Basil's hands twitched and he released his grip on the handgun, which dropped with a clatter to the throne room floor. His knees buckled, making him too heavy for the deputy to hold him up. Cain released the hilt, and the Chairman slid to the floor. Blood started to seep through the fabric of his expensive business suit.

Basil let out a long rattling sigh and rolled slightly so that his gray eyes met Cain's. One last breath gurgled from the Chairman's throat, as if he were trying mightily to utter some final expression of defiance, but he managed to find only one word before he died. "Disappointed . . ."

Cain looked coolly around the room, remembering how McCammon had bled across this very same floor. He spoke in a surprisingly loud voice.

"As deputy chairman, I hereby assume control of the Hansa." He withdrew the dagger from the Chairman's back, wiped the knife clean, flipped it over, and extended it hilt-first toward King Peter. "On behalf of the Confederation."

159 ☀ TASIA TAMBLYN

By the time Tasia and her companions got back to Earth and learned what had happened, the whole war was over — the Hansa and the Confederation, the black robots, the Ildiran Empire, the faeros, the wentals, the verdani. Everything. On their approach to Earth they intercepted numerous transmissions: Patrick Fitzpatrick's exposés, Confederation reports, and newsnet stories.

"Shizz, and we missed it!"

Hud Steinman made a sour face. "I can't complain about being left out of all that."

"We did our part," Orli assured Tasia. "And from the news stories, I'd say it had a pretty significant effect on how things turned out."

Kotto was still floating with excitement that his Siren had worked so well. Moving from world to world, they had found and completely knocked out ten of the separated sub-hives. That had been enough to topple the One Breedex.

Dodging the wreckage strewn like a metallic asteroid belt around the military ships in Earth orbit, Tasia flew toward the *Jupiter*.

"Admiral Willis," she transmitted to the Juggernaut. "Are you ready for some company? My team has very interesting news about the Klikiss . . . or what's left of them."

The responding voice did not belong to the Admiral, though. "You're always welcome aboard my ship, Tamblyn—even if you *were* off on a little joyride while the rest of us were saving the world."

"Joyride? Excuse me, *Commodore* Brindle, but we'd better compare notes before we decide whose accomplishments trump whose."

Robb laughed. "Come aboard the *Jupiter*. We'd love to hear about your exploits. Admiral Willis is on her way back here, too."

The reunion aboard the Juggernaut was a happy one. Kotto had never been on such a large EDF ship before, and he poked around the bridge, incessantly asking questions. Steinman wanted to find the crew's mess so he could have a meal that didn't come from self-heating packages, and Orli and DD went with him.

From the Whisper Palace, Deputy Cain had formally instructed General Brindle to cancel the guillotine-code commands and reinstate power and control to all the Confederation battleships. The EDF commander had been glad to comply. All the ships were now functional.

While King Peter remained at the Whisper Palace to prepare for the formal changeover of power, Admiral Willis headed back to her Juggernaut, resplendent in her dress uniform. Stepping onto the bridge and taking command again, Willis clapped both Tasia and Robb on the shoulder.

"Well, I sure am glad to be done with all this nonsense."

"The Spiral Arm's a big place, ma'am. I'm sure there's plenty of nonsense left."

Willis frowned. "Don't rain on my parade, Tamblyn."

When General Conrad Brindle's shuttle crossed over from the *Goliath,* the Confederation soldiers formally received him. "Some things should be done face-to-face," he had said, and Admiral Willis granted him permission to come aboard. Accompanied by an honor guard of ten (all of whom sported ceremonial sabres but no sidearms), Conrad wore his uniform immaculately.

Willis swiveled her command chair to face him as the General stepped out of the lift and saluted crisply. All of the bridge personnel remained hushed, wondering what the EDF's commander would say. She favored him with a kind smile. "A lot of water under the bridge, General."

He nodded stiffly. "Much of my fleet has been crippled or destroyed. A hundred ships lost to sabotage."

Tasia crossed her arms, not standing on ceremony. "Shizz, sir, we could get by with a lot smaller fleet if our ships stopped shooting at each other."

Conrad looked at her, then at Robb. "I've come to the same conclusion." He gave a half bow to Admiral Willis. "As commander of the Earth Defense Forces, I am here to issue our transfer of allegiance to the Confederation."

Tasia caught her breath. Willis blinked.

Conrad continued. "As a guarantee of our sincerity, I will volunteer the guillotine codes of all our ships." He withdrew a folded document from the pocket of his uniform, smoothed the creases by running them through his fingers, then extended the papers to Admiral Willis. "Here is my formal surrender of authority. You are now in command of the *Goliath* and all my remaining ships. May you guide them well." He took a step backward. "We could use some steady and rational leadership for a change."

"Why thank you, General. I accept your surrender." She cracked her knuckles. "There, now that the formalities are out of the way, we can talk turkey about how this is going to work—practically speaking, I mean."

Brindle, though, had something to do first. When he turned to his son, Tasia could see the warring emotions on the older man's face. "I just received a message from your mother, Robb. After all we've just been through, she'd be very grateful if you'd visit us at your earliest convenience. We have a lot to talk about as a family." He looked at Tasia. "And, of course, Commodore Tamblyn is more than welcome to join you."

With Estarra and Deputy Cain sitting across the table in a small Whisper Palace room, they discussed what to do with the deposed King Rory. OX stood ready with his uploaded databases to recite chapter and verse from his files on Hansa law or diplomatic tradition, but no decision was made.

"My family died in an accident . . . if it was an accident." Rory swallowed hard. "I just want my normal life back."

"We could see to it that the boy lives comfortably, with a new name and a new identity," Cain suggested. "If he disappears from public view, he'll soon be forgotten."

"I'm not sure that's a good idea. Considering what the people are used to from the Chairman, they'll probably assume he was killed," Estarra pointed out.

Peter looked sadly at Rory, who seemed out of his depth. "Sorry, but you're King Rory, for good or bad. But you can still help. You'll *need* to help."

"Perhaps find some ceremonial role?" Cain said. "Demote him, but don't brush him away in disgrace. Let him continue to have a following."

"The people have endured enough turmoil, and it would help with continuity," Estarra said. "He'll serve as a bridge between the old Hansa and the new Confederation."

Later, soldiers lined up to hold back the crowds and the newsnet imagers for the abdication ceremony. As he and Estarra stood with Rory under the bright lights, Peter could see that the young man was sweating heavily. He looked so much like Peter's lost brother that the cruelty of Basil's trick burned like salt in a wound. But it wasn't Rory's fault.

Peter spoke quietly, so no one else could hear. "I hold no grudge against you. Don't be ashamed."

"I didn't ask to be made King, you know." Rory still wore his royal clothes. "But that doesn't mean I don't regret some of the things I did."

"No one understands that better than I do," Peter said.

"I'm glad the Chairman is dead. I don't have to be afraid anymore." Rory's dark brown eyes looked up at him. "I don't know how you were strong enough to stand up to him."

"Sometimes I don't know either."

Basil's portrait in the boardroom had been labeled "the last Chairman of the Terran Hanseatic League." That room had been sealed off. Eventually, the gallery might prove instructive as a place of historical significance, but for now Peter didn't want anyone staring at Basil's portrait.

Earlier, he and Estarra had attended the subdued and poorly publicized funeral of Chairman Wenceslas out of a sense of obligation. As far as the King could tell, no tears were shed. Though Sarein had the opportunity to join them, she could not face returning to Earth yet and chose to remain aboard the *Jupiter*. She would soon go home to Theroc. Colonel Andez might have been the only person who *wanted* to attend the funeral, but she and her cleanup crew had been arrested and charged; they were locked up awaiting trial.

Now, in front of the crowds, Peter and Estarra took their seats on adjacent thrones, while Rory faced them standing. The boy had memorized his lines for one last public presentation. The audience fell into a hushed anticipation, and Peter gave the young man a slight encouraging nod. Rory removed the intricately worked gold crown that rested atop his dark hair and held it up as if a great weight had been taken from him.

He said in a loud, clear voice, "The Hansa and the Confederation must have one leader, one true King. I did my best to guide the Hansa, but now that we have sailed safely through those troubled waters, I yield to you, Peter. I abdicate my throne and give you this crown for safekeeping."

Peter accepted the crown and laid it on his lap. Applause swelled among the viewers, growing even louder as Rory dropped to his knee in a gallant, and unrehearsed, gesture of fealty.

Peter said, "The Queen and I ask that you continue to serve your people and help them feel welcome in the Confederation."

"Always, sire."

"Then rise with our blessing."

A gala reception took place with dignitaries and bureaucrats from the Hansa as well as representatives from across the Confederation. Green priests had already spread the word throughout the colonies.

Deputy Cain came up to Peter. Rather than seeking power, Cain was now more interested in acquiring, and enjoying, additional classic art for his Velázquez collection.

"What else will you need before taking over the Whisper Palace, sire?" he asked, holding but not sipping his champagne. "Will you reclaim your quarters in the old Royal Wing, bring your son here? The people of Earth would surely welcome you. They are ready to have their King and Queen back."

Estarra looked at her husband. "We didn't talk about that, Peter."

In addition to the occasional lunar fragments that still slipped through the vigorous search nets, the loss of the Moon had left the Earth unsettled, with sporadic tremors and quakes. Peter had assigned teams of Hansa scientists to make projections of the climatological and seismic consequences, and many Roamer scientists had already volunteered, eager to sink their teeth into another interesting, and extreme, problem. Eventually, the pieces of the broken Moon would settle into a broad and diffuse ring around the planet. In the meantime, though, there would be a lot of changes, many of them unpredictable.

But that wasn't the reason why Peter did not want to move back to Earth. He shook his head. "No, Deputy Cain. Theroc is the heart of the Confederation. That's our new capital, and that is the place from which I must rule. But I'll be back here often enough, and we'll have green priests and treelings so that direct lines of communication remain open."

OX, as always, accompanied them. "If I can be of any service in the transitional government, I would be interested in accepting the assignment, or any other assignment you deem appropriate, King Peter. I am eager to make many new memories."

Peter said, "You've proved your loyalty and your competence plenty of times, OX, but it still bothers me how much of your past is missing." He turned to Cain. "Mr. Deputy, I have a favor to request. It's a long shot, but I have to ask."

"Ask. Now you have me intrigued."

"As the Teacher compy here at the Whisper Palace, OX taught me, Prince Daniel, Old King Frederick, and all of our predecessors. Since he's such an important compy, I was hoping that someone in the Hansa had recognized his value."

Cain's hairless brow furrowed. "Certainly, we realize how vital the Teacher compy has been. What favor did you need?"

"OX purged most of his memory storage in order to fly the hydrogue derelict and operate its transportal. I can only hope and pray that Chairman Wenceslas was wise enough to keep a backup of all his memories. Otherwise, we have lost OX's vital experiences, as well as the wonderful personality that he developed over all those years."

The deputy sighed. "I know for a fact that Chairman Wenceslas never considered such a thing. He wouldn't have wasted the time or effort."

Peter's expression fell. "I had to ask."

Cain's expression broke into an impish grin. "I, on the other hand, was not so lax. There is indeed a backup of OX's memories. I did that myself shortly before you and the Queen escaped. We can install it without any difficulty."

Though he had become friends with the two technical compies, DD did not accompany KR and GU when Kotto Okiah returned to the Roamers. Instead, he chose to remain with Orli Covitz. Margaret Colicos had told DD to watch over the girl, and he liked being around her.

After Tasia Tamblyn put in a good word for Orli and Mr. Steinman, King Peter found them a place to live on Earth, and the Friendly compy joined her in their comfortable new quarters, with Mr. Steinman in the immediately adjacent apartment. After everything they'd been through together, they wanted to settle near each other. Though housekeeping and meals were provided, DD tried to be of service as much as possible. They all took care of each other.

Orli slumped onto the small bed in her clean bedroom. "I don't know what to make of my life, DD. For so long I've just been reacting to one disaster after another. Now I don't know what to do with myself."

"I should point out, Orli Covitz, that most girls your age have not yet begun to make big life decisions. At your age, my first master, Dahlia Sweeney, was full of dreams. She told me stories of what she wanted to do, places she intended to see, but they were just wishes. You remind me very much of her. She was very nice."

"Thanks for the compliment."

"It has been a long time since I last saw her. It has been

a long time since I saw Margaret Colicos, too. Do you think she is all right? The Klikiss are gone now."

"I'll see what I can find out, DD."

The next day the compy was delighted to receive word that Margaret was indeed alive and had returned to Earth. Once Orli told him the news, DD suggested that they contact her immediately; Orli was happy to do so, since she and the older woman had become close on Llaro.

They set up a time to meet, and DD was filled with excitement about the reunion, although Orli seemed somewhat hesitant. He couldn't understand why. "Don't worry, it's nothing," she said when he asked. "Margaret will want to see both of us."

He and Orli traveled to the university district where Margaret shared an apartment with her son, Anton. When the older woman opened the door, DD's optical sensors flashed. "Margaret Colicos, I am pleased to be reunited with you."

The woman threw her arms around his polymer shoulders. "Oh, DD, I wasn't sure I'd ever see you again." She gave the girl a hug as well. "And Orli! I'm so happy you're safe."

Anton invited them into his small apartment, then hurried to make tea. Out of habit, or perhaps by accident, the scholar brought out a cup for DD as well as the others.

"I have heard very much about you, Anton Colicos," DD said. "Your mother told me tales of how you grew up with her and Louis Colicos on their archaeological digs, and how you gave her the small music box that saved her life among the Klikiss."

"I'm still amazed by that." Anton flushed. "It wasn't much of anything."

"It was exactly what it needed to be," Margaret said.

"DD, we've been through so much, and truth be told, I'd just as soon we were done with our adventures. It's time to relax and recuperate."

Orli nervously cleared her throat. She hadn't touched her tea. "That's why I brought DD back to you, ma'am. He's your property. You should take him back."

DD suddenly realized that this was what had been bothering the girl. He hadn't even considered the consequences, hadn't understood why Orli was so worried.

The offer surprised Margaret. "I won't hear of it. DD is yours now, Orli. You two belong together."

Orli started to cry, though she quickly wiped the tears from her eyes, pretending that no one had noticed them.

"I am pleased with that decision, Margaret Colicos," DD said. "But are you certain you won't need my assistance? Will you not be doing other work?"

The old woman and Anton exchanged smiles. Margaret said, "Oh, we definitely have interesting work ahead of us, but we can handle it ourselves. Orli, you watch out for DD now. I don't want to worry about him. My son and I have places to go."

162 ☀ MAGE-IMPERATOR JORA'H

In spite of the devastation of Ildira, the Mage-Imperator found great cause for hope and gladness, especially with his Empire strongly connected once more. The faeros were defeated, and the treacherous Hansa Chairman dead by his own deputy's hand. The numerous soulfires stolen by the blazing elementals had safely found their way to the Light-source. Even the one burned-out sun in Ildira's sky now shone again.

The landscape of the universe had been forever changed, as had Jora'h and Ildira itself. Nevertheless, he was home, leading the remnants of his people, reconnecting the splinter colonies that had been adrift since the faeros invasion.

In spite of the rough conditions of the temporary camp outside the remains of Mijistra, Nira had mentally healed and strengthened, finally achieving a new peace. "Look at this as an opportunity, Jora'h. You have a chance to be the greatest Mage-Imperator the Empire has ever known. The slate is wiped clean."

Ildiran civilization had long rested upon old accomplishments. The people revered the past to such an extent that they changed very little. Now that the foundation of Mijistra had been swept away, however, the people had no choice but to make a fresh start.

Getting to know the human race better had changed

Jora'h's opinion about steadfast Ildiran ways. It would do his race good to be creative and inventive. Architects and builders, diggers and rememberers, medical kithmen and administrators—he could pull them all together in a project vastly more complex than anything ever chronicled in the *Saga*—re-creating the entire capital city in its glory. Maybe even make it better.

And they would do it.

From their camp on the outskirts of the ruined city, he and Nira watched the work continue. Yazra'h and Prime Designate Daro'h had shown amazing verve and independence. Rather than requiring detailed orders, they took initiative and lifted some of the burden from his shoulders.

Unlike Thor'h, who had shirked his duties as the leader in training, Daro'h clearly would one day become a formidable Mage-Imperator. The young man no longer looked reticent about his role, and the Mage-Imperator reminded him to begin breeding many, many new Designates. Attender kithmen, eager to follow the Prime Designate's instructions, followed him around as if he were already sitting in the chrysalis chair.

Teams of rememberers struggled to chronicle all those who had fallen, trying to tally the deaths caused by the faeros and mad Rusa'h. The names of the dead were etched on diamondfilm and made into structural plates that would be used to assemble a new Hall of Rememberers.

Cargo ships and cutters descended from the Solar Navy warliners in orbit. All of the Ildiran soldiers had been reassigned as workers, though they remained ready to defend the Empire, should the need arise. The Mage-Imperator was confident that his people would have at least some time to recover before the next crisis struck.

Designate Ridek'h had brought together all the survivors from the Hyrillka refugee camps and spoken to them. Now he approached Jora'h, bursting to talk. "Hyrillka is where these people belong, Liege, not Ildira. There is rebuilding enough for them to do there. With your permission, I shall lead them home."

"I give it gladly."

"And one other thing." The boy hesitated, then added quickly, "I believe I should take former Designate Rusa'h with me."

That surprised Jora'h. Though he was free of the faeros since his defeat and collapse, Rusa'h was a mere shell of himself. Because he was so unresponsive, it had taken the rest of them several days to discover that he was blind, like Tal O'nh, his sight burned out from within by the faeros. Utterly broken, unaware of his surroundings, he often sat trembling; Rusa'h did not seem to remember anyone or anything, as if his mind had been purged.

"We have lens kithmen and medical kithmen," Designate Ridek'h continued in a rush. "We should surround Rusa'h with Ildirans, enfold him in the true *thism* and through it allow him to see the brilliant light of the suns. Let him return to his home on Hyrillka."

Jora'h was skeptical. "My brother was in a sub-*thism* trance once before, because of his severe head injury. When he awoke, he was dramatically changed."

"And now he needs to awaken again—but properly. If there is a chance he may recover, then we are obligated to try."

Nira considered, then slowly nodded. "I think Designate Ridek'h's suggestion shows great maturity."

Jora'h thought of what he had done to his own son

Thor'h after his betrayal, keeping him drugged with shiing and locked in an underground chamber. He would not do the same to Rusa'h, no matter what crimes the mad Designate had committed. "Very well. I entrust him to you. It pleases me that your desire is not for vengeance, but for healing."

Then the Mage-Imperator saw one of the most hopeful signs of all: Giggling, and actually *playing*, Osira'h and her brothers and sisters ran through the camp, chasing a small mirrored balloon that drifted into the air and slowly bounced back to the ground. Muree'n seized the balloon and ran faster than the others, rushing up to her mother and Jora'h; Osira'h raced after her sister.

Nira looked immensely happy. "It's good to see them acting like *children*. They need this change."

"We all needed it," Jora'h said. "With my people here and my family around me, I feel strong . . . and the Empire will be as well."

163 ⚹ ANTON COLICOS

When he and his mother arrived at Ildira, Anton did not have to look hard for Yazra'h. Lean and sweaty, she strode up to him with a feral grin; her coppery hair flowed like the tail of a metallic comet. "Rememberer Anton, it is fortunate you have returned. Much history is being made here. You should record it for us."

The two Isix cats bounded forward, startling Margaret, but Anton laughed and scratched behind the big cats' ears.

Yazra'h looked scuffed, dirty, and ready to explode with energy even though she probably hadn't slept for some time. Anton doubted she'd ever been given so much responsibility in her life, placed in charge of so many major projects. "You look good, Yazra'h."

"As do you, Rememberer Anton." She touched his arm warmly, stood very close to him. Then with an almost dismissive glance at Margaret, she added, "And who is this woman?"

"My mother."

"Ah, the xeno-archaeologist. One of the discoverers of the Klikiss Torch. Your son has told tales of you." Yazra'h bowed slightly. "Anton is a great rememberer. He helped me see things in our *Saga* that few Ildirans noticed. My father holds him in very high esteem. Come, I will take you to him." Yazra'h marched away, giving them no opportunity for argument. The Isix cats bounded ahead of her.

Margaret asked, "Was she flirting with you?"

Anton was embarrassed. "She intimidates the hell out of me."

"I see."

Mijistra's construction continued all around them. Even with the advantage of their *thism*, the Ildirans seemed barely able to control the chaos of all the parallel efforts. A new headquarters camp had been set up on the outskirts of the old city. The camp held hastily assembled structures, interlinked shelters, the frameworks of new towers. Scavengers excavated raw materials from the rubble of Mijistra, while other vital components came from Ildiran colony worlds whose people had raced back to the central planet to help.

Margaret's face was wistful as she looked at the broad impact site. "Louis and I never went to see the Ildiran Empire. I wish we had."

After Yazra'h announced their arrival, the Mage-Imperator came out to greet them himself and led them into the new audience chamber. "Rememberer Anton, I am glad to see you safe. And I am sorry to hear about Vao'sh. I deeply regret that he was abandoned, that *I* abandoned him."

Anton had thought he was done crying, and the sudden tears welling up in his eyes surprised him. He tried to find some way to answer, but the words would not come out of his throat.

Chief Scribe Ko'sh looked distraught at the news. Anton had had previous difficulties with Ko'sh, who strenuously objected to changing the *Saga,* even after being shown the obvious historical errors. Now, though, Anton felt for the man whose Hall of Rememberers and all the ancient records had been smashed into dust. Ko'sh seemed overwhelmed, showing none of the hardness he had displayed before.

After a few quick formalities, the Mage-Imperator surprised Anton by offering a new assignment. "Some time ago, I asked you and Rememberer Vao'sh to perfect and rewrite our majestic story. Please stay with us now and help our rememberers reconstruct the *Saga of Seven Suns*. The Empire needs you."

Anton looked awkwardly at his mother, then back toward the Ildiran leader. "I'm sorry, sir, but I am under another obligation. My mother and I have a different calling." He glanced away. "I'll have to leave the task to your Chief Scribe. All rememberer kithmen memorize the entire *Saga,* and they know the stanzas a lot better than I do. Besides, I couldn't do it without Vao'sh."

He lowered his gaze, swallowing a lump in his throat. "However, I would like to record Vao'sh's place in the *Saga*—to tell of his final days. My friend would have been horrified to be portrayed as a hero, but he was one nevertheless. I want to make sure he's remembered that way."

"Tell his story," Jora'h said. "We will remember him."

Yazra'h squeezed his shoulder in a rough, comradely gesture. "If not to help us, then why did you come here, Rememberer Anton?"

He flushed again. "I came to say goodbye to you, for now."

164 ☀ ADAR ZAN'NH

The resort world of Maratha could once again be a glorious place, and Adar Zan'nh intended to make it so. The destroyed counterpart cities of Prime and Secda would be rebuilt in opposite hemispheres, with the work taking place during alternating halves of the year. The Ildiran crews could work continually through the months-long sunlight.

After the faeros were defeated, the Solar Navy had split apart to complete numerous vital tasks across the ragged Empire. Tal Ala'nh's cohort of warliners shuttled the Hyrillkan survivors back home with Designate Ridek'h, where they could reestablish the once-flourishing splinter colony. Other ships had gone to Dobro and to the worlds of the Horizon Cluster, helping to fortify the frayed *thism*. The Ildiran Empire might be changed, but it would still be strong. Perhaps even stronger than ever.

With King Peter's blessing, Roamer skymines delivered shipments of ekti at a heavily discounted rate, providing all the stardrive fuel the Solar Navy needed for their operations; in exchange, the Mage-Imperator promised commercial concessions for centuries to come.

Now Zan'nh assessed the operations in the ruins of Maratha Prime, the first Ildiran city that had been taken over by the deceitful Klikiss robots. After months of darkness, the dawn sun hung low and bright on the horizon, and he knew that over the next week the colors of the long sunrise would fill the sky.

Maratha Secda had been heavily damaged during the Solar Navy and Klikiss bombardment, and Ildiran surveyors had combed over the wreckage to determine what could be salvaged. Administrative kithmen worked diligently to develop a reconstruction plan for Secda; during the months of darkness in the opposite hemisphere, they would determine the most efficient way to complete the monumental task and be ready to go as soon as the slow day arrived on that side of the world.

Zan'nh thought of the human engineer Tabitha Huck, who would have found better ways to guide the Ildiran crews if the faeros had not killed her along with so many others. Sullivan Gold would be a welcome addition to the crew here, but the man and his family had gone elsewhere to help both Ildirans and humans.

That meant he would have to encourage innovation from his own people. It was a task that filled him with a mixture of nervousness and exhilaration. He was certain they could do it.

The Adar stood at the doorway of his temporary command post, watching heavily laden troop transports disgorge workers, engineers, diggers, attender kithmen, and more bureaucrats. At one time, Adar Kori'nh had expressed disappointment that he was forced to devote so much of his career to civil engineering projects and rescue missions; Kori'nh had wanted to experience military glory in order to earn a place in the *Saga of Seven Suns*.

Now Zan'nh found himself in the opposite position. He'd had his fill of space battles and destruction, of losing ships and uncounted crewmen, of constant tragedies and atrocities. He was perfectly content to devote the capabilities of the Solar Navy to the rejuvenation of the Empire.

He savored the simple act of watching the golden light of Maratha's protracted sunrise grow slowly brighter across the broad construction site.

Estarra took great pleasure in being home on Theroc and holding her baby again. Not surprisingly, Father Idriss and Mother Alexa had doted on little Reynald while his parents were gone.

"What have you been feeding him?" she asked. "He looks like he's doubled in weight!"

Her mother's expression puckered. "Is there something wrong with that? He's a growing baby."

Estarra cradled her son and looked into his bright eyes. They were brown, the natural color of Peter's eyes, as well as her own. The child's dark hair was already unruly.

She looked up at the magnificent worldtrees, some of which showed deep scorch wounds from the faeros flames. Now Theroc was abustle with Confederation representatives, Roamer workers, and visitors from Earth. Green priests sent excited messages back and forth to the interconnected colony worlds, disseminating news of all the positive changes. With the outpouring of support, much progress had been made in erecting a new ruling house—a combination of Roamer structure, fungus reef, and sturdy yet ornate Hansa architecture. The King and Queen felt it was important to show that the new Confederation was a synthesis of all parts of humanity.

Beside her, watching Estarra's wistful expression as she surveyed the thick forest and the people, Sarein said, "It's time for us to sink our roots deep." She looked around with an expression of contentment and a hint of awe. "I never imagined I could miss this place so much."

Idriss and Alexa had welcomed their oldest daughter home after her escape from Basil Wenceslas, not worried about what she had done on Earth or what political entanglements the Hansa had dragged her into. Estarra was proud of her sister, knowing how she and Deputy Cain had worked to bring about the downfall of the Chairman.

Celli ran to her sisters wearing a garland of flowers. A sash made of lavender and peach lichens hung loosely around her narrow waist. "Only a few more hours. All the trees are focused on it—I can tell. You should hear the buzzing across telink."

"Don't the trees have anything more important to worry about?" Estarra teased.

"Not right now, and not to me." Celli turned to her oldest sister. "Come on, Sarein—show some excitement! This is my big day."

Sarein seemed embarrassed. "I am excited—honestly. I wouldn't miss it for anything."

"You'd better not." Then Celli bounded off.

Estarra glanced at Sarein. "We'd like you to put on your ambassador's robes for the occasion. It seems appropriate."

"I'm not sure I should ever wear those again, considering."

"Yes, you should." Estarra lifted her chin regally, then broke into a smile. "Your Queen gives you permission to do so."

She went off to extricate Peter from his political meetings, insisting that he take the time to prepare himself properly. When they were ready, they ascended to the bright sunshine of the canopy where everyone had gathered to watch the wedding of Celli and Solimar.

Estarra carried the baby against her chest in a cocoon-weave net, while Peter reclined next to her in a mesh chair. The purple-and-black butterflies were hatching again, and clouds of them swirled around like winged amethysts in the open breezes.

Celli and Solimar stood together on the interlocked branches, beaming. Their emerald skin was marked with new dye-tattoos to signify their training, their accomplishments, and their betrothal to each other. The couple looked extremely young, Estarra thought, but she realized that Celli was now nineteen, a year older than she herself had been when she'd married King Peter.

"They look so proud to be together," Peter said, "as if they share one heart and one mind."

"Through telink, they've already joined their thoughts and emotions."

"We didn't have that advantage." He turned to her. "But I still would have chosen you, no doubt about it."

As green priests, Celli and Solimar had come to their decision and announced it to the other green priests through telink. Their comrades already knew of their deep commitment, and so the two needed to say very little aloud for the marriage ceremony.

Instead, Celli and Solimar did what they had been born to do. Rejoicing in their abilities, glad to be alive and moving, they demonstrated the acrobatic skills they had learned from other master treedancers. Solimar leaped out to grab a high branch, swung himself around, and folded his legs until he dangled upside down, just as Celli jumped behind him. Solimar caught her with his downstretched arms and swung her up to the next branch, where she pirouetted, barely seeming to touch her toes to the wood.

As the audience cheered and applauded, Solimar launched himself after her, and the two continued a spontaneous yet perfectly choreographed chase through the canopy. Their exuberant dancing had once awakened a new spirit in the devastated worldforest. Now the verdani reciprocated, bowing branches, fanning fronds, taking part in the performance.

As she watched the exhilarating spectacle, Estarra basked in the sunshine. Around her, she saw her parents and other Therons sitting comfortably with Roamers, colonists, and even Hansa representatives. The baby in her arms was warm, solid, and alive. Theroc was lush and in bloom again, and Estarra could smell the flowers in the air.

166 ✺ MARGARET COLICOS

Alongside the *Blind Faith*, the *Voracious Curiosity* took off from the sprawling Klikiss hive city on Llaro. The fully repaired *Curiosity* lifted into the air, her engines sounding like a sigh of relief.

Margaret watched the two ships go with a bittersweet feeling, uneasy at being left behind with the Klikiss again, though it was what she had requested. Anton stayed with her, looking somewhat uncertain about his decision, too.

The Klikiss workers, engineers, and scientists had used their technical skills to repair the damaged *Curiosity,* guided by the Davlin-breedex, who had now established complete and clear control of the remainder of the species. When Captain Kett had brought her two passengers to Llaro, she'd been skeptical at first about letting the bugs do all the repair work, but when it was finished, she was quite pleased to discover that her ship's systems were as good as new. The two captains flew away to meet their other obligations for the Confederation.

Margaret saw her son looking nervously at the thousands of clattering workers, high-crested warriors, and tiger-striped domates. "Don't worry, Anton, the Klikiss won't harm us. Not now."

"How could I argue with you? You've got more experience with the Klikiss than anyone in history."

"Are you just trying to convince yourself?"

He swallowed hard. "Yes. Yes, I am."

Margaret and Anton had brought their own supplies, and the breedex provided a hive tower for them to use as a temporary residence. After Rlinda and BeBob departed, she and her son settled in and began their work. They felt awkward at first, mostly about being together, but quickly formed a workable partnership. They grew closer than they had ever been. Margaret told him stories about his father, and Anton described his years of dealing with university politics and how he'd been accepted among the Ildirans to translate their *Saga of Seven Suns.* And he also talked a lot about Vao'sh.

"I'll get used to it," Anton said. "We've got plenty of Klikiss stories to record. That's the main thing."

"Then it's time for us to meet with the breedex again."

Of all the scattered subhives, the only Klikiss that remained functional were those that had been closest to the One Breedex aboard the swarmships at Earth. The rest of the bugs remained in hibernation, perhaps permanently. The Davlin-breedex had not been able to override the effects of the crippling Klikiss Siren, but Margaret wasn't sure how hard he had tried. The sudden attrition of so many parts of the hive mind had given Davlin the opening he had needed to take over permanently with his strong and independent personality.

Inside the putrid-smelling main chamber, the great mass of grubs and pieces formed itself into a swirling, seething sculpture of Davlin Lotze's face, much more concrete now than it had been before. Margaret stepped close to the terrifying visage. "The rest of humanity may not know it, Davlin, but you alone probably saved us all."

"I'll make certain to tell that part of the story," Anton insisted.

"There are other stories you must preserve," the breedex said.

"Indeed, there are," Margaret said. "You need to help us understand, Davlin."

"I will," he said in his eerie, overlapping voice. *"Listen."*

Together, they spent days in the hall of the breedex as the Davlin persona drew upon genetic memories. He told the never-before-heard history songs of the Klikiss, the former swarmings, the One Breedex, the creation of the black robots and their subjugation . . . and the treachery that had nearly exterminated the race.

Anton recorded and annotated all the tales, even capturing the alien melodies as background, while Margaret interviewed the breedex. Her son was engrossed, awed to know that he was setting down an untold epic to rival even the *Saga of Seven Suns*. With a sigh, he looked up from his datapad and flexed his sore hand. "I wish with all my heart that Vao'sh could have been here with us."

Margaret understood his affection for his old colleague. "And I wish Louis could be here." She smiled. "But we're together. That's enough of a miracle for right now."

167 ☀ SULLIVAN GOLD

Sullivan put on a brave face as the Solar Navy cutter landed on Dobro and opened its hatches to the dry, dusty air. Taking Lydia's hand, he stepped out and said, "Remember, I didn't promise you anything fancy, but there won't be any faeros here. And the hydrogues are gone. The Ildiran Empire and the Confederation are allies." His voice trailed off as he searched her face. "This isn't going to be so bad, is it?"

"Well, I can think of a lot of things I'm going to miss," Lydia replied, but she smiled. "And a lot of things I won't—Chairman Wenceslas and his cleanup crew, for one. We'll make the best of it, and we're together."

The rest of his family emerged, blinking. They had been through enough turmoil that they were glad just to set foot on solid ground again. "The Chairman's dead, and the Hansa's overthrown," said Jerome. "Things are getting better on Earth. We could always go back and pick up where we left off."

Lydia waggled a finger at him. "The fact that it happened at all should give you cause for concern. Similar things have occurred before. Secret police, rights trampled on, people afraid to speak up against injustice, neighbors turning on neighbors. The ones you thought were your friends are suddenly afraid to get involved when you need help." She sniffed. "I'm sure this place isn't perfect either, but it'll be a long time before I let down my guard again."

Sullivan looked hopefully at his family. "Give Dobro a chance. We can really make a difference here."

"If your father says this is a good opportunity for us, then the rest of you are going to give it your best shot," Lydia said, and nobody argued with her.

After so many generations, there was no love lost between the human descendants and Ildiran splinter colonists on Dobro, but they had agreed to bury the hatchet, to work and live together. Now Sullivan would use his administrative skills to cement the two groups into one cooperative colony. With the help of Lydia and his family, he was sure he could pull it off.

Benn Stoner, the leader of the *Burton* descendants, walked with a rolling gait across the landing field to shake Sullivan's hand. "So you're the professionals? We're pleased to have the help."

"The Mage-Imperator has his hands full at Mijistra. The Confederation will send cargo ships with a few necessities, but we'll have to do most of the work ourselves."

"We're fine with that," Stoner said. "We're hard workers—both humans and Ildirans."

Several of the nearby Ildirans nodded, knowing that Sullivan had the Mage-Imperator's blessing. Even if they were poorly trained in innovation, they were good at following instructions, and Sullivan felt that was a good start. "Before you know it, this place will be a model colony."

"I believe that Dobro will thrive for the first time in its history," said one of the Ildirans, a lens kithman.

Sullivan had his family unload their few belongings from the cutter. Stoner shouted out, "Stop sitting around and help the newcomers find a house to live in! Get them something nice—they'll be here awhile."

Although the original colony town had burned to the ground, new buildings made of freshly sawn wood had been built. The Gold family had more than enough space to spread out into three dwellings.

That first night, while he and Lydia relaxed in their new bedchamber, he patted her hand. "Sorry it's not quite a paradise."

She leaned over to give him a peck on the cheek. "You need a shave again."

"I know."

"We have running water, a heated home, and a pantry of food. I have all my family here with me. And we're safe." Lydia looked out the window at the dark sky and the dazzling blazers that illuminated the colony town. "It's not paradise, but it'll do."

Nira did not look forward to seeing the familiar yet painful landscape of Dobro. As the *Voracious Curiosity* came in to land, the dry brown hills reminded her of horrific fires. She scanned the main colony settlement and shuddered to think of the breeding barracks, the fences, and the many times she had been abused and impregnated as part of the Dobro Designate's experiments.

But Nira had a purpose in coming here. She had brought treelings to plant, to help the world heal from all the harm that had been done. Osira'h, Rod'h, Gale'nh, Tamo'l, and Muree'n had accompanied their mother on the pilgrimage, supporting her with their love. Together they would make a change.

"It'll be fine," Rlinda said, seeing her uncertain expression. "I promise."

"I'm the only one who can make it right. Coming here, facing the past, seeing these people . . . I need to do that before I can move on."

The *Blind Faith* flew beside the *Curiosity,* also carrying a load of supplies for the Dobro colonists. Rlinda said, "BeBob and I won't be staying long, so you and the kids better finish your business quick, unless you want us to sail off into the stars and leave you all behind."

"No, we won't be staying behind." Nira looked into the back section of the ship, where the children were occupying themselves with some Hansa entertainment vidloops Rlinda had loaded aboard. "We've all spent quite enough time here already."

Once landed, the *Curiosity* and the *Blind Faith* opened their cargo hatches like vendors displaying their wares, and excited colonists came to help them unload the new material. Rlinda supervised the workers, watching the stacks of supply crates diminish until the cargo hold was empty.

Holding a treeling, Nira hesitated at the bottom of the ramp until Osira'h took her hand and said, "Come, Mother. Do you need us to show you the way?" The girl carried another of the small potted worldtree fronds, as did each of the other children. Six new worldtrees for Dobro.

"I know it too well." Cradling the treeling in one arm, she smiled, and together the six of them stepped out onto the ground.

Nira walked with them away from the landing field and passed through the reconstructed colony town in a small procession. While the half-breed children expressed surprise at all the changes they saw, unshed tears welled up in Nira's eyes. The fences were gone, the breeding barracks burned down, the Dobro Designate's dwelling torn apart. She barely recognized the place. So many of its shadows and stains were mercifully washed away.

The once-segregated Ildiran settlement and human prison camp had now merged, the structures intermingled. Nira recognized most of the colonists, and she could see a genuinely changed attitude on their faces. The Ildirans really were helping them. She knew there were many scars to remove, both on the landscape and in the peoples' hearts, but they seemed to be doing it.

Perhaps this would work after all. Dobro could be beautiful.

The children seemed happy and excited, bounding along toward the nearest hills, drawn to a particular place. After the springtime rains, the weeds and grass had grown in lush, thick masses.

She was not surprised to find that her own grave was still there. Muree'n found it first and called the others over to the spot.

Looking at it now, Nira felt disoriented to see the polished geometrical stone that marked where Designate Udru'h had supposedly buried her. The holographic image of her face—much younger and more innocent—still shimmered there. Her children seemed captivated by the projection.

"You look beautiful there," Rod'h said.

Nira knelt in the rough grass and stared for a long moment, recalling all her years in the breeding camp. She knew that Jora'h, too, had come to grieve by this marker, believing the false story of her death.

It was time to remove the lie. Nira detached the data crystal and its power pack and took the holographic memorial with her. Although the gesture was symbolic, she felt lighter somehow.

The people on Dobro would be all right, and so would she.

"Why did you do that, Mother?" Osira'h asked.

Nira set her pot down on the ground. "Because we are here to make a new memorial, a much more important one." She began to scoop out a hole in the dirt so that she could plant her treeling. The children helped, and soon the small worldtree had been patted down in its new home. Nira stepped back to admire what they had done.

"And where shall we plant the others?" Gale'nh asked.

Nira marked off spots, separated widely enough to give

the growing trees room, but close enough for them to share their strength, where their roots could find each other and interconnect underground. "Someday there will be a fine grove here," she said.

Bringing the worldforest mind to this place was her way of forgiving Dobro. The trees would grow tall and strong.

When they were done, they walked back to the landing field where the two cargo ships waited. Happy and relieved, Nira was ready to put her bad memories of this place behind her. Feeling a strong wash of love, she reached out to gather all five of her children in a fierce embrace.

This was the only memory she needed of Dobro.

169 ☀ ORLI COVITZ

Though she doubted DD could interpret subtle expressions despite his many years with humans, Orli did her best to keep the impish excitement from her face. She could barely hold back a grin as she used special cloths to scrub and polish the Friendly compy's exterior.

"I have always done my best to maintain a clean appearance, Orli Covitz. However, I appreciate your attention to detail. My recent difficulties have left me somewhat worn and discolored."

"I have a surprise for you, and I want you to look your best."

"What is the surprise?"

"Now, DD, if I tell you, it's not a surprise anymore."

The little compy digested that. "By definition, you are correct."

She glanced at the clock and quickly finished with a last wipe across the compy's shoulders and the back of his head. "Time to go. Mr. Steinman has arranged transport for us."

"You have made me very curious."

"Good."

DD followed Orli out of her apartment, still chattering. "I can experience curiosity, you know. My programming is very sophisticated."

"I'm aware of that. You can experience lots of things that surprise me."

Mr. Steinman had shaved, showered, put on clean clothes, and combed his wet gray hair behind his ears. He could have used a haircut, Orli thought, but she was pleased that he had taken the trouble to make himself presentable. He realized this was very important to her—and to DD. Mr. Steinman was even wearing cologne. Lots of it.

"Everything's set," he said. "Ready to go?"

"You look as excited as I am."

The older man flushed. "Just doing it as a favor for you, kid."

"Where are we going?" DD pressed.

"It's a surprise," the two of them answered in unison.

"Whom will we meet?"

"It's a surprise."

"Will you answer *any* of my questions?"

"No."

"Then shall I stop asking?"

"Yes." The Friendly compy was as antsy as a child about to open a birthday present.

As they traveled across the city, Orli at last relented and offered a hint. "I did some research. You already know I couldn't find my mother, but I did find someone—someone for you."

"I do not want anyone else, Orli Covitz. Margaret Colicos told the two of us to stay together."

"This is different. You'll understand soon enough."

They arrived at a modest house with beautiful flower boxes out front. Orli smiled at the brown shutters and shingle roof, the pale yellow siding, the welcoming walk that led up to a front door surrounded by potted plants.

DD kept up with Orli's eager step as they passed blue-chip juniper shrubs on the way to the front door. Mr. Steinman followed a few steps behind them. As soon as Orli knocked, the door opened, and a striking old woman in a loose green dress answered it. She wore her pewter hair neatly pinned back, and a delicate gold bracelet encircled her left wrist. To Orli's eyes, she seemed about the same age as Mr. Steinman.

After a second of awkward silence, the old woman asked in a breathy voice, "Is that DD? Is that really DD?"

The compy stepped forward. "Yes, I am DD. I am pleased to meet you."

Orli thought she would burst with excitement. "DD, don't you remember Dahlia Sweeney?"

"Dahlia? My first master?" The compy was actually taken aback.

The woman laughed. "That was fifty years ago. But I

grew up and gave you to my own daughter . . . and she grew up, but decided not to have a family."

"You're so much older now."

"Yes, that happens over time. Are you glad to see me?"

DD chattered, his voice filled with delighted exuberance. "This is absolutely wonderful."

"Yes, it is." Dahlia opened the door wide. "Please come in. We have so much to catch up on. I'm going to cry, I'm sure of it."

Inside the house, Orli could smell cookies.

They spent hours that day just talking, and Orli realized how lonely the old woman must be. DD regaled her with his adventures over the years, and Dahlia gave him the story of her life since her daughter Marianna had sold him. Then Mr. Steinman talked of his own exploits, modestly downplaying his heroics. He seemed almost shy, for a change, and he covered it by showing excessive interest in her backyard garden.

They returned the next day for dinner. Then the day after that. There wasn't a single time that Dahlia didn't have tears in her eyes when they left.

Finally, on their next visit, the old woman primly sat down on the sofa. Instead of tea, she had made lemonade. "What I'm about to propose is the best solution. We're all orphans and loose ends. Orli, it sounds to me like you've been bounced around from place to place and are just looking for a home."

Orli forced a smile. "Well, it's not through lack of trying that I haven't settled down."

"Then I suggest you and DD stay here with me. I have plenty of spare rooms, and I could certainly use the company—as well as some help in the garden and a few odds and ends."

"I can offer my assistance," DD volunteered.

Orli, who felt no attachment to her little apartment, didn't hesitate for a moment before agreeing.

"The invitation extends to you, too, Mr. Steinman," Dahlia said. "If you would be interested."

"Call me Hud, please—especially if I'll be settling down here." The old man couldn't stop grinning.

"I am very happy about this," the Friendly compy said.

Orli realized that was exactly the way she felt, too. At last.

170 ☀ PATRICK FITZPATRICK III

Staring out at the gauzy pastel clouds of Golgen, Patrick no longer felt any threat inside the gas giant. The yawning gulf of emptiness did not make him dizzy, as if he were about to fall (having walked the gangplank, after all). Even the odd smell of chemicals from the upwelling gases didn't bother him.

"I could almost get to like this place," he said.

"Then should we keep your grandmother's mansion on Earth as a vacation home?" Zhett said. "Although compared to this sky"—she spread her arms wide—"even that big old house would seem cramped."

"I'm perfectly content to be wherever you are," Patrick said with a mixture of teasing and sincerity, so that she couldn't tell whether he was being corny or genuinely romantic.

Spiderlike cargo escorts took off from the skymine's lower decks, circled around the attendant satellite platforms, and ascended to the more rarefied atmosphere until they reached orbit and streaked away with their full canisters of ekti. Production had gone into overdrive. The Ildiran Empire and the Confederation fleet were insatiable customers for stardrive fuel.

Del Kellum joined them, putting his hands on his hips. "Every time I see one of those ships fly off, I can't help but think of all the profits coming back to clan Kellum."

Patrick stared upward, blinking into the bright light. "Every time I see one of those ships fly off, I'm just glad nobody's shooting at it, and that we don't have to worry about the hydrogues, the faeros, the Klikiss, the robots, or the EDF."

Zhett's father turned to her, looking stern. "Now, don't go expecting your husband to have a free ride around here, my sweet. He's got to pull his own weight, do as much work as I do—"

"Better yet, Dad, I'll make sure he does as much work as *I* do." She slipped her arm around Patrick's waist, knowing that he already put in long days at the facility. "I promised to make him spend at least two hours with me every day in the command center so I can explain how things work on a big skymine. We'll make him into an adequate administrator sooner or later."

Patrick gave her an indignant look. "*Adequate?* I was raised to be leader material—the head of the military, a captain of industry, a well-respected diplomat."

"Yes, but can you do any *work,* by damn? One of these days I'd like to retire, you know."

Zhett gave her father a scornful laugh. "You, retire? It'll never happen."

"Oh? Something wrong with settling down? Brewing my orange liqueur—maybe even taking it commercial? Getting a few new tanks of angelfish . . . hell, how about a whole aquarium center of my own? I could run it as a tourist operation. Most Roamers haven't seen a real live fish, you know."

Two more cargo escorts streaked off. Billowing exhaust gases continued to spew out of the funnels in the skymine's superstructure. Scout ships skated along the cloud tops, dangling long antenna probes deep into the misty layers to measure concentrations of valuable gases.

Across the gas giant's skies, numerous other facilities hung suspended against gravity, filling tank after tank of ekti. Fortunately, Patrick thought, the open vastness had room for everyone.

Over the course of weeks, the Davlin-breedex shared with Margaret and Anton all the story songs he deemed necessary, everything memorable about the entire Klikiss race. After hearing of the incredible conflicts, the rise and fall of numerous subhives, the cyclical Swarmings and subsequent consolidations and exterminations, Margaret felt breathless from the sheer volume of information.

Then one day, the breedex was finished.

In the hive city, all of the Klikiss marched briskly about, forming themselves into ranks, millions lined up in perfect order, all categorized by sub-breed.

"What's going on out there?" Anton asked.

She shook her head. "Something I've never seen before."

Through two of its warrior breeds, the hive mind summoned her and Anton into the yawning hall. The smells were thicker and the background buzz so loud that her teeth rattled.

Even before the myriad organism finished forming the crude human face, Margaret asked, "Davlin, tell us what's happening."

"In the distant past, the Ildiran Empire coexisted with the Klikiss. They avoided our colony worlds, and our hive wars remained irrelevant to them." The alien voice paused for a long moment. *"That will change now. Humans will not ignore us. The time will come when vengeful people will re-*

fuse to leave us alone. Thus, we can wait here and be exterminated . . . or we can go into hibernation and allow time to pass, perhaps another ten thousand years."

Margaret couldn't argue with the assessment. She doubted humans would ever leave the Klikiss in peace.

Anton said, "Those are your only two choices?"

"For a long time I thought so, but now I choose a different way to survive." The simulated face seemed sad and preoccupied. *"I am all that is left of the Klikiss. Therefore, as breedex, I shall leave. I will take what remains of my hive and go elsewhere—far, far from human and Ildiran civilization. I do not expect to meet any of my old race for thousands of years. Goodbye, Anton Colicos. Goodbye, Margaret Colicos. Thank you for gathering our songs."*

Davlin's enormous face collapsed into a shapeless mass. With scraping sounds, the eight looming domates marched into the hall of the breedex and waded directly into the writhing, squirming mass of the hive mind. For a moment Margaret thought this was the beginning of another fissioning, that all the grubs would devour the domates. Instead the squirming creatures crawled over the eight towering figures, climbing up their hard exoskeletons until they covered each domate with a living, twitching blanket. Then the laden creatures lumbered out of the hall, carrying the dispersed breedex with them.

Margaret and Anton followed them out into Llaro's bright sunlight and climbed to a tower opening from which they could observe the main city. Below them, Klikiss scientist breeds huddled around the transportal at the center of the metropolis. The tall trapezoidal frame shimmered, and the flat stone barrier melted away to reveal another world, a place of gray cliffs and steaming geysers under a dim indigo sky.

The ranks of Klikiss parted as the tiger-striped domates moved forward in a regimented march. Without pausing, they carried the dispersed breedex through the pulsing transportal.

As soon as the domates were away, the first ranks of warriors filed after them in a march that lasted more than an hour. Then came the workers, harvesters, excreters, scouts . . . one sub-breed after another, line after line in an awesome but orderly mass exodus from Llaro.

Margaret and Anton watched from their vantage. "Davlin is taking the seeds of the hive with him."

The Klikiss flowed through the transportal in an endless stream, evacuating to an unidentified new world. The scientist sub-breeds remained beside the transportal, watching the passage of all the insects until the last yellow-shelled borers scuttled through.

Then the scientist creatures fiddled with the engraved circuitry and controls at the base of the trapezoidal frame. Satisfied, the Klikiss technicians plunged through the frame—all except one.

When the others were gone, the sole remaining Klikiss touched the transportal controls, and the stone doorway melted back into solidity, cutting off the passage to the other world. Sparks flew from the circuitry network, and parts of the coordinate tiles melted, permanently disabling the transportal.

His work finished, the Klikiss scientist died.

When she saw the dead scientist crumpled next to the opaque trapezoidal wall, Margaret was reminded of the lone Klikiss cadaver she and Louis had found inside the cliff city on Rheindic Co, also lying beside a transportal. Now she understood how the last remnants of the insect race had escaped from the black robots and the hydrogues.

And she understood what Davlin had done.

Margaret and Anton made their way down to the stone frame and looked at the vast and empty insect metropolis all around them. "The breedex picked a new planet, one that wasn't marked on the normal coordinate tiles, so we'd never find them. Then the scientist sub-breeds destroyed the transportal to cover their tracks. I don't expect even our best experts could figure out where the Klikiss have gone now."

Anton nodded sadly. "It seems like a good ending to the hive song."

His mother agreed. Davlin was gone, the Klikiss were gone, and she finally felt that her work was done.

172 ☀ JESS TAMBLYN

Back at the ruins of Rendezvous, where the formerly inhabited asteroid facilities and artificial domes had once been strung together in a loose cluster, Jess gazed wistfully at the debris through his ship's windowport. Dozens of Roamer craft flitted around, locking onto the largest pieces of the wrecked governmental complex and using their powerful thrusters to nudge the rubble back to a common gravitational center. Others used momentum cannons to fire rock pellets into space, gradually easing the asteroids into place.

"At one time, we could have used wental power to re-align all of those pieces," Jess pointed out. "Now I feel . . . at a loss."

"Now we feel *normal*," Cesca said. "We're Roamers, and that's good enough for me."

Though they no longer had the presence of the water elementals inside them, the intimate mental touch had come to them one last time after they had left Ildira. *The wentals are exhausted, but we survive. The verdani sacrificed much, but they survive, as well.* Jess and Cesca had felt weary, but gratified by what they had accomplished. *The hydrogues are contained within their gas giants, and the faeros within their suns. Chaos has been controlled, life still thrives, and balance has been achieved once again, at last.*

"Yes, life thrives," Cesca agreed with a cryptic smile, pressing a hand against her belly.

"Then we've won," Jess said.

The wental voice was silent for some time. *The war is over, and all factions have survived*, it said. *That is our victory.* Then the voice was gone.

Jess and Cesca rode in a small Roamer ship that had been given to them, since they could no longer fashion a water-bubble craft whenever they needed it; nor could they survive in vacuum or stroll across the terrain of an airless planetoid. Now they were just average people again, real people. A man and a woman.

How Jess had longed for that. "I wouldn't change a thing." He reached over to stroke her long dark hair. "And our work isn't over—it's just going to be different."

"The work of a Roamer Speaker never ends. Isn't that what Jhy Okiah used to say? She was a smart woman."

Cesca grinned. "My new role as Speaker will be to help the clans fit in with the Confederation and to encourage plenty of cooperation."

As they approached the Rendezvous site, Jess and Cesca identified themselves, got clearance, and docked their small ship in a complex where the ambitious workers had established a rugged living dome. Tanks of spare fuel, water, air, and packaged supplies had been set out in a metal-walled oasis. After cycling through the airlock, they met several dozen men and women who had come back, working on a quixotic scheme to put all the pieces back together, as if that would make everything as it had been.

Cesca swept her gaze around, smiling at the people. "I recognize you—clan Rudyear, isn't it?"

An older woman nodded. Three teenaged boys stared at the two visitors. One short, stocky man paled as he recognized them. "Don't let them touch you!" He hesitated. "Can you two come in here? Is it safe?"

Laughing, Jess stepped forward and clapped the man on the shoulder. "Nothing to worry about. The wentals are gone from our bodies."

"We're nothing special anymore," Cesca added.

"I beg to differ," said the older woman. "We've heard plenty about the two of you. Even without wentals inside you, nobody's going to argue that Speaker Peroni didn't do what was necessary for clan survival during our hardest times."

Cesca hugged the old woman, who flinched from the embrace, despite her assurances. Jess threw his arms around two of the other people inside the dome. "I hope you don't mind. It's been so long since we could actually touch another person, we've really missed it." He shook the hands of the perplexed teenaged boys, who didn't seem to understand what the problem was.

"Speaker Peroni, are you going to return to Rendezvous when we have it completed?" said an obviously pregnant blond-haired woman.

"I'd like that," Cesca said. "The clans will always be independent, but we probably don't want a separate governmental center from the Confederation."

"I was just thinking of it as a nice place to live," said the short-statured man.

"We'll help spread the word," Jess said.

"Good. We could use any help the clans can spare," the old woman said.

"For a percentage, of course," the short man added.

"For a *small* percentage." She and the man eyed each other, and finally he backed down.

"Who knows," one of the workers suggested, "once we get finished here, maybe we'll figure out a way to reassemble Earth's Moon, too."

"Ridiculous," the woman said. "It would be easier just to haul in a new one from a planet that doesn't need it."

"Okay, we can do that, then."

Jess didn't think either plan sounded particularly easy. But then again, Roamers specialized in solving problems, regardless of the complexity.

He and Cesca stayed long enough to have a meal, and then flew onward. Their next stop was the Osquivel shipyards, and then Theroc, where King Peter had called a great meeting to relaunch the government of humanity.

Reveling in being among people again, he and Cesca

took every opportunity to shake hands or exchange embraces with friends, family, or new acquaintances, relishing the human contact.

They also relished their time alone in their journeys between destinations. "We have a new start," Cesca said.

"I'm glad we won't be starting at the beginning." Jess remembered how unhappy they had been for so long, with Cesca first betrothed to Ross Tamblyn, then to Reynald of Theroc. They had been kept apart, following what they believed to be their duty rather than their hearts, afraid to speak up for what their emotions demanded. They had been so miserable. "We belong together."

As the ship flew onward, Cesca gave him a kiss. "You're right. I don't ever get tired of feeling human contact . . . close human contact. Especially contact with you."

He glanced at the autopilot and the chronometer. "We do have several hours before we get to our destination. How do you propose we occupy our time?"

"For that, Jess Tamblyn, I suggest you follow your Guiding Star."

173 ☀ KING PETER

The great gathering of civilizations occurred on Theroc.

Condorflies buzzed overhead, as if trying to compete with the numerous Roamer ships that landed in a constant stream in the worldforest clearings. Celli and Solimar acted as the official green priests, and through them the messages and news spread everywhere throughout the telink network.

The representatives of Confederation colonies had used their own green priests to call for ships, so they could attend the convocation. Rlinda Kett, Branson Roberts, and Nikko Chan Tylar delivered as many visitors as their ships could carry. Those ambassadors who could not appear in person sent messages through telink, which were delivered and read aloud so that every attendee could hear the widespread and unwavering support across the Spiral Arm.

Sarein, dressed in the same ambassador's robe that ancient Otema had worn years ago, acted as a liaison with the former Hansa bureaucracy. Deputy Cain was also there, along with Fleet Admiral Willis, General Conrad Brindle, his wife, Natalie, Robb, and Tasia, all in seats of prominence.

Patrick and Zhett scolded Del Kellum, who continued to scribble messages, passing them to green priests for transmission as he waited through tedious delays before the final ceremony. Now that his skymining business and the gigantic shipyards were operating without hindrance, Kellum couldn't tear himself away from his administrative duties, but his daughter and her husband made him sit up and pay attention.

Overhead, forty-nine Ildiran streamers raced back and forth, creating sonic booms and leaving a crosshatched pattern of exhaust trails. Though reluctant to leave Ildira again himself—considering what had happened on his last innocent mission to Theroc—the Mage-Imperator nonetheless sent Nira, Osira'h, and Prime Designate Daro'h; through the *thism* he would know what he needed to know.

Next to King Peter, Estarra held baby Reynald in her arms. She didn't care that this was a formal government ceremony: She intended for their baby to witness the birth of a truly unified Confederation. Proud grandparents Mother Alexa and Father Idriss wanted to watch the child, but the Queen's word was final.

OX never allowed himself to be more than a few steps away from the King and Queen. His synthetic skin was polished and all his systems up-graded—especially his memory capacity, to accommodate the data that Deputy Cain had saved in the archives, as well as the new experiences he had accumulated since escaping from Earth with Peter and Estarra.

"Now I can store several more lifetimes' worth of memories," the Teacher compy had said when the restoration upload was complete. His optical sensors gleamed gold with excitement.

"You have a lot more work ahead of you, OX," Peter had said. "You taught me so many valuable things that I was hoping you'd teach our son, too."

"Will you be Reynald's Teacher compy?" Estarra asked.

OX did not hesitate. "I would be honored."

After the Ildiran skyparade wrapped up overhead, the streamers raced back to their warliner in orbit, and King Peter called for attention. "People of Earth and Theroc, people of the human race—whether former Hansa colonists or Roamers—and representatives of the Ildiran Empire." He looked around to see rapt attention on the faces of the large crowd that sat shaded under the green canopy of leaves. "Endings are often sad, beginnings usually joyous. Today we have both. After listening to an overwhelming majority of representatives, I exercise the authority vested in me as the leader of the Confederation to formally dissolve the Terran Hanseatic League."

King Peter listened to the surge of applause. Deputy Cain and Sarein clapped the loudest.

When the cheering died down, Estarra spoke. "The King and I welcome all peoples who wish to live in peace, so that a strong civilization can thrive in the Spiral Arm. We have seen the costs of enmity and destruction. Now let us reap the rewards of cooperation, commerce, and friendship."

Peter continued even before the applause had quieted. "Our past was built on the whims of tyrants, the blood of innocents, the embers of stars, and the ashes of worlds." Beside him, Estarra held the baby in one arm. He took her free hand. "Together, we build a new future for all, and together we can achieve the impossible."

GLOSSARY

Adar — highest military rank in the Ildiran Solar Navy.

Aguerra, Carlos — Raymond's younger brother.

Aguerra, Michael — Raymond's youngest brother.

Aguerra, Raymond — streetwise young man from Earth, former identity of King Peter.

Aguerra, Rory — Raymond's younger brother.

Ala'nh, Tal — one of the remaining cohort commanders of the Ildiran Solar Navy.

Alexa, Mother — former ruler of Theroc; wife of Father Idriss and mother of Reynald, Beneto, Sarein, Estarra, and Celli.

Andez, Colonel Shelia — EDF soldier, former Roamer captive with Patrick Fitzpatrick III, chosen to lead Chairman Wenceslas's "cleanup crew."

Andropolis, Dr. Tito — Hansa scientific adviser assigned to assist Chairman Wenceslas in creating technological "miracles."

Aquarius — Nikko Chan Tylar's wental-repaired ship.

Archfather — symbolic head of the Unison religion on Earth.

Barrymore's Rock — isolated Roamer fuel depot destroyed by Sirix's black robots.

BeBob — Rlinda Kett's nickname for Branson Roberts.

Beneto — green priest, second son of Father Idriss and

Mother Alexa, killed by hydrogues on Corvus Landing, returned in a wooden body as an avatar of the worldforest, then later joined with verdani battleship.

Big Goose—Roamer derogative term for Terran Hanseatic League.

blazer—Ildiran illumination source.

Blind Faith—Branson Roberts's ship, destroyed during an escape from Earth, rebuilt by Roamers at the Osquivel shipyards.

breedex—a hive mind of the Klikiss, which controls all the members of a subhive.

Brindle, Conrad—Robb Brindle's father, former military officer, returned to active duty; when Robb left to join the Confederation, Conrad insisted on remaining loyal to the EDF.

Brindle, Natalie—Robb Brindle's mother, former military officer returned to active duty.

Brindle, Robb—young EDF recruit, comrade of Tasia Tamblyn, captured and held prisoner by hydrogues after trying to contact them at Osquivel, rescued by Jess Tamblyn. With Tasia, Robb joined the Confederation and helps them build their military.

Burton—One of the eleven generation ships from Earth, seized by Ildirans at Dobro and its passengers used in breeding experiments for generations.

Cain, Eldred—deputy and heir-apparent of Basil Wenceslas.

cargo escort—Roamer vessel used to deliver ekti shipments from skymines.

Celli—youngest daughter of Father Idriss and Mother Alexa; she recently became a green priest.

Chan, Marla—mother of Nikko Chan Tylar, wife of Crim

Tylar. Marla was killed by Klikiss during the colonists' escape from Llaro.

Charybdis — primordial water planet, site of Jess Tamblyn's original dispersal of wentals. Charybdis was devastated in an unprovoked faeros attack.

chrysalis chair — reclining throne of the Mage-Imperator.

cleanup crew — elite watchdog security group given special orders by Chairman Wenceslas to quell dissent. They are led by Colonel Shelia Andez.

cloud harvester — ekti-gathering facility designed by Hansa.

cohort — Ildiran Solar Navy battle group consisting of seven maniples, or 343 warliners, commanded by a tal.

Colicos, Anton — son of Margaret and Louis Colicos, translator and student of epic stories, sent to Ildiran Empire to study the *Saga of Seven Suns*. He was captured with the Mage-Imperator's Ildirans and held prisoner on the Moon.

Colicos, Louis — xeno-archaeologist, husband of Margaret Colicos and father of Anton, killed by Klikiss robots at Rheindic Co.

Colicos, Margaret — xeno-archaeologist, wife of Louis Colicos and mother of Anton, vanished through transportal during Klikiss robot attack on Rheindic Co and lived among Klikiss. After helping colonists escape from Llaro, Margaret was recaptured by the new breedex.

competent computerized companion — intelligent servant robot, called compy, available in Friendly, Teacher, Governess, Listener, and other models.

compy — shortened term for "competent computerized companion."

condorfly—colorful flying insect on Theroc like a giant butterfly, sometimes kept as pets.

Constantine III—stormy, primordial planet, site of Roamer facility to extract polymers and raw materials from its thick atmosphere; known for exotic flame-proof materials.

Corribus—ancient Klikiss world where Margaret and Louis Colicos discovered the Klikiss Torch technology, site of one of the first new Hansa colonies. Eradicated by Klikiss robots; Orli Covitz and Hud Steinman were the only survivors.

Covitz, Orli—teenaged girl, one of two survivors of the Klikiss robot attack on Corribus. Later, she moved to a new home on Llaro, only to be caught in the Klikiss invasion. After discovering that her music could stun the Klikiss hive mind, she helped the remaining colonists escape.

Crenna—former Ildiran splinter colony, evacuated due to plague, and resettled by humans, then later frozen when its sun died in hydrogue-faeros battles. The colonist refugees resettled on Llaro, and were trapped by the Klikiss invasion there.

cutter—small ship in Ildiran Solar Navy.

Cyroc'h—former Mage-Imperator, father of Jora'h, poisoned himself so that Jora'h would have to take over the leadership.

Daniel—Prince candidate selected as a replacement for Peter, left stranded on neo-Amish world of Happiness.

Daro'h—former Dobro Designate-in-waiting but now the Prime Designate of the Ildiran Empire after the death of Thor'h.

DD—Friendly compy owned by Margaret Colicos, seized

by the Klikiss robot Sirix, before he escaped through a transportal to rejoin Margaret. Now DD serves as the companion to Orli Covitz.

Designate—any purebred noble son of the Mage-Imperator, ruler of an Ildiran world.

diamondfilm—crystalline parchment used for Ildiran documents.

Diente, Admiral Esteban—one of the four surviving grid admirals after the black robot uprising and the hydrogue war; he was ordered to capture the Mage-Imperator's Flagship.

Dobro—Ildiran colony world, former site of human-Ildiran breeding camps before a revolt shut them down.

domate—largest sub-breed of Klikiss, silver carapace with black tiger stripes. The domates acquire and provide genetic material to the breedex during reproductive fissioning.

drogue—deprecatory term for hydrogues.

Durris—trinary star system, close white and orange stars orbited by a red dwarf; three of the Ildiran "seven suns." Durris-B was extinguished in the hydrogue-faeros war, but reignited when faeros incarnate Rusa'h led an armada of faeros back through the star's transgate.

Earth Defense Forces (EDF)—Terran space military, led by General Kurt Lanyan, devastated during the black robot uprising and the hydrogue war.

Eddies—slang term for soldiers in EDF

ekti—exotic allotrope of hydrogen used to fuel Ildiran stardrives, primarily extracted from gas-giant planets.

Eldora—Confederation forestry colony.

Estarra, Queen—second daughter, fourth child of Father

Idriss and Mother Alexa, married to King Peter, recently gave birth to a son, Reynald.

faeros — sentient fire entities dwelling within stars.

featherviper — poisonous serpent from Theroc.

Fitzpatrick, Maureen — former Chairman of the Terran Hanseatic League, grandmother of Patrick Fitzpatrick III, nicknamed "Old Battleaxe."

Fitzpatrick, Patrick III — General Lanyan's protégé in the Earth Defense Forces, presumed dead after battle of Osquivel but captured by Roamers. Later, he abandoned the EDF, stole his grandmother's space yacht, and went in search of the Roamers; now he is married to Zhett Kellum.

Frederick — previous Great King of the Hansa, Peter's predecessor, assassinated by hydrogue emissary.

Freedom's Sword — outspoken protest group that is attempting to oust Hansa Chairman Basil Wenceslas.

fungus reef — giant worldtree growth on Theroc, carved into a habitation by the Therons.

Gale'nh — experimental half-breed son of Nira and Adar Kori'nh, third oldest of her children.

Gold, Jerome — Sullivan and Lydia's adult son.

Gold, Lydia — Sullivan's wife.

Gold, Patrice — Sullivan and Lydia's adult daughter.

Gold, Philip — Sullivan and Lydia's teenaged grandson.

Gold, Sullivan — former administrator of the Hansa's modular cloud harvester at Qronha 3, which was destroyed by hydrogues; temporarily held captive by Ildirans, then quietly returned to Earth by Rlinda Kett and Branson Roberts.

Gold, Victor — Sullivan and Lydia's adult son.

Golgen — gas giant where Ross Tamblyn's Blue Sky Mine

was destroyed; now it is the site of renewed Roamer sky-mining, particularly by clan Kellum.

green priest — servant of the worldforest, able to use worldtrees for instantaneous telink communication.

Guiding Star — Roamer philosophy and religion, an inspirational force in a person's life.

Gypsy — space yacht flown by Patrick Fitzpatrick III, renamed after he stole it from his grandmother to search for Zhett Kellum.

Hansa — Terran Hanseatic League.

Hansa headquarters — pyramidal building near the Whisper Palace on Earth.

Hobart — Roamer clan, operators of a skymine on Golgen.

Horizon Cluster — large star cluster near Ildira, location of Hyrillka and many other splinter colonies. Most of Rusa'h's rebellion took place in the Horizon Cluster.

Huck, Tabitha — engineer aboard Sullivan Gold's cloud harvester, held captive by Ildirans and turned her talents to helping in the war against the hydrogues. A devotee of the green priest Kolker's joined telink/*thism* philosophy, Tabitha was killed by faeros when they reemerged from the dead sun of Durris-B.

hydrogues — alien race living in the cores of gas-giant planets, allied with the black robots and defeated by a combined force of verdani, wentals, Solar Navy, EDF, and Roamers.

Hyrillka — Ildiran colony in the Horizon Cluster, from which Designate Rusa'h began his rebellion. When battles between faeros and hydrogues threatened to extinguish one of Hyrillka's suns, the population was evacuated and taken temporarily to Ildira. The current Hyrillka Designate is the boy Ridek'h.

Idriss, Father — former ruler of Theroc, husband of Mother Alexa and father of Reynald, Beneto, Sarein, Estarra, and Celli.

Ildira — home planet of the Ildiran Empire.

Ildiran Empire — large alien empire, the only other major civilization in the Spiral Arm.

Ildiran Solar Navy — space military fleet of the Ildiran Empire, much of which was devastated defending Earth during the end of the hydrogue war. Many warliners were being rebuilt in large orbiting shipyards over Ildira before the recent faeros invasion.

Ildirans — humanoid alien race with many different breeds, or kiths.

Isix cats — sleek feline predators native to Ildira; Jora'h's daughter Yazra'h kept three of them, though one was killed by faeros.

jazer — energy weapon used by Earth Defense Forces.

Jonah 12 — icy planetoid, site of Kotto Okiah's hydrogen-extraction facility, destroyed by Klikiss robots. Caleb Tamblyn was stranded on Jonah 12 after faeros destroyed his water tanker.

Jora'h — Mage-Imperator of the Ildiran Empire.

Juggernaut — largest battleship class in Earth Defense Forces.

Jupiter — Admiral Willis's flagship Juggernaut.

Kamarov, Raven — Roamer captain, destroyed with his cargo ship during a secret EDF raid. Patrick Fitzpatrick III gave the order to fire on him, following instructions given by General Lanyan.

Kellum, Del — Roamer clan leader, in charge of Osquivel shipyards and many Golgen skymines; formerly engaged to Shareen Pasternak, who was killed by hydrogues; father of Zhett.

Kellum, Zhett — daughter of Del Kellum; married to Patrick Fitzpatrick.

Kett, Rlinda — heavyset merchant woman, captain of the *Voracious Curiosity*, now serving as the Confederation's Trade Minister.

kith — a breed of Ildiran.

Klikiss — ancient insectlike race, long vanished from the Spiral Arm, leaving only their empty cities, recently returned to take over their former worlds.

Klikiss robots — intelligent beetlelike robots built by the Klikiss race.

Klikiss Siren — sonic device developed by Kotto Okiah.

Klikiss Torch — a weapon created by the ancient Klikiss race to implode gas-giant planets as a defense against the hydrogues; their design was rediscovered by Margaret and Louis Colicos, who tested the device at the gas giant Oncier, thereby unwittingly provoking the hydrogue war.

Kolker — green priest stationed on Sullivan Gold's cloud harvester at Qronha 3, held captive by Ildirans. Kolker discovered a way to unite telink and *thism,* thus forming a new pseudo-religion, but he also unwittingly created a pathway for newborn faeros to spread. He was killed during the faeros invasion of Ildira.

Kori'nh, Adar — leader of the Ildiran Solar Navy, killed in a heroic suicidal assault against hydrogues on Qronha 3; mentor of Zan'nh.

Ko'sh — Chief Scribe of the Ildiran rememberer kith; despite the Mage-Imperator's orders to correct and revise the *Saga of Seven Suns,* Ko'sh resisted all changes.

Kulu, Dr. Jane—Hansa scientific adviser, assigned to assist Chairman Wenceslas in creating technological "miracles."

Lanyan, General Kurt—commander of the Earth Defense Forces.

lens kithmen—philosopher priests who help to guide troubled Ildirans, interpreting faint guidance from the *thism*.

Lightsource—a realm on a higher plane composed entirely of light. Ildirans believe that faint trickles of this light break through into our universe and are channeled through the Mage-Imperator and distributed across their race through the *thism*.

Liona—green priest assigned to Del Kellum's skymine on Golgen and then to the Osquivel shipyards.

Llaro—abandoned Klikiss world, site of a human colony and also a POW camp for Roamer detainees. The Klikiss invasion overwhelmed this colony, killing many of the people; only a few colonists escaped.

Lotze, Davlin—Hansa exosociologist and spy, sent to Rheindic Co, where he and Rlinda Kett discovered how to use the Klikiss transportal system. Later, he left Hansa service and went in hiding to live on Llaro with other Crenna refugees. After helping the colonists to escape, he was captured by the Klikiss and consumed in the breedex's next fissioning.

Mage-Imperator—the god-emperor of the Ildiran Empire.

Manta—midsized cruiser class in EDF.

Maratha—Ildiran resort world with extremely long day and night cycle, abandoned since Klikiss robots took over.

Maratha Prime—primary domed city on one continent of Maratha, destroyed by Klikiss robots.

Maratha Secda—sister city on opposite side of Maratha, destroyed by Klikiss robots.

Mijistra—glorious capital city of the Ildiran Empire, site of the Prism Palace.

Muree'n—experimental half-breed daughter of Nira and a guard kithman, youngest of her children.

Nahton—court green priest on Earth, assassinated by Chairman Wenceslas when he tried to send a warning to Theroc about an impending EDF attack.

Nira—female green priest, Jora'h's lover and mother of his half-breed daughter, Osira'h. She was held captive for years in breeding camps on Dobro, then freed.

Okiah, Jhy—former Speaker of the clans, died on Jonah 12.

Okiah, Kotto—Jhy Okiah's youngest son, a brash and eccentric inventor who created many innovations to assist the clans during the hydrogue war, including the "doorbells" that destroyed warglobes and the wental-ice artillery shells that destroyed faeros.

old Battleaxe—nickname for former Hansa Chairman Maureen Fitzpatrick.

O'nh, Tal—second-highest-ranking officer in Ildiran Solar Navy, mentor to Hyrillka Designate Ridek'h. He was blinded by Rusa'h in a faeros attack on his septa of warliners.

Osira'h—daughter of Nira and Jora'h, bred to have unusual telepathic abilities. She was a special envoy to the hydrogues.

Osquivel—ringed gas planet, site of secret Roamer shipyards; also, the name of a new personnel transport built to retrieve Roamer detainees on Llaro.

Otema—former ambassador from Theroc, green priest sent

to Ildira, where she was murdered by Mage-Imperator Cyroc'h.

OX—Teacher compy, one of the oldest Earth robots, instructor and adviser to King Peter; his memories were mostly wiped during Peter and Estarra's escape from Earth.

Palace District—governmental zone around the Whisper Palace on Earth.

Palomar, Ronald—former Hansa Chairman who served between the administrations of Maureen Fitzpatrick and Basil Wenceslas.

PD—one of two Friendly compies formerly belonging to Admiral Wu-Lin, taken as "students" of Sirix during the black robot uprising.

Peroni, Cesca—Roamer Speaker of all clans, trained by Jhy Okiah. Cesca was betrothed to Ross Tamblyn, then Reynald of Theroc, but has always loved Jess Tamblyn. Nearly killed by the black robots on Jonah 12, she was saved by the wentals and is now infused with wental power; she has joined Jess in his work for the wentals.

Peroni, Denn—Cesca's father, killed by faeros near Jonah 12.

Peter, King—formerly Raymond Aguerra; Great King of the Hansa, married to Estarra; he escaped Earth and established a new Confederation on Theroc.

Pike, Zebulon Charles—one of four surviving grid admirals after the black robot uprising and the hydrogue war.

Plumas—frozen moon with deep liquid oceans, site of Tamblyn clan water industry, nearly destroyed by a tainted wental inhabiting Karla Tamblyn's body.

Prime Designate—eldest son and heir apparent of Ildiran Mage-Imperator.

Prism Palace—dwelling of the Ildiran Mage-Imperator.

Pym — abandoned Klikiss world resettled during the Colonization Initiative, now the site of a large Klikiss subhive.

Qronha — a close binary system, two of the Ildiran "seven suns." The system contains two habitable planets and one gas giant, Qronha 3, where all skymining was destroyed by hydrogue attacks.

QT — one of two Friendly compies formerly belonging to Admiral Wu-Lin, taken as "students" of Sirix during the black robot uprising.

Relleker — former Hansa colony, destroyed by hydrogues. Now resettled by Roamer clans and Confederation colonists, known for its new cutting-edge technological industries.

Rememberer — member of the Ildiran storyteller kith.

Remora — small attack ship in Earth Defense Forces.

Rendezvous — inhabited asteroid cluster, once the center of Roamer government before it was destroyed by the EDF.

Reynald — eldest son of Father Idriss and Mother Alexa, killed in hydrogue attack on Theroc. Also the name of King Peter and Queen Estarra's firstborn son.

Rheindic Co — abandoned Klikiss world investigated by Margaret and Louis Colicos; the central transfer point for the transportal network before the Klikiss recaptured it from General Lanyan.

Rhejak — former Hansa colony, an ocean world of reefs, medusa herders, and fishermen. Rhejak was the site of a planned EDF pogrom, but General Lanyan was foiled by the mutiny of Admiral Willis.

Roamers — loose confederation of independent humans, primary producers of ekti stardrive fuel.

Roberts, Branson — former husband and business partner

of Rlinda Kett, also called BeBob; his ship is the *Blind Faith*.

Rod'h — experimental half-breed son of Nira and the Dobro Designate, second oldest of her children.

Rusa'h — former Hyrillka Designate who degenerated into madness after a head injury and began a revolt against the Mage-Imperator. Rather than allow himself to be captured, he flew his ship into Hyrillka's sun, where he merged with the fiery elementals and has returned as the faeros incarnate.

Saga of Seven Suns — historical and legendary epic of the Ildiran civilization, considered to be infallible until Anton Colicos and Rememberer Vao'sh proved otherwise.

San Luis, Zia — one of the four surviving grid admirals after the black robot uprising and the hydrogue war.

Sarein — eldest daughter of Father Idriss and Mother Alexa, Theron ambassador to Earth, also Basil Wenceslas's lover; she helped Estarra and Peter escape from the Hansa, but chose to remain behind on Earth.

septa — Ildiran Solar Navy battle group composed of seven ships.

septar — commander of a septa.

shizz — Roamer expletive.

Sirix — Klikiss robot, leader of robotic revolt against humans.

skymine — ekti-harvesting facility in the clouds of a gas-giant planet, usually operated by Roamers.

skysphere — main dome of the Ildiran Prism Palace, equivalent to a throne room.

Solimar — young green priest, treedancer, and mechanic; Celli's boyfriend.

soul-threads — connections of *thism* that trickle through from the Lightsource. The Mage-Imperator and lens kithmen are able to see them.

Speaker — political leader of the Roamer clans.

Spiral Arm — the section of the Milky Way Galaxy settled by the Ildiran Empire and Hansa colonies.

splinter colony — an Ildiran colony that meets minimum population requirements.

Steinman, Hud — old transportal explorer, discovered Corribus and decided to settle there. After the black robot attack on Corribus, he and Orli Covitz were the only two survivors; they joined the Crenna refugees on Llaro before the Klikiss invasion there, and were rescued by Tasia Tamblyn and Robb Brindle.

Stoner, Benn — leader of former human captives on Dobro.

streamer — fast single ship in Ildiran Solar Navy.

Sweeney, Dahlia — DD's first owner.

tal — military rank in the Ildiran Solar Navy, cohort commander.

Tamblyn, Caleb — one of Jess and Tasia's uncles, stranded on Jonah 12 after the faeros destroyed his water tanker.

Tamblyn, Jess — Roamer in love with Cesca Peroni, infused with wental energy.

Tamblyn, Karla — Jess and Tasia's mother, frozen to death in ice accident on Plumas, revived by tainted wentals.

Tamblyn, Ross — Jess and Tasia's brother, betrothed to Cesca Peroni, killed in the first hydrogue attack on Golgen.

Tamblyn, Tasia — Jess's sister, who left the Roamers to join the EDF, captured by hydrogues at Qronha 3 and freed by Jess. Now she and Robb Brindle have joined the Confederation military.

Tamblyn, Torin—one of Jess and Tasia's uncles, twin to Wynn, currently running the Plumas water mines.

Tamblyn, Wynn—one of Jess and Tasia's uncles, twin to Torin, currently running the Plumas water mines.

Tamo'l—experimental half-breed daughter of Nira and a lens kithman; second youngest of her children.

telink—instantaneous communication used by green priests via worldtrees.

Terran Hanseatic League—commerce-based government of Earth and Terran colonies, also called the Hansa, managed by a Chairman and a figurehead King.

Theroc—forested planet, home of the sentient worldtrees, currently the center of the Confederation's government.

Theron—a native of Theroc.

thism—faint racial telepathic link from the Mage-Imperator to the Ildiran people.

Thor'h—eldest noble-born son of Mage-Imperator Jora'h; former Prime Designate who joined Rusa'h's rebellion; he died on Dobro.

torch trees—worldtrees possessed by faeros, filled with living fire but not consumed.

transgate—hydrogue/faeros point-to-point transportation system.

transportal—Klikiss instantaneous transportation system.

treedancers—acrobatic performers in the Theron forests.

treeling—a small worldtree sapling, often transported in an ornate pot and used by green priests for telink.

Troop Carrier—personnel transport ship in the Ildiran Solar Navy.

twitcher—EDF stun weapon.

Tylar, Crim—Roamer detainee on Llaro, father of Nikko, rescued by Tasia Tamblyn and Robb Brindle.

Tylar, Nikko Chan—young Roamer pilot, son of Crim and Marla; Nikko was one of Jess Tamblyn's first water bearers to deliver wental water; his ship is the *Aquarius*.

Unison—standardized government-sponsored religion for official activities on Earth, whose spokesman is the Archfather, a paid actor.

UR—Governess-model Roamer compy, formerly held at Llaro with other Roamer detainees; she lost one of her arms protecting several children during an attack by a Klikiss scout.

Usk—breakaway Hansa colony, populated mainly by farmers, site of a horrific pogrom led by General Lanyan and the Archfather of Unison.

Vao'sh—Ildiran rememberer, patron and friend of Anton Colicos, survivor of the robot attacks on Maratha; one of the only Ildirans ever to survive the isolation madness caused by separation from other Ildirans.

verdani—organic-based sentience, manifested as the Theron worldforest.

Voracious Curiosity—Rlinda Kett's merchant ship.

warglobe—hydrogue spherical attack vessel.

warliner—largest class of Ildiran battleship.

Wenceslas, Basil—Chairman of the Terran Hanseatic League.

wentals—sentient water-based creatures.

Whisper Palace—magnificent seat of the Hansa government.

Willis, Admiral Sheila—one of only four remaining grid admirals to survive the battle of Earth; she defected to the Confederation after refusing to slaughter colonists on Rhejak.

worldforest—the interconnected, semi-sentient forest based on Theroc.

worldtree—a separate tree in the interconnected, semi-sentient forest based on Theroc.

Yarrod—green priest, younger brother of Mother Alexa, a devotee of Kolker's telink/*thism* philosophy. He was killed by the faeros on Theroc.

Yazra'h—oldest daughter of Jora'h; his official guard.

Zan'nh—Adar of the Ildiran Solar Navy; eldest son of Mage-Imperator Jora'h.

ACKNOWLEDGMENTS

I've worked on the Saga of Seven Suns for nearly eight years, and even though I originally envisioned a vast epic spanning many volumes, the story has still grown and changed, thanks to the advice and expertise of many people. Among those who have helped me enormously over the course of these novels are Jaime Levine, Louis Moesta, Diane Jones, Catherine Sidor, Tim Holman, Kate Lyall-Grant, John Silbersack, and Robert Gottlieb.

KEVIN J. ANDERSON

returns with an incredible new adventure . . .

THE EDGE OF THE WORLD

BOOK ONE OF THE TERRA INCOGNITA TRILOGY

Terra Incognita – the blank spaces on the map, past the edge of the world, marked only by the words "here be monsters."

Two nations at war, fighting for dominion over the known, and undiscovered, world, pin their last hopes at ultimate victory on finding a land out of legend.

Each will send their ships to brave the untamed seas, wild storms, sea serpents, and darker dangers unknown to any man. It is a perilous undertaking, but there will always be the impetuous, the brave and the mad who are willing to leave their homes to explore the unknown.

Even unto the edge of the world . . .

Publication Date: June 8, 2009

extras

orbit

meet the author

KEVIN J. ANDERSON has written 46 national and international bestsellers and has over 20 million books in print worldwide in thirty languages. He has been nominated for the Nebula Award, the Bram Stoker Award, and the SFX Readers' Choice Award. Find out more about Kevin Anderson at www.wordfire.com.

introducing

If you enjoyed **THE ASHES OF WORLDS**,
look out for

THE EDGE OF THE WORLD

Book One of the Terra Incognita trilogy
by Kevin J. Anderson

These foreign seas looked much the same as the waters of home, but Criston Vora knew the lands were different, the people were different, and their religion was contrary to everything he had been taught in the Aidenist kirk. For a twenty-year-old sailor eager to see the world, those differences could be either wondrous or frightening—he wouldn't know which until he met the people of Uraba, which he was about to do.

The *Fishhook* had made this voyage several times, and Criston's captain, Andon Shay, was confident in his abilities to negotiate another trade deal with the Uraban merchants. The young man kept his eyes open and studied the unfolding coastline as the ship sailed far, far south of everything he had known.

From his fishing village of Windcatch, he had always felt the call of the sea, wanting to see what lay beyond the horizon, yearning to explore. Though he had signed on for only a short trading voyage, at least he was seeing the other continent: *Uraba*. A place of legends and mystery.

Though connected by a narrow isthmus, the world's two main continents, Uraba and Tierra, were separated by a wide gulf of history and culture. Ages ago, at the beginning of time, when Ondun—God—had sent two of his sons in separate sailing ships to explore the world, the descendents of Aiden's crew had settled Tierra, while those from Urec's vessel colonized Uraba. Over the centuries, the followers of Aiden and the followers of Urec developed separate civilizations, religions and traditions; despite their differences, they were bound together by ties of trade and necessity.

On a bright sunny day with a brisk breeze, Captain Shay called for the sails to be trimmed for a gentle approach to the city of Ouroussa, where they hoped to find eager customers. The hold of the *Fishhook* contained barrels of whale oil from Soeland Reach, large spools of hemp rope from Erietta, grain from Alamont, and, in a special locked chest in the captain's cabin, beautiful metal-worked jewelry made by the skilled smiths of Corag Reach. Though the bangles and ornaments would be sold to the followers of Urec, the Corag metalworkers subtly hid a tiny Aidenist fishhook on each piece of jewelry.

Captain Shay would sell his cargo at prices greatly reduced from what the other Uraban merchants and middlemen could offer. With fast vessels, intrepid Tierran sailors braved the uncharted currents and sailed directly to Uraba's coastal cities, bypassing the much slower overland merchants (much to their consternation).

Near the ship's wheel, Criston paused to look at the two compasses mounted on a sheltered pedestal, a traditional magnetic compass that always pointed north and a magical Captain's Compass that always pointed *home*. The silver needle of the Captain's Compass came from the same piece of precious metal as an identical needle in the Tierran capital city of Calay. These twinned needles remained linked to each other by sympathetic magic, as all things in Ondun's creation were said to be linked.

Now, as the *Fishhook* closed in on Ouroussa, the crew saw a flurry of activity in the distant harbor; a ship with a bright red sail set out to meet them, sailing toward the open water. Captain Shay gestured to Criston. "Go aloft and have a look, Mr. Vora." Shay's dark hair ran to his shoulders, and instead of wearing a full bushy beard like most ship captains, he kept his neatly trimmed.

Nimble and unafraid of heights, the young man scrambled up the shroud lines to reach the lookout nest. During the voyage, Criston had enjoyed spending time high atop the main mast overlooking the waters; he had even seen several fearsome-looking sea serpents, but only at a distance.

As the Uraban ship approached, Criston noted its central painted icon on its square mainsail, the Eye of Urec. He spied additional movement in the harbor, where two fast Uraban galleys launched, their oars extended, beating across the water at a good clip. They spread apart, approaching the *Fishhook* from opposite directions.

Criston scrambled back down the lines and reported what he had seen to Captain Shay. "I couldn't see many crewmen aboard the main ship, Captain. Maybe they just want to escort us into port."

"Never needed an escort before." Shay snapped orders

to his crew, and all twenty-eight men came out on deck to stand ready. "Once they know what we're offering, they'll welcome us with open arms, but don't let your guard down." He turned back to the young sailor. "This could be a very interesting first voyage for you, Mr. Vora."

"It's not my first voyage, sir. I've spent most of my life on boats."

"It's your first voyage with *me*, and that's what counts."

Criston's father, a fisherman, had been lost at sea, and Criston himself had served aboard many boats, working the local catch, but dreaming of more ambitious voyages. Though young, Criston owned his own small boat for carrying cargo up to the Tierran capital of Calay, but the prospect of paying off the moneylenders seemed daunting. So, when the *Fishhook* had passed through Windcatch on her way south, and Captain Shay asked for short-term sailors to accompany him on a two-month trip to Ouroussa, offering wages higher than he could make on his own boat, Criston had jumped at the chance.

Not only would it help him pay off the debt, but it would give Criston a chance to see far-off lands. And when he returned to Windcatch with his purse full of coins, he would finally be able to marry Adrea, whom he had loved for years. Once the *Fishhook* unloaded her cargo in Ouroussa, Criston could be on his way home. . . .

As the scarlet-sailed Uraban ship closed to within hailing distance, he spotted a man standing near the bow dressed in loose cream-colored robes, his head wrapped in a pale olba. Only five crewmen stood with the man on the foreign vessel's deck. The robed man shouted across to them in heavily accented Tierran. "I am Fillok, Ouroussa's city leader. What goods have you brought us?"

Shay lowered his voice to Criston. "Fillok . . . I know that name. I think he's the brother of the soldan of Outer Wahilir, an important man. Why would he come to meet us?" He frowned in consternation. "Men who consider themselves important sometimes do brash things, and it's rarely a good sign." The captain raised his voice and called back across the water. "We are on our way to port. I can give your harbormaster a full list."

"It is my right to inspect your cargo here and now! How do we know your boat is not filled with soldiers to attack Ouroussa?"

"Why would we do that?" Shay asked, genuinely perplexed.

If Fillok did not change course, his ship would collide with the *Fishhook* within minutes. Criston eyed the two swift war galleys coming toward them from both port and starboard. "This doesn't feel right, Captain. I'm going to have another look." He slipped away and scrambled back up the ropes to the lookout nest.

Tierran traders often made great profit from selling to Uraban cities, but many vessels vanished, more than could reasonably be accounted for by storms and reefs. If Fillok were an ambitious and unprincipled man, he could have attacked those traders and seized their cargoes. No one in Tierra would know.

When Criston reached the lookout nest and peered down at the foreign ship, he was astonished to see far more than just the five Uraban sailors standing at the ropes. At least a dozen armed men crouched out of sight behind crates and sailcloth on the deck; the hatches were open, and even more Uraban men crowded below, holding bright scimitars. Criston cupped his hands around his mouth and yelled at the top of his lungs. "Captain, it's a trap! The ship is full of armed men!"

Shay shouted to his crew. "Set sails! All canvas, take the wind *now*!" Already on edge, the men jumped to untie knots, pull ropes, and drop sails abruptly into place.

Criston's warning forced Fillok into abrupt action. The Ouroussan city leader screamed something in his own language, and hidden men burst into view, lifting their swords. Shrill trumpets sounded a call to battle. Ropes with grappling hooks flew across the narrow gap between the two ships; several fell into the water, but three caught the *Fishhook*'s deck rail. Answering horns and drumbeats came from the two closing war galleys, and the rowers picked up their pace.

Shay reached down to grab a long harpoon stowed just below the starboard bow of the *Fishhook*. The Tierran men armed themselves with boat-hooks, oars, and stunning clubs. Criston clambered back down to the deck, ready to join the fight. He held a long boat-knife to defend himself, though its reach was much shorter than that of a Uraban scimitar.

Criston ran to the straining ropes that bound the ships together, just as five Urabans jumped across the gap with an eerie inhuman howl. Ducking a wide swing of a Uraban sword, he sawed at the first rope until it snapped and immediately set to work on the second one.

The *Fishhook*'s sails were fully extended now, giving her a much greater canvas area than Fillok's small Uraban ship. The ropes creaked as the Tierran vessel tried to break away. One of the Tierran sailors went down, bleeding from a deep gash in his head.

Ignoring the mayhem around him, Captain Shay cocked his arm back and let the long harpoon fly toward the other ship—where its sharp iron tip plunged directly through Fillok's chest. The Ouroussan city leader staggered backward, grabbing the harpoon's shaft in astonishment, before he collapsed into a pool of blood on his own deck.

The Uraban attackers gasped, then howled in rage upon seeing their leader killed. They piled against each other, preparing to leap across and slaughter the Tierrans. Racing in from shore, the two war galleys closed in a pincer maneuver.

Criston sawed with his knife until he severed the third grappling rope, and like a freed stallion, the *Fishhook* lunged free, separating from the Uraban ship as many of the enemy fighters leaped across. A dozen men tumbled into the deep water, and only two managed to cling to the side of the *Fishhook*, clutching nets and an anchor rope. Leaning over the rail, Criston lopped off fingers with a knife slash, and the screaming men slid into the water.

Though he was white as a sheet, Captain Shay's voice did not waver as he shouted. "All speed—head north! Out to open sea!" The *Fishhook* began to pull away.

Only three enemy soldiers remained on the deck. Captain Shay's crew quickly dispatched them and dumped the bodies overboard.

With Fillok killed—the brother of the local soldan!—the remaining Uraban sailors were in a frenzy aboard his ship. The drums of the approaching war galleys beat furiously, but the *Fishhook*'s sails pushed the cargo ship faster. The coastline began to dwindle in the distance, but Criston knew the uproar would not die down. "Captain, what just happened? Why did they do that? We only came to trade."

"They wanted our cargo, and now they'll want our hides as well." Shay looked sick. "Fillok's brother will go to Soldan-Shah Imir and demand blood. I suppose the blood of any Tierran will do. We have to get to King Korastine as quickly as possible." He gave the young sailor a weary smile as he turned the wheel and aligned the course with the Captain's Compass. "When we pass Windcatch, I can drop you off, Mr. Vora. But for the rest of us . . ." He shook his head, still frowning. "I think we just started a war."

**Jo Beverley is
"one of the great names in the genre."***

Five RITA Awards

The Readers' Choice Award

The Award of Excellence

The Golden Leaf Award

Two Career Achievement Awards from
Romantic Times

Member of the Romance Writers of America
Hall of Fame

Member of the Romance Writers of America
Honor Roll

*Romantic Times

continued . . .

SKYLARK

Jo Beverley

A SIGNET BOOK

SIGNET
Published by New American Library, a division of
Penguin Group (USA) Inc., 375 Hudson Street,
New York, New York 10014, U.S.A.
Penguin Books Ltd, 80 Strand,
London WC2R 0RL, England
Penguin Books Australia Ltd, 250 Camberwell Road,
Camberwell, Victoria 3124, Australia
Penguin Books Canada Ltd, 10 Alcorn Avenue,
Toronto, Ontario, Canada M4V 3B2
Penguin Books (N.Z.) Ltd, Cnr Rosedale and Airborne Roads,
Albany, Auckland 1310, New Zealand

Penguin Books Ltd, Registered Offices:
80 Strand, London WC2R 0RL, England

First published by Signet, an imprint of New American Library,
a division of Penguin Group (USA) Inc.

First Printing, May 2004
10 9 8 7 6 5 4 3 2 1

To my sisters, Stella, Marian, and Eileen,
because sisters play a part in this book,
and sisters are special

Chapter 1

The Berkshire Informer, October 7, 1816:

We hail the return of Johnny Tring, despaired of by his family when lost at sea six years ago. As a result of the might of His Majesty's navy and the bravery of Britain's sailors, he, along with nearly two thousand other unhappy Christian souls, has been liberated from durance vile in the cruel hands of the Mahometan corsairs of Algiers. Most of these unfortunates were from hot Mediterranean lands. How much deeper must Tring's gratitude be to Him on high when now restored to Berkshire's cool and green Elysium.

More likely a nasty shock to the system, Laura Gardeyne thought, tucking her woolen shawl more closely around herself. The chancy sun had slid behind clouds again, and a cool breeze rustled the newspaper and the dying leaves in the oak above her seat.

But still, to be released from slavery and imprisonment must gladden any heart.

Her son ran up to her. "Mama, may I have my ball?"

As a child must gladden any heart. She smiled at three-year-old Harry and gave him the ball and a canvas bag. "Why not ask Nan to build a tower with your blocks? Then you can try to knock it down."

He ran back to his nursemaid, a sturdy bundle of energy in nankeen trousers and a short blue jacket. Free, as happy children are always free. As adults rarely are.

She gazed around this small piece of Elysium. The park of Caldfort House was lovely, even on a dull day, designed as it was in the natural style. The grass that ran from the house to the River Cald was kept neatly short by sheep and dotted with majestic old trees.

Caldfort House itself stood on a rise, square, pale, and dignified—the very picture of a modern country home.

What had Lovelace written?

Stone walls do not a prison make,
Nor iron bars a cage.
Minds innocent and quiet take
That for an hermitage.

It worked in reverse, too. An idyllic setting could be durance vile. In fact, she remembered where the phrase *durance vile* came from: Robert Burns, the Scottish poet.

In durance vile here must I wake and weep. . . .

Her son's laughter broke her mood and she shook herself out of poetic melancholy. It was not at all in her nature, and compared to most, she was a fortunate woman. She was a widow, to be sure, but that sadness was nearly a year old, and she had a handsome jointure that meant she need never fear poverty.

And she had Harry, the joy of her life.

She watched him roll his red leather ball again and demolish at least half the blocks. He was developing a good eye for a three-year-old, but then his father had excelled at every type of sport. Harry got his dark curls from her. The rest of him was pure Gardeyne—

square chin, brown eyes and hair, and the promise of height and strong build.

His next attempt sent the whole tower flying. Laura put aside the paper and applauded. "Well done, Harry! Well done!"

He hurtled to her for a hug, then back to roll his ball at the rebuilt target. It hit only the corner, but it made a sound like an explosion. He raced back to her again. "Mama! Mama!"

Laura caught him up, thinking, *Thunder?*

But crows had risen cawing into the gray sky.

It had been a shot!

Laura realized immediately what had happened, but she still held her son close. "Don't be frightened, Minnow. It's just your Uncle Jack enjoying some sport."

The maid came over. "Shall I take Master Harry in, ma'am?"

"No, of course not. Reverend Gardeyne would never aim his gun near us, and Harry's enjoying himself, aren't you, darling?"

After an uncertain moment, Harry nodded and scrambled off her lap to run back to his game.

With hard-won skill, Laura kept a slight smile in place as she watched, then as she let her eyes move to the coppice wood that spread between the house and the village of Cald St. Edwin's. The shot had come from there, but the wood offered no extra information. The crows had settled, and there was nothing to see.

Surely she'd spoken the truth. Her brother-in-law would not be careless about where he aimed his gun. Jack Gardeyne was vicar for the local parishes of St. Edwin's and St. Mark's, and a good one. As with all Gardeynes, however, hunting, shooting, and fishing were the true joys of his life.

In six years of marriage, Laura had grown accustomed to living among dogs, horses, and firearms. Guns hadn't bothered her until recently. Until she'd

begun to suspect that the Reverend Jack Gardeyne
would like Harry dead.

Now sweat trickled down her spine. She tried, as
she did all the time, to convince herself that no man,
especially a vicar, would wish harm to his innocent
nephew. Even if the child did stand between him and
a title, a fortune, and all the hunting, shooting, and
fishing he could want.

She wasn't convinced, and she couldn't stop herself
from hovering over Harry's play as if watching could
hold off disaster. No one could watch a child all the
time, however, and as he grew older it would become
impossible. A boy must be allowed to explore and
have adventures, but as things stood now, Laura didn't
know how she could bear to let him out of her sight.

She noticed that he was throwing the ball more
wildly and becoming frustrated. Time for his nap . . .

Then she leapt to her feet and ran.

Harry had hurled the ball right past Nan. It was
rolling down toward the river and he was chasing it,
but that wasn't what alarmed her. A black dog had
streaked out of the woods with the same intent.

The dog got there first and snatched the ball in its
sharp teeth. Harry had already reversed. He'd spun
around and was fleeing toward safety—toward her.
She swung him into her arms and held him close, mur-
muring reassurances that she could hardly hear over
her own thundering heart.

"Don't be cowardy custard, Harry! Bouncer won't
hurt you."

Laura glared over her child's head at the source of
the hearty voice. Jack Gardeyne was strolling toward
them, jolly smile in place.

How could anyone see him as a monster? He was
a fleshy man, portly around the middle, but strapping,
like all the Gardeynes, and full of vigor and bonhomie.
He carried a gun under his arm, but safely pointed
down.

In his casual country clothes he looked as harmless as could be, but his free hand gripped the legs of a dead pheasant, its limp head brushing the grass. Laura was not mawkish about dead animals, but at this moment the corpse made her shiver.

"Your uncle's right, darling," she said, hiding her tension. "His dog won't hurt you."

She made it a statement for Jack rather than for her son. When Nan hurried up, Laura passed Harry to her, then went to his retriever and grabbed the ball. "Release, Bouncer!"

Bouncer snarled deep in his throat.

Though fear leapt inside, Laura didn't let go. She wanted Jack to know that he faced not only a small child but her. She stared a demand at him.

His smile set a little. "Bouncer, release! Heel!"

The dog let her have the ball and turned to settle at his master's side. It was surely her imagination that saw a sneer in its panting expression.

Jack shook his head. "Laura, my dear, dare I suggest that perhaps you are a little overprotective of Harry?"

He'd started this line recently, trying in subtle ways to separate her from her son. She feared that he was slowly turning his father, Lord Caldfort, to his side.

"He's only three, Jack," she said, drying the ball on her handkerchief. "There'll be time to toughen him up later." She attacked back. "I'm surprised to see you out. We received word that Emma's confinement had started."

"Nothing for a man to do there," he said. "In the way, in fact. I've been through this three times before, remember."

"But I hope all is going well."

"Midwife said so. Hoping for a boy, of course, this time. Father would be pleased. Always good to have a spare as well as an heir."

Laura's throat tightened, but she looked straight at

his cheerful face. "I'm sure it is, though it's unlikely that anything will happen to Harry, isn't it? Children don't die as frequently as they used to."

"God be praised! But still, His divine will takes some innocents. Wise men pray for the best, but prepare for misfortune." He nodded. "Good day to you, Sister. I'll drop by to see how Father is, then get back home."

She watched him stroll toward the house, corpse dragging on the grass, trying to persuade herself that the threat was entirely in her imagination.

Jack Gardeyne was a man of God, and a good enough vicar in his way. He ran the services responsibly, preached excellent sermons, and organized the care of the less fortunate of the parishes. He was a good father and a kind husband. In fact, he seemed to care for his Emma more than Hal had cared for her once the first bloom was off their marriage.

She looked at Harry and saw he was limp in Nan's arms, his head on the maid's shoulder.

"Time to go in, Minnow," she said as if nothing unusual had happened, and bent to gather up the blocks and ball, wishing Jack hadn't been on his way up to the house. She didn't want another encounter.

She sighed. It was considerate of Jack to visit his ailing father so often, to talk with him, play cards, and perhaps laugh over wicked, manly jokes. Laura would have done the same—even the latter, but Lord Caldfort didn't care for the conversation of women. He also believed women should never gamble, and he enjoyed playing cards only for money.

She straightened, tightening the drawstring of the bag. Lord Caldfort was not an easy man to live with but she tried to be understanding. He'd been an active man for most of his life, and becoming an invalid had turned him sour. It had been particularly bitter that his health had failed just as his fortune turned, just as he had inherited a title and estates from his brother.

An unlucky family, the Gardeynes. Her father-in-law had come into the title because his brother's only son had drowned in the Mediterranean. Now his own older son, her husband, Hal, was dead at thirty-two.

Any ill luck wouldn't carry on to her son. Laura made a vow of it. She picked up her newspaper, checked that nothing else was left, and led the way back up the slope toward the house.

She had once thought Caldfort House delightful. It wasn't large, which was part of its charm for her, since she'd grown up in a modest house. Built only fifty-two years ago, it was perfectly designed for a private family home and occasional gracious hospitality. Its proportions were elegant and it had plenty of long windows to let in the light.

Yes, she'd liked it when visits had been an occasional respite from life in the fashionable whirl. Being stuck here forever with bitter Lord Caldfort and peculiar Lady Caldfort was another matter entirely. Add in Jack and her macabre suspicions, and the house was as appealing as a cell in the Tower of London.

Needing the comfort of her son in her arms, Laura exchanged burdens with Nan. Harry had his thumb stuck in his mouth but she didn't try to remove it. He only did that when he was upset and tired.

He was a sweet, trusting weight, the most precious thing in the world. Hers to raise. Hers to protect. Even if her fears seemed insane at times, she couldn't afford to ignore them. She'd never forgive herself if anything that she could prevent happened to Harry.

The closer they came to the house, the slower she walked. She didn't permit herself pointless regrets, but they settled on her now. She'd felt blessed by the gods on her wedding day, but she'd not found true happiness in her marriage and now her future was bleak.

She was only twenty-four years old, but she was a prisoner as surely as if she was in the Tower.

Lord Caldfort insisted, with some justification, that

his heir be raised here. She was allowed to take him away, but only for short visits to her family. Her movements were not restricted, but how could she leave Harry, even for days, when she worried about his safety?

She straightened her shoulders and walked into Caldfort House. Her prison until her son was of an age to take care of himself.

Chapter 2

As they entered the marble-tiled hall, Harry gave a little *hic* as if he might be crying. Laura moved him slightly to see, but he was fast asleep. She brushed a kiss across his forehead.

Had he detected something bad about Jack? They said children and animals were sensitive, and Harry had never taken to his uncle. She mustn't build monsters out of nothing, though. A snarling dog would upset any small child.

"What's the matter with him now?"

Laura started and saw Lord Caldfort, wheezing, bloated, and leaning on his cane, at the open door of his study.

"Nothing, sir. He's just tired."

"Jack said he ran screaming from his dog."

"The dog growled at him, sir."

"You mollycoddle him! Jack's right. The lad should spend some time with him. Learn manly ways."

Laura hoped her dread didn't show on her face. "What a good idea," she said cheerfully. "He's a little young yet, though, don't you think? He would benefit from your attention, sir, if you feel able to give it. You have raised two fine sons, so you know the way of it."

It was blatant flattery but he nodded, even preened a little.

"Might be something in what you say, m'dear. Not up to outdoor stuff these days, but I'll spend a bit of time with the lad. Get him in the way of things."

Laura thanked him, dropping a curtsy, then headed upstairs, hoping that her suggestion blunted the impression of Jack's. The trouble was that it was perfectly reasonable for an uncle to take his brother's place in guiding his son. In other circumstances she would have suggested it herself.

Laura climbed the stairs, praying that all went well with Jack's wife. She had offered to attend the birth, but Emma had pleasantly refused. Remembering her own confinement, Laura hadn't been surprised. She and Emma were always cordial but they were too different to be close. At such a time, a woman wanted harmonious companions.

She knew Emma longed for a son as much as Jack did, but as she entered the nursery and passed the sleeping child to Nan, Laura prayed that this child be another girl. If there was anything to her suspicions, then Jack having a son could be disastrous.

That prayer wasn't answered. When she went downstairs for dinner, she found Jack with her father-in-law, and both men were beaming.

Jack pressed a glass of claret into her hand, and Lord Caldfort raised his. "A toast, m'dear! To Henry Jack Gardeyne!"

Laura froze, glass at her lips. It was family tradition to call first sons Henry, but it was as if a replacement for her Harry was being prepared.

Jack smiled at her. "If you don't object, Laura, we mean to call him Hal."

"Of course not," she said, and found a smile. "Congratulations."

She was about to ask about Emma when Lady Caldfort wandered in, thin and vague as usual. She stared when given the news, as if she'd forgotten that her daughter-in-law was confined, then said, "How convenient. An heir in case the other one dies."

Even the two men seemed taken aback at this blunt statement of fact, but they were all accustomed to Lady Caldfort's ways. She tended to say exactly the words that others were too discreet to let out.

Laura wished she'd been watching Jack. She might have learned something from his reaction.

Lady Caldfort was a cold, angular woman who had little interest in other people and no facility for dealing with them. Apparently Major John Gardeyne, as Lord Caldfort had been then, had married her for her money.

Her only interest in life seemed to be insects, which she collected and arranged in display boxes. That wasn't unusual, but Lady Caldfort kept the boxes stacked in a spare room, never on display. Laura worried that one day her mother-in-law would become completely insane—and that she'd have to take care of her.

"Isn't it time to eat?" Lady Caldfort said, and headed for the dining room, even though the meal hadn't been announced. With a shared look, Laura and the two men followed.

As soon as they were seated, Lord Caldfort and Jack began a discussion of estate matters. As Harry's mother, Laura had an interest in his future property, but that was a battle not worth the powder at this point. She listened, as she always did, gathering knowledge. Eventually their talk turned to sporting details, and she looked away.

Lady Caldfort was frowning at the nearest candle. She might be angry because the food wasn't in front of her, but she could as easily be pondering some problem of entomology. Laura knew that an attempt to start conversation there was hopeless. She was a veteran of hundreds of dinners exactly like this, except that if Jack was not here, there was often no conversation at all. Even so, she was expected to attend.

How many such dinners?

Eleven months since Hal died. That would be about 330.

Since Harry's birth, she'd spent at least half the year here, because both Hal and his father had objected to her taking him away much, and she liked being with her son. She'd enjoyed visits to London, Brighton, and other fashionable spots, but happily sacrificed time at hunting house parties.

Hal had probably been here with her about half the time—a quarter of the year. Sitting opposite her. Looking at her with that look in his eyes that said he was already thinking of an early retreat to their bedchamber and his other favorite sport.

At thought of that sport, her body clenched like a hungry stomach. She pulled her mind back from those lost pleasures.

Calculations. Her antidote to lust.

Two years and five months from Harry's birth to Hal's death. Two times 365 plus about 150 equals 880. She had been here without Hal about a quarter of that time: 220.

Add the 330 since Hal's death: 550.

No, more, because Hal had left her alone here through much of her pregnancy. It had overlapped prime hunting season, after all. She hadn't minded. Her sister Juliet had been with her during the last months, and then her mother had come. Watcombes were powerful medicine against sourness and gloom.

She could add perhaps 50 to make it a round 600.

Six hundred of these dinners, with thousands still to come. Perhaps she would become as eccentric as Lady Caldfort, except in her case it would take the form of eating in her room with a good book or the newspapers. How crazy would she have to appear to get away with that?

Lady Caldfort suddenly banged her spoon on the table. "Where's the food? Why is there no service in this house? Lazy slovens, the lot of them!"

Thomas the footman dashed in. "It's coming, milady. Just a few minutes more." Then he dashed out again.

Lady Caldfort kept rapping the spoon on the table, such a grim look on her face that Laura feared she was contemplating violence.

"Take that damned spoon off her," Lord Caldfort growled.

Laura did so, grateful that at the same time he snapped, "Stop your folly, Cecy!"

Lady Caldfort gave up the spoon but scowled.

"Pour the wine, Jack," Lord Caldfort ordered, and Jack rose to fill all their glasses with red wine. Lady Caldfort took a deep draft and it seemed to pacify her. Laura tried to feel sorry for the woman, who had endured the Gardeynes far longer than she had, but it was hard. She was so totally selfish.

Like mother, like son? Laura wondered, for Hal had been selfish at bottom. Unlike his mother, he'd been blessed with good looks and a kind of jollity that passed for generous charm, but underneath . . . Fortunately, he'd had a kind of generosity in bed, for he took pride in pleasing a woman. A gentleman's duty, he would declare, but she'd suspected that if she were hard to please, he'd have neglected her. Fortunate for their marriage that she had not been at all hard to please.

The strangest thing was that she'd only quickened once.

No, don't think about the pleasures of marriage. Multiply the number of glasses by the number of plates. Add the number of candles in the chandelier. . . . At last, thank heavens, the servants hurried in with dishes.

"And about time, too!" Lady Caldfort snapped, lifting the lid off the nearest dish herself and spooning soup into her plate.

Laura smiled at the maid placing a tureen in front of her and thanked her. How lucky they were that Caldfort had a competent and forbearing housekeeper in Mrs. Moorside, who came to Laura rather than Lady Caldfort if any troubles arose. The soup, as always, was excellent. A good cook was another blessing, and Laura made sure to count them all.

She believed in people accepting responsibility for their actions. She had married Hal Gardeyne by choice, thinking herself the most fortunate young woman in Dorset. In the first years of her marriage she would have described herself as a happy bride.

She had made this bed and must lie in it, and she would do so with as good a grace as possible. She could even be content if she could only be sure that Harry was safe.

A gun, she suddenly thought. *A gun would be very useful.*

With that in mind, she welcomed Lady Caldfort's early and abrupt exit from the dining room and followed her, even though there was no question of the ladies taking tea together. Lady Caldfort marched upstairs. Laura picked up one of the spare candles, lit it at the hall fire, and headed toward the back of the house. Toward the gun room.

Hal had taught her to shoot. It had been amusement for him while living quietly here, and had amused her until he'd tried to get her to target a rabbit. She'd refused, and in disgust he'd given up the lessons.

She knew how to load and prime a gun, however, and Hal's were stored in the gun room, waiting for the day when Harry would be old enough to use them. Splendid hunting pieces, ornate dueling pistols, practical, deadly horse pistols. Her interest, however, was a smaller pistol that he'd carried in a pocket when out at night.

She went into the room and made a face. The former Lord Caldfort had dabbled in the new art of taxidermy in order to preserve his hunting triumphs. A stag's head loomed over the door, three foxes, one with a chicken in its mouth, ran along the tops of cabinets, and various predatory birds eyed her. She supposed they were all properly preserved, but to her the room always smelled of decay.

She hurried past the racks of big guns and put her flickering candle down to open the drawer where Hal's pistols were kept.

It was empty.

She frowned and opened the one to the left, but it held Lord Caldfort's pistols. The drawer to the right contained old ones, kept only for curiosity value. She slowly closed that drawer, guessing where Hal's pistols were.

Jack had taken them.

She stared at a beady-eyed hawk. Again, it was not unquestionably suspicious. Hal's guns were the best money could buy, and if his brother wanted to use them until his son was old enough, why not?

But it felt like a deepening of the threat. She considered Lord Caldfort's pistols, but shook her head. If she was discovered, what excuse could she make? With Hal's guns she had intended to say she wanted Harry to get used to one—unloaded, of course.

The bigger guns wouldn't be of much use to her, anyway. Her hands were small and she'd never really been able to handle Hal's ordinary pistols. Only the smaller one.

She picked up her candle and left the room, as weaponless as before.

Chapter 3

Laura didn't sleep well that night, despite trying to persuade herself that any threats were in her imagination. The next day brought a blessing in the form of a long letter from Juliet. After making sure that Harry was safe in the nursery, Laura took the letter to her boudoir to enjoy.

One benefit of marriage to Hal had been her ability to introduce her younger sister to London society. Their own family were county gentry of the most minor sort. Their grandfather had been a yeoman farmer until he made the transition to gentleman farmer. Hal Gardeyne, heir to a viscountcy, had been a brilliant match.

In London, Juliet's good looks and loving nature had won her, too, a man of excellent family. She'd had to wait two years for Robert Fancourt to rise high enough in the Home Office to afford a wife, but she hadn't seemed to mind. That thought troubled Laura now and then, but things in the past were past worrying over.

Juliet was certainly happy now. She adored her Robert and thrived on living most of the year in London.

Lines of social gossip and stories of comings and goings soon had Laura relaxed and smiling. Here at

Caldfort, it was easy to forget that elsewhere life went on its merry way, even in October.

Fashionable London would be quiet, but Juliet clearly found much to keep her busy. The bustle and hum almost rose from the page like an aroma, catching Laura's breath with longing.

She looked up from the letter and out at the tranquil countryside. It was doubtless shallow of her, but oh, to be in town, too. Walks in the parks, shopping, the theater, exhibitions, lively company, and the sheer fun of being with her favorite sister.

She shook off wistfulness and turned to the next sheet. Juliet never tried to economize by crossing her writing.

Can you imagine whom Robert brought to dinner not long ago? Sir Stephen Ball! He asked after you.

Oh? Laura felt a strange sensation, as if something had tugged at her insides.

I know he was only your friend's brother, but I did think you and he might make a match of it. Before Hal, of course.

Laura wondered how many other people had thought that. The idea had never crossed her mind—until the day Stephen had so inappropriately proposed. She'd already been betrothed to Hal. What had she been supposed to do?

But she shouldn't have laughed. . . .

She looked back at the slightly blurred writing.

I was somewhat taken by him myself. Do you remember him as Valancourt when you made a play of Udolpho? Blond and heroic. Fuel for ro-

mantic dreams. He could have been no more than
seventeen, but at thirteen, seventeen is a great age.

Laura had achieved the grand age of fifteen when
they'd performed that play, but to her, too, seventeen had
seemed a great age. Stephen had been one of those young
men who mature early, perhaps because of his serious attention to his studies and to issues of politics and law. He'd
never been dull, though. She remembered working with
him for weeks during his summer holiday from Harrow,
turning the dramatic novel into a short play. The taste of
it in her mind now was of challenge and pure, thrilling excitement, yet she'd not thought of it for years.

How strange. Had she deliberately wiped it from
her memory?

Staging the play had been pure, thrilling excitement
of another sort. She'd had the role of Emily and he
Valancourt. Daringly they'd written in a kiss, and
she'd come close to swooning with embarrassment at
that stiff and awkward press of lips to lips in front of
an audience of his and her families.

She laughed a little now at that, but what business
did Stephen have of asking after her? Their friendship
had faltered after his proposal, and died when he'd
maliciously pinned her with the name Lady Skylark.
They'd hardly met or spoken in six years.

Lady Skylark. She still didn't understand how he
could have been so cruel.

She'd gone straight from her wedding to London,
and instantly become a toast. She'd loved being the
beautiful Mrs. Hal Gardeyne, which had soon become
La Belle Laura. Heady stuff at eighteen, but she didn't
think she'd been insufferable.

Then someone—rumor said it was Brummell
himself—had turned that into Labellelle. It simply
meant the "beautiful *L*," but the unique construction
had seemed mysterious and sophisticated, everything
Laura longed to be.

But then, overnight, she'd become Lady Skylark.

Everyone thought it charming and a perfect fit, and so it had stuck.

She'd hated it.

People assumed she had a lovely singing voice, and she didn't, but the real problem was the other meaning. Overnight, she'd transformed from mysterious, sophisticated Labellelle into a feckless and immature child, because *skylarking* was a term used in the navy for lads who played dangerous games high in the rigging.

When she'd heard a rumor that Stephen had christened her that at some drunken, manly gathering, she'd known it was true and known it was malicious because *Skylark* had special meaning for them. A meaning connected to his absurd and embarrassing proposal.

She'd known immediately that she shouldn't have laughed, known that she'd hurt him, which she'd never wanted to do. He'd abruptly walked away from her and left the area until after her marriage, so she'd had no chance to make amends. She understood his pain, but there had been no call for such a cruel retaliation.

It was all in the past, all in the past, but if Stephen was asking about her now, she worried about his motives. Did Juliet have anything to say about that?

He's making quite a name for himself in Parliament, you know. A brilliant speaker, Robert says, though I have not heard him. Sitting in the visitors' gallery, no matter how fashionable it may be, is not my choice of entertainment. Robert says he may be offered a position in the ministry. At only twenty-six. That will be quite a stir at home, won't it? He's still unmarried. Perhaps not surprising when he's still young.

He's two years older than I am, Laura thought, and skimmed over Stephen's noble causes, Stephen's pithy quotes, Stephen's prospects of becoming Prime Minister, for heaven's sake.

Imagine that! Of course Pitt was a Member of Parliament at twenty-two and Prime Minister at twenty-four, which makes Stephen quite a sluggard. From my mature perspective, I'm not surprised that you didn't marry him. He's frighteningly clever, of course, and he can be terribly witty, but I find him daunting. I found myself in danger of being tongue-tied all through dinner. Me! Can you imagine it?

No.

Speaking of political advantage, which I was, dearest, if you will only look back up the page a little, Robert has gone on some mission to Denmark, which he says will have that effect, so I am returning home for a few weeks. Is it possible that you could join me there? I long to see you and little Harry again. I would come to you, but in all honesty, Caldfort makes me shudder!

Laura let the letter sag.

Go home?

Immediately she thought, *Why not?*

She hadn't seen Juliet since the wedding six months ago. She hadn't been home since then, either. She rose to her feet, folding the letter, a smile already tugging at her lips.

A week away! It felt like paradise and would restore her perspective. Perhaps she would see that her fears about Jack were gothic, and most important, in her bustling home in another county, Harry would be completely safe.

Eager to have it settled, she hurried downstairs and knocked at the door to her father-in-law's study. Silence. She knocked again, thinking that if she started preparations immediately, they could even leave tomorrow.

Tomorrow!

No reply.

She frowned at the door panels. Lord Caldfort lived between this room and his bedchamber across the hall. He preferred the study during the day, but he retired to bed if he suffered one of his bad spells. She couldn't pursue him there.

She turned away, but then heard a faint, "Come in."

She went in quickly, thinking he might be ill. Indeed, though he was sitting behind his desk with the postbag and letters still in front of him, he looked even pastier than usual.

"Is anything wrong, sir? Do you need your tonic?"

"Nothing more than the ordinary. What d'ye want? Disturbing m'peace. Everyone's always cutting up m'peace."

Laura abandoned concern. He wouldn't hesitate to summon the doctor if he felt worse. She made her request, hoping his mood wouldn't turn him difficult.

He surprised her. "Back to Merrymead, eh? Well, why not? It's a six month or more since you've been there. When do you want to go?"

This was a little more enthusiasm than Laura was used to, but she wouldn't complain. "I see no reason to delay, sir. We seem to be in a spell of dry weather. I would like to be off tomorrow, if that is agreeable."

Again, he made no objection. "Of course, m'dear. And why not make a nice long stay this time? A month or so, eh?"

Laura blinked at him, almost protesting out of shock. She conquered that insanity and quickly agreed. "Thank you, sir," she said, and curtsied and left before he could change his mind.

She paused in the hall, wondering if she should send for the doctor, anyway. Lord Caldfort was not his

usual self. She reminded herself to never look a gift
horse in the mouth and hurried upstairs to give instructions for the journey. Only when that was done
did she let herself return to the puzzle.

She retired to her boudoir, frowning over Lord
Caldfort's suggestion that she and Harry be away for
a whole month.

Did he want nothing to do with Harry now there
was another Gardeyne to inherit? That made no sense.
Harry was a Gardeyne, too. Why should Lord Caldfort favor one grandson over the other? He'd always
been fond of Harry, in his careless way.

Was it simply that the existence of an alternate heir
meant that the other one could be let out of sight?
She'd welcome that, but it wasn't rational. Babies
were delicate creatures, especially in the early days.
The longer a child lived, the more likely it was to
survive.

That reminded her that she'd not visited her sister-
in-law and should do so before she left. She put on a
warm spencer, but then thought of Harry.

Jack could sneak into the house and . . .

Oh, rubbish! She'd end up in an asylum at this rate.
He'd be safe with Nan.

She put on a bonnet, gloves, and sturdy leather half-
boots, then set off for the mile walk to the village,
enjoying the exercise and fresh air.

She tried to put her worries out of her head, but
her mind kept returning to Lord Caldfort's strange
behavior. He had looked decidedly unwell. But he'd
not sent for the doctor.

He'd been dealing with the day's post.

Had he just received bad news?

The instant she thought of it, she knew it was true.
Lord Caldfort had looked as if he had just received
very bad news.

The explanation should soothe her, for she couldn't
imagine how such news would affect Harry and her-

self. But then, it was as if the bad news had made him eager to have Laura and Harry away from Caldfort.

Disease in the area?

No. That news wouldn't arrive by letter, and the alarm would be more general.

She realized that she'd stopped and was staring blindly at a rambler covered with scarlet rose hips, and set off again. A lawsuit? Debts? Scandal?

In the months after Hal's death there had been awkward letters. Creditors had emerged like maggots, and two women had claimed to be carrying Hal's child. In view of her own difficulty in quickening, Laura had been skeptical, though she didn't doubt that Hal had been with many women when away from her. He'd been a lusty man.

Eleven months after his death was late for a new child to turn up, and in any case, another Gardeyne bastard would not upset Lord Caldfort. He seemed to see them as a mark of virility.

Scandal or lawsuit involving Jack? Even if he was a villainous uncle, that seemed unlikely.

Yet something had happened.

Wild investments failing, leaving them all penniless?

From what little she knew of the Gardeyne finances, they were managed cautiously. Lord Caldfort, to his credit, was satisfied with the wealth he had unexpectedly inherited.

Laura entered the village of Cald St. Edwin's having come up with no plausible cause for alarm. That was more worrying rather than less. Something strange had arrived in this morning's post. She was sure of it.

By the time she approached the green door of the red brick vicarage, she knew she had to try to find out what it was. She didn't want to leave Caldfort for a month ignorant of a possible threat behind her.

Chapter 4

Laura went up to her sister-in-law's bedchamber thinking that it wouldn't be surprising if Jack lusted after Caldfort House. The vicarage was small for his growing family, and it also lacked charm. It hadn't been built by the Lord Caldfort who'd commissioned Caldfort House, but by the previous one, who looked to have done it on the cheap.

She found Emma Gardeyne glowing, however, especially with the satisfaction of finally producing a son. Laura admired the sleeping baby, who was as mysterious and entrancing as all newborns, then sat to take tea and listen to an account of the birth.

Perhaps even there she'd been unjust to Jack. Emma claimed to have had an easy time of it and to have driven her husband out of the house.

"He would keep popping in to see if all was well, which is very distracting, as I'm sure you know."

Hal had never popped in, but Laura made vague noises of agreement.

The midwife came to check on the health of mother and baby and stayed to chat. Mrs. Finch was wife to the local blacksmith and had attended Laura's confinement, too.

Everything seemed perfect, but Laura thought she detected some strain in Emma's manner. Was she imagining that?

She must be. It was just barely possible to imagine

that Jack was plotting infanticide, but never that
Emma was part of it. Emma's gentle goodness and
firm moral beliefs frequently put Laura to shame,
which was part of the reason they hadn't become
close. Laura had to bite her tongue too often in order
not to challenge Emma's conventional beliefs, and if
she relaxed and spoke naturally of subjects that interested her, Emma was shocked.

And didn't hesitate to comment on it.

But Emma was truly *good*. Laura had never heard
her say an unkind word about anyone, and she would
not gossip. Which was a shame, since there was a delicious rumor circulating about the innkeeper of the
Red Hen and Dr. Trumper's housekeeper.

When Mrs. Finch left, Laura broke her news, unable
to stop herself from watching closely for any reaction.

"And Lord Caldfort says Harry and I may stay for
a month."

Emma's eyes widened, but only in natural surprise.

"How lovely for you, Laura. I long to visit my family, but it is so far to Durham and would cost a great
deal for a private carriage. Anyway, I'm sure Jack is
right that days on the road with young children would
be very difficult. And, of course, he has his duties to
the parish."

"You should persuade him to take on a curate."

Emma's face tightened. Was all not perfect here
after all? "It would be an expense, and there are so
many calls on his purse."

Not least his horses and dogs, Laura thought, but
didn't say it. Jack was no worse than any other man
in that respect. Perhaps it was unfair to think that a
vicar should be willing to economize on his own pleasures to provide his wife with a visit to her family.

Laura wanted to know if Emma had an explanation
for their father-in-law's strange behavior, so she said,
"I am puzzled to be allowed to take Harry away for
a whole month."

"Perhaps Father Caldfort is becoming more moderate." Lord Caldfort hated to be referred to like that. "After all, there is little Harry can learn here at such a young age." But then Emma fixed Laura with an intent look. "Jack does hope to take a father's place with Harry, Laura. It hurts him when you don't agree."

Laura's mouth dried and she sipped more tea. "Harry's too young yet."

"Would you say the same if Hal were alive?"

"That would be different."

"It's as if you don't trust Jack with Harry, Laura, but you must know he would be as careful of Harry as Hal."

What could she say? "I'm sure he would."

"Don't mind his way of talking. He doesn't mean what he says."

Laura stared. "What can you mean?"

Emma's color rose. She was pretty, with soft blond hair, and seeing her blush like that, no one would believe that she was a matron of thirty with four children in her nursery.

"It's just the thrill of a son. You know how men are about such things. Jack has said once or twice that if . . . if anything were to happen to Harry, little Hal would one day be Lord Caldfort, but it doesn't mean anything."

Laura found a light laugh. "Of course it doesn't! It's a simple truth, as if I were to say that if Lord Caldfort took a turn for the worse, Harry could end up being an infant viscount."

Emma's smile showed relief. "Yes, that's it. It wouldn't mean you were *wishing* for his death." But then she flushed a deeper red at the implication of her words.

"Of course not." Laura brushed over the moment. "I wish Lord Caldfort a very long life so that Harry can grow up without burdens. I fear it will not be. He seemed particularly unwell this morning. I think he may have received bad news in the postbag. Jack hasn't mentioned any concerns about the estate, has he?"

Emma was clearly grateful for a change of subject. "No. Well, there are the usual problems due to the depressed state of the economy and the atrocious weather. The harvest was sadly off, and many will feel the pinch. We intend to take a special collection to provide winter food for the desperate. I hope you will contribute."

"Yes, of course."

Emma could be guarding marital confidences, but Laura didn't think so. Emma lied no more than she gossiped. "You don't think the estate could be in debt?" she tried.

"I shouldn't think so. Jack would know, wouldn't he? And I'm sure he would tell me something like that. But if Father is unwell, has Dr. Trumper been sent for?"

Laura rose. There was nothing to learn here. "He never hesitates to summon Trumper if he feels the need, but I'll check his condition again when I return to the house."

She kissed her sister-in-law's cheek and left the room, feeling as she always did after time with Emma—like a lower form of womanhood.

As she arrived at the hall, the front door opened and Jack came in bringing brisk fresh air.

Laura searched him for any sign of evil and found none. "I've been visiting Emma and the baby. Congratulations, Jack. A fine, robust boy. A true Gardeyne."

"Aye. Nothing frail about *him*."

She kept her smile in place. "Emma seems well, too."

"Birthing's no trouble to her."

"Even an easy birth is a considerable challenge, Jack."

Perhaps he flushed. "Aye, well . . . Father says you're going to Merrymead for a week or two."

She caught a strange tone and braced for trouble. Would he try to stop it? "Harry should know his other family."

"True enough."

Laura was sure she heard a silent *but*. Her attention, however, was on the fact that he must have visited his father in the past hour. "Has Lord Caldfort sent for Dr. Trumper yet?"

He frowned. "Not that I know of. Why?"

"He seemed to have a funny spell, though he denied it."

His frown deepened. "I thought he looked a bit the worse for wear. His heart?"

"I don't know." She considered for a moment, then added, "It might have been something to do with a letter, since he was reading his correspondence at the time. He didn't say anything to you?"

He stiffened, doubtless at the notion that he would discuss estate business with her. "No. Therefore there can't have been anything of import. Summon Dr. Trumper anyway, Laura."

Laura bit back a sarcastic, *Yes, sir.* "I must be on my way. There's much to be done if we're to leave tomorrow."

"You'll bring Harry to visit his father's grave before you go?" It was phrased as a question, but sounded like a command. Laura was tempted to refuse for that reason, but Jack was right. She and Harry visited the grave every Sunday, taking fresh flowers, so they should do that before going away for weeks.

"We'll drive over later in the gig," she said, but then came to a resolution. "Do you have Hal's guns, Jack?"

Perhaps his ruddy cheeks grew a little redder. "Aye, why not? Don't want them rusting away up there."

"Of course not, but I was thinking of what you said about manly ways. If Harry had the little pistol—unloaded, of course—it would be a memento of his father and get him in the way of such things."

She was sure she saw hesitation, but then Jack said, "Not a bad idea. I'll get it."

He strode off and returned with the case. Laura opened it. She tried to make her scrutiny look like fondness, but she was making sure that all the essentials were inside. "Sad memories," she said, and it was true. Poor Hal, who'd enjoyed life so much and was no more.

She closed the case. "Thank you, Jack."

"Be sure to keep the balls and powder hidden. Boys get the hang of that sort of thing more quickly than you'd think."

"Of course."

Laura left and set off back to Caldfort, considering Jack's last words. She'd swear his concern for safety had been genuine. Thank heavens she was going to Merrymead. It could straighten the brain of a Bedlamite.

Once back at Caldfort, she plunged into the arrangements for travel. She sent a groom to order a chaise for the morrow, then supervised the packing, letting the excited Harry help with his.

"No, Minnow. You can't take flowers to Grandmama. They'd be dead before we arrived. Come to my jewelry box and you can choose something to take as a present."

Her valuable jewelry was in the safe, so she let him look through her box, which amused him for quite some time, as she wrote instructions for Mrs. Moorside.

In the end, he chose a pretty rose pin that her

mother would like. It had been a gift from Charlotte Ball, she remembered. For her eighteenth birthday. Stephen had remarked that pink roses were a strange choice.

From the depths of memory came a clear recollection.

She'd asked what flowers would suit her.

He'd said, "Poppies."

"Poppies? Weeds of the field?"

"Vibrant, beautiful, and a great deal more resilient than they appear. And then, of course, there's the type that provides a powerful drug that turns men mad."

She'd been startled and unsure whether she was being teased, flattered, or insulted. His gift, she remembered with a snort, had been a copy of William Wordsworth's "Ode: Intimations of Immortality."

"Mama?"

She started and looked down at a worried Harry. "Yes, dear. I was just thinking about when I received that brooch. Grandmama will be very pleased with it. Come along and we'll wrap it up prettily and tie it with a ribbon."

Where, she wondered, had that slim volume gone? It was a reminder, however, that Stephen had disapproved of her even then, before Hal Gardeyne had visited the area and changed everything.

Chapter 5

Harry chattered about his grandparents, his uncles and aunts and cousins. He seemed to remember them all remarkably well, when it had been six months since their last short visit. Laura couldn't help thinking that he could have a happier, healthier childhood at Merrymead but she was powerless to change his home.

Powerless.

In a right and just world, a mother should have more power, but in this one, Lord Caldfort was Harry's guardian. When he died, the power would transfer to Jack.

She stilled in the midst of tying a pink ribbon. She truly wished Lord Caldfort a long life.

She managed to eat enough lunch that Harry didn't notice anything wrong, then took him into the flower garden, which was not much cherished. He chose some Michaelmas daisies and stocks and some delicate grayish foliage. Laura gazed around, thinking that perhaps she should dedicate her life to gardening. But surely if that had been her calling, she would have felt it before now.

Her mood was certainly suitable for a visit to her husband's grave, but she didn't want Harry to be sad, so as they walked to the stables, she started a song he enjoyed. By the time she lifted him into the one-horse gig, her heart was lighter, which proved her belief that people could mostly be as happy as they tried to be. To have Harry to herself was certainly a delight, and soon she'd have him to herself for a whole month.

She never took Nan to Merrymead. There wasn't much free space there, and there were always plenty of people happy to look after a child. She didn't take her maid, either, for the same reason.

"Just you and me, Harry," she said as they rolled along the lane toward the village, the bells on Nutmeg's harness jingling.

"Just you and me!" he echoed, bouncing on his seat.

He was so excited—and at tomorrow's journey, not this one—that Laura drove slowly. They were in no hurry and she didn't want him to fall out. In truth, she'd rather not spoil his or her bright spirits by this visit to Hal's grave, but that was an unworthy thought. Poor Hal deserved to be remembered.

Harry pointed to cows, horses, sheep, and trees. They paused by Figgers Farm to watch some ducks. When she lifted him out by the churchyard, he beamed at her. Was there anything so magical as an excited, happy child? She planted a big kiss on his cheek before putting him down.

When the horse was securely tethered, she took Harry's hand. "Come along, Minnow. Hold tight to those flowers."

They walked through the gate and up the path.

"Church?" he asked, pulling toward the ancient building.

"Not today, sweetling. Today we're going to put the flowers near your father's grave because we won't be at church next Sunday. We'll attend St. Michael's near Merrymead."

"Merrymead!" he caroled, making her laugh.

She hastily controlled that. It was hardly appropriate for a widow visiting her husband's grave. Instead, she began to talk about Hal, as she did during

every visit, to try to keep his memory alive for Harry.
She knew it couldn't work, though. Poor Hal would
end up as only a grave and a stranger in some
portraits.

She couldn't even tell Harry the whole truth. Hal
Gardeyne had not been a particularly clever man, and
he'd inherited all his father and mother's selfishness.
There were positive aspects, too, however, or she
would never have married him.

"Your father was a strong man, Harry. Over six feet
tall and broad shouldered. I think that one day you'll
be the same. He had such energy it almost sparkled
around him, and he was generous."

In bed. Judging from the way some women found
their husbands' attentions a burden, she supposed
other husbands were not. She recognized, too, that if
she'd been highly fertile she might have been wary of
her husband's approaches herself.

She fought a smile. What would the world be like
if secret thoughts were heard by others?

"Here we are." Laura halted before the handsome
marble stone upon which Hal Gardeyne's life was recorded. Eldest son of John, Lord Caldfort of this parish, beloved brother of the Reverend John Gardeyne,
vicar of St. Edwin's. Sorely missed by his loving wife,
Laura, and his son, Harry.

Beneath was carved the phrase that Jack had insisted on. HE LEFT LIFE LEAPING.

The alliteration had always made it sound slightly
humorous to Laura, but she knew the words came
from a brother's understanding. Hal had indeed been
full of vibrant energy and had died doing one of the
things he loved most—flying over a jump in the hunting field.

Laura hoped there were horses and hedges in
heaven.

She looked down to see that Harry had already

taken out last Sunday's wilting flowers and was trying
to shove the new ones in. She went to help him. "Now
we need to get water from the pump, love. Come on."

Harry had sat down, however, and started to pick
a new bouquet of buttercups with the intensity typical
of a three-year-old. Laura shook her head and left him
to his work. The Gardeyne plot was close to the pump.

She worked the pump handle, keeping an eye on
Harry to make sure he didn't wander. Thin sunlight
lit the scene, but the wind was soughing through the
tall elms that shadowed the plot, creating a melancholy air. It seemed they were more sorrowful than
she.

She did grieve for Hal, but it was unselfish sorrow.
He'd been snatched from vibrant life so soon, and that
was tragic.

She recognized that her own sorrows were entirely
selfish. She resented being abandoned in this constrained and tedious situation, barred from both her
family and the fashionable world she'd enjoyed. She
grieved—had grieved for years—for the marriage
she'd dreamed of at eighteen.

Dazzled by an energetic, worldly man, she'd expected his courting attention to continue. Instead, he'd
drifted back to his manly sporting world. He'd seem
to enjoy her company when with her, but his heart
had been solidly elsewhere. Time tends to flow to
where the heart dwells.

She'd come to realize that they had nothing in common, not even their fashionable life. He'd preened
to be husband of Labellelle, but he'd liked being the
husband of Lady Skylark even more. He'd thought
Labellelle too highfalutin and suspect.

"Brummell," he'd said once. "Funny sort of fellow,
Brummell. Don't like to hunt because he gets mud on
his clothes. Lady Skylark, that's you, my dear. Happy
as a lark."

They'd been in bed then, relaxed and sweaty. . . .

How fortunate that an observer would not be able to read her thoughts. In all the sympathy about her widowed state, no one mentioned bed. She supposed they couldn't, but no wonder there were so many wicked widows.

Even that relief was not open to her. She couldn't imagine taking casual lovers, but she certainly couldn't risk scandal. A scandalous mother could be cut off from her children. If Jack was as evil as she thought, her misbehavior could seal Harry's death warrant.

He was still sitting by his father's grave, surrounded by massacred buttercups. She picked up the wooden bucket and set off back toward the grave, being careful not to splash her skirts.

Harry looked at something in his hand, then shoved it in his mouth.

"Harry, no!"

Laura started to hurry, and the water splashed. She dropped the bucket and ran. Buttercups weren't poisonous, but still . . . She grabbed his hand. It was covered with something brown.

"*Harry*! Don't eat that. Spit it out!"

He was chewing, looking mutinous, so at least it couldn't be dung.

"Open!" she commanded in her sternest voice.

Glowering, he obeyed, revealing a mess of brown and white. It looked like some kind of sticky bun.

"Harry, you know better than this!" she scolded as she scooped out as much as she could with her fingers. "You don't eat things you find on the ground. Spit out the rest. Immediately!"

Face crumpling, he did as she said, and she wiped his mouth with her handkerchief. Then she towed him over to the pump, grabbing the empty bucket as she went.

"Never, never, never eat something you find on the

ground! It could make you ill." She began to pump.
"Drink from the water as it comes out and then spit.
Try not to swallow."

She wasn't sure he could follow her instructions, but
he did, even though he got drenched in the process.

Laura's panicked heart began to settle, and she felt
dizzy and had to lean against the pump for a moment.
It had only been a sticky bun that someone had
dropped. At his age, Harry probably wouldn't put
something vile in his mouth, and if he did he would
spit it out.

She knelt and gathered him into her arms, wet
though he was. "I'm sorry if I frightened you, Minnow,
but you frightened me. You must never eat things you
find lying around, no matter how tasty they look."

Some of the wet on his face was tears. "I'm sorry,
Mama."

She kissed his temple. "I know, sweetling, and all's
well that ends well. Let's finish the flowers and get
you home and dry."

They completed the business quickly, then Laura
said, "Come along, now."

Harry dragged on her arm, so she picked him up
again, sorry to have alarmed and upset him. She definitely needed to get away from Caldfort and be restored to her usual sunny nature. She gave him a
special hug before putting him into the gig, and promised him another cake when they arrived home.

Evening was settling and the air was turning sharp.
Laura stripped off Harry's wet jacket and helped him
into his coat, which she'd brought in case. Then she
wrapped a shawl around herself, winding the ends
country-fashion behind her and knotting them there.

Harry leaned against her so she kept one arm
around him, but that meant she couldn't drive fast.
She wanted him home and into dry clothes, but she
couldn't deny him a hug. They had entered the park-
land around Caldfort when he whined, "Mama . . ."

A moment later, he threw up over the side of the gig.

She halted the horse and wiped Harry's mouth. "It must have been that bun, Minnow. Heaven knows how long it had been there. You'll feel all the better for getting rid of it."

She gathered the reins again, but he was crying now and clutching his stomach. Suddenly full of dread, Laura gripped his coat and urged the horse to speed.

They were in the stables in minutes.

She abandoned the gig, gathered her screaming child into her arms, and raced for the house, for her stillroom, where she kept her medicinal supplies.

The vomiting and pain could just be from excitement, but she must rid his stomach of any trace of that bun. She put him down and grabbed the infusion of ipecacuanha. Her hands were almost shaking too much to pour some into a glass and force it down his throat.

He fought her but she made him swallow. In moments, he hurled up all the contents of his little stomach, then burst into sobs again. She held him close, trying to soothe him, but ecstatic to see bits of bun among the vomit.

By then, the housekeeper and a maid were hovering.

"Whatever is it, ma'am?" Mrs. Moorside exclaimed.

"Harry picked up something from the ground and ate it. Could you make some lemonade for him, please, with lots of honey and a little brandy?"

Harry was hiccupping with tears and sucking his thumb as she carried him up to his room, where Nan cried out with alarm. Laura told the story again as they worked together to strip off his damp and messy clothing, wash him, and dress him in his nightshirt. Then they tucked him into a warm bed and Laura sat beside, watching for any further ill effects.

Mrs. Moorside herself came up with the lemonade,

and Laura coaxed Harry into sipping it. It was one of his favorite drinks, and soon half of it was gone. The brandy made his lids droop, and in a moment he was fast asleep.

Laura checked again to see that his brow was cool and his pulse normal. His tummy wasn't hard or showing any sign of distress, and her boiling panic settled to a simmer. If there had been danger it was probably over. Probably. It took great willpower to leave the room, to leave her son in Nan's hands even for a while, but she was wet and foul.

It was only when she reached her room that she faced her deepest fear. She leaned against the wall, legs shaking so much that they gave way and she sank to the ground.

Someone might have tried to poison her son.

Jack Gardeyne might have tried to poison her son.

Laura crawled to a chair and got into it, dirty as she was.

A bun, even if it was days old, shouldn't have such an effect. On the other hand, vomiting and pain could just be a nervous reaction. She might have caused it herself.

She couldn't make herself believe that. She couldn't afford to believe that. Thank heavens they were leaving tomorrow; otherwise she'd go mad from fear.

Her maid rushed in to take care of her and she had to pull herself together, to pretend to be only an upset mother as she stood to undress, to wash, to put on fresh clothing. As she sat to have her hair tidied, to be restored to perfect Laura Gardeyne.

By then a message had come up from Lord Caldfort demanding a report on what had happened to his heir. Laura collected the last disordered scraps of herself and went down to his study. He was in his big chair by the window, swollen legs raised on a footstool, looking distressed and haggard again.

"Harry's fine now, sir," Laura said quickly. "He's in no danger."

"But what danger was he in, eh?" Lord Caldfort demanded. "What were you doing to let him eat poison?"

"Poison?" she gasped, wondering what he knew.

"I hear you forced an emetic down him. Was that for amusement, woman?"

Laura sat down before her legs betrayed her again. "No, sir, of course not. But it may not have been necessary. I couldn't afford to take any risk. Harry ate something he found on the ground. A bun, probably."

"Rat poison, was it?"

She shuddered. Such deaths from poisoned bait were unfortunately common. "Who would put out rat poison in a graveyard, sir? Doubtless someone dropped the bun and there was nothing wrong with it, until my panic excited his stomach."

He narrowed his eyes at her. "But you don't think so."

She licked her lips and repeated what she'd said. "I couldn't afford to take the risk, sir."

He scowled, looking like a dyspeptic bulldog. "You're a good mother. Thought you were nothing but a pretty flibbertigibbet when Hal married you. Didn't the *ton* used to call you skylark?" He snorted. "Not for your singing, either. For your larking around. But you've turned out to have all your wits about you. Hal was fortunate."

It was the first time he'd said anything like that to her.

"Thank you, sir. I do grieve for him."

"Aye." He sighed. "He lived for hunting, though."

"He would have chosen that way to go," she agreed. He certainly wouldn't have wanted to outlive his ability to ride and hunt, as his father had.

"I suppose you'll want to put off your departure," he said.

Laura's stomach tensed. "I don't think that's necessary," she said as casually as she could manage. "Children get over these things quickly. Unless Harry seems worse, we will leave tomorrow as planned."

She braced for resistance, but he nodded. "Aye, that would be best."

Laura curtsied and left, relieved in one way but not in another. Did Lord Caldfort share her suspicions? Could his distress this morning have been due not to a letter, but to something Jack had said?

She paused in the hall to go over everything, and she couldn't make it fit. She was almost certain Jack hadn't visited that early, and everything pointed to Lord Caldfort being alone, reading his correspondence when the shock occurred. . . .

"Laura? Is something the matter?"

She started and whirled, hand to chest, to find that she hadn't imagined that distinctive, slightly drawling voice.

"Stephen! What on earth are you doing here?"

Chapter 6

Elegant, blond, lean, and quizzical, Sir Stephen Ball was indeed standing across the hall from her, though her stunned mind couldn't imagine how. It was as if he'd appeared in a puff of theatrical smoke.

"What am I doing?" he asked, strolling toward her. "Attempting to speak to Lord Caldfort on a political matter, but I gather there's a problem in the house. Cook's burned the sauce? A rat's invaded the larder?"

Stephen, here, sardonic as always. Wishing to speak to Lord Caldfort . . . ?

Her dazed mind suddenly sharpened. Was his arrival connected to Lord Caldfort's earlier shock? Had a letter heralded political scandal or disaster?

"Laura?" His brows had risen, and his lazy eyes were now sharp. As her shock faded, she realized that he hadn't appeared in a puff of smoke, but simply walked out of the reception room.

She gathered scraps of information. He'd come here to speak to Lord Caldfort and been shown to the reception room. Her drama had distracted all the servants and he'd been forgotten.

She managed a light laugh. "Stephen, I'm so sorry! As you say, we have all been distracted by a domestic matter, but how shameful that you've been neglected. You're here to see my father-in-law? I'll go and let him know—"

She began to turn, but he caught her arm, shocking her. As she turned back, she knew it wasn't just the outrageousness of it. It was a man's touch. It had been so long since she'd felt a man's touch like this.

But Stephen . . . ?

"Take a moment to settle your nerves," he said, letting her go. "I don't wish to intrude, but is there anything I can do to help? I'm quite a hand at catching rats."

To spill every detail to him now was perhaps the strongest temptation Laura had ever experienced, but she stopped herself. Once they had been as close as sister and brother, but once long ago. For six years, he had avoided her as deliberately as she had avoided him.

"Thank you, but the drama is over. My son ate something noxious and I had to give him an emetic. Lord Caldfort is upset because, of course, Harry is his heir."

"What did he eat?"

"A bun of some sort, dropped in the churchyard."

She managed to speak lightly, but shocked thoughts rushed in anyway. *And possibly deliberately laced with poison.*

An arm came around her and she needed it, needed assistance into the reception room and onto the sofa there. She couldn't afford to be so weak, but muscles and sinews don't always obey will.

"I'm all right. . . ." she tried.

"Going sheet-white and swaying is Lady Skylark's latest party trick, is it?" He went to the fireplace and rang the bell.

"All the rage in these parts." She managed to say it lightly, but was relieved to be sitting down. She even closed her eyes and leaned her head against the back of the sofa for a moment, listening as if from a distance as Thomas arrived, apologizing fervently for having forgotten the visitor.

"Never mind that," Stephen said with cool authority. "Mrs. Gardeyne needs a restorative. Sweet tea and brandy. Immediately."

Thomas left and Laura opened her eyes. Despite everything, she even found herself smiling. "How typical of you, Stephen, to be giving orders in someone else's house."

"Playing lord of creation. Do you mind?"

"Of course not."

But what if he'd come to tear her bit of creation apart?

A final act of revenge? No, she couldn't imagine Stephen sinking so low. They had been friends once, good friends.

He came to sit beside her on the sofa and she noted a new grace in him. He had grown into his height and strength, but that shouldn't surprise her. They had met now and then over the past six years.

He was in boots and leather breeches. Country wear, but London made, she noted. After all, they called him the Political Dandy. A riding crop lay with his hat and gloves on a table.

He'd ridden here. From where? People rarely chose to ride long distances—off the hunting field, that was.

His lips twitched. "As readable as ever, Laura. What am I doing here? I stopped by to speak to Caldfort about some Parliamentary matters."

She straightened and gathered her wits. "Yes, you said. But stopped by? Berkshire is hardly next door to Devon or London."

"A little out of the way. Am I unwelcome?"

Yes. But she couldn't say that.

"Of course not. It's only that I'm still shaken by the incident with Harry. I fear you've wasted a journey, however. I doubt Lord Caldfort will appear in Parliament again. He can hardly leave the house." She lowered her voice. "He may not last long."

"Unfortunate. He's always been a supporter of military reform, which is the issue in hand."

She tried to read his expression, but he'd always been skilled at concealing thoughts and feelings. Was the explanation of his presence that simple? No connection to her father-in-law's distress? She distrusted coincidence, but she supposed it did happen.

The tea arrived with the brandy decanter on the side. Stephen would have poured, but Laura insisted, even though the pot felt heavy in her still-unsteady hands. She stirred more sugar into her cup than she normally took, and let Stephen add some brandy. As soon as she sipped, her nerves began to calm and she smiled at him.

"This is exactly the thing. You must have thought me demented."

"Just distressed. A threat to your son is explanation enough."

She froze with her cup halfway to her lips. "Threat?"

His brows rose. "Possible poison is a threat, is it not?"

She forced a laugh. "Yes, of course. It's just that *threat* sounds deliberate, and of course it was not. An accident, that's all."

She was babbling, so she occupied her mouth with tea again.

When he didn't say anything, she grimaced at him. "This has not been a good day, but there's no mystery, so don't turn your gimlet mind to it."

"You know the source of the tainted bun?"

She should have known she wouldn't deflect him.

She gestured it away. "Oh, it probably wasn't tainted at all. Children's stomachs are upset by the slightest thing, including excitement. If I'm distressed, it's that I fear I forced the emetic on Harry for no reason, and he's wrung out, poor mite. If not, I'd take you up to meet him. So," she said, forcing the conversation back to his affairs, "what journey brings you past Caldfort?"

She thought he might reject the change of subject,

but he relaxed. "I've been in Oxford—a neighboring county at least—and I'm on my way home."

That route would bring him close. Relief unsteadied her almost as much as fear had, but she still had to deal with him.

Even in normal circumstances, Stephen's arrival would be a strain. Today it was close to intolerable. How quickly could she speed him on his way? Not until he'd spoken with Lord Caldfort. She would arrange that now. . . .

But then the clock chimed five.

"So late?" The words unfortunately escaped her.

He put down his cup and rose. "I've kept you with this idle chatter when you have a sick child. Forgive me. I'll put up at the local inn and return tomorrow to talk to Caldfort."

She rose, too, and acted as she must. "Of course, you will stay the night here, and I'm sure Lord Caldfort will be happy to speak to you now if he is able. He misses involvement in the world's affairs. I'll go and see."

This time he made no attempt to stop her, and Laura could escape.

She paused halfway across the hall, struck by a sickening new realization. Stephen did nothing without thought. He'd arrived here late in the day and then, yes, he had kept her talking when she had a sick child in the nursery. He'd made an invitation to stay impossible to avoid.

He and she had avoided each other for six years. He would never come to her home for a trivial purpose. Whatever the purpose was, however, she could see no way to prevent it.

She carried on to Lord Caldfort's study and watched his reaction to news of the guest. Pure delight. She took Stephen to him and would have loved to linger and find out more, but Lord Caldfort would never stand for that.

In the hall again, she shrugged. If a sword was to fall on the Gardeyne family, it would fall. She summoned Mrs. Moorside and gave instructions for the preparation of a room.

"And tell Cook there'll be one extra for dinner. A gentleman likely to eat more than the rest of us together."

Despite Stephen's slim build, he'd always had a healthy appetite, especially after riding. She remembered—

She blocked that. "Oh, and as there's no sign of a valet, tell King to be ready to assist Sir Stephen if needed."

King was Lord Caldfort's man and might enjoy attending to a man of fashion.

Laura wanted to check on Harry, but she took a moment to be sure that she'd done all that was necessary. There was one more task. She went to Lady Caldfort's room to inform her that they had a guest. Laura had taken over the running of the house, but she tried not to ignore the older woman.

"A *young* man?" Lady Caldfort asked, turning to face Laura, brandishing a beetle on a pin.

"Yes, I suppose so."

"Good. You should marry again. Get away from here."

Lady Caldfort turned back to her work and Laura left, wondering if that was a warning, but no one was less likely than her mother-in-law to know of secret plans. After all, she was clearly blind to the fact that Laura was pinned here like a beetle in a box.

Now, thank heavens, she could go up to the nursery. When she saw how much Harry was recovered, most of the knot of tension in her unraveled. He was awake from his nap and demanding his supper. Laura checked again for fever or pain, but no one would guess he'd been so unwell.

"Very well, but just soup with bread in it. And then some stewed apples and cream if you feel like them."

His bright eyes said he did. She played with him a while, but couldn't stay with him all evening when they had a guest and Harry was clearly recovered. She kissed his brow and went downstairs, but her mind wouldn't stop circling the events of the day.

Had she imagined Lord Caldfort's distress?

Had that bun really been poisoned, or had that been her own unbalanced interpretation?

Was Stephen's arrival an innocent coincidence?

One shock after another after another had caused a turmoil inside her that was almost as violent as the one caused in Harry by that bun. She could no longer tell truth from fiction.

She entered her boudoir and leaned back against the door, trying to reason away her fears.

Lord Caldfort's problem probably had nothing to do with her.

If Jack wanted Harry dead, why try such a clumsy way when better occasions would turn up in time? Boys will be boys, and in a few years Harry would be climbing trees, boating on the river, learning to ride, and even to jump fences. A fatal accident could literally be child's play.

As to Stephen's arrival, at least it must mean that he'd put old rancor aside. It might be time for her to forgive and forget, too. They were close to strangers now.

Laura's maid bustled in. "With a guest for dinner, ma'am, you need to change."

"Not for Sir Stephen, Catherine. We're old . . ." Laura sought the right word and in the end settled on "acquaintances."

"And that dress is likely older, ma'am! I only chose it because I thought you might need to do more sick-room duty."

Laura looked down and saw that she was indeed in one of her oldest, simplest dresses. It had been a favorite once and that was probably why she'd kept it, but only for the messiest household tasks.

Not one she'd have chosen for greeting any guests, let alone Stephen.

She spread the skirt. "You'd never know, but it was lovely once. A leaf-green stripe on white." And now the stripes were faded like tired leaves, the white yellowed. "I do believe this dates from before my marriage."

Before her marriage, indeed.

She'd been wearing this gown—the green fresh, the white pure—when Stephen had proposed.

Had he recognized it? What had he thought?

Chapter 7

"Come along, do, ma'am, or you'll be late!"

Laura went into her bedchamber but she couldn't stop memories breaking through the barriers she'd erected around them.

A June picnic at Ancross, hosted by Stephen's parents up on the hill that was crowned by the ruin of ancient Ancross Castle. Her whole family there and most of Stephen's, along with Hal and his hosts, the Oxholmes, and some other local families.

Most of the party had still been eating in a sheltered, sunny spot, but she, Charlotte, and Stephen had taken Hal on a tour of the ruins.

Charlotte had teased Hal to help her climb the crumbling stone steps to the tower. Had Charlotte been jealous that such an eligible gentleman had asked for Laura's hand? Laura had never considered that before, but it was probably the case.

She and Stephen had dallied on the ground. The ruins were familiar and held no great interest anymore, and perhaps she'd been thinking that she didn't want to risk her lovely new gown in the climb.

But they'd stopped while the other two had gone on.

Why . . . ?

Because they'd been caught by the song of a skylark.

It was as if she could hear the beautiful tune now. They were not so common around lush Caldfort, so it was a sound she associated with her home.

The bird had shot up not far from their feet, perhaps because they'd come too close to its nest. As skylarks do, it had soared up, singing to distract them, climbing and climbing. There was only one way to watch a skylark, so they'd sunk to the ground and lain back, eyes on the pristine blue sky as the bird became a dot too small to distinguish.

As presented by her memory, it had been one of those perfect moments when nature seems heavenly, with no hint of predators, blight, or storms.

Once a skylark was out of sight, the only thing to do was to wait for it to descend in the mad plunge that always seemed suicidal but never was.

She had never seen the bird return.

Stephen had sat up, then pulled her up to sitting. Then he'd asked her to change her mind, to marry him, not Hal. To wait a few years until he finished his legal studies . . .

Catherine began to undo buttons, pulling Laura out of the past. She swallowed and managed not to shudder.

Stephen could not possibly think she'd worn this dress to torment him. Coincidence again, which meant his arrival here was the same, and there was no particular significance to it. She had only to survive dinner. Tomorrow he would leave.

She washed, then put on her one silk mourning dress. A dull weave, as was appropriate, and an equally dull lilac color. She was suddenly desperately tired of these mourning shades. Even the bilious old dress was preferable.

For a moment she considered her wardrobe of rich colors, but then put that aside. She would give Hal his full twelve-month due, and she certainly could not feed Lady Caldfort's twisted mind by appearing for dinner in fine feathers. Heaven knows what she would say.

She could wear pearls instead of jet and steel, however, and so she did so. That raised her spirits a little, but the lilac-trimmed cap that matched the gown made them plummet. Purple shades had never suited her, but she'd given the matter no thought before tonight.

She glanced at the clock. She must go down to make sure all was in order for a guest. Not too soon, however. She always calculated her arrival in Lord Caldfort's study so that she would have to spend as little time as possible there before dinner was announced.

On the other hand, she suddenly thought being early might provide an opportunity to look for the cause of Lord Caldfort's distress. He always made the laborious journey across to his bedchamber to change, and he'd take especial care for a guest. If she hurried down now, the room might be empty and she could . . .

What?

Poke around in the desk? Read Lord Caldfort's correspondence? The very idea appalled her, but she steeled herself. She'd break into the Tower of London if it was necessary to protect Harry.

She glanced at the clock and hurried downstairs. The study door was open, as it always was from the time Lord Caldfort went to his bedchamber until they went in to dinner. She braced herself, feeling as if her wicked intent must be obvious, and walked in. Her struggle was for nothing. Lord Caldfort was there, in his chair by the fire.

He scowled at her. "Isn't it time for you to be in colors? That tired old thing you had on earlier was more cheerful than that."

How very peculiar that he was echoing her own earlier thoughts. It was hardly sympathy, however. He was complaining as usual, which was why she always avoided these moments.

"It is not yet a year, sir."

"Damn near enough. If I don't care, why should you?"

She met his pouched eyes. "I will give Hal his due." Before he could jab at her anymore she asked, "How are you, sir? I hope the day's alarms haven't weakened you."

"Alarms?" He stiffened as if he'd try to rise from his chair. "There's been more than one? And I haven't been told?"

"An exaggeration," she said quickly. "Sir Stephen's arrival was not an alarm, but it was unexpected."

He sank back down. "That it was. Pack of trouble, guests are, but he's a sensible man, for a youngster. Old friend of your family, I gather."

She was surprised Stephen had mentioned it. "His family estate lies three miles from Merrymead, yes. And, of course, he's member for our local town, Barham."

They talked of her home area without much interest on either side until Stephen and Lady Caldfort came in together. Not arm in arm, Laura noted, though she was sure Stephen had offered.

Lady Caldfort halted near the door to wait in her usual impatient silence, but at least she seemed willing to wait. Stephen shrugged slightly and came forward to converse with Lord Caldfort.

Since they spoke of military pensions, Laura seized the chance to stroll about the modest, book-lined room. She looked for letters, though she didn't expect to find any lying out in the open. More to the point, she studied the desk. Though shocked at herself, she faced the fact that she was going to try to search it in order to read the letters that had arrived today.

The inlaid, walnut, bowfront desk had seven drawers, three in each pedestal and one in the center. All had brass lock plates, and none had a key sitting in it. She assumed the desk would follow the normal pattern and one key would fit all the locks, but without that one key she would be at a loss. She could hardly force open the drawers. It would leave marks.

She looked casually over the top of the desk. No key was obvious. There were two small boxes—one of inlaid wood and another carved from onyx—but she couldn't poke around in them. Not now, at least.

Later tonight, when the house was quiet, she was going to have to return here and do just that.

It was possible that Lord Caldfort kept the key on him, but he frequently complained that getting anything out of his pockets with his swollen hands was a "plaguey nuisance." She strolled back to his side and confirmed at a glance that he didn't wear a watch chain or any fobs where a key could be hung.

He might give the key to his valet for safekeeping, but why? She didn't think he kept anything of value in the desk, and having to send for King to lock and unlock would amount to another plaguey nuisance. So where would it be . . . ?

"Laura?"

She started and found Lord Caldfort standing, braced by a hand on his chair and another on his cane.

"We are summoned to table," Stephen said, extending his arm.

She blushed as she took it, and they followed Lord and Lady Caldfort. For once, Lady Caldfort was keeping pace with her husband's slow progress.

Laura's blush wasn't just embarrassment at her distraction. There had been a question in Stephen's eye and she didn't want him alerted to mysteries. To distract him, she said, "I've been trying to remember when we last met. Some social occasion in London. A glittering one."

"The Arden wedding ball."

"Oh, yes!" She in red; he looking splendid in dark evening clothes. "The social event of last year."

"And a successful one. The Ardens are now blessed with a son."

"It was in all the papers. I gather the christening was magnificent, too."

"But of course. The next heir to Belcraven. Though Beth Arden seems determined to raise the child in as normal a manner as possible for a future duke."

She glanced at him, surprised that he seemed intimate with such an aristocratic family when his circle was more that of the political reformers. But then she remembered.

"The Rogues," she said. "Arden is one of the Company of Rogues, your group of friends at Harrow. You're all still close?"

Too late, she recognized danger. Talking of youthful matters, of more intimate days, felt like stepping near the edge of an unreliable cliff.

"Did I really bore you with stories of them that much?" he asked wryly. "But yes, Arden is a Rogue, and we keep in touch."

"Lord Darius Debenham was one, too, wasn't he? I thought of that when I read the news of his miraculous return. You must all be delighted."

They had reached the table and he merely said, "Yes," as he seated her, then went around to his place opposite.

"How is Lord Darius?" She glanced to either side. "We are speaking of the Duke of Yeovil's younger son, who was thought lost at Waterloo, but who was discovered recently, still suffering from his wounds."

"Fishy business," Lord Caldfort muttered. "Gone a year?"

"A head wound, sir," Stephen said. "That plus the effect of opium for the pain."

"Mad, is he?"

"No, sir."

Stephen's face and tone were equable, but Laura

could tell he was angry. Before Lord Caldfort could speak again, he said, "The treatment of soldiers maddened by war is one of the matters under discussion. . . ."

The conversation became safely impersonal.

Deft, but that didn't surprise Laura. Even when young, Stephen had been tactful and skilled at manipulating people. Which was why his awkward proposal had been particularly shocking . . .

She blocked that.

The conversation was now firmly political, however, which meant that Lord Caldfort was acting as if the women at the table didn't exist. Stephen glanced at Laura, and she sent him a reassuring smile.

Lady Caldfort was frowning, but at least she wasn't beating her spoon on the table or screaming for the meal. There was no need, anyway. Thomas entered with the soup. As it was served, Laura allowed herself to study Stephen.

The Political Dandy. When she'd first heard him called that, it had amused her, for he'd given no thought to clothes when young. But then she'd realized that he'd always made the simplest garments look their best.

When she'd next seen him in London she'd noted that his clothes were elegant in the subtle way made fashionable by Brummell. He wasn't precisely a dandy, even so, but it had become the thing to designate men who dressed well that way. The Racing Dandy. The Hunting Dandy. The Golden Dandy.

She chose stewed eels and surveyed Stephen's current style.

He was all muted colors, but there was no suggestion of mourning. His coat and pantaloons were plain black, his waistcoat a beautiful damask of beige, black, and silver. His cravat was tied in one of the complicated knots men prided themselves on and held in place with one touch of color, a swirling jeweled pin. Emeralds, sapphires, and diamonds, alive in the candlelight.

She suddenly remembered that pin. He'd been wearing it at the Arden ball. Wasn't something grand enough for that occasion out of place here?

As she ate, ignoring the conversation as easily as it ignored her, Laura considered that event.

Hal had been cock-a-hoop at being invited. He and Arden were hunting-field acquaintances, but no more than that. He'd wanted to show her off and urged her to order a new gown.

She'd chosen a gown of daring red, wide on the shoulders and low on her back, which was veiled only by a lattice of ribbons. Hal had given her rubies to wear with it. The gown had been a huge success, and she'd enjoyed the event until they'd encountered Stephen.

Hal had called him over, mentioning something about Melton. She'd been surprised that Stephen stole time from politics for sport.

Stephen, she remembered, had been perfectly polite. But he'd given them the courtesy a gentleman reserved for strangers or for those he did not like. She'd thought it was directed at her, but then she'd become aware that Hal had forgotten that he was in a ballroom in London rather than in the Old Club in Melton.

She'd steered him away from Stephen and guided him through the evening so that there'd been no disaster. But she remembered wishing that she'd not attended, even when Hal had crowned the event later with particularly vigorous lovemaking. That had been the first time that she'd felt ashamed of Hal, and she'd known then that it was because of that encounter with Stephen.

She'd not returned to London again that year, and in November, Hal had died.

This simple evening was beginning to resemble an estate riddled with gin traps to catch poachers. An idle question about where she and Stephen had last met had bitten her with steel-toothed jaws.

Chapter 8

At least Stephen could be trusted to manage conversation throughout the long meal. At first he tried to include Laura or Lady Caldfort, but was enough of a realist to give up. Laura confronted a pork chop without any appetite and wished Lady Caldfort would make one of her abrupt departures so she could leave, too.

"Do you have an opinion on electoral reform, Laura?"

So Stephen hadn't given up. Laura pulled a face at him, but replied, "It does seem wrong that some members are elected by a handful of people and others by thousands."

"Tradition," snapped Lord Caldfort. "Can't play ducks and drakes with tradition."

Laura took braised turnips and held her tongue.

Stephen took the same, but said, "Tradition had schoolboys holding the rank of colonel in the army, sir, and you approved of that reform."

Laura smiled as Lord Caldfort grunted and attacked his food. He liked to think of himself as a reformer, but it stopped short of anything that would damage his own interests. As Viscount Caldfort he controlled a so-called pocket borough, where the thirty voters elected whom he wished.

Stephen cut into his meat. "And tradition says that

all property owners should have the vote. What, then, of women who hold property?"

Laura watched in horror as her father-in-law turned puce. *"Women? Voting?"*

"Don't bellow, John," snapped Lady Caldfort. "You know it upsets my digestion."

"To perdition with your digestion!"

"Don't distress yourself, sir," Laura said, shooting Stephen a chiding look.

Lord Caldfort turned his glare on her. "Would *you* want the vote, woman?"

Laura was pinned like one of Lady Caldfort's insects, unwilling to lie but not wanting to tell the truth and distress him further.

"See?" he said, turning to Stephen. "She can't even make up her mind on a simple question! Women don't have the brains for these things, Ball, and if they do, they're unnatural. World would go to rack and ruin."

"Strange," Stephen said, looking at Laura from beneath his heavy lids. "As I remember, Laura could give me a good game of chess."

Lord. How long was it since she'd played chess?

"Games." Lord Caldfort dismissed that with a wave of his fork. "Anyway, how many women own enough property to qualify for a vote? Besides tavern keepers and such."

"Perhaps that's another area of the law that needs examination, sir. Women's control over their own property."

Though Stephen's expression was innocent, from long practice Laura recognized that he was deliberately stirring trouble. She wished the table was narrower and she could kick him.

Lord Caldfort let his fork fall. "Damme, sir, but you're a radical!"

"I fear I am." Stephen glanced at Laura and perhaps understood the look she was firing at him. "But I am firmly in favor of law and order," he added.

"Wouldn't you agree, sir, that the mob must be controlled for the good of sober citizens?"

Lord Caldfort returned to his meal. "Aye, there you speak sense. Bring in the military. Shoot a few."

Laura doubted Stephen had meant that, but he let it go and soon Lord Caldfort was comfortable again, especially when Stephen moved talk to sporting matters. But then that took a strange turn. From hunting to riding, and the old king's belief in riding for vigor, which hadn't kept him sane, poor man, and then on to other sorts of races.

"Running races," Stephen said as the main courses were removed and the sweets brought to the table.

"For footmen." Lord Caldfort's attention was on a damson pie. He shouldn't eat such things, but there was no stopping him.

"And occasionally for wagers. Lieutenant Naismith recently won five hundred guineas in a footrace over five miles. I assume that running would be as healthful an exercise as riding. Or swimming," Stephen added, glancing at Laura before turning to inspect the pie being offered.

Laura almost spilled wine down her gown.

He'd known that she and Charlotte had gone swimming, but something in his eyes suggested that he knew about the other.

"Swimming!" Lord Caldfort sneered. "Amusement for lads, but nothing more than that. Don't hold with that sea dipping, either. The king used to do that, and look at where it's led. Stark, staring mad! A gentleman should stick to riding and walking. I'd be a happy man to be able to do either."

Silence settled. Laura could have started a new topic but she was too distracted by wondering what Stephen knew.

One particularly hot summer's day when she'd been about fifteen, she, Charlotte, and some other girls had daringly cooled themselves in the River Bar near to

Ancross, in a spot where Charlotte said the boys swam. They'd carefully posted a maid to keep watch and only frolicked in the shallows in their shifts, but it had been both wonderful and wicked.

The next day Stephen had let slip—which amounted to a tactful warning—that the spot could be seen from the upper floors at Ancross. Doubtless he'd thought to deter such folly, but it hadn't worked. What's more, it had sparked something even more wicked.

She and Charlotte had kept watch, with the added weaponry of Sir Arthur Ball's spyglass. She had to struggle not to smile at how deliciously shocked they'd been to discover that the males swam naked! How intrigued to be able to study their mysterious bodies through the telescope.

An ache jolted inside her along with a sudden rush of embarrassing heat. She kept her head down as if damson pie fascinated her, but even the swirl of purple juice in rich cream seemed arousing. It was so long since she'd seen a man's naked body, since she'd pressed against one in her bed.

Hal's familiar body. Heavily muscled but lean in the hip, furred on the chest.

Stephen's body had been different back then. Even among other young men he'd looked slender, but he'd been swift as a fish through the water. Mostly he'd been in the water and hardly visible, but he'd stood once in the shallows, laughing, pushing wet hair back off his face, caught in a sunbeam, looking like a young water god.

Then she'd thought her reaction to be shock and embarrassment. Now she recognized that it had been arousal, prickling like heat across her skin, tingling in her swelling breasts, beating like a pulse between her thighs.

She picked up her wineglass and sipped from it, looking at Stephen through her lashes. If he were Hal . . .

Lady Caldfort stood, startling Laura out of her shocking thoughts. Without a word, her mother-in-law left the room, and Laura seized the excuse. She stood, murmured, "Gentlemen," and escaped.

She fled upstairs. Was she really as pitiable as that? Would her hungers surge every time a virile man sat opposite her at table? She heard a noise below and turned to look back. Jack was striding across the hall toward the dining room. He'd heard about the guest and come to enjoy a bit of company.

His arrival was as sobering as cold water.

She rushed up to the nursery to be sure Harry was safe.

Chapter 9

Harry was fast asleep, of course, with no evidence of the day's dramas. He was unguarded, however. Laura hadn't thought to tell Nan not to leave Harry alone. It wouldn't even be fair. Nan deserved a little time with the other servants.

Laura couldn't bear to leave until Nan returned, however, so she sat by his bed to keep watch, smiling at him.

He was so beautiful lying there in sleep that he could model for a dark-curled angel. He wasn't, and in time he would become as troublesome as most men. What fretted her was that he was already adventurous. He was Hal Gardeyne's son, after all—and hers. In her youth, she'd not been famous for being cautious.

That swimming expedition had been her idea, as had been the watch kept with the telescope—

No, she wouldn't let her mind return there. She had best cultivate the mind of a nun and concentrate on keeping Harry safe through a normal, adventurous youth. But how? To try to wrap him in flannel would be a disaster of its own.

Perhaps when she was home she could talk about this with her father and oldest brother, Ned. They were such bluff, honest people, though. They'd think her mad, or even worse, come straight to Lord Caldfort about it.

There was always Stephen. . . .

He had a complex mind, which her father and brother did not. He knew the law. She pulled a face. The time was long past when she could ask Stephen for help, but she could help herself by finding out what had disturbed Lord Caldfort.

The door opened and Nan looked in. "Oh, ma'am," she whispered, "is everything all right?"

Laura stood and went out into the corridor. "Yes, of course. I came up to check on Harry and decided to sit a little. Sleeping children are delightful, aren't they?"

"That they are, ma'am."

"Is everything ready for departure tomorrow?"

"Yes, ma'am."

Laura felt reluctant to leave, but that was carrying concern too far, so she went back down to her room. She couldn't resist pausing at the banister overlooking the hall and listening for Jack's booming voice.

There it was. He was in the dining room.

Laura retreated to her room and had her maid prepare her for bed. It was early, but she had the excuse of today's alarms, and travel the next. Once she was ready, she sent Catherine to bed.

She would sit up to make sure Jack didn't come upstairs, but also, when everyone was asleep, she would invade the study. She paced the room, watching the ticking clock, but then made herself sit and read the day's newspapers.

Her eyes read lines of print without taking in much of the meaning, but her attention was caught by a story in the paper about army officers whose minds had been turned by the horrors of war. Stephen had mentioned that.

They were now to be treated in their regiments for a year before being sent to an asylum, which would give a chance of recovery. Asylums for the insane were horrible places, likely to turn someone mad if they weren't so already.

As Caldfort House seemed to be deranging her?

She looked at the clock. Nearly half past nine. Lord Caldfort was often in bed by ten. Why wouldn't Jack go home! She opened her door a crack, but even from here she could hear his voice.

She sat again and moved on to a hair-raising account of the captivity of the English consul in Algiers during the confrontation there in August. The consul and his family, along with some naval officers who had tried to rescue them, had been chained, locked in a pit, and marched over long distances with only bread and water.

Another story of imprisonment, and one that put her own resentments to shame.

The prisoners' release was due to the efforts of the American consul, though the dey of Algiers had been humane enough to send the ambassador's child back to the safety of a British ship.

Wasn't it a universal rule to try to avoid harm to children?

Only if they were irrelevant to the issue. Other children had not fared well. The Princes in the Tower. Prince Arthur, who had stood between King John and the throne of England.

She forced her mind back to the paper. Two coaches had come to grief while racing to be first into Brighton. She shook her head. One of Hal's friends had died in a similar accident. Men seemed to need no reason to kill one another. Improve the roads so they were safer, and madmen raced on them.

She finished the paper and again looked at the clock. Though she felt it was an age since she'd left the dining room, it was only quarter past ten.

There was no point to sitting here watching the hands of the clock, so Laura settled to writing a letter to her sister, Olivia, who was wife to a naval captain.

Was that movement below?

She opened her door and—praise be—heard Jack
call his good nights. A little later, footsteps came up
the stairs. She closed her door and listened as someone, surely Stephen, passed and another door closed
down the corridor.

At last.

Lord Caldfort would be settling for the night in his
bedchamber. The servants would be clearing the dining room, then washing the last dishes before taking
to their beds. Lady Caldfort had been in her rooms
for hours. Laura didn't know when her mother-in-law
went to bed or went to sleep, but she'd never been
known to emerge after dinner.

As the house settled into silence, she itched to set
off, but she had the whole night. Though she fidgeted
and paced, Laura waited until the clock showed eleven
thirty before she would let herself leave her room.
Then, senses screwed for any sign of life, she carried
her candle downstairs and across the hall to her
father-in-law's study.

She had a story prepared, though it didn't stop her
heart from pounding. Lord Caldfort kept road guides
in his study. Her excuse would be that she wished to
study tomorrow's route. It was flimsy because she
knew the way well, but it would do.

She was, after all, an idiot woman.

When she arrived at the door, Laura paused once
more, ears pricked for any sound, but then she entered
the room without further hesitation. If someone was
watching, she must not look furtive, even if she felt
it. She couldn't believe that she was intruding into
someone's study intent on reading his private
correspondence.

She crept to the desk, put her candlestick down
there, and surveyed the surface again. Nothing had
changed since before dinner, except that now she

could open the two small containers on top of the
desk. The box held small coins; the bowl was empty.

She hadn't expected it to be so easy, but it would
have been a pleasant surprise.

Aware that she was passing from excusable to inex-
cusable, she went around and sat in her father-in-law's
chair. If anyone came in here now, she was sunk.

She tugged on the handle of the central drawer—
and it slid out. She almost laughed with surprise. It
didn't hold letters, however, but only the necessities
for writing them. There were sheets of paper, pens,
and some open boxes holding sticks of sealing wax,
sand, a penknife and such.

She closed that and tried the top one on the left.

Locked.

That was to be expected, but the center one had
given her hope. She quickly tried the others, but all
were locked. She muttered the sort of word that ladies
were not supposed to know and considered again
whether it would be possible to force the drawers
open. The locks did not look sturdy, but she couldn't
see how to do it without leaving marks.

She glared at the desk. Expecting difficulties didn't
make them any the less disappointing, but she re-
grouped and put her mind to work. If the key was
here, where would it be?

She lifted and examined every object on the top of
the desk, even peering into the inkwell. At that insanity, she reminded herself that the key wasn't hidden
in that sense. Lord Caldfort presumably used it every
day. He wouldn't fish it out of ink.

She felt under the kneehole and down the inner
sides. She was about to crawl under when she realized
that her father-in-law was incapable of that.

So where?

She looked around the room at a daunting array of
bookshelves and objets d'art. The key could be any-

where, but the more she thought about it, the more
sure she was that Lord Caldfort would not want to be
heaving himself up out of his chair to get the key or
to hide it.

So where?

It seemed too careless a place, but she opened the
center drawer again and explored it all the way to the
back. Nothing but dust. She poked through the box
of sand—nothing—then tipped out the box of sealing
wax into her lap.

A small ornate key glinted in the light of her candle.

Hardly able to believe it, she tried the key in the
lock of the top drawer on the left. It clicked sweetly.
Could she take this as divine approval? No. This intrusion was wicked, but she had to do it. She put back
the sealing wax and closed the center drawer, then
settled to her search.

The top left drawer contained ledgers and estate
portfolios. No letters. She closed that drawer and
locked it, then opened the next one down. A few more
ledgers. The bottom one was empty. Of course, bend-
ing so low would be difficult.

She opened the top one on the right.

Letters!

They were all folded, but the seals she could see
were broken. Ones received, not ones waiting to be
sent. This was what she was looking for.

There was more than a day's worth, however. Laura
tried to remember how many had been on the desk this
morning when Lord Caldfort had given her the letter
from Juliet. Perhaps six? She counted quickly. Eleven.

Did he keep the letters in order of arrival? She
wanted to intrude as little as possible in this search,
but she might have to at least glance at them all.

She picked up the top one and unfolded it, the rustle of paper sounding loud in the quiet house. A quick
glance showed it was about a purchase of a bull. She
couldn't see how that could be a cause for alarm.

The next was about a case before the courts in London, but nothing dangerous or controversial. Then a letter from France from an old friend. She read it all the way through, but saw nothing strange.

She continued opening and glancing at letters, trying not to read any more than she had to. Then she picked up one that was clearly on cheaper paper—thinner and less white. She tensed with excitement. Unlike the others, it had been sealed with a wafer rather than with sealing wax. It was addressed to Lord Caldfort, and the only indication of sender was the place of origin.

Draycombe in Dorset.

That startled her. She came from Dorset. Draycombe was on the coast near the western edge of the county and she'd never been there, but could this alarm have something to do with her?

Chapter 10

She unfolded the paper with unsteady hands, terrified of tearing it or doing anything else to show that it had been disturbed.

She expected uneducated writing to match the paper, but the contents were neatly written, though there was something a little strange about the handwriting. An angularity, perhaps. A weight in the use of the pen.

She looked first to the bottom, seeking the sender's name.

Azir Al Farouk.

What sort of name was that?

> *Great Lord,*
> *I have information of interest to you about a certain HG, connected to Mary Woodside. Having been for some years a guest of Oscar Ris, HG has now changed course and might trouble you. You will find enclosed an item of relevance.*
> *I would be happy to assist you in the avoidance of this trouble for payment of ten thousand guineas.*
> *I can be reached through Captain Egan Dyer, care of the Compass Inn, Draycombe, Dorset. I am in hopes of being your most humble servant, great lord,*
> *Azir Al Farouk*

Ten thousand guineas! That was certainly enough to give Lord Caldfort a nasty shock, but apart from the figure, the letter mystified her. This had to be the letter she was looking for, however.

HG. Henry Gardeyne?

Her Harry? Surely not. He'd not been anywhere for "some years" and certainly not with Oscar Ris, whomever that might be. The Gardeyne family tree was full of Henrys, however, in one form of the name or another.

She started to run through the recent ones in her mind, but stopped herself. She could think in a safer place. Fearing that she would forget some detail, she took out a sheet of paper, dipped the pen, and made a precise copy. When she was sure it was exact, she refolded and replaced the original.

She looked around the desk for the item of relevance. There was nothing there except letters, and she was sure there was nothing unusual in the central drawer.

She couldn't search further now. She had no idea what she might be looking for. A scrap of fabric, a button, a lock of hair, a picture. She might not know it even if she saw it. She was sure she'd found the troubling letter, but she glanced at the remaining three, just in case. They were all ordinary correspondence.

After checking that the pile of letters looked as it had before, she locked the drawer and replaced the key. Once she was sure that the center drawer was in order, she closed it with sweating hands, picked up her candle—and froze.

Was that a sound?

She stopped breathing to listen, but the house seemed dead around her. She was tempted to race up to the safety of her room, but she must appear innocent to the end.

She went to the shelf of road guides, found the one

that included the road to Merrymead, and slipped her copy of the letter inside it. With her excuse in hand, she left the room feeling as if guilt were stamped on her forehead.

If it was, there was no one to see it. The house slept except for the ticking of clocks. Even her slippered footsteps sounded loud.

She went up to the nursery again, compelled to check that Harry was still safe. He was sound asleep, but she realized that her arrival here had not woken Nan.

Just as easily, Jack could have returned to the house, come quietly upstairs, and smothered Harry with a pillow. Or thrown him out of the window with the explanation of sleepwalking. There were so many ways to kill a child without it clearly being murder.

She hated to leave, but she must. She would be thought unbalanced if she slept up here, and she needed to study the letter. She couldn't stop thinking that there was a connection between it and Lord Caldfort's insistence that she take Harry away for a month, and thus a connection to Harry's safety.

She slipped downstairs and was at the door to her room when a soft voice said, "Is something amiss?"

She turned, heart jolting. Stephen stood outside his room, dressed for the night in a blue banyan over his nightshirt. He looked fully alert, however, not roused from sleep. Laura felt as if he could see into the book she was clutching and identify the letter.

"I've just been up to check on Harry," she said quietly, astonished by the calm of her own voice.

"He's all right, I assume."

"Yes. Fast asleep. Good night."

She turned back to her room, but he said, "You went down earlier. To get that book in your hand."

She looked back at him. "Pray, what concern is that of yours? I wanted a road guide. We leave tomorrow for Merrymead."

A flicker of amusement spoke of skepticism. "And you don't know the way?"

"I wanted to remind myself of details along the way so I can amuse Harry with them."

He strolled closer, and she made herself not draw back as if afraid. She was not used to thinking of Stephen as so tall, however, or so formidable.

"You travel home?" he said. "I wish I'd known. I would have accompanied you. I'm on my way there, but I'm promised to a meeting in Winchester tomorrow."

"Alas," she said, but thought, *Thank heaven!* The pressure of his company for days would be intolerable. For some reason, she couldn't think clearly when Stephen, clever Stephen, was observing her. As he was now.

"So there is nothing amiss in the house? Nothing wrong with your son?"

She matched calm with calm. "No, nothing. I'm sorry to have disturbed you, Stephen. Good night."

She went into her room and closed the door.

Stephen regarded the closed door thoughtfully and then returned to his room. It was a perfectly adequate room with all that a guest could require, and yet it spoke in subtle ways of a place unused to visitors.

Caldfort House was architecturally elegant and efficiently run, but it was not welcoming. It was not a home. He wouldn't like to live here, and he couldn't imagine Laura liked living here, either. Did that explain her tension, her . . . fear?

No, that was because of the threat to her son. He didn't believe that she'd overreacted, and the only rational murderer was the boy's uncle, the hale and hearty Reverend Gardeyne. Thus Stephen had spent the after-dinner session evaluating the man.

Sporting mad, clever enough but not brilliant, and

the sort of man who put enormous stock in siring a son, as if it proved his virility.

Wanting a son was rational when a title was at stake, or any other inheritance that must go in the male line. But it would make no practical difference to Reverend Gardeyne.

Unless his little nephew died.

Despite hours of observation, Stephen had no certainty that Gardeyne was a potential murderer, but he was relieved to hear that Laura and her son would be leaving in the morning. It was only a respite, however, so no wonder she was wound tight with worry.

He smiled wryly. A fine time he'd chosen to come courting.

He'd planned it so carefully, too. Not earlier in her mourning, which would have been inappropriate, but before the end, just in case she moved back into society and the other men flocked to Lady Skylark.

To make his excuse ironclad, he'd arranged meetings with reformers in Oxford and Winchester, and devised a valid excuse to stop here. Pathetic cowardice, really. If she still regarded him as a brother, she need never know his intent.

So now what should he do?

Brother or lover, he could not abandon Laura when she was worried, perhaps terrified, especially when she'd been sneaking around the house in the night for some purpose.

The hospitality here didn't run to decanters of spirits for the guests, but he kept a small flask of brandy in his bag and he sipped from it.

Laura.

He'd expected the brilliantly fashionable Mrs. Hal Gardeyne, and come prepared to entice. Or Lady Skylark, who would appreciate wit and high spirits. Instead, he'd found Laura, in a dress he remembered all too well, her hair disordered almost to a girlish state, almost at point of collapse from fear.

It had almost unmasked him. Threat to her or hers enraged him. He'd tear the world apart to make it right for her, but . . .

He laughed again and drank more brandy. But he had clearly been nothing to her but an inconvenient guest. Not even a friend, dammit. Merely someone to be taken care of in the name of hospitality. He hadn't missed her exclamation at the time, or that she'd offered a bed at Caldfort House with reluctance.

Tempting, so tempting, to hurl the brandy flask at the wall, but the damn thing was metal and wouldn't even smash.

Just because he'd never forgotten her, because he had loved and desired her longer than he'd known and shamefully taken the news of her husband's death as a second chance, didn't mean she felt the same way.

And clearly she didn't.

He wanted to flee and lick his wounds as he had six years ago. To plunge into work, trying to persuade himself that Laura was no loss. That he didn't need a skylark for his wife, a social flutterer who would drag him from ball to rout to frivolous house party.

It seemed that common sense was being reinforced by reality. She felt nothing for him at all.

He eyed the brandy flask, capped it, and put it away. Even if Laura didn't regard him as a friend anymore, he couldn't abandon her.

If Reverend Gardeyne was a Wicked Uncle, there had to be ways to keep her son safe. If she was leaving to visit Merrymead, that gave him time to investigate the situation. He had a feeling there was more going on, however.

After coming up to bed, he'd stayed alert in case Reverend Gardeyne returned to the house. Instead he'd heard Laura leave her room. From the upper landing he'd watched her go into her father-in-law's study. A slight hesitation at the door had suggested that she wasn't entirely at ease.

A road guide? She'd remained there a lot longer than it would take to find that, and he thought she'd emerged even more tense than when she'd entered. She'd gone to the upper floor, presumably to look in on her son. When she'd come back down he'd decided to interrupt her, hoping she'd share her problem as once she surely would have done. Instead, again he'd been an intrusive nuisance. But she needed a friend, needed help. He was sure of it.

Six years ago he'd tried to rescue Laura Watcombe from folly and made a complete fool of himself. He'd been wrong, as well. He'd thought she was making a mistake, but she'd been happy as Mrs. Hal Gardeyne. Happy as a damn lark.

Now he was going to do it again.

With the same sickening sense of being about to make a fool of himself, and the same awareness that he had to try, he left his room. If Laura's room was dark, if she'd gone to bed, it could wait until the morning, at least.

But a light shone out from beneath her door.

Chapter 11

He knocked, not expecting the door to open instantly, but it did. Laura was wide-eyed, but when she saw him, fear turned to exasperation. "Is something the matter?"

He was nothing but a bother, but he was here. He might as well go through with it.

"I'm sorry. Did you think it was something to do with your son?" He moved forward and she stepped back. She was still frowning, but at least he didn't have to fight his way in.

Perhaps because this was not her bedchamber, but her boudoir.

Probably as well, though it whispered of her delicate, sophisticated perfume. Nothing from her girlhood about that. He'd heard that the famous perfumiers, Lascelles and Brun, had created a unique fragrance for Labellelle. The men were geniuses.

"This is an intolerable intrusion," he said, closing the door behind himself, "but we were friends once, and friends don't turn their backs on one another in need. Something's going on, Laura. Something that sent you down to your father-in-law's study—"

"The road guide."

He glanced at the desk behind her. "And a letter?"

She seemed frozen, so he moved around her to

where the sheet of paper lay open on the desk, bright beneath the candle. "May I?"

She didn't say yes but she didn't say no, so he picked it up and read it with increasing astonishment and—yes—interest. He delighted in puzzles.

"Clearly not a normal piece of correspondence." He turned it and saw no address or sealing wax. "A copy?"

"Yes." She came to life and gave him a look that reminded him of the Laura of old. "I suppose I do need help, if you promise to keep this confidential."

"I'm offended." He spoke lightly but was hurt.

Perhaps she colored. "I'm sorry, but it's a long time since we were friends."

He considered how to respond to that and settled on the truth. "I never stopped being your friend."

"Lady Skylark?"

His heart missed a beat. He hadn't thought she would know, or care, who had suggested that name.

"That offended?"

She shrugged. "I preferred Labellelle. More intriguing."

There was more to this than appeared on the surface, but now was not the time to delve into it.

"Then I apologize. But I stand your friend, I assure you. Tell me about this letter."

After a moment, to his immense relief, she sat down at her desk.

Of course, it would be better if she showed awareness of their being in her boudoir in their nightwear. It would be better, much better, if she weren't wearing an ugly nightcap over her lovely hair, but at least her robe was a pretty rose. The colors of mourning didn't suit her at all.

"I spoke to Lord Caldfort this morning," she said, "as he was dealing with the morning postbag, and he seemed distressed. With everything else that's happened today, and because I'm leaving tomorrow, I decided to try to find out what had disturbed him."

She met his eyes, chin set defensively. "Matters of importance to the estate are of importance to Harry."

"I agree." He picked up another chair, put it close her hers, and sat. "What do you make of it?"

Being this close by candlelight was a crumb to the starving.

"Thus far, little." She touched the letter. "Azir Al Farouk is an Arab name, I believe."

Stephen looked at the letter again, commanding his brain to his lady's cause. "It sounds like it. The English is good, though. Was it addressed to Lord Caldfort? This only addresses 'Great Lord.' "

She grimaced. "I should have copied both sides, shouldn't I? But I'm sure it was addressed to the Right Honorable the Viscount Caldfort."

"An Arab with a nice understanding of English protocol. Most intriguing."

Like her scent, which made it damn hard to think.

"Let's be orderly," he said. *Yes, do let's.* "HG. We assume that's your husband, Hal Gardeyne?"

She shook her head. "How could he return to trouble anyone? You may not know, but first sons in this family are always called variants of Henry."

"Ah. So Lord Caldfort is a Henry, too?"

"No, because he was a second son, so his name is John. He inherited when his older brother, Henry, died. That Lord Caldfort had a son—Henry, of course—who died at sea."

"Navy?"

"A scholar of some sort. He was traveling to Greece. But poke around the Gardeyne family tree and there are dead Henry Gardeynes by the bushel."

"But how many alive?" he asked.

Fear flickered in her eyes. "Only the two infants. My Harry, and Jack's newborn Hal."

He wanted to take her in his arms, and only to comfort. "HG can't be them, then, can he? *'Having been for some years a guest of Oscar Ris . . .'* So it must be something to do with a dead Henry Gardeyne."

He had his reward when she relaxed, even smiled a little. "Old debts? Old scandals?"

"Connected to a woman called Mary Woodside. Could she have been a mistress to any of the dead Henrys? Perhaps turning up with a bastard child in tow?"

Too late he realized that could embarrass. He knew Hal Gardeyne had been a notorious womanizer, but did Laura?

She didn't even seem conscious of it being a delicate subject. "A bastard wouldn't shock Lord Caldfort. He regards them as proof of manly virility. Do you know what nationality a man called Oscar Ris might be?"

"Spanish? Portuguese?" He looked at the letter again. "What about Captain Dyer?"

"Lord Caldfort has many military friends, but I've never heard the name."

"With a military man involved, it might be something to do with the war."

She sat back, shaking her head. "Lord Caldfort retired from the army nine years ago, and even then he'd been behind a desk for a decade. There've been no other military men for generations. The Gardeynes like the comforts of England. The only one I know of who's gone traveling was the old viscount's son, and see what came of it. A watery grave."

But then she came alert like a pointer sensing game. "Could it be? His ship went down in the Mediterranean, close to Arab countries. He was on his way to Greece. Could Oscar Ris be a Greek name?"

Suddenly, delightfully, she was the Laura of his youth—quick, bright, and soaring above reality.

"Not obviously," he said.

As always, she wasn't daunted. "But his return would certainly be a shock, wouldn't it? Because then Lord Caldfort wouldn't be Lord Caldfort anymore."

As always, her enthusiasm was infectious. "It's an idea. And this Farouk is offering to remove the inconvenience. Astonishing."

But then, unlike the Laura of old, she came back to earth. "It is, isn't it? Astonishing. Unbelievably so. How could anyone come back from the dead?"

"Lord Darius did so."

"But that was one year, not ten."

"True." Stephen looked back at the letter to focus his mind. "What do you know about this Henry Gardeyne?"

"Very little. He died—or whatever—long before I married Hal."

Her voice was enough to make thought difficult. Voices didn't change, and it was almost as if they were back in Ancross, working on a puzzle.

"There's a memorial to him in the Gardeyne plot," she said. "I think it says he was twenty-one. And a portrait of him hangs in the hall."

"Ah, I saw that and wondered if it was the vicar as a younger man, but there's something too dreamy about it."

"In his eyes, I think."

He made the mistake of looking up and was caught by *her* eyes. There was nothing dreamy about them, alas, but poets had praised Laura Gardeyne's brilliant sapphire eyes.

He'd known them all his life, but not like this, by intimate candlelight; she an experienced woman, he a desirous man. *Desirous.* What a pretty word for burning hunger that threatened his sanity, his reason, and his control over this situation. If he tried to move his hand, he feared it would shake. If he tried to speak, he could not possibly make sense.

"I've always thought that picture shows a romantic

zest for adventure rather than dreaminess," she said, seemingly unaware of the effect she was having. "It makes his early death so sad. I'd like him to be alive, but where could he have been all these years?"

He grasped the simple question like a lifeline. "With Oscar Ris, apparently." *Think. Think.* "But as you say, that makes no sense. Why would he linger abroad when a title awaited him in England?" He sought a suggestion as a courting bird might seek a worm to tempt his mate. "What if Henry sired a son before he died? A legitimate one."

Her lips parted in a delighted smile. "And the wicked Farouk is offering to kill the child for money? Brilliant, Stephen!" But then she sobered. "We have to prevent that."

We. What towers of hope a man could build on one word.

"Even if it deprives your son of his inheritance?"

Those eyes could spit fire, as he well knew. "You imagine I would blindfold myself to another child's death in that cause? What sort of monster do you think I am?"

He raised his hands. "I'm sorry. Of course I don't think that, but I'm a man of law, Laura. I'm accustomed to pointing out the legal consequences of decisions. As long as you understand."

"I do." Now she was cold, but it was a passionate cold. Everything she did was passionate. "So, a child, and the object enclosed must have been proof of his legitimacy. I looked, but I didn't see anything. Certainly not a document." She fixed him with her gaze, and even cold it burned him. "We have to do something."

We again. *If you insist,* he thought, as a worm of an idea uncurled, an idea he knew he should resist.

She was looking into nowhere now. "You're going to think me mad."

I know I am. He sucked in the vision of her, the

delicate perfume, the movements of her breasts with every breath. He should speak. "Why?"

"Because, I'm looking with hope at the thought of Harry *not* being the heir to a title." She turned those eyes on him again. "Stephen, if Henry Gardeyne is alive, or his legitimate son is alive, they are the key to Harry's safety." She reached out and grasped his hand. "If Harry isn't heir to anything, he's *safe*."

It took the strength of Hercules to keep his hand passive in hers, and his heart was thundering. "Many would think you mad."

She laughed. "So he won't have a title and he'll have to make his own fortune, but he won't have to grow up at Caldfort, and he will *live*!"

He turned her hand then, held it in both of his, longing to raise it, kiss it. "As your legal adviser, no matter how informally, I have to ask you to think before you act on this."

She snatched her hand back. "What became of Stephen the warrior for justice? How can I possibly permit a murder, even by inaction?"

Words escaped him for a moment, then he managed, "I don't mean that. This could all be a hoax, however, an attempt at extortion. Do you want to succumb to that for your own advantage?"

Yes, she did, he saw. Her angry frown came of guilt. "With so much evidence?" she demanded.

Now that this had become a legal matter of sorts, he regained some sanity. Her legal adviser. God have mercy.

"How much evidence is there?" he asked. "Someone knows that Henry Gardeyne existed. That could be anyone. He has sent some supposed proof of something, we know not what. Mary Woodside eludes us, as does Oscar Ris and any explanation of a ten-year absence."

"You're being coolly analytical again," she complained with a pout. Yes, definitely a pout that made him want to hug her, it was so part of their youth. Perhaps she recognized it, too, for her expression softened and she suddenly looked away.

Was that the first sign that she saw him as a man?

"My virtue and my flaw," he agreed. "Shall I attempt to awe you with my brilliance to compensate? I'd be willing to gamble that Mary Woodside is the name of the ship Henry Gardeyne traveled on. The one that sank."

She looked back at him, eyes bright again. "Oh, brilliant, indeed!"

"That's public knowledge, too," he pointed out. "A villain could have discovered it."

"But a villain would have to have a reason to look it up. Hence," she declared triumphantly, "contact with Henry."

He had to smile. This followed the pattern of so many debates of their youth. "A point, I grant you."

She smiled back, and he'd swear it was unrestrained, a smile she might have given him in the past, before Hal Gardeyne had come into their lives. No, before he had made a mess of everything while a skylark sang.

"I'm glad you happened to come here today, Stephen, and that you invaded this room. I think I'd be going mad without your steadiness."

Steadiness?

"Do you see that as aging?" she asked. Damn, she'd always been too good at reading him. "We're both past being wild, I think."

"Are we?" Quickly he added, "Yes, of course we are. I'm a responsible Member of Parliament, supporter of worthy causes, and you're a respectable matron and mother. Wearing caps, no less."

That bloody cap—plain, encompassing, and tied beneath her chin—should be illegal. She touched it as if suddenly conscious of it. And blushed. What the devil about her damn cap made her blush?

She grabbed the letter and read it again, though

they'd sucked it dry. Oh, the deuce, he'd as good as said she was an aged antidote.

"I'm sorry. You're still a young, beautiful woman, Laura. If you return to society, you'll be a toast again."

"Toast?" she echoed, still hectic with color. "Thank you, but I can't leave Harry as long as there's any hint of danger."

"Take him with you when you marry."

Her bright color faded. "Lord Caldfort will never permit that. He says his heir should grow up here, and he's right."

"Ah. But only as long as he is the heir. I understand better now."

"I'm not doing this for selfish reasons."

"Of course not." But it was certainly additional motive for him. If Laura needed to find a new heir for Caldfort before she could marry, he was heart and soul for the cause. What's more, it fit in with his plan.

"What we need is the truth," he said, "and that can only be found in Draycombe."

She smiled brilliantly at him. "You would go there and find out for me?"

"No."

Color rushed beautifully into her cheeks. "Stephen, I'm so sorry! Why should I assume that you have time to do that? You must be very busy—"

He raised a hand and stopped her. "I'm never too busy to help a friend." He couldn't help adding, "Especially you, Laura. I can certainly go and uncover some facts, but once we have them there may be decisions to make. Decisions only you can make."

"What decisions?"

He was telling the truth, he realized, which certainly made this easier. "I don't know, but I can imagine dilemmas. What if HG is Henry Gardeyne's son, but an idiot or impossibly corrupt? Do we inflict such an owner on Caldfort?"

"The law . . ."

". . . must always be tempered by common sense."

"Stephen, I'm shocked!"

He waited and she added, "I can't decide that."

"Who else? Your Harry is too young, and Lord Caldfort's desires might not be the same as yours. He could well pay Farouk's price. That's why you must travel to Draycombe and judge for yourself."

She stared at him. "How? It's impossible without explanation, and how could I explain?"

"You're about to visit your family, which is halfway there."

"But I can hardly arrive at Merrymead, then immediately leave."

She was right, but he thought he saw a solution. He needed to tighten and tidy his plans, but he thought they would work. In more ways that one.

"It's late," he said, standing, "and our minds are buzzing with tiredness and tangles. Let's sleep on it. I'll travel part of the way with you tomorrow, which will give us time to talk far from prying ears."

She stood, too. "I suppose I'll have to do something. Perhaps Father or Ned could go to Draycombe."

"I've always thought them rather conventional. Salt of the earth, et cetera, but if matters become . . . irregular?"

She winced. "You're right. But I don't like to impose on you, Stephen."

"Sleep on it," he said, suppressing all reaction.

But he could not resist taking her hand and kissing it. Lightly, but even that was more than he'd ever done before. Holding her hand, he said, "I stand your friend, Laura, and I will help you sort this out. It will be no imposition."

Her fingers tightened on his. "Then I think heaven did send you here today."

"There's an Eastern philosophy that says that nothing happens by chance. That we are ruled by destiny, which cannot be fought. Good night, Laura."

He made himself leave, having found less than he longed for but more than he'd hoped. And probably a great deal more than he deserved.

Chapter 12

Laura watched the door close, then sank into her chair. Stephen's last words hung in the air as if they had import, but that must be exhaustion speaking. She needed sleep, but it felt impossible. How could she sleep with her mind and her body in turmoil?

They'd been together in her boudoir in their nightwear!

That awareness had prickled over and through her, so it had been a miracle that she'd spoken a word of sense. It sizzled in her still, making even the movement of her cotton nightgown against her skin scarcely bearable.

She stood and went into her bedroom, stripping off her clothes, then scrubbed with cold water. Disgusting—that's what it was when carnal lust distracted her from matters of life and death. Life and death for Harry. She clasped a dripping cloth to her breasts and the cold water trickled down, gathering on her thighs.

The first unmarried, virile man to enter her orbit, and she had become a would-be whore.

She tossed the useless cloth back in the bowl, but the madness was cooling. When she was dry and back in her nightgown, it no longer tormented her skin. She looked in the mirror, fearing to see a slack-mouthed slut, but she was Laura Gardeyne, lady.

In her cap. She put her hand to it. Oh, Lord, her cap!

That had almost been her ruin.

Hal had made a game of her nightcaps. He liked taking them off, which was largely why she'd worn them. He'd saunter into her bedchamber saying, "Off with that cap, wench. . . ."

Her body clenched at the memory of the words, at the memory of what always followed. She pressed her hand over her mouth, then bit it. She missed it so much, so *much*.

She could relieve herself and she would, but it wasn't the same. It was more than a year since a man's strong body had pleasured hers, and it would be many more before one would again, and her tears marked a tragedy fierce enough for the Greeks.

She climbed into bed but it took a long time to fall asleep, and she woke twice in the night. The second time, unable to settle, she went up to the nursery to reassure herself that Harry was still all right. He was fast asleep and she stood there looking at him, wondering if he'd hate her one day if she managed to free him of a viscountcy.

That, not lust, had stolen sleep, but it wasn't as if she had any choice. If Henry senior or junior existed, Caldfort must be theirs. She couldn't try to prevent that.

But she would rejoice if Harry became safe and she became free. No lying about that. She wanted to be free to leave, to live, to love.

She returned to her bedchamber. As she passed Stephen's room she only allowed herself to think about important matters—the journey and the letter from Azir Al Farouk. Because she was concentrating on that so fiercely, she realized there was something useful she could do. She could sketch a copy of Henry Gardeyne's portrait.

Her drawing portfolio was already packed in her

coach bag, but she dug it out and slipped into the dim corridor again, candlestick in hand. What would be her excuse if she was caught now? She was almost beyond caring. She'd announce that she was as eccentric as Lady Caldfort, but devoted to nighttime portraiture.

She went down to the hall and copied the picture as best she could by the light of one candle. She paid particular attention to the bones of the young man's face, the line of his nose, and the shape of his one visible ear. Those things didn't change much over time.

She would have made a more finished job of it, but the clock struck six and she heard a rattle from the kitchen area. The staff was stirring. She hurried back to her room and closed the door with a shudder of relief. She almost felt as if her own life was in danger. Perhaps it was. What would the Gardeynes do if they learned that she knew this secret?

She wouldn't feel safe until she and Harry drove away. With Stephen as escort. Thank God for that. She could even imagine Jack riding after to kill them both. She wasn't sure what Lord Caldfort would do about the letter, but she felt certain Jack would not accept the return of his cousin.

After acquiring Hal's small pistol, she'd not done anything with it. Now she carefully cleaned, checked, and loaded it. She paused, thinking that if Hal was looking down from heaven, he'd approve.

"You're an unlikely guardian angel, Hal," she whispered, "but keep our son safe."

She packed the case in her trunk but put the pistol in her coach bag, feeling considerably more secure.

No chance of getting back to sleep now, but too early to ring for breakfast. She worked a little on the drawing, but then realized it was a mistake. Anything she added now might make a better picture, but would be less like the original. She put it in her portfolio and returned that to her bag.

She read over the letter again, but it gave up no more wisdom. Oscar Ris. They'd come up with possible explanations for everything else, but not that. Perhaps it had a private meaning for Lord Caldfort.

Dear heaven! Could Lord Caldfort have had a hand in his nephew's disappearance all those years ago? Consigned him to imprisonment with Oscar Ris?

She'd try the suggestion on Stephen, but she could see the main objection. If the then Colonel John Gardeyne had decided to get rid of his nephew, he would have killed him, not locked him away somewhere. And only in fairy tales did hired killers turn softhearted and spare the victim.

The clock struck half past six. The sun was up, so she could be, too. She rang for Catherine, and by seven was taking breakfast with a fidgety, excited Harry. Waiting until eight for the post chaise to arrive was clearly going to be a torment for him. She and Nan occupied him with last-minute packing and with the important choice of toys to take in the coach.

With half an hour still to go, Nan said, "Will I take him down to the stables, ma'am, to wait there? The horses and cats will amuse him."

It was an excellent idea, but with escape so close Laura didn't dare let him out of her sight. She felt as if Jack could be lurking, ready to pounce, and she couldn't warn Nan.

"No, I'll take him down to my room. You make sure everything goes down to be ready, then wait there to say good-bye."

Her bedchamber and boudoir did distract Harry a little, especially her mechanical singing bird in a cage—a favorite treat. She thought for a moment of taking it with them, but recognized in time that the winding and playing would weary her long before it wearied a child.

Even now it was making her sad. Hal had given it to her for her twentieth birthday, saying he'd bought it because she was Lady Skylark. Even then, when he could do no wrong, she'd recognized that it didn't fit. No one caged a skylark. What point, when it sang only when on the wing?

"The coach is here, ma'am!"

"Thank heavens," she said to Catherine, and they shared a smile. "Come on, Minnow."

He was already at the door and would have rushed down the stairs if allowed. She had no intention of risking a fall now, and made him go at a decorous pace.

Mrs. Moorside and Rimmer, the butler, were waiting to bid her farewell. She went first with Harry to Lord Caldfort.

If she needed proof that Lord Caldfort was not his usual self, she found it. He seemed paler and weary, as if weighed down by something. Or as if he'd not slept. Hardly surprising if he thought he was about to lose everything.

Or, she wondered, *is he burdened by the decision? Is he thinking of paying Farouk to remove the problem?*

He kissed Harry's forehead, holding him too close. Harry squirmed as he always did, and Laura didn't blame him. His grandfather smelled of snuff and camphor at the best of times, and today he smelled worse. Sour.

She did feel sorry for the old man. However he was thinking about it, Azir's letter must have been a shock, and it laid a terrible burden on him.

"You enjoy a good long holiday," Lord Caldfort said again to Laura as he let Harry escape. "No need to hurry back. Lad's too young to be learning estate management yet, you know."

Just how far would this stretch? "My sister Juliet is

at Merrymead at the moment, sir. Perhaps I might travel back to London with her."

She saw the struggle, but then he said, "Good idea, good idea. Just for a few weeks, though."

Why had that letter caused this peculiar behavior? If they found Henry Gardeyne's legitimate son, perhaps it would be a kindness to the old man, as well. His dilemma would be over and it might be possible for him to live out his life here.

She and Harry said farewell to the senior staff, then went outside. Laura sucked in the crisp autumn air as if it were freedom itself and let Harry run down ahead to the horses. He knew not to go too close.

The four horses looked fresh and healthy, jingling the traces as they shifted, ready to be off. The last trunk was being loaded into the boot, and in a moment the lid was slammed shut.

Stephen was already there, but a handsome bay horse was saddled and waiting for him. How were they to talk if he was riding? Mind you, how were they to talk with an excited Harry along?

Laura remembered that he hadn't met Harry and collected her son. "Come and make your bow to Sir Stephen, Harry. He's an old friend of mine who's going to travel with us a little way."

Stephen came to meet them halfway. Harry did bow and say, "Pleased to meet you, sir," in proper manner, but then added, "May I ride with you, sir?"

Stephen looked startled and Laura said, "He must remember doing that with Hal. No, Harry, not today. When we get to Merrymead, your grandfather and Uncle Ned will take you riding."

"May I get in the coach, Mama?"

"Of course. Off you go."

He raced to the coach as if speed would make the journey start sooner.

"A charming lad," Stephen said.

"Yes, but the next two days will take fortitude."

"No nursemaid?"

"I never take her. She's not needed at Merrymead. How far can you come with us?"

She meant, *When can we talk?*

"To Andover."

About twenty miles and two changes. It would do.

Harry was hanging out of the carriage and calling for her to hurry, so she did. She was as keen to be away as he. Nan took a tearful farewell, Stephen mounted, and they were off.

Laura looked back at Caldfort House as long as she could, but that was only for the relief she felt when it finally slid out of sight with no sign of Jack Gardeyne in hot pursuit. Harry was now safe.

Chapter 13

The novelty of the carriage and the passing scenery held Harry's interest for quite some time, and then the changing of the horses at the first stage fascinated him. Laura let down the window so he could lean out and watch.

Stephen rode over to chat, but this stop would be too brief for much. "All went well, I assume?" he asked.

"Yes, though Lord Caldfort is definitely in a strange state of mind." Laura kept a grip on the back of Harry's jacket as he leaned out, and spoke softly. As they say, little pitchers have big ears. "He even agreed to let us spend some time in London if we wished. Why would this matter of HG make him do that?"

"To be sure that you don't catch wind of anything he does about it?"

She nodded at him. "That could be it."

The new horses were in the shafts, their postilions in the saddles. Laura pulled Harry back into the coach, and Stephen said, "Call a halt at Andover and we'll talk properly."

She agreed and they set off again, fast enough to keep Harry glued to the window. Stephen rode beside them at a canter, and Laura was glued to watching him.

She'd always thought of him as a thinker more than

a sportsman. He'd certainly never been as sporting
mad as her brothers and the other young men of the
area. Or like Hal, but Hal had been an extreme case.
A blood, a buck, a Corinthian.

Being married to a Corinthian gave a woman an
appreciation of a fine rider, and to her surprise, Stephen was one. He was clearly riding because he enjoyed it, and she enjoyed watching him. There was
something sensual about a good rider on a good horse.
She'd never thought that before.

Not even with Hal.

Something was changing, as if the strange events of
yesterday had cracked a seal. If Harry was not the
heir to Caldfort, she could marry again. It would no
longer be wicked to view men as potential husbands.

Men like Stephen?

She grimaced. After the debacle six years ago, he
was the last man to be interested in marrying her. Last
night had proved it. Not a hint of interest in anything
but the letter and the mystery.

Despite the riding, he was clearly still a man of the
mind—and besides, she remembered Lady Skylark.
That showed what he thought of her. A foolish player
in the riggings of life.

There would be suitors, however. She'd been the
toast of Dorset before her marriage and a toast of
London after it. She was older now, but it would be
coy to deny that she still had charms enough to attract
a new husband.

She wouldn't pursue those thoughts yet. It would
make disappointment too sharp. But they lingered like
a distant but pleasant melody.

In Andover she told the postilions that she wanted
tea, and took Harry into the White Hart. Stephen
soon joined them, but Laura pulled an apologetic face
at him, because Harry was eager for refreshments and
wanted to chatter about everything he'd seen.

She'd brought his bag of carved animals, however,

and once he'd drunk his milky tea, eaten a cake, and talked for a while, he scrambled off his chair to play on the floor.

It seemed a minor miracle, and Laura thanked heaven for it.

She shared with Stephen her thought about Lord Caldfort having a hand in his nephew's disappearance.

Stephen saw all the problems she did. "I suppose it's possible to imagine that Oscar Ris, hired assassin, had a daughter who managed to marry Henry before her father carried out his wicked work. . . ." Eyes laughing, he shook his head. "No, it isn't."

"But I do think HG must be a child rather than a man," she said. "It explains the delay. His legitimate origins may not have been clear until recently."

"If true, it might be hard to prove his claim."

"There's whatever evidence was sent. I wish I'd found that."

"Caldfort may have destroyed it."

"I suppose so. I do have something, though."

She showed him her copy of the portrait.

"Clever woman. I tried to commit it to memory, but this is much better. I'd forgotten how skilled you are at drawing. You were always sketching us." He glanced at her. "What happened to those pictures? They must be a record of a misspent youth."

There'd been one, drawn from memory, of the swimming. "I don't know," she said honestly, "but they must be around somewhere. I would never throw them away."

"Ah," he said. "I wondered." After a silence he went on. "So if we come face-to-face with someone claiming to be Henry Gardeyne, we can check for resemblance to this, but if the claimant is his son it becomes harder. Resemblance to fathers is a chancy thing—for which, I'm sure, many women are grateful."

"Cynic!"

"Realist."

They smiled at each other, but then Laura sighed. "I still don't see how I can go to Draycombe, Stephen. Not, at least, in the next few days. I can't arrive home and immediately leave—"

Harry put an animal on the table by Stephen. "Cow!"

"Definitely," Stephen said, which fortunately seemed an adequate response as Harry returned to managing his farmyard.

"He'll be back with another one," Laura warned.

"If a similar response is all that's required, I believe I can cope. I can get you to Draycombe, too, if you're willing."

"How?"

"Definitely," he said in response to a presented "Hen!" Then he continued their conversation. "We have a little breathing room. Caldfort will have to investigate this Azir Al Farouk. Do we assume that he'll send the vicar?" He glanced down. "A baa-lamb. Assuredly, sir."

This slightly more complicated response caused Harry to frown, but he went back to his animals for a while.

"You could always make the appropriate sounds," Laura said, fighting to keep a straight face.

"*Baa*?" Stephen responded with horror. Feigned, she thought, though she wasn't sure. She couldn't interpret him as she once had. It shouldn't surprise her, but it did.

"He'd have to send Jack," she agreed. "Whom else can he trust? And that certainly gives us breathing room."

"Why?"

"Today is Thursday. On Sunday, Jack has two services to lead. He could get down to Draycombe and back in time if he pushed, but he'd have no time to investigate there."

"Curate?"

"He doesn't have one."

"Then you're right." He looked at the animal presented, glanced at Laura with a mischief that was familiar, and did a creditable imitation of a turkey gobbling.

Harry broke into giggles and turned back to his animals.

"Now you've done it."

"It was your idea."

"I never thought you would!"

"*Oink, oink,*" Stephen said to a pig, but caught Harry's hand. "Your mother and I need to talk a little without interruption. Then I will play barnyard animals with you. Yes, sir?"

Harry frowned mutinously, but if a battle of wills waged, Stephen won. "Yes, sir," Harry said, and wandered back to his toys.

"Well done."

"A short respite, I'm sure. Now, getting you to Draycombe. Would your family be suspicious if you claimed friendship with a Mrs. Delaney, living near Yeovil in Somerset?"

"Perhaps not. They don't know every detail of my life. But I don't know this Mrs. Delaney."

"You do now. Eleanor Delaney is the wife of a friend of mine—"

"I know. King Rogue!"

He winced. "I really did bore on about the Rogues, didn't I?"

"We were fascinated. Nicholas Delaney. King Rogue. Leader of your merry band. So he's married now?"

"Yes, and in the right place, but most of all, in a matter like this we can trust him."

Laura didn't like to express doubts, but she must. "This is a delicate matter, Stephen. Complex and private. I don't think it's suitable for . . . for schoolboy nonsense."

Instead of offense, he seemed to fight a laugh. "Oh, I assure you we're past that. Trust me, Laura, in matters delicate and complex, the Rogues are your men, and in totally adult ways."

"Rogues? Plural? This can't be broadcast around England!"

Any amusement faded. "You can trust all the Rogues, but if you don't wish to, so be it. I still recommend trusting Nicholas. I pledge my life that you can."

How could she respond to that other than by agreement, even though doubts lurked?

"His home is only a few hours' journey from Draycombe. More to the point, Nicholas and Eleanor will accept us as guests, lie for our cause, and if it comes to trouble, be useful support."

"Trouble?"

"We don't know how violent and desperate this Farouk is, or how many people he has with him."

The situation shifted. "I never thought of that. How foolish I am. I'm embroiling you in danger."

"You think me too delicate for it?" It was phrased almost as a joke, but Laura detected affront. She wasn't sure why he would feel that way, but she hastily reassured him.

"Of course not. But this is only your concern by accident."

That didn't seem to help, so she tried to smooth his ruffled feathers. "I don't know what I would have done if you hadn't turned up, Stephen. And I value your help in more ways than the practical. I know you'll advise me well. You know the law, and I trust your judgment. You've always followed the highest principles."

"Have I? It has cost me greatly at times."

What was that wry tone supposed to convey? He was an enigma, but she had no time for delicate male feelings just now. "I still can't leave Merrymead as soon as I arrive."

"No? What if you receive a letter explaining that your friend is about to travel elsewhere. That it's then or never. Given that you have a month at home, that should do."

She supposed it would, but his strange mood had her on edge. "Harry will have to come," she pointed out. "He won't be happy to be left for days, and I wouldn't want to leave him."

"The Delaneys won't mind. They have a daughter. She's younger, but they're accustomed to children."

"You seem very sure."

"I am."

She shrugged. "Very well, then, and we need to be on our way. If we travel to the Delaneys together—"

"That could cause talk. I will arrive separately."

"You could always pretend to be courting me." The words slipped out and her cheeks burned. "I'm sorry."

He smiled. "A useful excuse if we need it."

He seemed to feel no awkwardness about it, for which she was grateful. But his response proved that he no longer felt like that about her. For which she should also be grateful.

"Anyway," she said, "I wouldn't do anything so deceitful."

"Laura, Laura! We're going to have to lie, and possibly cheat and steal, too, for this cause."

She looked at him. "You're right, beginning with lying to my parents. I'm going to hate that."

"If you insist on perfect virtue, our enterprise stops here."

Virtue. That made her rethink everything. "Then it must stop here. I can't afford scandal, Stephen, and my being in Draycombe with you would be a terrible one. It would give the Gardeynes an excuse to cut me off from Harry, and if I'm right about Jack, that could cost him his life."

He frowned in thought. "Disguise, then. I should be myself. My position might be useful if we need to call in the authorities, and I'm also fairly well known to some gentlemen of the area. But you can be a distant relative. One in poor health, whom I'm escorting to try the sea air. Nicholas will arrange it. He's good at that sort of thing."

Laura felt as if he was dragging her into danger. "You're forcing this. *If* I agree to this plan, then I agree to the disguise. But I think I should stay at the Delaneys'." She saw his resistance and put a hand on his arm. "If it's only a few hours away, I can make decisions from there. And then I can stay with Harry. We can't take him to Draycombe if I'm in disguise, and I can't leave him with strangers."

His arm was tense beneath her touch. "You used to trust me more than this, Laura."

"We were children then. The consequences were minor."

"Were they? They seem to have brought us here. But come along. You'd best be on your way. You have two days to think over your decision."

Harry sensed liberation and ran over to them. "Horsey!"

Stephen whinnied, causing a peal of delight.

Laura knew there was no point in arguing further now and went to help Harry gather up his toys. He kept out a duck and ran to present it to Stephen.

"*Quack.*" Then Stephen swung Harry into his arms, and for a wonder, Harry didn't object to that, or to being carried out and placed in the chaise.

Strangely close to tears over many things, not least of them Stephen's animal noises and the sight of Harry in his arms, Laura hurried after.

Stephen handed her into the vehicle. "I'll send a messenger so that a letter from Eleanor will await you at Merrymead or arrive soon after you. I'll also reserve rooms at the Compass for three days hence."

"Stephen, I can't go!"

"If you can come up with a better plan, I will rejoice with you." A smile twitched his lips. "Don't pout."

"A look of resolve is not a pout. You're pressing me."

"Because there's need. Caldfort will probably take some time to consider his actions, but he might even now be dispatching Jack to investigate. You say his church duties will constrain him, but in the face of this disaster can you be sure?"

"No," she admitted. "I should be used to you winning every argument."

"That's not as I remember it."

She brushed that aside. "This is no time for the past. What if Jack arrives in the Draycombe area before me? I'll have to stop frequently on the way to Merrymead to give Harry a chance to run around."

She had the window down and was leaning out, one hand on the top. He covered it with his. "Am I not the efficient one? I intend to ride back and check on Gardeyne's movements. If he's still at home, we can assume you have at least the day's grace you need. If not, I'll go direct to Draycombe."

"My, my," he said to Harry, who was presenting a lion. He managed a ferocious roar that had Harry pealing with laughter and crying, "Again! Again!"

"Next time," Stephen said with a smile that seemed to encompass more than a child's games. Then he mounted and rode away.

Chapter 14

When Jack walked into Lord Caldfort's study without knocking, the old man quickly slid another letter on top of the one from Azir Al Farouk. "What is it?" he grumbled. His legs were swollen, he hadn't slept, and he felt as if he could hear his weary heart laboring in his breast.

And here was Jack, taunting him with life and vigor. Jack wouldn't feel so cocky if he knew what was going on. Tempting to tell him, but not yet, not yet. Not until he decided what to do.

"Just dropped by to see how you are, Father."

"Piss awful, but that's no news."

Jack paced the room as if demonstrating health in the face of illness, complaining about him letting Laura take little Harry away for so long. Preaching a damn sermon, but Jack was no saint.

Lord Caldfort knew he hadn't been a perfect father, but he'd always understood his sons because they were a lot like him. There was something cold about Jack, however, and he'd never been a cold man himself. Nor had Hal.

The boy probably got it from his mother. Thirty-five years ago it hadn't seemed to matter that Cecily was a bit strange. Her dowry had been twenty thousand pounds, and she'd been plain and peculiar enough for her family to be grateful for a younger son.

He should have remembered that you didn't breed a bad hound.

"A month at her home'll do Laura good," he said when the sermon ended. "She's been looking a bit worn."

"A bit demented, if you ask me. She'll smother the boy with her cosseting! All that fuss because he picked something up off the ground and ate it. I'm not sure she's a fit mother, Father."

So that was how it went. "Who would take care of the lad if not her?"

"Emma and I," said Jack, every inch the charitable vicar. "He'd be better off in the midst of a family, and he'd still be close enough to Caldfort to know the place. Or," he added, "we could all move here."

Ah. Jack would like that, but Lord Caldfort wasn't having a pack of noisy brats all over the place. One quiet one was bad enough.

"It'd be better for Laura, too," Jack went on. "She's still a young woman, and must be hot to marry again. She'd be free to take up residence in some lively spot. Heaven knows, her jointure's rich enough. Hal was besotted to increase it like that."

"I approved it," Lord Caldfort growled.

Jack looked at him sharply, but didn't let go of his bone. "Then you should let her enjoy it. She'd be welcome to visit Harry here as often as she wished."

So cogent. Lord Caldfort admired his younger son's way with words. He preached well to his parishioners, too. Not too long, livened with a bit of earthy humor, and making a worthy point. What he said about Laura made sense, too. She'd find another husband in no time, but Jack, typically, hadn't thought it through.

"She's still a beautiful woman, Jack, so she'd probably marry well. If a powerful man becomes Harry's stepfather, we'd find it hard to keep him here, where he belongs."

Jack's eyes narrowed, but then he shrugged. "We can face that fence when we come to it."

What fence? That was the question. Keeping Harry here, or getting rid of him altogether? But Jack wouldn't go that far. Not that far.

"This isn't the hunting field," Lord Caldfort growled. "Law be damned, a powerful stepfather for Harry would be a plaguey nuisance. Then there'd be no way to stop Laura mollycoddling the boy to disaster."

Jack smiled. "He's a Gardeyne, Father, and boys will be boys."

Lord Caldfort was sure then. As sure as he could be until the day Hal's boy lay dead, dead of some boyish enterprise gone wrong. But what was he to do? Dr. Trumper warned he could go at any time, and then Jack would be Harry's guardian.

Time to change that, but to whom? You didn't leave a woman as guardian to a peer of the realm. Laura's father? The man was little better than a farmer and lived days away. . . .

"Father? Are you all right?"

Lord Caldfort looked up into Jack's ruddy, healthy face. Did he see a glint of anticipation? If he died and then Harry died, Jack would have it all. Except that Henry Gardeyne might be alive. He felt a touch of glee at maybe having Jack's plans scuppered like that, but mostly he wished everyone would leave him alone.

" 'Course I'm all right. Or I was before you barged in here haranguing me. Go away!"

Jack pulled a saintly, forbearing face and took his leave.

Lord Caldfort pulled out the plaguey letter. Pain in the bloody arse, but it needed handling. How, how? If he put it in Jack's hands, he knew what would happen.

But perhaps he should. It would all be taken care of then, and he could have some peace.

Chapter 15

When the chaise rolled into Barham, Laura remembered that Friday was market day. Streets full of stalls and animals slowed their progress, but made her smile. Despite the noise and smell, she'd always loved the town in the market-day bustle, and loved exploring the wares of itinerant merchants.

Moreover, she and Harry would soon be home, where she could take action about HG. She'd had two days to think, and Stephen's rationale was inescapable. She had to go to Draycombe. Now her chief concern was to get there before Jack.

A post chaise with regular changes travels as fast as humanly possible, but she'd stopped last night when the light went and not started again until the sun was up. Someone on an urgent mission might not do that. Her hopes were pinned to Lord Caldfort's innate caution and Jack's parish responsibilities, but most of all to the fact that neither man could guess that anyone else knew about Farouk and HG. They had no reason at all to think there was urgency.

She hoped the letter from Redoaks awaited her at Merrymead, but even so, it was already late afternoon, so she could not leave until tomorrow. More delays. More danger for HG.

"A cock, Mama! *Cock-a-doodle-dooooo!*"

Laura looked. They were leaving the town, and a cock paced in male arrogance among his harem of hens.

Stephen's animal noises had made a lasting impression on Harry, which hadn't made the journey any easier. They'd passed all too many cows, horses, sheep, and pigs, not to mention ducks and chickens. No lions, thank heavens, but that hadn't stopped Harry from practicing his roar.

"Are we there yet?"

Laura laughed and hugged him. "Very, very soon, Minnow. Just around the next bend. Do you remember the lions at the gates?"

He nodded and pressed to the window, letting out his best roar. Oh, dear. Was he going to do that throughout their visit?

Stone lions guarded the entrance to Merrymead House, and on their last visit, they'd fascinated Harry. That was why she'd bought him the inappropriate lion for his farmyard animals.

The lions had been her father's contribution to the family's rise into the gentry. Merrymead Farm—three hundred years old—had become Merrymead House in her grandfather's time, masked by a new facade that included a pillared entrance. Her father had transformed the paddock between the house and the road into a garden and marked the entrance with low stone pillars topped with crouching lions.

Having been designed by her father, the lions did not snarl a warning. They grinned merrily, welcoming all, and seemed designed for children to pretend to ride. They probably had been.

Harry's nose was squashed to the glass, so she let down the window so he could hang out a little. "See the tower of St. Michael's? Merrymead's very close to there."

Laura was almost as excited as he was, and tempted to hang wildly out of the window to catch a first glimpse. The chaise turned the bend and Harry pointed. "Happy lions! Happy lions! *Roar!*"

Laura laughed as the postilions guided the horses carefully between the smiling guardians and up the short drive to the door.

Her mother and Juliet rushed out to stand under the classical portico, grinning and waving. Her mother was unchanged—round, gray, and beaming. Juliet looked to have reverted to younger years. She was wearing her brown hair tied back and a simple blue dress, and was bouncing with excitement like a mere girl. No one would imagine she was the wife of an important servant of His Majesty.

As soon as the coach door was opened, her mother swept Harry into her arms. Laura climbed out and into Juliet's arms.

"Oh, it's so good to see you, Laura! And for a whole month. We could hardly believe the message you sent ahead. And Harry's grown so much."

Juliet took Harry's face and planted a kiss on his nose.

Harry didn't squirm away, but he was looking overwhelmed, so Laura took him in her arms. "Where's Father?"

"In town for market day, of course," Laura's mother said, shepherding everyone inside and to the drawing room.

The so-called drawing room was large and part of a new extension, but despite the name it was as comfortable and informal as the old parlor next to the kitchen.

"Him and Ned both," her mother went on. "Aggie! Here's Laura home. Come and take their coats and such and find George to deal with the luggage. And they've taken Tom and Arthur," she added to Laura as the middle-aged maid rushed in smiling to take away the clothing.

"That explains the quiet," Laura said, putting down Harry and stripping off his warm coat.

Tom and Arthur were her brother Ned's seven- and ten-year-old sons. There was a thirteen-year-old, too—Edward, who was off at Winchester School. Merrymead was usually bursting with noisy life, and even with only the women at home, it completely lacked the chilly calm of Caldfort.

Dogs circled, and the two indoor cats leapt up from in front of the drawing room fire, possibly with an eye to escaping Harry. Laura watched for a moment, but they seemed willing to be stroked.

Her mother was ordering tea and chattering at the same time, as if she'd give all the news of the family and gossip of the county in a minute.

Laura sat down on the familiar red-striped sofa, feeling very, very happy. Even the smells were familiar. Wood smoke, baking, rose potpourri, and a hundred others that told her she was home.

"Laura!"

Her sister-in-law, Margaret, came in smiling, with her baby in her arms. Her four-year-old daughter, Megsy, was at her side, cradling a doll in solemn imitation. Mother and daughter looked so alike that it made Laura smile—both were sturdy, forthright, with bubbling brown curls, and dimpled smiles.

Megsy and Harry had played well together on their last visit, and he talked about her sometimes. She hoped it would work out now.

Megsy marched over and offered her doll to Harry. "But she's only to lend!"

Harry took it, nodding solemnly, and arranged it in his arms as Megsy had. Laura gave thanks the Gardeyne men weren't here to see Harry cradling a doll. She'd brought his bag of toys from the coach and wondered if she'd have to prompt him to share in turn. He sat down on the carpet, however, and tumbled out his animals with one hand.

After a hesitation, he chose the lion and offered it. "Only to lend. It's a lion, and it roars."

He demonstrated, which made the adults laugh.

Negotiations over, the two children settled to playing with the animals, the doll, and the cats when the cats allowed.

Laura turned to Margaret, who was beside her on the sofa. "She's becoming quite the little lady."

"Only when it suits her, I assure you. You're looking well, Laura."

"It's good to be home."

It was, but Laura saw her mother's flicker of alertness at the word *home*. She'd forgotten the other thing about home. Everyone had their nose in everyone else's business, and her mother knew all her children too well. Telling lies might be even more difficult than she'd imagined. Besides, having arrived, the last thing she wanted to do was leave.

For the moment she settled to enjoying a normal homecoming, including holding and admiring darling four-month-old Ruthie. Tears suddenly pricked her eyes. Why hadn't she realized how much she wanted more babies? Perhaps because she wasn't the sort to pine for impossibilities. As long as Hal had been alive it had been in God's hands, and since his death, it had seemed impossible. If HG was the true Viscount Caldfort, however, things could change there, too.

Escape from Caldfort.

A new home, one much more like Merrymead.

More children.

She tried not to hope, but it swirled in her as she tried to follow six months of news.

The baby stirred and demanded food, so Margaret took her and put her to the breast. Laura rose. "Come along, Harry. You must help unpack your trunk."

Anyone would think she'd suggested a penance. "Can't I stay with Megsy?"

"Leave him here," her mother said. "I'll keep an eye on him."

Juliet bounced to her feet. "I'll come with you. We're in our old room."

"He'll be indulged to death," Laura said as they went upstairs.

"Of course. It won't hurt him any more than it hurt us. He won't get away with brattiness."

Juliet led the way into the room they'd shared as girls and young women. It had been papered with red roses after Laura had left home, but otherwise looked just the same.

"I was so unhappy when I couldn't go abroad with Robert," Juliet said, "but this almost makes up for it. We'll be like girls again!"

"Except that we're now wicked women of the world."

Juliet grinned. "And isn't it lovely? Do you remember our whispered speculations about what happened between husbands and wives?"

Laura turned away to unlock her trunk. "I remember that book you got your hands on."

"Oh yes. It mystified us rather than enlightened. It makes more sense now."

"Yes." Laura lifted out a neat pile of shifts and passed them to her irrepressible sister.

"It is rather wonderful, isn't it?"

Laura caught her breath. "Yes."

"Oh, poor Laura. You must miss Hal dreadfully."

"Really, Ju!" Laura laughed, but she knew she was blushing.

"For more than bed," her sister protested. "But for that, too."

Laura abandoned stoical pretense. "I'm certainly young to enter a nunnery."

"Don't be silly. You'll marry again."

Laura took out a gray dress and laid it in a drawer,

wondering what to say. For now she might as well stick to the unchanged situation. "I doubt it. I can't leave Harry, and Lord Caldfort won't let Harry live away from Caldfort House."

"That's horribly unfair." Juliet was putting away stockings. "Don't you have any pretty ones?"

"I'm still in mourning, remember."

"Oh yes. I still think it unfair that they're trying to trap you at Caldfort House until you're as gray as your wardrobe. No lilac, even?"

"Voilà!" Laura took out her lilac dress. "If you'll remember, purples never suited me. Black does better, but lurking in black for twelve months would have been excessive."

"Lurking at Caldfort House for decades would be even more so."

"Ju, I have no choice. And Lord Caldfort is correct. Harry should grow up there. He could even be viscount soon. Lord Caldfort isn't well."

"Then perhaps you could marry a man who'd be happy to live at Caldfort. A scholar, or even a gentleman with no significant property of his own."

Laura stared at her. Juliet had always liked to find solutions to every problem. "A possibility, I suppose. I don't see how the Gardeynes could make any objection. But I'm not sure I'd want to marry a penniless man."

Juliet put away the lilac dress, looking pleased with herself. "He doesn't have to be penniless, just without a property. A nabob from the East, even. There, see. Now, what other problem can I waft away?"

Laura smiled at her, close to tears. "Oh, Ju, I have missed you. Do you solve all Robert's problems, too?"

"Whenever I can. So?" Juliet cocked her head. "I have the impression that something is weighing on you."

"Is it as obvious as that?" Laura closed the lid of

the empty trunk, realizing that her words admitted there was something. "I can't tell you at the moment. Perhaps later."

"Is it a man?"

"No!"

"It's a reasonable assumption. The Gardeynes don't want you to marry, but you've fallen in love. Romeo and Juliet . . ."

"I'm Laura, remember? Petrarch's beloved, adored from afar. No balcony kisses, but no death, either."

"To avoid death is to avoid life," Juliet stated, reverting to their lifelong debate about their namesakes. Their sisters, Beatrice and Olivia, both some years older, had claimed smugly to have more normal fates; Beatrice with her Benedick in *Much Ado About Nothing* and Olivia with her Orsino from *Twelfth Night*, a duke, no less.

Laura was in no mood to play, especially when the fate of saintly Laura seemed to fit her all too well these days.

"Let's unpack for Harry," she said to escape, and led the way to the smaller nursery bedroom where he'd sleep with Megsy. His things were soon put away there and Laura went to find him.

He was in the kitchen with Megsy and his grandmother, happily covered in flour and shaping dough into rolls, adored by the servants preparing dinner. He smiled at her, but he didn't seem to have missed her at all.

It hurt.

Her mother said, "He's no trouble, love. Go into the drawing room and have a nice chat with Juliet."

It was as good as a command, but Laura said, "Let's stroll around outside, Ju. Sitting in a carriage for two days leaves my legs feeling neglected."

They rambled the garden and orchard and then into the farm proper.

"There are kittens," Juliet said as they strolled by the stables. "Harry will like that."

"He'd like a cat, but Lord Caldfort doesn't like them."

"He's a sour old despot, if you ask me."

"He's a sick and bitter old man, but it is his home."

"It's yours, too."

"Not really." It came out because she was relaxed, and because she was tired of saying the right thing all the time. "Where's your home?" she asked Juliet as they passed through a gate to walk along the edge of a stubbled field.

"Wherever Robert is." Then Juliet pulled a face. "Well, not Denmark. Or at sea, which is probably where he still is. But yes, our London house is home. Perhaps it's because it's ours, not his father's."

"That would make a difference." Laura picked a rose hip from the hedge and broke it open to look at the seeds. "As it is, I feel . . . transient. The vessel for the next Lord Caldfort, but no more than that. Of course, when Hal was alive we didn't spend much time at Caldfort House. Or before Harry was born, at least." She shrugged. "Hal was not rooted anywhere. Home was where his horses were."

Too late she realized that sounded as if he loved his horses more than her.

"I always thought it a love match," Juliet said.

"It was, but love . . . changes."

She saw a protest form on her sister's lips and be suppressed.

"Not for everyone," Laura said quickly. "I believe in true love, lasting love. But I think it's hard to detect at the beginning. Like knowing gold from gilding. It has to be tested. Scratched—"

A bird burst up out of the nearby stubble and shot into the air, singing.

"A skylark!" Juliet said, shielding her eyes to watch it climb.

Laura did the same. "It can't have a nest at this time of year."

Memory stirred despite her effort to suppress it. Poor Stephen, but at least they were friends again now. She and Stephen had lain down to watch. They couldn't do that—

Then Juliet did. Right there on the rough ground. "Come on. Let's watch it return." She looked at Laura. "Come on! One advantage of wearing dismal clothes has to be that you don't care if they're stained."

With a laugh, Laura sat. "I've never thought of mourning clothes like that before."

She lay down, shifting away from some stubble that was digging into her back. The sky wasn't a perfect blue today. It was mostly cloudy, but the clouds were high. The ground was chilly beneath her, but at least it was dry.

When had she last lain back to look up into the infinity of the sky? Perhaps that last time with Stephen. It was a shame. Everyone should do this and be aware of . . . She contemplated it. Of the grandeur of the universe, in which mere mortals moved.

"That bird sees more of the world than we ever will," she said. "Perhaps that's why it flies so high."

"I think it flies and sings because it can. Out of sheer joie de vivre. Here it comes!"

First as a dot, then growing larger, the bird plummeted down, wings tucked, only spreading them at the end to circle around. It was as if the bird knew they were watching him.

Laura sat up, hugging her knees. "Can you imagine doing that? Deliberately falling from the sky, knowing you'll be safe?"

Juliet sat up, too. "Sounds rather like you-know-what."

"Ju!"

"Or the appeal of danger. People do take risks just for the thrill."

"Like hunting," Laura said softly, and quoted, "He left life leaping," perhaps understanding it for the first time.

Juliet reached over and took her hand, but Laura's doubtless grim expression was for another reason. The same passion that sent men into battle and over fences could drive a man to kill.

Chapter 16

The letter arrived the next morning. Laura's father came into the breakfast parlor with the postbag and sorted through the correspondence.

"One for you, Laury-love," he said, studying a letter before passing it on. "From Somerset. Didn't know you knew anyone in Somerset."

Laura managed her part, even though she felt as if *liar* must be written all over her. "It must be from my friend, Eleanor Delaney. I wrote to her hoping we could meet while I was here. We haven't seen each other since we became mothers."

Was she explaining too much too soon?

She read through the letter, expecting to have to lie about the contents, too, but it was a clever imitation of a letter between old friends, including bits about supposed shared acquaintances and their two children.

It made it easier to produce her next lines in the play. Better to think of it as a play rather than as lying to her parents.

"Oh, dear. Eleanor says they're to travel north soon." After a moment of supposed thought, she suggested, "If I'm to see her, I must go soon. Will you mind, Papa, Mama? Harry and I are here for a month."

Her father's bushy gray brows rose, but he said,

"No, no, love. If now's the only time to visit your friend, now it must be. You're thinking to go for a few days, then?"

"If you don't mind. I can't make it there and back in a day and have time for a proper visit."

"Of course we don't mind, dear," said her mother, passing around a platter of eggs and urging more on everyone. "It's such a treat to have you here for so long that we can afford to share. I don't think I've heard you mention this lady, though, have I?"

Squirming inside, Laura gave the story she'd prepared of a London friend who was now mostly a friend by correspondence.

"How nice to meet again, then," her mother said. "I'm sure it must have been dull for you at Caldfort after dear Hal died, so letters will have been a solace. But a real meeting is so much better. And Mrs. Delaney has a child, too, you said?"

"Yes. Arabel. But she's over a year younger than Harry."

"Still, someone for him to play with."

"I'll arrange a chaise for you?" her father asked.

"Yes, thank you, Papa."

Talk moved on to the best road to take, and Laura thought it all done. She hoped she was imagining a speculative look on Juliet's face.

After breakfast she packed again, but only a valise, since they would be away for a short time. When the post chaise arrived from the George in Barham, she went to find Harry. He was in the stables with his uncle and Megsy.

She took his hand. "Come along, Minnow. We're going for another little journey."

He stared at her, then ripped his hand free. "No. I'm not going!"

"Harry! Don't be foolish. Of course you're coming. You can't stay here."

"Well, he can," said her brother. "He's no trouble."

Laura glared at the traitor, took a breath, and knelt to explain. "It won't be a long journey, Minnow, and the Delaneys have a little girl to play with."

Harry's face set in mutiny and he shook his head.

"There'll be plenty of animals along the way."

He just scowled.

She couldn't believe it. He'd never behaved like this before.

Laura glared at her brother again, but as usual he was dense as a rock. "Leave him here, Laury. The traveling'll be easier alone and you can enjoy a holiday."

Holiday! She didn't need a holiday from Harry. Of course, Ned didn't know that Harry's life was in danger. She stood and grabbed Harry's arm. "Harry, you are coming. We'll be back in a few days."

He didn't protest, but he became a dead weight and she saw tears trickling out of his screwed-up eyes.

She let him go. "Harry, what's the matter with you?"

If Harry wouldn't come, she couldn't go, yet she had to. She had to find out the truth in Draycombe and make sure everything was done properly, but she couldn't explain to him or to anyone else.

Laura glared at her brother. "Ned," she mouthed. "Do something."

He shrugged. "He probably thinks you're dragging him off home. Every other time he's been here, he's climbed into a coach to go back to that house. Leave him. We're happy to have him here."

Laura went back on her knees, finding a bright smile. "Sweetling, we're not going back to Caldfort! We're going on to another house."

But Harry had reached a state of mutiny that was impervious to reason. "I'm staying *here*. You stay here, too."

Laura recognized a crucial moment. Apart from her

need to go, she couldn't let Harry dictate her movements to suit himself.

She got to her feet. "Very well. If you really don't want to come, you can stay here."

He grabbed her skirt. "No, you *stay*!" He even stamped his foot.

Controlling an urge to return temper for temper, she said, "That can't be, Harry, but you can stay here."

He glared at her in a way that could break her heart, but she didn't waver. In the end he let go of her skirt. "Stay here. Stay with Megsy and Uncle Ned and Aunt Margaret and Grandma and Grandpa."

Laura fought not to show her shocked betrayal. She'd never believed that in the end he would choose others over her. When she could speak through her tight throat, she said, "Very well, love. I won't be gone many days, and I'll write you a letter every day."

Perhaps he, too, had thought he'd win, for his lips trembled. "With drawings?"

Laura blinked away tears as she hugged him. "With drawings. You'll be good, yes?"

He nodded.

Laura realized that she was still waiting for him to change his mind, to declare, now he saw that she wouldn't falter, that he'd come with her. But he didn't. Instead he wriggled free, said, "Bye-bye, Mama," and ran back into the stables.

After a moment her brother said, "There's kittens."

Laura couldn't find anything to say to the traitor, so she turned and stalked back into the house, wavering, wondering if she shouldn't go after all. Stephen would go in her place. He could report back.

But a letter would be two days to and from, and matters could turn urgent.

Her parents and Juliet were waiting by the door

to wave her off, and she had to explain the change of plan.

"That's no problem," her father said heartily. "In fact, it's a treat for us." He and Ned were very alike.

Her mother understood. "They all go in the end, love. Particularly the boys."

"But he's so young."

"And he'll miss you dearly. But they become dictators if we let them, and it never serves. You go and have your little visit. It'll do you both good."

Laura hugged her mother, who meant well and was probably right, but—Lord!—it crashed in on her that she would be leaving Harry unprotected. She believed he would be safe here, but even so, she had to warn someone.

Her parents? Ned? But she knew them too well to think that would work.

Juliet.

"Oh," she said, "I have all Harry's things packed. I must undo that."

She commanded the valise unloaded and carried back into the house, then dug through it to extract Harry's clothing. When Juliet came to help, Laura looked for condemnation but saw none.

Even so, she said, "I have to go."

"So I gather. Don't worry about Harry. He'll be fine."

Perhaps I don't want him to be, Laura thought, then was ashamed of herself, but his content with the separation was a knife in her heart. He wasn't even here to see her off.

She grabbed the pile of Harry's clothes. "I'll take these back upstairs."

"No need. I'll do it."

Laura shook her head and Juliet caught the hint. She took half of the small pile, and they went upstairs together. Once in the room, Laura dropped the clothing on the bed and explained the essentials as succinctly as she could. She wanted to tell Juliet only about Jack, but she had to say something about Draycombe to explain leaving at all.

Juliet frowned as she followed it. "You truly think Reverend Gardeyne might come here to try to kill Harry?"

Laura put a hand to her mouth. "No. If I did, I'd never go. If Jack's doing anything other than writing his sermon, he'll be heading for Draycombe. That's why I have to get there first, but I couldn't bear to leave Harry here with no one alert for problems. I don't *expect* any, but I need you to promise that if Jack Gardeyne comes here, you won't let him be alone with Harry for a moment, no matter what pretext he comes up with."

Still looking skeptical, Juliet nodded. "I promise."

"And don't let him take Harry anywhere. Not even to church."

"Very well. But in that case, you know, I might have to tell Papa or Ned." After a moment, she asked, "Don't you think you should tell them now?"

From downstairs, Laura's father called, "Laura? Are you all right, love? Don't keep the horses standing."

She opened the door. "Coming, Papa! No," she whispered to Juliet. "They'd think I was mad, and you know what they'd be like! They'd want to go to the magistrates. I don't have time for that, and in the end I have no proof. Oh, if only Harry would come with me!"

"Into danger?" Juliet asked.

That caught Laura. "Heavens, you're right. I'd rather leave him here than with strangers at Redoaks."

"But what about you? Are you going into danger? Who is this Mrs. Delaney? Laura . . ."

At any moment, Juliet was going to decide that she had to tell their parents herself.

Laura had left out one detail.

"Stephen is helping me. Stephen Ball. The Delaneys are friends of his. He's meeting me there, and we're going to investigate this together."

Juliet's eyes went wide, but now with mischievous delight. "I *knew* there was a man involved! Go, go, and have a wonderful time!"

Chapter 17

It took three hours to travel to Redoaks, and three hours gives ample time for worry. Laura worried that Harry would already be missing her. She worried that he wasn't. It still hurt that he seemed able to wave good-bye to her without a care in the world. It hurt, simply, that each turn of the wheel separated them more. They had been so little apart.

Perhaps everyone was right. Perhaps even Jack was right that she clung too closely to her child. She would try to do better, but only when Harry was safe. She prayed that HG was Henry Gardeyne's legitimate child, and that she and Stephen would be in time to save him.

When the post chaise rolled up to the elegant brick house called Redoaks, she was ready to leap out and go on immediately to Draycombe. She knew that couldn't be. They would have to plan a little, and she would need some disguise.

Because what she was about to do was scandalous.

That awareness had grown in her. She and Stephen were old friends, once as close as brother and sister, but that wouldn't count for anything if they were caught together at an inn. It would ruin her.

The disguise had better be excellent.

The door opened and a couple came out, the man carrying a pretty infant in a pink dress. Eleanor Delaney, a handsome woman with auburn hair, came forward. "Laura! How lovely to see you again."

Laura missed her cue by a heartbeat, then realized that indeed they should act their parts, even before the indifferent postilions. She went into the other woman's arms. "It's been so long." Pulling free, she turned to the man and child. "And this must be Arabel."

She would have kissed the child, but the girl shrank back, face puckering as if she'd cry.

"She's shy," Nicholas Delaney said with an easy smile.

King Rogue. He didn't look regal or wicked, though there was something unusual about him—apart, that was, from the fact that his shirt was open-necked beneath a loose jacket. Informal, to say the least. Perhaps the uncommon impression came from his coloring, for unlike most fashionable gentlemen his face was tanned by the sun to a shade that almost matched his dusky gold hair.

"A pleasure to see you again, Laura," he said. "I'll attend to your luggage and the carriage. You go into the house. You must be ready for refreshment."

Laura went, but she couldn't help finding it strange that Delaney kept the little girl with him rather than passing her to his wife.

Eleanor Delaney didn't seem to mind. "No Harry?" she asked as they went upstairs. "Arabel will be disappointed."

"I'm sorry. He's enjoying his cousins, and there are kittens in the barn. No Stephen?"

"Not yet, but we expect him shortly."

Eleanor Delaney took her into an airy bedchamber with blue-and-white curtains and bed hangings. In this house Laura had an impression of casual elegance that made her long to settle in and enjoy. But there was also something as unusual as its owner.

Perhaps it was the colors, or even the scents. She

detected potpourri, but perhaps incense, as well. On the landing, she'd recognized a large pale statue of a laughing fat man as a representation of Buddha. She remembered Stephen saying once that King Rogue had gone traveling instead of to university.

So it would seem.

"I'll go and get some hot water for you," her hostess said.

She left, which was tactful, as Laura did need to use the chamber pot. She hadn't anticipated, however, how very strange it would feel to be foisted upon strangers with Stephen not here. Was she to carry on chatting as if they were old friends? When would she be allowed to stop lying?

She took off her black bonnet and gloves and her gray spencer, then relieved herself. As she waited for her washing water, she looked out at a pleasant, unpretentious garden, an orchard, and placid scenery beyond. A lovely spot, but not the setting she'd expected for daredevil Nicholas Delaney.

Stephen put great faith in him, but was he really able to help them? People changed. *Yes*, she thought, considering the past few days, *indeed, people do*.

Eleanor returned, carrying the jug of hot water herself.

"This is a lovely house," Laura said.

"We like it. May I call you Laura all the time? It's best to act a part completely—I have that from a master of deception. And you must call me Eleanor."

It would feel awkward, but Laura said, "Of course."

"And do call Nicholas, Nicholas. No one who knows him would believe that an old friend of mine wouldn't."

That would feel even stranger, but pouring water into the bowl, Laura agreed. As she washed her hands and face, she asked, "Is there need to pretend in front of the servants?"

"It's best to be thorough. Did you have a smooth journey?"

Laura followed that lead. She wouldn't be here long, after all, but she wished she knew how much Stephen had told his friends.

"I gather that you and Stephen intend a further journey," Eleanor said.

So he'd told them that much. "There's nothing improper about it. Well, there is, of course, but we do it only from necessity."

Eleanor's eyes twinkled. "Exciting necessity, I'm sure, Stephen being a Rogue."

Did it seem she was engaged in this for *amusement?* "Perhaps I should explain . . ."

But Eleanor waved a hand. "Oh, no, it will be more efficient to do it all at once. Now, would you like tea? We will have a lunch when Stephen arrives."

"Tea would be lovely."

Laura realized that what she really wanted was to be alone, to be free of pretending friendship and guarding what she said. She remembered a good reason.

"I promised my son letters. Deceptive, I know, but if I write them, will you send them each day?"

"Of course," Eleanor said, without a hint of disapproval. "I'll get you some of our stationery."

She left, and returned in moments with a portable desk containing everything Laura needed. "I'll send up tea and let you know as soon as Stephen arrives."

Laura sat at the table by the window, aware of feeling disgruntled and it being unreasonable. Eleanor Delaney was so very amiable and even tempered that it was irritating. Of course, Eleanor had not married a man like Hal Gardeyne. She was the type to have more sense.

Laura winced. She wouldn't be reduced to thinking mean thoughts about Hal. She'd made that choice and would live with it. He hadn't changed; she had. Or perhaps simply come to know herself better.

It wasn't even as if she wanted a life like this for herself. It struck her as much too placid.

She liked the bustle of Merrymead, and she loved London.

Thinking of that was a waste of time. She uncapped the inkwell and chose a pen. Stephen would be here shortly, and these letters must be written.

Tea came and she sipped it as she wrote. Soon she had five simple letters written, dated today and subsequent days, except that one was for both tomorrow and Monday. Neither people nor letters traveled on Sunday.

On Monday, Jack might set off for Draycombe, but it would take him at least two days to make the journey and by then surely she and Stephen would have dealt with the situation. She had four days. Four days that might solve her problems or land her in disaster.

She enjoyed gambling, but only for trivial stakes.

A clock somewhere began an interesting harmonious chime. Laura counted, but she knew it had to be noon. Where was Stephen?

She didn't want to join her hosts until he arrived. She remembered promising Harry drawings, so she began to illustrate the letters. On the first one, she drew a post chaise across the top, with herself at the window, waving. On the next one, she drew a church with her coming out with the Delaneys and little Arabel.

Such a pity the child was so shy. She gave thanks that Harry had a robust, sunny temperament. It made him trusting, however. Too trusting.

Juliet would keep him safe.

She drew the view from her window on Tuesday's letter, then, her imagination failing her, a meaningless border of flowers on the last. By the time Harry got Wednesday's letter, she might be home again.

There was a tap on the door, and Eleanor came in. "Stephen's here, and lunch is ready."

At last. Laura quickly folded her letters and sealed them. Sadness poked at her. "Harry usually does this. He loves it."

"Arabel, too."

They shared a smile and Laura felt more comfortable. Children were children and mothers mothers. It would not be long before Harry was sealing her letters for her again. She stacked the letters and gave them to Eleanor, then they both went downstairs.

Stephen was in the drawing room, seated on the sofa with little Arabel leaning trustingly on his knee, apparently showing him her doll. It was quite a plain one. A stick-and-rag doll. Stephen was smiling, and the little girl was smiling, too. He liked children and they liked him, even shy Arabel.

He would make a good father.

Then Arabel saw Laura and ran to her father.

He picked her up as if this were normal, but said, "Mrs. Gardeyne is a friend of Uncle Stephen's and thus a friend of ours. Make your curtsy, poppet."

He put the girl down. The child's look was so distrustful that Laura thought she might refuse, but she dropped a curtsy. Immediately afterward, however, she scrambled back into her father's arms.

Laura felt mortified to be terrifying a child so, but why? Harry had been terrified of one of his great-aunts, who wore red circles of rouge on her cheeks in the old style. She, however, was without face paint and wearing a simple dark gray gown and white cap.

She caught a flicker of something on Eleanor Delaney's face. Perhaps it was embarrassment at the way her child was behaving, or even unhappiness that Arabel so clearly preferred her father. All was not well in this house, after all.

Stephen greeted Laura in a casual sort of way. "Did everything go smoothly?"

"Perfectly. Our plans are in place."

"Yes, and when I left the Caldfort area a second time, the vicar was making no unusual moves."

Laura had thought that Stephen's arrival would make everything easier, but it was quite the opposite. She realized that she'd expected Stephen to be more struck by their reunion.

As she was?

Talk became general, then Stephen asked Nicholas, "How's Dare?"

"Coming along."

"Fit for visitors?"

"For you, of course." Nicholas glanced at Laura. "Lord Darius Debenham, a friend of ours who is still suffering the effects of a war wound."

"All England talks of the miracle. And, of course, Lord Darius is one of the Rogues."

Nicholas grinned. "Ah, you know all."

"I'm sure I don't, but I heard many schoolboy tales. Is there hope of full recovery?"

"Excellent hope, yes. I see lunch is ready. I'll take Arabel upstairs and join you in a moment."

At least he carried the child over for a mother's kiss before taking her away, but as Laura went to the dining room with Stephen and their hostess she felt uncomfortable about the whole situation. It was none of her business, but she couldn't help thinking that King Rogue indulged his daughter too much. As with letting Harry dictate to her, it would prove disastrous in the end.

Chapter 18

Servants placed dishes on the table and then left. By the time Eleanor was finishing the serving of the soup, Nicholas joined them. "So, who's going to dish up the story?" he asked.

Laura exchanged a look with Stephen. "You're the one with the gift for words."

He pulled a face at her, but then gave a succinct account that was over by the time the Delaneys cleared the soup plates and uncovered the next course.

"I can imagine your concern," Eleanor said to Laura. "It must have been so hard to leave your son behind in these circumstances."

Laura flinched from that reminder. "I'm sure Jack Gardeyne will not go to Merrymead, and my sister knows the dangers."

She explained that, and Stephen said, "Excellent. Juliet always had a clever mind and quick wits."

More so than herself? Laura wondered.

Nicholas ignored his pork. "Let's look at that letter."

Laura produced it, but Stephen said, "I don't think even you can squeeze more out of it. The answers lie in Draycombe. I did confirm that the ship that went down, supposedly taking Henry Gardeyne to the deeps, was the *Mary Woodside*."

"Well done!" Laura declared.

"And achieved in a couple of days on the road," Nicholas said. "Brilliant as always."

Stephen didn't seem particularly pleased by the accolade.

"You don't have a clue about Oscar Ris?" Nicholas asked. "Heaven knows there are strange names around the world, but it doesn't fit with any nationality I know." He passed the letter to Eleanor. "And how could he keep someone prisoner for ten years?"

"What if it were voluntary?" Eleanor suggested. "A flight from disgrace or scandal? Perhaps Henry's father cast him off and it was made to look as if he'd died."

Nicholas raised his brows. "I never knew you had such a gothic imagination, love. But if he wasn't disinherited, why not rise from his watery grave once his father was dead? The key question I see is, Why *now*?"

Laura was making an attempt to eat. "We think this HG might be his son. Raised by Oscar Ris, but newly discovered to be legitimate."

"Now that makes a fragment of sense," Nicholas said. "Azir Al Farouk is entrusted with the task of bringing the child to England to claim his inheritance—perhaps because of his excellent command of English. But the villain has recognized a chance to make his fortune."

"In league with Captain Dyer?" Eleanor suggested. "Could there be a band of ruffians involved?"

Stephen put down his knife and fork. "That's what worries me. I don't want to take Laura into danger."

"Then you shouldn't take her at all," Nicholas said. "Whenever there's villainy, there's the possibility of danger. Desperate people will do desperate things."

The words seemed to have a meaning that shadowed the room. Whatever that meaning was, they cleared Laura's mind. She couldn't send Stephen alone into danger.

"I want to go, and I won't be in danger. I'll simply be visiting a respectable seaside resort. I have no intention of skulking around in the dark or doing anything foolish."

Stephen gave her a look. "I believe I've heard that before."

She looked right back. "When we were children. You were right when you argued that any decisions are mine to make."

Nicholas finally cut into his meat. "I think we should involve Captain Drake."

"Oh, good idea," Eleanor said.

Laura looked between them. "Whoever he is, no. We can't involve any more people. Not when things might become illegal."

"She's right, Nick," Stephen said. "Who the devil is Captain Drake, anyway?"

Laura recognized Nicholas's smile as mischievous, which seemed horribly inappropriate. "He's the smuggling master who controls the coast round about Draycombe."

"Smuggling!" Laura gasped.

Stephen groaned. "Trust you to know the local criminals."

"It wasn't me. It was Con." Nicholas glanced at Laura. "Con Somerford, Viscount Amleigh, briefly Earl of Wyvern. Have you heard of the affair?"

"He inherited the earldom earlier this year and then someone else claimed it. It's being fought in the courts, isn't it?"

"It's being arranged amicably, but the stamping and sealing takes time. Crag Wyvern, seat of the Earl of Wyvern, is about three miles from Draycombe."

"But how does Con connect to the smuggler, Captain Drake?" Stephen asked.

Nicholas shared a look with his wife. "He's going to be upset with me."

"You always knew that," Eleanor replied.

Stephen put down his cutlery. "You've been up to something illegal again."

It was said levelly, but Laura tensed. Stephen was angry? Because of illegalities? Did he try to keep his irresponsible friends in line? If so, why had he involved them in her serious affairs?

"Not I," Nicholas protested.

"But as usual, you protected me from any dirt."

"Stephen," said Nicholas, suddenly serious, "you're the Rogues' secret weapon within the legal and political system. We can't have you tainted."

"For pity's sake—"

Eleanor stopped Stephen with a raised hand. "Before you two have a Roguish fight, you're going to have to decide how much to tell Laura. Private matters in public are not polite."

"I've had my knuckles rapped." Nicholas turned to Laura. "My apologies. Since you've told us your secrets, I have no problem with telling you ours, but I need your assurance that you will keep them in confidence."

"Illegal matters? I'm not sure. If I were to find them wrong, wicked . . . I'm not sure."

"Excellent. Honor should rule. How strongly do you feel about smuggling?"

"Not strongly at all. The taxes are iniquitous."

"Then you should have no difficulty. I've been wondering how Al Farouk and HG arrived in England, you see. There are formalities at official entry points. My guess is that they came ashore on a smuggling boat. If it was anywhere near Draycombe, Captain Drake will know all about that."

"I see, but can we get the information without telling him why?"

"Possibly, but I think we should involve him more. It's his business to be informed about any unusual people visiting his territory. In addition, he commands most of the people along that stretch of coast and can

even summon an army if required. If Farouk is part
of a vicious gang, Captain Drake can keep you and
Stephen safe."

A noise came from Stephen that sounded like a
stifled protest.

Nicholas looked at him. "Steve, you know I don't
approve of courting danger. It comes on its own easily enough."

"Not to me."

"Now that," his friend said, "is idiotic. As well ask
to break a bone."

Laura noted that Eleanor looked resigned, as if this
was an old battle. The Rogues tried to keep Stephen
out of dangerous activities because he was more useful
to them as a sober, respectable citizen? Clearly Stephen objected.

How much danger could a group of English gentlemen get into in the normal run of things?

Stephen turned to her. "It appears that this Captain
Drake might be of use, though I share your concerns.
He is a criminal, after all."

Nicholas said, "And before I say more, I must have
your word that you will keep this secret. I promise
there are no worse crimes to reveal."

After a moment, Laura said, "Very well. You have
my word."

"Captain Drake is also David Kerslake-Somerford,
soon to be Earl of Wyvern."

Laura knew her jaw had dropped.

Stephen exclaimed, "Good Lord!" But then he said,
"Yes, I am upset. I assume the Rogues had a part in
the rearrangement of the earldom and all know about
this but me."

"No. Con knows, of course. It was his affair—"

"And his wife is Kerslake's sister! I was at the wedding. I met the man. He's a gentleman."

"It's a long and complex story."

"When is it not?"

"And not surprising if no one wanted to burden your conscience with it unnecessarily, Steve."

Stephen went silent, but Laura saw that he took this matter of being protected hard. She remembered when she'd worried that she was dragging him into danger. No wonder he'd turned frosty.

Nicholas said, "Miles, Francis, Lee, and Luce are as much in the dark as you, I promise. And note, I *have* told you now that there's a purpose."

There was apology there, but the cool voice of command, too. Laura looked down at her plate, wondering why nothing could be simple anymore. She'd thought the Rogues were a close-knit, endlessly supportive group. She'd thought the same of her family, but in this extreme, she'd not confided in them.

"Let's return to Laura's problem," Stephen said. "So, Captain Drake might know when Farouk arrived, and what companions he brought. Perhaps even their whereabouts. You're right. That will be useful. I'm not sure, however, about making open contact. Smugglers have a rough way of keeping their secrets."

"You and Laura have agreed to keep the secrets, and David is a Rogue by association now."

"Ah, is he?"

"Too useful to be ignored."

"And," said Eleanor dryly, "now owner of a truly astonishing collection of strange books and artifacts."

"Are you ascribing base motives to me, my love?"

She grinned. "Just practical ones." She looked at Laura. "I know David quite well now, and he can be trusted. Because of his responsibilities he cannot always act legally, but he will always act honorably. Once he understands this situation, I'm sure he will feel about it just as you do, and he's perfectly placed to rescue HG and deal with trouble."

Laura felt a strange pang of disappointment, as if a

daring adventure had been snatched from her, and she understood Stephen's mood. How silly. Safety and a quick resolution were what they needed.

"Then I agree. How will it be managed?"

"I'll send a discreet note," Nicholas said, "asking him to contact you at the Compass."

The sonorous clock struck one.

Laura pushed back slightly from the table, ashamed of how little she'd eaten, but eager to be off. "We've done all we can here, I think."

She realized that it sounded rude, but with talk of armed gangs and smugglers, she couldn't linger. Not when there was a child at risk.

Everyone stood, but Stephen said, "There is one thing. We can't risk Laura's reputation. If she were to meet anyone she knows, it would be disastrous. I was hoping for a disguise."

Nicholas turned to eye her. "As what?"

"An older, sickly cousin."

Humor sparked in Nicholas's eyes. "A pity to cloud such beauty, but I think it can be done."

Chapter 19

Not long afterward, Laura looked in the mirror, still disconcerted by her appearance. She knew she'd need something, but she hadn't imagined a change as thorough as this.

Nicholas had produced a faded blond wig as if it were the kind of thing every house contained. The wiry curls bubbled excessively around her face, which was rendered sallow with a tinted cream. A darker cream around her eyes made her look dismally unwell. As the coup de grâce, a large mole now squatted on the edge of her upper lip. She'd heard such marks called "beauty spots" but there was nothing beautiful about this one. There were even a few hairs sticking out of it.

She'd lived with her beauty for so long that it was unsettling to have it gone. She could tell, however, that anyone meeting her would see only mousy curls, ill health, and mole.

She'd thought her mourning clothes dull enough, but Nicholas had decreed they were too stylish. She and Eleanor were stripping off some trimming, but Laura thought half the work had already been done when she'd abandoned her corset.

They'd realized that she couldn't use a maid to help her undress, because there was no way to make her body fit her face and hair. Eleanor had lent her a kind of bodice that hooked up the front. It was decent, Laura supposed, but didn't raise and support the breasts as she was used to.

A glance at her hostess suggested she was wearing such a garment herself. Comfortable, Laura granted, but . . . well, it was a good thing Eleanor's dress made no attempt at fashion.

All in the cause, she told herself, and sat to rip off a belt of ruched gray silk. "It's as well I'll soon be out of mourning. I'll be able to give these to my maid, except that I doubt she'll want them."

"They'll bring her a little in the secondhand shops." Eleanor was unpicking a white lace ruffle from around a neckline. She glanced up with a twinkle in her eye. "So wickedly frivolous, ruffles."

"And I thought I'd been dressing so plainly."

"You're used to high fashion. I was green with envy of the gown you wore at the Arden wedding. Low in the back with crisscross ribbons. Rubies, and red feathers swirling through your hair."

Laura was surprised to feel embarrassed. "I don't remember meeting you, I'm afraid."

"Oh, you didn't. But you were one of the bright lights. I haven't offered my condolences on your husband's death, have I? It must be especially hard when a husband is taken so young and suddenly."

"Yes," Laura said, unwilling to even look at her increasingly muddled feelings about Hal. "Do you visit London often?" she asked, to steer talk to safer channels.

Stephen had been left alone for a while. Nicholas had decreed that he must not witness the transformation so that he could give an honest first impression.

Time to think.

Time to doubt.

Looking out at the plain but pleasant garden, he tried to decide whether his recent actions had been

heroic or villainous. They certainly hadn't been wise—
or unavoidable. There were other ways of dealing with
this mystery. He had framed this plan to get Laura to
Draycombe, to create time together and alone. Perhaps even to compromise her.

He wasn't consciously planning that, but he couldn't
ignore the fact that if they were caught, if the world
discovered them together at Draycombe, they would
have little choice but to wed. The damnable thing was,
as a man, he wouldn't suffer much from the scandal,
but her reputation would be smirched forever.

When Nicholas came in, Stephen wasn't sure how
much time had passed. He turned from the view.
"Beauty transformed?"

"Excellently. It's an insubstantial quality, isn't it?"

"I don't think so."

Nicholas smiled. "Nor do I. But we're speaking of
deeper beauty, I assume. A saber through the face has
ruined many a man's beauty. Laura and Eleanor are
attacking her clothes."

Nicholas sat, so Stephen did, too. "They're devilish
dull as they are."

"But far too stylish for Mrs. Priscilla Penfold. Mrs.
Hal Gardeyne has always had an unerring instinct
for style."

"I didn't know you knew her."

"I don't, but we do visit London. I was there exten-
sively in 1814, if you remember."

"I could hardly forget." That was the year Nicholas
had played a dangerous game of counterespionage,
married Eleanor, and almost died. "But Laura wasn't
there as often after her child was born."

"One only has to see Olympus once. She's a rare
specimen. I assume you wish to collect her?"

Stephen reacted to the hint of disapproval. "I'm
helping an old friend." When Nicholas raised his eyebrows, he said, "Devil take you. Very well. I want
her, but I don't like the word *collect*."

"Nor do I, but I think it's what women like that stir in some men. A desire to own, to bask in reflected glory. No, not even that, alas, but to bask in pride of possession. Hal Gardeyne was like that. Puffed up like a cock to own her."

Stephen found himself driven to defend the man. "What's the difference between that and being an adoring husband?"

Nicholas thought. "What is valued, I suppose. What did Gardeyne truly value?"

"His hunters."

Nicholas nodded. "In the end our true love will rule. His was sport. They were destined to drift apart. A man with a passionate avocation should be careful where he weds."

Stephen tensed. "You refer to me?"

"I would claim it to be a universal truth, but yes. If you are not passionately devoted to the political life and noble causes, you've been doing a remarkable imitation of it."

"I should give up my life upon marriage, as you have given up yours?" Stephen flinched at the sharpness of his own attack, but didn't retract it.

"I've given up nothing. Once I traveled, but I'd already wearied of it when circumstances brought me home. You can hardly think that London enthralled me."

Stephen was suddenly angry at being advised. "You and Eleanor are not markedly alike."

"Lock and key don't have to be identical. In fact, it would defeat the purpose. I'm a mental magpie. She's interested in some of the treasures I bring to the nest. She's a practical countrywoman, and I'm learning the joys of being in one place. She is restful, which I find a blessing. She enjoys being excited now and then. We can be as silent as a starlit night and blessed by it."

"You're saying I should *not* marry a woman who is interested in politics and reform?"

"Steve! You're a cleverer man than I am, so don't sink to that level. You should marry a woman who will bring joy to your life in many ways, because if she's of value to you in only one way, what when that changes? What if Laura's beauty is ravaged by smallpox?"

"She's been inoculated." Stephen recognized that as irrelevant, however. "I don't know."

"Find out. And be sure that you can give joy to her, and without sacrifice. Sacrifice is a galling burden."

"How very unchristian."

"I didn't say it isn't good for us to be galled sometimes."

Stephen rose and walked to the window, trying to sort through what Nicholas had said. Did he simply want to possess Laura's beauty, as if she were a vase or a painting?

"Do you know her?" Nicholas asked.

He turned to stare. "She was my sister's closest friend. We were almost like brother and sister."

"Are you the man you were six years ago? If not, why assume she is that woman? My advice . . . Damnation, I took a vow to stop giving advice."

"As well tell Coleridge to give up opium."

It was a sharp enough cut to draw blood, but Nicholas merely smiled. "I would if I thought it would do any good. He's too far gone, poor man."

"And Dare is not?" Stephen asked, to change the subject.

"No. He was never dependent on it for escape, you see." But Nicholas wasn't deflected. "I've wondered what was amiss with you. I think I know now, but old passions can prove poisonous when stirred. My advice is to try to forget the past and to discover Laura as if you were meeting her now. Perhaps her new appearance will help. I think I hear them coming."

They went into the hall, and Stephen was glad to have that encounter over, even if he felt he carried it with him like splinters buried in his skin.

He didn't know Laura?

Once prompted, he recognized truth.

Vibrant Laura Watcombe. Brilliant Mrs. Hal Gardeyne. Labellelle, toast of society. Even Lady Skylark, which he knew now hadn't been fitting even five years ago. . . .

He looked up the stairs and saw a sallow, sickly woman.

The dress was the same, he thought, though it had somehow become frumpy. Beneath the plain black bonnet, a close cap was tied beneath her chin by ribbons as narrow as string. It hid all of a faded blond wig except for a frame of tight curls that created the impression of a low forehead. A disfiguring mole ruined her lovely mouth. She was even wearing beige net gloves to hide her elegant hands.

The whole effect was sealed by a remarkably ugly shawl in yellows and browns that managed to clash even with the gray spencer.

"Where do you find these things?" he said to Nicholas.

"Oh, Nicholas collects like a magpie," Eleanor remarked as she and Laura arrived in the hall.

Stephen flicked a glance at his friend, but Nicholas merely said, "It is the virtue of the magpie to be undiscriminating."

"Virtue?" Laura asked, and at least her voice was the same.

Eleanor laughed. "Don't encourage him to expound on the virtues and dangers of discrimination. He says you never know when his indiscriminate collections will be of use. And as usual, he's right."

Stephen was still trying to absorb Laura's appearance. "That mole . . . What we will do for the cause."

She stiffened. "Do you think I wouldn't give up all

my looks for this cause? To save two young Henry Gardeynes?" Then she winced. "I'm sorry. I'm on edge."

"So am I. But it was only a joke, Laura."

They might have apologized back and forth, but Nicholas interrupted. "Don't forget to move and speak like a plain woman, Laura. Be uncertain in your speech, and don't expect people to pay attention to you. Efface yourself. It will be useful anyway if people hardly notice you. Such a light disguise is an illusion rather than a perfect concealment."

"I've never thought of these things before."

"Do. I've sent word to Kerslake, Steve. We're sticking as close to the truth as possible, so if you need to explain the connection, you're a friend of a friend. Con's friend, of course."

"Right."

Discover the real Laura. Nicholas was right. He held out his arm. "Come along. It's a game, an adventure. Don't I remember a time when you put blue streaks on your face and stuck feathers in your hair in order to be a Red Indian?"

That brought back a smile that was pure Laura. "With a bow and arrow. I shot your hat off."

"Damn near killed me. Thank heavens you're not armed now."

"Ah," she said as they left the house. "Did I forget to mention my pistol?"

He looked at her, about to object, but remembered Nicholas's advice. Learn about her now. "Can I assume Mrs. Hal Gardeyne knows how to use it?"

"Of course you can."

As he handed her into the curricle, Stephen reckoned he deserved a medal for self-control. Speaking the man's name had almost choked him.

Chapter 20

Laura thought her cheerful manner deserved a medal.

She looked awful, but she'd hoped that in some way Stephen would be able to ignore it. Clearly not, but the pain of that had made it dawn on her—literally, like the crack of dawn opening in the dark sky—that she was attracted to him.

Perhaps just physically.

Perhaps not.

Whatever her feelings were, they demanded that he look at her with appreciation and admiration.

This made her newly unsure about this enterprise. She didn't understand her own emotions, and she didn't have time to ponder them, but she knew they made this journey doubly, triply hazardous. Yet she must go, not just to uncover the truth and possibly rescue a child, but to explore these mysteries. Her life teetered on a balance point, and the issues at hand extended beyond the future of the viscountcy of Caldfort.

They were using Nicholas's curricle, which made transport to Draycombe simple. As Laura and Stephen drove away, they waved back at the three Delaneys. Little Arabel had reappeared and was again in her father's arms.

"He's a devoted father," Laura remarked.

"Yes."

"Unusually so."

They swung into the road at speed, showing impressive skill. "You disapprove?" he asked.

Her thoughts had shown and she grimaced. "I'm sorry, but having recently forced myself not to cling to Harry, I'm sensitive to such things. It can't be wise to encourage a child to cling like that, particularly to a father."

"Do you really find a devoted father so unusual?"

She almost said a blunt yes, but then considered the question. "Hal certainly wasn't, but he might have become so when Harry was of an age to share his interests. I suppose Ned dotes, but he leaves most of the care of the little ones to Margaret, particularly the girls. It's the usual way."

He negotiated another bend and then they were on a straight stretch and he could give the horses their heads. "Nicholas is unusual in nearly everything he does, but there's a special reason. I don't think they'll mind me telling you. Arabel was kidnapped not long ago."

Shock hit like a fist. "No! How?"

"By a woman who hated Nicholas and wanted money. It's left Arabel shy and anxious when she used to be the most cheerful, trusting child. Ah, I should have realized."

"What?"

He glanced at her. "She's particularly wary of strange women in dark clothing. That must be why she shrank from you. As for her clinging to Nicholas, he was the one to rescue her. Unfair to Eleanor, of course, but a child's view of the world is simple."

As Harry's was. Coaches meant change, so having arrived at a place he liked, he refused to get in one again. Harry was safe, but Laura had to ask, "How was she taken?" What had she forgotten to guard against? What might lure him into danger? "Tempted away by a stranger offering a treat?"

"She was snatched from her bed."

"In her own *home*?"

Stephen halted his horses and turned to her. "Laura, what is it? She was rescued."

"Harry!" She clutched his arm. "I'm sorry. I can't do this, Stephen. Turn around. You must go to Draycombe to rescue this other child, but I have to get back to Merrymead. I never thought to warn anyone about that. About him being taken from his bed . . ."

He freed his sleeve from her hands and gripped them. "Laura, this was nothing like Harry's situation. Arabel was held for ransom. If Jack Gardeyne tries to harm Harry, he has to make it look like an accident. How could a child being stolen from his bed be that?"

"Sleepwalking?"

He shook his head. "At Merrymead, and no one will notice?"

"That's true. Mothers have an extra sense for children stirring in the night."

"And remember, Gardeyne isn't a lunatic. He has to know there'll be better opportunities."

"He tried with that bun. If I didn't imagine that."

"Perhaps he panicked when he heard you were going away for a month. I doubt he'll do that again."

Laura began to settle, aware of great comfort from Stephen's hands around hers, from his steady eyes.

He smiled slightly, which eased her heart even more. "And he'll not have a chance to harm Harry with Juliet on guard."

"That sounds as if you admire her more than me."

The smile deepened. "Don't be a goose."

She found herself laughing. "*Honk*?"

"In my experience, they hiss and then attack. Nasty creatures, geese."

"But they end up on our dinner tables. Perhaps they have reason for anger."

"Perhaps they do, at that. All right now?"

She nodded and slipped her hands free. "I'm sorry for panicking, but the poor Delaneys. I feel for them."

"As do I. Especially as I wasn't around to help or even support." He put the horses into motion again.

She could use that as an opening to ask about his grievance with the Rogues, to discuss the allure of adventure and the wisdom of avoiding it, but she was wound too tight for a serious topic.

"Tell me more tales of the Rogues, Stephen. I assumed it all ended with school days."

He amused her with stories, though she suspected most of them were carefully edited. A horse race at Melton seemed innocuous enough, but clearly some espionage in 1814 had not been. Even when there was no need for action, the Company of Rogues seemed to have regular gatherings, mostly in London or Melton, but apparently marriage and progeny were making such meetings more difficult.

"It's doubtless time for me to marry," Stephen said, eyes on the road, for they'd passed the one-mile marker to Draycombe and the way was now rough and narrow.

His words caught at her heart in a way that was a warning. She watched him as she said, "I hope this business of mine isn't interfering with your plans."

"Plans?"

"To marry."

Was that a smile? "How could it?" he asked.

They might as well be talking of the weather. "You could be courting someone," she pointed out, "instead of squiring a quiz of a relative to a watering place."

He seemed to find that amusing. "Don't concern yourself. This doesn't interfere with my plans."

"What if we end up in a scandal? That might cause difficulties."

"Hold on." He slowed the horses for the descent down a long, steep hill into the small town strung along a bay. "If we end up in a scandal, we can always marry."

She could read nothing at all from tone or expression. "All the more reason to be quick and careful."

"As you say."

Aware of something that might be annoyance, Laura welcomed their first glimpse of the sea and of their target, Draycombe.

It looked to be more of a large village strung along a bay and hemmed in on both sides by headlands. It had probably been a simple fishing village before seaside visits became fashionable. Boats were still drawn up on the pebbly beach and whitewashed fishermen's cottages clustered where this steep road met the sea.

Newer buildings had spread in both directions. To the left, Laura saw a church spire, and to the right, the tiled roofs of modern houses mingled with the thatched ones of the past.

When they reached the cottages, the road split. Stephen halted and asked directions to the Compass Inn. He was pointed to the right and they turned that way, past a row of shops that must mostly serve the visitors, and a square, modern inn, the King's Arms.

Laura took it all in, searching for an obvious foreigner, a military man, or a stray child with Gardeyne features. "There seem to be many invalids, even this late in the year," she said, seeing two blanket-swathed elderly people being pushed along the seafront in long wheeled chairs.

"Draycombe's noted for its sheltered climate and healthy air." Stephen flicked her a look. "Yes, I read up about it. My fatal flaw."

"It's not a flaw. Look. Two military men—one navy, one army. We don't know which Captain Dyer is, do we?"

"We know nothing but his name. No turbans?"

"Do you really think Farouk will be so obvious?"

"From his name, I doubt he can pass as an Englishman, and foreign servants, especially from India, are not unheard of."

"In Draycombe?"

He grinned at her. "It does seem to be a sleepy backwater, doesn't it? Speaking of which, the Compass looks ancient. But decent."

The inn's long and wavering two-story front held only small windows, but they were plentiful and clean, and one on the ground floor was bowed.

Stephen steered his team through open gates into a large coach yard. Stables and other such buildings formed three sides of the square, and there were few windows on the back of the inn. Laura deduced that the Compass had a single line of rooms on the upper story, all facing the front.

No sign of a military uniform or anyone who looked foreign in the coach yard. So tempting to immediately ask about their quarry, but they must seem merely guests. In such a small inn, however, they should soon encounter Dyer and Farouk.

Chapter 21

As Stephen helped her down, he murmured, "Frail antidote," and Laura remembered to move like a woman of uncertain health with no high opinion of herself.

They entered the inn and were greeted by the innkeeper, Mr. Topham, who immediately produced a letter for Stephen. "From Mr. Kerslake-Somerford of Crag Wyvern, sir. A gentleman very much in the public eye these days."

He was clearly bursting to tell the extraordinary story, but Stephen quelled him. "Yes, we know of his situation."

The innkeeper deflated and led them up to three adjoining rooms. They were pleasant and already warmed by fires, though this being an old building, the rooms were small, with only one modest window in each. Those windows looked out at the bay, however. Laura chose the bedchamber on the left of the central parlor, thinking that she might enjoy a visit here if so much wasn't at stake.

Laura had tried to count doors, but as their rooms were close to the stairs she couldn't be certain of the number of rooms up here. Eight, she thought, so if Farouk, Dyer, and a child were here, they must be close.

The innkeeper was about to leave so she asked, in

the manner of a perpetual worrier, "What other guests are there here, sir? My nerves cannot take disturbances."

"Only one, ma'am," the innkeeper assured her. "A military gentleman and his servant. Both very quiet."

As soon as the door closed, Laura turned to Stephen. "They're here!"

"It would seem so, but we can hardly pelt anyone with questions immediately. Not without raising suspicions."

She sighed. "You're right, and there was no mention of a child. But it should be simple enough to stage an encounter, and then nosy Mrs. Penfold can quiz the servants to her heart's content. What's in the letter? When can we meet the smuggler?"

Stephen had already broken the seal and was reading. "He'll call tomorrow, for lunch."

"Tomorrow!"

"A smuggler-earl must be a busy man."

"But now we're here, I want to *do* something." Then she laughed. "I'm flapping, aren't I?"

"Like a skylark."

It was said with dry humor so she really couldn't take offense, but it made her resolve to be calmer.

"As for doing something," he said, "I suggest a stroll to learn more about this place and stretch our legs."

Laura had been thinking more of knocking on doors in order to meet their fellow guests, but she knew he was right. "Very well, but we should delay long enough to unpack. Dashing straight out might look strange."

He smiled at her. "I should have known you'd be an effective criminal colleague."

Laura returned to her room better pleased with that response. Skylark, indeed. Was that how he saw her, even now? It stung particularly sharply when she was beginning to feel differently about him.

Was this fluttering inside her the same excitement she'd felt when she'd first met Hal? Or was it solely because of this risky adventure? Or was it because she'd been stuck at Caldfort like a nun in a convent and was giddy at being with any handsome man again?

Had she felt anything for Nicholas Delaney? She didn't think so, but she'd always had a disciplined nature. She didn't think she'd allow herself to feel anything for another woman's husband.

"Oh, perish it," she muttered, and tugged on the bellpull.

A sharp-faced but smiling young woman arrived with washing water. She curtsied, gave her name as Jean, then quickly set to deal with Laura's valise. Laura gave occasional instructions and decided she could safely ask some general questions.

"Such a pretty place," she fluttered. "I hear the air is healthy here."

"Very bracing, ma'am. We've had invalids come here and leave again dancing."

"Remarkable. I don't suppose there are many here so late in the year, however."

The maid hung Laura's dull gowns on hooks in the armoire. "Oh, not so bad, ma'am. We get mild winters here, you see, so some stay all year round."

"Really? Do you have any notable visitors?"

But the maid pulled a face. "Not to speak of, ma'am. I reckon they all go to Lyme Regis, see, it having a royal connection."

Laura thanked the maid and gave her a tip, though she hadn't revealed anything useful.

Laura hadn't taken off her outdoor clothing, so she had only to pull on gloves over her tiresome net ones before being ready to go out. A habitual last glance in the mirror almost made her yelp. She'd forgotten what an antidote she looked. No fear of anything amorous happening as long as she looked like this.

When she joined Stephen, he instantly asked, "What's the matter?"

She must remember that he was ferociously observant.

All the same, his question sparked a laugh. "What's the matter? Until a few days ago, my main complaint was boredom. I was afraid for Harry, but I thought it was probably in my imagination. I was mainly in the doldrums because Caldfort House did not present an exciting future.

"Now I seem to be teetering on the edge of danger and disaster. Even the Delaneys turn out to be not just allies but a lesson in the vulnerability of children. And here I am, pretending to be someone else—an ugly someone else—and if I'm recognized, my reputation will be in shreds, my access to Harry might be threatened—"

"Laura." He reached for her.

"And soon I'm going to be lunching with a smuggler!"

The absurdity struck her as it did him, and she collapsed into a chair, laughing. He was grinning at her, looking so much like the Stephen of the past. She held out her hands to him and he pulled her up.

"I'm sorry," she said.

"For laughing? Certainly not in character for Cousin Priscilla . . ."

Did he remember at exactly the same moment as she did?

It had to be spoken of. "I'm sorry for laughing all those years ago—when you asked me to marry you."

His laughter died, but perhaps it lingered a little in his eyes. "It was all those years ago, Laura, and we were both very young."

"I was old enough to marry."

"And I wasn't."

But Juliet had waited for her Robert.

"I suppose you weren't, but truly, I never meant to hurt you. I never . . ."—she sought the right words—"I never thought your offer ridiculous. I want you to know that."

They were still holding hands, and looking into each other's eyes.

"I won't say it was pleasant," he said. "I was young, every emotion raw. But I knew you hadn't meant to be cruel. I knew, even when 'screwing my courage to the sticking point' that it was an idiotic thing to do. . . ."

"Not idiotic."

He let go of her hands and stepped back. "Yes, it was. I thought you didn't know your mind, but Gardeyne was exactly what you wanted."

Laura shocked herself by almost denying it. She fussed with her gloves. "If we're going, we should go."

"Yes."

He extended his arm. She was tempted to continue the conversation, but she knew it would be unwise. They left the room and descended the stairs with no sight of any other guest and walked out of the inn into the damp, sea-tanged air. The sky was overcast now, however, and the wind cut.

"Bracing, the maid called it," Laura said with a shiver.

"Blows the cobwebs away."

"I am not inhabited by spiders. Do let's walk, and briskly."

"You forget. You're frail Mrs. Penfold."

"Oh, a plague on it."

He chuckled. "Tut-tut."

"Don't make me laugh. I'm sure it's not in character."

They walked back as far as the steep road into the village and then retraced their way. No one in a turban, and both military men had disappeared. Everyone was probably heading home for their evening meal.

They dawdled past the windows of the shops, for Laura hadn't seen any even as minor as these for months. There was a promising bookshop and an apothecary advertising ALL MODERN CONVENIENCES FOR THE FRAIL AND INVALID.

"I'm sure I should be interested in that establishment," she said, "but this is much more to my taste." She stopped to study the dressed dolls in the window of a mantua maker. "Are skirts really being worn shorter in London?"

"To the gentlemen's delight, yes."

She gave him a look. "There have always been ways to display an ankle, and it's more effective when they're normally veiled."

To demonstrate, she eased up her skirt slightly as she raised a foot onto a step.

He looked down and smiled. "I see—but not perhaps the behavior of my sickly Cousin Priscilla?"

She pulled a face at him but dropped her skirt. "Do you have a cousin called Priscilla Penfold?"

"No, but then your name would have been different before marriage. You must have married into the Penfolds of Warwickshire. A sober, studious bunch."

Where she would have once thought he fit perfectly, but now she was too aware of the ready laughter in his eyes, not to mention his remarkably fine looks and what she was coming to see was a strong, athletic body. A few days ago she would have said she knew Stephen very well. Now she was not so sure.

"I'm not sure I can play that part," she said. "Sober and studious."

"Look absentminded and mutter something about empiricism and Hume."

He clearly thought she wouldn't understand, so as they walked on toward the inn, she said, "Oh, that I can do. I've read Hume's essays."

His look of surprise was not unexpected, but it stung. She didn't confess that boredom had led her to read nearly everything in the limited Caldfort library except the sporting almanacs. "I have interests beyond the length of skirts, you know."

"Do you support Hume, then?"

Was he testing her? "He has many interesting ideas, but I cannot agree with his attacks on God and religion."

"Religion can sometimes be a vehicle for evil. Look at Reverend Jack."

"His evil, if true, has nothing to do with him being a vicar. True religion is virtuous by definition."

"Even if it demands that a widow throw herself on her husband's funeral pyre?"

She frowned at him. "No, but is that truly a religious belief or a social one?"

"You're trying to define religion to fit your premise. . . ."

When they neared the inn, Laura realized that she was enjoying a spirited philosophical debate. Her first instinct was to flutter and protest that these subjects were of no interest to her, but it was obvious Stephen didn't dislike her for it.

But really, anyone would think her a bluestocking!

Because of that, she did explain about boredom and the Caldfort library. "I didn't think the works had made such an impression on my mind. Perhaps one day I'll join your sister Fanny's philosophical circle."

She meant it to be flippant, but he said, "Why not?" But then added, "Cousin Priscilla."

With a suppressed exclamation, she remembered to be dull and awkward, which was probably helped by a feeling of depression. Was that the sort of woman he admired—a bluestocking?

Lady Skylark's only accomplishments had been high spirits, beauty, and charm.

Perhaps—and the thought was truly depressing—becoming physically plain changed everything, including Stephen's impression of her. Was it worse to be assumed feckless when beautiful, or to only be taken seriously when plain?

She paused to frown at him. "I don't see why an interest in philosophy should require being unfashionable."

"Nor do I," he drawled, and she had to fight a laugh. Of course he didn't. He was the Political Dandy. Even his plain traveling clothes were the height of fashion and beautifully made.

"Thank heavens for that, for I do enjoy pretty clothes."

"You'll be back in them soon."

"Will you still talk philosophy with me then?"

His brows quirked. "Now, what do you mean by that? I will talk anything with you, Laura, whatever you're wearing." As he opened the door for her, however, his smile was merely polite. The connection that had spun during their discussion had disappeared.

Laura moved to enter the inn, but a man was about to come out. A man in a long black robe, a three-quarter-length coat of sorts, and a bright blue turban. He stepped back to make way for her.

Laura felt her effort not to stare should be palpable—but then she realized that she *should* stare, at least a little.

She slid a glance to the side as she passed and took in the strange clothes, mahogany skin, strong, austere features, and impassive brown eyes.

And yet she felt that he had studied her just as keenly as she had studied him.

Chapter 22

She had to almost bite her lips until they were in their parlor with the door shut. Then she could exclaim, "Farouk. Now we have our excuse to gossip!"

"So we do," Stephen said, pulling the bell, but Laura sat, suddenly unsteady.

"He's real. I wasn't sure until now."

"Nor was I. Or at least, that Azir Al Farouk was the Arab he sounded like, not a strange device."

"And staying here. There aren't many rooms—"

She broke off as the door opened and Jean came in to curtsy.

"We'll order our dinner now," Stephen said with unusual coolness.

The maid curtsied again and listed the various dishes available. Stephen gestured for Laura to select and she did so, wondering if he was going to ignore this opportunity for questions.

Of course not. "We encountered a foreign gentleman on our way in," he said. "Is he a guest here?"

His tone had shifted from cool to icy, and the maid's eyes turned wary. "He is, sir, yes. But he's no trouble. Farouk's his name. From Egypt. Servant companion to a sickly gentleman, Captain Dyer."

"Does Captain Dyer have a number of such servants?" Stephen asked with an astonished hauteur that made Laura want to giggle. She'd never heard him put on such an intolerably superior manner.

"Oh, no, sir! Just the one. Farouk does everything for his gentleman. Won't even let us in to change the sheets or build the fire."

Excitement began to fizz. Because they had a child confined in their rooms?

"Are they staying long?" Stephen asked. "I am not pleased to be sharing a roof with a *heathen*."

The maid's fingers were tugging at her apron now. "I'm sure I don't know, sir. They've been here only a week and show no sign of leaving. The climate here is very healthy, you know."

Perhaps Stephen sniffed. Searching for a heathen odor? Laura pursed her lips, praying not to laugh. Surely Priscilla Penfold would purse her lips at this horror.

"Do these people have rooms near us?" Stephen asked at last.

The poor maid turned pale. "Well, sir, the captain's parlor lies next to your bedchamber, sir, but there's no adjoining door! There's no other way, sir, for Captain Dyer's taken the center rooms, you see, and we only have the eight up here and two down below, but an elderly couple has those on account of him needing a chair to go out." She ran out of breath and asked desperately, "Shall I get Mr. Topham, sir?"

Stephen appeared to consider it. "That will not be necessary at this time. At least assure me that there are no children around. My cousin cannot abide a childish racket."

"Oh, no, sir! No children other than the boot boy."

Laura longed to soothe the maid, but suspicion and affront gave a better basis for curiosity. She was relieved when Stephen, radiating disapproval, sent the maid off to get their dinner.

As soon as the door closed, she laughed. "You were insufferable."

His eyes twinkled. "Yes, wasn't I? But we know our men are here and nicely close."

"But where's the child?"

"There may not be one, Laura. That was only supposition."

She realized she'd built young Henry Gardeyne in her mind to point of reality. "Then who is HG? I know, I know, this could all be a hoax, but it may not be."

"Perhaps HG is hidden somewhere else. This is all speculation. We need more facts, and we'll find them in time."

She almost spit back, "Time!" but suppressed it. Stephen seemed to bring out the child in her.

He turned to look toward his room. "So, we share a wall."

That was more like it. Laura rose. "You think we might be able to hear something. Do let's try!"

But he raised a hand. "Patience. Dinner will be here soon, and you can hardly be found in my bed-chamber."

"We could switch. I don't think it's fair that you have that one."

"What? Would I let my frail cousin sleep next door to a heathen savage? I'll go and listen while you wait for the meal." When she would have protested, he added, "There's doubtless no point yet, Laura. Farouk has just left, so who would Dyer be talking to?"

Accepting that, Laura only pulled a face at his back, then went into her own bedchamber to remove her outer clothes. She really must stop acting like a girl—and yet it was as amusing as sharing a bedroom with Juliet at home and chattering as they once had.

She turned, smiling, for her habitual check in the mirror, and remembered. She snarled at Priscilla Penfold and returned to the parlor. Stephen was already there.

"Silent, as expected." He eyed the door to the corridor. "I wonder if their doors are locked."

She grabbed his arm. "Now who's being rash?"

"I will merely be checking out these suspicious characters for fear that they might attack my poor cousin in the night." His smile was boyish as he slipped free and left the room.

He was back in moments. "Locked, which is certainly suspicious if Farouk is merely a servant."

Laura frowned in the direction of the next room. "I'm not normally impulsive, but I wish we could break in."

"Not impulsive? Don't I remember a prizefight you attended, dressed as a lad?"

"I was twelve. And you took me!"

"Even so. And the time when you and Charlotte went swimming in the river without thought to the view from Ancross."

"A gentleman wouldn't have looked. I could remember some of your childish scrapes, you know."

I could remember watching you swimming in the river, too.

"I indulged in no scrapes to match yours," he said, strolling to the window to look out. "What about the time you bribed the gypsy at the Barham fair to let you take her place so you could give most peculiar predictions to your friends and neighbors?"

Laura covered her mouth. "I thought no one but Charlotte knew about that. Did she tell you?"

He looked back. "No, but when I heard some of the fortunes I kept watch, so I saw you slipping out of the back of the tent. So don't tell me, Laura Watcombe, that you are not impulsive."

"That, sir, was a carefully thought-out plan."

But he'd called her by her maiden name, as if he, too, were back in the past.

He didn't seem to notice. He was looking out of the window again, and said, "Farouk!"

She ran over to look. "Now can we listen? If dinner arrives, you can emerge to deal with it."

To look out at Farouk, she had pressed close to Stephen's body. A tingling awareness washed through her, almost causing her to gasp. She slid away, trying to make it look natural.

"You always get your way," he said, but his voice sounded strange. She glanced at him and saw a tight expression. Disapproval of her impulsive manner, probably. Or disgust at her appearance. Or both. She couldn't tell. It was most peculiar to inhabit a different skin, to make different ripples in the world around.

They turned together and hurried into the adjoining room, past his nightshirt hanging on a rack before the fire to warm. Through a faint aroma of spicy soap, and him . . .

The shared wall was mostly taken up by the head of the bed and a chest of drawers. He moved into the available space and beckoned her to join him. She could hardly refuse. Or perhaps she didn't want to, even though she had to squeeze against him there. That frisson dazed her again, and now she was aware of his scent.

She knew about the arousing smell of men, but Stephen's was both new and familiar. She wanted to press closer to his chest and inhale, but had willpower enough to instead press her ear to the rough plaster wall.

Chapter 23

Stephen pressed his right ear to the wall, but his mind could not escape Laura. She was facing him, and they were squeezed into the small space available, her back to the bed. She was almost where he wanted her.

In his arms.

In his bed.

Had she just looked at him with awareness that he was a man, not just her old friend? He was used to assessing situations and making quick decisions, but now, in the midst of the most important situation of his life, his brain seemed like a soggy pudding.

"Can you hear anything?"

Laura's soft question pulled him out of the pit and he concentrated. "Only a faint murmur."

"Me, too."

So hard not to press his body against hers, hard to look anywhere except at her breasts, swelling softly beneath her dull, high-necked gown. Impossible to avoid that perfume.

The one created for Labellelle.

Careless, that. It wasn't at all the scent for Priscilla Penfold, but he wouldn't ask her to change it. He tried to remember what scent she'd used as a girl. Something light and flowery, he thought, probably made in the Merrymead stillroom from garden flowers. This was a complex masterpiece.

As she was.

Nicholas had been right.

To all the other Lauras he was aware of, he must now add philosopher and quick-witted partner. He shouldn't be surprised—Laura had never been stupid or silly.

Something about her appearance was twisting his mind, as well. Would he have even mentioned philosophy to her without her sallow skin and faded hair? On the other hand, the way he was reacting now had nothing to do with Priscilla Penfold.

He swallowed and concentrated again on the voices beyond the wall. Frustratingly, they were almost distinct, so he felt that if he concentrated hard enough he would be able to distinguish words. Either that was untrue or concentration was beyond him.

"Well?" he asked.

She shook her head.

That gave him an excuse to move away. He didn't want to, but for sanity's sake, he must.

When they were safely back in the parlor—people could make love in a parlor—she said, "It sounded like a normal conversation, though, didn't it? No anger or fear? And adult voices."

He tried to recollect and couldn't. Devil take it, being squeezed close like that had clearly had no effect on her. Would he have to watch as she again married another man?

"Stephen?"

He pulled his wits together. "Probably."

She spun away and took a tempestuous turn around the parlor. "How frustrating this is. Is there *nothing* we can do?"

His hungry mind put a different interpretation on her words, and her sizzling energy burned him.

"Stephen? What is *wrong* with you?" She'd stopped and was frowning at him, hands on hips.

"I was thinking. Wait a minute."

He fled into his room to collect himself, taking a deep breath to try to sort out his wits. Now he needed an excuse for his abrupt departure. Some result of his brilliant thoughts. Some action.

He opened his valise, took out the long leather case, and returned briskly to the parlor to show it to her. "A telescope. Nicholas lent it to me. Tomorrow, if nothing else avails, we can spy on the windows from the beach."

"What a clever idea!" She glanced out of the window. "We could do it now."

"Impatient again."

"Do stop throwing my heedless youth in my face."

"I liked it."

He had, too. It occurred to him that his love was rooted in the Laura he'd known until her marriage. That he hadn't disapproved of her then, even if he'd teased.

She frowned slightly. "Do you like me less now?"

"Devil take it, Laura, don't take me up on every word. I like you now. I liked you then."

I didn't like you when you were married to Gardeyne. But he managed not to say that.

"Good. And," she added, "there's no reason not to go out now to look for boats through a telescope. Dinner can be held."

"It's almost dark."

She grinned at him. "We're impractical landlubbers. The local people will only laugh at us."

He found himself smiling back. It was exactly what the Laura of his youth would have said. "Then let's go and amuse them."

They headed out again, pausing to tell a servant that they would dine in fifteen minutes. Stephen could feel Laura's excitement bubbling beside him. Unfortunately, his baser nature translated it into another context.

As they headed into the wind, down onto the pebbly beach, he knew she would be a magnificent lover. That bit like shark's teeth, because she must have been a magnificent lover to Hal Gardeyne. ·

As they crunched close to the rippling waves, she held her bonnet in place and raised her face to the wind, reveling in the sensual elements.

"I don't think Cousin Priscilla would do that," he warned.

"It's the latest medical advice. To inhale the vigor of the wind off the sea." She turned an invigorated smile on him. "It's wonderful here, isn't it? I've only been to the sea at Brighton, and it's so busy there. Here it's more elemental."

The breeze pressed her clothing against her body. He didn't need that to know that it was lovely. Her breasts looked soft, as if she wasn't wearing a corset. The sight didn't help his sanity. Her mind was on nature, however, not on him, so he tuned his senses to hers. "The sound of the sea on the shore is a complex music, isn't it?"

She was back to inhaling, eyes closed. "Exciting and soothing at the same time. It's as if nothing terrible could happen by the sound of the sea."

People die in the sound of the sea, he thought, but he didn't want to spoil her pleasure.

"Yet the sea can be brutal," she continued. "It can smash and kill, as with the *Mary Woodside*. I wonder how many died then."

It was as if she'd picked up his feelings. Or, he thought with hope, as if their minds were more in tune than he'd thought.

She turned to him. "You're very quiet, my friend."
Friend.

"Appreciating everything around."

She looked around, missing his meaning. "Some of the inn windows are lit. We might see something. Where's the spyglass?"

He took the telescope out of its case, wondering if

the damn woman really felt nothing but the magic of the sea and the intensity of her purpose. "To have an excuse to look at the inn, we'd better pretend to admire the ships out there first. Here, you can be the idiot."

Her laughter danced on the wind. "Very well. Give it to me."

She dutifully studied the distant bobbing lights. "Do you think we could see France in daylight?"

"I doubt it. My turn." He took the spyglass and turned it on the inn.

"That's not fair. I thought we were supposed to pretend."

"We've pretended."

"Cheat. So what do you see?" She pressed close, as if she could share the view piece.

Devil take it. He could hardly keep the telescope steady as he scanned across windows. "That's one of their rooms, but the curtains are down." He could feel her warm breath on his jaw. "Ah!"

"What?"

"Their parlor curtains are open."

"So what do you see? Talk, Stephen, talk! Or let me have the glass."

He couldn't help but grin. "I see Farouk in his blue turban, standing, bowing slightly over the other man, who is sitting down."

"Dyer is described as sickly. What does he look like?"

"His back's to the window. Lightish brown hair."

"Let me see."

She gripped his wrist and tugged. Her touch, even through gloves, sent such a jolt of raw desire through him that he froze. It was that or grab her into his arms, tumble her down onto the beach, even.

Damnation, he'd never expected this to be so challenging. He'd never expected the fire to burn so fiercely. He was a man of the mind, wasn't he?

Not the slightest damn bit.

She seized the glass from his hand, stepped apart, and put it to her eye. He watched her. He couldn't not do so, but at the moment she was unlikely to catch him at it.

A hint of light from the inn and other buildings sketched in her perfect profile, which curls and cream could not distort. Straight nose, but just a little short. Lips full and slightly parted with concentration. Neat, determined chin.

"Farouk's moving around," she said. "There could be a child there, out of sight. . . . Oh, no, he's lowering the curtain."

She turned to give him the spyglass. "I had quite a good view of Farouk, but we've seen him, so we achieved nothing."

"To solve everything within hours is too much to expect."

"But we can hope." He heard a smile in it as she turned back to face the wind and sea.

Over time, the most wrought emotions have to mellow. As Stephen slid the glass back into its case, he felt surprisingly content to be here in the clean wind, soothed by sea music, with Laura at his side.

"If Dyer is a cripple, he can't be a henchman," she said. "So we have only Farouk to deal with."

"We?"

She turned to him. "I will have my part in this."

"It could turn dangerous."

"I gave you no permission to protect me."

"I need none. A gentleman does not let a lady fall into danger."

"So a gentleman automatically takes command?"

"Yes."

He could sense rather than see her frown. "You forget our past."

"I remember it all too well. You were always recklessly impulsive."

"And you have become intolerably stuffy!"

"Adult."

"Timid with age!"

Something snapped. He pulled her close and kissed her, quickly, but hard. When he let her go, he said, "I am not so aged as that."

Her eyes were huge, but in the darkness, he couldn't read her reaction at all. He had probably just destroyed any chance he had.

"So I see," she said, and turned to walk back to the inn.

Chapter 24

Darkness, Laura thought, was a friend to the embarrassed and the confused. In daylight, who knows what Stephen might have seen? She certainly didn't. She didn't know her own feelings.

She didn't know whether to laugh or weep. What did it mean when a man kissed a woman in anger? What would have happened if she'd kissed him back?

To the music of the sea rolling rhythmically against the beach and the crunch of feet—his and hers—through pebbles, she made herself accept that to kiss him back would have been disaster. She didn't even know this man. She hardly knew herself. She'd thought the young, wild Laura past and done with, but now she danced inside her like a possessing imp.

By the time they arrived at the sanctuary of the inn, she could face the light. She had no idea what to say, but as she hoped, Stephen didn't refer to what had happened. All the same, when Topham popped out of a room, it was a huge relief.

"Sir Stephen, Mrs. Penfold, I want to assure you that Mr. Farouk has created no problems in the week he has been here."

"It was something of a shock to my poor cousin," Stephen said haughtily. "Her nerves are not of the best."

Laura tried to look frail and fearful when at this

moment, fresh from sea air and that kiss, she felt anything but.

Topham wrung his hands at her. "I assure you, ma'am, that you have nothing to worry about."

"So alarming. After all," she added, dropping her voice to a whisper, "Mr. Farouk cannot be a Christian."

"Alas, I fear you are correct, ma'am, but I assure you he behaves like one."

As they seemed to have a perfect opportunity for more questions, Laura asked, "And his employer? What sort of man is he?"

"An English officer!" Topham said triumphantly. "Sadly frail, but an Englishman born and bred. Been in the India service, I gather."

"Frail, you say? Elderly, then?"

"Oh, no, ma'am. Quite young. Very sad. A war injury, I suppose. His man had to carry him up to his rooms, our ground-floor ones being already taken."

"Oh, the poor man. I do hope Mr. Farouk takes him out to enjoy the sea air. After just two short strolls, I am feeling much restored."

"I rejoice, ma'am," said Topham, beaming. "I'm sure Captain Dyer would be well advised to do the same, but thus far he has remained in his room."

Laura hid dismay. That would make things much more difficult.

"And doctors?" she asked, deciding that it would be useful to establish Mrs. Penfold as intolerably nosy. "Does he see excellent doctors?"

"Again, ma'am, not so far."

Laura couldn't resist a glance at Stephen. Surely a genuinely sick man would consult a doctor.

"But if you need medical advice," the innkeeper went on, "permit me to suggest Dr. Nesbitt. A most excellent physician and a particular favorite of the ladies."

"Thank you. So kind," Laura fluttered, then added,

"Do you think poor Captain Dyer might want company? My cousin and I would be happy to take tea with him."

Topham bowed. "You are the soul of kindness, Mrs. Penfold. I will suggest it to Mr. Farouk, though I must warn you that Captain Dyer has not entertained whilst he's been here. Your dinner is ready, sir, ma'am, as soon as you wish it."

"Serve it, then," Stephen said, and offered Laura his arm.

She placed her gloved hand on his sleeve and they went up the stairs. For the first time, she was nervous to be going into a private room with Stephen, but he acted as if that kiss had never happened.

Very well. If he could act that way, so could she.

"It may be harder to encounter Dyer than we thought," she said as she stripped off her leather gloves.

"But his staying in his rooms fits with him being a prisoner."

"So he could be HG! Or if there is a child, someone must stay with him."

"I doubt they could have a child here with no one aware of it."

"I suppose you're right."

He said nothing else so she escaped to her bed-chamber, where she tore off her dull bonnet with a degree of rage. She didn't understand him, she hardly understood herself, and this matter of HG was likely to be a great deal more difficult than they'd thought. What were they going to do if Dyer remained closeted in his room? How were they to compare him to the portrait?

She puffed out a breath and commanded herself to be sensible. Or at least patient. They'd only been here a matter of hours. She checked her appearance—

Perish it! Perhaps she'd stop looking in mirrors for the duration.

Laura returned to the parlor, where Stephen was leaning on the mantelpiece, staring into the fire. He looked up with a slight, impersonal smile. Some lingering hopes she'd not really been aware of popped like soap bubbles.

"I've been considering what we know," he said. "Dyer's apparent frailty might be because he was drugged or bound."

"But unless he's kept drugged at all times, wouldn't he cry for help?"

"Then perhaps he's kept drugged at all times."

She considered it. "That might make rescue difficult. Someone will have to carry him."

"As Farouk apparently carried him up to his room, I should be able to do the same. He and I are of a similar build, I think."

She considered his physique, which was no penance. "Yes, so do I." Both men were lithe but strong. Farouk was probably wider in the shoulders, but not by much.

She began to pace the room. "Do you think there's any chance they'll accept the invitation to meet? It would solve everything. Probably not," she answered herself.

"Especially," he said dryly, "if Dyer is HG tied to his chair."

He was looking at her strangely.

"Was that a bad idea?" she asked. "To suggest tea? They have no reason to suspect us."

He moved away from the fireplace. "It was an excellent idea. Just what a kindhearted lady would do, not to mention a nosy one. But be careful. Keep in mind that Dyer could be both confined to a chair and part of the plot, which is a simple attempt to fleece money from Lord Caldfort." After a moment, he added, "I don't want you taking risks, Laura, or letting your hopes rise too high."

She bit back an instinctive protest. "I know."

Their dinner arrived then, which was a relief. When the servants left and they sat to the meal, Laura became aware of a new discomfort.

A meal for two, she thought, serving oxtail soup. How very matrimonial—except that she couldn't remember ever sitting to such a meal with Hal. Whenever they were at Caldfort, his parents, and often others, ate with them. Elsewhere, they'd rarely eaten at home. Only when they were playing host to others, in fact. It made this simple meal at a small table awkward, especially with that fierce yet impersonal kiss still ignored between them.

"So," she said, when she'd consumed half her soup, "what do we do tomorrow?"

He smiled. "Tomorrow is Sunday, so as a Member of Parliament and a respectable widow, we go to church. It's always possible that Captain Dyer will be God-fearing, too, but if not, there should be opportunity to gossip."

She found herself smiling back. "Of course! Draycombe is bound to be in a ferment about a heathen in their midst. And the smuggler is coming to lunch. He will have much to tell us."

Her smile faded. He was looking at her in a way that did not seem connected to church or smuggler.

"You surprised me with your knowledge of philosophy," he said.

"I being a mere woman?"

He laughed dryly. "Remember my sister Fanny."

"Then why assume I'm a feather wit?" But she knew. "Because I never showed great interest in such matters when we were young, I suppose. That's probably more truly me than what happened today. I told you, there's not much to read at Caldfort."

He put aside his soup plate and uncovered a meat pie. "I assume you could have ordered novels if you'd wished to."

"And I did. But one cannot read novels all the time."

"Charlotte manages to."

He served her pie. She served him vegetables. "Charlotte and I are much alike."

"You were. But you and I rubbed along pretty well, too, I think."

Laura picked up her knife and fork, considering his sister. "Perhaps Charlotte and I are quite different now. Perhaps that's why we're no longer close."

"We drift apart from people over time. It's a natural force."

"And drift toward others."

"I would say you hurtled toward Gardeyne."

"He was a very attractive man."

"Wealthy and heir to a title."

She speared a carrot. "There was more to him than that."

So much for matrimonial, or even friendly, harmony. They abandoned conversation by agreement, and finished the meal quickly. That was easy for Laura, as she'd lost her appetite. To her surprise, Stephen ate little, too.

Surely they could do better than this. She pushed away most of a pear tart. "Why are we fighting?"

"I was not aware that we were."

"I know you never liked Hal."

"I would prefer not to talk of him. It seems disrespectful to the dead."

"Only if you say disrespectful things."

His brows quirked in a way that suggested that there was nothing else to say.

"You can't deny that he was a brilliant rider."

"So are most jockeys."

She pushed away from the table and stood. "You're right. We shouldn't talk about Hal. We should talk about our plans."

"We're here and have gathered some information. Any further discussion would be repetitive."

Let's talk about that kiss, then.

She almost said it, but knew it would be disastrous. If it had meant so little to him, what was there to say? If it had meant more, she wasn't ready to explore those depths.

She tugged angrily at the bellpull and soon Jean arrived to clear away their dinner. Perhaps the picked-at meal would confirm her sickly status. She wanted to question the maid further about Dyer, but couldn't think of a reasonable question. Patience was probably best, but what were they going to do now? It was only eight o'clock, a ridiculously early hour to go to bed, and she didn't want to. She wanted to explore Stephen, infuriating as he was.

When the maid left, she suggested, "Cards?"

"By all means. What?"

"Bezique. Piquet?" She tossed out the gambling games deliberately, and added, "I was married to Hal Gardeyne, remember?"

His lips tightened. "Piquet, then. Do you have a pack? If not, I'm sure Topham can provide."

"I do, as it happens. Sometimes I play simple games with Harry." She went to get them, then sat at the table and opened the wooden box. "How good are you?"

He sat opposite. "Good enough. I was raised among Rogues."

"Excellent." She sorted out the lower cards, aware of a simmering annoyance that lent edge to the game, and of enjoying it. "Do we play for paper points?"

"Not at all. I want you in my debt."

A shiver went through her that was surely not what he intended, though if she were willing to permit herself fantasy, she could imagine a vivid scenario.

She passed the reduced pack to him. "You want

to use my poor widow's mite to fund some reform, I assume."

He shuffled with those promising, long-fingered hands. "Certainly to bring about a significant change." He put the cards in front of her. "Cut."

She did so, exposing a ten. He cut to show a six.

"Your deal," he said, and they settled to the game.

Chapter 25

Guttering candles forced the end of play. When they'd completed the last *partie*, Laura leaned back, aware that anger had transmuted into a peculiar and unexpected pleasure. For the past hours everything had disappeared except the game. Stephen had simply been Stephen, the sharp-witted player she wanted to beat.

Now he was more than that, as if the hours of intense play had burned away dross, leaving clarity.

"Who won?" she asked, without great interest. They'd been evenly matched and the points had gone backward and forward.

He was calculating on a piece of paper. "You," he said, looking up. "By one hundred and fifteen. Guineas?"

"Lord, no. I'd never play for guinea points. Shillings."

"Five pounds fifteen, then. I assume you'll take my word for it?"

It was an idle pleasantry of a conversation and the strange idea came to her that it was like the words spoken after coupling, contented and dreamy.

"Of course, and I'll give you time to pay."

He passed the paper to her, but she didn't bother to check it. "That was an excellent game."

"You're very good."

"As are you."

With her mind stuck in bed, it was . . . stimulating.

He rolled the paper and threw it accurately into the fire. "Too late for more, I assume."

She bit her inner cheek to control a smile. "Could you rise to the occasion?"

"It's past ten, but I'm not exhausted. I was merely thinking that we should be up with the larks to spy on our neighbors."

Up amused, but *lark* sobered. She looked down for a moment, then met his eyes again. "I forgive you for Lady Skylark."

He stilled. "I never thought you'd mind."

"You didn't mean it to be a constant reproach?"

"Ah . . . Perhaps I did. What I meant was that I didn't think you'd mind being Lady Skylark."

She wished he hadn't misjudged her so, but she only said, "It was too light. It doesn't matter anymore. Thank you for coming, Stephen. For helping. For being you."

"And who is that?"

He pinched out one wallowing candle, which turned his features shadowy. In childish competition, she licked her fingers and did the same to the other. Now only firelight lit the room.

"Stephen the thoughtful, the observant," she said, but then saw a flicker of distaste. "Stephen the fighter for those who cannot fight."

It was the right thing to say. He took her hand. "I will fight for you, Laura. You have my promise on that."

"Thank you." Her heart pounded deeply, a beat that seemed to pulse through her body. *Will you also kiss me again?*

But he held her left hand, and Hal's wedding ring glinted in the candlelight. It no longer bound her, but it gave her strength not to speak her thought.

She didn't want to go, didn't want to break this

moment, but she made herself free her hand, rise, and say good night. In the privacy of her bedchamber, she closed the door then leant against it, breathing deeply and trying to sober her heated mind.

When she realized that she was rubbing her hands over her body, over her breasts, she stopped, but she couldn't stop desiring Stephen in a direct and feverish way.

If he were Hal, she could go to him, touch him, kiss him, and get exactly what she wanted. If he were Hal, she wouldn't feel quite this way.

She puzzled over that as she took off her cap. When she looked in the mirror, however, she saw the sallow skin, the ugly mousy curls, and the mole. She tore off the wig so roughly it hurt, then sat, head in hands. What was she *doing?* What had become of her orderly life? She'd always coped, always created a way to be content. Why this turmoil now?

Because of Stephen. Her feelings now were nothing like feelings she'd ever had with Hal, but Stephen was Stephen. She was no suitable match for a future Prime Minister!

She took out the remaining pins and shook her own curls free, then realized she still had to ring for her washing water. She did so and put the wig back on, stuffing her own hair roughly under it.

To put distance between herself and the door, she stood by the window, realizing that she hadn't lowered the curtain. If someone was out there with a spyglass they could have seen everything. She let down the balloon curtain, then went to her empty valise.

When the maid knocked and entered with her hot water, Laura said "Thank you" without looking up.

"Was there anything else, ma'am?"

"No, thank you. I can undress myself."

When the door closed, she straightened and began to undress. The substitute corset was very comfortable. As her fashionable days were over, perhaps she'd have some made.

Rational clothing. Rational actions.

Somewhere inside, the old Laura laughed.

Chapter 26

Laura awoke from a restless night overhung by inconvenient hungers and an awareness of just how perilous her situation was. Urgency had carried her to Draycombe, but now it seemed like a headlong, heedless rush into danger and temptation.

Last night she'd scraped and washed off her disguise—except the mole, which was glued so firmly she wondered how she'd eventually get rid of it. Putting her disguise on again was tiresome, but she tried to take reassurance from it. Priscilla Penfold would never do anything scandalous.

When she ventured into the parlor, she found Stephen already there, eating his breakfast. He'd ordered enough for two, and immediately poured her coffee. Laura surreptitiously studied him, wondering if he, too, had suffered a restless night, but she could see no sign of it.

Abandoning hope that he, too, was seething with restless and confused desires, she turned her attention to food. The delicious smell of warm rolls was already reminding her that she'd picked at her dinner last night. She remembered why, but all the same, a body must eat.

She buttered a roll, and the first delicious bite settled her nerves somewhat. "Do we know what time the service is?"

"Am I not the epitome of efficiency? The church is St. Peter's, and the service is at ten."

"Bravo, but I assume you simply asked the servants."

His smile acknowledged it.

"If Dyer attends, we could rescue him then. Claim sanctuary, even."

"That's protection from the authorities, not villains." He was still smiling. It was strangely comforting to be back to friendly ease.

"But in the midst of a staunch English congregation, Farouk would be powerless," she pointed out, then sighed. "Which almost certainly means Dyer won't be there."

"Remember, we don't know that Dyer is a prisoner, or that he is Henry Gardeyne. We need more information before we act."

He sounded apologetic, but as Laura ate another bite of roll, she recognized that she was pleased. It was wicked of her, but she didn't want this adventure over just yet. It was as if she'd turned the first few pages of a fascinating book—about Stephen and about herself. She couldn't bear to abandon it.

Once they'd finished breakfast, they both dressed for the cool weather and set out to walk to the church at the other end of town. It was small, simple, and quite full. Three worshippers arrived in wheeled chairs pushed by servants. None, however, was a young man, and, of course, there was no turban.

The vicar preached a sermon that mentioned the holy duty to be hospitable to visitors, then touched more delicately on the need to convert the heathen by showing Christian charity. They'd been right to think that some of the local people were uneasy about, or even hostile to, Azir Al Farouk.

As she and Stephen filed out of church, Laura murmured, "It would have been more politic of him to wear normal dress."

"I believe the turban is part of the religion."

"Even so, with a normal jacket and trousers, he wouldn't stand out quite so much."

They had to break off then to speak to the vicar, who confirmed that some of his parishioners were angry about Farouk, especially with the news not long ago being full of the horrors of Algerian slavery.

"Fear for the honor of their womenfolk is also good excuse for deep drinking," remarked the worldly vicar. "May I invite you and your cousin to dine with us, Sir Stephen?"

Stephen extricated them from that, then had to do the same with the rotund, jowly squire, Mr. Bartholomew Ryall, who knew him from London. Next, a Mr. Frobisher wanted to shake his hand. Of course, Laura had to be introduced—a problem she hadn't foreseen. She blessed her concealing bonnet, and used her sickliness as excuse to keep her head and voice low.

She was part of each encounter, however, and realized that a great many people here knew Stephen, or knew of him. He was a Member of Parliament from Dorset, even if his constituency was on the eastern edge, but that didn't account for the attention. He was a well-known, and well-admired, man.

It was no surprise to her that Stephen had a flourishing political career and that, as Juliet had written, he was even spoken of as a potential Prime Minister, but she'd not understood the extent of his reputation until now. In her mind, he'd remained the childhood friend with too deep an interest in books.

The military captain, Trainor, shook Stephen's hand and thanked him for his support of better treatment for injured officers. Mrs. Ryall praised his work to reform the Poor Laws. A frail elderly gentleman in a chair turned out to be the Dr. Grantleigh who with his wife had the ground-floor rooms at the Compass. Unfortunately, he had been one of Stephen's tutors at

Cambridge and went on and on about how he'd always predicted a brilliant future.

"Not like the rest of them," the old man said, "Arden, Cavanagh, Debenham. Using an ancient college as a club for drinking, gaming, and worse. You, sir, used the opportunity to learn!"

Laura sucked in her cheeks to stifle laughter, for Stephen was looking uncomfortable. No gentleman, no matter how clever, wants to be known as an ink-nose.

As the Grantleighs were staying at the Compass, there was nothing for it but to walk back with them and the manservant pushing the chair. The road was rough in places, so progress was slow. Stephen walked beside the chair, apparently amusing the old man. Laura was paired with Mrs. Grantleigh, who said not a word.

"I do hope Dr. Grantleigh is finding benefit in the sea air," Laura said, to break the silence.

Mrs. Grantleigh sighed. "I'm not sure how, as the weather is generally too inclement for him to enjoy it. But our doctor insisted, and my husband chooses to do what his doctor says. Dr. Nesbitt here is encouraging. But after all, time cannot be halted, nor age reversed."

Laura approved of stoicism, but only to a point. She wanted to suggest that if the case was hopeless, the couple should move to a place where they would find the setting and company more congenial. Instead, she tried for information about Dyer and Farouk.

"Such a shame that there are so few guests at the Compass. Only ourselves and Captain Dyer, whom the innkeeper says never leaves his rooms and never entertains."

"A sad case," Mrs. Grantleigh agreed. "I saw him arrive, you know, but not a glimpse of him since. I must say that I didn't think him quite so unwell as that. No worse than my husband, I'm sure, and yet Captain Dyer did not attend church."

The older woman had pursed her lips, so Laura did the same. "I noticed that, Mrs. Grantleigh, and I could not help wondering if that *heathen* in some way prevented him."

Mrs. Grantleigh looked startled. "I don't see how he could."

"Sometimes servants can gain an unhealthy power over their employers, my dear lady."

"Why yes, I have known such cases. . . . But alas, there is nothing to be done."

Stoicism could definitely be carried to extremes, and Laura had seen a way to use this situation. "I believe I might mention the matter to the vicar when next I see him. If he were to pay a visit, I don't think he could be denied."

"What a good idea." Mrs. Grantleigh seemed truly admiring, and rather surprised that anyone—or perhaps just a woman—might come up with an idea at all.

Laura feared Mrs. Grantleigh was the sort of woman who had depended all her life on her husband for guidance—which is what most people would think right and proper. But see the result. With her husband failing in body and mind, she was adrift, unable to form firm decisions and unused to considering what was truly best for them both.

Laura couldn't help seeing that her situation had been somewhat the same. She had felt lost and powerless after Hal died, but she had recovered, even if it had needed an emergency to shock her. She decided that when her current problems were dealt with, she would find some way to help the Grantleighs. Stephen was acquainted with them, so it must be possible.

"Sir Stephen is an admirable young man," Mrs. Grantleigh suddenly said, and went on to tell some stories of his virtues as a student. Again, it was probably the sort of praise that he would blush over, but it alerted Laura to a completely new aspect of their situation.

She'd thought that if this deception were uncovered, it would only be disastrous for her. But Stephen was at risk, too. He wouldn't be ruined but he would lose some of the respect of these people.

Most men of fashion, even MPs, wouldn't care about being discovered in an assignation with a widow, but Stephen might. He was held in high respect not because of rank or wealth, though he had a modicum of both, but because of who he was. She searched for the best word and settled on a Biblical one. He was a *righteous* man.

He worked hard, and not only for selfish ends. Most MPs were in Parliament to increase the power of family or faction. Stephen, it would seem, was working to make life better for people of all sorts. Once she might have made a joke about anyone in her circle being "righteous." Now the realization weighted her with a sense of inadequacy.

What place did Lady Skylark have in the life of Sir Stephen Ball? She could win him votes at the hustings by lively charm, but she'd lose him as many from those who disapproved. He didn't even need that kind of help. Barham wasn't a rotten borough, but the voters there would return him to Parliament as long as he was willing to stand.

She could run his household and throw glittering parties that might sway important people he wanted to influence, but she suspected that wasn't Stephen's way. She had only rarely seen him at *ton* affairs.

Could she fit into the mold of his life? Live quietly, helping him with his research and arranging occasional dinners for groups of serious-minded men who would regard any woman at the table as a distraction. She supposed, with a sigh, that she could chair committees of ladies working to support worthy goals.

She'd been on such committees—it was expected of any lady of fashion—and she'd liked being useful, but she knew she couldn't dedicate her life to that. She liked parties and balls and musical soirées. She liked laughing and flirting and charming men. She liked being at the center of the fashionable world.

If she had to live quietly at Caldfort in order to take care of Harry, then she would, but she couldn't imagine choosing to live a sober, serious life in London, not even with Stephen. It would be like forcing a gourmet to live on gruel within sight of fine cuisine. That made her a despicable, shallow woman, but it was better to know it now than too late.

The Grantleighs invited them to lunch, but they could plead their other engagement.

Laura entered their parlor and studied Stephen, trying to blend the handsome man of fashion with righteousness. "Perhaps you should be in disguise, too," she said.

"I certainly didn't anticipate Grantleigh. Are you all right?" Was that question because he knew holding to her character had been a strain or because he detected something?

She turned away, fussing with her gloves. "Yes, of course. I don't like to live a lie, however."

"Nor do I. We should be able to be done with this soon."

He sounded eager to escape. So, in a way, was she. She turned back and related Mrs. Grantleigh's remarks about Dyer. "If he wasn't particularly ill, it lends weight to him being a prisoner."

He frowned. "Yes, it does. Damnation, but this is frustrating. I'll go and check the wall."

He strode into his room, and Laura smiled wryly. He must be driven crazy by this situation to swear in front of her. Or perhaps he was simply relaxing back into friendship. That was better.

He was back in moments. "Mumble, mumble, mumble. If only they'd fall into a shouting match, I might be able to understand something."

He paced restlessly to look out at the street. That provided an opportunity for Laura to study him some more, but to do so would be folly so she broke the silence. "Were you nervous the first time you stood to speak in the House?"

He turned his head toward her. "No, but only because of the brash arrogance of youth. I'm more nervous now sometimes because I want to make my arguments in a way that'll carry others with me."

"I'm sure you do."

A smile expressed wryness. "I am a good orator, but not golden-tongued. I haven't yet reduced the house to tears as Sheridan and Fox did. In any case, I prefer to make my arguments to reason rather than emotions." After a moment, he added, "For that I am doubtless a fool."

"Reason is gold, whereas emotion is gilding, soon worn away."

"A strange observation from Labellelle."

She met his eyes. "Beauty and reason being antagonists?"

"Unfair, wasn't it? I'm sorry."

They had no time to progress from there, for a knock at the door brought Topham. "Sir Stephen, here is your guest, Mr. Kerslake-Somerford!"

The innkeeper spoke as if he could take credit, and certainly the new arrival was someone to take credit for. Laura couldn't have said what she expected of a smuggling master, but it was not this handsome young man with glowing vigor and an open, unguarded smile.

Topham bowed again. "I'll have your lunch brought up, shall I, Sir Stephen?"

Stephen agreed, and the man left with yet another bow, seemingly directed to the smuggler-earl.

"You're an important person, sir," Stephen said, shaking hands. "May I present Mrs. Gardeyne, currently masquerading as my cousin, Mrs. Penfold."

"Ma'am." Kerslake-Somerford bowed to her. "I

gather the Rogues are up to something again. I must say, association with them is enlivening my life."

More boyish enthusiasm. "I wouldn't have thought your life short of livening, Mr. Kerslake-Somerford."

"Different kinds, Mrs. Gardeyne. Most of my . . . professional activity is no more exciting than book-keeping. The whole point, in fact, is to keep enliv-enment to a minimum."

"Ah, I think Mr. Delaney said something similar. That danger comes of its own."

"Precisely. It's those who lead dull lives who seek it out."

Laura made sure not to look at Stephen. A dull life? Surely not. "Excitement comes in many forms," she said. "I'm sure politics can be hazardous."

"Not anymore," Stephen said dryly, perhaps guess-ing her intent to soothe his feelings. "No one's been beheaded for opposing the monarch in generations."

"Prime Minister Perceval was shot," Kerslake-Somerford pointed out cheerfully.

"By a madman," Stephen said. "That sort of thing could happen to anyone."

"Not just anyone. Perceval was shot because the assassin thought the Prime Minister the creator of all his problems. The danger of being a figurehead."

Foolish to fear for Stephen, but Laura couldn't help it. "You are a figurehead, too, Mr. Kerslake-Somerford."

"For my sins. Please call me Mr. Kerslake, ma'am. It's how I've been known all my life. I've only adopted the other as part of my claim to the earldom."

Their lunch arrived and was spread on the table. Once the servants left, they sat and got down to business.

"What's amiss?" Kerslake demanded. "And how may I assist you?"

Chapter 27

Kerslake had drunk two cups of tea, eaten bread, ham, pie, and fruit, interspersed with pertinent questions before all was clear. Laura was uncertain at times about telling this man everything, but he had been vouched for by Nicholas Delaney, and they needed his help.

"I've known about Azir Al Farouk since he landed. Drew Chideock brought him in from France on the *Long Jane*. Now we're at peace, we don't get many such passengers, so we were all curious. But"—he shrugged—"as long as a man pays we don't ask questions. In fact, it's easier now. During the war we tried not to carry spies."

"Just Al Farouk?" Laura asked.

"Him and Captain Dyer."

"No child?"

"None was mentioned. You expected one?"

She shook her head. "Please, tell us what you know about the arrival."

Kerslake took a plum. "Despite the rank, Dyer wears no uniform. He's some sort of invalid. Can walk a few steps with a cane, but Farouk had to carry him from the boat to the cart that stood ready to take away the cargo."

"Carried him upstairs here, too, apparently," Stephen said.

"So it wasn't temporary. Chideock took them to Lyme Regis and fixed them up with Paul Wey's coach, which brought them here. All part of the price." Kerslake looked at Laura. "What about the child?"

Laura shared a look with Stephen. "He might have come separately. A boy, perhaps nine years old."

"I've heard of none, but I'll ask."

"What about a party of men?" Stephen asked. "Or no. Nicholas would flay me for assuming the villains are all men, especially with a child involved. It could appear to be a family group."

"That would certainly make them harder to detect, but we don't have many visitors this late in the year. Do you mean a group arriving normally, or by a smuggling vessel? I'm almost certain no child has arrived here recently that way."

Laura shared another look with Stephen as she tried to fit these new pieces into the puzzle. "If there was a reason Farouk and Dyer came in surreptitiously, why would they send HG openly?" It struck her like a loss, a death. "I suppose I must accept that there is no child. He's become so real in my mind, I'm loath to let him go. It's as if he's imprisoned without anyone even knowing about it, and I must set him free."

"I'll make enquiries, Mrs. Gardeyne," Kerslake said kindly. "I can find out what strange children are in the area, too. I mean ones not connected with local families. There probably won't be many this time of year, but it will take a few days to have the tally."

"Thank you."

Stephen took her hand. "It's better not to have a child at risk, Laura. What's more, this means that if anyone is Henry Gardeyne, it must be Captain Dyer himself."

That revived her. "Yes, of course. Tied up. Behind locked doors."

"We still have the puzzle of a ten-year absence," Stephen warned, "and as Nicholas asked, why now?"

"I know, but if it's true, it's better. If it is Henry, he'll be able to prove his identity without any difficulty, and we have his portrait to match him with." She turned to Kerslake. "I have a drawing of Henry Gardeyne. Do you think Mr. Chideock and his men might recognize whether he's Captain Dyer?"

He pulled a face. "It all happened by night, and their attention was probably more on their cargo. I could ask them, but to be frank, I'm not sure it would be wise. I trust them to a point, but only to a point. They'd likely let something slip, and then it would snake around the area and reach the people here. After all, you're here, next door. It shouldn't be hard to get a look at the man."

"You'd think so," said Stephen, "but it's proving tricky for law-abiding citizens."

Kerslake laughed. "I'm no dab hand at breaking and entering, but if you can't manage it legally, I'll have someone help you. Shame old Elsie Musbury's dead. She owned this place before Topham and had been hand in glove with smugglers all her life. Topham's a new man from Exmouth way. He knows what's what, but I can't trust him as I would Elsie."

Stephen nodded. "What if Farouk has supporters standing by? Would you know of unexplained bullyboys in the area?"

"Certainly, but would they be that? As you said, they could masquerade as a family or as other orderly visitors."

"You mean they could be anyone?" Laura asked, thinking of the various people they'd met today.

"Not anyone. Most people here now are local or long-term visitors, but sensible villains announce their identity no more than smuggling masters do. In fact, it seems strange to me that this Farouk is creating such a stir."

"He could never pass for an English gentleman," Stephen said.

"True, but from what I hear, he's almost making a point of being peculiar."

"That bears thinking on. But who in this area could be called suspicious?"

"No one," Kerslake said. "It's my business to know of possible preventive men."

"Do the forces of law and order sometimes prowl around in disguise?" Laura asked.

"They do anything they can to catch us."

"I saw two military men as we arrived," Laura said. "One army, one navy."

"Captain Sillitoe, RN, cousin of a local family. Captain Trainor of the Buffs, attending his grandmother. We're keeping an eye on both just in case, but neither has acted out of character."

"I'm impressed," Stephen said.

"I told you, knowing these things is my business. I keep the trade going because it's the main means of support for many along the coast, especially this year, with the poor harvest and the economy going to hell with the peace. My main intent, however, is to avoid violence and keep my people out of jail."

Laura was beginning to have considerable respect for young Captain Drake.

Kerslake rose. "I need to be off. I'll find out about children and other unexplained strangers, but I suspect the action is all here. Do you have a plan? If you want to break the prisoner out now, I can arrange it."

Stephen smiled. "Not yet. You see, we don't know what we should do. Even if Dyer is Henry Gardeyne, we have an unexplained decade of absence. We also have a cripple. In body only, or in mind? He might not be the sort of man who should be given control of an English estate and all the people dependent on it."

"Ah."

Laura studied the man. "You don't seem shocked, Mr. Kerslake."

He turned to her. "My predecessor as Earl of Wyvern was insane, Mrs. Gardeyne, but not enough to be confined, which was unfortunate. He did considerable damage. If someone had prevented his reign, it would have been a blessing."

"Then you understand why we have to try to find out more before taking any action. Because . . ."

"Because when you liberate him, you might wish to cage him elsewhere. I'd offer Crag Wyvern except that it might tip a delicate mind into madness all by itself. I do know some safe places, however."

"Why am I not surprised?" Stephen murmured.

Kerslake's lips twitched. "There's a farm not far inland from here where the people are completely trustworthy. If you liberate Gardeyne but don't want him on the loose, take him to Stonewell Farm. I'll draw a map."

He took out a tablet of paper and drew roads and signs. On the back he scribbled a note of introduction. "I'll stop by Stonewell on my way home and warn the Huddlers. No details, just that they might need to keep a man confined for a day or two."

Laura found herself again feeling that she'd landed in an unreal world where these shocking things were taken as normal.

He passed the paper to Stephen. "They'll be happy it's not smuggling business. That's getting risky. That's one problem about the end of the war," he said, putting away his tablet and picking up his riding cloak. "Too many ex-officers willing to become preventive men, and the navy with not enough to do, creating trouble all over the place. That's the only reason the slaves of Algiers were liberated, you know. A fighting navy with nothing else to do."

"And that expedition cost a shocking number of lives for little direct value to Britain."

"Freedom," Laura protested. "Thousands of Christian slaves were freed, and one was from Berkshire."

"A handful were English, yes. But only a handful."

"So we should care less about foreigners?"

"Resources are never infinite, Laura, so they must be used with discrimination."

Kerslake swung on his cloak. "I'll leave you to the ethical debate and pursue the practical." But he added to Stephen, "The key to ending smuggling is to lower taxes to reasonable levels. I intend to apply myself to that when I'm in the House of Lords. Will I have your support in the Commons?"

"Certainly." The two men shook hands. "And now you're associated with the Rogues, there'll be others."

"So I gather. Life takes strange turns, doesn't it? Less than a year ago I was an estate manager with no weightier responsibility than that."

He turned to bow to Laura, and she thought of one more thing.

"Could you alert us if the Reverend Jack Gardeyne arrives in the area? Lord Caldfort will probably send him here at some point."

"Of course."

He left, and Laura said, "A very impressive man."

"I certainly look forward to working with him in London. So, what do we do now?"

"I'm puzzling over something," she said. "Something about Kerslake . . ."

"What?"

But she'd realized what, and it wasn't something she wished to speak about. The oddness was that the young man had never once looked at her with the interest, or just the acknowledgement of beauty, that she'd come to accept as her due. How terrible that she was so accustomed to it. Perhaps this time in disguise would be good for her. Like a penitential fast.

She moved on to other matters. "So we have only Farouk and Dyer to deal with, and our hypothesis, that Dyer is Henry Gardeyne. I was thinking about that during the sermon."

"Tut-tut."

She grinned at him. "I was thinking that if Henry is alive, he must have changed. I'm going to reproduce my copy of his portrait and try to age him."

"An excellent idea."

Did he seem surprised?

She went to get her drawing portfolio and returned to find Stephen gone. He reappeared from his room. "Just checking the wall, but I think that's hopeless. They'd have to bellow for us to hear what they're saying."

"We might hear more through the doors."

"I thought of that, but didn't you notice how the boards in the corridor squeak? Embarrassing to be caught out there. More to the point, it might make them suspicious. We don't want them to make a run for it before we've sorted it all out."

She sighed and sat in a chair that caught the light. "It seems such a simple problem, doesn't it? But it has us stumped." She took out a clean sheet of paper and set to work. "When I've done this, we still have to find a way to compare it to Dyer. Perhaps when Farouk goes out . . ."

"Locked doors," he reminded her.

"They could be locked from the inside."

"Why?"

"Ah-ha! So you do think he's a prisoner. Thus, he's Henry Gardeyne!"

He laughed. "Checkmate. But I'm not willing to make any assumptions."

"Nor am I . . ." An idea occurred. "I think what I need to do is 'accidentally' leave the altered picture where people can see it. Mrs. Grantleigh, Topham, the servants."

"An excellent idea!" He leaned closer to look at her work. "What would ten years do to a man? Surely they can't have been comfortable ones. Adventuring. Imprisonment?"

Laura looked up from the light outline she'd drawn.

"Didn't the maid say Captain Dyer is pale? Some English people were imprisoned in France."

"But they were all released in 1814."

"Perhaps he was badly injured and has only just made it home."

"With an Egyptian servant? That is damned peculiar."

"It all is," she complained. "But I won't give up hope. Sit for me, Stephen. I need to see how a man's face changes."

He obliged, moving a chair opposite, but said, "I must point out that I'm not Gardeyne's age. I'm only twenty-six."

She smiled as she studied him. "I promise you, I do not see you as aged. Or," she added, "stuffy."

Their eyes met in wary acknowledgement of that kiss, but they weren't ready to talk about it yet.

Laura seized the excuse to make a quick sketch of Stephen, capturing the elegant lines that his body seemed to fall into so naturally, his long hands, and his high, intelligent forehead. She conveyed his features with a few strokes, unwilling to linger there. Long, straight nose, high cheekbones, flared brows, and clever lips.

She wasn't sure why that word came to mind, but it did. He'd always had expressive lips. When he saw her studying him, they turned up slightly in a guarded question.

"How do you see me, then?" he asked.

As the man I want naked in my bed.

That thought startled her with its brutal honesty, but Stephen—any man—deserved better than to be used to slake a widow's hunger. She returned to the drawing of Gardeyne and chose a safe response. "As a very good friend."

When she looked up again it seemed to her that Stephen's lips had hardened. Did he want to be more? Would a quiet life with Stephen not be so dull after all?

Later. There would be time enough later to work through all of this. She blinkered her mind on the task of creating a picture of an older Henry Gardeyne. That youthful roundness would have gone. Would he be as lean as Stephen? Frail, someone had said. She thinned the face close to the bone, hinted at sunken eyes, then turned the happy smile bitter. The hair?

Men wore their hair shorter now, so she removed most of the poetical locks. She fiddled with it, then passed it to Stephen. "I think he looks too old now. It's all guesswork."

"Older, but perhaps not too much so if he's had a hard time of it. He's even slightly familiar. More of a resemblance to Reverend Gardeyne, perhaps."

Laura moved the drawing so they could both see it. "I don't see that except in the general Gardeyne features. Jack is fleshy. A bit more like Hal, perhaps." But then she pulled a face. "It feels lifeless to me. I've never tried to do an imaginary portrait before. I don't know how."

"It'll do. We know what we're looking for now, and perhaps a glimpse in a window will be enough. Let's get you out for another dose of sea air, spyglass in hand. Sooner or later the man must obligingly sit at his window."

"It will be more difficult to study the inn during daylight."

He rose and rang the bell. "Heroes relish a challenge."

"Heroes?" she queried.

"We are equal in this enterprise, I think."

That warmed her, a warmth that lingered as she put on her outer clothing. Equals. For much of her life she'd not even considered that. She'd accepted that women, for all their qualities and abilities, were not the equals of men.

When had that changed? Perhaps some time in the past year when she'd had no husband, and when his

substitute, Lord Caldfort, had been so obviously frail
in mind and body. But perhaps the final straw had
been Jack.

Jack was the sort of man who expected to command
women by right, but she'd never felt any inclination
to bow down. Once she'd suspected that he wanted
to harm Harry, he'd become her enemy. One could
not feel subservient to an enemy.

Chapter 28

When they left the inn, Stephen kept his mind fixed on their purpose, but it was an effort. Moment by moment, Laura was shredding his sanity. He was even beginning to read wicked interest in her friendly glances.

"Let's move behind that wooden rig," he said. "We can probably study the Compass from there without being too obvious."

She agreed and they ambled down onto the beach in that direction.

"What is this?" she asked as they moved into position.

He looked at the tall timbers. "Perhaps something to support a boat in the building?"

From within the ugly, concealing bonnet, framed by faded curls and dark circles, her blue eyes sparkled. "Does it hurt to admit to ignorance about something?"

He smiled back. "Of course not. There are vast fields of human knowledge that have escaped me."

"Really? I've always been in awe of your knowledge."

A rational man would appreciate being admired for his mind.

He turned toward the Compass and focused the lens. "The curtains are up, but I see no one." He turned the telescope back out to sea. "Plenty of ships."

He passed the glass to her and she scanned the waves. After a while, she swung the spyglass around, pausing on one building after another until she could settle on the inn.

"You're right. Nothing to see." She lowered the glass and gave it to him. "We can't stay here doing this for long without being thought peculiar."

"Let's do one brisk walk along the front," he said, putting away the telescope. "That will be expected."

"Not too brisk," she reminded him as they walked back up to the road. "I'm frail."

"Perhaps I should hire a chair. I could wheel you up and down."

She grinned at him. "That might be fun."

"Cousin Priscilla," he said with a quelling look, "does not enjoy fun."

"Yes, she does. She finds her fun in gossip and nosiness."

Laura found it was hard to be Cousin Priscilla while strolling in the autumn sunshine arm in arm with Stephen, especially when the rustle of the waves seemed to whisper of wickedness.

"I'm not at all surprised that seaside visits have become so popular."

"Invigorating, isn't it?"

That's one way of putting it.

She'd expected to be comfortable with Stephen, especially once they'd dealt with the embarrassment of his proposal and her unfortunate reaction. They'd even cleared the lingering sourness of Lady Skylark. She'd expected a return to before, when they'd been living in the remains of youth, still like brother and sister.

Now, despite occasional teasing, they were man and woman, and this—a stroll, arm in arm—was the sort of thing a man and woman, not a youthful pair of friends, would do. It had the same effect as eating a meal together had, just the two of them.

They passed a notice about an upcoming assembly, a sight that reminded Laura of how she'd used to avoid dancing with Stephen. She'd not disliked it, but it had seemed too like dancing with a brother. Everyone knew that no young lady would do that if she could obtain a real partner.

How very, very strange.

They arrived back at the inn and were snared by Topham bearing an invitation to take tea with the Grantleighs. It was impossible to completely refuse, but Laura made the excuse of tiredness and sent Stephen down alone. She spent the time migrating between listening at the wall and watching through the window, and achieved precisely nothing except even more tangled thoughts.

By the time Stephen returned, she'd abandoned vigilance and was reading a book. "Did the Grantleighs know anything about the other guests?" she asked.

"Nothing new. As you said, Mrs. Grantleigh saw them arrive. Dyer was pale and swathed in blankets, and Farouk carried him upstairs." He looked over her shoulder. "Ah-ha! A novel."

"I never denied reading them."

"*Guy Mannering*. It's good."

She cast him a look of exaggerated astonishment. "Sir Stephen Ball reads novels!"

"We took turns reading from *The Mysteries of Udolpho* once."

"When we were very young." But she smiled. She was coming to love these returns to the past. "We even made a play of it, remember? You were noble Valancourt, and I was Emily because you refused to act love scenes with your sister."

"It would have been most unnatural."

"You could have romanced Juliet."

"She was too young for such things." But he was

smiling in an interesting manner. " 'Ah, Emily!' " he quoted. " 'I have then little cause to hope. When you ceased to esteem me, you ceased also to love me!' "

"You remember that? Wait, wait . . ." The words popped into her memory. " 'And if you had valued my esteem, you would not have given me this new occasion for uneasiness!' Said, as I remember, turned away, with pale and faltering hand stretched back to dissuade insistence." She stood and took the pose.

"Exactly. 'Is it then true, Emily, that I have lost your regard forever?' "

"I turn, hands clasped to trembling bosom. 'Oh, sir, explain yourself.' "

" 'Can any explanation be necessary?' I demand imperiously. 'Oh, Emily, how could you so degrade me in your opinion, even for a moment!' "

"I believe you skipped some there," she complained. "It was a long speech."

"He did prose on a bit. That was the crux of it. She should have trusted. If these feather-witted heroines would only trust their heroes, all would be simple."

"If men were not so pestilential, it would be easier for heroines to trust despite the evidence!"

"On with your part, wench."

"I'm not sure I remember it." But she knew her lips were twitching. "Oh, very well. 'Valancourt!' " She stretched out her hand to him. " 'I was ignorant of all the circumstances you have mentioned—' "

" 'All,' note. Even she thought he went on a bit."

" 'The emotion I now suffer,' " she quoted sternly, " 'may assure you of the truth of this. Though I had ceased to esteem—' "

"Fickle . . ."

" '—I had not taught myself entirely to forget you.' "

"Weak willed . . ."

"Say your next line, sir."

He laughed. " 'Am I dear to you, then, still dear to you, my Emily?' "

"Dense dolt. Well might she demand, 'Is it necessary that I should tell you so?' And then she says, 'These are the first moments of joy I have experienced since your departure. . . .' "

Though there were no similarities between the dire tale of Emily and her Valancourt, those words drew special meaning from the air.

"And then," he said softly, taking her hand, "we kissed, as I remember."

"As tentatively as if our lips were flame to gunpowder."

He drew her closer. "We could do better now."

She saw all the dangers, but said, "I would hope so," and cooperated as he lowered his lips to hers.

It was as chaste a kiss as that they'd dared all those years ago, on a stage in front of their families and a few guests, but it was not tentative. They both knew kisses now, and their lips brushed and played with delicate experience.

The effect rippled down through Laura like warm wine, pooling as desire, then flaring into intoxicating fever. Though it took all the strength she possessed, she did not press closer, did not tighten her hand on his arm, did not open her mouth to taste him fully. But her heart pounded and her legs began to tremble . . .

He broke the kiss and stepped back. "Ah, youth. Ah, drama."

His lids were lowered, concealing his expression, but color had risen in his cheeks. She thought to check what else might have risen, but he turned away to look out at the restless sea. "Astonishing what lurks in our memories."

"Yes." She tried for a light tone to match his, but how could she manage that when aware of his body as if he wore no clothes at all? Her hand itched to explore his long back and taut buttocks, his chest, his muscled abdomen, and more. . . .

"I might as well go out again," he said, "being healthy and restless. I should check at the King's Arms to see if they know anything there. I can use the excuse of considering a move from this heathen enclave."

Sanity was returning and his absence would make self-control easier. "What do I do? I tell you, I'm tempted to break down HG's door."

In lieu of other passions.

"Patience. This is only our first day."

He meant only the first day of their enquiries here, but Laura's body clenched as if that were a promise. Considering the changes in the day since they'd arrived, what could happen in two or three more?

What should she allow to happen? Flame to gunpowder, which could destroy them both.

He walked to his bedchamber door but paused there and turned. If there had been any physical reaction, it had been controlled. "Promise me you won't rush into action while I'm gone."

"Rush into action?"

"I know you. If Farouk goes out, you'll be tempted to act on your own and try to see Dyer. Don't. It's too dangerous."

Laura sighed. "Very well, sir. I will try to restrain my mad passions."

If he caught the double entendre, he gave no sign of it as he left.

Chapter 29

Laura settled back to her book, promising herself that she would indeed practice restraint. Matters were too important for self-indulgence. The novel could no longer hold her interest, however, when thoughts of Stephen dazzled her mind.

Three times they'd kissed, now. First awkwardly, then angrily, then . . . truly. Yes, though nothing had been said, that had been a true kiss, one that in any other circumstance could have led to more.

She put the book aside but saw the dangers of sitting here sunk in such thoughts. She had to be sensible and in control. There must be something useful to do, something distracting. She went into Stephen's bedchamber and listened at the wall.

A murmur of voices as indistinguishable as the murmur of the sea. No sign of fear, anger, or pain.

She glared at the wall and even checked it for a crack at the top, bottom, or sides. The Compass Inn was in unfortunately good repair. She turned to go back into the parlor, but instead she drifted to the bed as if pulled there by a magnet.

She trailed her hand over the rough wool of the blue coverlet, inhaling, finding Stephen in the air. She couldn't resist pulling the coverlet down from the pillows so she could touch the place where his head had rested.

Maudlin nonsense.

Yet she picked up the pillow and inhaled, pressing her face into it. She'd not been aware before of knowing Stephen's smell like this, but she did. It was as distinctively his as his signature, and it trickled into her body, exciting every part of her.

She held the pillow closer, sinking to sit on the bed, igniting at the thought of being here with him, of breathing in his skin, licking his sweat. . . .

With a gasp, she scrambled off the bed. What did she think she was *doing*? Desperately she put back the pillow and tidied the covers, smoothing them over and over to erase any trace of her idiocy. Then she fled back through the parlor to the privacy of her own room, feeling, when she closed the door, as if she'd shut out the devil.

After a minute or so, she peeled herself away from the door and went to the mirror. She didn't look deranged—but then she saw a smudge of the dark around her eyes and realized she must have left some trace of her face paint on Stephen's pillow.

"Perish it!" she muttered, ripping the cover off her own pillow. She raced back to Stephen's room and dashed to the window to check for his approach. No sign. *Please heaven, keep him out for a while longer!*

As she'd feared, smears of brown marked the pillowcase. Heart thundering with urgency, she stripped it off and replaced it with hers, then straightened the bed again. Would he notice any difference? She'd normally think not, but Stephen was infernally perceptive.

She hurried back and put his pillowcase on her pillow. Only then did she feel safe.

The feverish energy lingered and she paced her room, multiplying the miles to Redoaks by the year, 1816, by her age, by the time. . . .

It didn't help. She was tempted to clutch and inhale her own pillow now. She forced herself away from her bed. In fact, this would be an excellent time to go down to the public parlor and exhibit her picture. She might learn other gossip there, too.

She wrapped her virulent shawl around herself, picked up her drawing portfolio, and left the room, assembling her persona of Priscilla Penfold. In fact, Priscilla Penfold would venture down the creaking corridor, just in case she might overhear something. It did her no good, however. The adjacent rooms could be uninhabited for all she could tell.

She headed downstairs, trying to appear timid. However, as she descended the stairs she decided Priscilla Penfold wasn't timid at all. She was the sort of woman who pretended uncertainty as a disguise. She would flutter and hesitate in order to hide the fact that she was a weasel in search of eggs of gossip.

She would worry out loud that she was bothering people so that everyone would have to assure her that she wasn't. She would timidly declare that she was just a silly woman so that everyone would have to pay attention to what she said.

Laura struggled not to laugh. She was describing a particular person she knew, someone who had exasperated her for years.

She crossed the hall and entered the small, bow-windowed parlor. It was painted a pleasant yellow, perhaps to suggest sunshine even on a dull day, and warmed by a large fire. It even seemed free of drafts. The only occupant, however, was a sinewy gentleman in a chair to the left of the fire who was drinking tea and reading a newspaper, pince-nez on his long nose.

He rose when she entered, but then resumed his seat and occupation.

Laura sat by the window and looked out, but the wind was rising and few were taking the air. The sea was steel gray and choppy, and she wondered if they were in for a serious storm. She opened her portfolio on a small table and took out a clean sheet of paper, leaving her aged sketch of Henry Gardeyne exposed.

The gentleman was engrossed in his newspaper.

Laura began to sketch, trying to catch the feel of the gathering clouds as she waited for someone else to come into the room. A lad came in with a bobbing bow and put more wood on the fire. He hardly raised his eyes and certainly didn't look at her drawing.

Laura drew boats tossed by the growing waves, and did a quick sketch of a man chasing after his tumbling hat. She silently cheered when he caught it just short of the sea. But it was becoming clear that she was unlikely to encounter anyone here except the newspaper reader.

To speak to a strange man was somewhat improper, but she was a dull widow, not a brash flirt.

She started with a timid clearing of the throat. When he looked up, she said—hesitantly, of course, "I fear we are in for a storm, sir. Are you, too, staying here for your health?"

He lowered his paper and looked at her over his glasses. "Only in a manner of speaking, ma'am. I am Dr. Nesbitt of this town, and I have been visiting a patient here."

She remembered Topham mentioning him. This could be exactly what she'd hoped for!

"Poor Captain Dyer?" she asked.

"No, ma'am." His look had become alert. "The captain requires medical care?"

Laura suppressed disappointment and fluttered. "Oh, I'm sure I don't know, sir. But the innkeeper said he is an invalid, and it seems he never leaves his rooms. They're next to ours, you see. Those taken by my cousin, Sir Stephen Ball."

"Ah. Sir Stephen." He beamed. Clearly her status had immediately risen.

"So kind of him," she simpered. "For my health, you see. But Captain Dyer has only the one servant, it would appear, and he is a foreigner." She lowered her voice as such people often do when about to criticize. "He wears a *turban*—the servant, sir—and I fear he is dosing the poor captain with *foreign nostrums*."

The doctor removed his spectacles. "My, my. That certainly raises alarms, ma'am." He rose, putting his newspaper on a table. "I shall have a word with Topham and see if I may tender my services."

With a bow, he left. Laura supposed it was too much to expect that if he attended Dyer he'd return and report to her, but if she remained here, she might learn something. She eyed Dr. Nesbitt's newspaper, tempted to read it, but it would be out of character for Mrs. Penfold. In her experience, nosy gossips were never interested in important matters.

She returned to her sketching but heard returning footsteps and turned to the door, wearing an anxious, questioning look.

"It is as you described, ma'am," Dr. Nesbitt said, shaking his head. "But from what Topham says, Captain Dyer is in a chronic rather than an acute state. Sad to say, medicine often has little to offer such cases other than rest and fresh air. Bleeding and cupping sometimes, but I am not in favor of those when the patient appears pale, which is as Topham describes him. I will, however, send over a bottle of my patent restorative, which might assist his return to health."

He had come over and now looked at her drawing. "Why, ma'am, you are quite an artist!"

Laura realized that her artistic ability was out of character with Priscilla Penfold, too, but there was no help for it now. She simpered. "So kind. Just my little hobby."

He had turned to the sketch of Henry. "Now there's a man who looks in need of my services, ma'am. Consumption?"

Laura was caught unawares, and any fluster was completely natural. "Oh, dear, I do hope not, sir. That is my brother. He . . . er . . . suffered a serious accident in the hunting field, but is recovering well now."

"I'm glad to hear it, Mrs. Penfold, but if he were my patient, I would want him to take my restorative draught. For now, however, I must take my leave. Another patient awaits."

With that, he drained his teacup, tucked his paper under his arm, bowed, and left. In a few minutes she watched him struggle against the wind down the road until he turned into a nearby house.

She waited. A young couple came in, windblown and laughing, to take tea. It turned out that they had driven from Seaton with no care for the weather. Laura suspected that they were on their honeymoon, and that perhaps wind and wild sea was exactly what they wanted, which made them positively irritating.

They left, rapt in one another, and Laura hoped the young man could manage to keep his mind on the road. She was about to give up and return to her room when Mrs. Grantleigh came in. What good fortune that she hadn't yet put away the picture.

The elderly woman paused. "Mrs. Penfold. Do you mind if I join you? My husband is dozing, and I like a change of scene but cannot go too far."

"Not at all." Laura pointed encouragingly to a nearby chair, remembering to be Priscilla Penfold when she would much rather befriend this poor woman. "I fear a storm is rising."

"I fear so, too," the older woman said, sitting by the picture but looking out at the sea. "So dismal."

Laura liked storms, but she fervently agreed. "I just met Dr. Nesbitt. He seemed an excellent man."

That set Mrs. Grantleigh off on an account of the doctor's kind but ineffectual treatment of her husband, along with the other doctors consulted back home in Cambridge, and in Bath.

Then, at last, she looked down and started. "My, that is an excellent portrait, Mrs. Penfold." She glanced around, clearly not believing what she saw. "Your work?"

Laura simpered again. "Just my little hobby."

Mrs. Grantleigh's glance was shrewd, and perhaps even suspicious. No fool after all. "A talent, Mrs. Penfold," she said firmly. "You should not hide it under a bushel."

Laura felt herself flush beneath her sallow cream. It was partly because she was caught in a lie, but also because she hadn't done anything in particular with her talent.

Mrs. Grantleigh was studying the picture, however. "There is something slightly familiar about this man," she said, "and yet I do not know. . . . Perhaps I might have known him before he was so unwell?"

She looked up, demanding an answer.

Laura had to tell the same story. "My brother, Reginald," she said, cheeks so hot she feared they'd melt the paint. "He suffered an accident in the hunting field. We . . . er . . . feared we might lose him, so I did that sketch. But he is much recovered now. I don't think he has ever visited Cambridge, however. He lives year round in the Shires."

Mrs. Grantleigh pushed the picture away with a moue of distaste. "Then you are doubtless correct, Mrs. Penfold. I have no patience with men who use their lives for nothing but sport. How refreshing to know a man like Sir Stephen . . ."

Laura let her sing Stephen's praises and slid away the picture. What was she to make of that moment of recognition, however? Did the picture look like Dyer, but too frail? After some thought, she tidied her portfolio and let the original copy of Henry's portrait flutter to the floor.

"Oh!" she exclaimed and grabbed for it. Then she turned it toward Mrs. Grantleigh. "My dear younger brother, Cedric. So scholarly."

The older lady smiled. "And he looks more robust and happy for it, Mrs. Penfold. May he be saved from the ways of dissipation and vice. Oh, my, look at the time!" She rose. "But it has been most pleasant to chat with you, Mrs. Penfold. I hope we can do so again."

She left the room, and Laura frowned at her pictures. Mrs. Grantleigh had shown no recognition of the picture of young Henry. None at all. If only she'd been able to ask if the familiarity with the aged one had anything to do with Captain Egan Dyer.

Topham. He was the other person most likely to have seen Dyer. Laura thought up and discarded a number of cunning ways of getting the man in here, but then shrugged and pulled the bellpull. A maid—a young, plump one she did not know—bustled in. "May I help you, ma'am?"

Laura willed her to come over to the table where the drawings still lay, but she stayed by the door.

"I wish to speak to Mr. Topham," she said.

In moments, the innkeeper was there, bowing. Laura stayed seated by the window and the man did come over. "What may I do for you, Mrs. Penfold."

"Oh, dear, oh, dear," said Laura with a hand to her chest, "I have been watching the storm rise. Are we safe, sir? Are we safe?"

He put on a beaming smile. "Safe? As houses!" He chuckled at his own joke. "Certainly a little storm is rising, but the Compass has weathered a hundred such."

She gave him an uncertain smile. "If you are quite sure. I was thinking that the King's Arms . . . it being constructed out of stone . . ."

He bridled. "Not at all, ma'am. Only been there ten years. Not stood the test of time."

"Oh, I see. Thank you. That does make me feel safer. Perhaps you could help me gather my papers, Mr. Topham. My hands are quite unsteady."

He quickly did so, flattering her artistic abilities but showing no recognition. Then he tenderly escorted her upstairs and left to arrange a steadying brew of brandied tea.

Laura sat at the table and spread the two portraits in front of her. "Did Mrs. Grantleigh recognize you, Henry, or was it some other fleeting resemblance? Are you dead, or are you Dyer?"

She frowned over that, wondering if the name Dyer was some complicated play on *die*. They had never solved the puzzle of the name Oscar Ris.

A gust of wind rattled the windows and she rose to look out, wishing Stephen would return. The light was going now and she wanted him here, safe. She smiled wryly at that, knowing her feelings flowed deeper and deeper by the moment.

She started at a knock, and called for the person to enter. It was Jean with the brandied tea. She watched carefully as the maid went to the table and put her tray down there, carefully away from the drawings. The maid paused, looking at them for a moment.

Laura hurried over. "My little hobby," she said.

"They're very cleverly done, ma'am."

Laura tittered. "People keep saying they recognize them, but they are my brothers who have never been here. I do find, however, that sometimes strangers look like people we know."

"That's the truth, ma'am. I went right up to someone in Seaton who I thought was a woman who used to live next door. And I must say that one"—she nodded to the aged one—"does put me in mind of someone."

"A guest, perhaps?" Laura prompted.

The maid shrugged. "I can't bring one to mind, ma'am. Likely it's just as you say and he reminds me of someone else. Folks aren't so different in the end, are they? Now, shall I pour your tea? And do you want to order your dinner, ma'am?"

Laura sighed. "No, thank you."

When the maid had left, she sat and poured herself tea. She could smell the brandy already. She supposed smuggling country had an ample supply. She sweetened it and sipped, enjoying the strong taste and the warmth, then carried the cup over to the window to watch the storm grow.

She drained the cup and found clean paper to do rapid sketches of wind and weather, reveling in the raw energy of the storm as shown in roiling clouds, whipping waves, and people fighting to make their way to their homes.

A blue turban caught her eye. Farouk! He was striding down the street away from the inn, robe flapping around his legs in the wind. Where could he be going? Because she had her pencil in her hand, she sketched him.

He was a fine figure of a man—tall, straight, and vigorous. What was he doing here, writing letters to an English lord, offering to kill for pay? She drew in palm trees behind him, bent in the wind, trying to imagine going to Egypt and attempting such a crime. Impossible. She and Stephen must be missing pieces of this puzzle, but she couldn't even imagine what they were.

If Jack wished to kill Harry, that was evil, but she understood why. An Egyptian coming to England to offer out of the blue to kill Henry Gardeyne, a man supposedly dead ten years ago? It was a fairy tale.

Then she saw Stephen emerge from the King's Arms, spot Farouk, and plot a course that would intersect. She sketched him, too. Merely the sight of him flushed heat through her body. How was she to cope with this?

The two men met and exchanged a few words, before Stephen turned toward the Compass and Farouk walked on, past the King's Arms. Where on earth was he going?

At least Stephen would know how good Farouk's

English was. Every scrap of information could be useful. As she thought this, she drew Stephen walking back toward the inn, clutching at his hat. Suddenly he gave up, and she saw his grin as he took it off and let the wind whip through his hair.

She smiled in sympathy, wanting to run out and let the same wind blow her hair and clothes, down by the edge of the wild sea. Alas, alas, that she was Priscilla Penfold and not Lady Skylark.

When he came in, bringing crisp, salty air with him, she said, "The windblown, I assume," referring to the fashionable hairstyle.

He grinned. "Definitely."

"I saw you speak to Farouk. Is his English good?"

"Fair, though heavily accented. He confirms he's from Egypt. His master is not well but improving. They plan to stay here indefinitely. That's it."

"I tried the pictures on the visiting Dr. Nesbitt, Mrs. Grantleigh, Topham, and Jean, the maid. Jean and Mrs. Grantleigh thought they might vaguely recognize the older picture, but surely if it looked like Dyer, whom they saw recently, it would be more than that. Nothing at the King's Arms, I assume."

"Just the expected rumbles about heathen savages."

"Then there's nothing for it but invasion. Farouk's out, though where on earth is he going?"

"Not far in this weather. It's too risky," he added. "Invasion, I mean."

Laura twitched her shawl into place. "Nonsense. I can try sociability. Priscilla Penfold would do that as a cover for her nosiness. Should I send a message through a servant? No"—she headed for the door—"simply knock."

"Laura." He caught her on the way to the door, as he had in Caldfort. His hand sizzled on her arm.

Perhaps he'd meant to stop her, but he let go and stepped back. "Very well. But be careful. I'll be on guard. Don't hesitate to scream."

"I am the best one to do this," she said, understanding. "Priscilla is precisely that sort of curious meddler."

"I know."

She smiled her thanks, then, correct manner in place, ventured into the corridor. As there seemed to be no other guests up here, she wasn't surprised to find it deserted. All the same, she stayed in character and minced along to tap on the door next to Stephen's.

Hearing nothing, she knocked harder. Ear to the door, she thought she heard a faint movement. "Captain Dyer?" she called in a fussy voice. "It's Mrs. Penfold, a fellow guest. I wondered if you would like some company, sir."

Silence.

She'd expected that.

"Are you all right, sir?" Having given reason for her concern, she turned the knob.

Again, the door was locked. Disappointing, but it supported her hopes. If Farouk locked the doors when he left, Dyer was a prisoner. If Dyer was a prisoner, he must be Henry Gardeyne, Harry's savior.

She glanced behind and saw Stephen watching her. She waved him back. If this was the parlor, then the next door must be the bedchamber. She walked along and tried that one.

It, too, was locked.

She returned to the parlor door and tried another knock, but heard nothing to indicate anyone was there at all.

She returned to Stephen. "He made one slight noise."

"If he wanted to be rescued, don't you think he'd make more? And you're only just in time. Farouk only walked down to the sea, as if wanting air. He's almost back."

Chapter 30

Stephen was sure he would be a lunatic soon. Enacting a stage kiss, when he wanted Laura in his arms with passion. Letting her go into danger, no matter how slight. Sharing these rooms, assailed by her perfume and her body.

Even his bedroom now seemed to carry a ghostly hint of her fragrance. He was going to have to spend another night in that bed, surrounded by it, aware of Laura so close with nothing between them—except honor.

A sane man would want to be free of this torture as quickly as possible, but he dreaded the end of the brief adventure. It was clear that Laura, however, was desperate to be done with it.

"They might be becoming suspicious," he said. "That was the second time we've tried the doors."

"They don't know who it was the first time, and since I gave my name, I should seem innocent. Anyway, if Dyer is a prisoner, he may not tell Farouk. But we're getting nowhere! Let's go out again with the spyglass."

"Out? The light's going and I think a storm is rising."

She turned to the window as if doubting his words, but surely she could hear the wind, feel it beat against the windows? Outside, dark clouds were pouring into the bay and the storm whipped the sea into white-edged blades. Anchored boats were tossing so wildly some of them might break free in the night.

"Oh, perish it," she muttered, but then moved closer to the window. "I love storms."

"I remember."

He remembered her habit of running out to dance in torrents of rain, hair and clothes plastered to her. Strangely, he didn't remember being aroused by it, only concerned that she'd catch her death of cold. Perhaps he had been a dull dog.

"I've only been close to the sea in a storm once before," she said. "At Brighton. I danced at the edge of it, flirting with the crashing waves."

"I know. It was written about in the newspapers."

He'd been furious. Furious that she was still so foolish, that she might have been in danger, that Gardeyne had probably egged her on. That she'd frolicked as good as naked before the world.

She turned to him with a sane and rueful smile. "So they did. They disguised me as 'a wild-spirited Thetis of fashionable society,' with sly hints about the way the spray plastered my gown to my body. Hal was angry for some reason."

"Perhaps he feared you'd put yourself in danger." For the first time he felt some fellowship with the man.

She seemed surprised. "Perhaps he did. At least Thetis was famed as a good mother. Dipping Achilles into the River Styx to make him immortal. Of course she botched it, missing the heel she was holding him by."

Was she thinking of her own son, worrying that she'd not done enough to safeguard him?

"I believe the oracle said that if any part of her touched the water it would blacken and die."

"That shouldn't have weighed with her. Or she should have used a rope."

"But what if the rope dissolved? The gods never make things easy for humans."

" 'As flies to wanton boys are we to the gods,' " she quoted. " 'They kill us for their sport.' The Christian God is supposed to be more thoughtful and kind, yet Shakespeare was a Christian."

"Perhaps we all have times when we doubt the benevolence of God. As during any war." But then he grimaced. "This is too weighty a matter for a stormy night."

"Especially when I'm out of sorts because we've done a paltry day's work. Jack could be on his way tomorrow."

"But is not likely to be. Remember, he and Lord Caldfort have no reason to think there's urgency. Caldfort may not have told him yet. He may never tell him. Tomorrow the town will be busier. I'll go around and see what I can find out. And if necessary, we'll enlist the smugglers and invade."

He was rewarded with a smile, but then a powerful gust shook the whole house, making Laura look around anxiously. "It won't be so hard to play nervous Priscilla Penfold tonight. I love storms, but I have no taste for having a building blow down around me."

He wanted to take her into his arms, to comfort and protect her, but that would raise a different kind of storm. "Look on the bright side. If the walls come tumbling down, presumably we'll finally see Captain Dyer."

"At the gates of heaven."

She was truly anxious, and he might have gone to her, but with a knock the maid entered with wood for their fire.

Having built up the fire and filled the box with logs, she asked, "What will you like for your dinner, sir? We have a Flemish soup, and cock-a-leekie, and good fresh sole, poached or fried. There's the capon as was cooked with the leeks and a kidney pudding, and to follow, a ratafia dish and a bullace pie."

"Not the kidneys, please," Laura murmured, and he remembered that she'd always disliked them. He also thought he heard her stomach rumble. He could at least feed his lady.

He ordered the leek soup, fried sole, capon, and both pastries. She had a sweet tooth. "And Topham's best claret," he added, "with port and brandy to follow with cheese."

When the maid had left, he smiled at Laura. "I trust that will do."

She laughed. "You heard my stomach's demands. Perhaps a storm stimulates the appetite." She gave him a strange look and hurried on, "Shall we read *Guy Mannering* aloud? We can take turns."

"If you wish."

She went to her bedchamber to get the book.

An occupation that would bar any personal conversation, Stephen thought. That kiss had clearly alarmed her, though he thought he'd controlled himself heroically. If he'd managed any true heroics, she might be more impressed, but she was right; it had been a paltry day's work. He was at a loss how to better it without resorting to crude measures, such as breaking down a door. Under cover of the storm, perhaps?

Laura took a moment to collect herself. Stormy appetites, both for food and for a man. The wind rattled the building but it was the deep-throated roar of the sea that shook her, and the pounding beat of it that she felt from her feet up.

She remembered that time in Brighton. Hal had run out to her and swathed her in a cloak, berating her. But when they'd reached her bedchamber, their loving had been some of the best and fiercest ever. She almost felt it now, a fierce, pounding pleasure to the rhythm of the sea.

She swallowed, straightened, and returned to the parlor.

Stephen was sitting in one of the two chairs that bracketed the fireplace. She took the other.

Like a married couple, she thought, but again, she and Hal had rarely if ever spent quiet, domestic evenings. If Hal was sitting opposite her with nothing to do, he'd already have that look in his eye. . . .

She hastily opened the book and began to read, doing her best to slide away to Sir Walter Scott's Scotland. The plight of orphaned Lucy and the return of Guy Mannering from India seemed to meld with the storm, however, whispering of forbidden desire.

After a while, she passed the book to Stephen, hoping listening would be more calming, but she'd forgotten how well he read. He put on no airs and didn't try to act out the parts as if on the stage. He simply read the words, letting them spin out the story in her mind, though soon she was hearing him rather than the drama. Simply him.

The arrival of the meal was a relief, though Laura wasn't sure she could eat. At soon as they sat at the table, she realized that they needed a safe topic of conversation. Safe. Was anything safe tonight? Politics! A dry enough topic for a convent.

"Tell me about your adventures in Parliament."

"Adventures?" he said, serving her soup. "Hardly that."

"They must excite you at times."

"But they would bore you."

She halted her spoon between bowl and mouth. Moments ago she'd thought the subject dry, but she was hurt by that.

Perhaps he colored slightly. "Let's say that I don't know how to make amusing stories out of it."

He thought her nothing, a mindless *skylark.* "Why don't we talk about military reform?" she said briskly. "I know that many of our brave soldiers are now left in a sorry state."

"Yes, but that's a separate issue except in the matter of pensions. They are inadequate and often hard to obtain."

"Can't that be changed?"

"It's all tied in to the purchase system. . . ."

By the time they moved on to the main dishes, they were talking back and forth about issues of importance and Laura was no longer trying to prove a point. She was fascinated. When Stephen said, "We have to do something about the situation of children in factories and mines," she heard the *we* as acknowledgement that they were talking as equals.

Not lovers, and she was weak enough to feel a pang at that, but mental equals. "Factories are certainly terrible places."

"Yet industry is beneficial," he said, taking more meat. "It creates wealth and employment and leaves workers less dependent on the elements for survival. Consider this storm. Such a wanton act of nature ruins crops and blows away winter fodder."

She pushed aside her plate, frowning at him. "You think factories are better? People work such long hours and are often injured in the machinery. Even children."

"You are surprisingly well informed."

It was like a shock of cold water. "Surprisingly? Why do you persist in seeing me as having a head full of feathers? I beat you at chess, remember."

He suddenly smiled. "Yes. But can you claim to have been an eager consumer of information about social hardships and legislation back then?"

She wanted to, but it would be a lie. "I am truly interested now. Children not much older than Harry are put to work. That cannot be right."

He nodded. "That's why we need legislation. We've brought in laws to control the cotton factories somewhat. They're the worst offenders. Little fingers, they say, are nimbler. But there are so many others. Pudding?"

Laura was not much interested in more food, but she took a little ratafia pudding as he served himself to bullace pie and thick cream.

She ate a spoonful, smiling at him. "So you're charging in there, lance lowered."

"I hope you're not seeing me as Don Quixote, tilting at windmills."

"Sir Galahad, at least." She abandoned the pudding. "So what other Grails do you pursue?"

"Nothing so insubstantial, I hope." He, too, put aside his plate. "Port? Brandy?"

"Port, please."

Laura accepted the glass of ruby red liquid, recognizing, with a deep beat of her heart, that he was about to speak of the things most important to him.

He poured himself brandy and cut a piece of Stilton cheese. "My prime interest," he said, "is legal reform. Did you know that there are hundreds of capital offenses on the books? It's a hanging matter to damage London Bridge, or to destroy any tree not one's own. A man was executed for that only two years ago."

She stared at him. "How is that possible?"

"Because it's the law. I gather he was a petty criminal of long standing, but the authorities hadn't managed to catch him. When they snagged him on this one, they used it as a means to get rid of him."

"Good lord. But is it wicked of me to see the temptation?"

He pulled a face at her. "Honest, as always."

"But I do see your point. It shouldn't be possible to use the law like that."

He nodded. "Bad and outmoded laws have to be swept from the books because they create opportunities for injustice, but there's more. They also lead to lack of respect. It's not overenforcement that's hurting us, but underenforcement. Most people don't want to see others hanged for trivial crimes, so juries let criminals off entirely."

She drank a little more port, feeling the rich wine weave dangerously into her already fevered mind. "What punishment would you ordain? Whipping?"

Even that sent a tingle through her, though she'd never been interested in that vice.

"Barbarous," he said.

"Transportation? That seems as barbarous to me."

"But you have a good life here, Laura, with friends and a loving family. Many criminals have nothing to hold them and a taste for adventure. That makes the threat of transportation a weak deterrent. In fact," he added with a wry smile, "the army in India has a problem with men deliberately getting into trouble hoping for free transport to Australia."

Laura chuckled, aware that politics wasn't an antidote to arousal at all. In fact, this talk had stimulated her in a new and deeper way. Stephen was a Galahad, a hero, and his clarity and purpose built a hunger in her, a hunger to have him—brilliant mind, generous heart, and virile, handsome body—for her own.

She recognized what had turned sour in her marriage, what had made even passion unsatisfying in the end. Hal's idle, self-indulgent life had drained her respect.

Though her mouth was dry, she had to say something. "So, what do you suggest?"

He sipped his brandy, his eyes on hers, shadowed in the candlelight as if he was wondering what she was thinking. She hoped he didn't know.

"Criminals must be deprived of liberty and idleness."

"In prisons? They are rife with sin and scandal."

"Reformed prisons, where they're kept in separate cells and obliged to work. Meaningful work, too, not tow picking or the treadwheel."

She rested her elbow on the table and her chin on her hand. "It's a shame to have to confine people at all. Can we not rid the world of crime? So much of it arises out of poverty and unemployment. We see that now. Hard times have pushed even respectable people to vagrancy and theft."

"Thus," he said, with a warning glint of triumph, "we need industry and prosperity. Give a man hope of a better future for himself and his family and he won't risk it through crime. Give him property and he will support the laws that protect property."

She relaxed back, laughing. "I should have known you'd win a debate in the end."

The low candles showed how long they'd talked. They'd never rung for the dishes to be cleared, but Stephen had risen a couple of times to build up the fire. It seemed to her to have been the most perfect evening of her life.

"This has been wonderful," she said.

"Talk about Parliamentary committees and social reform?"

"Talk about something important. I don't know when I've last done that."

"When you were in London, did you not take part in some of the more serious female salons?"

She felt her cheeks color and laughed to cover it. "Heavens, no. There were too many other things to do. Oh, dear." She seized on her abandoned port and sipped. "That sounds as if I only discussed serious matters here out of boredom. I assure you that isn't true."

"I never thought that."

She put aside her port again, needing him to understand. "What I mean, Stephen, is that I was not serious-minded then. I *was* Lady Skylark. For me, the term *haute volée* was appropriate. I loved flying high. But we all change, and now my interests and occupations are different."

"You now prefer the quiet of the country?"

She grimaced. "Are you deliberately misunderstanding me? It was the tedium of the country that stirred an interest in politics and the issues of the day." She shook her head, seeking honesty because suddenly honesty was all-important.

"Why do we grow as we do, change as we do? If I had not had Harry, if Hal had not died, perhaps I would have continued on course to be a fashionable matron all my life. A patroness of Almack's, even, believing that who is let in and who is excluded is important. I was not unhappy before. You know I have never been as serious-minded as you."

"Yet you've just held your own in a challenging discussion." He rose and rang the bell. "Do you want tea or coffee now?"

She stared at him, shocked by his indifferent tone. She'd thought they were sharing thoughts and ideals, coming together on a deeply intimate level, but clearly he'd just been passing the time.

"Tea," she managed.

Two maids came to clean away the dishes, and soon Jean returned with the tea tray. Stephen asked her for a chess set.

"Chess?" Laura queried, wondering if she could reasonably plead tiredness and escape to her bed. It was only minutes past eight.

"Cards being inappropriate on a Sunday, don't you know."

"I don't remember you observing that extreme propriety before. I think you want a game at which you think you can beat me."

"Can I?"

"Almost certainly. I haven't played in years." She remembered the last game, and after a moment, spoke of it. "The last person I played was you."

"In that case, the last time you played, you won."

Jean returned with the set, and Stephen moved a small table between the fireside chairs. Seared by frustration, Laura set to work to beat Stephen again, but this time she was completely outmastered.

When the game was over, she could escape, ragged by the lashings of the storm and the snarl of the hungry sea, but above all by needs and hungers she'd never expected to feel for Stephen. It was more than physical. Tonight she'd become aware that she might after all enjoy a life of quiet dinners and political discussions by the fireside, but Stephen showed no sign of feeling the same way.

Was it just her ugly appearance? She peeled off her disguise and studied Labellelle in the mirror. Would Stephen want her again when she was beautiful? Would she want him on those terms?

She crawled into bed, still tormented by the storm that seemed to rattle the beams of the old building, and by her pillowcase, which whispered to her of the last head to lie on it—Stephen's.

No amount of calculations seemed to help, and she prayed that tomorrow they could solve the mystery of HG and escape the tortures of this jagged intimacy.

Chapter 31

Laura rose the next morning feeling she would hardly need her disguise to look haggard. Her mirror showed her familiar face, however, except for the ugly, glued-on mole. She traced brow, nose, and lips with one finger, wondering what beauty was and what the lack of it did.

Would Stephen have talked with her about political matters if she'd been Labellelle? Even faced with sallow skin and faded curls, however, he'd thought the matters that enthralled him would bore her.

He'd kissed her in the dark the first night.

He'd kissed her again when he could see the Penfold plainness, but only after their playacting as Valancourt and Emily. She was used to more from men and she didn't know this abode.

The inn clock struck, and she counted nine. Though she hated to do it, it was time to restore her ugliness before Jean came knocking with her water. She applied the cream and darkened around her eyes. The mole was still so firmly fixed that she was beginning to think it would be permanent, as her mother had always told them sour faces would become.

It occurred to her that it was quiet outside, and she peeped around the edge of the curtain. The sky was heavy with clouds and the sea still rippled with rough waves, but the storm had passed. Seaweed and wood littered the beach where there'd been none before, and down near the church a boat lay on its side, tossed up by the storm. She hoped no one had been aboard at the time.

It was relatively calm, however, and it was Monday. As Stephen had said, shops would be open and people about their business. Today they should be able to sort out the mystery, and if not, there was always armed force. She was in a fit state for leading the invasion herself.

She put on her wig, replaced her nightcap, then rang the bell.

Jean came promptly with the hot water. "Such a night of it, ma'am! Roof tore right off Farmer Tully's barn."

"I thought there was no danger."

"Not here, ma'am, but Joss Tully, he's a lazy man as doesn't keep his property as he should."

"I saw a boat up on the beach."

"Aye, the *Cormorant*. Broke its moorings, but it's not too badly off. Anything else, ma'am?"

"Has Sir Stephen breakfasted?"

"Not long ago, ma'am."

"Then bring my coffee and bread, please. And I'll have boiled eggs, as well, today."

"That's the spirit, ma'am! I told you as how the air here'd soon have you as right as a trivet."

When the door closed, Laura smiled. It seemed the whole town fancied itself a doctor. She dressed quickly and joined Stephen, finding him frowning at the letter from Farouk as he sipped his coffee. She sat and shared her thought about Dyer and *die*.

"Intriguing," he said with a quick, careless smile at her. "Wordplays?" He looked back at the letter. "But what does that give us for Oscar Ris? *Riz* is rice in French."

"And *ris* is part of the verb to laugh. This is all a joke?" she asked.

"In Latin, *os* means mouth. They have come to eat us all?"

His eyes were twinkling and she returned it. "The scarred mouth is eating rice?"

They laughed together, and Laura was suddenly certain that she would love to take breakfast with Stephen for the rest of her life. But that was for later, she sternly told herself. When they were safely away from here.

She took a boiled egg and a slice of toast. "You plan to wander the vast metropolis and ask questions? What am I to do?"

"As you imply, it won't take me long to squeeze Draycombe dry. You could keep watch in case any opportunity arises to see Dyer."

"Unless I walk along the outside wall like a spider to peer in the window, I doubt I'll achieve that. I think I'll station myself downstairs again with my pictures."

He rose. "Very well."

She buttered her toast. "Did you mean what you said about calling on Kerslake's men to force an entry?"

He hesitated for a moment, looking at her. "I'd prefer that to be our last resort. How long can you stay here?"

Something made her want to say *as long as you wish,* but she said, "I think I should return to Redoaks, at least, tomorrow, then return to Merrymead. To stay away longer would appear very strange, and Harry will be missing me."

She certainly hoped he was. She didn't wish him unhappy, but surely he must be missing her. "We've rarely been apart," she added, "and not at all since Hal's death."

He nodded. "Let's see what the morning brings and then make our plans."

He left, and she carried her slice of toast to the

window to watch him stride away. The wind was still brisk and he had to hold on to his hat like all the other men. Women's hats with ribbons were much more practical, perhaps because the women often had baskets and children to manage. They needed both their hands.

A group of small children played on the beach, hunting among the mess left by the storm. Harry would like it here. He'd never been to the sea. An ache told her how much she was missing him.

She could write him another letter. Send him a picture of the effects of the storm. She turned to do that, but realized it was impossible. She wasn't supposed to be here. She was supposed to be at Redoaks, inland.

Tears threatened, and some of them were from shame.

She wasn't ashamed of being here trying to solve the mystery of HG. She wasn't even ashamed of her passions, as long as she didn't succumb to them. But she hated to lie to her son.

She shook herself, put her half-eaten bread back on her plate, and went to get her drawing materials. She had little hope of recognition now, but what else was there to do?

A good part of the morning passed as she'd expected, with only Dr. Nesbitt joining her in the parlor. In conversation she learned that he was a single man and liked to stop at the inn for an occasional cup of tea as a break from his house. He admired her drawings again, but his only reaction to the picture of the older Cousin Henry was to remark how fortunate the gentleman had been to recover from what had clearly been a crisis.

Laura decided to modify the picture a little and try to make Henry a little less ill.

She was startled out of her work by that sixth sense that tells us that someone is staring at us. She looked up to see Farouk just outside the parlor door. Shockingly aware of the younger picture lying on the small table, Laura tried to give him a cold, forbidding look.

Perhaps it worked, for he turned away. A moment later, she saw him striding down the street. Why had he stopped like that? Had her attempt to enter the rooms yesterday raised his suspicions?

Was she in danger? If Farouk was the villain he appeared, he might not hesitate to dispose of a meddlesome woman. When she saw Stephen approaching the inn, delight surged into her for many reasons. She gathered her papers and hurried up to their parlor. She had only put her portfolio away when he entered, carrying a small brown box and looking very pleased with himself.

"What is that?" she asked.

"A present," he said, but she recognized a tease, so she wasn't surprised when he added, "But you'll have to wait."

Because he clearly expected her to be impatient, she merely said, "Very well," and sought a completely different topic of conversation. Ah, yes.

He'd gone into his bedchamber to discard his outer clothing, but left the door open.

"Yesterday, Mrs. Grantleigh and I were clucking over the fact that Captain Dyer didn't attend church, perhaps prevented by his wicked heathen servant, and I suggested that someone should tell the vicar. Farouk can hardly bar him at the door."

He emerged smiling. "Very good! As is your patience." He gave her the box. "Not precisely a present, though I hope you'll be pleased with it."

Laura opened the box and stared at the object inside. It looked like a metal cup with a long spout, but the spout came out of the bottom.

She picked it up and peered into the cup part. She could see out through the small hole at the end of the spout, but she looked at him in puzzlement. "A different way of spying? Do we apply it to the keyhole?"

"An interesting idea, but no. Though you're close, in a way. The other way around."

She put the end of the tube to her eye and looked at him. "I'm not impressed."

"Put it to your ear. It's an Auricular Enhancer."

"That sounds risqué!"

His eyes sparkled. "Only if I whisper improper suggestions down it. If you were hard of hearing, you could hold the spout to your ear, and when I speak into the wide end, my voice would be, by some magic of science that I didn't entirely understand, loud enough for you to understand me."

"Stephen, how brilliant! Where did you find it?"

"Remember the apothecary shop with a selection of helpful devices for the sick and elderly? I was hoping for information about something bought by Farouk for Dyer, but no. By then, I had been trapped into a guided tour of his wares. He's admirably enthusiastic. The Auricular Enhancer is his latest delight. I purchased it . . ."

"Not for me, I hope. I can't be both nosy and deaf."

". . . for my grandmother."

"If you mean the Dowager Lady Ball, she wasn't deaf last time I met her."

"Don't be distracted by details." He gestured toward his room. "Shall we try it out?"

"Yes!" But then she pulled a face. "Farouk's out, so there'll be no conversation."

"Blast. You're right. Let's try it, anyway. I'll go into my bedchamber, shut the door, and orate. You listen at the wall."

He left, and by the time she had the wide end pressed to the wall, he was already into some poem.

"Last noon beheld them full of lusty life,
Last eve in beauty's circle proudly gay;"

It was Lord Byron's passage about the Battle of

Waterloo from the latest part of his ongoing work
Childe Harold's Pilgrimage.

> *"The midnight brought the signal-sound of strife,*
> *The morn the marshalling in arms, the day*
> *Battle's magnificently stern array!*
> *The thunder-clouds pour o'er it, which when rent,*
> *The earth is covered thick with other clay,*
> *Which her own clay shall cover, heaped and pent,*
> *Rider and horse—friend, foe—in one red burial*
> *blent."*

She stayed there a moment, remembering men she'd
known who'd fallen in that terrible victory, then
pushed straight as he returned to the parlor.

"You lost friends, too?" she asked.

"Everyone did. But one, at least, returned from
the grave."

"Lord Darius."

"Yes. It worked?"

She shook off the solemn mood. "Excellently,
though I think you were in orator mode. I don't know
how clear an ordinary conversation would be. What a
shame Farouk is out."

"We have only to wait for his return. Then we might
finally discover what they're up to."

She sat and smiled at him. "I always knew you
were brilliant."

He bowed. "Thank you, fair lady. Now, I intend to
seek some reward in lunch." He pulled the bell.

"I'm hardly fair at the moment."

"Fair at heart."

It was an admirable sentiment, but it didn't satisfy
her.

"Did you learn anything in town?" she asked.

"Everyone's aware of Farouk, of course. It's not
wise of him to be so noticeable, but I've not come up
with a cunning purpose for it. I suspect he simply

doesn't understand the effect he has in a small English town."

"The vicar was concerned enough to mention it in his sermon."

"Let's hope it did some good. We don't want our business complicated by a riot."

"It might give us a glimpse of Dyer."

He smiled in acknowledgement. "Farouk's movements are noted, but all he seems to do is go for long walks. The only purchases I could uncover were a chess set, a pack of cards, and, believe it or not, a copy of Byron's *The Corsair*."

"Good heavens! Checking it for accuracy about the Arab world?"

Stephen shrugged, and Jean arrived then to take their order for lunch.

"And your morning?" he asked, when the maid had gone.

"Virtually nothing, though Farouk did stop and stare. My heart was in my mouth in case he came in and saw the pictures. But then," she added, "he probably wouldn't recognize them, either."

He gave her a commiserating smile. "Don't lose hope."

"I want so desperately for Dyer to be Cousin Henry. It means everything!"

"There are other ways to keep Harry safe, Laura. You can't think I would let anything happen to him."

She held out a hand and he took it. "I don't, but . . . A child cannot be kept safe, Stephen, as long as someone wants him dead. Wants it badly enough."

When he didn't argue, she knew that he saw that, too.

Their lunch arrived then, but Stephen waited by the window as the maid spread it on the table.

As soon as she left, he announced, "Here he comes."

Ignoring food, they both ran into his bedchamber.

He gave her the instrument and she smiled her gratitude for his letting her go first. She pressed the wide end to the wall and put the small end in her ear, waiting for Farouk to arrive.

Stephen was over by the corridor door. "He's coming. I hear the squeaks."

"It works," she whispered. "I heard the door open and shut."

Say something, she thought, concentrating fiercely. *Say something that makes it clear that Captain Dyer is Henry Gardeyne.*

Then she heard another click.

She moved back from the wall. "I don't believe it. After all this, Dyer must be in the bedroom, and Farouk's gone in there."

Stephen came to take the instrument and try, but then he shook his head. "Infuriating, but they can't stay there forever. Let's eat."

"What if Captain Dyer's taken ill and is confined to bed?"

"Then we sneak into the empty room farther down the corridor."

"Of course!"

She moved toward the door, but he stopped her. "Not yet. Give them a little time, and have your lunch."

Laura had a strong urge to act like the tempestuous girl she had once been, but he made sense. Sense would be easier all around if she wasn't in his bedchamber, so she went to the parlor and settled to bread and sliced ham.

Both of them, however, ate little and quickly, then Stephen rose. "I'll take first turn at the listening post."

It would be madness, besides being pointless, to crowd against him there, so she paced the parlor helplessly.

"Laura."

She started and whirled to find him at the door.
"They're there." He held out the listening device.

"You're a saint!" she exclaimed as she seized it,
and unthinking, she kissed him quickly on the cheek.
She was halfway to the wall before she realized what
she'd done. She carried on, anyway. What was there
to say?

She pressed the device to the wall and applied her
ear to the spout. "I can hear them!"

He came close, though not, she noticed, too close.
"What are they saying?"

"They're not orating. Hush."

She and Stephen were both whispering, even though
the men next door could not possibly hear what
they said.

"Nine?" she guessed. "Or mine? There's so much
silence."

"Only natural." He did come closer then to speak
in her ear. "It's unlikely, anyway, that they'll neatly
lay out their history and their plans for us. They must
both know them well."

She swallowed against the effect of his voice and
his breath, almost on her skin. "Except that if Dyer
is Henry, he doesn't know Farouk wants to slit his
throat for money."

She made herself be noble and passed the device to
him. As they exchanged places, their bodies brushed
together for a brief moment. He seemed not to notice.

"Anything?" she asked.

"A rattle."

"A *death* rattle?"

He grinned. "Of course not. Like dice. No, chess.
He bought a set, remember. Farouk has given Dyer
his choice of colors, and he has chosen white. Conversation has ceased. . . ."

Laura allowed the situation to give her permission
to lean against him, one hand on his shoulder. He was

so beautiful in his concentration, his features still as a classical statue, perfectly made.

In London his hair had always been carefully arranged. Now it was windblown, and not in the elaborate artificial manner of that fashionable style. She longed to comb it with her fingers, to brush a wave from his temple.

To run her hands through his hair.

To cradle his face.

To kiss. To kiss with all the passion burning inside her.

Stephen kept his eyes closed, as if that might aid hearing, but in truth he could not let Laura glimpse his emotions. A moment ago, she'd even leant against him, her whole body brushing down his side, her hand resting lightly upon his shoulder.

Through shirt and jacket, he shouldn't have been able to even feel that light hand, but it had burned. She'd moved now. Inches, at least, separated them and the world was colder. The temptation to turn and drag her into his arms almost broke him.

He moved away from the wall, put the Auricular Enhancer on the chest of drawers, and gestured her back into the parlor.

"I don't think they're likely to say much at the moment," he said. "They have all the feel of long familiars, with no need to talk. I confess to disappointment. Despite what I said before, I did hope they would immediately reveal something to make the situation clear."

"We have to keep listening."

"I suppose so." He couldn't bear it. "Perhaps I should put your plan into action, as well." When she looked puzzled, he added, "A visit to the vicar."

"Oh. It seemed so clever at the time, but is it necessary now?"

It was necessary to escape again. At this rate, he would be rushing out every half hour.

"Do you mind keeping vigil for a while?" he asked.

"No, of course not. Dividing our forces."

"Right." He grabbed his hat and gloves. "But remember, no matter what you hear, don't do anything rash."

"Stephen."

He turned at the door, alerted by her tone. Her severe tone.

"Stephen, I'm not a girl anymore. I know that sometimes these past days I've acted it, but it was . . . a sliding into what we were, I suppose. No more than a game." After a moment, she added, "I don't want you to treat me like a girl."

What did that mean?

"I'm sorry if I have offended you," he said.

"Of course not. We're friends beyond trivial offense."

Friends.

"I'm merely pointing out that I must do what I think best. I'm a woman full grown, which I believe to be in all practical ways the equal of a man."

"You denied being a bluestocking. You didn't tell me you were a radical."

"I'm not sure I was aware of it myself. But here I am, shaping my fate and my son's, and unwilling to give that over to anyone else. Even you."

He had never expected this. Never expected to discover in Laura a woman like this. He hadn't thought he could love her more, but it threatened to shatter him.

He felt he should say something eloquent, but he simply escaped.

Chapter 32

Laura bit her lip. She'd probably just destroyed any hope of happiness with Stephen, but without warning she'd come to a point of truth, a point of choice. She'd recognized herself for the first time and had to speak. And she had meant every word.

She felt as if the world had changed, but of course, it hadn't. Nothing had except her. It was as if she was settling into a new home and must make it comfortable. Whether Stephen was part of it remained to be seen. They would get nowhere useful in this hothouse of emotions, however. They needed to solve the mystery and return to normal life—ideally a life where Harry was no longer heir to Caldfort.

She headed for Stephen's room, but then thought of something. She found paper and pencil to record what was said, then went to the wall.

She paused at the end of his bed, but more in thoughtful contemplation than in rash passion. She knew now what she was, and she knew what she wanted. As a woman full grown and responsible for her actions, she must be careful.

She put a chair by the wall, grateful that it fit in the space, then settled herself as comfortably as possible. The irritating men still said nothing except for the casual comments on the game.

She began to record the conversation anyway,

though it was awkward with one hand required for the listening device. She hoped she could decipher her scribbles later.

Dyer: Check!
Farouk: I should have seen that.

Thank heavens the two voices were distinctive. Farouk's was deeper and stronger, not in volume but in character. HG's was higher and less certain. Did that fit Henry Gardeyne?

Silence settled, so she marked it with a line. She wished there was a clock here. She would note the time and length of the silences. Pointless, but it would feel as if she were doing something.

Dyer: You devil!

Said admiringly, warmly. If Dyer was Henry Gardeyne, he had no suspicion that his head was on the block.

She didn't like calling him Dyer. She wanted him to be Henry Gardeyne, key to Harry's safety, but she compromised on HG, who according to the letter had sailed on the *Mary Woodside* and been the guest of Oscar Ris.

Scarred mouth rice, she thought with a twist of the lips. She feared she was clinging to cobwebs. What could explain Cousin Henry staying away for ten years?

Do you sometimes miss it?

Laura started out of her thoughts. Miss what? She grabbed the pencil and tried to nudge her paper straight. That had been HG.

F: Strangely, I do, but freedom is better.

Freedom! Laura felt as if her heart was bruised. They had been *convicts?*

HG: *Yes, but I miss the sun.*
F: *I believe the sun does shine in England.*
HG: *Laughs. I think I remember that. Faintly.*

Sun. New South Wales, the penal colony, had a hot climate, didn't it?

The men settled back to their game and Laura ignored their occasional comments. She was reading over those few, hope-destroying words.

HG had lived in England once, but was now more used to a hot climate, which was linked with imprisonment. It seemed that they'd been imprisoned together. She'd thought only British people were sent to New South Wales, but perhaps they had only to break British law.

She realized something then. Farouk had spoken perfect English, not accented at all. He must have been educated under British rule, probably in India, and Stephen had mentioned men in the Indian army committing crimes in order to be sent to New South Wales.

She pressed her hand to her head. It seemed horribly clear that the two men next door were criminals intent on extortion, but how did this link at all to Henry Gardeyne? He could not have ended up a convict, and he'd been nowhere near India!

She stilled, listening. Had that been a clink in the parlor? Their parlor!

She rose in shock. Had Farouk somehow realized what she was doing and crept around to attack? And—stupid!—she'd left her pistol in her bedchamber.

She put down the hearing device and crept, heart hammering, to the door. Eased it open . . .

To find only Jean, filling the log bin. The maid saw her, however, and her eyes went wide.

Oh, Lord! Here she was, emerging from her male cousin's bedchamber.

"Sir Stephen is out," she said, fluttering. "I . . . I saw a tear in his handkerchief and thought I would repair it while he was gone."

The maid didn't look impressed, but she didn't seem much interested, either. She probably assumed that nosy Mrs. Penfold had been poking around in her cousin's belongings.

Merely to stay in character, Laura asked, "Do you take wood to Captain Dyer?"

"No, ma'am. That Farouk collects it himself, which is a blessing, for they use a lot."

"Because they come from a hot climate, I assume."

"Nothing wrong with a bit of brisk English weather. As I hear it, those hot places breed diseases."

"It seems they do."

"And it's wrong that the captain stays in his stuffy room all the time, ma'am. Sea air is *good* for you. Everyone says so. I hope their letter comes soon."

"Letter?" Laura inquired, merely to keep the conversation going.

"Captain Dyer expects a letter, ma'am. Farouk asks about it every day. Says he's to be told as soon as it arrives."

"From family, I suppose." From Caldfort, in fact. It was good to have confirmation that Lord Caldfort had not yet responded, though if Dyer and Farouk were the villains they appeared to be, she was inclined to let Jack murder them!

The maid shrugged, indicating ignorance. "Likely they're awaiting news before traveling on. Always wise, that, ma'am. My auntie went all the way to Nottingham to visit her sister, and when she arrived her sister'd gone off to Wales!"

"What a confusion. Yes, very wise to wait."

The maid left and Laura returned to her listening post, praying to have her earlier conclusions proved wrong. She caught Farouk saying a clear, "Yes."

She hissed with annoyance. If only she'd heard the question. But they were talking again. She grabbed her paper.

HG: I'm so tired of this, Fellow.

Fellow? It sounded like a name. She put a question mark against it. Perhaps she'd heard it wrong.

F: Not much longer.
HG: Then Paris?
F: It's no warmer there, you know.
HG: Greece, then, or Italy. Do you want to stay here? You said it was too dangerous.
F: Yes, you're right, Des. South Carolina, perhaps. Or even Florida. I hear the Spanish are welcoming.
HG: Farther away from British influence?

Voices dropped and she couldn't catch words.
Des? Laura underlined that. Desmond? An Irish name? She didn't think HG had an Irish accent. Despard, Desford, Desalles. Certainly not short for Henry or Gardeyne. It was like the last nail in a coffin, especially with that mention of wanting to be away from British influence. She hadn't thought convicts escaped from New South Wales, but anything was possible.

HG: I'm frightened, Fellow. This isn't going to work.
F: It will, nuranee. Trust me.

Nuranee. An Arabic term—or what language did they speak in Egypt? She couldn't care. These men were clearly not what she had hoped. She made herself read the words as the conversation of two petty criminals intent on a swindle. They fit all too well. Get some money from Lord Caldfort—though HG was afraid the plan wouldn't work—and then flee the country because it would be too dangerous to stay.

She tried to make the conversation fit HG being Henry, but shook her head. Close to tears, she put aside the paper. Whatever these men were up to, Henry Gardeyne was long dead and so Harry's destiny would not change. If she didn't do something, her son would soon be dead, too!

She rose, hands gripped together. She'd do *anything*, but she couldn't imagine what. She knew Stephen would help, but as she'd said, all his intelligence, influence, and legal knowledge couldn't keep a small child safe.

He would bring the Rogues with him. Her brief time with Nicholas Delaney told her that he would support her cause, but there were stronger forces. Lord Arden, heir to a dukedom, and some other titled gentleman.

Even they couldn't help, however, as long as Harry was in Jack's power.

She drew in a breath.

She had to remove Harry from Jack's power, and the only way to do that was by marriage, marriage to a man powerful enough to override Lord Caldfort's will, whether it be his purpose now or his testament when he was dead. Why hadn't she seen it before? The right stepfather for Harry was his best protection, and now she understood Stephen's reputation, the choice was clear.

How could Lord Caldfort argue that Harry would learn less by living with Stephen than by living at Caldfort? And when Lord Caldfort died, Stephen would know how to work with Harry's trustees to remove Jack from the local living. Find him a better one, but far, far away. In the north, near Emma's family. She deserved some blessings.

Then Harry would be able to visit his property without much danger. It wasn't a perfect solution, but it might work especially with the Rogues brought into play. Surely Jack would understand that once Harry was surrounded by powerful protectors Jack would never survive murder.

All she had to do was marry Stephen.

She stirred and fidgeted about his bedroom, trembling with hopes and doubts. Once, so recently, she'd thought marriage impossible. Now it looked like a necessity, but it was also wrong—wrong to be planning to snare a man whether he wanted to wed her or not.

She could seduce him. She knew she could, and she knew that once he'd compromised her, Stephen would feel honor bound to offer her marriage. It would be easy. Whatever he felt for her, he was not immune to lust.

But she still wasn't sure that she could make a good wife for him. She wanted to. She would try. But trying was not always enough.

She'd enjoyed a political discussion with him, but she knew herself. Lady Skylark still fluttered inside her, longing to be free. She wouldn't be happy in a cage of propriety, but could he cope with her soaring flights? She thought of another political man, William Lamb, constantly embarrassed by his half-mad wife, Caroline. She wouldn't be as bad as that, but she might be a burden to Stephen. When he'd christened her Skylark, he had not meant it to be complimentary.

She considered their brief time here. At times he'd seemed loverlike, but at others only the old friend. Occasionally he'd been distant and even disapproving. She'd been hoping to explore this more when they left, to find the truth of what lay between them, but with Harry's life at stake, she could not allow Stephen any chance to escape.

She'd never had to hunt a man, and she'd never

had to seduce one except in play with Hal. It was the last thing she wanted to do, especially with Stephen, because . . .

Because he was a friend, and friendship required trust. She'd come here without a thought that she might be putting herself at risk because she and Stephen were friends. She didn't think men worried about being seduced or raped, but perhaps they should.

She leaned against a bedpost and considered Stephen's bed in an entirely new way.

Chapter 33

Laura returned to the parlor and closed the door temporarily on temptation. Now that she accepted that Henry Gardeyne was dead, she saw no point in further listening at the wall. She tried to distract herself with *Guy Mannering,* but such dramas lacked weight now. When a letter arrived from Kerslake, she didn't open it. It was addressed to Stephen, but she might have read it if she thought it carried news of importance.

She put wood on the fire from time to time, and as the light faded, lit two candles, wandering constantly from window to fireplace, trying to avoid her thoughts. Night was approaching, however, the classic time for lusty wickedness.

Stephen came in. "I'm sorry for being gone so long. Reverend Lawgood wanted to talk about the Speenhamland system." But then he asked, "What's the matter?"

Was her mood so obvious? She hoped her thoughts and plans weren't.

At the very sight of him, she'd jolted inside. She wasn't sure if it was from guilt, lust, or both, but it shook her. She did lust, but that made her plan more wicked rather than less. She'd rather be planning a noble sacrifice to a man she did not want.

She found a slight smile and gestured to her notes on the table. "They talked somewhat. It's clear they're in this together, and both have been convicts, probably in New South Wales. Dyer can't be Henry Gardeyne."

She watched him read, praying even now that he'd find some other interpretation. But he looked soberly at her. "It does sound like that. I'm sorry, Laura." He came over and took her hand. "Don't be afraid. We can find other ways to keep Harry safe."

She knew he wasn't referring to her plan, but it felt as if he was reading her mind. "Yes, I know."

Tonight? It might be my last night here. What excuse do I have to stay?

She gently pulled her hands free and tried for a light tone. "I do hope that one day I will know the whole story, though. It's exasperating. Why have that unlikely pair come up with this plot? And why, as Nicholas Delaney asked, *now*?"

"And who the devil is Oscar Ris? That really niggles at me. My impression is that nothing in that letter is meaningless."

"It doesn't relate to convicts or the antipodes?"

"Not in any way I can see, and I've studied the matter a great deal in my investigation of the legal system. Oh, to the antipodes with the lot of them. The wind's dropped. Let's go out and watch the sunset before dinner. Without a telescope. For nothing but pleasure."

It delighted her as she'd not expected to be delighted here, and perhaps she could encourage a proposal rather than forcing it. A glance in the mirror as she put on her bonnet gave her great doubts. Seduction would have to be for the night, when she was Labellelle.

It was lovely to be out, however, breathing in the fresh briny air as they walked down the beach admiring the last of a sunset that was fiery instead of gray. A sunset that turned the rippling waves bloodred.

Laura closed her eyes to that and inhaled. "Perhaps the sea air is healing."

"Now the storm's passed."

She turned to look at him. "Benign and destructive. Two sides of the same thing." *Like love, and desire, and two writhing bodies in a bed.* She tried to read his every look and word, seeking the truth of his desires—and his points of vulnerability. He was a mystery to her, but moment by moment, she wanted him more.

They strolled on, just out of reach of the sea's eternal lick. Like a bloodred lover lapping at skin or at hot, secret places. She swallowed, trying to control the ripple of sensual awareness, but feeling the rumble of the sea up through her shoes, up, up . . .

Their only contact was linked arms, the only permissible contact between a sickly woman and her escort. She longed to turn into his arms, to imitate the sea by kissing, licking, and it was nothing to do with maternal purpose. . . .

"We'd best turn back," he said, doing so, speaking as if they were only invalid and escort.

The sun's last fire was fading, darkening the sky and stealing passion from the sea, but that did nothing to the way she felt. He didn't share her desires, however. That was obvious.

"What will you do when your mourning is over?" he asked.

She was expected to make practical conversation? "I expected to live on at Caldfort."

"Keeping Harry safe will be easier if you live elsewhere."

"I know that." She heard her own snappish tone. "It will not be allowed."

Could she put the situation to him honestly and make a marriage of convenience? If he refused, however, it would alert him.

"Influence can be brought to bear. So, where would you choose?"

She let a silence linger, hoping he might make a

suggestion, a proposal. Then she said, "At Merrymead, I suppose."

"Not London?"

"My jointure is generous, but it won't stretch to *ton* life, and Lady Skylark can't subsist on the fringes."

"You could live with Juliet until you marry again." He was discussing it as if it were a dry matter of law.

"So I could," she said tartly. "Once I can leave Caldfort, finding a husband should be no problem at all."

No problem at all.

As they climbed the shallow slope up to the road, Stephen wanted to smash something or force a kiss on her, wanted to fall to his knee and beg her to marry him, him! But she wasn't following any of his leads and he didn't want to press the matter now. Not now, not here, where she had entrusted herself to him. Not when she had no easy escape if his proposal was once again an embarrassment.

Not when she might have said that she no longer cared for life in London, where his work required him to live for most of the year.

"I probably would like to live in London again," she said, making him wonder if he'd spoken his thought aloud. "If I had Harry with me and a fashionable establishment."

He couldn't give her the pinnacle of society or a peerage title, but he could manage fashionable.

Before he could put together the right response, she continued. "As for marriage, I take the matter of providing the perfect stepfather for Harry very seriously."

"And who would that be, the perfect stepfather?"

She glanced at him, but in the gathering gloom even the light from the windows of the inn couldn't reveal her expression. "Someone with enough power to over-

rule Lord Caldfort, of course, and stave off any threat
from Jack. Someone able to fight for Harry's welfare,
but also able to love him, to be a true father. And,"
she added, sounding strangely rebellious, "someone
with enough money to support Lady Skylark's new
flight. If I go to London, it can only be to fly."

He didn't understand her tone and it unnerved him.
Had she guessed his feelings and was trying to warn
him away from repeated folly?

"Only a fool would want to cage a skylark," he said,
and opened the inn door for her.

A few moments later, Laura swept into her room
and clenched her fists. Stephen had turned cold as the
sea at the mention of Lady Skylark. Why, oh, why,
had she been driven to honesty? Why hadn't he taken
her hints about marriage?

She felt torn into warring pieces. She was Harry's
mother, who needed Sir Stephen Ball as a weapon,
primed and loaded. She was Stephen's friend, who'd
chase off another woman who wanted to use him as
she did. She was a wicked woman who desired him—
honor and sense be damned.

And tonight she must decide, and act.

Chapter 34

She composed herself, straightened her wig, and returned to the parlor to find Stephen at the table, scribbling on a piece of paper. It reminded her of so many times in their youth that a wash of pure warmth soothed her.

She smiled and went to look over his shoulder. He had the copy of Farouk's letter open, but was writing on another piece of paper. "What are you doing?"

"Hunting for a meaning," he said tensely, pencil circling the name Oscar Ris. "The mouth of Carris. Or perhaps in distorted Latin, the mouth of love?"

"HG has been in thrall to the mouth of love?" As soon as Laura said it, a lewd image filled her mind. Quickly she added, "Backward it's Sir Racso."

He flashed her a grin. "That sounds like the villain in a farce. With a few more letters we could be looking for Scarred Boris."

She sat beside him, suddenly surprisingly happy for this lighthearted moment. "Rascal? I like rascal."

"You're missing an *a* and an *l*," he pointed out. "Osiris? An Egyptian connection."

"You're missing an *i*."

"It has to mean something," he muttered, tossing down his pencil. "I can't help thinking that it's key to everything."

Laura picked up the pencil and wrote herself. *Sir Acros. Sir Scora. Sirra Soc.*

He burst out laughing. "Sirra Soc? A buffoon in a pantomime."

"Definitely . . ." But then the letters rearranged themselves. "Stephen!" She gripped his hand. "It *is* an anagram! It's *corsairs*!"

Hope blossomed. "That explains the ten years! It explains why *now*. It explains freedom. It explains everything! Ever since the *Mary Woodside* went down, Henry Gardeyne has been a slave on the Barbary Coast, one of the ones recently freed from Algiers by the navy!"

He stared at the paper. "Good God, and look. Egan Dyer is an anagram of Gardeyne." He turned to frown at her. "But there were hardly any Britons among those slaves. And an aristocrat? He'd have been ransomed years ago. The corsairs always took ransoms if they could."

"But it has to be. It can't be coincidence."

"It must at least be the story behind it. The one supposed to trick Lord Caldfort."

She instantly saw what he meant but didn't want to think it could be true. "You're being sensible again," she complained. "It is possible, I grant, but it's equally possible that Henry Gardeyne's been a slave, isn't it? After all, why would Dyer—or whoever he is—and Farouk talk about freedom when they didn't know anyone was listening, unless it was true?"

"As you said, convicts?"

"Who have escaped from New South Wales?"

"Or served their time and returned."

"I find it hard to imagine Farouk as a convict, but I will consider it later. For now, let's assume that when the *Mary Woodside* went down, Henry Gardeyne wasn't drowned, but captured by the corsairs. Perhaps ransom was demanded and not paid."

"By his loving father?"

She frowned. "No, that's not possible. He was apparently so devastated by his son's death that it hastened his own. But there might be some explanation."

He took her hand. "I know you want to believe this, Laura, but let me play devil's advocate. If by some mischance Henry Gardeyne was enslaved in Algiers for nearly a decade, when he was freed, he could have commanded every service and comfort from the navy. He'd have been brought home on the best and fastest ship and lionized throughout the land."

She grimaced at him. "Instead he sneaks in on a smuggling boat with only an Arab servant. Farouk could be Algerian, though, rather than Egyptian."

"But it that case, Dyer—Henry, whoever—is more likely to have been servant to him. And why would an Algerian—and an educated one, since he speaks and writes English—take such efforts to bring his slave back to England? And again, why not simply deliver him to Lord Exmouth, as he was supposed to?"

Laura sighed. "The devil has an excellent advocate in you. It doesn't make sense. But it doesn't make much sense as a hoax, either. Why has educated Azir Al Farouk sneaked into England to attempt a rather feeble extortion?"

Stephen thought for a moment. "The loss of his slaves has been a financial blow. He encountered Henry Gardeyne once. Yes," he said to her, "I'll work with the idea that Henry survived the wreck long enough to end up in the hands of the corsairs. In fact, Farouk purchased Henry, and was about to demand ransom when Henry died. He wrote it off as a loss, but in this current situation he remembered Henry and also some possession that could establish a claim. He found someone resembling Henry and brought him here to try to squeeze money out of Lord Caldfort."

"It holds together," Laura said, "but it would hold together if HG really was Henry, wouldn't it?" She answered herself. "No, because then he would have been ransomed. And besides, everyone says Dyer is pale. How could he be pale after ten years in Algiers?"

He squeezed her hand. "I'm sorry, but I think all we have discovered is the explanation behind the hoax. Perhaps there was an enclosure with the letter laying this out for your father-in-law."

"And if Lord Caldfort pays, Farouk will report the deed done, and he and his accomplice will go off to South Carolina or wherever. Oh, dear. Perhaps he really does intend to kill his dupe and leave a body for Lord Caldfort to find."

"Perhaps drowned. That can make bodies hard to identify."

"I refuse to feel sorry for the wretch," Laura said, but she did. Farouk sounded so strong, and Dyer so weak. "Do you think he's really a cripple?"

"What? Do you want to rescue him? I doubt he'd cooperate."

Laura realized that she'd drifted to accepting the worst possibility, not the best. "I won't give up until I'm sure," she said. "Imagine if it is Henry and we leave him to Farouk's or Jack's mercies. Yes, if Dyer is Henry he should have announced himself to Lord Exmouth, et cetera, but he would have spent ten years as a slave. They were horribly punished, and he is injured in some way. Perhaps Farouk befriended him and persuaded him that this quiet return was a better idea than being, as you said, lionized."

He picked up the piece of paper and rolled it into a ball in his hands, something he'd done in the past when struggling with a decision. "You want it to be so, but the evidence doesn't point that way."

"I must be sure. I can afford to stay another day. Even if Lord Caldfort has told Jack and Jack left this morning, he can't arrive until late tomorrow."

He nodded and tossed the paper accurately into the

fire. "Very well. We still need a way to compare HG to that picture. Such a seemingly simple matter to thwart us."

"We could set the inn on fire." She raised her hand. "I know. I'm not even considering it."

"You make me consider a little smoke. . . . But it's too risky. I could try to pick the lock."

"Do you know how?"

He smiled. "Yes."

"Stephen! And you never told me? Or showed me, for that matter."

"Heaven knows what you'd have done with a skill like that."

She pulled a humorous face, but inside it hurt.

"Or I could break down the door, with or without the assistance of Kerslake or Topham."

"Oh, I forgot! Kerslake sent a message." She leapt up and brought it to him. "Perhaps he has something to contribute."

He broke the seal and read, but then passed it to her. "Only confirmations."

He was right. Kerslake wrote that the details of the landing were as he'd said, and that the two men had arrived alone. He'd found no word of a likely child in the area, or of people who could be in league with the two.

"He does reiterate the offer of help," she pointed out. "I'm sure that with his help we can pop HG out of that room like a nut out of its shell."

"But once we do, the subterfuge is over. We have to be ready to take them prisoner, possibly against armed resistance. People could get hurt, and if we muff it in any way, they could escape. What do you want to do? I told you that in the end, the decisions would be yours."

That weighed on her, but at the same time she felt liberated. She wouldn't need to seduce Stephen tonight, to steal his freedom. There was still hope.

"We try patience for just a little longer," she said. "We listen at the wall in the hope of clarity. Perhaps tomorrow will be warm, and HG will sit at an open window. Perhaps, oh, perhaps something will happen. For tonight," she said, taking his hand, "let's simply enjoy this time together. We were apart too long."

His look was quick and searching, but he said, "That sounds delightful. Shall we order our dinner served now?"

She agreed and watched as he rang the bell and then gave the order. Simply watching him, listening to him, gave her such joy. And now she had hope. Some deep instinct told her that HG was Henry, so both Harry and she would be free. She would move to Merrymead for the time being, and if Stephen didn't come courting her, she would go courting him.

Not force, not seduction, but courtship, where they could both learn about each other and make the right decision.

They waited for the meal in the relaxed pleasure of old friends. "You said Farouk purchased a copy of *The Corsair*," she remembered. "That fits now. Perhaps he likes the fact that it portrays the corsairs as heroes."

"Quite possibly. It's said Byron based it on some adventures of his own, and of course he liked to dress up in the costume."

"Which was nothing like Farouk's costume."

"My money's on Farouk being authentic."

"Mine, too. He is certainly the real thing."

When the servants had spread the meal, Laura and Stephen sat and continued to talk about the famous poet and his stormy, scandalous life.

" 'Linked with one virtue and a thousand crimes,' " Stephen quoted. "Many think Byron was describing himself."

Time, talk, and perhaps wine had eased tension.

"His virtue being his art?" she asked, watching the play of candlelight on her glass of claret. "Is not one great gift enough?"

He studied her across the remnants of their meal. "And what is your great gift, Laura?"

She looked at her glass, sipped from it. "Harry."

"I don't think a child, even children, can be the prime purpose of a life. Your art is above the common standard."

"I have no wish to become an artist." She met his eyes. "Perhaps my art is to be a bird."

She saw no particular reaction. "And fly high? There's nothing wrong with that. The skylark gives a great deal of innocent pleasure." He put down the glass he had been merely toying with. "I will regret this, but I must tell you something."

"Don't." It came out without thought, and she frowned over it. "I mean, don't tell me something I must keep secret. I'm not sure I'm trustworthy at this moment."

"It's not a secret. I want you to know. I did not arrive at Caldfort by accident."

She stared at him. "You are part of Farouk's plot?"

"Damn it to Hades, Laura. Of course not."

Such swearing didn't shock her, but it startled her when it was Stephen. "I'm sorry. Why, then?"

His lips tightened as if to hold back words, but then he said, "I fabricated a reason to visit Caldfort because I wanted to court you."

She realized her glass was tilting and hastily put it down. She almost said *Why?* but that would be silly. "And found me in a fuss and flurry. But you said nothing later."

She should be relieved, ecstatic. It was such a shock, however, that she felt numb. And he had given no sign until now. Or no clear sign . . .

"The fuss and flurry seemed continuous," he said.

"I think I had the notion of snaring your attention through heroics, but it would seem that I'm not the heroic sort."

"Nonsense. I wouldn't have wanted anyone else by my side through this."

He smiled. "Which isn't quite the same thing."

She wasn't sure what to say. If she could believe this—and why shouldn't she?—it was everything she needed and desired.

If she could only be sure that she was the right wife for him. She didn't doubt his words, but she'd seen many men choose wives from desire and discover disaster.

"At times," she said, "I haven't been sure that you like me."

"We've talked over this. I like you."

"But do you *love* me?" She shook her head. "I shouldn't ask that."

"I don't see why not." He picked up his neglected glass and drank. "I am resolved to be nakedly honest. I'm uncertain what love is, Laura. I want you. Blunt, but there it is."

Blunt enough to hurt. "You want to possess Labellelle?"

He considered it. "Only insofar as she is the external of you."

That was better. "I'm not at all serious," she warned.

"I think you can be very serious. If not, I'm sure I can be serious enough for two."

She shook her head. "I don't think you're serious. I mean, you are, but not too serious." She rose from the table and walked away. "I can't seem to find the right words."

"A sensation I'm familiar with."

She knew he was still in his chair, which was impolite, but the right thing to do.

"You could tell me how you feel about me," he

said. "I think we are friends. I think we trust each other, enjoy each other's company. But we need more than that."

Nakedly honest. She could agree that they were only friends. She could tell him that she wanted him as much as he wanted her, simply physically, his body joined to hers. She could tell him that she wanted him as husband so he would protect her son.

But she sensed that none of these things were needed here. Thank God that there was hope that HG was Henry Gardeyne, and she didn't need to betray his trust. As it was, she was too fraught at the moment to sort out her own mixture of need, desire, and fear. She'd experienced an impulsive, inadequate marriage and wanted more—especially for Stephen.

She turned and faced him. "I don't know. It's more than friendship, believe me. I don't see you as a brother. But . . ." She opened her hands helplessly. "There's no hurry, is there? I'll be at Merrymead. We can . . ."

She couldn't find the right word. *Court* did not seem to fit.

"Continue to relearn each other," he said. "No, to learn the people we are now." He rose and came to her, took the hands she still held out. "You don't mind that I went to Caldfort with intent?"

"No, of course not. Why, though? We'd spoken so rarely over six years. Why did you think you wanted to marry me?"

Slowly, he brought both her hands to his lips and kissed each one. "Because I wanted to marry you six years ago."

"When you proposed? But I thought . . ."

He smiled. "What?"

She had to give him truth. "That it was gallantry. Logic, even. You thought I was making a mistake and offered to rescue me."

His smile deepened. "Not so far off. I didn't realize

myself how much I really cared. Perhaps if I had, I would have been able to persuade you."

"I doubt it," she said honestly. "Hal dazzled me, and anyway, I would have balked at the scandal of jilting him."

"Even if you'd loved me?"

She pulled free of his hands. "I'm not sure I could have recognized another love then, but the scandal would have terrified me. I was only eighteen. And," she added deliberately, "I wanted Hal."

"I know. And once you had him, you were happy. I accepted fate. I wasn't really angry at you, no. My needs were my concern, not yours."

"But that's the problem. I wasn't aware of you that way!"

"I know, but does that mean you never can be? We could test the hypothesis. . . ."

He drew her into his arms. She raised a hand between them. "Stephen, I'm not sure this is wise."

"Trust me."

She let him draw her close because she wanted this so much. Willingly, she molded to his body for their first real kiss, sliding her hand up and into his silky hair, opening her mouth to taste him, sighing with deep, revealing satisfaction.

Different, so different to Hal in every way, but right. This part, at least, was right.

And thus it was dangerous. She felt his arms tighten, his mouth demand, and clutched back at him as hunger burst into flame. She dragged free, tore away, faced him at bay.

Saw his devastation.

"No!" she cried.

Swiftly, he put his fingers to her lips, but in his eyes she saw pure pain. She clutched his hand to her lips and kissed it. "No, I'm not offended," she murmured against his skin. "No, I didn't dislike it. I liked it too much. As did you."

"God, yes. Come to my bed, Laura. I'd like it even more."

She laughed against his hand, pressing it to her cheek. "We mustn't."

"You know I want to marry you."

"That's why. If we make love, we're committed." Before he could make the obvious comment, she said, "I can't believe I'm the one preaching restraint, but I am. Desire is not enough, Stephen, even desire as powerful as this. I may not be the wife you need."

"Do I have no say in that?"

"Only half. Do you really know me?"

"I think I do."

"I'm still Lady Skylark."

"Are you?"

Strange that sadness could make her smile, but it did. She kissed his hand again and let it go. "We need time. We have time. We can bill and coo in the usual way and be sure before we make commitments."

Silence settled, marked only by the steadily ticking clock and never-ending rumble of the sea.

"You're right," he said at last. "I can't believe that you're the one preaching restraint. It probably means that you're right in other ways. That your feelings are not as deeply engaged as mine."

She could protest—it felt as if her heart was breaking—but she knew where that would lead. There was only one way to end this.

"Good night," she said and retreated to her room.

Once there, she sat in thought, but thought did no good. Goodness knows who Stephen had wanted when he'd gone to Caldfort, but now he wanted the woman who could debate philosophy and discuss laws.

He thought Lady Skylark was a person of the past.

Laura wasn't sure that was true, or that she wanted it to be, so she had to continue to be strong.

*　　*　　*

Stephen looked at the remains of the meal with disgust. Scraps, smears, and congealing fat. A good representation of his hopes. For one moment as they'd kissed, he'd thought he held heaven in his arms, but then he'd been hurtled back to earth.

She could sweeten it as she wished, but the kiss hadn't held her, her desire hadn't compelled her, and she'd retained full control of her reason.

He allowed himself a glimmer of hope. Perhaps it was this situation and all the stresses of it. He would court her in proper fashion from her parents' house, and perhaps it would all work out in the end.

He picked up his abandoned glass and drained it.

He didn't believe it.

Not for one bloody moment.

Chapter 35

Sunshine woke Laura to her last day at the Compass. No matter what happened today, she must leave early the next. Jack might turn up, but even if he didn't, she must return home.

She didn't want to. Oh, she wanted to be back with her family and she ached for Harry, but she didn't want this special time with Stephen to end. It must, however, or they would plunge into disaster. In the middle of the night she'd had to fight the temptation to go to him, to taste him, feel him, burn with him.

And bind him.

She prepared for the day, trying to armor herself against folly, longing and fearing their next encounter, but when she went into the parlor, he wasn't there. The remains of his breakfast replaced the remains of their dinner last night, and a note lay by her place.

Out for a walk. Back soon. S

She picked it up, realizing that it was the first letter she'd ever received from him. It seemed absurd, but he'd never written to her from school or university. Why would he? He'd spilled all the news during holidays. Any messages from Ancross had come from Charlotte. After her marriage, there had certainly been none.

She handled the sheet of paper as if it were precious, tempted to tuck it away and treasure it. Instead she rolled it into a ball between her hands and lobbed it at the fire. It raised her spirits to see it land accurately in the flames. With a wry smile at herself, she rang for fresh coffee and settled to eat.

When she'd finished, she went to listen at the wall. Solving the anagram had given reason to believe that Dyer was Henry Gardeyne, but she wanted certainty. Proof. Did he need rescuing from Farouk or not? In fact, she'd be delighted to hear anything that clarified the situation and guided her about what to do next.

She immediately knew that being in this room was dangerous. The smell of Stephen's soap and of him was just as powerful, if not more so. The mere sight of his brush and comb stirred her longings, and she touched his book simply because he'd probably held it last night. When she looked at the title, however, she found it was the bound report of a committee investigating the country's prisons. She must not hide from what he was.

The chair was still by the wall, so she sat and listened. They were talking. She sat straighter, annoyed not to have brought paper and pencil, but then she realized it was one voice—HG's—and he was reciting.

". . . But still from room to room his way he broke,
They search—they find—they save: with lusty arms
Each bears a prize of unregarded charms;"

Laura recognized *The Corsair*. No doubt the copy Stephen had discovered that Farouk had bought.

She listened, enjoying the desperate battle back to the boats. There was nothing else to do, and HG read surprisingly well.

". . . The Pasha wooed as if he deemed the slave
Must seem delighted with the heart he gave;
The Corsair vowed protection, soothed afright,
As if his homage were a woman's right . . ."

Those words startled her and she moved away from the wall. The first described Hal perfectly. He'd assumed he was doing her a great honor, and she'd thought the same.

It was true. He could have married higher.

Was Stephen the Corsair, wanting to protect and soothe?

She heard a noise and Stephen came into his bedchamber, halting briefly when he saw her, then continuing, stripping off his gloves.

"You look amused," he said easily, as if nothing awkward lay between them. "Are they telling jokes?"

"HG's reading *The Corsair*. Do you think a man's homage is a woman's right?"

"Hardly. Why would a woman—or man—wish to be worshipped?"

She recognized that he'd put his finger on the problem she'd sensed. "Why, indeed?"

But perhaps, she thought, she'd been as bad as Hal. She'd been gratified by his proposal, but hadn't she thought it her due? She, the beauty of her area, desired by all?

He was looking at her. "There are few things more worrying than a thoughtful woman. Are you concerned about last night? Don't be."

His calm, direct reference exasperated her, but she was also touched by his honesty. She would match it as far as she could.

"I'm concerned about many things, Stephen, but I'm not distressed. Were you out doing something useful, or simply walking?"

"Walking." He leant against a bedpost facing her. "Do you want to return to Redoaks now? It might be best."

Indeed it might, but she said, "No. I'll give it one more day. But if we have no clarity by this evening, I'd like to arrange an invasion then. Settle it once and for all."

He nodded. "I'll send a message to Kerslake. No, I should ride over. It's not far, and it's no matter to put bluntly in a letter."

Another way of avoiding her?

"No clever codes?" she teased.

"I have some and so, I'm sure, does he. Unfortunately, we neglected to coordinate."

He continually surprised her.

"Can it wait until after lunch?" she asked. "The sun's shining and I'm cooped up in here without an escort. We could have a walk, and then you might as well eat."

"By all means. We can take the telescope, in case our elusive quarry is sunning himself in the window."

The sun was pleasant, the breeze light, and the air as crisp as ever. Laura had come to love it and was hard-pressed to play her sickly part. They plied the spyglass, and she enjoyed watching a ship with full, rounded sails speeding east along the Channel.

"Coming home, probably," she said. "Soon making land at Portsmouth, or going around to London. Being on a ship like that must be almost like flying."

"One of the fishermen here could take us out." But then he added, "Sometime."

They returned to the inn, encountering people they knew. As they eluded Captain Sillitoe, Laura said, "It's definitely time for me to leave. Soon some of these people will be familiar enough with my face to perhaps remember it undisguised."

"True."

They ate a light lunch, and Laura wondered if Stephen, like she, was thinking about when next they would do the same.

Then he rose. "It's only three miles, so it shouldn't take long. I worry about leaving you here."

"I have my pistol, remember?"

"And know how to use it, yes. But don't do anything rash." He raised a hand. "I understand. But I'd prefer not to return to your corpse, you know."

"And I'd prefer not to have your corpse brought back to me, so ride carefully. I assume the route goes along the cliffs."

His lips twitched, then relaxed into a smile. "Very well, but *I* will not be in the company of villains."

"I doubt I will be, either, but if I see a chance to glimpse HG, I'll take it. But carefully. Very carefully."

He sighed. "As you will." He pulled her to him for a quick kiss. "Be safe."

Then he left through his bedroom, and shortly afterward she watched him ride away on a horse he must have hired from Topham. It wasn't as good as the one he'd ridden on the journey from Caldfort, but she still enjoyed watching him.

When he turned out of sight, she went into her room and took out her pistol. Her simple round gown had pockets beneath the skirts and she put the pistol in one, but it was heavy there. Instead she put it in her reticule and carried that with her.

She checked at the wall but it was quiet there now. She was walking away when a loud *bang*! made her jump. She looked back at the wall. A shot?

She'd only ever fired a pistol outdoors, so she'd no idea what a pistol shot in the next room would sound like, but it didn't seem likely. More like a mallet banged on a table. A chopper on a chopping block?

She couldn't ignore this. She opened the door to the corridor to peer out—and looked straight into the dark eyes of Azir Al Farouk. A quick glance showed no bloodstains.

She knew she'd started at the sight of him, so she built on that. "Oh, Mr. Farouk!" she exclaimed, hand on bosom. "I thought I heard a shot. Is everyone all right?"

"A shot, madam? I heard no shot."

"A bang, then? Most alarming! It sounded as if it came from Captain Dyer's rooms!"

"Ah. I killed a cockroach with one of my master's boots."

A likely tale.

"Oh, I see. You must excuse me."

"No, madam, you must excuse me for disturbing you." Austerely polite, he bowed and went on his way.

Laura watched him go. His accent had definitely been stronger than when she'd heard him through the wall. Now, why would he play such games? To allay suspicion? English people were inclined to think foreigners less clever than themselves. It made her all the more determined to learn the truth.

She walked along the squeaky corridor and knocked at the first door. Not the faintest sound. Was it possible that Farouk had received his payment and that bang had been the execution?

She began to tap continuously, remembering to behave like Mrs. Penfold. "Hello? Captain Dyer? Are you all right? Hello? Oh, dear, oh, dear, what to do, what to do . . ."

She kept on tapping and twittering. Surely if he was there, if he was alive, he would have to respond.

And then she heard something. A scrape. A . . . shuffle? Was the wounded man crawling toward help?

Suddenly the lock clicked and the door opened a crack.

"What do you want?" a pale-faced man whispered.

Chapter 36

Laura's first, crushing thought was that this was not, could never be, Henry Gardeyne.

Her next was that he *was* wounded and he'd staggered to find help.

Her third was that no, there was no blood, but the young man was truly an invalid and he'd exhausted his strength in reaching the door. He was clutching at it desperately.

She quickly put an arm around him, grateful that he was shorter than she. "My dear sir, I'm so sorry! Please, let me assist you back to your chair."

It was at the table, where cards were laid out in a game of patience.

"I apologize for causing you to rise, sir," Laura said sincerely as they reached the table and he could clutch it. "I was merely concerned because earlier, I heard such a loud noise."

The young man sank back into his chair with a wince of pain.

The too-young man. HG couldn't be the thirty of Henry Gardeyne. If that weren't enough, he was completely the wrong type. Henry Gardeyne at twenty had possessed some fine-boned features, but not as delicate as these. Both men had brown hair, but HG's was lighter, a dark honey, and frothed in irrepressible curls.

Most impossibly of all, this man's eyes were as clear a blue as a summer sky. Gardeyne eyes were usually brown, and that portrait had shown dark eyes. An artist might take liberties, but not to this extent.

He readjusted his position in his chair with another wince. "I'm sorry if the noise disturbed you, madam. It was only F . . . Farouk killing a cockroach. He hates such things."

He sounded anxious and nervous and Laura wondered why, when he was clearly part of this plot. After all, he'd been able to unlock the door, so he hadn't been locked in. Was he afraid of punishment? Something about him summoned her protective instincts.

She made some more quick analyses.

He spoke well, but not quite well enough for the highest birth. There was the hint of an accent, but she couldn't place it. He looked an unlikely type to be a military officer, but she knew she shouldn't make that judgment. War could turn strong men weak.

Whoever he was, however, he wasn't Henry Gardeyne.

All hope died.

"Ma'am? Are you all right? I'm sorry if you were alarmed."

She supposed she should still try to find out what was going on, if only for Lord Caldfort's sake. And for Harry's. If these criminals succeeded in extorting ten thousand guineas, it would come out of his inheritance. She sat down, remembering to be Mrs. Penfold, which she feared had slipped when she'd assisted him to his chair.

"No, no, sir. Well, only a little. Much better now. So sad to be sick when so young, Captain Dyer. A war wound?"

His eyes fluttered uneasily. "Fever. And an accident. I'm getting stronger."

"I see you are playing patience. A pleasant occupation, but it becomes tedious over time. Would you care for a game? Casino, perhaps, or cribbage?"

He glanced at the door and she knew he was worried about Farouk's return. She couldn't do this to him. "I am sorry to have intruded, Captain. Would you prefer that I left?"

She began to rise, but he said, almost shyly, "No, if you don't mind. It *is* tedious here and I'd like to learn a little more of . . . things. I . . . I've been abroad for many years, you see."

She could see why Farouk kept him in his rooms. He was a terrible liar. But then she remembered that he might have been an Algerian slave, poor man.

Then brought here to pretend to be Henry Gardeyne? Whom he didn't resemble at all.

And he certainly hadn't recently done brutal physical work, or lived under a hot sun. His skin was as delicate as the most fussy beauty's, and his hands, though manly in shape, as soft.

She simply had to try to solve this conundrum.

She settled back down and put her heavy reticule on the table close by. "Foreign air can be so very insalubrious," she clucked. "But then, you cannot have been in the tropics, sir."

When he looked alarmed, she added, "You have not been browned by the sun, sir. I pride myself on my powers of observation!"

He smiled, and she wondered if it was a suppressed laugh at her idiocy. He certainly hid his eyes with lowered lids. "No, no sun."

"An icy clime! Equally harmful. England is ideal because it is *temperate*, you see. It avoids tropical and arctic extremes. Are you receiving good treatment here, Captain? I understand that there are many excellent doctors in Draycombe."

"Oh, Farouk takes care of me."

Laura pursed her lips. "Your turbaned servant, yes.

But forgive me, sir, a British constitution requires a British doctor. I met a most amiable one here. I believe he sent up a restorative potion."

With another glimmer of humor, HG gestured to a dark glass bottle on a sideboard. "Farouk doesn't trust it, and when I sniffed it, it smelt awful."

Laura put on the stern expression of the Merrymead nursery governess. "The best medicines always taste the worst, sir."

"Farouk says that's why the doctors make them taste so foul."

Farouk says, Farouk says. No, this young man had never been an officer. He sounded as if he was scarcely out of the schoolroom, though he looked to be about the same age as she.

"Besides," he said, "the doctors say I need only rest and recover. It's damned boring." He flushed and apologized. "I'm so sorry, ma'am."

She waved a gloved hand. "Oh, I make allowances for a gallant soldier, sir. I don't think I introduced myself, did I? I am Mrs. Penfold, a widow, you see. We are in a similar case, for I am here for my health, though I fear I have no noble excuse for my state. Since my dear husband's death, I have been in a poor way with my nerves and so my dear cousin offered to escort me here for a little while. If it suits, I may take rooms . . ."

She burbled on in this way for a while about fictional plans for the restoration of her health and saw the man relax.

Time to pry. "So, sir, what of Mr. Farouk? Such an interesting appearance. He is Indian, you said?"

Often an error elicited truth.

It worked. "No." Then he stopped. "He's . . . er . . . Egyptian."

"Egypt! All the rage, sir. Pyramids, crocodiles, and the Sphinx. Were you posted in Egypt? Was that how he came into your service? Oh, no, you said otherwise. Russia."

She tried the error trick again, but he said, "Perhaps we could play cards, Mrs. Penfold. I don't know the games you mentioned, but I would like to learn."

It was clearly a deflection, but his eyes were bright with interest. It presented a new puzzle, however. He didn't know casino? It was played in every household, even in schoolrooms.

Laura hesitated. If she stayed here long enough, Farouk was certain to catch her, but did it matter? HG would tell the man she'd been here, and her excuse should hold. In fact, being found here innocently playing cards with the invalid would be safer than retreating after a few questions.

She gathered the cards and shuffled, explaining the rules of casino, then dealt. To allay suspicion, she asked no questions as they played, but simply tried to understand this strange young man. He learned the game quickly, so he wasn't simple, and yet his amusement with it seemed juvenile.

Eventually she mentioned playing casino with some fictional nieces and nephews, and gained the response that his family never played cards. "Methodist," he explained, with a twitch of the lips that might be a grimace.

An explanation. There, at least, she'd constructed a mystery out of nothing. "Well, to be sure, that is a worthy practice," she remarked, "but I cannot see any harm in a simple game of cards. One need not play casino for money, not even for farthings."

"Cards are a first step toward damnation, all the same," he said with a smile.

She saw an opening and probed. "Are you perhaps estranged from your family, Captain? Is that why you are not recovering at your home?"

"Yes, that's it." He said it too quickly, though.

"So sad when families are divided. If you have been serving abroad it is perhaps some years since you have visited your home. They might be more tolerant now."

His quick look startled her with its amused cynicism. "I doubt it."

And oh, those wicked eyes. What sturdy, Methodist home had produced this fey creature? It was hardly surprising that they'd parted ways.

"How very sad," she said. "So foolish to cling to old estrangements, but it is their loss, I'm sure. So what will you do once your health is restored? Will you return to military service or have you sold out?"

"Sold out?" he asked, as if the term was new to him.

"Sold your commission in the army. Retired."

"Oh! Of course. Er . . . yes."

"Because of your injuries." She nodded sympathetically, but wanted to roll her eyes. Army, indeed. He didn't know the term, and captains who left the army didn't use their rank thereafter.

She dealt a new hand. "Will you return to your home area to live, sir? You must have friends there. Where did you say it was? Cheshire?"

"Suffolk."

"A country estate, or in town?" she asked as if all her attention was on fanning her hand.

He didn't answer, so she looked up to smile a bland query at him.

"Er . . . Ipswich."

He mumbled it, however, and was becoming uneasy. She pretended to be puzzling over her play as pieces began to form a pattern.

A port town. A sailor? Had he run away from his stern home and gone to sea? She supposed he could be a naval captain, and naval captains didn't purchase or sell their commissions. But if it was hard to imagine him a captain in the army, it was impossible to imagine him lord and master of a ship. There was no trace of command in him.

No, if she had to lay money, she'd bet on him having run away from home as a lad to be a sailor, and a sailor could then have been captured by Barbary pirates. He could even, she realized, have served on the *Mary Woodside.* . . .

"You must have visited many fascinating foreign places, sir," she prompted, putting a three on a four. "Seven."

"No."

She glanced up politely and saw him swallow as he tried to think what to say next. "I . . . I didn't find them fascinating."

"Oh, I see. You, like me, would prefer to live at home in England."

"Or France," he said, and she remembered hearing him say the same yesterday.

She pursed her lips. "A fascinating country, I'm sure, but I cannot forget that until so recently they were our enemy and cost the lives of so many brave men."

"Or Italy," he said, somewhat desperately. "Or America. Oh, Azir! See, Mrs. Penfold has been teaching me casino."

HG's voice had risen in pitch.

Laura turned and felt a spurt of fear herself, perhaps because of the icy look on the Arab's blade-boned face.

She rose by instinct, and had no difficulty in appearing nervous and unsteady. "Mr. Farouk! I have been enjoying such a pleasant game with Captain Dyer, and he does admit to being bored alone here, so you must not hesitate to request my company whenever he wishes."

She picked up her reticule, taking comfort from the weight of the pistol inside. She thought the Arab did hesitate a moment, as if he might not let her leave, but then he stood aside.

Laura minced toward the door, and only turned

back when halfway into the corridor. HG was looking like a puppy that expected a scolding. But a devoted puppy.

"Do let me know whenever you wish to play cards again, Captain Dyer."

With that she tottered to her own parlor door. Once inside, however, she raced into Stephen's room and pressed the listening device to the wall.

Farouk's voice was low and angry, but she caught bits of it.

"Foolish . . . dangerous . . ."

HG's voice was high and clear. "She's only a silly woman, and I'm so bored here. When can we leave?"

"We must hear from the Caldforts soon."

No contact yet.

"Then we can go where it's safe?"

"Yes."

"You're angry at me," HG said in a little-boy voice.

"No, no. No harm done, *nuranee*. I know this is hard for you."

"Is . . ."

The voices sank into muffled murmurs. Could HG be crying? She should think him pathetic, but instead she felt the urge to protect him. He was clearly in some sort of thrall to Azir. Perhaps he *had* been Azir's slave. Slaving underground, far from the sun . . .

But then she remembered his hands.

She growled, tired of trying to make these mismatched pieces fit. The soft voices faded even more, and then a door closed. They'd gone into the bedroom. Or HG had been sent to bed like a naughty boy.

Laura straightened and abandoned her post. She went to look out at rippling sea and sunny sky. Not a scene to match her thoughts. There was no longer any hope that HG was Henry Gardeyne.

Stephen was on a wasted journey, for there was no need to raid the room. But then she changed her mind. They'd do it in order to liberate HG from Farouk and give him a chance to live his life as he wished. She'd have to leave that in Stephen's hands, however, because she really must return home.

But then it truly sank in that Harry was as vulnerable as before. That she must return to her previous plan. It was perhaps not quite so bad now. Stephen had said he wanted to marry her, so there was no need to seduce him. She had only to say yes.

As for suitability, she would make sure it was an honest bargain. After all, she loved him, so it surely wouldn't be difficult to be what he wanted and needed—informed, concerned, serious, decorous. There would be no trace of skylarking. She'd enjoyed their quiet time here and their complex, interesting discussions . . .

She wasn't paying any attention to the scene in front of her, so it took her a moment to realize what she was seeing.

Jack Gardeyne. Riding up to the Compass!

Chapter 37

Laura shrank back out of sight. How had Jack made it here so quickly? He must have ridden like the devil, and half through the night. She shouldn't have under-estimated a sporting Gardeyne. Of course, there was nothing for him to find other than a fraud, but there'd be hell to pay if he discovered her!

She edged forward just enough to watch him. Was he planning to take rooms here? How was she going to avoid him then? She didn't believe her disguise would fool him for more than a moment.

When he turned his horse, she let out a fervent breath of relief. He'd only been checking out the Compass.

What would he do now?

She watched him ride back down the street and into the yard of the King's Arms.

Oh, thank heavens. Here came Stephen. She waited impatiently, keeping a cautious eye on the street. As soon as Stephen walked in, she said, "Jack Gardeyne's here!"

He was instantly alert. "At the inn?"

"No, but he rode past, studying it."

He smiled. "Then things could become interesting."

"Interesting!" She sank into a chair, realizing that Stephen didn't know what she knew. "HG isn't Henry Gardeyne."

"What?"

She told her story.

He'd taken the station by the window and was looking out, so she couldn't see his expression. "Don't tell me it was too big a risk," she said at the end.

"I wouldn't dream of it." It was flat, possibly sarcastic. He turned to look at her. "You're sure? He could be very changed."

"Including the color of his eyes? What's more, I'd lay money that he was a common seaman once. It's there, even though he's been educated. And how can that have happened, when he was a slave in the Algerian mines? Which he obviously wasn't. His hands and complexion are finer than mine."

"Impossible," he said with twitching lips.

"Wait until you see him."

"Will you be jealous?"

She realized where that might take them. "*Nothing* about this makes sense. Nothing! But I want HG freed from Farouk. He . . . he dominates him, and I'm sure he can be cruel."

"Of course." He seemed lost in thought. "And we want to see what Jack Gardeyne does. We might be able to make some use of it. You'll have to stay in these rooms, though. He might recognize you."

"You're right. And when the sun is finally shining. As for Jack, what do you think he'll do?"

"Investigate, I assume. And have as much trouble seeing HG as we did."

Stephen, however, had a look she knew of old: deep thought. "What if Lord Caldfort shared his worries, and Jack decided to act on his own?"

She straightened. "Strike without warning and get rid of the problem altogether? It would be like him. And his principal target would be HG. Until he sees him. Then, I assume, he'll ride home laughing."

"Thus HG's seclusion. They could never know when an investigator would arrive, so Egan Dyer had to stay

out of sight. Strange that Farouk didn't find someone
a little more likely."

"Oh!" she cried in exasperation. "It *still* doesn't
make sense. My brain feels like scrambled eggs. I
should leave for Redoaks now."

But then she realized that would leave Stephen
unbound.

"Don't you want to be here to catch Jack Gardeyne
in mischief?" he asked. "It could be very useful."

"As a weapon over his head? You're like the snake
with the apple."

"Hisssss."

She laughed, shaking her head, but inside she knew
she was the snake, or Eve, ready to tempt him, perhaps into misery.

"What of Kerslake's men?" she asked.

"I reached Crag Wyvern—and I don't envy Kerslake that place. It's like the grimmest medieval
keep. Nothing on the outside but arrow slits—to find
him away at Bridport. So I left a message hinting at
the situation. He probably won't get it until it's too
late to come here today, but that doesn't matter
now."

No, nothing matters now.

She found herself fretting about HG, however. He
seemed so defenseless. "What if Jack's come here prepared to pay the money, and Farouk then slits HG's
throat? Just because HG seems devoted to Farouk
doesn't mean that Farouk isn't a deceitful villain. And
the young man is strangely sweet."

Stephen gave her a look. "I approve of a tender
heart, but yours is becoming mushy. What exactly do
you want me to do?"

"If Farouk goes out again, can you follow him?
Make sure he doesn't rendezvous with Jack?"

"I can, but I don't like to leave you alone. I know,
I know, but if Jack Gardeyne is a murderer, he'd wel-

come a chance to kill you, too. That would leave Harry completely in his power."

A chill swept through her. "You're right. I'll lock the door while you're gone, and I do have my pistol."

She took it out of the reticule, and he came to inspect it. "A nice piece. Does it fire straight?"

"I could hit things with it. I stopped practicing when Hal wanted me to hit a rabbit."

She caught a flicker of a grimace. "Stephen, I cannot and will not stop talking about Hal. He was my husband for five years, and some of those years were happy. Harry is his son, and I'll do my best to keep Hal's memory alive for him."

There she was, warning him off again.

"I was simply wondering if you'll be able to fire at a man."

"Oh," she said, deflated. "Have you ever shot a man?"

"Touché. But I have shot rabbits and various other creatures."

She put the gun back in the bag. "I can only hope I'll do what I have to do."

He returned to watching through the window, and Laura paced anxiously. Though serious, this venture had not seemed truly dangerous before. She wasn't even sure where the danger came from—Jack or Farouk, or both—but she truly believed it now.

She didn't want Stephen out there, even though Jack could meet him and be not at all suspicious.

She paced into Stephen's room and listened at the wall.

Silence.

And anyway, what was the point? She knew the truth, and she knew what she had to do.

Hidden from Stephen, she leaned for a moment against one of the bedposts. She wanted him so much, in earthy ways and others, that she felt weak with longings. Only see how calm he was, though. Perhaps her warnings had taken root and he'd come to his senses. And how could she seduce her beloved out of that? Scrambled eggs, indeed.

A noise startled her, and then she knew what it was. Squeaks in the corridor. She hurried into the parlor. "I think Farouk's leaving."

Stephen picked up his gloves and hat, and Laura took his station at the window.

Stephen paused at the door. "What are you going to do if Farouk is going to the apothecary for corn plasters, and Jack sneaks in here?"

"Run out with my pistol and throw myself between HG and death . . . Don't be silly. I think I'll screech, *Fire!*"

"Do that. This is no time for skylarking. Remember, Jack might want to kill you. I'd see him in hell by tomorrow, but he may not know that until too late."

His cool intent quivered in her like desire. She couldn't resist. She went to him, cradled his face in her hands, and kissed him. "Take care. I value your safety, too."

She moved to let him go, but he pulled her to him and kissed her, a full, passionate kiss more staggering than before. Then he was gone. She touched her lips, still sensitive from his searing kiss, knowing she was smiling like an idiot.

He was not cool. Not cool at all.

What was she going to do about this? If she could believe he felt true love, she would be as carefree as a skylark, but what if he was deluded by her sober appearance? Even at Caldfort, he'd encountered Laura Gardeyne, mourning widow and devoted mother.

Within weeks she could bring out her old finery and be Labellelle. Was that who he wanted? Was that who she was—now?

She sat by the parlor window to watch for Jack and consider true honesty.

A number of people were taking advantage of the late afternoon sun, promenading to and fro for health and pleasure. Dr. Grantleigh was out there in his chair, his wife beside him, holding his hand. Captain Sillitoe was chatting to another gentleman. Jean was hurrying back from some errand.

They were all, she assumed, living relatively uncomplicated lives.

What a blessed state.

Chapter 38

Stephen followed the blue turban, trying to concentrate on the dangers from different parties and anticipate them, but his mind seemed stuck in that kiss. He kept losing control when he was supposed to be winning Laura with care and restraint. Giving her time to think. Not pressing her. Certainly not seducing her!

He'd gone to Caldfort with the aim of stealing her freedom by courting her before anyone else had the chance. Proof of how low desperation could push a man. It had been even worse. Nicholas was right. He hadn't even recognized the nature of the prize he wanted to possess; simply been desperate to correct the old loss.

Now he knew, however, knew the remarkable complexity and strength of Laura Gardeyne, and for the first time he recognized how sane, intelligent men could be driven beyond all limits by desire, by need, of such a woman. He would not be pushed into dishonor, he vowed. He would do nothing to force her choice.

How the devil could she be expected to make any rational choice now, amid the danger and mayhem that circled her precious child?

Farouk approached the King's Arms and Stephen watched, praying that the man did not go in, for that would mean an appointment with Reverend Gardeyne. The Arab walked on and Stephen paused to think.

Farouk and Gardeyne might have already appointed a meeting elsewhere, but in so little time? If he followed Farouk, he couldn't watch for the vile vicar. He decided to stay near the King's Arms, where he could watch and guard Laura.

The vile vicar. He felt coldly certain that Gardeyne was a villain, and that his plan was to kill and leave. He could see the sense of it. As far as Gardeyne knew, no one else except his father had a hint of this affair. Eliminate any threat from a resurrected Henry Gardeyne and there'd be only one small boy to dispose of.

He didn't know that small boy had a resolute protector. No, two. Stephen was sure that Gardeyne greatly underestimated Laura.

He loitered near the Arms, buying a newssheet from a lad for an excuse, but after a couple of encounters with people who wanted to chat, he strolled down onto the beach. He could continue to observe from there.

He found his attention wandering too often to the upstairs windows of the Compass, not looking for Dyer but for a glimpse of Laura. He even wished he had the telescope. Madness, but in normal circumstances, of the sweetest kind.

He couldn't lose her. In a fair and just universe, he could not lose her again. Everything about Laura was precious to him. The turn of her hand, the line of her back, that omnipresent perfume, so subtle yet so magical. Her sparkling laugh.

She didn't laugh enough, and he didn't think it was just this situation.

He could make her merry as a lark.

He could seduce her.

Despite all his resolve, the thought returned, winding itself in false colors. He'd be saving her from another mistake, making it easier for him to protect her son.

Despite the somewhat wild reputation of Lady Skylark, he knew Laura was not the sort of woman to take intimacy lightly. She would feel she should marry a lover. She might even get with child, which would clinch it.

Unfair. Unethical. Base. But would it really matter, when it was clear she desired him, too? When they were old friends and newly delighted in one another?

"Hissss," he said, recognizing the snake in his thoughts and trying to stamp it into oblivion.

Laura had seen Stephen halt outside the King's Arms while Farouk went on. She'd watched him buy a newssheet and read it, then walk down onto the beach. She wished she were there with him, arm in arm, breathing in the sea air, walking with Stephen.

She remembered to look away, to check the wider scene for threats, to her, to him. No Jack, no Farouk.

She went to listen at the wall when there was no point, simply to be in Stephen's room.

She wouldn't let herself repeat her previous folly and disturb the bed, but she didn't seem able to control herself entirely. She wandered the room, exploring with eyes and sometimes with fingers. His valise— plain leather, well used, and with a small brass plate engraved with his name.

His greatcoat, hanging on a hook on the wall, rough to the touch, delightful to inhale, even though it mostly smelt of wool.

That book lying beside the bed, the place marked with a strip of cloth that must have been embroidered by a child. By one of Charlotte's little girls, she supposed.

The washstand containing his brush, comb, and shaving equipment. Shaving was so particular to men that it had always pleased her. She'd sometimes liked to watch Hal being shaved, which he'd indulgently thought peculiar.

The results had been predictable, which was part of the reason she'd done it, but it had made the smell of shaving soap and the sight of a razor quite stimulating.

Blond hairs were caught in his brush. She teased one free, and blushing at her own folly, tucked it down between her breasts.

If only she'd been wiser when young. Would it have been so dreadful to stay unmarried for a few years until Stephen was in a position to take a wife? As Juliet had done.

She shook her head. She understood too well the Laura Watcombe who'd thrilled to have caught the most eligible man in the area, and who'd thought she'd found a like spirit in Hal Gardeyne. They had been happy for a while. She would never let herself pretend that wasn't so.

She'd been a different person then.

She had, indeed, been Lady Skylark, immediately at home in the *haute volée*. Would that girl have been able to tolerate life in rooms in London, playing hostess to other lawyers and politicians who wanted to debate reform until the candles guttered?

Such thoughts seemed to violate some ideal, but people changed. Perhaps that was the cause of many unhappy marriages.

Ah. She went over to Stephen's window to look out at the setting sun. If she was facing hard truths, she might as well accept that in the end, she and Hal had been in an unhappy marriage.

Not miserable, not tortured, but providing none of the joy they'd shared earlier. After Harry's birth, she'd wanted a more domestic life, but he hadn't. However, the tonnish social life no longer appealed to him. He'd clearly played there to please her, but reverted to form so that he spent most of his time with his Corinthian set.

They'd lost their meeting points.

No, they'd had one. They'd both wanted more children. She wasn't sure why she'd not quickened again. Hal had sired bastards, but not that many, considering. It seemed natural that such a vigorous man would be vigorously fertile. With a wry smile, she wondered whether a lifetime spent as a "bruising rider" as they put it, had an effect.

Oh, dear, she really shouldn't think of these things or one day she'd speak of them in public. The *ton* might be amused, but the sober lawyers and reformers would not.

Backward, forward, her mind swung like a pendulum. No, like a weight on a string. She'd seen a demonstration once at the Royal Society. Something to do with the movement of the planets, she thought, but to her merely a weight on a string, set to swing in a circle but slowly falling in until it was stationary in the center.

A force of nature, which made it very like the force that kept circling her back to Stephen's bed, to touching smooth wood, rough wool, firm pillow. That sent her mind circling down to what she and Stephen could do there, and the consequences. . . .

She became aware of someone knocking on the door.

The parlor door!

She hurried into the other room, but then hesitated. "Who is it?"

"Mr. Topham, ma'am. There's a woman here wishing to speak with Sir Stephen. A woman with child."

Because of her thoughts about Hal, Laura immediately wondered if a pregnant mistress of Stephen's had arrived. What a laughable complication that would be! And the thought hurt, though she didn't imagine he'd lived like a monk.

She opened the door a crack. "Who does she say she is?"

At least the uncertainty fit Mrs. Penfold.

"A Miss Capulette, ma'am." The man looked concerned. "I'm not at all sure she's what she seems, ma'am. Arrived with Tad Whipple's vegetables. And as Sir Stephen is out . . . But she was most insistent, and speaks like a lady."

With coins, no doubt. Now what?

But then Laura was hard put not to gasp. Montagues and Capulets? *Juliet*?

"Oh, indeed!" she twittered, opening the door. "I know just who she is. Do please bring her up. And tea. I'm sure she will want refreshment."

His brows rose, but he left. Laura would have rushed down with him, but she made herself wait. Juliet. Had she brought Harry? What had happened? Jack was *here*, not creating danger at Merrymead.

Then Juliet came upstairs, with Harry asleep in her arms.

Laura took him, and could have wept with relief. Thank heavens he was asleep, though, or he would surely have called out "Mama!"

Juliet looked exhausted, and momentarily astonished at Laura's appearance.

"My poor dear!" Laura gushed, drawing her into the room. "You must have had such a journey." She looked back to where Topham was hovering, probably to check that everything was truly in order. "Thank you. Tea, please."

Harry stirred, but by heaven's grace he didn't let out a sleepy "Mama?" until the door closed.

Laura gave him a long, close hug. "Yes, it's me, Minnow! How wonderful to see you. As you see, I'm playing a little game and have disguised myself, but it's nothing to be afraid of."

She looked over his head at Juliet, however, her gaze asking fearful questions.

Harry was knuckling his eyes, so she carried him over to the window and put him down there. "The sea, Harry. Isn't it splendid?"

"Can I go out there?" he asked, waking up enough to press his nose to the glass.

"Perhaps tomorrow, love. It's too late now."

Oh, Lord. What would an inquisitive, restless child do to their plans?

Harry tugged at her. "We traveled on a cart, Mama."

"So I heard. I'm sure that was a splendid adventure."

"It smelt of pigs."

"Oh." Laura wrinkled her nose. "I think you smell a little bit of pigs, too. Why don't we take you into my bedchamber for a wash?"

She saw no sign of a valise or even a bundle. What had happened? She took him into the bedchamber and Juliet followed, to collapse wearily onto a chair.

"I thought we were going to have to walk the last miles, but we were taken up by a man bringing vegetables here. He was very kind, but a bit whiffy."

Laura heard the door open to the parlor and waved her to be quiet. "Let Aunt Juliet wash your face and hands, Minnow, and then there'll be cakes."

She returned to the parlor, closing the door behind her.

Jean had entered without permission—Mrs. Penfold wasn't the only nosy one—and was placing pots, cups, plates, and cakes on the table.

"A surprise visitor, ma'am," the maid said with a smirk. "I'm sure Sir Stephen will be pleased."

Laura knew the maid, probably the whole inn, was leaping to the same conclusion that she had, except with a child, not with child.

"Very pleased," she said, "at the arrival of his sister, though it is most unfortunate that her coach lost a wheel."

A story that wouldn't hold up under the slightest scrutiny, but it was all she could think of at the moment.

The maid left with an insolent twitch, and Laura hurried back to the bedroom. She halted at the door, however, realizing that this ruined any wicked plans for the night.

Juliet and Harry would have to share her bed.

Though the results could be disastrous, it felt like salvation.

Stephen forced himself to analyze Jack Gardeyne's mind. The man was clever enough and a well-respected vicar. How could he be willing to murder an innocent nephew? How could he remain so jovial? Where was Macbeth's haggard torment? How did the man preserve his image of himself as a righteous man?

Perhaps he told himself that he was taking care of his family, especially his newborn son. How could he condemn the infant to life as a parson's son when he could so easily be heir to a title?

He might even have persuaded himself that Harry was not his brother's son. Yes, that was likely. Thus, he could see himself as correcting Laura's wickedness in foisting the child on the Gardeynes. Deceiving his poor old father.

Which put Laura even more at risk.

He must return quickly to the inn—

But perhaps he'd left it too late. The vicar had walked out of the Arms and was heading purposefully toward the Compass. *Purposefully* was exactly the word, and Stephen realized that he himself was a little farther away.

He hurried after, but the shifting pebbles fought his boots and he could hardly run without causing a commotion. He was only a few yards behind when Gardeyne reached the Compass, however, and then the vicar turned into the inn yard.

Stephen paused, letting his heart rate calm, but then walked in after him. If he was seen, so be it. He must know what Gardeyne was up to.

Two men were unloading a cart, which gave some cover but also prevented Stephen from hearing

Gardeyne's conversation with an ostler. The ostler took Gardeyne into the stables.

Stephen followed and heard what sounded like an inspection of the facilities. Was Gardeyne using moving as a reason to ask questions, just as Stephen had done at the Arms? Was he here, after all, as an honest investigator? Was he even willing to welcome his lost cousin home, if he truly lived?

Stephen retreated to a side door into the Compass and let his objective mind evaluate. It could be true. Laura could have imagined the earlier danger, and Jack Gardeyne could be an honorable man.

Soon Gardeyne emerged and walked out of the inn yard to turn left. Stephen strolled after and watched, but the vicar did nothing suspicious. He simply returned to the King's Arms.

Stephen searched the street for Farouk, but didn't see the blue turban. But then a touch of blue drew his eye up to the grassy headland beyond the bay. He wished he had the spyglass, but it would probably tell him nothing extra. The Arab had completed the steep walk and was looking out to sea, blown by the wind. An active, vigorous man who was finding the waiting irksome.

He was still waiting, however. He wouldn't be up there if he knew Jack Gardeyne was in Draycombe.

Chapter 39

Harry and Juliet ate like the starving, but at least they both seemed none the worse for their adventure. By silent consent, Laura and Juliet said nothing of importance while Harry was with them, but eventually he abandoned the remains of a cake and wandered back to the window. Laura thought he'd fall asleep on his feet soon, poor lamb, but her immediate concern was a full explanation.

"I probably acted too dramatically," Juliet said, "but there was no time to think." She glanced at Harry and lowered her voice. "Lord Caldfort sent two men to take a certain *enfant* back to his house."

"Back to Caldfort?" Laura said, astonished.

Juliet nodded, taking another scone. "They arrived with a letter, full of authority. They expected you to be there, of course, and to go with him. But your absence didn't dissuade them. Mother was in distress over it, for Father wasn't at home, but I could see she was likely to give in. I was in a dither, because you didn't tell me not to let *l'enfant* be taken there. I decided it couldn't be what you'd want, so the only thing was to come here to you, and to leave immediately. I took what money I had, but it wasn't quite enough."

"Lord above! Mother must be frantic."

"I left a note, of course, begging her to tell the men

that we were out somewhere. She must have, for they didn't catch us . . . Oh, dear."

"What?"

"I don't think I said where I was going. Just that I was taking Harry to you. It seemed obvious, but they'll think I've gone to Mrs. Delaney's."

"Lord, what a tangle. What could Lord Caldfort have wanted? Jack's here. In Draycombe."

Juliet paled. "So I've brought Harry into danger?"

"Not particularly, but it complicates everything. But you did do the right thing, love. Thank you. I wouldn't want Harry at Caldfort House without me. But now we'll have Father or Ned here soon, and look what they'll find. We should all return to Redoaks. . . ."

But Laura looked out at the setting sun and knew it would be folly to attempt the journey now, especially with Juliet and Harry so weary.

"First thing tomorrow morning," she said.

Despite his nap on the journey, Harry's head was drooping, so Laura went over and scooped him into her arms. "Come on, Minnow. More adventures tomorrow."

She peeled him out of his grubby clothes and washed crumbs off his face and hands without much help from him, poor darling. Then she tucked him into the big bed. She snuggled with him for a while, singing the songs he liked.

He opened his eyes and frowned. "You look strange, Mama."

"I know, Minnow. But it's just a game."

He wriggled closer. "I missed you."

She fought tears. "I missed you, too. A lot."

"Go down to the sea tomorrow?"

Laura almost said yes, but she didn't make promises she couldn't keep. "Maybe, love. But if we can't, we'll come back to the sea very soon. *That's* a promise." She stroked his hair. "Go to sleep, Harry. There'll be many more adventures."

And that's a promise, too.

She sang some more until he was sound asleep, warm and precious in her arms. She settled his head on the pillow but her hand lingered on his hair, unwilling to break that final connection. She wanted to stay here all night but she couldn't. There were plans to make.

Especially as her bold venture had failed.

No, failed was too harsh. Chance had been against her, but Henry Gardeyne was not alive and Harry was still the Caldfort heir. Even if no one tried to force it, he would have to spend some time at Caldfort House because once Lord Caldfort died, it would be his property and his home.

Apart from all the other problems, he was too young for that. If it didn't oppress him, it could spoil him.

She could protect him from that, but the greatest threat would always be Jack. She wished she were the sort of woman who could shoot the man in cold blood.

No, no, that would be evil, and she still had no proof. Even if he'd come to Draycombe to kill HG, that was only slight evidence that he would kill Harry. Jack might be here simply to investigate the letter, in which case he, too, would eventually discover that HG was a fraud and everything would return to the way it had been.

Except that she and Harry now had Stephen on their side—especially if Stephen became Harry's stepfather.

She smiled wryly. After working herself up to settling it by seduction, she'd left it too late. Did one get credit in heaven for forced virtue?

She leaned down to brush the lightest possible kiss on her unwitting chaperon's forehead, then eased away. She locked the door into the corridor to keep him as safe as possible, then returned to the parlor.

"Dead to the world," she said, but then winced at that expression.

"What have you discovered here?" Juliet asked. "Is Henry Gardeyne alive?"

Laura sat with a bit of a thump. "Alas, no." She told the tale, which made no more sense than it usually did.

"So what will you do now?"

Laura was tempted to lay her ethical uncertainties about marrying Stephen before her sister, but they were even more complex and peculiar than the situation with HG and Farouk.

"Stephen will help. Perhaps Jack can be convinced it will be too risky to try anything."

"And you and Stephen?"

"Are living in perfect virtue."

"What a shame."

"Ju!"

"I'm sorry, but this is a perfect situation for . . . adventures."

"For follies. And look at me."

Juliet pulled a face. "I'd rather not."

"Precisely."

"I assume you take it off at night."

"Ju," Laura warned, but added, "Except for the mole. It's stuck like a barnacle."

Juliet reached over and squeezed her hand. "He'll be more enthusiastic when you look your normal self."

More enthusiastic than that searing kiss? Heaven preserve her.

Chapter 40

Laura went to the window, searching for Stephen, but the light was going and she couldn't tell if he was still out there on the beach. Avoiding her.

"I wish he'd return," she said. "We need to sort out our plans. You, Harry, and I need to leave at first light, but I wish I could see HG safe first."

"It's the sort of thing you can leave in a man's hands."

"But I want to see this adventure through."

Stephen walked in then and stopped dead. "What on earth . . . ?" Then he closed the door. "Trouble?"

Laura, heart suddenly spinning, tried to tell him the story but her words became tangled and Juliet took over. Stephen's return seemed to have changed the air in the room. There was either too little or too much.

"Caldfort?" he said, sitting at the table and helping himself to a scone. "I don't believe he would want to harm Harry, but even so, you were right, Juliet. Though this certainly puts some extra knots in the rope."

"Especially," said Laura, coherent again, "as my father, my brother, or both are doubtless on their way now to Redoaks, expecting to find me there. I can't get there before they do."

Stephen thought for a moment, then rose. "I'll send a message to Nicholas telling him to report that you're visiting . . . Crag Wyvern, I suppose. Another message to Kerslake to cover that. You can go there first thing tomorrow."

"Goodness," Juliet said. "Instant brilliance. I *am* impressed."

So was Laura, but she told him with only a smile. "But what about Juliet?"

He'd brought his traveling desk into the parlor and was beginning to write. "Can't smooth that over entirely. You'll have to tell your father about your fears. When Juliet turned up at Redoaks, Nicholas sent . . . No, I think Nicholas had better theoretically escort Juliet to Crag Wyvern. If he can't, he'll send her with a groom. Check it over to see if it makes sense," he said, and settled to writing.

"I think so," Laura said. "So I was never here." But then she asked, "Why did I go to Crag Wyvern alone?"

"Blast. All right"—he rolled a paper and tossed it into the fire—"Nicholas, Eleanor, and Arabel will have to travel there tomorrow and have their servants say they went today. Thus you went with your hosts to visit the peculiar place. Juliet was taken on by a groom to join you."

"But Stephen," Laura protested, "that's a terrible imposition."

He looked at her. "They're Rogues."

Laura shared a look with Juliet, but she supposed if the Delaneys cooperated the plan might work. Her time here as Priscilla Penfold would never be known.

He finished the letters, then sealed them. "I'll take these down and send them by grooms."

He was soon back. "That's done, and Topham says that tomorrow, assuming the weather's fine, the best way to Crag Wyvern will be by boat. It's true that it's either a long road inland or a rough way over the top." He let out a breath. "Right. Anything happening next door?"

"Nothing. But of course, Farouk went out. HG was hardly likely to take to soliloquy. 'Oh, what a rogue and peasant slave am I,'" she quoted from *Hamlet*, but the combination of *rogue* and *slave* made her chuckle.

"What are you talking about?" Juliet asked.

Laura rose. "Come and see."

Juliet was delighted with the listening device, but soon lost interest when there was nothing to be heard. Laura led the way back into the parlor, astonished at how this latest turn had already settled into a sort of normality.

Juliet yawned. "I think I need to go to bed, too."

"We can all share my bed, Ju."

"No."

Laura stared at Stephen.

"You snore, Juliet—"

"What?" Laura exclaimed, looking between the two of them.

Stephen burst out laughing, and after a moment, Juliet joined him. Clearly they hadn't been lovers, but Laura didn't like being laughed at.

"Don't be a goose, Laura," Stephen said. "I was creating a convenient excuse. Juliet snores, and you, as Mrs. Penfold, can't abide that. Therefore Juliet and her child, which is how it must appear, will have a separate room."

"Oh, I see . . . But Harry's already asleep in mine."

"Then you can move into mine, and I will move down the corridor."

Was he, Laura wondered, attempting to make it possible for them to tryst in the night? It both tempted and shocked her. To do that with her sister and her child so close?

"That," he continued, with wicked delight in his eyes, "will mean that I will share a wall with HG's bedchamber. Perhaps they talk of secrets there."

"Oh, how clever!" Juliet declared.

Oh, how damnably practical, Laura thought.

"What is the point in listening?" she demanded. "We know enough."

"There's no such thing as knowing enough."

In moments, it was arranged. Juliet joined Harry in Laura's bed and was almost instantly asleep. Stephen, along with his clothing, his brush, and his shaving things, moved down the corridor.

But his essence remained. Laura had deliberately brushed aside any question of changing the sheets. At least tonight she would be able to nuzzle his pillow without need of explanation.

They ordered dinner and sat to it, just the two of them again. They ate in companionable harmony, reviewing their plans.

"At least we solved the mystery posed by the letter," she said at the end, and raised a glass to him.

He drank, but said, "Without finding a new heir to Caldfort."

"Knowing HG isn't Henry Gardeyne is important."

"Your work entirely."

She understood then that he wanted to be the dashing hero.

"You found the Auricular Enhancer."

He didn't swell with pride. "Which actually revealed little of that we didn't already know."

"It confirmed Algeria."

"Which you'd already discovered in *corsairs*." He toasted her. "You are the hero of this story, Laura."

She reached for his hand. "Heroes. We are equal. Or are you demanding the greater part by nature of being a lordly male?"

As she'd hoped, that brought a touch of humor to his eyes. "Checkmate?"

"I could have done none of this without you. Without you, I would probably have stayed at Merrymead, worrying to no purpose."

He turned his hand to hold hers. "I suggested this plan almost entirely to get you here alone with me."

She blinked at him. "That was very clever."

"Clever, I am."

"I like clever. And you know, comparisons are hardly fair. You're here as Sir Stephen Ball, MP, watched, admired, and having to take tea with the Grantleighs and the vicar. I'm infernal Mrs. Penfold, able to poke, pry, and pester. If you'd come here as a warty groom, you'd doubtless have had a lot more fun."

"I would have liked to be that kind of hero." But he stood and paced away to look down into the fire. "That is irrational. My friends—particularly Nicholas—have suffered in their heroics. It has sometimes spilled over to hurt their dearest ones, as with Arabel. I would never want that."

She was trying to think of the right thing to say when he turned to her. "But I wish they wouldn't exclude me."

She recognized a secret feeling offered to her. " 'They also serve who only stand and wait,' " she said, quoting Milton.

"That, if you remember, was a bitter commentary on his blindness."

"You are Sir Stephen Ball, MP. It must be a wearisome burden, but it's a noble calling and the Rogues recognize that."

His lips were tight. "Is that how you see me? As a saint to be preserved from taint? Would you be acting differently if I were sinful Hal Gardeyne?"

"Of course I would." Before she could continue, words spilled out of him.

"Hal Gardeyne! One among hundreds of English sporting bucks who are as much use as drones in a hive. They create a new generation, then kill themselves in one stupid activity or another."

She was speechless.

He turned away, pressing hands to his face. "I'm sorry."

All kinds of soothing words rose to her lips, but she had to remind him, "Hal was Harry's father, Stephen. He must be allowed to be proud of his father."

He lowered his hands, but stayed staring into the fire. "I know. I apologize. I would never say such things to your son, but it is probably as well that this is over."

Laura thought of arguing, but what was there to say? Walking backward, trembling slightly, she retreated to her room, his room, and closed the door.

Stephen's assessment had been cruelly accurate, but what did that make her? A queen bee? No, just a skylark, another creature with no purpose except to sing and breed.

But what was so wrong with that? Anger stirred, and she turned to go back, to debate, but thought better of it. He was right. People were not animals and should contribute more to the world.

She knew that wasn't even the point. Stephen's uncontrolled outburst spoke of his feelings for her, feelings even more intense than she had guessed. Like a stick roll on a drum, they resonated in her, especially here where his presence lingered. She hugged herself, trying to confine a pounding desire that combined physical want with a need for everything that was Stephen.

Chapter 41

When he heard a door open and shut, Stephen turned
to confirm that Laura had gone.

That had certainly done it.

How peculiar that he'd thrown away the one thing
he'd dreamed of for years. The one thing that he'd
devoted a year of careful thought and planning to winning. Better his opinion of Gardeyne had spilled now
rather than later, after he'd cleverly coaxed her to
the altar.

He laughed. His bitter words had been accurate, but
quite unwarranted. He knew dozens or more of such
drones and hardly gave them a harsh thought. Sometimes he even enjoyed their company.

Hal Gardeyne's sin had not been his wasteful way
of life. It had been marrying Laura Watcombe.

Stephen settled to duty, since it would seem he had
nothing else left. He summoned the maid to clear
away the dinner. He considered staying on guard here,
but there was no need. Jack Gardeyne had no notion
that Laura and his nephew were here, so he wouldn't
creep in to attempt murder.

Stephen knew that he wanted to hover near Laura,
but he wouldn't embarrass her by being here if she
came out of the bedchamber. He put out the candles
and made sure the logs in the hearth were safe, then
left the parlor. After consideration, he took the key

and locked the door as an additional safeguard, but
pushed the key back under the gap beneath the door.

In his new room, which totally lacked that hint of
Laura that had tormented and delighted him for days,
he rang for his water. When it came, he stripped and
washed. Not the faintest likelihood of being disturbed
tonight, so he didn't bother with a nightshirt and just
put on his banyan.

Now what?

All that remained was duty, so he picked up the
Auricular Enhancer, though he doubted the two extor-
tionists would reveal anything new. The instrument
worked as well from this wall, and the two men were
in the bedchamber. Their voices were muffled, however. Perhaps they had the bed-curtains drawn.

They slept together?

Personal servants often shared a bed with their employers, though he'd have expected Farouk to sleep
on the trundle bed. Because, he realized, Farouk was
dark-skinned and therefore inferior. It was an attitude
Stephen fought. Shameful to be caught by it here.

People did often reveal more in darkness in a bed
than they would in daylight, so Stephen strained to
hear what was said.

He only caught fragments.

". . . fair . . ."

". . . when . . ."

". . . care of you, *nuranee*." Stephen assumed that
must be Arabic. A term of respect? Or how an owner
addressed a slave?

Oh, what did it matter?

". . . love . . ."

Love? It was then that Stephen interpreted the pattern of what he was hearing, and it was confirmed by
a gasping cry.

He stepped back, staring at the wall.

Great Zeus. HG was a *woman*? Laura had said he
was delicately made, but it must be a brilliant imper-

sonation to have convinced her, convinced everyone.
It explained a lot—Captain Dyer's lack of knowledge
of military matters, for example—but made other details more mystifying than ever.

An Englishwoman who'd been a slave in a harem?
Had she been rescued by Farouk? It ran too close to
the storyline of Byron's *Corsair,* but he supposed it
was possible.

It might explain why the pair had avoided Lord Exmouth, who would want to return the lady to her
proper home. No matter how heroic, Farouk would
hardly be acceptable here as a husband. Especially if
HG's home really had been a stern Methodist one.
Stephen laughed at the thought.

Perhaps the situation wasn't so mystifying, except
for this attempt to defraud the Gardeynes.

As he put away the Auricular Enhancer, he supposed this might make sorting out the situation simpler. If the lady wished to be with Farouk . . . but
marriage between a Christian and a Mahometan?

Lord above.

And what would they live on, lacking Lord Caldfort's ten thousand guineas?

It wasn't his concern. He needed to cow Jack
Gardeyne, then guard Laura and Harry.

From afar.

Then watch her marry another man.

He took out his brandy flask, which he'd had the
foresight to have Topham refill, and took a deep
drink. Damn good brandy. Not surprising, in the heart
of smuggling country. He drank the next mouthful
more slowly in homage. He couldn't afford to get
drunk, but a little haze would be welcome.

He hadn't lit the candles, but firelight was sufficient
for drinking and regrets. He sat by the window, sipping from the flask, watching the faint glimmer of
waves rippling eternally to kiss the shore.

Kiss.

So few kisses he and Laura had shared . . .

The door opened and he turned, cursing the gloom, the brandy, and the fact that he was half a room away from his pistols.

Laura?

She must be a drunken dream.

Laura, her beauty radiantly unconcealed, her dark curls loose, wearing the rose-pink robe that had almost stolen his wits at Caldfort House. As he pushed to his feet, she closed the door and walked toward him.

Opening her robe.

Letting it slide off her shoulders and down her arms, to reveal perfect, breathtaking nakedness.

Full breasts. The sweet curve into her waist. Flare out to her hips, thighs . . .

He quickly looked up at her face, free even of the mole.

"You need to know," she said, eyes brilliant, "that I am not at all shy."

He opened his mouth and absolutely nothing came out.

"Or hesitant."

She unfastened one, two, buttons of his banyan.

He found a word then—"Laura"—as he grabbed her hand.

"Don't be silly." She slipped free with a smile that was alarmingly like the Laura he'd known years ago. The Laura who would never have stroked him through the heavy silk as she was doing. Or continued to undo the buttons and open the robe.

"Of course, if we go too far," she said as her hand closed around his pulsing erection, "we'll have to marry. Remember that, Stephen."

Remember . . . His temples were throbbing and he wasn't sure he could see.

He was somehow back in the chair, and the red glow of the fire revealed her perfect face and perfect body as she straddled him.

"Are you shocked? This is who I am, Stephen."

In no more than a rasp, he said, "I have to be able to think to be shocked."

She smiled, captured his head, and kissed him, a deep, clever-tongued kiss, but when she drew back, her expression was serious. "You *have* to think. This is who I am. A lusty woman. A demanding woman. A woman who enjoys a man and knows how to pleasure him."

It was as if her words rushed straight to his penis. He gripped her hips and shifted to enter her, but she slid away and went to her knees. Her hand enclosed him and her hot mouth slid over him.

"God . . ."

Her tongue, playing games as she gently slid and sucked. Her teeth, startling him, but only teasing. He vaguely thought he should protest. Laura? But he sank his hands into her silky curls and closed his eyes. He'd never even dared dream of something like this.

But something blocked him. He looked down, then pulled her up by the hair. "I want you. In you."

Her eyes seemed impossibly full of stars. "If you come in me, we marry."

"Damn it, I *want* to marry you, remember?"

"Do you want to marry this woman? Be sure, Stephen."

He laughed. "Are you mad?"

He picked her up and carried her to the bed, tossed her there, then shed his trailing robe. He fell on her, vaguely aware that the efficient woman had pulled back the covers and was lying on the sheet.

He found the strength to halt at the brink. "Are *you* sure?"

She laughed. "Are *you* mad?"

She grasped him, guided him, and he plunged home. Thoughts of elegance bumped at the distant edges of his mind, but he was too far gone. He slid in and out as slowly as he could bear, eyes open, every sense quivering to fix this miraculous moment so it could never be taken from him.

Laura.

His.

Even more wonderful than he could ever have imagined.

She smiled back at him, lips parted in clear ecstasy.

"At last," she gasped. "Oh, Lord, but that feels so wonderful. More, Stephen, more! Harder!"

Her hands, her nails, demanded, and he obeyed, feeling her clutch of pleasure as his mind exploded into bonfire stars.

He rolled to one side, gathering her close, kissing her hair, her neck, her shoulder, whatever part he could find. Filling his hand with a magnificent breast, assuring himself that this was real.

"Shush," she said, a hand stroking him, and he realized he was weeping.

"Oh, God . . ."

"Don't you dare be embarrassed, Stephen. I'm weeping, too."

He touched her cheek and found it wet. Licked a delicious, salty tear.

"It's been a long time for me," she whispered. "Over a year."

"Then why weep?"

"For joy. Are your tears for sorrow?"

He smiled and met her eyes. "No, but a man should weep when he experiences a miracle, shouldn't he? It's been a long time for me, too."

She looked a query.

"Since I heard you were a widow."

She raised a hand to cradle his face. "Yet you waited."

"Was I supposed to rush up to you at the graveside?"

"But later?"

"I meant to wait the full year. My will wasn't strong

nough. I was afraid some other man would snatch
ou away."

"One might have done, and simply because I had
no idea how you felt. Or," she added, tracing his brow,
his nose, "how I felt. What a tragic mistake that could
have been."

Did she accept that Gardeyne had been a mistake?
That was irrelevant now, now that she was his at last.

Then he remembered what he'd said about
Gardeyne earlier and recognized that her coming here
had been an act of faith that humbled him.

"Why?" he asked.

She moved farther away, but wove her hand with
his. "To capture you if I could. But fairly."

She wanted to talk seriously, but he couldn't resist
tasting her breast, her full, dusky nipple. "What do
you mean?"

"I wanted you. I needed you." She grasped his hair
and pulled him up to look at her. "Pay attention, Stephen. I want you for myself, but also for Harry. Marrying you will be best way to keep him safe."

"You expect me to object?" He savored her breast
with his hand. "It's true."

"But I meant to tell you before you committed
ourself," she protested, stopping his hand. "I wanted
to explain that I'm still Lady Skylark. I'll want fine
clothes and parties and light company at times. I won't
be happy spending all my time on politics and philosophy—"

He caught her words in a kiss that lingered, but
then he brought it to an end. "Laura, you goose, what
sort of dullard do you think I am?"

"You don't like fashionable affairs."

"Don't I?"

"I hardly ever saw you at one."

"Because I worked like a nervous general to avoid
you. I want to marry *you*, Laura. Are you trying to
claim that I don't know you? That I don't know that

you love fine clothes and dancing and parties. That you're impetuous and free-spirited? That you're beautiful, inside and out. And I've learned even more these past few days. I want to marry skylarking Laura, who has some understanding of Hume, and a lot more of social rights and justice. And who can probably beat me at chess with a little practice."

He suddenly thought to look at her left hand and found it ringless, though the mark showed. He touched it.

"It didn't seem right to wear it here, but I'll have to put it on again."

"Until I replace it with mine." He looked up. "When?"

He recognized that it was a blunt proposal, but they were past pretty speeches.

"It's three weeks until the anniversary of Hal's death." She frowned slightly. "I'm sorry, but . . ."

"But it would look crass to marry the day after. I can wait, love. Until you're comfortable."

"I don't want to, but we must." Her hands were wandering his body, perhaps unconsciously, but with exquisite skill. "We could announce our betrothal then, perhaps. I meant what I said. I'm using you to protect Harry. Lord Caldfort won't be able to refuse to make you Harry's guardian, and then we can keep him safe."

She looked anxious, or perhaps even guilty, so he kissed her again. "Everything I am, everything I have is yours to command."

"The balance seems unfair."

He laughed against her breast, awash in her warm mysterious perfume. "Our pleasures here have been a little unfair. I must correct that. As for our future . . ."

He slid his hand down her body, into the hot moistness between her thighs. "My life has felt incomplete for six years. I'm no tragedy. I've lived my life well, enjoyed most of it, but I've always been aware of the missing piece. I need you. All that you are. Nicholas mentioned the lock and the key, and that's it—quite apart from any erotic connotations," he added with a smile, sliding fingers into her and seeing, feeling her quick response.

"What is a key without the lock it fits?" he went on, and tongued her nipple. "What is a lock without the key that turns it?" He rotated his fingers inside her. "Once, I would have laughed at the idea of fated partners, but we are that, Laura. It means that I can make you complete, as you complete me. Tell me what you like."

"Press harder." When he obeyed, she gasped and rose up to kiss him. "You do complete me. I've felt that ever since we arrived here, Stephen. Love. As if I was discovering the whole of me through you." Her lids lowered and she exhaled. "Ah, yes, yes . . . But your fingers aren't the true key, you know."

She grasped his erection and he let her guide it again between her thighs.

"You're a very demanding woman."

"You noticed," she said with a sultry, teasing smile as their hips joined. "Click."

Chapter 42

"A miracle," Laura said much later, rousing out of a light sleep to sweet darkness, "cannot by definition be so substantial."

"And if we bring Kant into it, should not be so delightful."

She laughed, returning to the pleasures of licking his salty skin. "I don't want to think of stern Herr Kant. How suitable that is, that his name form a negative. I'm sure he'd say that we can't do this."

"That would be to deny reason entirely, since we are."

"No philosophy," Laura protested, tickling him.

"You started it."

"I—" But then she pushed him away. "Do you smell smoke?"

"The fire?" he said, sitting up, but she knew it was dead by now. Not even the slightest glow.

"I'm sure I smell smoke." She scrambled out of bed in the dark and fumbled her way to the door. "It is!"

She heard the scratch as he tried to make a light, but she opened the door. The corridor had night lamps, and in their light she saw wisps of gray smoke coming up through the floorboards.

"Fire!" she cried, then gasped, "Harry! I locked the doors."

She almost ran as she was, stark naked, but took

the seconds necessary to scoop up her robe from the floor. The tinder flared then, but she was already racing barefoot down the corridor, grabbing the key to her bedroom from the pocket.

Behind her, Stephen was yelling, "Fire! Fire!" and banging on doors.

No flames yet. Her hands fumbled the key, but then she got it in, turned it, and was through. Through the bedchamber, through the parlor, to her son.

Juliet was just stirring. "What . . ."

Laura grabbed Harry. "Fire! Wake up, Ju!"

Juliet came alert. "God save us!" She was out of bed and into slippers and cloak in moments. Laura had already unlocked and opened the bedchamber door, which faced the stairs. Praise God, they looked clear, though smoke swirled around there, too.

Then she heard a distant crackle of flames.

Not in this part of the building, and she was shoeless and almost naked. She thrust the crying Harry into her sister's arms. "Take Harry and get out."

"Mama!"

"You come, too!" Juliet cried.

"I'll only be a moment. I need to get shoes!"

Juliet looked as if she'd argue, but then she raced down the stairs and out of sight.

The excuse was real. There could be broken glass, anything, but Laura also couldn't bear to leave Stephen. He was still pounding on HG's door. She dashed into her dark bedchamber, shouting at him, "Leave them! Perhaps they're already outside."

But then she heard voices. So the two men were awake now, and would get to safety. She looked desperately around the room for her shoes. Where?

A bell began to clang, and she could hear yelling voices along with distant crackling flames. Then smoke made her cough.

Stephen bellowed, "Laura! Where are you? For God's sake, get out!" He appeared in the doorway.

"Come on. The whole place could go up at any moment."

"I need a nightgown and the wig if I'm to escape scandal."

"To hell with scandal." He hauled her up, but she wrenched free.

"No! Only a moment."

Shoes. On. Nightdress on bed. Shed robe, pull it on. Stephen came to help her with the robe, then slammed the wig on her head, coughing. The clanging bell was a clarion of urgency.

"Come on!" he yelled. "Smoke can choke before the flames reach you."

It was danger to him as much as to herself that had her racing to the open door. So much smoke now, and a glow, as well, down the end of the corridor. The first flames, licking up from below.

Stephen's arm came around her, but they almost collided with Farouk, running out of the smoke in his robe, but turbanless, carrying a clinging, nightshirted Dyer. They let him by, then fled down the stairs after.

Laura heard a roar and thought it was a crowd or the sea, but then she realized it was another element—fire. Roaring in triumph as it began to consume the inn.

They reached the hall and she saw safety beyond the open door. Farouk raced through it, but the Grantleighs were staggering out into the hall, the old woman trying to support the coughing, hunched man. Stephen rushed to assist them.

Laura hesitated, but she wasn't needed there. She ran out into clean, fresh air in search of Harry and Juliet.

"Mama!"

She saw them then, by the ruddy light the fire was already casting over the growing crowd. She raced over to take him in her arms, to hug him close, to soothe him, to assure herself, kissing his hair, his face, that he was all right. Juliet tugged on the wig, straightening it. Heaven knows what she'd looked like.

Laura turned quickly back, seeking Stephen. Then she finally relaxed. He was safe, attending to the Grantleighs. Other people were helping. Townspeople, rushing to see what they could do.

A bucket line was forming to bring seawater to the fire. She'd run to help, but Harry was clinging. "It's all right, Minnow. It's all right."

She prayed that everyone was out of the old building, for the fire was raging now at one corner and behind, in the stable area. Men were climbing up ladders to the roofs of the neighboring buildings, ready to try to beat out new fires. The chandler's to the left had a tile roof, but the house to the right was thatched like the inn. Dangerous.

Harry was becoming excited rather than scared. She supposed the brilliant sparks flying into the air looked like a bonfire to him.

Then she realized Stephen wasn't with the Grantleighs anymore. They were being helped away, probably to some house, but where was he? Up on a roof?

She put Harry back in Juliet's arms. "Stay with Aunt Ju, Minnow. I need to find Sir Stephen."

"He might be helping with the horses," Juliet said. "Look."

Laura turned to the arch into the inn yard, which seemed only a frame for flames, and saw people and horses in there. Oh, the fool. No, the hero.

She ran forward, dodging through the crowd, seeing some horses to one side. Most of them must be out. But she couldn't see Stephen.

Then against flames and black smoke, she saw him leading out two blindfolded horses. Controlling two huge beasts that could crush him if they tried.

A scream whipped her head toward the Compass and a great gasp came from the crowd. Someone was hanging out of one of the tiny dormer windows in the thatch and screaming for help. It even sounded like a child. A kitchen maid or the boot boy?

Somewhere in the crowd, a woman screamed, "Jemmy!"

As if to frame the moment, the fire bell went silent.

Men rushed toward the burning building. One grabbed a ladder from the next-door building, propped it against the Compass, and began to climb. Other men held it, despite the growing danger. Flames could be seen, now, through the lower windows.

Laura pushed closer, as if that could somehow help. She tore her eyes away to search for Stephen and saw him handing off the horses to other men. She ran over and grabbed him before he could go back.

"The stables are hopeless!" she shouted.

"The horses are all out."

They both turned to look at the rescue.

Then Laura gasped, "Stephen! It's Jack!"

She knew his shape at the top of the ladder, reaching to pull the lad out through the small window. Knew his voice as he called, "Stay calm, lad, you're strangling me!"

Jack—a hero? Had she misjudged him all along?

The lad didn't stay calm. He clung, screaming, and the ladder began to topple. As if everything slowed, Laura watched the men at the bottom try to keep it up, and it tilt inexorably sideways.

Everyone went silent, so only the roar and crackle of the flames accompanied the child's scream as the ladder crashed down.

People rushed forward. Laura would have gone, but Stephen held her back. "You have to stay out of sight. Go back to Harry. I'll take care of things here."

He was right, but she feared Jack and the child were dead. But as she backed away, someone burst out of the crowd carrying the sobbing boy to his screeching mother.

Then someone bellowed, "Watch out! It's going!"

The crowd around the ladder ran, some carrying a bulky shape, as the fire poured sideways like a burning river through the rooms at the front, the rooms where Laura and Stephen had been. Behind, it ran even faster along the stables, where the upper floor was probably full of hay.

With a roar louder than any lion, the fire caught the thatch and became one enormous bonfire. Appalled silence fell on the crowd.

But then she heard Stephen. "Get those buckets moving. Wet down the buildings to either side!"

As the bucket line swung into action, a cheer greeted men running down the road with a hose and pump on wheels. Draycombe had some provision against fire after all, and she supposed it was mere minutes since the fire bell had first rung.

But no one seemed to be in command except Stephen.

And he was magnificent.

In breeches and flapping shirt, he was organizing the buckets to soak the tile-roofed house to the left. He directed the pump to soak the thatched one to the right.

Reaction was setting in, and Laura started to shake. It was partly the cold night air, but it was so many other things, as well. She'd left her wedding ring in her room, which was now a furnace, and that seemed a terrible sin.

Jack. What had become of Jack? She should stay out of his sight, but he was Hal's brother. She moved cautiously to the huddle around someone on the ground.

She managed to push in far enough to see. Thank heavens. He wasn't dead. He was babbling. "Sorry, so sorry. Never thought . . . Is the boy all right?"

"The boy suffered no more than a fright, thanks to you, sir." That was Dr. Nesbitt, kneeling and feeling

Jack's leg. "But you have a badly broken leg, at the least. Stay still, if you please."

"So sorry, so sorry," Jack kept saying, but then he let out a scream of pain and lost consciousness.

"As well," said the doctor. "Let's move him to my house so I can attempt to save his leg."

As men grasped the blanket to carry Jack away, Laura huddled into her robe. Perhaps the others would hear Jack's babbling as meaning he was sorry the ladder had fallen, but she knew differently.

He'd started the fire, perhaps only meaning to smoke out the rats. The same plan had occurred to her once, but been instantly dismissed for exactly this reason. Fire was too dangerous to play with. Jack's had burst out of control.

She was sorry for his pain, but to her it looked like divine justice.

Speaking of justice, where were the rats?

Over there.

She checked that Juliet and Harry were all right—they both waved—and went over to the couple who were the root and cause of all her problems. And pleasures, she must confess.

HG was sitting on the ground, Farouk on guard.

"Mr. Farouk," Laura said, "I will take care of Captain Dyer if you wish to help fight the fire."

The flames cast enough light for her to see the flat rejection in the man's dark eyes. For her also to see that without his turban, he looked different. His hair was cut short. Didn't Mahometans keep their hair long beneath their turbans?

"Captain Dyer needs my support, madam."

He was speaking in that heavy accent again, but she wondered now if he was Arab at all.

Laura turned to a respectable-looking woman. "Do you live nearby, ma'am? Could you give refuge to this poor gentleman?"

"Of course, of course!" The woman seemed delighted to help and called for a man with one of the wheeled chairs to come over.

Laura was sure Farouk would have liked to protest, but HG said with surprising dignity, "I will be safe. You go."

The touch they exchanged was strange—Farouk's hand on Dyer's shoulder and Dyer's hand covering it. What was more, Laura would swear that Farouk was saying thank you for being allowed to help. She liked the man more for that.

He lifted HG into the wheeled chair and fussed the blankets around him, but then he strode off. Despite wearing what was, in effect, a dress, he climbed nimbly up a ladder to the thatched roof to help the men there beat out fires. The most dangerous job.

Another unexpected hero.

Laura wouldn't have been surprised to find Stephen at the same task, but he was still on the ground, organizing. He probably wished he had a more daring role, but he was Sir Stephen Ball, MP, and thus in charge. Many here might not know who he was, and they certainly couldn't tell from his rough appearance. They simply recognized command.

As if feeling her eyes on him, he looked away from his duties. She waved and saw his relieved smile, teeth white in a sooty face. Then he returned to his work and she knew she was out of his thoughts, as she should be now he knew her to be safe.

She, in turn, looked back toward Harry.

Thank heavens for Juliet.

Laura turned to see where she could be of most use, but then a group of horsemen thundered down the street, lanterns waving.

Laura heard "Mr. Kerslake!" but she also heard some people whispering, "Captain Drake." A new spirit of confidence surged like another fire. The leader they knew and trusted was here now. What a burden it must be to carry such authority when so young.

Kerslake swung off his horse, his five men doing the same behind him. Local men hurried to speak to him, and he gave rapid orders. Stephen joined him and the two men clasped hands, accepting and acknowledging each other's authority. They began consulting like officers on the deck of a warship and directing the action in partnership.

After consideration, Laura slipped over to join them.

Stephen's eyes kissed hers, but he didn't do or say anything revealing. Kerslake looked at her blankly a moment, then said, "Mrs. Penfold. I hope you're not hurt."

"Not at all, but I'm relieved to see you here. We need to talk when things are under control."

His look was understanding. "Where are our mysteries?"

"Farouk's up on the roof, and the other man's in a cottage. My sister and child are here, however, and Stephen made some complicated arrangements that included your Crag Wyvern."

"I received the message. That can go ahead. When things are under control here, a boat will take you all there, the two mystery men included." He flashed her a smile. "I, too, want to know the whole story."

Then he turned back to business, and Laura, suddenly exhausted, went over to take the wide-eyed Harry.

"He wants to get down," Juliet said, clearly exhausted, too, "but I neglected his shoes."

"And you're in your petticoat and cloak. It occurs to me that none of us have a stitch other than what we're wearing. How are we going to explain *that* to Father?" She kissed her son's cheek. "Another adventure, Minnow. You'll have a great deal to tell Nan when you get back, because soon you're going in a boat to a castle."

Chapter 43

It was a while, and Harry went to sleep in Laura's arms. They were offered blankets, so Laura bundled him up. They were offered shelter, too, but she explained that they were soon to go to Crag Wyvern. A woman brought them mulled cider, and that was certainly welcome.

How were they going to explain an almost total lack of possessions? Perhaps she'd have to tell the truth. She'd prefer that, and it wouldn't matter so much now that she and Stephen were to marry.

Despite weariness and Harry's weight, she smiled.

Poor Juliet was sitting down, huddled in a blanket, clutching a pottery beaker of cider, so Laura was deeply relieved when Stephen came over.

He took Harry from her, and that was a relief, too. "We can leave now. Squire Ryall's arrived, and Captain Sillitoe. There's a boat at the jetty. Kerslake's own, apparently. The *Buttercup*."

"Shouldn't a smuggling master's boat have a more awe-inspiring name?"

He gave an arm to help Juliet up.

"Remember, the point is not to look significant. And besides, I doubt he brings in cargo anymore than Wellington holds the line in battle."

They made their way to the wooden jetty and along to a fishing smack and a cheerful fellow called Ham

Pisley, who helped them aboard. Laura looked back for a moment at the fire, hardly able to believe that it was so little time since she and Stephen had been making love in that inn.

It was mostly a blackened skeleton now, angry red in places, with flames still licking hungrily in search of new food. The adjacent buildings had been saved, thank God, and as far as she knew, no lives had been lost.

She went into a cabin that was small but comfortably appointed. There was a narrow bunk, and she encouraged Juliet to collapse onto it, Harry beside her, tucked against the wall.

Laura turned into Stephen's arms and rested against him. "You must be as tired as I am."

His arms were strong around her. "We will cope. We're alive and betrothed, yes?"

She looked up and smiled. "Yes."

"So this is perfect."

"No," she said with a chuckle, "but it will do for now."

"You lost your wig somewhere."

She put her hand to her head. "Perish it. Ah, well. I'm too tired to try to piece together a story to cover all this."

"As am I." He kissed her. "I have to get Farouk and HG, then we'll be off."

"You're a hero. I'm not sure I can keep my eyes open."

"You gave up the bed, which makes you a heroine." He opened some cupboards and found an extra mattress. It was thin, but Laura gratefully sank down onto it.

"Definitely a hero," she said, her eyes closing even as she felt him tuck an extra blanket around her.

"Jack started the fire," she managed to mumble.

"I suspected as much. He was here under a false name—Mr. John Dyer, if you can believe it—so we might be able to slither through it all without connection to the Gardeynes."

She probably should discuss it, come up with plans, consider what all this meant to Harry's future, but instead she surrendered to sleep.

Laura was only blearily aware of landing and being carried to some sort of vehicle for a rather rough ride. Then she was carried again to a bed, and knew no more until opening her eyes to daylight.

She, Harry, and Juliet were in a large bed in a large bedchamber that seemed to be decorated in a pale, classical style. One wall was taken up by a mural of St. George and the dragon. Strange, but not as peculiar as she'd been led to fear. A fire burned in the massive hearth, but the room still had a chilly feel and perhaps even a touch of moldy disuse.

Laura sat up, careful not to wake the others, and smiled. Clothing! There was a small pile of boy's garments, and spread over the backs of two chairs, ladies' garments. She slipped out of the bed to inspect the treasure. Juliet would not be thrilled. Both dresses were of a severe gray and plain cut, and the shifts, stockings, and corsets, while white, matched. The housekeeper's clothes? Or was there a Puritan in the house? Laura didn't mind. She was used to mourning dullness, anyway, and any decent clothing was a treasure.

In fact, dull might be excellent today, as her father would arrive demanding explanations. What could she tell him that would make sense of all this?

Then she remembered last night deciding to tell him the truth, or almost all of it, and her heart eased. Her dislike of lying made her a very poor conspirator, but Stephen had agreed.

And they were to marry.

She went to the window and looked down on an enclosed garden. From the season, and perhaps from neglect, it was not a thing of beauty, but it could be made pleasant. Some sort of fountain stood in the center, dry and unused.

They were to marry.

Memories of the night, of the earlier part of the night and their lovemaking, swept over her, making her smile and hug herself. She rubbed her hands up and down a body whose appetites had been stimulated rather than sated even by those intense hours of pleasure.

It had been a kind of madness to go to him. She'd known it at the time. And a kind of wickedness. But she'd lost the will to resist, the will to be restrained and sensible. Apart from any need of Harry's, she'd realized that she wanted Stephen more desperately than she'd wanted anything in her life and could not bear to part in case she might lose him.

But she'd had to warn him. After that last kiss, she'd thought she knew him, knew him to be passionate, but she'd also known that they would make a sour marriage if he preferred modest propriety in a wife, even in private. She simply couldn't do it. She'd enjoyed a lusty marriage, and the fires of desire burned fiercely in her.

She smiled, and perhaps she blushed. No doubt now that he was an equally lusty man, and skilled. More skilled than Hal in ways, because he had more control and patience. Perhaps even because he was more clever. She'd never before appreciated the wonders of a brilliant lover. . . .

She shook herself. She couldn't spend the day mooning over Stephen, and much more of this and she'd be hunting him down to leap on him in passion!

And their life would not be totally smooth. She brought trouble as her dowry. She turned to look at Harry, sleeping so innocently, sprawled on his back. Wicked to wish Jack dead of his wounds, but she did. It would make everything so much simpler.

There was no clock here, and the Crag Wyvern

walls made it difficult to judge the hour from the sun, but it was not particularly early. Time to be up and about and find out what was happening. The first requirement was washing water. They were all grubby and smelt slightly of smoke.

She inspected the room. There was a door in one wall, but it was locked. Another opened into the corridor, and that did startle her.

The corridor was gloomy because the only light came from the arrow slits Stephen had mentioned. The walls appeared to be rough stone with green spots that indicated damp. When she touched one, however, she realized it was all paint. Trompe l'oeil.

Kerslake had said the previous earl was mad. If this was his work, he'd certainly been eccentric. There were even weapons hanging at regular intervals along the wall, and they weren't a trick of paint.

She retreated back to the classical setting. She'd have to keep a close eye on Harry. This place might frighten him, and heaven knows what other peculiarities it contained.

She found the bellpull and tugged on it, wondering about Stephen's complex plans. Hadn't Kerslake implied that they'd been put into effect? Could the Delaneys already be here? That would mean she could spin the story they'd prepared. . . .

She pushed the temptation aside.

A bone-thin maid with wide, pale eyes came in carrying a large, steaming jug of water. She put it on the washstand and curtsied nervously. "Will there be anything else, mum?"

She looked like a scared, emaciated sheep.

"Do you know what other guests are in the house?" Laura asked. "And where breakfast will be available?"

The young woman blinked. "Mr. Kerslake's here, mum, and Mr. Delaney, and a Sir Stephen Ball, and two other gentlemen what I don't know the names of, mum. And you, mum, and the lady and the lad in the bed there. I think that's it, and breakfast's in the breakfast room, mum!"

The maid came to the end of her recitation, looking as if she'd just attempted a test. Then she gasped, dug into a pocket, and produced a folded piece of paper.

"Mr. Kerslake said to give you this, mum! It's a map, on account of there's short ways and long ways here, see, and you'd probably better not take the short ways. And he said to say sorry if the skeleton scares your little boy."

Laura was struggling with laughter and perplexity, but she managed a sober "Thank you," and the maid left.

Shaking her head, she unfolded the paper to find a hand-drawn map of two levels of Crag Wyvern. The place was a square with the garden in the middle. The rooms all looked into the garden and corridors ran around the outside wall. A cross marked the George and the Dragon Room on the upper floor. Another marked a drawing room on the ground floor. That sounded pleasantly normal, but she'd believe it when she saw it.

Not far from the drawing room was the breakfast parlor, which also sounded normal. Perhaps the peculiarities were kept for the upper, more private floor.

There were circular staircases in each corner of the building, but she was directed by arrows past one of those to a wide, straight staircase down to the hall.

Lady Skylark stirred, suggesting that the inadvisable spiral staircase might be fun, but responsible Laura shooed her away.

"What's that?" Juliet asked sleepily. "And where are we?"

"Crag Wyvern, for which we apparently need a map." She handed over the paper.

Juliet sat up, rubbing her eyes, and took it. She chuckled. "Extraordinary and intriguing."

"You can explore later. For now, we'd best be up and dressed—we have clothing—and meet the others to sort all this out." She faced her sister. "I'm going to tell the truth, Ju."

"Oh, good. I don't see how I could keep a story straight that would cover all of this."

They shared a smile, then washed and helped each other to dress. Juliet, as expected, grumbled about the plain gowns, but she was only teasing. Laura realized that though she'd be dressed again in plain clothes, she didn't have to wear a disguise. Tidying her hair in the mirror around her familiar features was a delight. No hairpins had been provided, however, so she had to leave her hair loose, as did Juliet.

"We look like girls again."

"From a very severe school."

Harry woke up, wide-eyed. "Where are we, Mama?"

She went to lift him out of the bed. "In the castle I told you about. It's called Crag Wyvern, and it might be a little bit frightening, but there's nothing here that can hurt you."

As she said that, she remembered the weapons. Yes, Harry would have to be under someone's eye all the time.

When she put him down, he ran over to the picture. "That's a scary dragon," he said, looking not at all alarmed. "*Roar!*"

Laura laughed, delighted that he seemed no worse for his adventures.

Chapter 44

All the same, when he was clean and dressed and they were about to leave the room, she took his hand. "This is a castle, Harry, so the corridors are dark and a little frightening, but you are safe with us."

To her surprise, from the security of her company, Harry was thrilled by the gloom and the weapons. The skeleton hanging in one corner, close to the arch into the forbidden stairs, was a particular wonder.

"A real little Gardeyne," Laura said to Juliet. "No wandering here, Harry. You must stay with an adult at all times."

The recommended wide stone staircase led down to a baronial hall full of dark oak furniture and hung with enough medieval weaponry for a small army. Harry was wide-eyed and had to be towed along to the breakfast room, which clearly disappointed him, though it was hardly in normal modern style. Instead it made Laura think of a medieval refectory with its white walls and long oak table, but it was of moderate size and lacking blades other than table knives.

Food was clearly some compensation, however, as he ran to the table and climbed into a chair. One next to Stephen, in fact. Harry looked at him and said, "Good morning, sir. There's a dragon in my room. *Roar!*"

Everyone laughed, but Laura said, "No more animal noises at table, Harry."

She had the choice of a seat beside Harry or beside Stephen. With regret, she sat beside her son, but the smile she and Stephen shared was almost enough for now. She had to suppress another smile because though he was normally dressed, it was not to his usual standards. She suspected the clothes were Kerslake's, and he had a taste for country clothes as well as being more heavily built. All the same, Stephen gave them an elegance they'd probably not known before.

She gathered her wits and introduced the other men—Nicholas Delaney and David Kerslake—to Harry and her sister.

"My apologies about the map," Kerslake said, "but there's only a small staff here at the moment, and mostly unused to serving guests. I'm still living at my uncle's house nearby, Kerslake Manor."

As Stephen was Stephen and Nicholas Nicholas, Kerslake was soon David, even to Juliet, who looked delighted with all this informality. In fact, she was looking delighted with everything. She'd always enjoyed handsome men.

They settled to reviewing their strategies.

"Eleanor and Arabel are at Kerslake Manor," Nicholas said. "We thought the Crag might be a bit much for her yet. Perhaps Harry would like to go down there."

Laura looked at her son, who was building a tower from "logs" of toast supplied by ingenious Stephen. "You're right. He will become bored soon, but I doubt he'll want to leave me."

"He'll go with me," said Juliet, giving Laura a wry smile. "Yes, I'd like to stay, but this is your adventure, not mine." She turned to David. "Are there animals at the manor?"

"Certainly. Even ponies small enough for him to ride."

Harry looked up. "Ponies?"

Juliet came round the table. "Ponies. Come along, pet. Mama will join us soon."

Harry gave Laura a doubtful glance, and she had to admit that she was pleased he was less careless about parting from her this time. She gave him a hug. "It's not far, Minnow, and I'll join you there soon."

He hugged her back tightly. "Promise?"

"Promise, sweetheart."

With that assurance, he slid off the chair, took Juliet's hand, and towed her away, already chattering about ponies.

They all chuckled, and Laura found his happiness didn't hurt. He didn't love her less for being happy to go with others, and thanks be to God, he was in no special danger at the moment. Jack Gardeyne was not plotting harm right now.

She was about to ask about Jack when Stephen said, "We have to assume that your father and perhaps Ned will be here soon." He met her eyes. "It probably would be best to tell him the truth."

She nodded and saw his relief. "Or most of it," she amended.

A grin twitched his lips. "Indeed. Fathers will be fathers."

"But what about Jack?" she asked, unable to put into words her hope that he was dead.

"Reports from Draycombe say he'll live and probably keep his leg, but he'll never walk as easily as before and may have trouble riding."

"Oh, poor Jack." The words escaped and she looked around at the men. "Does that make me feeble? I have been thinking how much easier everything would be if he were dead."

Nicholas smiled. "It makes you compassionate, but he deserves punishment, especially as he'll doubtless escape other justice. It would be hard to prove anything, even starting the fire. And it would be inconvenient for you to have a Gardeyne on trial."

"It would probably kill his father."

"Which is why," Stephen said, "it's useful that he was in Draycombe as John Dyer. Clever move, really. It could have given him a way to get to a possible relative, Captain Egan Dyer."

A chill went down Laura's back. "He so *cunning*. I never would have thought. How are we to keep Harry safe? I want Jack away from Caldfort. Far away."

Stephen took her hand. "That can be done, I think. Maybe not until Lord Caldfort's death, but now we're promised, I believe I can persuade your father-in-law to make me Harry's guardian."

"And perhaps he'll let me stay at Merrymead until the wedding. I wonder if he suspected Jack, or if it was just the mysterious letter that made him want me out of the way."

"Perhaps a combination of both. He's a lazy man who likes his own way, but he's not stupid, and not without insight."

"If Caldfort proves difficult, there are many ways to exert pressure," Nicholas said in a pleasant manner at odds with the cool purpose in his eyes. "When do you plan to marry? Sooner would be better."

Stephen explained the discretions of propriety. Laura thought Nicholas had little patience with it, but he didn't argue. "Then stay at Merrymead, Laura. Even if Caldfort objects, any attempt to drag Harry away by legal force will take more than a month or two, especially with Steve handling the legal end. Why not marry on Gaudete Sunday, the third Sunday in Advent, devoted to rejoicing? An ecclesiastical calendar would give us the exact date."

David pulled a humorous face, but he rose. "I'll go and see if the library here has such a religious tome."

Nicholas rose, too. "I'll help."

"Anything to poke around in the books here again," Stephen said with a grin, but turned to Laura. "And to tactfully leave us together for a little while."

He moved to the chair next to hers and took her into his arms. It felt, thought Laura, like coming home. She opened her mouth to him and let her hands explore the body she had learned well and would learn even better, but she remembered where they were and eventually gently pushed free.

"They'll be back soon."

"I doubt it." His eyes smiled at her. "I thought you were not at all shy."

"There's a difference between shyness and propriety!" But she was smiling, too, mostly at memories stirred by his words. She ran her fingers back through his hair. "I never had the chance to tell you what a wonderful lover you are."

He colored slightly, but his eyes darkened. "Whatever I am, you are my match. It's more than that, though—"

She slid her fingers over his lips. "Yes, of course, but it's a delightful icing on the cake, isn't it?"

He laughed with her and they kissed again. She forgot propriety, and it was he who broke the kiss and moved away. "They're coming. Very noisily."

Laura was fighting laughter and blushes and knew she must look well kissed, and she saw a hint of humor on the two men's faces as they came into the room, but nothing was said.

"December fifteenth," Nicholas declared.

"And a day of rejoicing," Laura said. "I like that. We have much to rejoice for, and we can celebrate our first Christmas at Ancross and at Merrymead, Stephen. I have so missed Christmases there."

Stephen smiled, but then he looked at Nicholas. "How many Rogues do you think we can assemble for the wedding? I would open Ancross to them, of course."

"A house party!" Nicholas declared. "A splendid idea. And I take your point. If Reverend Gardeyne clings to his plans, he needs to see just how powerfully young Harry is protected. Me, of course, but I'm a mere commoner. Luce and Beth may be willing to travel. The baby will be about six months old. In fact, Luce could be your groomsman. Unsubtle to wield the heir to a dukedom like that, but there are times when a sharp battle-ax is an effective deterrent. If not, an earl will do, especially when well supported by minor titles."

"Lee? Good idea." Stephen turned to Laura. "Earl of Charrington."

"My, my."

"And," said Nicholas, "we could possibly persuade the Duke of St. Raven to grace the event."

"My, my, my! The whole Barham area will be in ferment for weeks."

Kerslake spoke. "A notorious almost-earl pales by comparison, but if my presence will add weight, I'm happy to oblige. I have a personal score with the vicar for causing damage in my territory, and I admit, I'm curious to meet more of the Rogues."

Laura was considering other matters. "In addition to all this," she said, "I still want Jack away from Caldfort. Harry will have to visit there, more and more as he grows up, and I will not have Jack nearby."

She had all their attention.

"What do you have in mind?" Stephen asked.

She looked at him. "Once Harry is the viscount, he—or his guardian and trustees, rather—have control of that living. It can be taken away from Jack."

"That will cause talk."

"Not if we find him a richer one elsewhere."

"A promotion," Stephen said. "Very clever, though he doesn't deserve it. I'd rather he end up in the roughest parish in a city."

"I know, but it seems he will live with his punish-ment, and I think he truly was horrified by the results of his actions. Also, it wouldn't be fair for Emma and his children to suffer from his actions. They are inno-cent. In fact, if a living could be found in the north, she would be happy to be close to her family."

"You have a very kind heart," Stephen said, and his smile was like a kiss, "but yes, that should be possible."

"There we are, then," Nicholas said. "The only thread remaining is our mysterious villains. I can't leave without understanding what they were up to."

"Where are they?" Laura asked.

"They were shown to a room last night and locked in," Stephen said. "None of us was up to a confronta-tion then. Nicholas and I took them breakfast, washing water, and clothing a while ago—armed, in case—but they volunteered nothing but thanks."

He looked at her. "I had begun to wonder if HG was a woman in disguise."

"Oh, no," Laura said. "Or if so, a very manly one." She puzzled over it. "It would explain a great deal, but I really don't think so. He's fine boned for a man and has those soft hands, but they're a man's hands. Much bigger than mine."

"I agree," Stephen said, but there was a strange expression on his face.

Perhaps he'd noticed what she'd noticed, but she didn't see why that should make him look almost embarrassed.

"I don't think Farouk is Arab," she said. "Last night, without his turban, and in the strange firelight, he could have been an Englishman." No one seemed surprised. "But why the masquerade? Were they pre-tending to have been slaves to the corsairs, and if so, why? If that part is true, why did he dress as an Arab? And why try to extort money from Lord Caldfort?"

"Perhaps they met Henry Gardeyne in the Mediterranean before he died," Stephen offered, but he obviously didn't like the hypothesis.

"The only way is to ask them," Nicholas said. "We nobly decided to wait until you were ready, Laura."

"After all," Stephen said, "any decisions are still yours to make."

She frowned. "Why? It's not a matter affecting Harry or Caldfort anymore."

"It has to be something to do with Caldfort. That letter can't have been a shot in the dark, and it enclosed something that persuaded Lord Caldfort of the claim." Stephen rose, drawing her to her feet. "Let's go and find out."

Everyone rose. "They're in the Jason room," David said. "It has mazes on all the walls, which seemed suitable. If you don't mind, however, I will leave the questioning to you. I should go to Draycombe to give assistance."

"If you can," said Stephen, "get Jack Gardeyne away from there before he says too much."

David nodded and left, and the rest of them went upstairs and along more of the strange corridors. Stephen unlocked a door and they went in.

Laura had a vague impression of walls decorated entirely with mazes, but she paid no attention to them, only to the human puzzles. "Farouk" was standing beside the bed upon which HG lay right on the edge, propped up with pillows. They were almost touching, as if HG couldn't bear to be far away. From his protector or his master?

There was absolutely no doubt about one thing. In jacket, shirt, and breeches, Farouk looked exactly what she'd thought him—an Englishman who'd been exposed to too much sun. In Algiers as a slave? Why, then, was HG so pale?

HG wore similar clothes, and to Laura's eyes there was no doubt that he was a man. Despite pale skin and soft hands, she could sense a strong body and see quite broad shoulders. Then he gave her one of his fluttering, wicked smiles and she was confused again. "You're beautiful, Mrs. Penfold."

"It's Mrs. Gardeyne," Laura said, and saw Farouk start, then stare at her.

She stared back, and her artist's eye absorbed what she was seeing. She'd been entirely wrong in aging that portrait because she'd been focused on frail Dyer. There was nothing frail about this man.

"*You're* Henry Gardeyne!" she exclaimed, and heard the stir around her.

The dark-skinned man made no comment, but Stephen said, "Ah, the final piece of the puzzle. I'm Stephen Ball, by the way, sir. This is my friend, Mr. Delaney. Will you introduce us to your friend?"

When Henry stayed still and silent, Stephen added, "Believe me, we wish you no harm. Quite the contrary, in fact."

"I find that hard to believe." Henry Gardeyne spoke in perfect gentleman's English, as he had when Laura had been listening through the wall, but now she thought there was the slightest trace of an accent after all, or a foreign intonation, something burned into him as the sun had burned his skin.

For nine years, Laura thought, shifting all she knew and trying to make a new picture. Why had Henry Gardeyne lingered in the Barbary States for so long when he could have bought his release at any time? Having done so, why—as Nicholas had asked before— decide to come home *now*? He hadn't needed liberating by the British navy.

She was dazzled, however, by happiness. Henry Gardeyne was alive, and so Harry wasn't the Caldfort heir anymore. He was safe!

"I'm sure you've lived where truth doesn't serve, sir," Stephen said, "but it is different here. Unless you have committed a serious crime, you have my word that you and your companion will be safe."

"And you can trust him," Nicholas added lightly. "You can trust us all, but Stephen's the most impeccably honorable."

Henry Gardeyne bowed his head then. "In Draycombe, I heard people talk of Sir Stephen Ball with great respect."

Laura smiled up at Stephen, seeing, as she expected, embarrassment.

"We can't help you without the truth, though," Stephen said. "Why did you try to extort money from Lord Caldfort when everything he possesses is rightfully yours?"

Laura saw HG grasp Henry's hand, pale against dark. "You didn't tell me, Fellow."

Henry spoke without looking at him. "It didn't matter, Des. It still doesn't. I don't want the title and estates, but we need money and I don't see why I shouldn't have part." He looked coldly around the room. "I still don't. I assume Lord Caldfort will pay to keep what he has."

"Then why not approach him that way before?" Laura demanded. "Why the offer to kill the rightful viscount?"

The hint of a smile touched Henry Gardeyne's features. "Perhaps I have spent too long in a land where indirect ways are favored over the direct. It seemed neatest. Once done, no one would ever know that Henry Gardeyne still lived."

Laura glanced around, wondering if she was exceptionally dull, if the situation made sense to everyone else.

"You were depending upon your relatives' lack of honor," Stephen pointed out. "Perhaps with reason, but you underestimated it. Your cousin set fire to the inn."

"Hal?" Henry said with a frown.

"Hal's dead. Mrs. Gardeyne is his widow."

"*Jack?* He was studying for the cloth."

"And is now the vicar of St. Edwin's, but carried away despite that on a wave of wickedness." Stephen sketched the recent events.

"Like most such people," Nicholas said, "he found himself in waters far rougher than he'd intended. He will be a concern to you, but I think his fangs are drawn."

Henry had relaxed somewhat, but now he became cold again. "He is nothing to me. I repeat. I will not claim the viscountcy. All I want, all we want," he amended, with a look at "Des," whose hand he still held, "is enough money to live in peace somewhere on this earth."

Laura looked at the two hands, absorbed the tone of Henry's voice, and understood.

"Oh." It escaped before she could stop it and she felt her cheeks burn. "I am *not* embarrassed!" she protested. "Just startled."

When Stephen laughed, she turned on him. "Do you mean you knew?"

"No. Well, not exactly." He winced and looked across at the two men. "My deepest apologies, sirs, but you see, we had the means of listening through the walls. And last night I had to move to the room beyond your bedchamber."

Henry looked outraged, but HG laughed with a faun's guiltless merriment. It made Laura smile, too, but how had these two very different men come together?

"I assure you," Stephen said, "that I stopped listening as soon as I realized, and even then, I thought you man and woman. I hadn't seen you then, sir," he added to the younger man.

"I'm glad there's no doubt," Des said with a coy flutter that was obviously put on for effect. He was a bewildering mix of masculinity and beauty that Laura found hard to fit into any slot in her mind. She abandoned the effort.

"I'm learning a great deal," she said, "but I still understand nothing. Could we perhaps have a name? Des, I think?"

He cast a questioning glance at his lover, then said, "If you wish. It's short for Desdemona, though."

Another piece clicked into place. " 'Thello, not 'Fellow,' " Laura exclaimed. "The moor and his fair wife."

For some reason that did embarrass her, especially when her mind began to fill in some of what she'd listened to. She'd known that some men preferred male lovers. She'd even known some men who were clearly of that type. She'd never before thought about it as another form of marriage.

The moment was interrupted by a knock on the door. Nicholas opened it.

The thin maid bobbed a curtsy. "There's a Mr. Watcombe here, sir, looking for his daughters!"

Chapter 45

Suddenly panicked, Laura sucked in a breath and looked at Stephen. "I'd forgotten Father. Here comes our need to explain everything."

"I admit," said Henry, not without an edge, "that I am curious as to why my cousin's widow was staying at an inn in disguise, with a lover."

Laura grabbed Stephen's arm before he could react to that. "Don't cast stones, sir. You are dependent on our goodwill."

"It seems I have a weapon to hold against you, however."

"Not equal to ours," Stephen said grimly. "Our sin is not a capital crime."

Henry jerked as if hit, and Des paled.

"You see, then, why I cannot become Lord Caldfort. I will not separate from Des. I will not marry and beget an heir." He rested his hand on his lover's shoulder. "We have come too far and suffered too much to be separated now."

"But—"

Nicholas cut Stephen off. "Not now, Steve. You and Laura have to go and pacify her father and get his blessing. We will leave Mr. Gardeyne and his companion in peace to talk things over, and resume this later." But he added to Henry, "It would lend more dignity to your companion for him to have a full name."

Henry's dark skin hid it, but Laura suspected he blushed. "You're right." He looked down at the blond man. "What name do you want to use, Des?"

"Not the one I was born with. I like being Des."

"Despard," Laura offered. "It was one possibility I came up with to fit with Des. Egan Despard, perhaps? The anagrams were very clever."

"We played with them," Des said. " 'Thello and I. I'm very good at it. Draycombe, for example, throws up both *my brocade* and *cream body*. Which," he added, in that lid-lowered, wicked way he had, "are very pleasing images."

Laura couldn't help thinking of him as a naughty child, and she shook her head at him before leaving with Stephen to face her father. "What's going to become of him?" she asked as they hurried down a corridor. "He seems both wicked and unworldly."

"Gardeyne will look after him, I assume. You're not too shocked?"

She stopped to look at him. "I thought I'd shown you last night that I'm no delicate bloom. I was never wicked, Stephen, and I kept my marriage vows, but Lady Skylark moved in racy circles."

He smiled and drew her close for a light kiss. "I can't complain, but it will take me a little while to adjust. Be patient."

To prove her point, she deepened it, pressing him against the wall, moving against him, feeling his response. . . .

Father!

She pushed back and straightened her stern gown.

"I know," he said, "your father's waiting, and we probably shouldn't appear looking too thoroughly kissed. But," he added, "I don't think I can wait until Gaudete Sunday to rejoice again."

She smiled and suspected she blushed, not with embarrassment but with desire.

"Me neither. We'll find ways."

Breathless with need, she pulled him on and down the stairs.

They found her father in the drawing room, which was surprisingly normal, with silk wallpaper and plaster cornices and inoffensive landscapes hanging on the wall.

Her father, however, was in a stern mood.

"What's this all about, Laura?"

With a gulp, Laura plunged into the truth, leaving out only the fact that she and Stephen had anticipated their wedding.

Fortunately, he latched on to Jack's behavior. "Such wickedness! Are you sure, Laury?"

"As sure as I can be."

"And there's little doubt that he set the fire in Draycombe, sir," Stephen added.

Her father shook his head. "What a terrible thing. But to be poking around in someone's desk, Laury . . ."

"If I hadn't, heaven knows what might have happened, Father."

"But why couldn't you have told us? You always were impetuous."

Laura managed not to look at Stephen. "I wasn't sure, you see. I had no evidence, and I knew you'd be too fair-minded to act without."

She prayed that would appease him, and it seemed to. "Well, that's discreet, I suppose. And you were wise enough to disguise yourself. But if you'd been detected, love!"

"We were very careful, and see, this has brought Stephen and me back together. I hope you'll give us your blessing, Father. We hope to marry from Merrymead in December."

That turned his mind to much happier channels.

"It'll be grand to have you close, Laury. You'll be refurbishing Ancross, then, Stephen?"

The two men talked a little of such practical matters.

Then her father looked at Laura. "You'll have a complicated life, Laury, what with Stephen's political work and two estates to oversee. Those men of Lord Caldfort's said that he's in a bad way. If he had wind of his son's wickedness, it's not surprising, but Harry may be Viscount Caldfort sooner than you thought."

Or perhaps not, Laura thought. Surely Henry could be persuaded to claim the viscountcy.

"Together, Stephen and I will manage."

"Even if you end up as Prime Minister, Stephen?" her father demanded. "That's what some predict for you."

Stephen shook his head. "I have no desire for it, and it will be a long time before an uncompromising reformer leads the country. If ever."

Laura couldn't help but be pleased about that. She would enjoy being Stephen's partner in politics, but that degree of responsibility would be a burden.

Her father stood. "Well, I think I'll go back down to Kerslake Manor. I don't care for this place, and Sir Nathaniel Kerslake mentioned some bean crops that sounded interesting. You'd best come with me, Laury."

Laura was feeling as if she was back in the schoolroom, but she managed to say, "I will come down in a little while, Father. I promised Harry. But there are a few things I need to take care of here first."

She saw him begin to ask what and stop himself. Perhaps he remembered that she was a grown woman, or he may have decided that she should be allowed to do a little courting. He nodded and took his leave.

Laura blew out a breath. "Now to convince Henry to assert his claim to the viscountcy."

"I'm not sure how we can if he's resolute."

She frowned at him in dismay. "But it would be wrong for Harry to become viscount now—quite apart from the danger it puts him in."

Stephen shrugged. "We might as well continue our discussion in here. I'll go and get the others. Remember, though, that the Rogues can defang Jack Gardeyne and I suspect that events in Draycombe may have shocked him to his senses."

Laura paced the room as she waited, realizing that this room was peculiar after all. It had only one small window and thus needed lamps in the morning. She didn't envy David Kerslake the possession of this place.

But surely there was a way to persuade Henry Gardeyne to claim the viscountcy. True, his . . . intimate relations made things difficult, and as Stephen had said, what they did was a capital crime. She thought she remembered a case involving some men of the upper class, and though they hadn't been hanged they'd been put in the stocks. The mob had been so outraged that they'd killed one by throwing stones before the guards had stepped in and put a stop to it.

But if he was discreet . . .

The others came in, Henry carrying Des. He put the younger man on the sofa. "Let us be clear from the start," he said, as Laura, Stephen, and Nicholas took seats. "I will not take up the role of Lord Caldfort."

"Please be seated, Gardeyne," Stephen said. "You're not a prisoner in the dock."

Henry sat but did not relax. Des smiled slightly and took his hand, obviously attempting to soothe him.

"Perhaps you could tell us your story," Stephen said, "and help us to understand. Then we can help you."

"Why would you wish to?"

"We're a philanthropic society," Nicholas said,

"particularly dedicated to the succor of rescued slaves and reluctant viscounts."

Henry studied him. "Why?"

"For right and justice, but also I'd like to learn more about Arab ways."

Stephen groaned. "Don't pander to him. He'll pick your mind dry."

For some reason, this seemed to release all the tension. Henry relaxed at last. "Our story is one of medium length."

"We have time."

Henry shrugged. "I assume you know that I traveled to the Mediterranean, despite the difficulties in sea travel at the time. I hoped to visit Greece and Egypt. A strange Gardeyne, I, being seriously interested in antiquities.

"I took passage on the *Mary Woodside,* whose master hoped to make the Ottoman lands and bring back a rich cargo. Des was the cabin boy." He touched Des's arm, his face softening with obvious love. "His real name is Isaiah Wissett, by the way."

Des winced, laughing. "Did you have to tell them?"

Henry smiled, then sobered. "I assure you I respected his youth. He was only thirteen and astonishingly innocent, even though he'd run away from home. He could read and write, but had never read anything except the Bible and knew nothing of the world. It quite terrified me, so I read other books with him and taught him geography, history, and the like. I'd never imagined that I'd like to be a teacher.

"We made it past the British and French blockades, but were felled by a storm. The ship went down, but a few of us got away in boats. Perhaps the other boats made land, but after days adrift, ours fell into the hands of the corsairs. I need not bore you with the details. It was the usual thing, which has been described in detail in the papers here."

"We wondered," Stephen said, "why you did not announce yourself a gentleman and arrange ransom."

"We had been some time in the boats, and I'd taken to it in my nightshirt, so there was nothing gentlemanly about me by then. I could have proved my status in time, but for the moment I stayed close to Des. Being so young, he was very frightened, and I assumed that when I arranged my freedom, I would be able to arrange his, too. Unfortunately, I didn't understand the value of his type—young, fair skinned, and beautiful. He was instantly purchased for a harem."

Even though Laura wasn't naive, it took a moment for her to understand quite what that meant. A male harem.

"Des did not go calmly to his fate. He was only thirteen, and he screamed and cried for me. His owner whipped him, but when he wouldn't calm, Abdul-Alim bought me to pacify his new 'pearl.' Like a pet. Like a dog. I was kept in the yard like a dog, but provided with shelter from the sun and given adequate food. Des was allowed to spend time with me as long as we did not touch and were in full sight of the guards."

"Couldn't you have revealed your identity and been ransomed," Stephen asked, "and then bought the boy's freedom?"

"That would have been delightful, but I soon learned that Abdul-Alim let no one else have his pearls. They were never sold. When they ceased to please, whether from bad behavior or from growing coarse with age, they were killed. So," he said with a shrug, "I stayed."

Laura stared at him. "What of your father? Your apparent death broke his heart."

Henry looked down for a moment, but then met her eyes. "I would have broken it sooner or later, Cousin. I would not have been able to hide my tastes forever, and he would never have been able to accept it. He was a Gardeyne, after all."

"So are you."

"Any family can produce an oddity. It's why I went abroad, to spare him and to try to find my place in the world. Ironically, I did, after a fashion."

"Go on with your story," Stephen said.

"I was allowed to continue Des's education, and Abdul-Alim soon came to see that I wasn't a common sailor, though he assumed me a lowly scholar or clerk. It amused him to have me to turn his English Pearl, as he called Des, into a gentleman. He even purchased European clothes for him to wear on occasion, though not quite of the sober style favored these days. It didn't matter. All that mattered was that we had more time, and even English books to read together.

"But," he said grimly, "Des was being educated in other ways. Trained for the harem. He turned to me for advice. What could I do? I advised him to cooperate, to do everything that Abdul-Alim required."

"It wasn't so bad," Des interrupted, clearly to reassure. "I liked the music and dancing, and I miss swimming in the warm pool, and the massage afterward. I made friends with other boys, and," he added with a genuine smile, "there was never any work. I could lie in bed as long as I wanted, and had servants to do everything I asked."

Laura supposed that for a child of a stern Methodist family who'd preferred the hard life of a cabin boy, this could have seemed like heaven.

But then he shrugged. "Or almost everything. We were never allowed to leave the palace. There were grilled windows, though, so we could look out."

"As you see," Henry said dryly, "Abdul-Alim was never needlessly cruel, and in our first years there, Des was one of his favorites. He doted on him, and thus became kind to me."

"Did he not suspect your feelings?" Nicholas asked.

"Probably, but if so, it would have amused him. He was quite sure that nothing could happen. Which was true. We were never alone and we both knew the punishment would be extreme and not at all quick. We witnessed it a time or two."

Des's lashes were lowered, but his lips formed a grim line. For the first time Laura wondered with horror what had caused his infirmity.

"I was gradually given better quarters," Henry went on. "By a year after our arrival, I was living in a small house close to Abdul-Alim's compound with a slave of my own. Ironically, a Greek girl with no knowledge of classics at all. I was allowed to move around Algiers freely and meet Des almost as often as I wished, but only in the palace courtyard, in sight of the guards. So there we were. I decided that I might as well use my spare time to study the place to which fate had taken me. It proved satisfying."

"But for nine years?" Laura asked.

Henry shrugged. "I learned a suitable acceptance of fate. Apart from one thing, it was not an unpleasant life. The culture, at its best, is gracious."

"And then the British came to set you free," Stephen said.

Henry's face returned to Farouk's coldness. "And then the bloody British came to set us free. No, I shouldn't be bitter, but I was furious at the time. I knew that Abdul-Alim would kill his pearls rather than let them go. Thus I would have to try to get Des out of there. Which would doubtless lead to a slow and excruciating death for both of us."

His hand had become a fist, and Des gently covered it.

"Des and I talked of escape, though he was as doubtful as I was. I delayed, hoping the British would fail." He spread his hands as if they'd accused him. "We had no hope of success in escaping, and had long

ince decided that the life we had was better than
nothing. But then the bombardment began, and I
knew the British would prevail. The slaves would be
freed, as they had been in other corsair states.

"Abdul-Alim began to smuggle his most precious
pearls out of the city. Des was not among the first,
for he was older so not quite as valued, but we knew
it would be soon. He was still beautiful and skilled at
pleasing. I was desperate for any plan that had the
slightest chance of success, but I hadn't found one
when they came for him."

He looked at Des, who was looking away now, his
expression not so much grim as lifeless, as if he did
not wish to remember this part.

"He was the brave, resourceful one. He hid. It was
the height of the battle and he hoped that Abdul-Alim
and his men would give up the search and flee. But
he was caught. He was beaten. Tortured. Not with the
usual refinements, for lack of time, but they would
have killed him if a shell hadn't broken down a wall
to the harem. All was panic, wounded, and dead, so I
took my chance and ran in to find him. What they'd
done . . ." He closed his eyes for a moment. "But he
was alive. He was in such pain as I carried him away,
but he never made a sound."

Tears escaped the young man's eyes and he suddenly turned his face into Henry's shoulder. Henry
put his arm around him. Laura felt that she should be
embarrassed but she wasn't. This was a remarkable
love story.

"If he was so badly injured," Stephen asked, but
even his voice sounded gruff, "why not take him to
the navy?"

Henry's look was pitying. "The battle still raged,
but besides, I could get better medical help in Algiers
if my friends would take the risk. They did. They hid
us and tended to Des until he could travel, then
helped us to a boat that would take us to Spain. I'd

carried Des away still wearing a collar and bracelets of jewels, and they helped us find a place where we could rest for a while. We had our freedom at last, and it seemed Des would live and be whole in time, but how were we to survive? The jewels wouldn't support us forever.

"So I decided to return to England. I would find a place for Des to live and then present myself at Caldfort, the dutiful son returned from the grave. Once reestablished, I would find a way for Des and me to be together as friends. You see, at this point I wasn't sure that Des's desires were the same as mine or simply part of Abdul-Alim's training. He deserved the chance to choose."

Des moved then and looked up at Henry, shaking his head. "He took some persuading, if truth be told."

Henry gave him a look, but wrapped it in a smile. "As it was, the briefest enquiries showed that it was too late for the return of the son. I was Lord Caldfort by right, but would have to wrest my property from my uncle. If I wanted it, which I didn't. Once I knew that Des shared all my feelings, I saw how that life would be torture. We would live under constant scrutiny and the *ton* would question his origins. I would be hunted by ambitious young women and under endless pressure to marry, as well as living in the shadow of the law. We would be almost as severed as in Algiers. So I decided we would make a new life, but I needed part of my heritage."

"What did you send as evidence?" Laura asked, fascinated by the couple, who had lived a romance more dramatic than anything Byron had written.

"A detailed description of the house, including places unlikely to be seen by outsiders."

"So simple. I am truly sorry you had to go through so much, Cousin Henry, but are you *sure* you don' want the viscountcy?"

He hesitated for the slightest moment, and his eyes flickered away, but then he said, "Completely sure."

Did part of him long for England and his home? She hoped for a moment, but then he became strong again.

"I have lived a long time in a foreign land. England seems strange to me now, and the climate is far too cold."

"This is autumn," Stephen pointed out. "You may like summer better."

"But there is autumn, and winter, too." He gave a theatrical shudder, but a smile lightened his lips and Laura saw a hint of the Henry Gardeyne of the portrait, but only a hint. He was right. He was a different person now.

She wanted him to take up the viscountcy to make Harry safe, but she could not try to impose it when he and Des had been through so much and would risk so much here.

"Where will you go?" she asked.

His smiled his thanks of her acceptance. "Somewhere warm. Perhaps we will wander the equatorial regions until we find a home. But," he added, "we do need money."

Her decisions to make. Laura looked around, then said, "My father says that Lord Caldfort has taken a turn for the worse, so there seems no purpose in distressing him. He must soon learn of Jack's injury, but it can be presented that Jack went to find out the truth, that the fire was complete accident and he a hero. If you are determined not to claim the viscountcy, Cousin Henry, then I would like you to write a letter admitting that your purpose was fraud and giving up your plan out of fear. That will lift a burden from him, allowing him to die in peace, for I fear it will come to that."

"Certainly, but we still need money. Des and I are

now destitute. What small amount of money we had left went with the fire. We don't even own our clothes."

"I agree that you are entitled to support from the estate, but I can't see how to arrange it now. I have very little." She looked to Stephen for help.

"A lump sum now," Stephen said, "and quarterly payments thereafter? My friends and I will arrange it until such time as it can be drawn on the estate."

Henry looked between him and Nicholas. "A philanthropic society dedicated to the succor of rescued slaves and reluctant viscounts?"

"Something like that. You will have to take my word for it."

After a silent communication with Des, Henry inclined his head in thanks. "We are free to go?"

"Of course."

"But," said Nicholas, "you would much oblige me sir, by paying me a visit at my estate of Redoaks. It is not far away, and as you said, you are temporarily embarrassed for funds. I would only ask to learn more of Algeria and Arab ways."

Henry looked a little nonplussed but then said, "We would be most grateful for your hospitality, sir."

"The gratitude will be entirely on my side. I will make arrangements."

He went out, leaving Laura and Stephen with Henry and Des.

It would seem that they were thoroughly Rogue entangled, but Laura was glad of it. "I am happy to know you, Cousin Henry," she said, "and sad that we will see little of you in the future." She hesitated, then said, "Would you like to visit Caldfort House before you leave England? I could discreetly arrange that."

His face softened. "You're very kind. Yes, I would. I was happy there as a boy, and I would like to show Des my old home. There are few things I would treasure, too, if they are still there. Nothing of any particular value."

"Of course."

"And I would like to visit my father's and mother's graves."

"You have a stone there, too, you know."

He laughed, and she realized it was for the first time since she'd met him. "How strange. I should definitely see that."

Laura turned to Des, who was looking brightly, if hesitantly, happy. "Is there hope that you will walk again, sir?"

He smiled. "Oh, yes. If I rest," he added, reminding her with a mischievous look of their discussion in Draycombe. "I can walk a little now, but it pains me and I hate to hobble in public. So ungraceful. But it gets better day by day." He cocked his head. "Do you think anyone at this Redoaks knows how to play casino?"

"*I* know how to play casino, Des," Henry said. "Is that what you were doing with Mrs. Penfold? I can teach you more complicated games. Piquet, for example."

"I will enjoy that. I will enjoy exploring everything in the wider world." He smiled up at Laura in a frank, delightful way. "Thank you, Laura Gardeyne. You were kind to me even when you thought me a villain. You have a legendary aura."

"What?" she asked, wrinkling her brow at him.

"She has," said Stephen, equally puzzled. "She is known as Labellelle."

But Laura had realized. "It's an anagram!"

In a little while, Nicholas took Henry and Des down to Kerslake Manor to arrange transport to Redoaks. Sharing a secret smile, Laura and Stephen had made an excuse to linger, and no one had argued.

They went back up to the George and the Dragon Room.

"This is very wicked," she said as he locked the door.

"And everyone will guess," he agreed. "Do you care?"

"Not at all. But, sir, this dress fastens down the back, so I will need your assistance . . ."

He came to her and turned her, and then she felt his fingers working at the buttons for the first time. Another matrimonial moment, and sweet.

"A corset, too," he said, as if his throat was tight.

"Yes." Her heart was speeding and breath seemed precious. "An inconvenience. Perhaps I should take to wearing the soft garment Eleanor favors."

"If you wish." He spread her gown so cool air touched her back. "But there are times when a corset is part of the pleasure. I confess, however," he said, his fingernail scratching down plain linen, "that when I allowed myself wicked dreams, I imagined your intimate garments to be somewhat more adorned."

Laura chuckled but then felt herself sway, felt his hands catch her, support her. "Silk," she breathed. "And lace. Ribbons." She swallowed so she could attempt coherence. "I have a corset of red silk, very low in the back."

He began untying her laces and loosening them, taking his time, each touch sweet torture. "To wear under that red dress? I hope you still have that."

"Yes, but it's very grand. Not suited for a quiet life."

"You plan to live a quiet life?"

She remembered their earlier discussion and smiled. "Now and then."

He tugged on her corset laces, more urgently now. "And now and then, I will expect my wife to host brilliant parties in fine plumage, flying high."

"Whether I want to or not?" she asked, knowing he would hear the teasing pout.

"I will be the proud possessor of Labellelle, and will expect you to play your part."

"Tyrant."

"Master. Consider yourself my slave, required to please me in every way."

Her corset loosened and her clothing began to slide. She wriggled to help it as she turned so she stood before him in only shift and stockings.

"Indeed?" Laura began to tear the clothes off him, buttons flying, cloth ripping. "Or I could make you my slave in all things."

"Do you think so?" But his breathing was deep, his erection strong, so she laughed as she tossed away her shift, backing toward the bed.

"Come to me," she commanded, and he obeyed.

When the bed hit her thighs, she lay back on it. "Now pleasure me, sir, and pleasure me well."

He lowered himself over her. "Tyrant."

"Mistress." She ran her nails lightly down his flanks.

He shuddered and smiled. "Beloved."

She smiled back, swept suddenly through by pleasure so intense that she could weep. "Come to me, Stephen. Love me and let me love you. Let us be one."

His eyes closed for a moment, but then he looked at her again. "Always, and forever. I promise it. Ah, Laura . . ." he sighed, watching her in daylight as they did indeed become one.

If you are new to the Company of Rogues series, I hope you want to read more. Here is a list of the other titles. They are all available now except for *Dangerous Joy,* which will be reissued in December 2004. If your bookstore doesn't have them they can order them for you, or they are available through online stores.

An Arranged Marriage. Nicholas and Eleanor
An Unwilling Bride. Lucien and Beth
Christmas Angel. Leander and Judith
Forbidden. Francis and Serena
Dangerous Joy. Miles and Felicity
The Dragon's Bride. Con and Susan

Connected books from NAL are:

The Devil's Heiress
The novella "The Demon's Mistress" in *In Praise of Younger Men*
Hazard
St. Raven

"The Demon's Mistress," *The Dragon's Bride,* and *The Devil's Heiress* will be reissued in June 2004 in an omnibus trade paperback edition, *Three Heroes,* with the most perfect cover. Look for it.

For details on these and my other books, please check my Web site www.jobev.com. There is an author's note on the next page with background information on *Skylark.*

AUTHOR'S NOTE

The seed for this story came while I was writing *Winter Fire*, my most recent Malloren book, set in 1763. The heroine of *Winter Fire* is a naval captain's daughter and has spent time traveling with him. Now and then people will mention that Miss Smith "fought Barbary pirates."

Of course I did some research about this but I wasn't planning on using it again——until I set to write Stephen's book and realized I was in the autumn of 1816.

The newspaper item at the start of *Skylark* is my invention, but there was excitement and furor in the fall of 1816 over the liberation of the Christian slaves of Barbary. Since my tentative storyline already required the return of a lost heir—bingo!

Barbary was the old name for the states of the north coast of Africa—Morocco, Algeria, Tunisia, and Tripoli—that had been notorious for centuries for piracy. The corsairs, as their maritime pirates were called, hunted down ships for cargo, but especially for slaves.

The harsh lands of North Africa required a lot of cheap labor, but the corsairs' religion, Islam, forbade the use of Muslim slaves. As they were close to Christian Europe, the solution was obvious, and as well as raiding shipping, the corsairs raided the shores, scooping up young, healthy workers.

In the sixteenth and seventeenth centuries they raided more widely, even pouncing on the shores of Britain, but improved navies put an end to that. By the early nineteenth century the Barbary states limited themselves to attacking crippled ships and the coasts of the weakest Mediterranean countries. In fact, by then most of their wealth came from ransoms and from protection money.

Most countries paid the Barbary pirates to leave their shipping alone, including Britain and the United States. For example, in 1812, Portugal paid over a million Spanish dollars for release of Portuguese slaves held by the corsairs and for immunity. The latter was guaranteed by an annual payment of twenty-four thousand dollars.

However, in 1815, the United States was the first to realize the weakness of the Barbary states and turned the tables. They refused to pay protection money and sent a fleet with a demand for the return of all American slaves and property. They were victorious.

There were not many American slaves, however, and the countries who had lost the most people to the corsairs had no naval power to use. It was Britain, Europe's naval champion, who was called upon to continue the fight.

The Annual Register for 1816 says: "It has long been a topic of reproach, which foreigners have brought against the boasted maritime supremacy of England, that the piratical states of Barbary have been suffered to exercise their ferocious ravages upon the inferior powers navigating the Mediterranean Sea, without any attempt on the part of the mistress of the ocean to control them, and to reduce them within the limits prescribed by the laws of civilized nations."

You have to admire such a long but coherent sentence, don't you? The writer goes on to point out that competition with the upstart America was one of the motives for action. There were others, however. The end of the war meant that Britain had time, a war-trained navy without much to do, and a leadership position to cement.

In late 1815 Britain sent Lord Exmouth to begin negotiations, backed by the threat of force, on behalf of some of the smaller and more vulnerable powers such as Sicily and Sardinia.

Tunis and Tripoli were "persuaded" to abolish Christian slavery and release all their captives, but diplomacy went out the window in April 1816 when a Tunisian corsair raided Sardinia. Not only did this violate the agreement, but Caroline, Princess of Wales—yes, the estranged wife of the Regent—happened to be there and only just escaped.

With British guns trained on Tunis, the dey of that country signed a treaty totally abolishing Christian slavery. Tripoli followed suit. Exmouth and the navy moved on to the toughest nut—Algeria.

The dey of Algiers resisted, and as mentioned in *Skylark*, treated the British consul and his family, and some naval officers sent to aid them, badly. This was an affront that could not be tolerated, and battle commenced on August 27, 1816.

The city of Algiers could not hold out for long, and soon the dey had to surrender and sign a treaty that ended Christian slavery in Algeria and released all those then held as well as repaid recent security monies. There were 1,642 slaves, most of them Italian.

The number of British is uncertain. Some sources say none, some up to eighteen. I failed to find any account of a returning British slave, which makes me think that none is the correct number, but for the purposes of this story I chose to go with a few, even though it doesn't affect the situation Henry Gardeyne found himself in.

As Stephen says, the Battle of Algiers was not particularly popular in Britain because the slaves were nearly all peasants from southern Europe, and Catholic to boot, and the cost, especially in casualties, was quite high. However, a victory is a victory, and when it was presented as Britain liberating the downtrodden that everyone else had abandoned, it went down well enough.

Is Henry and Des's story likely?

It is certainly possible.

Young male captives did become sex slaves, so a male harem is likely, and conditions there would be luxurious to an English farm lad.

As for Henry, slaves were used for everything from the hardest labor in the salt mines to housework. Generally constrained by an iron ring on their right ankle and a heavy dangling chain, some slaves were allowed to move about the area and even to run small businesses on the side. Some ran taverns for other slaves, even though devout Muslims do not consume alcohol.

In a strange way it was a tolerant society, and some slaves who earned enough from their enterprises to buy their freedom chose to stay. Don't forget that conditions at home were harsh for many, as Stephen points out when telling Laura that some soldiers in the army in India tried to get transported to Australia in hope of a better life.

The Christian slaves in Barbary had their own hospital and even chapel. They were not persecuted for their Christian religion, but if they chose to convert they were automatically set free. It was, however, slavery. Some slaves were kept in harsh conditions and worked to death, and the punishments for disobedience and especially for attempting escape were cruel.

So that is the background which I found waiting for me as I began to discover this story, and it created a fascinating story for Henry and Des as well as Stephen and Laura. I hope you enjoyed it. If you want to catch up on the other Rogues stories, and my other novels, please check the page before this author's note.

I also write romance novels set in the 1760s, centered on a family called the Mallorens. The titles are:

My Lady Notorious
Tempting Fortune
Something Wicked
Secrets of the Night
Devilish
Winter Fire

I have written a few medieval romances:

Lord of My Heart
The Shattered Rose
Dark Champion
Lord of Midnight

Now for something different. In February 2004, I had a science fiction romance novella, *The Trouble with Heroes*, published in a trade paperback collection called *Irresistible Forces*. This will be published in smaller paperback early in 2005.

There is more about all my books on my Web page, www.jobev.com.

I enjoy hearing from readers. You can write to me c/o The Rotrosen Agency, 318 East 51st Street, New York, NY 10022, in which case I appreciate an SASE, or you can e-mail me at jo@jobev.com. Ask to be put on my e-mail list.

All best wishes,

Jo

About Heroes

Glorious spring sunshine beamed through the open curtains, and the raised window let in courting birdsong. Nearby, people chattered amidst their busy lives, and wheels rattled as a horse and cart hurried down the back lane. The golden light danced on the silky, disheveled hair and ravaged classic features of a young man lolling in the faded armchair beside the window. It glinted off half-lowered lashes, and golden stubble that suggested a night without sleep or orderly waking, and dug deep into a jagged scar down one cheek that told of more dangerous adventures in the past.

His legs, in breeches and well-worn boots, stretched before him, and a half-full wineglass tilted in his lax, long-fingered hand.

On a round table by his elbow stood a decanter with an inch or so of pale amber wine, and a plain, practical pistol.

He raised the glass and sipped, seeming intent on the small garden outside the window, but in fact Lord Vandeimen's gaze was directed at nothing close or visible. He looked at the past, both recent and far, and with increasing, slightly fretful curiosity, at the future.

Switching the glass to his left hand, he placed two fingers on the cold metal of the pistol barrel. His father's pistol, used for the same purpose nearly a year before.

So easy.

So quick.

So why was he waiting?

Hamlet had had something to say about that.

In his case, he decided, he was pausing to enjoy this particularly fine wine. After all, he'd spent nearly all his last coins on it. He must be careful not to drift away under its influence and waste this moment of resolution. One bottle hadn't put him under the table since he was a lad, though.

So long ago, those days of wicked youthful adventures. Was it really less than ten years since he'd been a carefree youth, running wild on the Sussex Downs with Con and Hawk?

No, not carefree. Even children and youths have cares. But blessedly free of the weightier burdens of life.

The three Georges. The triumvirate.

His drifting mind settled on the day they'd tired of having the same patriotic name and rechristened themselves. Hawk Hawkinville. Van Vandeimen. It should have been Somer Somerford, but Con had balked at such a effete name. He'd taken a variation of his second name, Connaught. Con.

Con, Hawk, and Van. They'd grown up like brothers, almost like triplets. Back in those days they'd not imagined a time when they'd be so apart, but Van was glad the other two weren't here now. With luck, they'd hear of his death when it was history, the pain of it numbed. They hadn't seen each other since Waterloo.

Con had returned home directly after the battle, but Hawk and Van had lingered awhile. Hawk was still with the army, tidying up Europe. Van had been in England for six months, but he'd carefully avoided his home and old friends.

He drained the glass and refilled it, his hand reassuringly steady. It was strange that Con hadn't hunted him down. Any other time, that would have worried him, but not now. If Con didn't care, that was good.

No friends. No family.

Once, in another life, there had been so much more. When he'd left at sixteen to join his regiment, mother, father, and two sisters had waved farewell. Ten years later, all were shades. Did they watch him now? If so, what did their ghostly voices cry? Wouldn't they want him to join them?

"Don't protest to me, old man," he said to his ghostly

father. "You took the same way out when you were left alone. And what have I—? Oh, devil take it!" he snapped, slamming down the glass and seizing the pistol. "When I start talking to ghosts, it's time."

Impelled by some mythical urge, he picked up the glass and poured the remaining wine to stream and puddle on the waxed floor. "An offering to the gods," he said. "May they be merciful."

Then he put the long barrel cold into his mouth and with a final breath and a prayer squeezed the trigger.

The click was loud, but a click didn't kill. He pulled the gun out and stared at it with wild exasperation. A flick showed him the problem. The flint on the old-fashioned pistol had worn and slipped sideways.

"Shoddy work, Van," he muttered, hands trembling now, desperately trying to think whether he had a fresh flint anywhere in his rooms. If he had to go out and find one, the moment might pass. He might try again to pull his life out of the pit.

He knew he didn't have a fresh flint, so he poked out the old one, sweat chilling his brow and his nape, and tried to fix it so it would work. He'd drunk enough to make him clumsy. "Plague and tarnation, and hell, and damnation, and—"

"Stop!"

He looked up, dazed, to see a figure standing in his doorway, draped in white, crowned in white, hand outstretched, looking like a stern Byzantine angel . . .

Smooth oval face, long nose, firm lips.

A woman.

She swept forward to grip the pistol barrel. "You must not."

That's the beginning of a novella called "The Demon's Mistress," which was first published in 2001 in the collection *In Praise of Younger Men*. It's also the beginning of the book *Three Heroes*, which brings together this story and the sequels, *The Dragon's Bride* and *The Dev-*

il's Heiress in a unique volume that will be published in June 2004.

The novella and two novels form a trilogy of connected stories about three friends from birth who go to war together at sixteen and return ten years later divided. You may have read one or more of these stories, but I think you'll want to add this edition to your collection, because in this form the three stories come together to make one long story of wounds healed and friendship restored.

Look for this trade paperback edition (a larger-sized paperback) if only to admire the absolutely stunning cover showing the three soldier heroes.

As a romance writer, I'm always interested in heroes, and by that I mean more than the man who gets the woman. Heroes—and heroines, too, of course—stand tall and fight for something, whether it be liberty, security, honor, or justice.

As you saw, *Skylark* has much to do with the nature of the hero. Stephen wants to be the dashing sort but instead is called to work through the law and politics to try to put the world right. In a way it can be harder to fight the quiet fight rather than the guts and glory one, but outright war always takes its toll, as it did on the men of *Three Heroes*.

This is the direct theme of my story in the SF-romance collection *Irresistible Forces* (NAL, February 2004). The novella is called "The Trouble with Heroes" and the phrase is completed at the end of the story. "The trouble with heroes is that they want to come home. But home is also their just reward." War changes the warrior, and it is often hard for them to return to and fit in with the home they have struggled to defend. Sometimes, as with Dan in "The Trouble with Heroes," the skills and qualities they have learned in order to defeat the enemy make them unwelcome back in their community.

I originally wrote that story in 1999, before we all became more immediately aware of the debt we owe to heroes and the price of war. With *Irresistible Forces* arriving now on shelves, I'm hearing from readers moved by the way the story applies to their feelings about our times.

In her review of the collection for *Romantic Times*, Donna Carter said, "The jewel in the crown is Beverley's 'The Trouble with Heroes,' a moving exploration of the consequences of war and power on the those who fight as well as those left behind."

As for the warriors in *Three Heroes*, George, Lord Vandeimen, has seen too much war and lost too many friends, so when he returns to find his parents and siblings dead and his home falling apart, he has no more will to fight. He decides on suicide, and it takes a beautiful, rich, determined widow to stir the ashes back into flame and give him a reason to live.

George, Lord Amleigh, has been flattened by the war, no longer able to truly enjoy life or live it to the full, but he's working to put his life together, including plans to marry the very suitable Lady Anne Peckworth. But then he inherits the title and property of the mad Earl of Wyvern and meets again the woman who as a girl had crushed his youthful heart. The meeting, the passion, and the restoration of life and love take place in *The Dragon's Bride*, set against the exciting backdrop of smuggling in Devon. Yes, the same backdrop as *Skylark*, featuring the same bizarre house, Crag Wyvern, and "Captain Drake," Susan's brother.

The third George is Major George Hawkinville, a man of the mind who is like Stephen in many ways, equally uneasy about being left on the fringes of the action, even though he knows that is where he can serve best. Today Stephen would probably still be a reforming politician but I think Hawk would be a computer genius. He has a gift for the organization of information.

He went into the cavalry to fight but he was soon moved into the quartermaster's division and accepted that he could do more good by moving armies efficiently and arranging for adequate food and supplies to be where they were needed. His work sometimes involved investigating fraud, thievery, and profiteering, so when he returns home to find a swindle affecting his home, he's the right man for the job.

In *The Devil's Heiress*, Hawk sets out in cold pursuit of the adventuress who's stolen his father's money, but finds the seemingly innocent Clarissa Greystone. His struggles to find the truth and do the right thing embroil him with the other two Georges and with Con's friends, the Company of Rogues. Soon Clarissa is his heaven and his hell, and everything is complicated by the return of an enemy who will do anything to get that money.

The Devil's Heiress in particular grows out of some earlier Rogues books, *An Arranged Marriage* and *An Unwilling Bride*. *An Unwilling Bride* was set around the time of the Battle of Waterloo, which was a glorious victory over Napoleon Bonaparte shadowed by a shocking loss of life—more than ten thousand in one battle. It was after that grim and gruesome victory that the Duke of Wellington, commander in chief of the allied forces, said, "Nothing except a battle lost can be half so melancholy as a battle won."

In *Skylark*, Stephen quotes from Lord Byron's verses about that terrible battle, which impressed itself upon its age as 9/11 has impressed itself on our times. In *An Unwilling Bride*, when the first casualty lists arrive in London, showing the loss of one of the Rogues there, Nicholas Delaney proposes a toast:

> "To all the fallen; may they be young forever in heaven.
> To all the wounded; may they have strength and heal.
> To all the bereaved; may they feel joy again.
> And please God, may there one day be an end to war."

I was deeply touched when in October 2001 a reader asked permission to include these words on a 9/11 quilt she was making. You can see it online here: www.geocities.com/spenycjo/goldendoor.html

In praise of heroes, who are usually the youngest and best of our times,

Jo Beverley

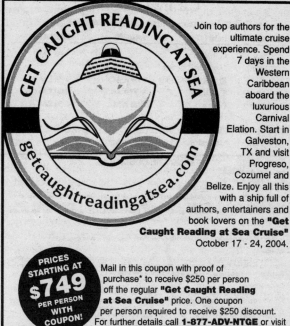

Join top authors for the ultimate cruise experience. Spend 7 days in the Western Caribbean aboard the luxurious Carnival Elation. Start in Galveston, TX and visit Progreso, Cozumel and Belize. Enjoy all this with a ship full of authors, entertainers and book lovers on the **"Get Caught Reading at Sea Cruise"** October 17 - 24, 2004.

PRICES STARTING AT $749 PER PERSON WITH COUPON!

Mail in this coupon with proof of purchase* to receive $250 per person off the regular **"Get Caught Reading at Sea Cruise"** price. One coupon per person required to receive $250 discount. For further details call **1-877-ADV-NTGE** or visit **www.GetCaughtReadingatSea.com**

*proof of purchase is original sales receipt with the book purchased circled.

Carnival
The Most Popular Cruise Line in the World!

GET $250 OFF

Name   (Please Print)

Address   Apt. No.

City   State   Zip

E-Mail Address

See Following Page For Terms & Conditions.

For booking form and complete information go to www.getcaughtreadingatsea.com or call 1-877-ADV-NTGE

Carnival Elation

7 Day Exotic Western Caribbean Itinerary

DAY	PORT	ARRIVE	DEPART
Sun	Galveston		4:00 P.M.
Mon	"Fun Day" at Sea		
Tue	Progreso/Merida	8:00 A.M.	4:00 P.M.
Wed	Cozumel	9:00 A.M.	5:00 P.M.
Thu	Belize	8:00 A.M.	6:00 P.M.
Fri	"Fun Day" at Sea		
Sat	"Fun Day" at Sea		
Sun	Galveston	8:00 A.M.	

For booking form and complete information
go to **www.getcaughtreadingatsea.com** or call **1-877-ADV-NTGE**

Complete coupon and booking form and mail both to:
Advantage International, LLC,
195 North Harbor Drive, Suite 4206, Chicago, IL 60601